Summer Hill

S 02.

Joseph Hone has written a number of novels, starting with
The Private Sector, and travel books, the most recent of
which was *Children of the Country*. He is a regular broadcaster,
and lives in Oxfordshire.

By the same author

Joseph Hone

Summer Hill

Pan Books

London, Sydney and Auckland

The author gratefully acknowledges the help
of the Virginia Center for the Creative Arts in
the preparation of this book

First published in Great Britain 1990 in a
single volume by Sinclair-Stevenson Ltd

This edition of the first three Books of the original edition
first published 1992 by Pan Books Ltd, Cavaye Place,
London SW10 9PG

9 8 7 6 5 4 3 2 1

ISBN 0 330 31732 6

Photoset by Rowland Phototypesetting Ltd,
Bury St Edmunds, Suffolk

Printed in England by Clays Ltd, St Ives plc

'Audaces fortuna juvat'

For Geraldine
and for
Sally & Stanley

book one

I

It had been ominously still and cold all morning under a leaden sky, where the mountains, Brandon and Leinster, remained just visible, grey against darker grey. But, by early afternoon, heralded by the smallest stir of warmer air, these peaks disappeared and the snow storm, broaching the high passes and spreading out along the upper flanks, suddenly rolled downwards, an avalanche engulfing the hunt – hounds, horses, riders all caught in a vicious, windswept drive of blinding flakes.

Frances Cordiner, unable to control her impatience at the slow hunt that morning, had run well ahead and below the field. But now, finding herself quite alone on the bare mountain, she turned in the saddle, hoping to see where the others had got to. Instead, as it seemed just above her, she saw the storm poised, like the crest of a great white tidal wave, about to fall on her.

Defiant then, smiling, she dug her heels in, spurring the mare forward, galloping furiously down the slopes as she tried to outpace the rushing blanket that rolled after her. She took every short cut home, heedless of danger or obstruction, clearing gates, walls, ditches in a dazzle of mad jumps, hooves drumming against the cold earth, a scarlet jacketed blur against the foamy white sea that raced behind her.

But eventually, held back at one point by an impossible hurdle, the storm outran her. Snow stung her eyes, enveloping, blinding her – so that seeing the steeple of the local parish church ahead she wheeled the mare down a farm track, making towards it for shelter.

The small church, near the village of Cloone, lay quite isolated at the edge of the Summer Hill estate, some miles from the great house. Frances knew it well. It was the Cordiner family church. She had been baptized and would hope to marry and perhaps even be buried there, in the family vault behind the building.

Soundlessly, the mare's hooves muffled on the snowy path, she rode up to the porch, dismounted, and, taking the horse with her, sheltered inside. There was room for both of them. But the mare, instead of relaxing, clear of the biting storm at last, became nervous, swinging her rump, tossing her head, whinnying softly.

'Easy, girl – what's the matter?' She tried to calm the animal, peering out into the graveyard. The branch of a great elm, behind the tombstones near the gate, creaked alarmingly in the white storm. 'Silly, it's only a tree.' She stroked the mare's nose again. But she remained uneasy. Then Frances, looking out again, saw the reason and felt a vague tingle of fear pricking her spine.

Across the graveyard, beyond the hollow where the Cordiner vault was, she saw, between the vicious snow flurries, a saddled but riderless horse, quite visible for a moment before the driven flakes swirled back over the vision.

But her fear remained. The beast had been so unlikely, so still and large, a black stallion, come and gone in a moment, invisible now in the bitter white drifts. But it must be real, she thought, steadying herself.

Taking her whip she set out into the storm, dodging between the tombstones, making for the sharp slope that ran down towards the vault. The stallion was no vision. She saw it clearly now, standing on a ditch beyond the line of old elms, reins hanging loose, as if it had broken tether in the storm from somewhere nearby and had come to find its master.

Indeed, it seemed to have found him, Frances thought, with increased alarm, when, turning and looking in the same direction as the horse, she saw the iron barred door leading into the Cordiner vault slightly ajar. The great door was always locked. Someone was inside. An icicle of fear pierced the back of her neck.

Moving diagonally towards the vault door, she noticed the broken lock – then, with infinite care, she peered slowly round the stone jamb. A short brick passage opened into the vault itself and in the bright reflected light from the snow the scene was sufficiently lit. She took it all in, almost at a glance, before recoiling in sheer horror, trembling violently.

The man, with his back to her, some rough tinker type to judge by his torn clothes, had already ransacked two or three of the dozen heavy oak, lead-lined coffins set in tiers about the vault, the lids wrenched off, a debris of old bones and frayed cloth strewn about the place. But, worse than that, at the very moment when Frances peered in, the grave robber had been manhandling the skull of some recently deceased Cordiner lady – her great-aunt Margot, it might have been, for the flaky brown, parchment-like skin and wisps of long white hair were still attached to the death's head – a woman whom the man had pulled up from her tomb, a broken skeletal doll in her plain shroud, jaws forced open hideously as the man prodded about for gold in her teeth.

Frances, dizzy with horror, eyes closed against the stinging snow, leant back against the wall beside the vault. When she opened them, she saw the second tinker, standing looking at her, not twenty yards away.

He was a much larger man than the first, swarthy, aggressive-looking, with florid, puffy features and strangely protuberant staring eyes under a battered black hat. Taking a knife from his belt, opening his long arms wide and crouching now, so that his hands nearly touched the ground like a baboon's, he approached Frances, moving forward across the snow very slowly, ready to spring to either side as if he was cornering a hen.

Frances, back against the vault, with the sheer ground to either side and the boundary wall immediately to her right, had only one path of escape. She must go left along the earthworks, then up into the main graveyard and back to the church.

She ran for her life – and with a sudden curse he followed, surprisingly agile, a great tattered figure, spring-heeled, pursuing her through the driving snow. She stumbled as she turned, trying to climb the gentler slope further down, slipping on the white-powdered grass. And now, his companion in the vault alerted, the two of them were after her. They nearly caught her before, finding a grip, she clambered out of their way at the last moment, when they slipped themselves in their frantic efforts to catch her.

But now, with the advantage of the high ground, Frances turned and used her riding crop on the two struggling figures beneath her – the whiplash cracking through the snowflakes, mercilessly, repeatedly, as she threw her whole body into the attack, drawing the crop right back, throwing it out from her shoulder, whipping the line straight at their faces, where the cord opened great livid weals on their cheeks, the smaller tinker's eye suddenly pulped and bloodied as the lash bit into it, tearing across his forehead. Time and again, exultantly, she smote them. But the bigger man finally put an end to her attack, catching the lash in his hands, and pulling the crop from her, so that she had to turn and run once more.

Now she was in the graveyard proper, dodging and slipping among the tombstones, racing for the porch. But she fell once more, cracking her shin on a metal tomb rail. And this time, as she lay spreadeagled over the hard grave, the larger man, on his feet now and up the slope, seemed certain to capture her.

He lunged forward, arms outstretched again, about to pin her down. But, as he stumbled, she twisted away suddenly, and saw him fall instead on the metal spike at one corner of the tomb, spearing him somewhere high up, between his legs.

He doubled up, bellowing in pain. She had time then to run for the church door, open it and ram the bolt home on the far side before she heard the man throwing himself against the heavy oak, then hammering on the outside. There was no vestry or other entrance to the church, she knew. Only the high windows might offer access – and indeed as she ran back from the door she saw the dark hat and protuberant eyes of the second tinker rising above the sill of the plain east window at the end of the church – a face that raged and glowered at her, as he started to break the glass, continuing his pursuit.

But she soon put herself out of harm's way by climbing up the ladder to the belfry, slamming shut the trap door there, and standing on it firmly before pulling at the bell rope that ran down through a hole in the floor.

The bell tolled violently, a haphazard, ill-rung chime. But riding with the snowstorm, carried by the wind all over the parish, down the river valley, to the village of Cloone, it was soon heard at the great house of Summer Hill.

Several days later, though the storm had passed the village, the frozen snow still lay thick on the bridge above the salmon traps, blanketing the river mall and the small tree-lined green behind, preserving a filigree of icicles down the Cordiner memorial in the centre.

The collie dog outside Mrs Ryan's post office sniffed the steaming fresh horse droppings from Hennessy's cob, but feeling the cold soon left his explorations and returned to the post office where he whined against the door. Neither of the two people inside took the least notice of him.

John Hennessy, the grocer from Thomastown, five miles north, dallied over his small delivery – a quarter pound of Lipton's tea, a dozen candles, a small bag of sugar – as he tried to engage the unforthcoming Mrs Ryan in conversation.

'Sure and wasn't that a terrible thing up beyant at the church the other day,' he told the old, yellow-haired woman. She made no comment. 'Did you ever hear the like of it?' he went on knowingly, though in fact he had gleaned little of the events in question, hence his assumed familiarity with them, as a means of putting himself on an equal footing with the old lady and getting her to talk.

Finally she spoke – slowly, with great measure and emphasis. 'Indeed, a terrible thing, Mr Hennessy. A *terrible* thing.' Then, thinking better of it, she stopped.

'And? . . . what happened at all?' Mr Hennessy was forced into a more direct approach.

'Oh, and I wouldn't rightly know now . . .' Silence.

Mr Hennessy took another sugar bag from his basket and put it on the counter. 'A little Christmas box for you, Mrs Ryan.' He patted the heavy brown paper bag, then leant over, offering the old woman a whiskery, cold blue ear.

Mrs Ryan laid a heavy hand on the sugar, as no more than her right in the matter. 'Well, now, mind you I've said nothing, but there were ructions, *ructions!*' she whispered to him. Then she paused.

'What happened? – what happened at all?' Mr Hennessy could barely restrain himself. But Mrs Ryan, even though the appropriate overtures had all been observed, was still loath to ring the curtain up. Finally, she launched into the drama.

'Well now . . . didn't the young Missy take the whole *eye* outa one of thim tinkers, the little fella, all in wan *lash* o' the whip, like an oysther it was, dripping blood, all out on his cheek and he in the county infirmary now, till they *string* him up—'

'Sure an' now they'll hardly do that, Mrs – wasn't the oul' one dead already and she in her coffin?'

'Well, now, I don't know about that.' Mrs Ryan was affronted at this imputation that she might have confused the quick with the dead.

'And what about the other lad that went for her and she inside in the church?'

'Ah, sure, an' didn't he run for it, when thim bells got going and the lads from the estate above went for the church. Got clear away.' Mrs Ryan stood back, disappointed. 'Though he took the lash, too, be all accounts, before he went – and he with a great knife on him as well.'

'She's a tough one all right, that young Miss Cordiner.'

'Oh and tough's not the word for it, Mr Hennessy! Clare to God she's – she's the divil itself when she's a mind to it.' Mr Hennessy stood back himself now, licking his cold lips, in awe. 'You wouldn't tangle with *her*, John Hennessy, nor *iny* man, I tell ye!'

'I hadn't the mind to, Mrs—'

'Ah, sure, and wouldn't she take the skin off you as soon as look at ye – just like her oul' mother.'

They leant closer, delving deeper into every aspect of the gruesome business.

Outside the cob shifted its weight, back feet clattering on the cobbles, shaking its bridle with a sharp tinkle of bit and chain. The sudden noise might have disturbed the snow on one of the old elms above the village green, for some flakes fell now, floating down through the bare trees, as if through water, confetti against a seaweed of dark branches.

Mr Hennessy finally emerged from the post office, climbing up on the bench of his van to continue his grocery rounds – the last and major delivery to Summer Hill before he returned to Thomastown: a small, red-faced man with wisps of reddish hair peeking out from beneath a worn bowler – his face glowed like a lantern against the white pall. He'd made these deliveries every Friday to Summer Hill for nearly twenty years, and today the usual mug of tea in the warm basement kitchen of the big house, while Mrs Martin checked the order, would be more than welcome.

Pulling a mackintosh rug over his knees, he took the reins, murmured to the cob, and they set off up the steep, twisting hill that led to the demesne gates at the top. It had started to snow again, very lightly – it would come to nothing, Mr Hennessy thought. But, by the time the van reached the top of the rise, the cob slipping on the flint stone past the estate cottages on either side, huge moist flakes fluttered in the air, side-slipping, circling, icing the stone pineapples on the gate pillars, dusting the fretworked gable ends and diamond window panes of the little Gothic lodge.

About to drive through the gates he was startled to see a thin, dark-coated figure ahead of him, shuffling past the lodge, a sack round his head, one empty sleeve pinned to the back of his jacket, tin cans jangling at his belt. For a moment Mr Hennessy feared he might be another dangerous tinker. But when the man turned abruptly, half-raising

9

a stick, his wounded, noseless features staring upwards, shrouded by the sacking, a skull-like vision in the white flurry, Mr Hennessy recognized him: everyone in the locality knew him simply as Snipe – from his fluttery, darting speech and equally unexpected movements – a tinker of sorts, but quite harmless, a man of the roads, maimed years before in some harvesting accident and now a regular traveller in these parts, in every weather, who sold tin billy-cans and told fortunes from tea-leaves for a few pence. He, too, now and then, was welcomed at the back door of the big house. The cob stopped and Mr Hennessy helped him up on the bench beside him.

The front avenue led due south for over half a mile between white railed fences through the large demesne, past great bare clumps of oak and chestnut, up a slight incline for most of the way so that the house itself was not visible until almost the last moment. To the east, for a quarter of a mile, the pasture fell gradually, before giving way to the steep, forested slope of the valley, the river hidden beneath it as it wound through the limestone walls and buttresses at the bottom of the escarpment.

Ordinarily, in any decent weather, the chain of hills moving against the distant blue mountains on the far side of the valley filled this approach along the high ridge to Summer Hill with wonderful, changing perspectives. But that afternoon in the white drifts nothing was visible beyond the line of tall beech trees – the Beech Walk, a screen which ran diagonally from the brow of the hill down to the first of the thick woods on the lip of the gorge.

The great demesne was foreshortened everywhere, without length or breadth, where none of the spacious eighteenth-century landscaping showed, curtained now by the gentle spirals of snow which muffled every sound, the cob's feet falling on the crunchy flakes, so that the van seemed to be moving through a huge crystal ball, a vast toy, a glass ornament shaken out of its liquid translucent peace, the snowflakes dancing in the orb then, where soon the two travellers would reach the centrepiece of the conceit: the pinnacles and towers of some Gothic fairytale castle.

Summer Hill itself, though, was flat-roofed in the Palladian manner, with a stone balustrade all round, like a fence enclosing a flock of chimneystacks, built in the early eighteenth century from chiselled local limestone – a vast mansion set in the plan of a capital E, designed by David Bindon in his best Irish period for the first Baronet, Sir William Cordiner, on a site set back from an earlier Cordiner castle which had stood there for centuries on the edge of the hill commanding the river and its bridge. Though finely built and proportioned – its flanks, cornices, porch pediment, pillars, sash windows and stacks all precisely balanced, so that it was nowhere heavy, there was little romance in the present building. It was classically elegant.

Summer Hill was very much there on the high plateau, not as ostentation or memorial to colonial plunder, for it was in fact set on land which had been a gift from the Irish themselves: the house dominating this whole middle river valley of the Nore which the Anglo-Norman Cordiners – invited to Ireland with Strongbow by the Irish Chieftain Dermot MacMurrough, hard pressed in wars with his own subjects and rivals – had been given as their reward over 700 years before. And, though the present building had nothing of this blunt medieval age in it, it reflected, in its graceful certainties, the same proprietorial confidence and agreed purposes that had first brought the family to Ireland and had sustained them ever since.

The Cordiners had been Old English originally, Norman Knights in the reign of Henry II – always loyal to the Crown and then, as Barons of Cloone and Kilclondowne, more loyal still to what soon became for them their undivided Irish heritage. More Irish than the Irish themselves, there was nothing of a later plantation family here, no taint of Cromwellian arrogance, loot or murder.

Now, as the snow lay on the house, coating the roof balustrades, edging the long window frames, Summer Hill had the air, not of fairytale romance, but of something very real, a dream writ large, graciously but most realistically cast. Tucked about behind by a semi-circle of dark trees, the house, taking light from the snowy lawns, glowed along its eastern flank, where the flakes glittered on its walls, seeming to fire rather than chill the blueish limestone – a building that triumphed in every weather.

At the back, hidden to the north, a recently built wing in quite a different neo-Gothic style closed the letter E, where first it offered additional bachelor and servants' quarters, and then formed one side of a new coach and stable yard. And it was here, turning right off the main drive and going through an archway, that Mr Hennessy and Snipe arrived a few minutes later. The yard was empty. But many windows about the house, already lamp-lit in the gathering winter twilight, confirmed considerable occupation inside.

Lady Cordiner took off her pince-nez, letting them fall on a capacious bosom. She stood up from her desk at the heart of the house, a boudoir of sorts, though furnished rather more as an office, a busy nerve centre that lay beyond the long drawing room.

'But, Mrs Martin, how *could* she have thought to clean the knives in such a manner?' Lady Cordiner spoke angrily of Bridget, a new scullery maid from one of the tenanted farms nearby.

'I really don't know, your Ladyship.'

'Pushing them up and down in the soil!'

'It's a country way, Ma'am. Some of the old men, with pocket knives . . .'

Mary Martin, the housekeeper, understood the enormity of this act in Lady Cordiner's eyes, though in her own mind it was hardly more than a peccadillo. It was one way to remove obstinate stains and the knives had not suffered. But her mistress was not Irish and had never understood such things. She looked at Lady Cordiner, a dumpy, formidable silhouette standing against the white beyond the window – a sixtieth birthday celebrated that autumn, but still well preserved, still tightly, fashionably waisted in a long, black, bell-shaped dress whose heavy pleated satin rustled over the carpet as she moved impatiently about the room. Her dark hair, scraped up from behind and piled high in a bun, was only just tinged with white; her skin a soft olive-ivory shade – with plump little hands and small feet that moved dexterously and quickly and lips that were rarely still either, even when she was not speaking; above all the challenging glitter of the eyes which made her face still beautiful, orbs always seeking release from the heavy lids, caged but dangerous, as if, in this small room, here was a hungry animal sensing prey moving about elsewhere in the forest of the house.

Mrs Martin had seen something of the same features and complexion among a few people from her home in County Galway: descendants of Spanish sailors, it was said, wrecked on the coasts there in their Armada hundreds of years before. And for a moment she pitied the woman, as an exile, far from her real home, and so unable to come to terms with Irish nature. But the sympathy was brief for she knew, in her years as housekeeper here, how well this woman, even if she did not understand local ways, imposed herself on them, reshaped them entirely to her own purposes.

Mary resented this – or rather resented the means, not the ends. For she had to admit that Lady Cordiner ran Summer Hill superbly well. A house, which thirty years before, when she had first come to it as a seamstress, had been quietly deteriorating, was now run vigorously, appropriately, in a way Mrs Beeton herself might have envied.

It was Lady Cordiner's overbearing manner that grated – not an aristocratic thing, Mrs Martin thought. It was more cunning in its form, the attitude of a wardress, so long versed in the wiles of those under her that she knew the likely misdemeanours of the servants in advance, the small tricks which local tradesmen might play, her family's ploys against her – where she would attack first, routing the opposition before it had any chance to order itself.

And yet, although she was high-handed, she was rarely

unjust – Mary had to admit that, too. And she never used her power or position distantly. She involved herself intimately with the affairs of the household and before any reprimand or sentence she took great pains to establish the guilt. She was fair in that way, like a hanging judge. And to those servants and tradespeople who did not offend, who accepted her sharp scrutiny and abided by her rules, Lady Cordiner was equally constant – and generous, for she paid better wages and settled her accounts more promptly than any other lady in the county. Thus Summer Hill had become an exception to the rule, or misrule, of the country – and Mrs Martin recognized this and was happy enough in her service, while most of the other retainers, whose backgrounds had been truly poverty-stricken and disordered, were more than grateful: fearful of the ruler, they all appreciated the benefits of the reign.

Lady Cordiner continued with her household business. 'Well, Mrs Martin, the knives are hardly important – beside these household thefts. Nearly three months now. And you tell me the little crystal snow-dome – with the model of the house here inside – that's gone now, from the drawing room mantelpiece?'

'Yes, Ma'am. Yesterday, some time in the afternoon it must have been. As you know, I see to all the small items now, morning and evening.'

'Chinese vases, figurines, silver snuff boxes, candlesticks, Meissen shepherdesses, Baccarat paperweights . . .' Lady Cordiner pondered this depredation of small antiques about the house.

'Perhaps it must finally be a matter for the constabulary,' she said. 'Though hardly at this moment, with all our house guests and the others about to arrive. We must simply watch and wait, Mrs Martin. But I wonder who it is?' she added, glaring at the housekeeper, venting her annoyance, though she knew it was not her. Mrs Martin was a Presbyterian.

That same afternoon Frances Cordiner, quite recovered from her drama with the tomb robbers the week before, and now impatient for further action, knelt by the window, alone in the great hall, looking at the small pane of stained glass which her Aunt Emily had made, inset at the bottom corner of the tall window – her family arms: a spread-eagle perched on a visored helmet with a scroll beneath and the inscription: 'Audaces Fortuna Juvat'.

'Fortune favours the brave,' she murmured aloud, looking out at the frozen snowscape, in the white twilight. The pleasure garden terraces, the sharp lines of the enclosing walls, steps, and box hedges, the exactly charted paths – all these had been smoothed and hidden in the fall, covered in a fluffy white eiderdown now, obliterating the strict patterns which Lady Cordiner, destroying an earlier and wilder Irish garden, had instituted. But the weather, at least, was immune to Lady Cordiner's brutal regimentation, and her daughter was suddenly happy that at least she had an ally here.

Beyond the ascending steps and terraced lawns to her right she saw the huge, white-dusted, Canadian maple, its lower branch just a stump now, no longer reaching out over the frozen croquet lawn. In summer, through many summers, the swing had hung there and she had been happy on it – pushing out, faster and faster, tummy left behind, toes in the leaves, then slowing down in a long glide. But her mother had had the swing removed some years before. 'You are no longer a child, Frances,' she had said. 'And, besides, the branch must be cut back in any case. It's beginning to overshadow the lawn.' That had been only very slightly true.

She had spoken to her father, Sir Desmond – pleaded with him, reminding him of this heritage of exotic shrubs and trees which his great-grandfather, a British Consul in the East, had brought back with him as seeds and cuttings and planted at Summer Hill: how this would be a desecration, a beginning of the end for the maple. And he had spoken to her mother about it. But the branch was cut down none the less. Her eldest brother Henry, a botanist and zoologist, might have successfully championed the cause, she thought, but he had been away on one of his long expeditions. Or would he have taken a victory there? She loved him but knew how little stomach he had for battle with their mother – hence his long absences from the house.

Frances changed her focus and tried to find her reflection in the window pane. But there was nothing to be seen. She was not there. It made her uneasy – at a loss already, house-bound now for the afternoon. She breathed on the window instead, clouding the glass – then, with her finger, wrote the word 'me' in the condensation. Then she rubbed it out.

She turned impatiently. She must seriously consider the shape of her afternoon. Time for her was a quicksand which would suck your life away unless you fought it, filled it with brave acts, overwhelmed it by force of will. You could stop the clock with one bright deed, she knew. Frances pondered the coming hours, the minutes even, considering their fitness to her purposes as a commander allocates troops in a plan of battle. There were nearly three hours left before her other brother Eustace, his friend Harold Perkins, and the rest of the Christmas house guests arrived off the Dublin train.

She smiled, remembering how little favour any of her purposes had ever found with her mother, closeted just then in her boudoir beyond the drawing room. Frances's schemes, though she was a woman of twenty-two, were still often those of an adolescent, so that they were necessarily secret – her real life, like that of a child's, lived in shadow. Well-born, not tall but beautiful in rather a gypsy manner, with short glossy dark curls, blackberry eyes, full lips, and a very straight nose, versed in every young lady-like manner, beneath these surfaces she harboured quite unexpected appetites: a greedy, inquisitive, uncompromising taste for life. But it was not at that moment any mere animal hunger which she wished to appease. It was a longing for the inanimate, a craving for the spirit of place, a suit which she offered to Summer Hill itself, a house like the Frog Prince now, where she alone, knowing its secret, could work the miraculous transformation.

She wanted to storm the dark and overstuffed place, clearing it of all that her mother had brought here – the massive damask-covered Victorian furniture, heavy grey serge curtains, all the dull red and brown colours that hid the gleaming Italianate stucco of the previously classical interior – now crammed with every kind of fiddly knick-knack and vulgar ornament: wax flowers under domes; small sentimental pictures in fussy gilded frames set like postage stamps all over the walls; gothic-lettered samplers, heavily beaded and embroidered cushions, velvet foot-stools, Benares brass coffee tables, wrought iron fire-screens, starched antimacassars – all in hideous taste.

The house, as she had seen from old aquatints of the hall and reception rooms, had once been spacious, set off in a clean blue and white geometry. It was a musty ware-house now, where most of its fine Chippendale and other Georgian furniture languished in outhouses and attics. Lady Cordiner had laid heavy hands everywhere. Even the white marble statues of Cupid and Psyche in their hall alcoves, considered immodest, had been replaced by togaed busts of Roman worthies. Frances wished Summer Hill a freedom which it no longer had, where she could bring back its true household Gods, rescue these divinities, kiss the sleeping stones into new life.

And it was only during such winter afternoons, when the ground floor was usually empty, that she could offer herself to Summer Hill, when she liked it best. She loved the silence of the great shell then, when she could speak and listen to it, in full possession of it, where she could wander the rooms and corridors, poke into all its nooks and crannies, be possessed by them in turn.

She looked at the long Flemish tapestry at the back of the hall, anchoring her arm about one of the great pillars there, letting her body swirl slowly round it, so that, as she turned, the chivalrous stories in the weave came alive, an animated panorama of fearless hunters and their prey, of medieval courts, of invulnerable Kings and Queens. Summer Hill seemed hers then, where she found faith in these Royal emblems of derring-do, a blessing for her own adventures. She tiptoed away, a wraith moving soundlessly over the floors and carpets, knowing every creak in the wood, where cover lay in each room or corridor, which doors groaned and which were mute.

Upstairs on the top floor, in the first of a suite of rooms which had been the old nurseries, now commandeered for his animal and butterfly collections, Henry Cordiner carefully speared a huge mauve-winged swallowtail with a large pin. Then he fixed it delicately into a glass display case, along with some dozens of other brilliantly winged insects in this particular collection of Nymphalinae. On top of the display, in fine copperplate, was the legend: 'North African Lepidoptera. Morocco, Tunisia, Egypt. March–June 1898'.

He picked up a magnifying glass and carefully examined this last specimen – a thick-set, stooping man in his late twenties, with an attractively broken nose and reels of dark loose curly hair that fell over his brow, partly obstructing his vision. He brushed the strands aside impatiently, trying to smooth them back behind his ears, licking his fingers quickly in the attempt.

'*Nymphalia jason* – best of the lot,' he said at last to his companion, sitting on a high stool next to a work bench where bell jars, glass retorts and ether bottles were ranged along the surface. 'You remember, in Egypt, that sweltering afternoon in the delta? Near Zagazig. We chased this one all over the cotton field before it escaped into the old man's pigeon loft. What a rumpus – fellow thought we were after his pigeons with our nets . . .'

The younger man on the stool, Dermot Cordiner, a lieutenant in the Hussars and a distant cousin of Henry's, smiled but said nothing – a generous smile flooding his thin pale face beneath the neatly parted frizzy straw hair: a neat young man in everything, a brushed moustache, with the piercing cornflower-blue eyes of most Cordiners, sitting very upright on the tall stool as if he was still on parade and not on leave from his regiment in England.

Henry turned to him, saw the smile and accepted it as

an entirely adequate response. The two men either talked a lot or very little. And, that mid-winter afternoon, the warm coals in the grate, together with the permanent rumour of ether in the room, had made them both drowsy and disinclined for conversation.

They seemed an unlikely pair at first – this burly, dishevelled, rather Byronic scion of Summer Hill and his meticulous, frail-looking cousin. What they shared was not obvious but lay near the heart of their relationship, a love of the great outdoors, for adventure there – new worlds to be mastered: lakes, rivers, mountains, deserts and forests to be traversed and charted, rare flora and fauna to be taken and catalogued, where all that they did in this way together was carefully planned and vigorously executed. It was Dermot, with his intuitive grasp of military tactics, who supplied the plans and Henry the scientific vigour. Together they were a happy and formidable combination.

Henry closed the display case, took it up and put it in line with a dozen others on a shelf at the end of the room. An open doorway here led into the old day nursery, a room now given over to much larger glass display cases, filled with stuffed animals and birds.

'Where's Gretel got to?' Henry moved through the doorway, searching the room beyond. On top of one of the glass cases – quite motionless, apparently one of the exotic exhibits – a strange animal lay curled. 'Ah, Gretel – too hot for you in the other room? I'm surprised.'

Henry touched the silky white hairs above a protuberant ear. A round fire-brown eye opened from the middle of a circle of black fur; a smooth, jet-black, puppy dog nose emerged from between prehensile paws – and then a wonderful tail uncurled, fluffy thick, ringed all the way in black and white, longer than the animal itself, before the ring-tailed lemur jumped on her master's shoulder and he took her back to the other room.

But the animal was unhappy there, fretting, chattering in soft clucks and chirrups, nose sniffing, her huge round eyes darting about, searching every corner of the room.

'It's obvious,' Dermot said.

'Yes, I know, Gretel.' Henry spoke consolingly to the animal, picking up half an apple, offering it to her, which she would not accept. 'It won't be long now. Just he's off colour, you see – needs the warmth here and the regular meals. But we'll have him out by morning with any luck, unless the snow stays.'

Henry took Gretel back to the other room, with a basin of cut fruit, setting her on an old patchwork blanket in a club chair at the far end of the room. Closing the door on his return he went to a large, hinge-topped tea-chest near the fireplace. Opening it he looked down into the sand inside. A slow, faint hissing noise rose from the olive brown and yellow coils; a very prettily patterned scaly head moved a fraction.

'Feeding time, I think.' Henry moved to a smaller box nearby where he kept a supply of live mice. Dermot remonstrated with him. 'If your mother knew.'

'She *won't* know.'

'But it *is* poisonous.'

'Yes. But it's only a sand snake, Dermot: African Beauty – and isn't he! The fangs are right at the back of the jaws, so he's quite unable to strike with them – has to almost swallow his prey before he can kill it. Absolutely no danger to humans.'

Henry washed his hands in a ewer, then moved over to a large central table where maps were laid out at one end and on the other a Mauser .375 sporting rifle had been dismantled, the mechanism neatly laid out on an oilcloth.

'Shall we take a look at possible routes again?'

Dermot joined him at the head of the table and together they pored over the large army ordnance map, headed 'British East African Protectorates and Territories'. The Arab ports on the Indian Ocean coast were clearly marked – Mombasa, Malindi, the island of Lamu. But the interior, most of the hinterland to the west, was almost entirely blank, apart from two roughly charted red lines, later inked-in additions, running from Abyssinia south-west across a vast space marked 'desert' towards some equally vague shapes marked 'mountains'.

The two men became engrossed in the map, planning their long journey, next year, into the heart of the dark continent.

Emily Cordiner, Sir Desmond's younger sister, maiden aunt in Summer Hill and long resident there, gazed at the snowfall from her studio-cum-bedroom on the west wing of the house. Her windows gave out onto one of the great features of the Summer Hill gardens – long alleys of clipped yew and beech hedging, interspersed with pleached hornbeam arcades, a tall maze of walks, offering surprising vistas, leading to secret bowers and stone grottoes, past antique statuary to little pavilions, a dovecote, an artificial waterfall – each walk terminating at the centre at a great oak tree, beneath which, in summer, pastoral comedies were sometimes presented by the house guests.

Emily loved this permanent conceit just outside her windows, which the snow made all the more baroque, bearding the statues, powdering a folly of broken Corinthian pillars, icing a little Palladian bridge in the distance: the baroque of Vanbrugh perfectly accentuated now in the white glitter, encompassed by this fluffy, pearl-topped regiment of hedges.

Her bedroom decor seemed more rococo. A passionate student and gifted interpreter of the period, she had decorated it herself, adorning the walls with a series of exquisite trompe-l'oeil paintings, turning one end of it, where her big brass four-poster bed seemed a stage now against the wall, into a representation of the little Residenz Theater in Munich, a place which had excited her to a pitch of frenzy when she had first visited it, as a young woman, over twenty-five years before. So here, on either side of the bed, she had faithfully repeated some of those tiers of boxes, exactly mimicking the carved wood and plaster in white and gold, the draped crimson curtains beneath with gold tassels, the cherubs swarming over them supporting coats-of-arms – and above the royal box a vast Imperial crown with glittering gold palm trees rising up each side. These perfect three-dimensional effects, though reduced in scale, gave the room an air of always-impending theatre, where a Mozart overture might break out at any moment.

But now, in the faint white light from the windows, with the help of a tall oil lamp, Emily sat facing away from the stage, intent on another pleasure, bent over her sketch-book – skilfully colouring a pen-and-ink drawing there, one of many in the book, the latest in a series of secret books in which, over the years, she had charted her vision of life at Summer Hill, the airs and graces, follies and foibles of its inhabitants. In this instance she had drawn the crowned figure of a Queen, elaborately wigged, processing under an ostrich-feathered canopy up one of the snowy walks outside the window – a rather dumpy, fat-legged but surprisingly confident Queen, since she was dressed only in an indecently short petticoat, followed meekly by her courtiers in their splendidly fussy eighteenth-century costume. The Queen was quite clearly Lady Cordiner, her followers other members of the Summer Hill household, family and retainers. Finishing the watercolour she entitled it 'The Empress's New Clothes' – on a swirly gilt scroll held between the mouths of the two Summer Hill terriers, Monster and Sergeant, trotting in front.

Emily had worked on the painting all day and now that it was complete her body went limp, the earlier animation left her face, the deft hands fiddled uselessly on the table. She was another person, unseeing, vague, released now from the source of her vitality. She said to herself, 'Did I wake at five o'clock this morning? – or was that yesterday evening?' She was worried by the uncertainty of this, day and night confused for her, where she seemed to be slipping out of time, no longer part of its light and dark, lost to the natural rhythms of clock and calendar, adrift without her sketchbook in a world where she had no anchors.

She heard the knock and the key moving on the outside of her door – the door to one side of her bed like a stage entrance – and turning the gilt chair round, facing the bed, she assumed the pose of a spectator in her theatre. Of course – overture and beginners, she thought, seeing the dark tail-coated man enter the room: the conductor, *The Marriage of Figaro*, her favourite.

Pat Kennedy, the young under-butler, came towards her with a tea tray, setting it down gently near her work-table, serving her early as he did most afternoons, giving Molly, her own personal maid, a rest. He smiled broadly, a friend of this thin, bird-like woman in her always-dark wool cardigans – eager-faced and happy with darting blue eyes when she was working, but who now looked up at him vacantly. He knew how, in this state, she would never complain at her incarceration, lost to the real world. But he could not understand why – when he had seen her busy and alive over her sketchbook – why she did not leave her paints and pens and ink, storm the locked door and quit the house. For in that vital mood – and he had seen the results of it, sometimes peering over her shoulder – Emily Cordiner struck him as an oasis of sanity in the great house.

Of course he knew why she was restrained here. Apart from her general vagaries she had recently, when Sir Desmond and Lady Cordiner had gone to Dublin for the Horse Show, run riot with her colours in several reception rooms at Summer Hill, starting to decorate them as she had her own bedroom: barely-clothed nymphs and shepherdesses – unsuitably bucolic murals in the dining room; then a witty trompe-l'oeil, a village band – a collection of quite obviously inebriated old men in bowlers with flutes and fiddles and crates of porter bottles – on the wall behind the Blüthner grand in the drawing room. Lady Cordiner had not been amused.

Sir Desmond Cordiner, in his dark-panelled, rather scruffy study beyond the morning room, considered the shape of the six-bladed propeller set up on a shaft attached to the wall. He turned it sharply, happy with the gust of air that penetrated his short beard, only half-listening to his farm steward speaking on the other side of the desk.

'. . . there's Cooper's wood,' Michael O'Donovan was

saying. 'And then the two fields beyond: the ten- and six-acre lots. I believe the price would be right.' O'Donovan leant forward, consulting a map of the Summer Hill estate with its bordering farms. 'The land drops on that west side of the hill – and it's damp, it's poorly at the bottom. But it could be drained. It'll go to auction certainly, but you might consider an earlier offer, sir.'

Sir Desmond half-turned. 'Yes,' he said. But his mind was elsewhere. The propeller wasn't the problem, he thought. This one, in light ash, together with one like it, would certainly give the required push. It was the engine, as always, that mattered in these heavier-than-air machines. And the petrol engine he was adapting, taken from a new Benz 3½-horsepower motor car delivered that autumn, simply wasn't reliable enough yet. His linen and wire-strutted machine, he knew – partly set up in one of the coach houses – would certainly glide with a man strapped beneath it, just as an earlier model had done, some dozens of times for up to half a minute on the slopes beneath the house. He was confident about that. He had been in touch with Otto Lilenthal in Germany on that score, using the same concave, bat-like, superimposed wings that the German had done, much more successfully over thousands of glides. But Lilenthal, in a sudden gust of wind, had been killed in his glider two years before.

'The auction is on the 17th of next month, sir. In Thomastown,' O'Donovan said. 'I'd say it'd go as high as £18 or £20 an acre.'

'Yes.' Sir Desmond nodded absent-mindedly. Of course, what one wanted – and he'd recognized this some time before – was a vertical air rudder like a boat's, where the wind would act like a flow of water against it, though only if the machine was propelled fast enough into it, since of course you couldn't tiller a boat in a calm. And besides such a rudder, which would only take you to port or starboard, there would have to be another means to manoeuvre the machine in its horizontal plane, a rudder that would push it up or down. He had foreseen that, too, and had been working on just such a scheme that afternoon, his plans lying beneath the Summer Hill estate map so that he was mildly impatient now with O'Donovan.

'Make an offer, O'Donovan – do what you think best. Be fair, of course. Be more than fair, indeed,' he added, suddenly thinking of something, looking carefully at the map this time. 'That hill the far side of Cooper's Wood,' he asked. 'It's steep enough, isn't it? And westward.'

'Yes, sir. But there's good pasture there, if it were drained.'

But Sir Desmond had quite other ideas for it: steep, with an open run from the top, westward into the prevailing winds . . . Perhaps that's what he needed, when the time came to try his new machine. Westward Ho, he thought. And a secret spot, too, away from the roads, with the cover of the wood, for there had been nosy-parkers enough, bystanders and newspaper men coming to the village recently, eavesdropping on his experiments. It would be a disaster, now that he thought himself close to success, if some rival were to pre-empt him. For more than anything else Sir Desmond, though nearly sixty, longed to be the first man in the world to soar aloft in powered flight.

In quite the second best guest bedroom, with its dark, very slightly threadbare velvet curtains, and darker wallpaper, Bunty Cordiner moped and fretted. She would not rest on the plain double bed nor read a society magazine by the low coal fire as her husband, Austin Cordiner, had suggested. Instead she paced the large room, a fidgety, over-dressed, competent little woman, fiddling with her excessive necklace, picking up ornaments from the table, dressing table and mantelpiece – gazing at them with annoyance, talking to her husband the while through the open doorway to their dressing room, where he was at work on some papers, matters concerning his own much smaller house and farm at Wellfield, sixty miles north in Queens county. These Cordiners, Sir Desmond's younger brother and his Ulster wife, had come to spend Christmas with their three children at the family seat.

'And *why* we must spend every Christmas here, I can

not understand,' Bunty said. Her husband, a taciturn man, much given to serious agricultural thought, remained silent, considering the rotation of next year's crops. 'Your sister-in-law treats me like dirt,' Bunty went on. 'The servants are haughty and the talk is either of these infernal flying machines, or grand opera. Or some quite unsuitable trek among the African heathen. Nothing else, nothing *sensible*. This evening, for example, I hear we are to be regaled by a ballad singer, no less, some saloon bar entertainer.'

Her husband demurred, speaking at last. 'Not *quite*, my dear. This Mr O'Meara is something rather more than that, I understand. Spoken very highly of in Dublin. The *Irish Times* had a very favourable critique of his RDS recital—'

'I should prefer bridge.'

'I think *not* – given Sarah's feelings about card games.'

'See! – how she chivvies you in everything, and you bow under!' Bunty was roused, coming to the dressing room door, holding a little Chelsea shepherdess in her hand.

'My dear, we are guests in her house.'

'*Her* house, indeed! It is your brother's house; and *why* are we always guests? – in the second best guest room to boot.'

'A family gathering at this season . . . is appropriate: besides being a welcome change of scene for both of us, and the children.'

'I should prefer to stay at home.'

This was untrue. Bunty disliked Lady Cordiner intensely, but envied her smooth running of the household, the grandeur of the place, the clever, wide-ranging conversations – envied here all that she did not understand, did not possess, or could not promote in her own home. Summer Hill was thus a continual affront to her lesser status, her inabilities, a permanent frustration, an itch. Yet it offered her a delicious *frisson* as well, a challenge to her social ambitions. It was a prize only just out of reach, which she dreamt about like a lover. So that to be here, living amidst its wonders, forced her to condemn the house, to sully it, since she could not possess what she wanted.

'Well, if we are not put down here,' she said aggressively, 'why do we spend afternoons lodged in our bedroom? Tell me *that*! We are all of us whip-handed by your sister-in-law,' she spat out. 'Cowering from her like beasts, hidden in our rooms – your brother, sister, nephew, niece – all of you afraid to face her – without a fire in the drawing room till teatime, so that we must lurk upstairs as if in some seaside boarding house in Bundoran.'

Her husband, removing his gold-rimmed spectacles, looked up at her at last, wary of her in this mood. 'Bunty, my dear – you are free to wander where you will. You exaggerate, you imagine. Sarah is no ogress . . .' But he let his words die, doubting their truth. Bunty glared at him pointedly, then with equal purpose dropped the little Chelsea figurine; it broke, a mass of splintered colour scattering over the floor. 'Oh, how clumsy of me,' she said, turning away, leaving the bits where they were. 'How clumsy.' Austin turned to his papers. He would like to have sighed, a very audible sigh, but he thought better of it.

Elsewhere in the house, in a distant playroom, Bunty's two sons, Neill and Robert, played snakes-and-ladders under the beady eye of their cantankerous old governess, a Miss Wildeblood from Manchester. Both boys, at twelve and thirteen, would have liked to be outside snow-balling. But that had been forbidden and they were a docile, obedient pair. Bunty's seventeen-year-old daughter Isabelle, though, was not so dutiful. She sat by the playroom window, pouting, pulling her blonde ringlets about, a secret thumb-sucker, her embroidery forgotten on her lap. She gazed out at the snow – not seeing it, seeing something else, thinking of the Honourable Harold Perkins, Coldstream Guards, her cousin Frances's young man, due off the Dublin train with the other guests in a few hours. She had met him earlier that year when he had first visited

Summer Hill and had not forgotten one single thing about him.

In his pantry, sitting in an old leather armchair, by the big silver safe beneath the tall green baize shelves with their vast collections of plate and glass, Flood, the ageing butler, stirred in his doze, woken by the sound of horses' hooves on the yard cobbles outside the window. Hennessy's van had arrived. Pat Kennedy, his deputy, was still upstairs with Miss Emily. He would have to check his part of the delivery himself, the consignment of lesser wines, and the spirits, ordered for Christmas.

Mrs Molloy, down in the basement kitchen preparing dinner, heard the van, too, stopped her supervision of the duck-trussing with the three kitchen maids and moved a kettle onto the hotplate of the big range. Mrs Martin was still with her ladyship and Maureen Molloy was pleased that she would have Mr Hennessy to herself, checking the groceries with him. Not that she objected to the house-keeper. No, she was a fair woman who did not interfere. But, like Flood, she was different, quite different. They were both Protestant: there were jokes and gossip with Pat Hennessy which she could never make or share in Mrs Martin's presence.

When she saw Snipe, however, coming into the kitchen as well, she was momentarily put out. Her own girls, and the other scullery and house maids, who would soon hear of his arrival, were always unduly excited by Snipe – as he told their fortunes in the tea-leaves, forecasting unlikely romance, putting all sorts of nonsense into their heads. Well, fair enough, she thought. They had worked like blacks all day: the half-dozen ducks were almost oven-ready, with their braise of chestnuts; the Béchamel Aurora sauce for the sole would not take a moment – the mock turtle soup had long since been prepared and the Kaiser pudding was already gently steaming on a slow plate. The girls deserved their fun.

Flood joined her then, and Snipe sat down among the tittering girls, big earthenware teapot and cups at the ready. Pat Hennessy went to and fro, up and down the steps outside, bringing the order: tea, coffee, cocoa, sugar, candied peel, dried fruit, preserved and canned provisions of all sorts, household requisites: 'Bath brick, beeswax, a dozen blacklead, six plate powder, six polishing paste, a dozen Colman's starch, two dozen carbolic soap, four quarts malt vinegar, one gross candles . . .'

Mrs Molloy ticked off the items, while Flood, more slowly, accounted for his Christmas wines and spirits: 'Two cases Tullamore whiskey, two cases scotch, one case Holland gin, one London gin, two cases sweet sherry, one pale, two Montilla, one Tarragona. One case ginger wine, one orange, two cases Seltzer, two Polly water. Six dozen Smithwick's ale. One nine-gallon stout in cask – can you manage that, Mr Hennessy?' he asked. 'Pat Kennedy will be back in a moment.' But Mr Hennessy could manage it well enough – anxious for his tea and then to be away in case the snow got worse.

Snipe's thin darting voice rose over the end of the kitchen table then, the girls already in his thrall, as he took a first empty tea-cup, inspecting the oracle of wet leaves inside. 'You,' he said, looking at Nelly, one of the parlourmaids, 'you will meet a stranger, from beyant – from over the sea: yes, I see – a dark stranger . . .' The girls were spellbound, as much by the information as by the scarred and wounded face of the young man who offered it, a face which, reflecting such grim tragedy, must have wisdom in it, they thought, and so more certainly speak the truth in these happy fortunes.

The following morning Lady Cordiner, at her desk, was looking at papers from her family brokers in London, considering financial matters. One of her investments in a Transvaal gold mine had continued to depreciate, but the letter recommended that she hold her stock pending, as her broker put it, 'a settlement with the rebellious Boers'. This was sure to come, the man had added, 'by treaty, not force'. There was nothing to worry about. Lady Cordiner was not so sure. As a Jewess, an outsider herself, she knew the destructive energy and tenacity of the dispossessed from whom, as she saw it, one had everything to fear. She knew this of her own race, of the Irish, too, and so of the distant Boers.

It was a feeling in her blood, not drawn from any first- or second-hand experience – since her own family, the Sephardic Halevys, had been successfully established in England since the Napoleonic wars. Timber, coal, diamonds, gold – the Halevys had not been usurers. Like the English gentry, with whom latterly they had sometimes merged, they had taken their money from the land. Unlike them, in the recent steep agricultural decline, the Halevys had seen their stock rise in every quarter. They were rich indeed, though not obtrusively so, living apart from the other greater Jewish clans in England, less orthodox than they, in their Spanish origins, their faith and in their muscular businesses.

Sarah's father, old Basil Halevy, with his mansion outside Leytonstone, not far from his ships and great warehouses on the Thames, had only brief doubts about her marriage over thirty years before to Desmond Cordiner, then a successful mechanical engineer – a brilliant innovator – as well as heir to the baronetcy, house and estates of Summer Hill. Basil Halevy, a Jew of liberal and expansive vision, with two elder sons to secure his own commercial titles, had thought of his daughter's happiness first – and then of other advantages in the match: here was a possible lever, a means of broaching fresh business territory in Ireland.

Besides, he had taken to the young Desmond Cordiner at once, admiring qualities in him which he had not met with in the upper reaches of the English gentry: Desmond's down-to-earth, scientific approach to affairs, yet his gifts of improvisation and lack of stuffy formality, an airy inventiveness. He liked the energy and quick wit of the man, among an Irish landed class that he had previously thought to be merely witty – and lazy. This Cordiner, he had decided years before, might well have been one of his own – one of the Magic People – and he had happily settled £100,000 on his only daughter as a dowry.

The investment, as far as his own business ambitions were concerned, had not prospered: few Irish markets were opened up to him. The Cordiners and their like had no association with, and no need of, the mining industry – coal or precious stones. They burnt their over-abundant wood, and their jewels were more precious family heir-looms. On the other hand Basil Halevy was quite happy to see how his daughter had subsequently made very solid use of her dowry, where the money had brought needed repairs and improvements, including, he thought, a most handsome new yard wing – in the recent neo-Gothic style – to Summer Hill.

On the death twenty years before of Desmond's father, the eighth Baronet, when, as Lady Cordiner, she had become mistress of Summer Hill, she had at once pro-moted this extra house room as a much-needed addition in familial space, for her own visiting relatives, and for the many other Cordiners – uncles, aunts and cousins of this extended family – who lived elsewhere in Ireland and over-seas: a strong Jewish sense of clan, she made clear, which she happily shared with the Irish – it was this which she wished to prosper in her expensive renovations and exten-sions. In fact what she wanted much more was social advantage, bricks and mortar which would underpin a rampant social ambition.

For what her father or Mrs Martin or few other people had recognized in Lady Cordiner was a vehement desire not only to be accepted by Irish society but more to be seen by them as a great hostess, opening shutters on what for her was a dark outpost of empire, where she would make Summer Hill a glittering beacon of culture and elegance – quite throwing off her mercantile background among the Wapping warehouses – creating a new dynasty of Cordiners, in the hands of her eldest son Henry, who would show the Irish how there was far more to life beyond squabbling with the Land Leaguers and arguing over Home Rule.

Sir Desmond himself had never resisted her ambitions here. He had no interest in them. For him, though he took little active part in the matter, the running of his farms and large estate was everything and the heritage he hoped to pass on to his son was one of well-maintained and endowed lands, not a taste for Schubert duets by candlelight.

His peers in the county shared identical hopes for their male progeny, though few were as likely as he to pass on so fruitful an inheritance. Sir Desmond, unlike his immediate forebears and almost entirely through his wife's money and her restless, dictatorial energy, had become a highly successful landowner. And that, besides his own aeronautical work, was all that mattered to him. His wife's rampant sociability, stamina and zealous interference in all the affairs of Summer Hill left him free to pursue his mechanical obsessions. It mattered little, whenever he had to admit it, that Lady Cordiner had come to bully and dominate him to an extent where, in the running of his own house and estate, he had become hardly more than a figurehead.

Lady Cordiner meanwhile remained entirely committed to her sophisticated hopes, and to this end now, leaving her financial papers, she turned to the guest list for the New Year's ball – climax of the seasonal festivities at Summer Hill. The Waterfords had accepted, but not the Ormondes, and the Devonshires would be away in England. She had not yet reached the top of the social pinnacle. But she would, she thought. Her will, together with her money and social flair, would eventually prevail here, as they had in every other sphere of her life. It was simply a matter of time, of maintaining an unsullied reputation and a strict selectivity in her guests, where she would so increase her social cachet that these other Dukes and Marquesses would readily exchange hospitalities with her – if not Royalty itself.

A moment later she turned suddenly, startled by a noise in the big drawing room next door – the sound of something falling: some small glass ornament, a figurine, a silver snuff box? She rose from her chair quickly, silently.

The heavily furnished drawing room, lightened only by a blaze of snowy sunshine, was deserted. There was no time to discover what might be missing or broken there, for the door at the other end was closing slowly. Someone had just left the room. But the hall, when Lady Cordiner got there, was empty, too. She glanced up at the first-floor balustrades enclosing the stair well: a shadow brushed behind them, disappearing along one of the landings running back into the house. This time the culprit would be caught red-handed, Lady Cordiner thought, picking up her skirts and running as fast as her small legs would allow up the staircase. Once in the corridor, without knocking she stormed into each of the bedrooms, occupied or not, astonishing Bunty and Austin Cordiner and receiving a dazed look from Emily, but without seeing anything suspicious. At the end was her daughter's room. Latterly, she had come to suspect Frances of these thefts. Now, as she flung the door open, impending confirmation of this filled her with a lovely bitter energy.

The pretty bedroom, with its apricot walls and frieze of primroses, was empty – apart from Marquis, Frances's red-tailed African parrot, a gift from Henry, on its perch by the window, cocking its head at her now and eyeing her impertinently. 'Three bags full, I say!' the bird croaked at her malevolently. She heard the splash of water in the dressing room beyond. Moving to the half-open doorway she saw her daughter, muddy riding clothes on a chair, naked under the portable shower, with its round tank on top supported by three mock bamboo metal poles. Frances's young maid, Eileen, half-way up a step-ladder, was pouring warm water into the tank from several brass cans, where the flow cascaded down through the small holes, straightening and plastering Frances's curls against her head, running off her breasts. Eileen stopped. Frances half-turned, quite unabashed, looking at her mother.

'Yes, Mama – what is it?'

The parrot squeaked from the other room – 'Water

biscuits! Water biscuits!' – infuriating Lady Cordiner, so that for answer she turned back into the bedroom and started to ransack the place, stripping the bed, lifting the mattress, peering under it, then pulling drawers out, curtains aside, spilling clothes from a great mahogany wardrobe, tossing and pawing at everything in the room like a bull in a china shop, while the parrot, flapping about on its perch, became equally roused, adding to the furore. 'Nuts! Nuts!' the bird screamed.

Frances came into the room, a towelled figure, curls dripping, her damp face radiant. 'Mama, what *is* it?'

Her mother threw a mauve feather boa on the floor. 'I know it's you,' she shouted. 'You thief!' – and she strode past her into the dressing room.

'Me *what*?' Frances called back to her, picking up the feather boa, putting it on, and doing a little strutting dance, so that Eileen, emerging from the dressing room, could not suppress a giggle.

'It's you!' Lady Cordiner shouted, running amok in the dressing room. 'You who have been taking all these little objects.' Frances and Eileen exchanged looks. Eileen was clearly frightened. But Frances simply smiled at her, putting a finger to her lips. Finding nothing among her daughter's toiletries, Lady Cordiner returned to the bedroom.

'Mama, you are unhinged,' Frances told her, while the parrot shrieked 'Nuts! Nuts!', seeming to add insult to injury, so that Lady Cordiner, goaded beyond endurance, unwisely made for the bird, attempting to sweep it off its perch, perhaps even to strangle it. But the bird pecked her sharply on the wrist, drawing blood, and that was an end of it. Lady Cordiner retreated.

'Be warned, this is *not* the end of it,' she said, confronting her daughter, trying to rescue some dignity in the matter, while staunching her wound.

'No, Mama, indeed not. I think you should lie down. And perhaps I should call Dr Mitchell?'

When Lady Cordiner had gone the two women went back into the dressing room – the petite, rather plump and dimple-cheeked Eileen, normally calm and collected, considerably flustered now. 'Miss, I can't go on with it,' she said. 'She nearly caught me then, downstairs.'

'Nonsense, Eileen.' Frances took her by the shoulders and gazed at her intently, smiling. 'It's my turn next, in any case. And if you like we'll drop it all for Christmas.'

'Yes, Miss.'

'Please don't call me Miss. I told you – I'm Frances.'

'It's dangerous, though – I'd never work again, *any*-where, if she caught me.'

'You will *always* work with me, Eileen, wherever I am.' Frances successfully consoled the girl, looking at her so openly and confidently that Eileen's fears subsided. This sort of persuasion was one of Frances's great gifts – an intimate, illicit thing which she could bring to bear against any resistance: a candour of regard which allowed Eileen to feel completely her equal, where at the same time Frances had made it clear to her that what she was offering was something the girl had never dreamt of, a partnership in some vastly exciting adventure. For it was not a simple, flirtatious, one-sided guile, this. Frances always in the end shared in what she willed, made people helpless accomplices in her desires. Like an unsprung trap her mischievous gaze seduced them before they knew it.

As she climbed the step-ladder now, her hair still dripped and glistened – water skating down over the oils of her skin, hesitating on the sudden slopes, finding diversions round her small conical breasts with their retroussé nipples, tickling the dark areolae there, trickling over her long midriff before swamping the towel at her waist and seeping down her creamy flanks.

Opening a brass water can she picked out the one prize she had for so long coveted in the house and finally gained – a lovely Baccarat snow dome, a paperweight, with an ivory model of Summer Hill, caught for ever in the drifting flakes inside.

She dried the crystal with the hem of her towel, the cloth slipping from her waist – so that, naked now, she held the snow dome up before her like a chalice, the Holy Grail, the secret essence of the house which, in default of possessing the real thing, she would take to now like an adulterous lover.

Then she showed the crystal to Eileen, holding it out, a great victory. Finally she put it away in the empty water tank on top of the shower, among her store of other hidden booty – glass overlay snuff bottles, enamelled colour twist wine glasses, silver snuff boxes, glazed porcelain figurines.

Eileen looked up at her. What's it all for? she wanted to ask – these useless bits and pieces, for a lady who had everything? Eileen did not understand but she marvelled at the cheek of it all. Being with Miss Frances was more exciting than listening to Snipe down in the kitchen: Snipe with his always-hopeful fortunes which for her, at least, had never come true.

But downstairs that previous afternoon, in a last throw of tea-leaves, Snipe had seen an unfavourable pattern. He had not said anything. The girl whose cup it was had looked at him nervously. 'No,' he'd said at last. ''Tis not for you, for there's no spread in it. You see,' he went on, showing her the little compacted hillock inside the cup. 'The leaves – they never moved at all.'

'Glory be! I have no fortune then!' the girl moaned.

'No, 'tis not that.' Snipe looked doubtfully about him, then up at the ceiling. ''Tis the fortune out of the house itself, that won't move the leaves, d'ye see? The air in the place.'

Mr Hennessy had called Snipe away then, when he had put his few pennies in his pocket, and the two of them had gone out into the snow, which had eased a little, a soft crunchy carpet over the yard, where Snipe looked back curiously at the great house in the white dusk, the holes in his face where his nose had been twitching sensitively, trying to sniff something in the air, an omen of some sort which he could not interpret at all.

2

'Down, Sergeant! Down, Monster! – down!' Sir Desmond roared at the Jack Russell terriers, leaping through the snow like tiny deer towards the guests, barking furiously, jumping waist high at Eustace, remembering him. As he picked them up, they promptly started a dog fight from beneath each arm.

Two flaming braziers on the porch steps illuminated the scene. The snow had returned with the night, coming thinly out of the darkness, falling into the circles of yellow light as Molloy with the other footmen attended to the luggage wagonette while the household waited to greet the new arrivals from the carriage – Mr O'Meara, the young opera singer, fur-collared, handsome and rather pleased with himself, clasping a small music case; the stoutish, owl-faced Eustace Cordiner and his aristocratic army friend, the Honourable Harold Perkins with the effervescent, well-bearded Mortimer Cordiner, Queen's Counsel and Member of Parliament – Dermot's father – bringing up the rear.

Behind the carriage, from two more hackney traps which had just drawn up, further and obviously unexpected guests were now emerging, small uncertain shapes congregating outside the splashes of light, being marshalled by a tall figure in a very long overcoat. Lady Cordiner gazed anxiously into the night before a stentorian voice made her gasp a fraction.

'God bless all here!' She heard the mock Irish brogue in the darkness, before an elegantly middle-aged man in an astrakhan greatcoat and hat, brandishing a silver-topped cane, strode into the light, followed by a group of strangers, five shawled and shivering young women and a young man.

Eustace turned towards Lady Cordiner. 'A surprise for you, Mama – they were all on the train from Kingsbridge.

It's Humphrey, with a troupe of Spanish dancers, can you imagine!'

A boisterous figure approached his mother, arms out-stretched, cane in one hand, doffing his astrakhan hat with the other. He enveloped Lady Cordiner in a theatrical bear hug, did the same for Frances, then pumped Sir Desmond's hand, while Bunty Cordiner looked on askance.

'But, Humphrey,' Sir Desmond said, 'we thought you weren't due down here till after Christmas. Our *Colleen Bawn* date at the Kilkenny theatre is still on the 29th, isn't it?'

'My dear fellow, with what I've brought now, I simply couldn't wait – knew you'd want to see them first, Rodrigo and his five girls, something quite sensational: flamenco dancers – ever heard of it? Found them out of an engage-ment in Dublin – absolutely first rate! A rat-a-tat-tat dance to a throbbing guitar – make your blood boil, old man. Saw them at the Olympia last week, brought them down for the date in Kilkenny. But I was sure you'd want to see them sooner. Put a show on here for you – here, on the steps, why not? – tomorrow morning—'

'But, Humphrey, where are they all to stay?' Lady Cordiner interjected.

'Oh, anywhere, Sarah.' And he looked at her, a knowing smile on his weather-stained face, where the snow was melting on heavy eyebrows, running past candid, roving eyes, down whiskery cheeks to a pointed chin. 'These are real Spanish gypsies – stables would probably do, long as they're well fed and watered.' He laughed, a deep belly chuckle, quite at odds with his thin frame, over which the folds of his enormous greatcoat flapped like sails in the chill air. 'In fact, I shall want the best bedrooms for them: your *own* people Sarah, you must remember, from Andalu-cia – nothing but the best!'

'Really, Humphrey.' Lady Cordiner, taking his point, none the less continued to remonstrate with the gaunt, gay figure, the rich and eccentric Englishman, Humphrey Saunders – amorist, actor, traveller, poet, pamphleteer, practical joker, Irish nationalist and wayward friend for many years: one of the very few people, even though he had loved her once, whom she had never managed to dominate.

'They will have to share quarters in the back wing. But you should have warned us, Humphrey.'

'My dear – surprise! The essence of life, is it not?' He flourished his hands, then warmed them quickly by the brazier, before introducing the troupe, beckoning each to the fire in turn. 'Maria, Concepta, Carmen, Consuela . . .'

The girls, darkly shawled, gave minute rigid curtsies – unsmiling, uncertain but proud, the flickering light showing their cold beauty now, the black eyes motionless, set in the cowled white faces, giving them the air of nuns, untouchable, brides only of a passionate spirit.

Rodrigo, small, with foxy good looks, in his twenties, but with the ease and air of a much older man, took off a wide-brimmed flat hat and bowed slightly, his darkly brilliantined hair, parted straight down the middle, glistening in the light.

'We are . . . honoured,' he said, slowly, with a heavy accent, opening his arms a fraction to include the girls, looking at Humphrey first, then at Lady Cordiner, whose hand he took, brushing his lips above it for an instant. But that was all he said, looking round at the assembled company without a trace of emotion, without pleasure or doubt in the meeting – simply an acceptance of it as something entirely natural and expected.

Frances, forsaking her small talk with Eustace and Harold, stared at the young Spaniard; Henry looked at him – everyone gazed at him in the sudden silence, as if trapped and warmed by his coldness, waiting for a further explanation or greeting. But he gave none, clearly implying that his very presence there said everything that needed to be said, that he ordered things without words. And indeed it seemed at his unspoken command, when he turned away to see to the girls' baggage, that everyone moved indoors.

'And what do you think of *that*?' Bunty Cordiner spoke to her husband later as they dressed for dinner. 'A band of

Spanish gypsies, I ask you! Led by that cheeky ruffian – we shall have our throats cut in our beds, I tell you. And as to those *women* in the house with us, proposing some indecent dance – women of the easiest virtue, I'll be bound – you can hardly think them suitable company, at *any* season – let alone Christmas. It's preposterous! Your sister-in-law is turning the house into a common music hall.'

Her husband rubbed his glasses. He had rather liked what he had seen of the women on the porch steps, but did not care to admit it. 'My dear, you exaggerate. They are merely dancers and musicians of some sort. Sarah is a cultured woman – and of Spanish extraction herself, you must remember, an old and distinguished family there. She will know what she's doing. Besides, it was not her idea – the guests were forced upon her.'

'Yes – by that horror of a man, Saunders: that unprincipled nationalist busybody who so viciously attacked poor Lord Kingston in the *Pall Mall Gazette*, taking sides against his own class, supporting Kingston's blackguardly tenants. I can hardly believe that I must sit at table with him.'

'I believe it was the matter of Kingston's over-zealous evictions in his Rosscommon estates which Mr Saunders complained of there. And he may well have had a point. It does no good to exacerbate the peasantry in that manner – no good at all in the present political climate, where we may see an end to strife in Ireland – with appropriate legislation.'

Bunty knew what he referred to – the distinct likelihood of Home Rule in the new century. 'There can be no "appropriate legislation" which takes control of the country out of the hands of us Unionists,' she proclaimed roundly.

'Yes, dear – a topic you might care to raise with my cousin Mortimer, just back from Westminster. He has a great deal to say on that issue.'

Austin was happy to pass responsibility on to Mortimer in this matter. Mortimer was an astute and vociferous Home Rule MP in the House, as Austin's own wife was an equally vehement, if not so sensible, opponent. He himself preferred not to take sides, though on balance he secretly favoured the Irish Home Rulers at Westminster if only because, loving the land, he despised the absentee landlordism which Unionism encouraged.

'That renegade Mortimer!' Bunty snorted. 'Another fouling his own nest. I can hardly be civil to him. I cannot imagine a more uncongenial house party – gypsies, ballad singers, poetasters, traitorous politicians. Really, Austin, it's too much . . .'

'He *was* rather handsome . . .' Frances, in petticoats, looking into the mirror, spoke to Eileen who was combing her hair. 'He plays the guitar.'

'A sort of fiddle?'

'Yes. But you play it with your fingers. Perhaps you'll see it tomorrow – I encouraged Mr Saunders in the idea.'

'And your young man, Miss Frances? – the other one, the fair-haired young man, with that . . . that sly look! Isn't he gorgeous.'

'Yes, Harold. I hadn't thought of him as sly—'

'Oh, I didn't mean sly in a bad way.'

'No, I know what you mean.' But Frances did not quite know. She rose and Eileen helped her into her dress, a long light blue silk skirt with a low bodice trimmed in narrow white lace, a broad, royal blue belt at the middle.

Her eyes sparkled in the lamplight as she flounced her soft curls, adjusted the blue amethyst pendant round her neck, before turning in profile to the mirror, judging the effect. Sly, Frances thought – in a *good* way? Was that possible? She had seen that sometimes supercilious look in Harold's eyes as something commanding and mature rather than sly – a natural attribute of such a man, Lord Norton's eldest son from Oxfordshire, whom her mother hoped she would marry, one of the very few wishes she shared with her. Now the slightest touch of uncertainty crossed her mind in the idea.

*

Lady Cordiner dressed with more speed than usual, chivvying her maid as she placed the cloth pads on her scalp, before back-combing, building her hair over them into an elaborate hillock. She was impatient to be downstairs with Mrs Martin, to see the Spanish contingent suitably cared for – by being made invisible. It was too bad of Humphrey, but impossible now to do anything about it. They would have to share rooms in the back wing and eat in Mrs Martin's pantry, no question of having them at table. Tomorrow, after their performance, she would send them on their way, no matter what Humphrey said: the Commercial Hotel in Thomastown or the Club House in Kilkenny could look after them.

Yet there were advantages to be derived from their arrival, she thought. Humphrey, like her, never made cause with the second-rate in culture. The flamenco dancing was likely to be good, another feather in her cap, fresh evidence of her wide and sophisticated tastes. Besides, the whole thing, she knew, would infuriate Bunty Cordiner.

After the ladies had departed, the men took port after dinner, passing the decanter round the evergreen decorations, picking nuts and dried fruit from the delicately latticed baskets that hung from two silver George III epergnes, set in beds of moss and maidenhair fern towards either end of the long table. It had been a tactful dinner with the ladies, Bunty being placed at some remove from both Humphrey and Mortimer Cordiner. But now Mortimer, the port flaming his usual energy and nervous attack, speared the air with his fingers, holding court, altogether the skilled and passionate advocate, whereas the other men rather held their tongues.

'You see it's *land* in Ireland – and the good management of it – which is what really counts. Land is the only gold here. But it's badly used and farmed, without profit, where what little of that there is is simply taken as rent from the hapless tenantry and used to finance a spendthrift, absentee class. For our *own* good, you see, one cannot properly have our vital interests controlled from London. We must have the yea and nay ourselves – must *live* here too – if we are to survive as a class.'

Humphrey Saunders bristled at this word 'class'. 'But it's the rack-rented tenants, along with the rest of the impoverished native Irish who must rather survive, Mortimer – not people like you and Desmond, who do very well, if I may say so.' Humphrey took a large Havana, inspected it pointedly, then returned it to its cedar box.

'*Survive?*' asked Sir Desmond in considerable surprise. 'I was quite unaware it had come to that pass for us – or the tenantry either for that matter, especially with all these new land acts where they'll be able to buy their holdings outright. And there's a point – no government in Dublin would have the money, the financial reserves, to underwrite such land loans as Westminster is planning to do.'

'With Home Rule all sorts of additional funds would be available *within* the country, Desmond – not leaked out straight away to absentee landlords and the Treasury in London. There are a hundred and one inevitable financial and other advantages for *everyone* in Home Rule. But there will be no advantage until we control our own destinies here, free of Whitehall's dictation. We are Irish after all, not English.'

'I grant you that,' Sir Desmond said. 'But it's unlikely that we should remain in control under Home Rule. The butchers, bakers and candlestickmakers would soon be in the saddle then.'

'Well, that would be entirely our fault, Desmond – as it precisely is already, that we have abdicated our responsibilities. And unless we rapidly change our ways it will be our end—'

'Abdicated?'

'Oh, perhaps not you, nor you, Austin. Responsible landowners, no doubt. But the majority of the others have long since done so.' Mortimer looked round the company. This was complete news to them. 'And you do not see it?' Mortimer went on, shaking his head. 'That these latter generations here – the Arrans, Kingstons, Clanricardes, people like King-Harman – where they have not been cruel and selfish, have been quite indifferent, irresponsible over their heritage: fecklessly indifferent – and they will lose it, let it slip from their hands before they know it. Indeed it's these very people, fighting blindly to maintain the Union now, who, through their lazy short sight will make Home Rule inevitable – and, more than that, violent as well as likely as not, a revolution among the butchers and bakers, Desmond, which won't be at all to your taste or mine. Unless we all change our ways our class in Ireland is doomed – finished – a decade or so hence. Mark my words.'

'Agreed entirely,' Humphrey said. 'Only wish it had happened sooner,' he added with smiling malice.

Sir Desmond looked round the great room hung with its rows of solid Cordiner family portraits – rather as Snipe had looked at the house a few days before, doubting something he could not identify, dissolution hidden in the old walls, decay in the rich smell of vintage port and fine cigars, an apocalyptic genie that might rise from the lovely Waterford decanters. But it was not difficult, given reassurance by his ancestors' commanding faces and surrounded by these vigorous, talented men who were his living progeny, relatives and friends, to put all doubts from his mind.

'You exaggerate, Mortimer,' he said easily. 'As you must do, playing to an audience of Fenians and Land Leaguers whose votes you require. But we are not that audience – and so not to be swayed by your cries of "Wolf".'

'My audience *is* the wolf, Desmond, make no mistake. I see it clearly every day, roaming the country, a hungry beast . . .'

There was a moment's awkward silence before Sir Desmond suggested they join the ladies.

But all in Summer Hill, present and future, seemed even more well founded and secure when afterwards they listened to the young tenor, Mr O'Meara, accompanied on the Blüthner by Humphrey, Renaissance man, casually gifted in so many things.

Mr O'Meara's voice, perfectly modulated, floated over the room – a sentimental Thomas Moore ballad which moved his audience for quite another reason, where the sentiment was made believable by the singer's great artistry and control, the over-sweet romance of the words transformed into a pure emotion, almost icy, by the classic voice.

'There is not in the wide world a valley so sweet,
    As that vale in whose bosom the bright waters meet.
Oh! the last rays of feeling and life must depart,
    Ere the bloom of that valley shall fade from my heart.'

Lady Cordiner, with a genuine love and appreciation of music, was moved as much as pleased, glancing at Henry, then at Eustace: Eustace, her chubby, owl-faced son – one might have liked a leaner mien there – doing so well with his regiment in Aldershot. His friend Harold, too – they were both fine men. What a future there was there, she felt, before she remembered that the future of Summer Hill, at least, lay in her eldest son Henry's hands. Of course, it was his ridiculously extended travels to all the wrong places, among savages and infidels instead of Society in London or Baden-Baden, that made him unavailable, kept him away from a suitable wife. But he must know of his responsibilities as eldest son, would accept them eventually, even if only in a marriage of convenience. With Frances on the other hand – well, she would soon be off her hands. Harold was suitable in every way – quite apart from the fact that they seemed in love as well. She looked at her daughter then, sitting on a little gilded chair beside and a little ahead of Harold, watching how he gazed tenderly at her now and then, lost to the song, or perhaps inspired by it.

'Tell me the witching tale again,
    For never has my heart or ear,
Hung on so sweet, so pure a strain,
    So pure to feel, so sweet to hear . . .'

*

Yes, Frances and Harold would be all right, she thought, Eustace, too – even Henry. There was nothing, indeed, in Summer Hill which, through her own efforts and skills, would not be absolutely fine in the end.

Outside in the hall, Pat Kennedy, making last rounds to see that the shutters and outside doors were secure, stopped a moment by the drawing room door, sunk in race memories, before he pulled himself together and moved towards the back of the house. A camp bed had been put up for him in the butler's pantry, where he slept – as guard for the big safe, which he unlocked now, carefully putting the more valuable silver plate and cutlery away. Flood had retired to bed earlier. The little room was his for the night, warm with the embers of a coal fire in the small grate. He was sorry he had to go out later, a cold tramp through the snow down the drive to the nearest of the estate cottages on the brow of the hill, where he had a meeting. He pulled back the blanket and sheet on the camp bed until the thin mattress was exposed. Then, putting his hand into the side where he had cut the seam, he drew out the RIC Webley revolver, checked it, before hiding it again behind his trouser belt.

Later only Eileen saw him leave the house, a shadowy figure against the snow stealing through the yard, as she watched him from her bedroom window in the servants' quarters. What risks he took, she thought. But then they both did.

The snow had finally moved away in the night, bringing a morning of brilliant blue sky and sun, almost hot, which soaked down on the landscape – an enchantment of pearly folds and meringue twists, a crisp glitter on the garden terraces, nursery slopes pushed up against the windbreak of low hedges, creamy glaciers running down the lawn to the valley where the trees were canopied in powdery foam. It was a day so unexpected in an Irish winter – buoyant, tingling, where land and sky made one vast empty canvas. There seemed no end of things in the air.

'Ah! Where are the pranksters then?' Mortimer said,

the company assembled around the breakfast table. He looked at Henry and Dermot, then at Harold and Eustace. It was probably the latter two, he thought, as revenge for his home truths the previous night after dinner. 'The most painfully judged apple pie bed last night indeed! I nearly broke my toes.' He looked firmly at Harold and Eustace who made a poor job of promoting their innocence in the matter.

'Come, Papa – the Christmas spirit!' Dermot, gently ironic, consoled his father – as he did when this could be done quite unobtrusively: an apple pie bed was a poor substitute for a wife, his mother Matilda, who had died two years before, with his younger and much-loved sister Molly, both drowned in a boating accident on the Liffey, above Islandbridge, near Dublin, where they lived. He would have liked to have snubbed Eustace and Harold in some way for their childish jape. He – and Henry, too, he knew – found them both tiresomely juvenile. But it was not the moment.

Humphrey was about to produce his flamenco dancers and, with his unfailing sense of the theatrical, he had arranged the show outdoors on the flagstoned porch, warmed on either side by the two braziers again; and now the household, in fur capes, hats and mufflers, sat with their backs to the hall door and windows – the stage set in front between the great pillars, against a backdrop of intense white and blue, sky and land sparkling like warm enamel, seeming to vibrate in the crystal air.

Rodrigo, without his hat, but with a cape, polka dot shirt and high riding boots, took a stool with his guitar to one side, playing a guarded, tremulous introduction, which gradually rose in sound and pace – until suddenly, on a stamped signal, the five girls, arms high, came in a streaming dancing line through the hall door and out on to the flagstones.

The effect of this sinuous, vigorous arrival, with the increased volume of music and the quick stutter of high heels on the flagstones, quite startled the audience, so that their heads drew back as if from fire – the girls in a weaving semi-circle, closing in around the spectators now, seeming to threaten them in their long bell-shaped skirts, which they picked up, flicking them arrogantly close to their faces as the music gathered tempo. Rodrigo nursed the guitar, bending to and fro over the strings – challenging, stroking, bullying, seducing the instrument as he drew a mounting run of chords from it, only to stop them all suddenly, with the flat of his hand, when the girls a moment later embarked on another, more startling, viciously staccato rhythm with their feet. Dressed in red and black cotton print skirts with tight-laced bodices, they arched their heads back, arms raised, palms facing down, fingers moving intricately, starting to snap them, punctuating the frenzied pace, forming patterns together, then breaking them, advancing on the audience, dark furies against the gleaming snow.

The girls were flagrant and yet indifferent. Their elegant sensuality was quite cold, almost with hatred in it. And when they started to sing, in vicious whiplash voices, the tone, the song, was full of longing and enmity. They revelled in their contradictions. For the audience, as they swirled against the dazzle, they were an insult, a predatory race apart. Most were trapped by their overwhelming physical spell, rabbits facing stoats. But a few others were enchanted, drawn to them, moths to candle flames. And Frances was one of these. She felt their scintillating vigour, passing in the keen air, brushing her face, stirring her blood, bringing a delicious tremble to her whole body. She wanted to emulate them, join the sensuous dance. Their passion – so great but so tantalizingly withheld – provoked her towards some unknown fulfilment of her own. In the rising, maddening rhythms she craved some release, through them, which they achieved in their thrilling finales, but which she did not. She sat there, vastly excited, frustrated. Then she found herself staring at Rodrigo – the fountain head, she realized then, of her excitement. And though, in his surly humour, he had barely glanced at the audience, suddenly he looked up, staring at her in return, with just the ghost of a smile.

Lady Cordiner was alternately rabbit and moth – stirred by it all, then appalled. For her, too, in this music, there was a race memory here which quickened her blood. But a latter world of inhibition and propriety stifled her natural impulses. What would the servants think? She was certain they were there, hidden behind the windows, gazing out. Still, she could hardly make a scene over it. And so, as in all things which she espoused, where she had taken action, she did not retrench, but went forward, undeterred by any qualms – showing all the more appreciation of the dance, the dancers whom, whatever their suitability in polite society, she recognized as being first-rate. Humphrey had not let her down.

'Splendid,' she said as an aside to her husband. 'Really splendid.' Sir Desmond barely agreed. It was not his cup of tea; few of his wife's cultural enthusiasms were. He found this particular business strident and lacking humour. But he was interested in the guitar strings. He would ask the surly Spaniard about them. Drawn from Toledo steel? A stronger, finer wire perhaps for the struts and controls of his flying machine?

Emily, in a high-backed cane chair, with pencil and sketch-book, attempted to catch the wild swing of the dancers, thrilled by the swirling movements, the vivid contrast of their dark dresses against the shining backdrop of snow and sky beyond. The air, icy, but shot through with wafts of heat from the braziers, was electrifying. Indeed, when Lady Cordiner rose, after the applause at the end, this combination of heat, cold and excitement proved too much for her. She swayed dangerously on her feet for a moment, before tumbling back into her chair, overcome, in a half-faint. A mild furore ensued, the dancers forgotten, as she was finally helped indoors to a drawing room sofa. Smelling salts and brandy were offered, but refused.

'It's nothing,' she said. 'Don't fuss. The dancing seemed to take me, quite dizzy-making, splendid.' She was pleased thus to make a profit out of her little turn, blaming it on an aesthetic, not a physical, weakness. When the others had left, Humphrey talked to her, drawing a chair up to the end of the sofa.

'Ah, my dear Sarah – I knew it would take you: a true *aficionada*. In Spain last summer, down in the south, I lived with some of these gypsies . . .'

'*Lived* with them?'

'Oh yes – quite wonderful! Wished you could have been down there with me. Too stuck here, you know, Sarah, shut away in this Irish backwater. Such a lot to offer, and not appreciated here.'

He looked at her earnestly – and she returned the look fondly, all the possibilities of another life, which she might have had with him, coming back to her.

'Yes, that would have been nice,' she said, avoiding the issue of her long parochialism, but remembering the woman she had been with him more than thirty years before, a softer, more pliant creature, no doubt. 'But you could hardly expect me to live in some tent!'

'In *caves*, my dear. They live in caves in the rock, not tents. Come back with me to Spain, and see it all again . . .'

'Caves?' She shuddered a fraction. 'Humphrey dear, I think a little brandy *would* do me good.'

The memory of the dance, of Rodrigo and the girls, kept intruding on Frances's thoughts throughout lunch. She longed to get closer to them in some way, talk to them, learn more about it. Humphrey would have given her detailed information, she knew. But she wanted some first-hand explanation of why she had been so intrigued and disturbed that morning on the porch. And it was urgent – the dancers were to be sent off later that afternoon on the train to the Club House in Kilkenny. The men meanwhile were proposing a rough shoot after lunch, which would leave her free – free of Harold, who was likely at any moment to press his suit. She was sure he was going to propose to her at the first suitable opportunity. And there was another urgency – she wanted to be able to say yes, but did not feel any true enthusiasm for the idea now. She must find the right frame of mind before he asked her, a more settled demeanour which she knew she did not possess: there was some itch to be satisfied before she found that.

It was quite simple, of course: she would go to the girls' rooms after lunch – no matter that they did not speak each other's languages. Sign, gesture, smile – these would be sufficient communication to assuage her curiosity.

An hour later, when the men had gone out and the house was quiet, she made her way to the back wing, knocking on one of the bedroom doors where Eileen had told her the girls were quartered. There was silence – until the door suddenly opened and Rodrigo was there.

'Oh, I am sorry – wrong room! I wanted to see the girls before they went. I was so interested – in the dance . . .'

So surprised was she, that she retained the inviting smile she had prepared for the girls, staring at the man, almost mesmerized. He stood there calmly – barefoot, half-dressed, a big carpet bag stuffed with black satin capes and frilly shirts open on the floor behind him.

'Come on in.' The familiar tone was not at all Spanish, clearly English – and common at that. 'Thought you might come round . . .' He held his arm out, gesturing her inside.

'But –?' Frances, in her greater astonishment at this deception, was barely aware of crossing the threshold. The man closed the door behind her, his every movement swift and decisive, as if, indeed, he had been expecting her. He leant against the door then, staring at her in return, a wise smile lighting up his dark features.

'But I thought you were Spanish!'

'Oh, I am. My mother was at least. I've never been to the place. Come from London. Cockney born and bred. Sound of Bow Bells.' He kept his voice at the same even, ironic level, almost *sotto voce*, and his eyes never left hers – arrogant, inviting, dismissive all in the same hard glance, like an animal trifling with its prey. 'But what was it in the dance that you were so interested in?' he asked intently, without irony, his lips continuing to move after he had spoken, as if he was whispering something to her then, offering some urgent, delicate, thrilling invitation.

The room was hot and oppressive, filled with a smell of brilliantine. Frances's head began to swim as the man approached her. She felt dizzy – trapped by his steely regard, which never left her, a beam of piercing light which she was enthralled by, could not escape from. She stared at the great cleft in his frilly shirt, open almost to his waist. She could not take her eyes off the shapes and colours there, the dark curly hillocks of his chest, the sloping snowy midriff. Eventually she cast her eyes down, only to be confronted by his perfect, alabaster-smooth bare legs and feet.

She backed away, stumbling against the bed, nearly falling before he caught her adroitly in his arms, half-pulling her up to him, holding her there, spellbound. And in those long seconds, winded, almost overcome, she felt she had stopped breathing, as she watched his long delicate fingers rise towards her neck, disappearing over the far side and down her back, deftly undoing the buttons there, as he pulled her to him then, gripping her fiercely with his other arm before kissing her neck, opening the dress now, bearing her down on the bed.

She half-struggled, trying vainly for some leverage against him as he lay on top of her. But for some reason she did not scream. This entirely confirmed the man's initial expectations of her, so that he redoubled his advances, tearing at her collar, pulling the dress right down about her shoulders now, so that her arms were pinned to her sides and her small breasts lay half-exposed beneath her camisole top. With both hands engaged he kissed the nipples through the silk, before taking the material in his teeth and tearing it down, displaying the erect shapes, taking one of them in his lips, while with his other hand, moving it quickly up between her legs, he grasped her sex, his fingers rising into her like a warm knife.

And then she screamed, struggling viciously, clawing,

scratching at him. Surprised now, he desisted, rising, letting her free. She stood up, red-faced, gulping air, breathlessly furious.

'You – you filthy brute!' She pulled her dress back up, settling herself. 'I'll have you out of here in two seconds!' She made for the door.

'Will you?' he asked, entirely calm, the dark thin smile still there. 'Don't forget, Miss, it was *you* who came to me. And I'll tell them that. What were you doing in *my* bedroom? – they'll wonder, won't they?' She tried to slap his face, but he held her arm easily. 'I wouldn't tell them if I were you – you little flirt. You really liked it all – before you started yelling!' He laughed as Frances rushed from the room.

She stood outside the door for a moment, chest thumping. She was shocked, horrified by his behaviour – felt dirty, defiled. Of course she would tell, there and then. With her dress torn, there would be obvious proof of his assault. She ran down the corridor, through the great interconnecting oak door, back into the main house.

But then she paused. What *had* she been doing in his room? Harold, inevitably, coming to know about it, would ask just the same question. The whole thing could only result in yet more embarrassment. She went to her room instead, stripping off her clothes and sponging herself all over by the wash basin. Flirting? Had she been doing that? Of course not! – she had simply gone to see the girls, she reminded herself.

'Flirting?' she said out loud. 'No, never!'

But the thrill, renewed now in her mind, and in her body, was undeniable. Standing stock still by the mirror and looking at herself, she started to tremble – at the rashness of her behaviour and its pleasure. She smiled then. She had, at least, an answer now to her curiosity about the dance, the dancers, about Rodrigo, too. Her itch was satisfied. Or was it? Had it only just begun? Frustrated once more, she decided, as a distraction, to visit Aunt Emily.

'Aunt Emily? It's me.' She knocked on the door, before turning the key.

Emily was half-way through a detailed sketch – not of the dancers but of their audience – when Frances came into her bedroom. Emily did not look up, completely absorbed in her work, while Frances stood behind her.

'Why not the dancers, Aunt?'

'Couldn't catch them, you see,' Emily spoke, still bent over the sketchbook. 'And, anyway, I wasn't really interested. Don't know them. Have to *know* the people in my drawings, you see.'

Frances saw how well her aunt knew the people in this instance – her usually uncomplimentary interpretations given a further twist here in that, while featuring their clearly recognizable faces, she had dressed all the household in Spanish costume. So Bunty, with an outraged Presbyterian face, had become the flagrant seductress, a gypsy Carmen in a flounced skirt, and her mother something of an Andalucian crone in a lace mantilla. Harold, she saw, in a stiff gold-braided military tunic, was transformed, lugubrious and long-faced, into a pompous Spanish grandee.

'Aunt! Is Harold really like that?'

'Oh yes.'

Frances, with her aunt, had a fruitful relationship in that Emily spoke to her, at least, as she did to few if any other members of the household. She recognized the cutting honesty and reality in this quite unreal woman. And in return Emily allowed her, alone among the family, access to her bedroom, her drawings, and her startling confidences whenever she wished.

'Should I not marry him then?' she asked. 'Is he pompous as well as sly?'

'Sly? I didn't know it. But quite possibly. Shall I make him sly as well?'

'Oh, Aunt – don't joke. You know what I mean. Trouble is, how can one tell what a man is really like until one lives with him—'

'Excuse yourself, girl!' Emily interrupted with a start of

54

her head, the slight brogue in her voice more noticeable now. '*Living* with men – the very idea! – an impossibility in any case. Don't even consider it. They are all far gone, entirely far gone.'

'In what?'

'In imbecility. *Tout court.*' Emily began to transform Isabelle, with her blonde ringlets, into a spoilt and pouting Infanta.

'What should I do then?'

'Take to your heels, girl. There's a place in London I used to stay at. Or was it Paris? Respectable accommodation and near some quite decent shops, too. Hotel Crillon, was it? Near our Legation, so it must have been Paris. Go there. The manager was less offensive than they usually are. You'll find it quite to your taste.'

'Yes, Aunt. It's an idea—'

'Excuse yourself again, girl – it's the *only* idea. Won't even need spending money either – found them all very accommodating on that score.'

'Yes, Aunt.' Frances knew, indeed, how accommodating so many tradespeople and hotel managers had been towards her aunt over the years – knew something of her earlier peregrinations about Ireland and further afield, to places like the Hotel Crillon and the shops in the Faubourg St Honoré, where lavish bills had been run up, which her father's solicitor in Dublin had forever to chase and settle, in person often, since he usually had to escort the spendthrift miscreant home as well, so that in the end doors were locked on her in Summer Hill.

Then, looking over her aunt's shoulder, she saw how, in her own case, Emily had dressed her in virgin white – a frou-frou, many-flounced Spanish bridal dress, her face a study in provocative devilry.

'And who am I supposed to be?'

'Carmen. One of the better operas. She came to a bad end. But they always do in operas, don't they? Have to, wouldn't be much point otherwise.'

Frances returned to her room, slightly chastened by this idea of a bad end. She took out her diary, a secret album *consolatum*, hidden in her dressing table: a locked leather-bound book with a sprig of gilt shamrock embossed on the cover. Opening it, she looked at the last entry: 'I intend *not* to be a good and useful person.' Taking a pencil she crossed out the word 'not' – then, after reflection, wrote it in again. Then she added the sentence, 'I also intend *not* to tell lies about myself,' before closing the book and hiding it once more.

She looked out over the valley, a bright glitter in the afternoon light, where long shadows were creeping down the slopes, the shape of the house darkening the lawn. But Mount Brandon, away to the east, still caught the sun full on, a dazzling, snow-covered peak against the pale blue sky. Did she want all the world out there, beyond the mountains – London, Paris – taking to her heels? Yes, part of her did, and certainly if she married Harold some of all that would be hers – but only intermittently and formally, where the major portion of her life would be spent, eventually, as Lady Norton, mistress of his Oxfordshire home. But, if she lived in the country, she wanted it Irish country, not English. She wanted the country of Summer Hill. What would Harold say to that? He would laugh outright – as it had already amused him that she should want to spend so much time here, with a mother whom she so signally failed to get on with. Harold would offer her the world – he would never understand why she really only wanted this small corner of it.

But why did she? It was love of the place, of course – the house, gardens, river, woods, the secrets she had found and fed on here – a love made the more intense since, perforce, it had been pursued behind her mother's back, against her will. And so her wish to stay here was also partly a matter of revenge; she realized and accepted that. She wanted to pay her mother out for her lack of warmth towards her as a child, her cruelties in such matters as the swing, and many others, small and large – above all for her inability to see and release the true spirit of the house, which she had made into a fortress where everyone was prisoner of her wishes. She had suffered, so had her father and two brothers. But the men had avoided the issue where they had not, literally, like Henry, run away. So it was up to her to stay. Instead of taking to her heels, where she too would share in their defeat, she would remain on the field of battle, waiting her chance somehow to spring a surprise victory.

But how, in what way? Did she unconsciously hope for her mother's early death, she wondered, remembering the curious spasm of excitement she had felt at her mother's faint that morning – a death which, in some measure at least, would make her mistress of the house? Certainly she could see no other way which would allow her victory – such a death seemed the only means, for in a dozen years or so the house would belong to Henry, and he would have his own bride to manage things, not her. Or was Henry a confirmed bachelor, she wondered, so that in time, unmarried, she would keep house for him? But time – that was the bugbear there, time that sucked your life away. She had no wish to wait that long. Besides, what she really wanted of the house was someone loved to run it with. And that, in Harold's terms, would be impossible. Harold would have his own inheritance in England to concern him, to share with her.

So there was the problem, she realized, looking over the waning, clear blue light in the valley: inheritance. The house outside Stow-on-the-Wold in Oxfordshire would never be hers, whereas Summer Hill *was* hers, as a shareholder at least – part of the blood, and the fact that she was a woman should make her no less a partner, she felt, in its future. And that, she knew, was exactly the sort of thing which Harold or any other man would never understand.

The men, coming home from their rough shoot, crunched over the snow that rimmed the high woods beyond the house, moving through a silver beech glade where the slanting light dazzled against the timber, finding tints of blue in the bark, where the woods were silent after the sporadic gunfire, several brace of pheasant, some rabbits and a hare accounted for. Harold was happy – he had taken the swiftly running hare. The shooting wasn't as good as at home, he thought, though it wasn't bad. He was pleased with the idea of home then, of England, where really everything, except the fox hunting perhaps, was so much better than things in Ireland. Frances couldn't fail, in the end, to see that. He would ask her to marry him that evening.

'But you don't follow, do you, Harold?'

'Can't say I do, darling.'

'I don't *want* to marry just yet.'

'You are over twenty-one after all.'

Impasse, she thought – just as she had expected. She closed the bound copy of *Punch* on her lap with a louder thump than she had intended. They were alone in the morning room, where it was cold without a fire. 'There are things for me to do here – still,' she said.

'But *what* things, when you might more often be in London – or at home with me. Oh, apart from Christmas and during the summer now and then – I understand your being here then. But why *live* here?'

'It's my inheritance, I'm part of it—'

'But, my dearest, it's Henry's inheritance, not yours. Yours would be my house, when I have it, and our children's inheritance.'

'It's not the same—'

'But you're at hammer and tongs with your mother here all the time. You've told me – and I can see that. So all the more—'

'Well, it's *not* all the more reason. I don't *want* to be at loggerheads with her. I want to settle that somehow, before I marry. I don't want to leave here with that shadow of ill-will.'

'You will surely only increase the ill-will between you both by staying here, for it's that very thing which annoys your mother most – your *being* here all the time.'

'Yes, perhaps. All the same, I have to make the effort. To be on better terms. Perhaps – next year? I simply couldn't marry now, not absolutely *now*. I want to wait, can you see?'

Harold sighed, not seeing. She had been honest with herself, she thought – why couldn't she be the same with him? She was lying to him, of course. She didn't expect to make things up with her mother – rather the opposite: she expected to contend with her for Summer Hill. That was the one thing – hopeless cause or no – that she was set on. The house was her love, and how could she explain that to Harold? What man could reasonably accept bricks and mortar and landscape as his rival in marriage?

A day later, the 24th, when the holly was set up and a tall, green-needled spruce brought into the great hall, Christmas descended on the house. Mr O'Meara had returned to Dublin, the Spanish dancers banished to the Club House in Kilkenny – the artistes had gone. Now, apart from Humphrey and Harold, the family reigned secure from further interruptions – tensions and difficulties put aside, if not forgotten, in the general aura of goodwill.

Though it did not snow again, a sharp frost maintained the earlier fall everywhere, so that on the Sunday Christmas morning, beneath a chilly blue sky, the younger members of the household walked to the little church near the village over the hard earth, their feet sinking into the snow with a crisp cutting noise.

Like stepping through an iced cake, Frances thought, moving a little ahead with Harold in tall buttoned boots, beneath a long sable-trimmed coat and matching Russian hat. They took a back avenue, directly across the lawn, where it twisted down through the forest gorge and met the river before turning sharply along the bank under a heavy canopy of trees towards Cloone. Here the branches above were festooned with icicles and the little rivulets and waterfalls, normally spurting from the steep rocks to their left, were frozen solid, long blueish fingers running down the granite face, with star-encrusted ferns beneath, that had doubled their size in the frost, become solid lacy crystal ornaments.

She loved this walk in every season, this river walk up to the village, or turning right down the bank to the octagonal stone boat house further on – that was a summer walk, where, if one did not take the boats out, the tree-shrouded river avenue went right on for several miles, before cutting up the hill by the southern edge of the estate, back to the house through the long avenue of monkey puzzle trees.

She was so much a tree person, she knew – loved these endless woods and forests that rose up in circles round the house, holding it, a jewel on the hill above, like the lattice work of a crown. In the Cotswolds, beyond Stow, where Harold lived, there was nothing like this. It was all manicured, neat and bare – open sheep pasture, set high up in the winds, with only a few spinneys of breeze-bent beech or elm in the folds. There were no secrets in the landscape there. She needed secrets, needed places to hide. And that was a problem with Harold, too. He was so open and honest, really – and she was simply not used to dealing with such people, where, exposed to their obvious good nature, a similar response was demanded. Her subtleties made that almost impossible for her.

She had been marked by her devious battles with her mother – just as she had by the covert Irish landscape, with its deceptive vistas, hidden views, sudden ruins, screaming rook-filled trees, its wild ragworty fields and moist creeping growths, where so much would always be ungoverned and any imposed order a mere holding operation, a temporary clearing won from a ragged and voracious nature: a restless, cloud-swept landscape, where the colours changed all the time in the wind. It had marked her by her love for it and by her wariness of it, for behind the most placid vision here, she knew, there was always a sense of surprise, disruption, violence. It was a world which had put her too much on her guard, perhaps, so that she thought then that she had been over-severe with Harold the previous evening.

'I'm sorry – if I seemed stubborn yesterday.' She turned to him, neither sly nor pompous in his muffler and greatcoat – just a tall, a nice young man with a good face set against the river light.

'No, no. I wouldn't wish to force you in anything. It must be your own free choice, of course.' His reply seemed entirely felt, reasonable and open. So that she was ashamed of her deceits with him over her mother, and was tempted to tell him so, to explain it all, what her true feelings were.

'Really, in fact, I'm sure it's just a passing phase – these feelings I have for home, for Mama. And a sort of cowardice about the great world perhaps.'

'Perhaps.' He seemed almost uninterested.

'I shall have to embark on it at some point.'

'Indeed.' He looked away, up-river, toward the salmon traps and the approaching bridge.

'You seem – somewhat unconcerned?'

'No, no, my dear.'

But he was, and of course it was probably intentional, understandable at least, Frances thought. He had been hurt by her refusal to marry him at once and was taking mild revenge. And no doubt she deserved it. Yet she did not feel like telling any truths then: he was unreceptive. And, besides, admission here could be weakness; it might mar her relationship with him ever after. At such vital points in life it was always wise to maintain any position of strength.

As they passed the little Gothic lodge, old Mr Kennedy, a widower now, out on the step, took his cap off to the party, wishing them many Good Mornings and Happy Christmases. Behind the small diamond-paned windows, his son Pat Kennedy, with the day off, saw the company pass, then turned to Eileen, watching with him.

'You'd hardly credit it, would you – Miss Frances, with that butter wouldn't melt in her mouth expression, and that eejit Perkins wrapped round her little finger. She's a flyer all right, I'll give her that! Leading him on with the one hand and thieving all that stuff from about the house with the other – and you helping her. Mother of God, if her Ladyship catches either of ye, there'll be ructions!'

'If they catch you, Pat Kennedy, with your Fenian

friends and guns and drilling and schemes, there'll be far worse ructions, so you needn't talk.'

He turned from the window. 'No, indeed, you're right there. The both of us,' he added, looking at her very pointedly, 'we'd better keep our mouths well shut.'

Christmas soon overwhelmed the household: triumphant carols in the church, presents unwrapped over cherry brandy before lunch, a vast turkey then – before Mrs Molloy, as was the tradition, carried in the two flaming plum puddings and was suitably congratulated on the gargantuan meal. In the afternoon the younger members tried to skate on the ornamental pond at the top of the terraced garden. But the ice cracked when the tubby Eustace launched himself forth on it, pursued by Sergeant, who sank in the freezing water with him, until half the company found themselves dancing about among the ice splinters in the shallow pond. More cherry brandy and hot hip-baths were forthcoming back at the house.

On Boxing Day, at nightfall, the Christmas tree was lit, when the servants, estate workers and their families, well over a hundred of them, accepted their presents from Sir Desmond and Lady Cordiner, the candle flames warming the green needles here and there, filling the hall with an intoxicating smell of burnt wax and pine.

The following evening they played charades in the drawing room, the teams of actors emerging on stage from the hall, where trunks of old theatrical costumes had been taken down from the attics. Sir Desmond particularly excelled here, at this one time of year when, forgetting his flying machines, he gave himself entirely to these seasonal recreations, leting his inventive spirit flow for once in quite another direction, preparing, in these charades, for his own part in Humphrey's production of *The Colleen Bawn* at the Kilkenny Theatre two days hence.

And, when that came, all the Summer Hill household assembled in their boxes in the little velvet and gilt theatre, Frances thought her happiness complete, realizing all the more sharply how little she wanted to live in Oxfordshire.

She gazed, rapt, at the romantic cavortings on stage, the vivid mix of Boucicault's Irish wit and malice, saw Humphrey excel as the hero, Hardness Cregan, and her father make a splendid fool of himself as the comic rogue, Myles na Coppaleen – the two cheered to the echo by the local populace.

What would Harold, the future Lord Norton, offer by way of similar entertainment, she wondered? Nothing. English county society, she knew, lived at many dull removes from such theatricals, without a spark of this élan, bound up in stuffy isolated formalities. In her life here she had access to any amount of expected or forbidden adventure. England was simply dull, she thought – the people, by comparison with the Irish, quite without character. That was it, that was the worst of it: they were grey, where here, with every sort of person, she basked in always unexpected lights. Was she to spend the rest of her life among dullards?

It was altogether a serious problem. And the only person who might offer sensible advice on it was Henry, her brother, with whom she had shared so many confidences. She would talk to him at the next suitable opportunity.

But when she did, the next day up in his work rooms, after Dermot had gone out for a walk with his father, Henry's answers were not encouraging. He was tinkering with the gruesome cadaver of some oversized bat on his work bench – the slimy furred animal, just released from its alcohol preservative, disembowelled, splayed out with pins on a board, where he was prodding at it with a scalpel and tweezers. The room stank of the chemical, along with some other, even more unpleasant odour, like a freshly suppurating drain.

'Francie, my dear Francie.' He bent over the scalpel, squinting. 'What can I say? – it's so much your life.'

'But you don't really like him, do you?'

'No – I mean, no, it would mean nothing, my liking him or not. Only you can be the judge there. Though, since you ask me about it all, you must have some doubts about him.'

'Not him. Just life in Over Norton House.'

'But that *is* him, or will be.'

'Exactly.'

'You marry the man, though, not the house. If you're really in love – the house, the place, the country doesn't matter. That must be pretty obvious, Francie.' He looked up at her now, the cadaver forgotten.

'But it's not as easy as that – that's in the "blind love" department. And I'm not. That's surely pretty obvious, too, isn't it, Henry?'

'*Touché*.' He left his dissection and moved over to wash his hands. 'But all the same, if it isn't, at least, pretty much in the blind love department, I shouldn't pursue it.' He stopped, arms resting on the basin, thinking of something.

'What?'

'Nothing.'

'Why haven't you anyone, Henry?'

'How do you know I haven't?'

'Some dusky African Princess . . .'

'As likely as not, you think?'

'I've no idea. I suppose it's Mama, makes it difficult for all of us.'

'Not for you. She's keen as mustard on Harry.'

'Yes. And that rather worries me, that we agree over something.'

Henry suddenly drew himself together, dried his hands and moved briskly away from the wash-stand. 'Which is another good reason for moving on from here, Frances.'

'But I don't *want* to move on, you know that. That's really the whole problem – this feeling I have about the place.'

'Yes, I do know. You have the sort of love for Summer Hill that I ought to have, but can't.'

'But why? Mama won't live for ever. And it'll be yours—'

'Yes, yes.' He was frustrated now, almost roused. 'But . . . it's not Mama, it's me.'

'Your wanderlust.'

"Yes. Of course – it's that,' he said, his expression softening, surprised and grateful, as if she had been the first person ever to identify his problem. 'That's what I love, travelling with Dermot,' he went on, more easily now, free of some burden.

The New Year's ball was a sensation, though not in a way anyone could have anticipated. A small string orchestra had been engaged from Dublin which played at the back of the hall, while the dining room had been made over into a buffet where the long table, elaborately decorated with ferns and evergreens, groaned with devilled lobster, oyster patties, galantines of turkey, fillets of sole in aspic and Neapolitan ice-cream.

Flood ministered over a drinks table at one end, and blue-and-gilt-liveried footmen dispensed a sweet champagne cup in long flutes from silver salvers, with whiskey-sodas less obviously available for the men. The drawing room, cleared of most of its bric-à-brac, became a redoubt for the older women, while their husbands commandeered the morning room on the other side of the house as a retreat. The younger company swirled to waltzes or danced vigorous polkas and intricate Scottish reels, under the great candlelit Waterford chandelier in the hall – Frances, rather the belle of the ball, in a ravishing white silk dress with spotted tulle, red velvet bows and streamers. But she was not the sensation.

It was the dog Sergeant who, once more taking aggressive initiative, announced the new revel in a cacophony of furious barking, the sounds first emerging from the landing above the hall, where soon the dog was seen worrying at something behind the balustrade – advancing but as quickly retreating from an invisible enemy on the floor, a rat it seemed, which the dog had cornered, or rather failed to corner, in some vicious game of hide and seek above the company. Eustace, breaking with his partner – he had been dancing with Isabelle Cordiner – remonstrated loudly with the terrier, bellowing above the music.

'Sergeant! Stop that – and come down here at once, you brute!'

For answer, the dog barked more loudly still, while yet making no appearance, leaving that honour to his intended prey, which came in sight just then – first a scaly head, then yellow and brown coils pushing through the landing balustrade, before the reptile suddenly dropped into space, swinging there ominously for a moment as the beast fought to maintain a grip with its tail, unsuccessfully in the event, for it fell sheer away then, onto the floor right in front of the orchestra, lying there stunned, immobile for a moment or two before raising its head with a loud and angry hissing noise.

The men took it mostly in good part, but the shrieks of the women might have been heard in the next townland. Though Lady Cordiner, appearing at the drawing room doorway then with Bunty, remained dumb, unable to credit her eyes. 'It's a menagerie – nothing but a menagerie this house,' Bunty murmured before turning on her heel and fleeing.

Later, when Henry had captured the snake, the ball proceeded – and Isabelle finally achieved her ambition by dancing a waltz with Harold. 'What *can* one think?' she said in a superior tone, currying favour. 'It could only happen in Ireland.' Harold agreed with her in an only slightly less patronizing manner.

At midnight arms were linked to 'Auld Lang Syne' and the New Year was toasted in. 'To the year of the snake!' Henry, in high good humour, raised his glass to a doubting Frances.

3

The valley had been wet at first, after heavy spring rains, so that, when the first long days of heat came suddenly, the greenery exploded in wild tropic growths, the daffodils on the lawn below Summer Hill replaced by rampant meadowsweet and cow parsley, while in moist-damp places by the river angelica, pennywort and saxifrage bloomed inordinately. The horse chestnut trees on the lawn and along the estate wall became brilliant green with white candelabra almost overnight; the beech and oak budded early and the grass gleamed, turning glossy sides to the wind.

The house in summer looked over the valley where all this green abundance rising up the slopes seemed to attack it, hoping to overpower it. But such a victory remained a hopeless cause. Gardeners scythed or mowed the grass without remission, woodmen hacked at ungainly branches and overgrown shrubs, gullies were cleared, fences mended, hedges vigorously clipped, weeds viciously attacked and uprooted: armies of men, under Lady Cordiner's obsessive direction, went forth each day to prune, transform or repulse nature.

On the rough pasture, ragged copses and gorse slopes of the small farms across the valley, leading up to the navy-blue mountains, the wind and damp of immemorial Irish weather had long since triumphed, leaving a wild and lovely land. But at Summer Hill, a formal enclave cut from all this indiscipline, the beauty, man-made, was rigorously maintained and manicured.

In front of the house, beyond the gravel surround, the elaborate terrace gardens, with their bedding plants, herbaceous borders and geometric multicoloured box hedges, were most exposed to Lady Cordiner's strictures. She inspected the lobelias, roses, salvias, geraniums and much else each morning with Appleton, the English head gardener, a commanding officer and sergeant major at a drill parade where the smallest irregularity or blemish was pounced upon, noted and subsequently set right or eradicated.

It was sometimes a longish tour for there were four sunken gardens within the main terrace, a good acre of land, perfectly square, divided by a cross of raised red marble chip paths. In the middle of the terrace, replacing a naked statue of the goddess Ceres, a large bronze-ribbed astrolabe had been set up, science ousting myth, the toy of some earlier Cordiner, a man of the Enlightenment, now become a central point for Lady Cordiner's more mundane but no less acute observations.

To the west of these pleasure gardens, a well-shaved lawn led up in a succession of gentle terraces and flights of steps to the tennis and croquet lawns and the walled vegetable garden hidden by the great trees beyond – for this was the area planted out over a hundred years before by Sir Archibald Cordiner, with glades of Japanese cedars, Canadian maples, Spanish chestnuts and American redwoods, trees now reaching some maturity in a spread of perfumed bark and exotic leaf.

Lady Cordiner was not a regular visitor in this higher domain. She disliked the overhanging gloom, the sense of impending jungle, the fact that here was growth in these great trees which she could never control. But, most of all, in the longer grass and thicker shrubs at the top of the rise here, she secretly feared a meeting with one or other of Henry's wild animals or reptiles, for it was against the vegetable garden wall, in a series of wire enclosures, that he had built his small zoo, a menagerie of dik-diks, porcupines, hyraxes, Colobus monkeys, civet cats, mongooses, snakes – and worst of all a Giant Pangolin from West Africa, a dragon-like mammal with a long tail and horny scales big as a man's hand: entirely harmless, slow-moving and confiding, Henry had assured her, with a diet of termites which it searched out in their nests with a long sticky tongue . . . This beast gave her waking nightmares so that she thought no pen strong enough to hold it and always expected the brute to erupt at her feet in these high glades.

But by and large Lady Cordiner managed to dominate these open spaces as much as she did the interiors of Summer Hill, so that for privacy beyond their own bedrooms the household was forced well away from the house and its immediate environs, down the steep sides of the valley or into the wilder woods, to other secret places, or ones inaccessible at least to Lady Cordiner.

*

Frances stood on the watchtower of wooden scaffolding below the bridge, looking down-river to where the white water, scurrying out from between the bridge piers, gave way to darker pools beneath the trees. She could just see the other men from the estate, up to their waists in the river, standing in to the bank on the same side, hidden by the trees, with the net.

'The flow is smooth enough – and the sight good,' the water-bailiff said to her. 'But will they come at all?'

It was mid-June, an early overcast morning after a night's rain, with a fair depth but with no great current on the river: ideal conditions for the start of the annual two months' salmon netting below Summer Hill, a right which the Cordiner family had enjoyed here since the dissolution of the monasteries, where the fish, when they came upstream in sufficient numbers, could be seen and trapped in the pools, before the others went on up to their spawning grounds: opportunity netting, a patient, skilful business where the water-bailiff or one of his men stood guard on the watchtower for hours each day waiting for a run.

Frances could make out very little in the first of the darker pools thirty yards or so down-river of them. If anything moved there she doubted if she would see it. But Matt Carney, the Summer Hill water-bailiff, gazing on these brown waters for years, knew every calm space and ripple and hidden stone in the reaches below the bridge. And it was he who, some few minutes later, saw signs of the first of the big fish, just the slightest spear-headed disturbance on the surface cutting upstream, so that he raised his hand smoothly to the men lower down on the bank – no noise above the chatter of the river in the silent early morning where the ground mists had only just left the valley.

Behind this first faint chevron on the water other lesser ridges and eddies sprang up, moving slowly upstream. It was a run. They let the fish come right into the last of the pools, Matt with his hand still raised, the men waiting for his signal. Frances could see vague shadows and shapes now, a flash of silver beneath the little curdling movements on the calm surface.

'Yes?' she whispered.

'Yes – a fair run, not big ones, but a dozen or more, I'd say.'

A moment later he dropped his hand and pandemonium ensued. The two men holding the net at either end, up and downstream, threw it out over the pool, so that most of the fish were trapped in a sudden fury of dancing water, jumping and spinning in the air, trying to leap free, as the weighted cords closed over and round them.

Matt was down the steps of the tower now, Frances following, both of them running along the bank towards the commotion. The other men, hands thrust deep in the pool, were muffling the fish, forcing the net down on them, before circling it together, making a bag out of it, so that they could pull the catch onto the bank.

Frances saw the fish clearly then, arms of reddish silver thrashing about, gills moving furiously, the water a turmoil, as the net closed and the men, up on the bank now with Matt, pulled it ashore. She joined them, heaving the catch in, glorying in the sheer animal energy of it all, clutching, struggling with the fish through the net with her bare hands, touching their fight as they spun and arched, feeling their slippery weight, the chilled scales in her fingers, a fight for life against her own flesh, the thrash of water drenching her, so that she became exultant, carried away by the battle, shouting out, 'It's mine, I have it – I have them!' as if these fish from the bridge of Cloone were hers, not her father's.

The men were not surprised at her force and competence – the way she tussled with the net, threw herself into the fray. For years, in their other work about the estate, she had joined them, watching, helping, as a child – always something of a tomboy. But now, today, as a young woman, they found this passionate involvement strange, that she should so take up with them, keeping no distance, like a man, one of their own. They appreciated her interest, yet were wary, not knowing the reasons behind it.

There were something less than a dozen fish, and most of them smallish peal. But there was one fully-grown salmon, she saw, thick as a man's thigh, with a great hooked underjaw, that fought to the end – a monster. She turned away as they clubbed it with lead-topped sticks – and then, ashamed, turned back to watch the killing. If you watched, then you watched to the end, she thought: you do not turn away.

They took the fish laid on ferns in a dog cart up to the yard of the house, to Matt Carney's office, where he put them out on a marble slab, weighing them, accounting for each in a big ledger.

'A fair start, Miss Frances. And that one at the end.' He looked at the largest salmon, with its lovely silver and blue sheen, the scales still jewels. 'That's one we've been waiting for – he's been around a time, many a season up and down. Will ye look at him – twenty-six pounds and ten ounces. Ye'll have that for your dinner, I'd say.'

Happy in the business, excited by it, for several weeks afterwards, morning or evening, Frances kept watch on the tower by the river, learning all the signs on the water from Matt or one of the other men, until she became almost as adept as they in spotting a run. As a child she had sometimes watched this netting distantly, the first catch usually, as a family 'event'. But now she took a lonely passion in it, to Matt's surprise and that of some of the villagers looking down from the bridge, who saw her in these early mornings as she stood on the watchtower, a motionless figure, intent on the wavering patterns on the water, in riding breeches and dark hacking jacket, a scarf hiding the ends of her dark curls, so that she might have been a man standing there, a young man, a dark sentinel on the tower emerging from the white mists. 'I am of the trees here,' she wrote in her album *consolatum*. 'And the river too.'

Sometimes Henry came with her, sharing the small wooden platform, where above them, set into the steep slopes of the gorge, they could see the ruins of the old

Cordiner castle with its stubby Norman tower, later Gothic arches and mullioned windows – appearing mysteriously as the mists cleared, catching the rising sun in a flash of old limestone, wrapt all round by the sheer green woods: a Lorelei vision commanding the river.

'I look at that old Norman keep,' Henry said. 'And wonder how it's mine.'

'You don't see all the family stretching back? . . .'

'Mailed knights and maidens – and the rough Irishry storming the slopes? Not really.'

'Remember that splendid battle here, when there was no proper bridge, just a ford, and they threw stones at each other across the river – the Cordiners against the Deanes, the rival Knights from Graig. We won.'

'Did we?' He turned to her, surprised, amused.

'Yes. I can see it all – the Cordiners getting their boats back across just in time, then throwing rocks at each other all day, till the Deanes retreated, "bootless home" as the account has it.'

'Homeric,' Henry said.

'But you must have heard the story?'

'Yes, yes – must have done. Simply forgotten it.'

'You really are always somewhere else,' she told him. 'Aren't you?'

'No. I've been thinking about this African journey.' He leant on the rail, not seeing anything on the water, pondering quite another landscape. 'And now that Dermot has got himself attached to Milner's staff it may not work out. One of "Milner's young men".'

'What is he? – some sort of military attaché?'

'Yes, exactly. At the War Office in London for the moment. But he'll have to join Milner in South Africa. So he won't have any real leave till next year, if then. All a perfect bore.'

'Does he think so?'

Henry looked at her ruefully. 'You're always so sharp, aren't you? I don't know,' he went on seriously. 'It's all a great honour, no doubt.'

'Well, he *is* keen on his career.'

'Of course.'

'And perhaps running round the African wilds with you doesn't help it.'

'Perhaps. But—'

'But that's *your* trouble, Henry – not really having a career.'

'But I do, I do—'

'Just stuffing the old nurseries full of dead beasts and butterflies. And live snakes. You don't work *with* anyone else, quite isolated, like Mama. You ought to do something with *other* people. You're too stuck in yourself.'

'It's not quite like that, Francie,' he said, quietly. 'I *do* do things with other people – with Dermot.'

'Except that you can't now – if he's to pursue his army career in London or the Cape Colony.'

He admitted this with a nod. 'Rather like you, with Harold – both faced with an impasse at the moment. He's coming over next week, isn't he? What will *you* do?'

'What will he do, rather.'

'You can't keep him on tenterhooks for ever.'

'No. All a perfect bore, isn't it?' She smiled hugely.

Lady Cordiner considered the summer season – the second annual visitation of uncles, aunts, cousins, friends and fiancées arriving intermittently at Summer Hill throughout the coming months, where they would stay until the Dublin Horse Show, or at least until the grouse shooting opened in Scotland in mid-August.

Meanwhile there was much to be organized. Bunty Cordiner had written a very nearly impertinent letter saying she and Austin, with the children, were expecting to travel to Clifden on the Galway coast for a seaside holiday that year: how the Summer Hill dates offered might clash with this. Lady Cordiner would put paid to that in her reply, by making no allowances to Bunty over her Galway arrangements – knowing full well how she would come to heel in the end, as she always did. Lady Cordiner was entirely aware of Bunty's social envy – her covert admiration, her longing for all the ordered summer events and niceties of the great house: the tennis and croquet parties, boating trips, fishing excursions, the spirited afternoon tea with the local gentry and more sophisticated foreign visitors on the lawn terraces. Indeed, Lady Cordiner thought, she might well pay Bunty out for her presumption by putting her and Austin in the third best guest room this year.

Frances, on the other hand, she had decided to treat more gently. A wrong move or too much pressure on the girl at this point might destroy the match with Harold – Harold who had explained to her, confidentially last Christmas, how Frances wished to wait before making any formal announcement of their engagement. But they were as good as engaged, Lady Cordiner felt: it was simply a matter of tactfully seeing it through. An announcement, she was sure, would come before the Dublin Horse Show.

But why the waiting in the first place, she wondered? Harold, quite obviously, had so much to offer; and, besides, they were surely in love. Harold had offered no explanation at the time and she herself was none the wiser. What was Frances waiting for? She knew, though without any definite proof, that her daughter had taken the little *objets d'art* about the house, simply thieved them. What did this signify? What did Frances want of and in Summer Hill that had made her so unaccountably tardy with Harold? Lady Cordiner, quick to identify hidden motive in everyone else, was at a loss here, and it annoyed her considerably that she simply did not know her daughter, a shadow moving quickly about the house and estate, always there but rarely seen, an ominous presence almost, watching, waiting. It was quite unnatural – a girl of her beauty and accomplishments, that she should not be in Dublin or in London for the season, among her own kind. Yes, she was very much banking on Harold taking the girl in hand without more ado. That was what was wanted really: a little male force and decisiveness in the matter and the girl would come to heel. Harold, no doubt, had been too tactful and restrained in his suit.

*

They arrived, over a week in late June – Eustace with Harold again; Mortimer Cordiner; a distant American cousin of Lady Cordiner, a genial railroad magnate, Wilbur Quince, from Brewster, Pennsylvania, with his pretty wife Mary Ann and her aunt, Mrs Chauncy, a sprightly widow from Lynchburg, Virginia – together with the Austin Cordiners, their two spotty sons and Isabelle, an older, more gracious girl now, just nineteen, her puppy fat gone, less prone to thumb sucking, her adolescent pouts and ringlets transformed and clipped, becoming tools of a flirtatious guile, making her an attractive, if deceptively mature, young woman, for she remained a child.

The dog Sergeant disgraced himself on the arrival of the Austin Cordiners by being sick on the porch steps, just as Bunty emerged from the wagonette, disgorging the gruesome remains of a half-digested rat almost at her feet. Bunty took the greeting generally in bad part.

Sergeant had caught the rat, with Monster, in a spate of furious digging into the bank behind the tennis court that morning, so that the chalk on the base line had been half-obliterated by soil and the end of the court itself partly undermined. The dogs, severely reprimanded, were locked in the stables for the rest of the day and the tennis tournament arranged for that afternoon delayed while repairs were effected.

But when it started Isabelle and Harold, drawing lots as partners, showed themselves dab hands at the game, beating the other mixed doubles, including one with the local curate, the agile and overweening Timothy Birch, who had played for Trinity College and was thus always expected to win, no matter how bad his partner was, in this instance Frances, who hardly played the game at all.

The Reverend Mr Birch took their defeat rather gracelessly and there was a *frisson* of ill-will in the air before fresh iced lemon-juice was served under the maple tree and the older spectators prepared themselves for an elaborate cream tea, superintended by Flood and Pat Kennedy and carried out by two footmen in their light summer livery.

Lady Cordiner, looking at the willowy Isabelle in her pleated ankle-length skirt and tightly bursting bodice, was surprised at the skill, at the development of the girl in every sense.

'How pretty you look, my dear,' she told her, as she and Harold came off the court before tea. 'The little embroidery there—' She pointed to the trim of daisy chains round the neck and cuffs of the bodice. 'Most becoming. Did you do it yourself?'

'Yes, Aunt – yes, I did!' Her face was peach-coloured, hot and puffed with excitement. Eyes wide, glorying in all her various accomplishments, Isabelle was visibly leaping into life that afternoon. Unladylike, no doubt, yet how attractive such excitement was, Lady Cordiner thought. Yes, Isabelle was undeniably attractive.

It was after tea, as one victory followed another for them, that Harold started to flirt with her – at first tactfully, then quite openly. Frances, on the sidelines, was simply curious to begin with, then astonished: the shouted encouragements, admiring smiles, even the little endearments which he tossed towards Isabelle after a good volley or when she ran like a startled deer for a drop shot – his general ease, his intimacy with her, for it was no less, became so obvious it was shocking. So that Frances blushed when she overheard Cousin Wilbur's tactless remark to Lady Cordiner – 'What a fine pair they make! Shortly to become engaged, I understand?'

Lady Cordiner turned to him, frowning. This mistaken thought of Isabelle as Harold's fiancée quickly alerted her. She had noticed and accepted Harold's fervour towards the girl as mere high spirits. Now, at once, she saw the real purpose behind it. Not male arrogance – Harold was playing quite a different game: raising a little jealousy in Frances by these new attentions, pointing out to her a potential rival, how there were other fish in the sea. How clever of him.

But Frances felt nothing but a growing anger, a fearful

indignity, a hatred of this man who could so openly humiliate her. She had never felt like this before – a hot flush of iron resentment rising in her, against Harold, then herself, that she could ever have thought to love someone so ill-mannered and insensitive, so that she snapped at Mr Birch when he offered her a meringue, and later, at the end of the match, was quite unable to control herself – storming away, most pointedly, back to the house, just as Harold and Isabelle left the court after a last victory. Harold's plan, if plan it was, had misfired.

Frances went to her room. On reflection, she was amazed yet proud of her behaviour. It had changed her life, a bright deed certainly, which this time had really stopped the clocks. It was the end of Harold, of course. She would accept no apology – the man was a Lothario, that was it. He was not for her. She could never live with such a person.

In her enthusiasm for her action it did not cross her mind that he might simply have been baiting her in his behaviour – or further, that she had, perhaps, deserved just this, that she had never really loved him. She had been publicly dishonoured. That was all – and that was that.

Insects hummed in the creeper outside her open window. She looked out at the soft, late afternoon sun slanting down the valley, over the lawn with its heavy trees, the cows below in the pasture moving in a long line towards their evening milking, the slabs of light and shade stealing over the blue flanks of Mount Brandon in the distance: the whole, abundant, settled world of Summer Hill.

And she was happy suddenly, wildly happy with a sinking feeling in her stomach, that all this – the land, the house – could remain hers, in secret at least. She would not now have to live in Oxfordshire – blown about, a cold, dull life on those high wolds, among a witless nobility and peasantry. How happy she was – it had really all worked out for the best.

And how unhappy, angry her mother became. Though

at first, when she spoke to Frances, she temporized.

'But, my dear, one must expect young men to flirt a little.'

'I do not, *will* not, expect that, Mama.'

'You will find life somewhat difficult then.'

'So be it—'

'Complete fidelity – you will rarely find it, I must be frank with you. Besides, you are not yet actually engaged to Harold. He was simply – how shall I put it? – encouraging you. He didn't mean anything with Isabelle – I'm sure, not for a moment.'

'People *should* mean what they say – and do. I cannot abide such trickery.'

'You have too much pride – lack experience of the world. You are too rigid, my dear. It was nothing – see it as no more than a little tiff on the tennis court. Make it up with Harold. I assure you, he has no real concern for Isabelle, none whatsoever. How could he? She is simply a child.'

'Mama, that makes his behaviour all the more reprehensible – leading the girl on.'

Her mother had no ready answer to this. And it was from then on, annoyed at herself and seeing this splendid match dissolving in front of her eyes, that she became alarmed and thus angry.

'Frances, you cannot throw your life away just because of a little misunderstanding on a tennis court—'

'I'm not throwing it away. I'm regaining it—'

'Don't interrupt. You must pull yourself together – be your age, for once. No more of this childishness. It's all far too serious a matter.'

'Exactly! And I am not to become engaged to a flirt!'

'Harold is a great deal more than that – you know perfectly well – a most distinguished family: Lord Norton himself, peer of the realm, eminent in so many fields, a beautiful house—'

'I was not to have married a *house*, Mama!' Frances rounded on her mother, becoming as roused as she was.

'You were to marry *into* one, a great house. You must not be so literal.'

'I have a great house here – and I prefer it.'

Lady Cordiner looked at her curiously. 'I do not quite understand? You cannot live here for the rest of your life.'

'Aunt Emily does – and will.'

'Your Aunt Emily is – she is touched.' Lady Cordiner was uncertain how to describe her condition.

'With genius, yes.'

'My dear, she is ninepence in the shilling.' Her mother was abrupt and dismissive now, still firmly believing that her daughter could be brought to reason if she spoke firmly, even ruthlessly to her. Frances simply lacked an intelligent grasp of the whole affair – a child who needed some brusque advice on the ways of the world. But this idea that the house, Summer Hill, might lie at the heart of Frances's aberrant behaviour was new to her and worried Lady Cordiner. 'In any case,' she went on, more brusquely still, 'you cannot compare yourself with Aunt Emily – not in genius or vagary. You are a young woman with many qualities' – she went on acidly – 'but not with either of those, I'm pleased to say. And you must go out into the world and express your gifts suitably, which naturally means marriage. I cannot think why you mention the house here as a bar on your life. You dishonour it in no way by marrying Harold. Just the opposite – nothing would make your father and me more pleased.'

'You misunderstand me, Mama.' Frances looked at her, stared at her bitterly. 'I love the house here—'

'But of course, as we all do—'

'No, it's something a great deal more than that.'

'But you would always have it, to visit.'

'More than that.' Frances fell silent. And for the first time, in her daughter's fiercely set expression, Lady Cordiner felt some intimation of her daughter's real desires. She could not identify them, but she saw whatever it was as a threat, to herself as mistress of Summer Hill. And now she was no longer angry, but more afraid, a moment's fear in the pit of the stomach, as when a commander, always victorious in unimportant local skirmishes, is brought news of a whole great army arrayed over the hill.

Harold, despite Lady Cordiner's best endeavours, left the house shortly afterwards – Frances remaining quite adamant. Even her father spoke to her, but to no avail – mumbling about the 'disgrace' of the matter. 'The disgrace is his, not mine,' she told him roundly, before he thankfully retreated to his machinery, the screw propellers, wire struts and rudders of his flying machine in the yard workshops.

The disgrace, too, was her father's, Frances thought. She neither loved nor hated him – he had simply never impinged on her life when she had needed him, another outcast of her mother's, as she had been, where Henry had been so much the favoured person, a cosseted little boy, the pet in old photographs dressed in girl's clothes. Her father had become so distant a figure that she was not even able to pity him now, seeing in his familial cowardice, his lack of warmth towards her, wounds which her mother had imposed, but which he ought to have resisted. That was his disgrace. She at least, she swore, would never suffer such indignity at her mother's hands – and no one would so stunt her warmth either, for she thought that to be her mother's worst crime, the way she proscribed all emotion at Summer Hill which was not her own.

Bunty and Austin Cordiner curtailed their visit, too, amidst a great many self-satisfied cluckings from Bunty, happy that Lady Cordiner should have been so exposed and embarrassed, and that Isabelle had been the cause of it – a much more suitable match for Harold, she thought, in any case, which the events on the tennis court had simply proved. She felt, indeed, that she might well further her daughter's cause in Harold's direction by taking her to England – to Oxford, Stratford and Stow, a little Cotswold tour – in September.

Only Henry showed sympathy for Frances. Indeed, he was obviously happy for her at this turn of events.

'Of course, you were right about Harold: you never did really like him,' Frances told him late one afternoon while up helping feed the animals in his menagerie, the two little dik-diks scuttling about nervously, inspecting the cabbage stalks suspiciously before retreating to their hutch.

'Not so much that, Francie. I was worried about you. You wouldn't have been happy. He was too dull a chap for you.'

'Yes. It was only a dream—'

'So you really knew it too?' He turned to her quickly. 'You were simply playing with him?'

'No. I just know it now.'

'But, Francie, you do flirt yourself, you know. You used to with him, with others as well. I've seen you—'

'Did I – do I?' she asked, only half-innocently.

'Yes, you know you do. You've got great gifts that way. But be careful. Lasting with someone is more important – and more difficult.'

'You speak from experience, do you?' she asked with pointed mischief.

'Yes.'

'Who is she, Henry? Do tell me!'

'She's no one. I just know.' He turned away then, moving towards the brick-floored cage where the Giant Pangolin slept in a box. 'Supply of anthills is getting scarce. Though there are some beyond Cooper's Wood, in Papa's new fields. Come with me and help get some this afternoon?'

Frances followed him, thinking of something else. 'Mama's furious, of course,' she said absent-mindedly, not caring.

'Yes. Obviously. And there's another problem – are you really going to stick it out with her here, in the present chilly circumstances?'

'What else?'

'Oh, a hundred other things, Francie. Go to Dublin, the Horse Show, stay with Mortimer at Islandbridge, he's home for the summer. Or to London. I'm going on there.'

'To see Dermot?'

'I hope so.'

'I might go away – but only for a bit. And what about your African journey this winter?'

'Doesn't look likely – if Dermot can't come.'

'Can't you go on your own?'

'No. Needs two people.'

'Stanley went on his own, looking for Livingstone.'

'Really, Francie, you don't know the first thing about it. It's much more complicated. I need Dermot.'

The Giant Pangolin, curled in a perfect circle like a huge scaly coil of rope, stirred a fraction in its bed of sandy earth, then continued its slumber. Henry closed the door. 'Must get some more anthills, else I'll have to give him to Bill Lawrence up at the Dublin zoo.' Henry moved on to the porcupine in the next cage. It, too, was half-asleep in the drowsy heat, showing no interest in the chopped carrots which Henry offered.

'Why are they all asleep?' Frances asked.

'The heat or they feed at night. And it's not their natural habitat, of course. We should all be out of here, Francie,' he went on, checking the water, leaving the food. 'It's not natural – clinging to home.'

'Not natural only because Mama makes life such a *prison* here. A caged zoo for us – as much as for them.' Frances gestured back towards the menagerie as they walked away between the glades, the Spanish chestnuts and cedars. When they stopped beneath one of these, Frances scratched some bark out with her nails, crushing it between her fingers, putting it to her nose, breathing the faint perfume deeply. She looked down the sloping emerald lawn to where the house basked in the late sunlight, the old limestone mellow, the gardens in front empty, innocent, with Lady Cordiner somewhere indoors.

'Oh, it really could be such a perfect place,' Frances said impatiently. 'All this – one could fill it with so much *real* life. You could, Henry, with whoever you marry.'

He smiled tartly. 'Don't know that I'm the marrying kind.'

'You see, there's some wonderful spirit hidden there,'

Frances went on. 'A frog prince, waiting.' Her eyes gleamed with frustrated emotion.

'All right then, but why do *you* have to release it, with all your own life to lead?'

'Because no one else will! And because it's here – somewhere – my life. That's why. I feel it. I'm tied to the place. Oh, not so much because of what I've had from it as from what I've *not* had from it, what Mama has prevented us from having.'

'But, Francie, it's not really Mama who prevents you from having it: it's the law of primogeniture, the eldest male descendant and all that nonsense. It's Papa and me and Eustace who prevent you from having it, if anyone does.'

'Yes,' she said shortly, turning away from him so that he would not see how unhappy this accident of birth had made her, how much she would so like to have been a man, and the first born at that. 'Well, in any case,' she went on, 'if I can't bring that life to the house, then you must. Which is why you'll have to marry, Henry. What will become of Summer Hill if you don't?'

'Eustace – Eustace can take it over.'

'Henry, that's nonsense. You'll simply let Mama have a final victory over you if you do that.'

'Mama . . .' He paused. 'You always see everything as her fault.'

'I do! She's killing the place, don't you see? And the people – Papa, you, me. There has to be a future, a real life here. And unless we stand and fight her there won't be.'

'A real life?' he asked vaguely. 'What?'

'Oh, don't be so obtuse, Henry! – anything that isn't so neatly and coldly ordered. Chatter, laughter, anything *quite* inconsequential. Nothing so serious, not this spying, this barracks life Mama goes in for, running the whole place like an army. "Do this, do that and you can't do the other thing." – she's always been like that. Can't ever simply relax and *enjoy* it all. You know, how she hardly ever says anything that isn't an instruction, a command or an interruption – and nearly always on some entirely banal matter, like one's dress or hair or being late for tea, just when one's talking about or doing something really interesting. And she kills it. Kills it stone dead,' Frances added, with bitter finality.

'A little hard—'

'But it's true, Henry – you know it is, which is why you disappear abroad so often, won't stand up to her. Oh yes,' she rushed on before he could interrupt her, 'much as I love you, you *do* know that, dearest Henry. You let her ride roughshod over you and I despise her for that.'

'Why not rather despise me?' he asked calmly, a little coldly, not looking at her.

'I told you – I am so very, very attached to you, so the faults don't matter. Attached, more so than ever.' She looked at him gently.

'Why?'

'Confidences – that I can only really ever share with you. And after Harold, well . . .'

'You weren't honest with him?'

'Not entirely. I never told him my real feelings about Mama for example.'

'Never really loved him then?'

'Oh, I did, in a way – and he loved me. But it must have been a game. It wasn't real,' she added quietly. 'Yet if only I could be *sure* I was right in what I did.'

'You were entirely right, Francie,' Henry told her promptly. 'Not because Harold is a flirt but because he is a fool. Oh, a nice enough fool, for dozens of other foolish women. But not for you. That will be your problem – finding some very very *un*foolish young man. Such men tend to come much older, when they come at all.' He reached out and touched her hand, shook it an instant. 'You really are so like me in that way – uncompromising. And you're right. It's painful, but it's the only way in the end.'

'But what are you so uncompromising about, in "that way"? – I didn't know.'

She looked at him intently. But he didn't reply.

'Oh, Henry, you are sly!' She smiled, kissing him impulsively. 'I really, honestly don't know what I'd do without you. All the same, I do wish you'd tell me who she is.'

Frances went to Dublin for the Horse Show, staying with Mortimer Cordiner in his pretty house beyond Islandbridge on the river. Henry came with her, before going on to London to meet Dermot.

By the time he and Frances met again, a month later in mid-September, her brother had changed. He was no longer sly or literal or prompt in his replies to her: he barely spoke to her at all, or to anyone else. And when they did talk he was fidgety and morose, giving little away. The reason for this decline was obvious. Dermot, apparently a considerable success at the War Office, would have no extended leave until the following year, if then. Their long-planned African trip together that winter had been cancelled.

The two men drove up in a hackney sidecar one September afternoon just as the trees were beginning to turn – a thickset man, neatly moustached, in a dark bowler with an unsuitable winter greatcoat, the other smaller, rat-faced, dressed like an undertaker's clerk. They came in by the yard entrance, so that Eileen, up in the servants' wing, saw them arrive and was immediately suspicious. She recognized the hackney driver, old Seamus Newman, who waited on the trains at Thomastown station. The two men weren't country men; they had come some distance. She rushed to find Pat Kennedy, to warn him – there was something wrong, for the men weren't tradesmen or gentry either. But she was too late. Pat, at the back door just then, coming up from the kitchen, was already facing them. She saw the look of fear in his eyes, his whole bearing, as he stood there, trapped.

'Afternoon.' The heavier man spoke, bowler forced down like a helmet over his bushy eyebrows. 'Mr Henry Cordiner – we'd like a word with him, if we may.' The accent was English, Eileen thought. Why hadn't they come by the front door?

Pat Kennedy relaxed. 'Who shall I say, sir?'

'We're from Dublin. Just a word with him, if you please.'

Pat led them away into the cook's parlour. When he returned to Eileen he confirmed their worst suspicions.

'Police,' he whispered. 'For sure.'

'Not you?'

'No. Nor you either, mercy be. The young master,' he added sarcastically.

'What is it, what is it?' she asked urgently.

'No idea. But something serious – all the way from Dublin Castle, I'll bet.'

'Glory be – what's he been up to?'

Pat shrugged. 'What mischief wouldn't they get up to? – any of these people, with the world in their hands.'

It turned cloudy an hour later when the two men had left. A wind got up and stayed there, coming in gusts and whines before blowing hard from the south-west, the first of the autumn gales getting under way, bending the trees in Cooper's Wood beyond the house, spots of rain starting to fall from a running sky. Summer was ending.

Henry did not appear for tea. But he was often absent then, busy in his workrooms in the old nurseries at the top of the house.

'Who were those men?' Lady Cordiner asked, after Pat Kennedy had brought the tray in, raising a bone china cup, then considering a tiny egg sandwich on the frilled doily.

'What men?' Frances hadn't seen them.

'Kennedy – you saw them in, didn't you? Came by the back door, Mrs Martin said.'

'Yes, ma'am.'

'Well?'

'I don't know, ma'am.'

'Something to do with his wretched animals, I shouldn't be surprised,' Sir Desmond grunted. 'Saw Henry walk up there with them. From the Dublin zoo, I shouldn't be surprised. I saw old Newman's sidecar in the yard.'

'Why didn't they come round by the hall door then?' Frances enquired.

'Tradespeople, dear, that's why,' Lady Cordiner said sniffily.

The rain spattered now against the glass, the windows shaking in their frames. Sir Desmond looked glumly out. 'What a wretched change,' he commented. 'Just when we were finishing the harvest so well.'

They forgot about Henry. But, when he did not appear for dinner either, they remembered him again.

They found him later that night, after a frantic search with lanterns, in the howling wind and rain, stretched out in the reptile house attached to his little zoo. At least one of the snakes, a puff adder, had escaped from its glass-sided box, for when Molloy, the coachman, carrying a lantern, with Simpson the head gamekeeper, came through the doorway, they saw the unlocked pen and the brute, in a corner, inflating itself, hissing malevolently, so that they dared not enter, waiting outside in the rain until Simpson's shotgun was fetched and the snake killed.

By this time some of the household – Sir Desmond and Frances with Pat Kennedy – alerted by the commotion, had gathered round the enclosure. But Simpson held them back. 'Wait, Sir Desmond – there may be others escaped.' Sir Desmond pushed him aside, moving in, kneeling by his son, holding the lantern up. Henry had been dead for several hours, his face darkly blotched already, twisted in pain, two clear marks by his swollen chin where the fangs had sunk in, as if he had embraced the reptile. There was an unpleasant smell in the air, so that it was Sir Desmond now who, standing up, prevented Frances from entering.

'No, my dear, no!'

She struggled with him. 'But why?' she shouted. 'Why?'

'The brute escaped – and bit him, simply bit him,' her father shouted at Frances, raising his voice over hers as she fought hysterically in his arms.

The other snakes were summarily executed by Simpson

that night. A massacre of innocents? Pat Kennedy wondered. For he had clearly seen the fang marks on Henry Cordiner's cheek. Had he somehow let the snake kill him, as a result of his interview with the two detectives?

The men were identified as such by Sir Desmond the following morning – in a flurry of telegrams, a talk with old Seamus Newman at Thomastown station and a trip to Dublin that same afternoon, where he had a meeting with the Police Commissioner at the Castle. But the details of this he did not reveal to anyone, returning that night a very shaken man.

'It is something I can't discuss with you, my dear,' he told Lady Cordiner, confined to her bedroom, in a state of agonized collapse. 'Believe me, it would be far better not. Suffice to say that Henry got himself into some trouble while he was in London. All charges have now, of course, been dropped.'

Lady Cordiner, the more heartbroken still for hearing some crime linked to her son's death, did not pursue the matter. Frances on the other hand, told the same thing by her father, pursued the reasons behind his sudden, shocking death vigorously. An early opportunity arose with Dermot Cordiner's arrival, among other family members, two days later for the funeral. Knowing him, liking him, she spoke to him at once, outright, going into his bedroom just after he'd got in from the Dublin train with his father.

'Dermot, Dermot, what has *happened*?'

He did not reply. She had cried hysterically at first at her brother's death, astounded, unbelieving. But now, though no calmer in her heart, her emotion had been transformed into a hard-eyed enquiry into the mystery, the injustice of the event. She looked at Dermot in amazement now when he said nothing, thinking that he alone, as Henry's closest friend, must have some explanation for the horror. Dermot moved away from her in his neat dark suit, ruffling his frizzy, straw-coloured hair, then smoothing it nervously. Finally he turned and shrugged.

'But, Dermot – you must know something. You *saw* him in London.'

'Yes. Yes I did.'

'And?'

'And nothing, Frances, nothing.' Dermot coughed, choking a moment, got a handkerchief out, fussed with it. His bright blue eyes flittered about nervously.

'Nothing?'

'He was disappointed, of course, by our African trip not going through.'

'But these two men – two policemen that came to see him, just before the accident?'

'Policemen?' Dermot looked away again. 'I didn't know.'

'About some criminal charge he was involved in, Papa said.'

'I knew nothing of that. Henry mentioned nothing.' Dermot paid full attention to Frances now, bending down, his neat frame leaning over the table, knuckles whitening on the mahogany. 'But I had to be at the War Office a lot. I didn't see as much of Henry in London as I'd have liked—'

'Dermot, something's not right, someone's hiding things – I know it. And the snakes, too. Henry would never have been so careless—'

'He killed himself? Let himself be killed –?'

'Oh, God, I don't know. It's possible. But no one will say, or help. We must find out, we must!'

'Why? He's dead. What difference will it make, Frances? It won't bring him back.'

Frances faced him across the table now, a Gladstone bag open between them. 'It matters, because I want to know why he killed himself – if he did.'

Dermot sighed, picking some stiff collars from the bag, then drew himself up suddenly. 'He loved me, Frances,' he said simply, fingering the collars, moving away to the chest of drawers.

'Of course,' she answered, surprised at so obvious a statement. 'As I loved him. But why should that have anything to do with it?'

'I really wanted my army career,' he said slowly, dully.

'More than the travelling, the exploration. Wanted to make a real career of it – and, when I was offered this position at the War Office, well, I jumped at it – when Henry wanted me to make this East African journey with him.'

'So?'

'Can't you see?' He turned to her.

'Loving you, why should he so mind that?'

'Well, he did, you see.'

'But love is a good thing, he must have wanted your success.'

'With him, though, not with the army or Milner in the Cape Colony. Henry felt I'd betrayed him.'

'Betrayed him?' Frances remembered her angry, agonized feelings when Harold had done the same to her. 'But it wasn't that sort of love – you weren't going to *marry* him!' Frances was astonished.

'It was, Frances,' he told her simply. 'It *was* that kind of love.'

Frances stood back from the table, head swimming. 'Oh, Dermot, how awful, how terrible. I see – I do see now, which is why he wouldn't marry. *You* were the person – when I used to ask him who she was.' She looked at Dermot now in a wholly new way. It was strange, yet it made perfect sense to her. She could entirely understand the feelings between them; she understood, she thought, any kind of love.

Dermot blinked, still standing with his back to the chest of drawers. 'And you, Frances – he told me, if you hadn't been his sister: how you were the only woman he could ever have thought to marry . . . He told me that. And I can see why. He was right.'

The two cousins looked at each other across the room in the dull light, vague ghosts in mourning clothes, before Frances rushed across, embracing him. 'Dear Dermot,' she said. 'How awful – *awful* for you.' He held her briefly.

'How very right he was about you,' he told her again, looking over her shoulder, sadder still now, yet warmed, amazed at this woman's innocent understanding.

'But why the police?' Frances asked, suddenly moving back from him, looking at him so bluntly that he could not prevaricate.

'I don't know, but I suspect he may have taken up with some unsavoury – some rough company in London after I left him.'

'I don't understand? Is that a crime?'

'It can be, Frances – between men,' he said reluctantly.

'I'd no idea!' She shook her head in disbelief, curls dancing, eyes wide and staring, so that Dermot saw himself accused then.

'I shouldn't have told you.' He spoke with cold resignation, acknowledging his own guilt and accepting the worst for himself in the whole matter.

'But of course you should, Dermot – if you think it's the truth.' She saw his unhappiness, moved towards him again, touched his hand. 'That's what I wanted, the truth – not lies, from Papa. It's always been lies and evasions here. One must tell the truth.'

'Even if it hurts?'

'But it doesn't. It's the lies that do that.'

'In any case, I feel entirely to blame,' he said, turning away, walking towards the window. She looked at his retreating back intently, as if summing him up in his absence.

Then she said quickly, vividly, 'No, Dermot, loving someone – is not to give your life up entirely for them, to throw away everything of your own. You were right to want to pursue your own career, of *course* you were.'

He turned, surprised. 'I least of all expected to hear that from you, Frances, a woman. You're simply being kind—'

'No, I'm not! That was why I wouldn't marry Harold. I know it myself, because I'd have lost *me* – and all this, here, at Summer Hill, which I love, which is my career, in a way. So I know exactly how you felt – and you were right to do as you did. And Henry was weak – that was the really awful thing. I saw it with Mama over the years. And I told him. I loved him, but I told him and he knew it, yet he went on doing these weak things so that finally he killed himself,' she rushed on. 'And that's what happens when you're weak, it goes from bad to worse and you can't stop it. You have to make a stand against it, from the beginning, and Henry never did. In that way Mama killed him, if anyone did – and that's the truth, too,' she added viciously, working herself up into a state. Dermot looked at her in astonishment. 'You are not to blame for your strength, Dermot,' she went on. 'How can you be? It's what he loved in you,' she added, looking at him now with candour and affection. He returned her gaze in the same way.

'I love you for just the same quality,' he said quietly.

In their shared loss a great bond, a bond of strength, was struck between them then.

The funeral, at which Frances insisted on following the hearse and the plumed horses with the men across the autumn fields to the family vault behind the church at the edge of the estate, was tediously and unnecessarily pompous, Frances thought – the Bishop of Ossory, all the way out from Kilkenny, addressing the packed congregation, offering endless platitudes, both spiritual and temporal.

Lies again, she thought – more concerned than ever now to live her life without them. Dermot had told her the truth about Henry and it had been a breath of fresh air which, though she knew she could not share it with anyone but him, gave her added confidence in all her natural assumptions. She no longer regretted, for an instant, her uncompromising temperament. She missed Henry desperately. But she saw his death, his weakness, as something imposed on him. What a price he had paid to convention – his mother's, his family's, the world's. She would never pay that price, would never contemplate it.

She looked at her father, a broken figure at the end of the pew, then at the porky Eustace, awkwardly mourning. They were living victims of the same impositions. And Summer Hill as well, which Henry would have inherited – the house, she saw then, would not have been freed by him but would simply have come to reflect his weaknesses, to hold his unhappiness and frustration, as it did her mother's now, remaining frigid, unfulfilled. She looked at Eustace, then. The house would come to him. What would he make of it? He was subservient to his mother, in a childlike, disingenuous way – and like his meek father, but lacking Sir Desmond's inventive gifts. He made the worst of both worlds, Frances thought – without Lady Cordiner's culture or authority or his father's flair. He was conventional – steady, easy-going, biddable and unthinking, largely unaware of others or his surroundings: a model officer and a gentleman. And that was what Summer Hill would come to reflect.

With an equally placid wife, lots of children, army friends and the duller horsy people of the county as visitors, the house would become like a thousand others of its kind in Ireland: staid and unimaginative, a bastion against all real life and feeling. For it was her mother at least, Frances knew, with her intelligence, money, vivacity and arrogance – yes, her Jewishness – who gave Summer Hill its purpose, its glitter and originality now. With Eustace, it would revert into anonymity, a shell echoing with platitudes, with everything conventional.

She held Dermot's hand rather pointedly as they walked back from the church, while she looked east to the clouds running over Mount Brandon, sudden shafts of sun and cloud shadow rolling over the gorse, the valley tinged everywhere with reds and orange, the leaves turning in a soft fire. When the house came in view at the top of the rise she squeezed Dermot's hand and said, just as she had said to Henry a few weeks before, 'Look!' And she gestured towards the graceful limestone rising from the tinted autumn trees, lines of tall shuttered windows mirroring the scudding clouds and sunlight, patterns moving across the glass like changing thought in human eyes: a house so secretly alive, rising so easily above death, offering life. 'Just look at it,' she said again, breathlessly, a pit of emotion opening in her stomach.

'Yes,' he said at once, seeming to know what she felt

about Summer Hill. 'And you mustn't see it all as an end, Frances. But a beginning.'

'Oh I do. I *do*,' she answered quickly, as if she was approaching a marriage, not leaving a funeral.

'Open the curtains and shutters, Pat. Where's Flood? – should have been done first thing. And all this black crêpe taken down, too.'

Frances spoke to Pat Kennedy in the darkened hall next morning beneath the covered chandelier. The reception rooms had remained shuttered for the funeral. And afterwards, the evenings drawing in quickly now, it had not been worth opening them again – or so Frances had assumed. But the day was fine and bright, the windows ought to be opened, and Frances in the absence of her mother still upstairs in bed – too unwell to attend either the funeral or the tea – relished the thought of taking temporary charge of the household.

'I'm afraid her Ladyship left strict instructions, Miss Frances, not to open anything or remove—'

'She *what*?' Frances picked up the pile of black-bordered mourning cards and letters of condolence on the hall table, about to put them away.

'Not to touch a thing, Miss Frances.' Pat Kennedy looked at her uneasily.

'That's nonsense. Have Mrs Martin come and see me, please.'

'She's upstairs with her Ladyship at the moment—'

'Never mind. I'll open them myself.'

Pat Kennedy looked at her, amazed, almost fearful, while Frances moved to the hall door, opening it, letting in the brilliant light from the porch, the fresh air of a tingling-sharp autumn day. Attached to the door was a large funeral wreath of glum evergreens. She tried to take it down, but it was firmly nailed to the wood. Returning to the drawing room, she was depressed at the vision. Black sashes hung from all the curtain rails; pictures had been masked with crêpe, every bright thing put away, dustcovers over all the furniture. It was the same in the dining room, the long table entirely obscured by a dull serge undercloth, all the family portraits sashed and shrouded.

In the general emotion of the day before, the crush and heat of people, Frances had barely noticed these exaggerated funerary mementoes: a far too lavish and tasteless indulgence of her mother's, she thought now. It was nonsense. Henry was dead and gone, entombed in the family crypt among his ancestors. He could only be mourned now in thought, not in curling evergreens, tatty black crêpe and black-bordered stationery. She would have it all removed.

Meanwhile, thinking of Henry's effects, and suddenly remembering his pet lemur Gretel, she strode quickly upstairs to his bedroom on the first landing. The door was locked – as was his suite of work rooms in the old nurseries on the top floor. She came downstairs and spoke to Pat Kennedy again in the butler's pantry. Flood was with him now.

'Flood, what is all this about?' She was brusque. 'All this nonsense. My brother's rooms are locked, the whole house like an undertaker's parlour. And Gretel – where has she gone?'

'To the young master's zoo, miss. And, for the rest, it was her Ladyship's clear instructions, miss—'

'Yes, yes, I know that. But what?'

Flood looked abashed. 'That – that everything in the house was to stay exactly as it was, miss, and that nothing was to be touched in Mr Henry's rooms, the doors locked. A period of mourning, her Ladyship said. Some months at least, she said—'

'Some *months*? Is this usual, Flood? You were here when my grandfather died, weren't you?'

'Well, miss, not entirely . . .' He stopped.

'And? Was the whole house shuttered up – for months?'

'No, miss, it wasn't. Though her Ladyship wasn't here then—'

'That's all. That's all I wanted to know, Flood. We shall have the house opened again—' She turned. Mrs Martin had just arrived outside the pantry door.

'Miss Frances, her Ladyship would like to see you, with Mr Eustace, in her bedroom.' Mrs Martin, she saw, was still in widow's weeds.

Frances looked at her severely. 'Mary, this is absurd . . .' she started, then thought better of it, looking at the cowed and unhappy faces of the three servants. Her mother had obviously given them the most strict instructions; it was not their fault. She found Eustace and went upstairs.

The bedroom, completely shuttered, was dark but for one small oil lamp on the bedside table next to a crêpe-bordered photograph of Henry – Henry as a young boy, curly-haired, dressed almost as a girl. Her mother lay propped against an uncomfortable mountain of pillows in the great curtained four-poster – a reduced figure, half in shadow, so that her face was almost invisible. Lady Cordiner, a black lace napkin over her head and black shawl round her shoulders, lay perfectly still on the bed, so that here it seemed was the corpse, the reason for all this mourning. The room, shuttered and airless, smelt of camphor, smelling salts and lamp oil: like a hospital – or a morgue.

'Mama? – are you all right?' There was no reply. 'Mama, we're here. Are you all right?' Eustace stood awkwardly behind her. Finally her mother stirred, leaning forward with a great effort.

'Children,' she began haltingly, a reedy voice emerging from behind the veil. 'We are all quite heartbroken – a tragedy that cannot be overcome, cannot be forgotten, cannot be put right, which we must all suffer . . .' Her voice became stronger as she spoke, more exact and formal, as if she had memorized the words.

'Mama, it's not—'

'Quiet, girl! You will not interrupt,' she snapped. 'A death that has struck at the very heart of our lives, the life of Summer Hill, the whole future – which has been destroyed in a trice, where we cannot make amends other than by our own suffering, where we must share each other's lasting grief . . . I want both of you to realize that, to join me in this deep mourning . . . mourning for a dear soul departed . . .' Her voice, with these Old Testament tones and admonitions, came haltingly again now, seemingly stricken with emotion.

Frances was astonished. Her mother had clearly lost her wits. She looked at Eustace, but he did not react, standing, head bowed, like a penitent at the end of the bed.

'Mama,' she said. 'Of course we mourn dear Henry. But—'

'Quiet, I said, girl. I shall have more to say to you – you,' she added bitterly, 'you who must bear the brunt of responsibility for this tragedy—'

'Me, Mama?'

'Yes, you! – You think I don't see it all quite clearly now? You, who drove Henry away from here, so often in the past, so that he would not stay with me. You, with your thieving designs on the house, as if it were yours and not his, so that he felt unwanted—'

'Mama, I had nothing to do with it. And he was killed by one of his snakes – you know that! I shall hear no more of this nonsense! You are overwhelmed with grief, I perfectly realize. But you shall not accuse me in such a manner. I will hear no more of it. We must get on with our lives now. The house must be put in order – it cannot be kept as a mausoleum, a shuttered, blackened—'

'How dare you! You will do nothing of the sort,' Lady Cordiner shouted, finding her usual strident voice suddenly. 'The house will be kept exactly as it was! Eustace, I charge you with seeing that *nothing*, but nothing, is altered in the present setting and manner of things. And as for you,' she said simply, turning her livid face to Frances, 'you will go from here! Go from this house, which you have so desecrated.'

'Yes, Mama,' Frances indulged her mother, looking back at her with condescending pity as she left the room.

'She has clearly lost her reason,' Frances said, describing this meeting to her father and Dr Mitchell, the family doctor, who had come out from Thomastown that afternoon. They met in Sir Desmond's study, where her father wandered aimlessly round the gloomy room with its death's head fox masks set above the bookcases, a wraith-like figure himself, clearly less able than ever to cope with these household disasters and disputes.

'Well, I'd not go so far as to say that, Miss Frances,' Dr Mitchell, a bluff middle-aged Protestant from Munster, spoke with a rich Cork accent. 'It's only temporary – the shock has taken your mother that way. Sometimes does, when they imagine all sorts of things—'

'That *I* was responsible for my brother's death?' Frances interrupted vehemently.

'Oh, yes, all sorts of sheer illusions.' He was a big, jolly, horsy type in gaiters and a broad-check suit. He knocked his pipe out now on the grate. 'The maddest sort of things – fire and brimstone, the lot. Seen it often enough before.'

'Come, Dr Mitchell,' Frances continued on the attack. 'My mother has always been malicious – but in an entirely sane and practical way. No hint of such ravings. And they were just that – the ravings of a mad woman. How could she so change overnight?'

Dr Mitchell humphed. 'Oh, indeed she could, just that. Exactly what happens – with some sudden, terrible event like this. But you mustn't take any notice of it. She doesn't mean what she says—'

'Oh, but she does! Tell Dr Mitchell, Papa, what she said to you, when you say she was quite calm, before I saw her this morning.' Her father, over by the small window, winced. 'Go on, Papa.' She glared at his back.

'Well, that you ought to leave the house, dearest. But I'm sure—'

'There – you see!' Frances almost shouted at the doctor. 'And she was quite composed at that point. I have to leave – because I was the cause of Henry's death. She's mad, but she means it all right!' Frances was roused now, bitter at the injustice of it all, barely able to control herself.

The two men, shocked at her outburst, looked at her doubtfully. Finally her father spoke. 'My dear, it would probably be better, just for the time being, if you left for a while . . .'

Frances turned to Dr Mitchell. He was nodding his head – avuncular, wise, understanding. 'The great thing is for her to avoid any upsets. I'm sure you don't want to aggravate your mother, if you can help it—'

'You could go and stay with Cousin Mortimer at Islandbridge, just for a month. Or a few weeks perhaps,' her father temporized. He was more enthusiastic now.

'Indeed,' the doctor said. 'Indeed you could – a grand girl like yourself, find plenty of things to do in Dublin. And that'd be the best of it certainly – from your mother's point of view.'

The two men appeared very reasonable. Yet there was a clear hint in their eyes – of condescension, certainly, as well as mistrust and suspicion – which told Frances that they did not really judge her mother wrong or mad at all in so banishing her. Of course, Frances thought, her father and the old family doctor – they both knew of her longstanding antagonism towards her mother, the temperamental clashes between them over the years. And of course they secretly took Lady Cordiner's side in the matter. Frances, in their view, was an unruly, ungrateful, insensitive daughter – a thorn in her mother's side, much better out of the house indeed, which she ought to have left long before, not hanging round forever exasperating her mother. She was in the wrong. Her mother, prostrate but still wicked as ever, had won. Frances was absolutely furious, her anger erupting now, uncontrolled.

'Well, if you think that, if you've been taken in by my mother, I really don't know what to say! That preposterous old fraud up there in bed with her evil imaginings. And you don't see it! It was she, if anyone, who brought my brother's death about, with her constant cosseting and nagging; she who drove him away from the house and made him what he was – unable to cope with life, just as she wants to do to me now; get rid of me, too: she, who dominates you, blackmails and bosses you, and both of you submitting to her every whim, every nonsense, like shutting the whole house up with black crêpe for months. And you just stand there, grown men, letting her get away with it, pandering to her! All I can say is – is you ought to be absolutely ashamed of yourselves!'

She glared at them, before turning abruptly and walking imperiously out of the room.

'Tut, tut,' Dr Mitchell said when she had gone, getting out fresh tobacco for his pipe, relaxing. 'The little vixen! But she'll see sense, Sir Desmond, she surely will.' They discussed matters further in a desultory way. However, it was not long before they looked up in alarm, hearing the first of the shutters banging open in the big reception rooms beyond.

Frances threw herself methodically at all the curtains in the drawing room first – dragging them wide, spinning the shutters back, clattering them against the wood, opening the windows, letting the light and air stream in. She tore the black sashes down, took the crêpe from the pictures and flicked off most of the dustcovers before moving into the dining room where she did the same, freeing all the family portraits. Then she tugged the serge mourning cloth from the great table in one vigorous movement, scattering salts and candlesticks before shredding the rest of the grim paper decor. Back in the hall she opened both the great doors wide and simply tore the laurel wreath from its nails. Then, standing on a chair, she tugged away the bag from around the chandelier so that the crystal danced and tinkled. As she worked obsessively, her face reddening, a gusty autumn breeze blowing leaves in from the porch, the house, with its doors and windows open now, became an airy, wind-blown place, small gales coursing through the heavy rooms.

While she gathered together a pile of mourning cards on the hall table, her father and Dr Mitchell appeared, Mrs Martin with Pat Kennedy standing alarmed behind them.

'Here!' she said to her astonished father, throwing the black-bordered cards and envelopes at him so that they streamed through the windy hall like tiny kites. 'Mourn him in paper, if that's all you want.'

She left the two men, moving towards Mrs Martin and Pat. 'Eileen? Have you seen Eileen?' But she did not wait for an answer, striding past them into the back of the house, then taking the stairs down to the basement and kitchen.

'Eileen?' she called. The girl appeared at the kitchen door. 'Eileen, will you pack my things, please? I shall be leaving for Dublin at once.'

'Yes—' Eileen was startled. 'Yes, I will surely.'

'I'll be staying in Dublin for a bit, with my cousin Mortimer. Will you come with me?' She gazed at her forcefully, wide-eyed, happy, offering the girl one more great adventure.

'I—' Eileen was uncertain.

'Not for long – a few weeks. I'll be coming back, don't worry.'

'I will, then, miss—'

'*Frances*, Eileen.'

'Yes, Miss Frances.'

'Good. Splendid.'

As she turned back along the passageway, Frances saw the long line of sprung room bells on the wall above her. She reached up, hitting each one vigorously as she passed, so that immediately, the metal tongues giving voice one after the other, a great joyous cacophony of sound rose from the basement, filtering up through the house.

Lady Cordiner heard the sounds faintly in her shuttered room, before pulling viciously at her own bell. Aunt Emily heard them, stopping in her grimly baroque drawing of the plumed horses and hearse of Henry's funeral procession crossing the demesne. Eustace heard them in the gun room, morosely oiling his twelve-bore. Nearly everyone in Summer Hill heard the wild bells ring out, felt the breeze flow through the house, the sound and wind of liberation. Mrs Molloy and Flood, parlour, kitchen, scullery and still room maids, laundry maids and footmen – all stopped in their work, or woke from a doze, surprised or alarmed. Some thought there was a fire, others that Lady Cordiner had risen from her bed in vengeance, a few of the more superstitious believed it was the spirit of the young master himself returned to haunt the place. Only Aunt Emily, when Frances came to explain and say goodbye, understood at once what it was all about.

'Well done, girl!' She congratulated her niece. 'Just what I'd have done myself – in better times. So you're off at last. Well, remember that hotel I told you about in Paris, near the shops. The manager is less offensive than they usually are. And entirely accommodating – you won't need any cash.'

Frances kissed her softly. 'Yes, Aunt. But I'll be back – I will. To see you.'

'Of course you will, girl. Now excuse yourself, before you miss the train.' When Frances had gone she looked at her funeral sketch, scowled at it, laughed quickly, then tore it up. 'Yes, indeed, we'll have no more of that nonsense – and quite right too,' she said to herself.

Frances looked back at Summer Hill from the waggonette as Molloy frisked the horse along the avenue. A scatter of rooks rose from the trees around the house, blown about in the sky like tea-leaves, their harsh chatterings thrown to her on the wind – the rooks of Summer Hill, which for Frances had always seemed like household deities, the very spirit of the place, so that for a moment, for the first time, she felt the heartbreak of her departure and thought she was going to cry. But she didn't. She must not. She would not allow herself to be sad. Leaving the house was a defeat, but in a battle not the war. And at last, she further consoled herself, she had nailed her colours firmly to the mast. The endless temporizing, the frustrations, evasions and prevarications of her life at Summer Hill were over. Everyone there now knew where she stood. Someone had had to make a stand against the cruel lifelessness of the place, the dictatorship of her mother – she had done that and she was right, she knew. Life was the thing, not death, not mourning.

Frances looked across at the pensive Eileen on the opposite seat, smiled at her, a candid tenderness in her eyes. 'A penny for them, Eileen?'

Eileen, with a glum face, had been thinking of Pat Kennedy, the conversation she had just had with him – the obvious fact that he did not seem very much to mind her leaving Summer Hill. He didn't love her, she decided, or at least he was more concerned with a stronger love, his own secret rebellions, the meetings and drillings in the woods with the other rebels in the area. He had ditched her, that was what it amounted to. So now, in answer, taking courage from her mistress's devil-may-care behaviour, she burst out, 'It was brave of you, Miss Frances. It was a brave thing you did this afternoon – that's what I was thinking.'

'We can't be sad, Eileen. Life's not for that. And it was just as brave of you – to come with me. And fortune favours the brave, so they say.'

Eileen nodded vigorously – and suddenly there were tears in her eyes, tears in the smile as she said, 'Oh, what a lark, Miss Frances – I can't believe it, out of that stuffy old house . . .'

Frances offered her a lace handkerchief and the two women turned then, looking expectantly up the valley, where the wind and the sun fell on the yellowing leaves, rustling them in a lovely dazzle, the cob's hooves echoing in the crisp air, smacking on the hard road now as they drove smartly out of the gates, making for the Dublin train.

Frances had telegraphed ahead, so that, when they got to Islandbridge House that evening, Mortimer – and Dermot, who had not yet returned to his work at the War Office in Whitehall – were expecting them. Mortimer stood by the mantelpiece in the small drawing room, Dermot in the bay window, half-open against the twilight so that the sounds of the weir by the bridge some distance away came clearly across the lawn, the engines chuffing in and out of Kingsbridge station further downstream on the other side of the river, the city itself a faint hum to the east. A busy metropolitan life lay just beyond the house and it excited Frances, seemed to justify all her actions at

Summer Hill: life – that had been her cause there; and now here she was, almost touching it.

The forthright and caustic Mortimer, when she had told her story, supported her, but with reservations. 'Your mother has never had enough scope for her gifts down there – a frustrated sense of the dramatic among other things, I've often felt, which accounts for her taking to her bed and playing Queen Victoria in a nightcap, trying to turn the place into a mausoleum for poor Henry. But I don't know that you should have so publicly attacked her foibles, dear Frances!'

'I was furious, at the spinelessness of everyone there—'

'Yes, yes – I see that. I've felt the same in my time. But *your* behaviour, look at that a moment, Frances. It simply shows your frustrations as much as anything – keeping yourself stuck down there, head against brick walls, when you should be out and about in the world. You surely see that, don't you?' Mortimer's small blue eyes glittered aggressively with this well-meant advice. He smoothed his extensive beard, eased a thin leg on the fender, picked his sherry glass up.

'Yes, I suppose so,' Frances said at last.

'Simply not good for *you*, Frances, this eternal combat with your Mama, because it's not *producing* anything for you.'

'I suppose not. Except that what I want to produce is for Summer Hill, not for me.'

'Be honest. The fact is you really want to run the house down there yourself, don't you? And that's always *bound* to clash head on with your Mama.' He emphasized the vital words, the voice rising theatrically, as was his habit in the privacy of his own drawing room or in the House of Commons. Trained originally in the law, and a lawyer still, in substantiating his point of view, he followed it up with sharp insight, a seemingly irrefutable argument – and always a brisk energy to drive the nails home.

But Frances was tired, remaining silent now. It was not the moment to explain what she really wanted at Summer Hill, all the myriad feelings she had about the house, her need, her love for it – the house like a lover now whom she had deserted.

Dermot turned in the bow window. 'The obvious answer then, Papa, is for Frances to come with us to London – and help run your little house there, isn't it?' Frances looked from one man to the other. 'You've only got Mrs Moxon coming in in the morning at the moment – the place might do with some running when you go back to Westminster. Why not?'

'Oh, Frances wouldn't want that,' Mortimer said. 'Poky little house . . .'

There was silence, indecision in the air, before Frances filled it with a firm small voice. 'Oh, yes I would,' she said. 'I'd love it, if you'd let me – I really would.'

A train started out from Kingsbridge, a few great bellows from the chimney first, then the fainter, regular rhythm of the wheels and pistons as it got under way.

'Very well, Frances.' Mortimer reached for his sherry. 'It'll be wonderful to have your company in any case. To London, then!'

They all raised their glasses.

4

The sun had dropped behind the roofs of Kensington Palace leaving a blowy chill over the deserted park. The leaves scattered in great drifts across the grass, the wind catching them, chasing them round the Albert Memorial, pursuing them over the Serpentine bridge, along Rotten Row towards the empty bandstand where the last concert of the season had finished several weeks before. Now there was only the notice: 'The Park gates will close at five o'clock or sunset, whichever is the earlier.'

Frances shivered, drew her fur collar closer, and turned quickly home. She had lost all track of time in her walk about Hyde Park – an outing which she had made almost every afternoon since her arrival in London with Eileen and the two men a week before. And now, once more, she was astonished by the city, in seeing the notice, that a park – the countryside to her – should ever close. She had not adapted herself to the loss of these freedoms – to roam wherever she wanted, at whatever hour, which she had loved at home. Indeed, more than that – Dermot had warned her not to walk in the park alone at all, at this season and late hour, when almost no one else did: there were rogues and footpads about. Or, at least, she should take Eileen with her. But Frances had wanted to be alone – to think what she might do with her life. But now, all thought abandoned and fearing that she might be locked in for the night, she quickened her step towards the gates.

A great charge of broughams, hansom cabs and omnibuses streamed round Hyde Park Corner, sweeping like chariots into Knightsbridge. She felt safer now among the clatter of hooves, the crowds everywhere hurrying on the pavements. Yet here again, very soon, she found herself losing touch, mesmerized, rooted on the brink of the street crossing, where urchins swept the leaves and dung at intervals between the rush of traffic. A man pushed and jostled her, before leaping past into a gap between the flow of vehicles. One of the ragged boys in the gutter whistled, beckoning her on, gesturing rudely. Now, among so much noise and movement, she was suddenly overwhelmed, at a loss, just as she had found herself in the empty park. London was all hot or cold, frenzy or emptiness, extremes. You took your chances . . .

Lifting her skirts she rushed out into the traffic without really looking – so that a hansom cab, bearing down, swerved at the last moment, the horse viciously reined in, rearing up in front of her, the cabby swearing. She ran for her life blindly, putting her foot in a pile of dung in the other gutter, the waif there laughing at her outrageously. London, this vast throbbing imperial city which she had only been to once three years before, was wonderful yet terrible, she thought – unless you attacked, controlled, dominated it. But how, in her present circumstances, was she ever to do that? As a debutante, it had been very different. With parties and dances arranged for her every day, she had had the support of her mother, a bevy of hired servants and carriages, and a large house in Mayfair which had been taken for the Season. Now she was more or less on her own.

Walking down Knightsbridge, she left the crowds, turning into the quieter Wilton Place. The gas lights had come on in the early twilight and the Italian organ-grinder with his monkey was there again, she saw, near Mortimer's house, on the other side of the street, opposite the church. She was calmer now. She liked the gay music – a polka, then a waltz – echoing in the distance, a touch of coming frost in the air sharpening the piped notes, the footfalls, the coachmen's voices in the ale house on the corner. London was suddenly human again in these quiet little crescents and mews behind Belgrave Square – where she seemed to have entered a village, a hidden intimate place, the music like an overture promising excitement in the sudden dark in which the street lamps were beacons, directing people home to all sorts of pleasures in the lamplit drawing rooms behind the curtains. London, which they had come to control, was theirs behind all the secret windows. She put a threepenny bit into the bowler that the monkey offered – almost the last of her ready cash – before turning up the short pathway to her cousin's house, getting her latchkey out. She had become accustomed to the key, at least, she thought, with doors everywhere securely locked here: locked against her for the time being, she felt, where she was shut out from all the life that surrounded her.

The smartly painted house – one of a line in a neat Georgian terrace running down to Wilton Crescent – was small but not poky. The front was narrow, certainly. But it was tall enough, rising three storeys over a basement with servants' rooms on the top floor. And the rooms, though narrow, were high-ceilinged and cleverly spacious – lengthy rooms, leading back to a long garden with the coachhouse in the mews behind.

Eileen slept at the top. Frances and the two men occupied bedrooms on the second floor, with a long, light-panelled drawing room-cum-library, divided by sliding doors, beneath – and a similarly gracious dining room with a shiny Chippendale leaf table and silver candelabra on the ground floor. A bijou residence, Frances thought, letting herself in, shouting to Eileen down the stairs in the kitchen before going up to her bedroom.

Neither of the men was home yet. The new session at Westminster had just begun; Mortimer rarely returned before midnight. Dermot was often delayed at the Ministry of Imperial Defence. And that was one of the problems, Frances thought, taking her jacket off in the prettily decorated bedroom: there was little enough house-running to do here, and little to occupy her outside.

She frisked the fire up in the small grate, taking a chair beside it, leaning forward, staring into the brightening coals – not the vast log fires she was used to. And yet it was warm in the house, especially with this new central heating they had. She loosened her high collar, got up and turned the magic electricity on above her dressing table mirror – gazed into the glass carefully and critically, turning her head one way, then the other. She needed some new image for herself in London. A new hair style – new accents, with rouge or silk, in her face and clothes? A new something, she thought. What was it? Clothes, of course, would be one answer. And there were so many of them, lovely new winter fashions in the big stores further down the road in Knightsbridge. But they were expensive and she had little money.

She ran a finger from her forehead down her nose. It was all too straight, the one leading to the other almost without interruption. She longed for a more broken nose, more fashionably retroussé. The forms there now, in brow, high cheek bones and nose, were too stern, regal. It gave people the wrong impression, as her skin probably did, too, with its faint olive tinge, a smoked ivory touch from her Spanish ancestors.

She bit in her too-full lips. They seemed better that way,

but her chin rose and flattened in an ugly manner when she did this. Her hair might be the easiest thing to alter, it would add a touch of refinement, make her less a country bumpkin. She ran her fingers through the dark helmet of loose curls. They had lost their country gloss in the grime and autumn fogs of London. She would bath – and wash and experiment with her hair then and there, rearrange it, have it ready for Dermot's opinion when he came back for dinner.

Dermot, she thought, as she lay submerged, luxuriating in the deep hot water, arching one knee, then the other, above the soapsuds, flattening her back right down on the bottom of the bath so that the water rippled comfortingly over her small breasts – Dermot intrigued her: that pale skin, austere face, crinkly straw hair; the delicate bones, slim body; the feeling of something sensitive, almost feminine there, hidden beneath a more obvious masculinity, a careful force. There were contradictions. And they lay in his spirit too. What sort of man was he? What, exactly, had he meant when he talked of 'that kind of love' between men? Only men and women could love each other in that way. He had spoken inaccurately or she had misunderstood him. She might ask him about these things, in time.

She lay still for a while, then raised her flanks and stomach, holding her breath, so that with this buoyancy the water fell away, in rivulets, across the oils of her skin, and she rose from the depths. She looked down her smooth, moistly steaming body where it narrowed dramatically at the waist before splaying out again over her hips. Then she took a fold of skin there, beside the navel, gently pinching it: a ready inch came up in her fingers. Too much, she wondered?

She washed her hair later and had Eileen help her rearrange it – flattening the curls, trimming some of them, pinning them back severely to the sides above her ears, letting the others on the crown of her head stand up as they had been.

'What do you think?'

Eileen stood behind her at the mirror. 'Well . . .' She was undecided.

'Go on!'

'Well, you look a bit scalded, Miss Frances . . .'

'It's the fashion.' She turned and looked up reprovingly at the girl.

'I'm sure it is. Just – you look strange, not like you.'

'Never mind. One must change you know, now we're in London.' Eileen helped her on with her dress then – in red velvet with turned-back white lace, an under-dress in ruched green silk – the only really decent costume she had with her, and even this was out of date, she knew. The *Journal des Modes*, which she had bought the day before at Woolland's in Knightsbridge, was crammed with far more fashionably tantalizing things. And more than that, she thought, as Eileen tightened the waist, this dress was too small for her – or was she too fat? The waist really pinched now as Eileen tugged at the back buttons. The twenty-two inch waist, like a wasp's, which she had had the year before, was no longer there. Yes, she had to admit it now – that was what was wrong; here was the real problem which lay against her London ambitions: she was too *fat*, already beginning to take on her mother's plumpness. She had avoided the fact in the bath. But now, with the evidence of the dress, there was no doubt where the trouble lay. She went down to dinner less confident about herself than she had ever been in her life.

Dermot sat opposite, at the far end of the table, the lit candelabra between them. He moved it aside the better to see her.

'Ravishing,' he said, with a touch of irony. 'But then you always were.'

'And the hair?'

'Not quite certain. You . . .' He paused.

'All right, all right – Eileen said it: that I looked scalded.'

'Yes, well . . .' Dermot paused again judiciously, before

continuing with sudden enthusiasm. 'But you see, Frances, you really don't need to be other than you are. Absolutely not.'

'But I do! I have to do something – change things over here. And I've discovered I'm getting fat as well.' She was downcast then, fiddling with her cutlery. 'And you know perfectly well – I can't lurk here indefinitely "running" the place. Runs perfectly well without me. You were being kind, that's all, having me here.'

'But of *course* we were being kind – all of us to each other. Distant cousins maybe, but part of the same family after all. You'll find your feet – no great hurry—'

'Oh, but there is!' Frances grasped a knife impulsively. 'I have to *do* something.'

'Well, you can't join the army.' He smiled at her curiously. 'Always so ambitious – thrusting away, when most women would be quite content with needlework and idle chatter.'

'Well, I can't be – even if I wanted to – since Mama will certainly cut me off now, "without a penny".' She resumed her ironic tone. 'And I'm not going to marry,' she went on decisively. 'That's another thing I won't consider. Like you.'

'Like me?'

'Well – like Henry, you're not the marrying sort, are you?' She looked at him with the flicker of a smile.

'Who knows?' he answered brightly, returning a much fuller smile, a touch of flirtatiousness in his eyes. 'Who knows?' he intoned in a deeper mocking voice.

A day or two later, Frances embarked on a regimen of physical training, designed to pare her weight and narrow her waist. Dermot obtained two sets of dumbbells, Indian clubs and a chest expander from the gymnasium at the Household Cavalry barracks – and together, each morning before breakfast, taking over one of the top-floor rooms, they lay on the boards lifting their feet, swirling clubs, and vigorously pursuing various other muscular tortures taken from an army manual. Frances obtained what looked like a circus tight-rope costume for these occasions: thin white woollen stockings that came right up to the tops of her thighs, a tight bodice in the same material, and an indecently small silk skirt that married these other garments together.

Eileen was shocked. Dermot found the whole business diverting. Mortimer, rising late, knew little of it until one morning, curious about the noise over his head, he came upstairs in his dressing gown and discovered them both, in what seemed to him a state of almost complete undress, writhing about on the floor.

'Good God,' was his only wry comment, before he turned back at the door. 'Reputation's bad enough at Westminster as it is,' he added.

'*One*, two, three – *One*, two, three . . .' Dermot sang out the stages of the exercise as they lay on their backs, pushing up from the waist, pausing, then tipping their toes. Now and then, he glanced at this vigorous woman, beautifully flushed, matching him step for step, lying beside him, her whole trunk arching back and forth in a wonderful rhythm. One made love in something of the same way, he thought – with a woman. At least, one might with this woman. The idea, against all his inclinations, excited him vaguely.

Frances hired one of the new safety bicycles, took hair-raising lessons on it at the Royal Cycle School in Euston Road, and, instead of walking morosely about the park in the afternoons, she now rode round its perimeter, much more happily, the wind in her hair, skirts flying. Sometimes she shrieked with joy at the sheer fun of it all so that only the odd horseless carriage, spluttering and back-firing along, attracted more attention from the passers-by. And later, through Dermot's good offices at the Cavalry barracks, she took the loan of a well-tempered chestnut mare called Rosie, and together, on other mornings, before breakfast, they rode in the park.

'What is it about your father,' she asked him one blustery, rain-threatened day as they moved along the Row, 'you both being so opposite – he with his Home Rule business, you so supporting the Empire – yet you get on so well together?'

Dermot looked up at the lowering clouds. 'Simple enough: we beg to differ. Home Rule in Ireland – he sees that as the right of a nation to do what it wants. And he thinks the same way about individual people. He never objected to my army career – and I like him all the more for it.'

Frances lowered her head against the sudden squall. 'Wish my parents were like that.'

'Frances, you'll have to make it up with your mother – at some point. Why not now? Why not write her a nice letter?'

'If it were that easy – I might. But it would make no difference,' she added, a sudden disgust in her voice. 'You don't know her. She sees me as more than just a wretch: I've despoiled the house, Henry's memory. It's a war – perhaps you should advise me on the tactics.'

'I have. Make it up with her. What other victory can there be?'

Coming to the end of the Row, Frances saw Kensington Palace beyond the Albert Memorial. Suddenly the clouds in the distance parted for a moment and a shaft of watery sun fell on the red brick, spreading a gold halo over the Palace for half a minute. 'The victory of my going back to Summer Hill one day,' she answered firmly. 'And living there.'

'Of your "winning" the house? But I don't see that. How?'

'Nor do I. I don't know "how" at the moment. But that's what I see myself doing in London – finding out. There must be a way,' she added quietly, more to herself than Dermot. He looked at her curiously, wondering at this obsessive longing which could not, he felt, ever be fulfilled, so that it gave Frances, for all her patrician self-confidence and forthright commonsense in other matters, the air of a woman touched, damaged in some essential. But then she had been damaged, he thought – a broken engagement, Henry's death, banishment from the family home by her mother.

All the same, he had seen in the last weeks how, when faced with these setbacks, she had quickly recovered and taken the initiative – with these exercises, the bicycle and horse-riding. And these were surely not prompted by her increased weight which was barely perceptible, mere puppy fat. It was an energy encouraged by a dream of Summer Hill, where she was preparing herself now, just as an army commander might, for a return engagement against the house. He could appreciate all the tactics here; they were straight out of the army manual: retreat in good order, re-form, consolidate a reserve position, renew stores and ammunition, set pickets and observation posts, prepare variations of original attack . . . This was what Frances had come to London for, he saw then: their house in Wilton Place was for her a headquarters in exile where she would plan a victorious return to Summer Hill, on behalf of the true monarchy, when the Pretender would be put to flight. What nonsense it all was, he thought, what sad nonsense – Frances was worth so much more.

'But really,' he said to her as they rode home, the rain dying now. 'All this Summer Hill thing – you're trying to regain a position you've never actually held. The house is your father's and will go to Eustace now. You're behaving as if you were a man, a son being denied your inheritance. It makes no sense.'

'I suppose not. But I love that house. I just wish I were a man,' she added defiantly.

He smiled at her distantly, hiding the compassion, the tenderness he felt for her in her wrong-headedness. And then he suddenly realized it was just this misguided, do-or-die male quality in her that he found most attractive.

But Frances, despite her physical regeneration through these vigorous activities, found no ease in her mind. She had not heard from her parents, and was not prepared, as Dermot had advised, to write to them herself and make things up. Nor, in this aggrieved mood, would she admit how she missed Summer Hill – missed its populated energy and familiar consolations: its friendships, domestic timetables, seasonal events and rhythms. Summer Hill had been for her a magic city, as London was not, and she would not face this fact. Instead she brooded on things – these contradictory rural and metropolitan hopes – resuming her lonely walks in the park.

She had noticed the rug-swathed invalid half a dozen times before, on brighter mornings or in the afternoon if the sun was still out: a restless young man being pushed along the edge of the Row in a bath-chair, gazing longingly at the Life Guards out exercising in their scarlet tunics and glittering helmets. His visits always seemed to coincide with these equestrian manoeuvres on the Row, so that she thought he might be a cavalry officer himself – and that the heavily bandaged leg propped up at the end of the chair could be the result of some service wound.

Yet the women who took him out on these autumn perambulations – and she had seen two of them – did not appear to be nurses. His family perhaps? There was an older lady, aristocratic-looking, with a fine long handsome face beneath a sensible hat, and someone a little younger, smaller and stouter who yet shared the same rather sallow skin, the same severe features on a reduced scale. Sisters, she thought? Like her mother, there was the same rich dark hair and skin. Were they Jewish, too?

They seemed an exceptional couple, in any case – the older woman especially, with her distant but kindly hauteur, her unfashionable but expensive clothes, her air of cultured regality. They were not nurses, surely – more women of the evening, Frances thought, made for salons, conversaziones, lamp-lit dinner parties; not outdoor women, people of the park, here seen solicitously tending a young man who, Frances saw when she got closer to him one afternoon, did not resemble them at all: an open-faced, fair-haired young man with a wispy beard and a badly scarred cheek, where the women were dark – and mysterious.

Idly curious as to their identity and the arrangements

between them, she followed the man and the younger woman that afternoon as they left the park by the Apsley House gate. They crossed Knightsbridge, then turned right into Grosvenor Crescent, then right again into the mews. Frances saw the wheelchair disappear through an open coachhouse doorway, and walked on down the mews none the wiser. The coachhouse and the small garden beyond presumably backed on to one of the huge and gloomy Crescent houses. Still intrigued, Frances made a long detour through the mews, round by the Grenadier public house, so that eventually she emerged at the bottom end of the Crescent, walking back up the street, glancing at the houses as she passed.

Which house had they gone into? All of them were vast terraced family mansions, with steps leading up to massive doors, sombre grey blinds drawn down over the windows. Only one house, she saw, half-way up on the left, had the blinds raised; indeed some of the windows were ajar here.

And now she heard the music, a piano – something from Mozart – coming from one of the open windows on the first floor: the delicate, precisely struck notes running forwards and upwards, hesitating, the phrase repeated again and again, before all the themes were gathered together in a thrilling run of sound, echoing forth on the sharp November air.

This, Frances thought, must be the house they had entered: number 23. She stood there on the pavement for a minute, spellbound, listening to the music. And suddenly an extraordinary sense of *déjà vu* or precognition came over her. The music, this Mozart theme, this great grey house with its windows open to the pale November sunlight – somehow she had heard these same notes, stood in front of just this house, at some time before or in a future not yet lived. A sweetness, a lightness, filled the air around her, seeming to emanate from the house – which was offering her something, a gift forgotten from a previous life or, as yet unwrapped, about to be handed to her. This feeling of lost or impending bounty was so strong that she had no hesitation in walking up the tall steps, there and then, and ringing the doorbell.

A rather dwarfish young man in a white coat, flat-headed, owl-eyed with a dank kiss-curl, opened the door, letting her in at once, as if she was expected.

'Excuse me . . .' Frances stood there, at a loss.

'Come this way,' he said immediately and rather uppishly, not the servant type at all, she thought, more like an impatient café waiter. 'Let me take your coat – Sister Ruth has only just begun the recital.'

Beyond her, in the sudden gloom, Frances made out an imposing Florentine staircase, in elaborately cut stone, with rectangular flights leading from the marble floored hall. Tall Chinese vases, filled with dried bulrushes and fluffy pampas grass, rose to greater heights from red marble pedestals. The house was warm and there were strange odours in the air, both brisk and sweet. A touch of carbolic mixed with violets – or orchids, could it be? Warm and heavy. Yet the mood, despite this exotic hothouse atmosphere, the dark and pompous decor, was not oppressive.

'I'm sorry—' She was flustered now.

'Not at all, madam,' the young man interrupted with a confident smile. 'You're not too late at all. Let me show you up.'

She followed him up the dark staircase before turning right along an equally shadowy corridor towards open double doors at the end, where the man suddenly brought her into a dazzle of winter light – sunlight and brilliantly white walls – as if she had come from night to day. She was standing at the back of what must originally have been a large drawing room, or even a ballroom, with a parquet floor and a pillared colonnade down one side facing the tall windows that gave out on to the street: again, a sumptuously decorated room, but here in the Louis XV mode, with stucco walls and ceiling on which gilded sunbursts, cherubs and cornucopias of flowers had been set in bas-relief.

But it was no longer any sort of reception room. At intervals between the pillars lay over a dozen beds, invalid men propped up in them, with a small audience on gilt chairs in the middle of the room, facing the other end, listening to the severely handsome woman whom Frances had seen in the park, playing at a grand piano. Had she arrived in a hospital or at a recital?

Tiptoeing forward, confused yet strangely happy, she took one of the little chairs at the back of the room, which the owlish young man offered her. It was extraordinary, she thought, listening to the sharp cascade of notes, the elegant woman with her back to her, bending to and fro over the piano, nursing the keys, extracting glorious arpeggios: the whole thing had been meant. She was expected here.

The sun slanted through the tall windows, raising delicate motes, falling in yellow shafts against the white walls, picking out the gilt in crowns and cornucopias. There was a swansdown lightness everywhere, a soft glitter, an air of bright repose filled with the scent of orchids which Frances noticed now, hothouse blooms in vases set against the windows. She took her bearings, her arrival barely noticed, sitting behind the fashionably dressed audience, perhaps a dozen other women, admiring their creative hats. But then she lost herself in the music so that after some time her eyes closed in the warmth and she fought to keep awake . . .

'Well – and which young man have you come to visit?'

Frances had woken with a start a few minutes before, and now, the recital over, the tall woman, having moved among the others in the audience, since dispersed to various bedsides, spoke to her kindly, standing with her by one of the tall windows. Frances should have felt awkward, but she did not. The middle-aged though beautifully preserved woman in front of her was so obviously warm, offering her such a genuine smile, so evidently interested, that Frances felt quite at ease, an immediate sympathy flowing between them.

'I do apologize. You won't believe it, but walking along outside I heard the music – you do play so very well – and I simply walked in. I know nobody here. Do please excuse me – my name is Frances. Frances Cordiner. I'm over from Ireland, staying with my cousin in Wilton Place . . .'

As she spoke, the woman's expression changed. At first a rather governessy frown appeared, which alarmed Frances. But then, at once, she smiled more broadly still, the dark eyes crinkling up, almost closing in amusement. 'Forgive my frowning – not at you, I assure you – simply embarrassment at your praise. I hardly play *that* well! More expression, at best, than any technique. But certainly I am honoured that you thought fit to come off the street and tell me so.' Was there a touch of irony in this last statement? Or was this a permanent feature of the woman's hooded, lustrous eyes, a wry and kindly detachment always there? Frances could not decide. The woman, plainly dressed in black silk without any jewellery, offered a long arm, the cream skin running out into delicately elongated ringless fingers: 'I'm Ruth Wechsberg. How do you do?'

They shook hands, the woman's grasp held for a few moments longer than necessary: warm fingers, firm but not as any imposition. 'You really must excuse me,' Frances rushed on. 'I don't know what came over me. You won't believe it either, but something beckoned me – as I stood out there in the street – so that I simply *had* to come into the house, as if I was *meant* to . . .' Frances shook her head vigorously as she spoke, anticipating the other woman's likely disbelief.

But Ruth Wechsberg simply said to her, 'My dear, why shouldn't I believe you? Stranger things have happened. And perhaps something *is* meant. I wonder what, though?' she added as an aside. 'But come, since you're here – let me show you round, let me explain.'

Her voice was easy, low-toned, almost a drawl – again with a colouring of irony in it, knowledge or laughter withheld. The tone, with its very slight German accent, was wry and detached, not in the manner of haughty society chatter, Frances thought, but through knowledge, culture, experience. She touched her dark hair then, where it spread out on either side of a central parting in full gleaming waves. And now Frances saw the polished, strangely shaped black stone which she wore as a brooch – a charm or amulet, she thought – with a silver inset cut in the shape of a Star of David.

Ruth Wechsberg noticed Frances's interest. 'A fragment from the Wailing Wall in Jerusalem,' she commented, fingering it gently. 'An heirloom.'

'It's so simple and nice,' Frances said enthusiastically. 'My mother is Jewish. Are you . . .?' She hesitated.

'Yes – a small clan, over here since my paternal grandfather left Vienna, many years ago.' They moved away from the window.

'That music you liked,' Ruth Wechsberg went on. 'Well, I try and play a little every week for the patients. Though their relations seem to enjoy it more, I'm bound to say. But, to be frank, we need to make an impression here, make ourselves known. It's a nursing home, you see. Oh, in only a very small way so far: my family home,' she continued as they walked down the room by the end of the beds. 'My father, Nathan Wechsberg – he is a stockbroker and since my mother died and we've grown up – my sister Agnes, you've not met her yet – well, the house has become rather too commodious for our needs! So I persuaded my father to let me open part of it as a nursing home, for officers – there are surprisingly few such facilities for them in London. I completed my nursing examinations at St Thomas's Hospital last year, with Agnes. But I don't know if it will work out. The expense – well, it may be even more than we bargained for!'

They had stopped at the last bed where a middle-aged man, his entire head swathed in bandages, was being talked to by two young women. Ruth turned back. 'Major Williams,' she said softly. 'And his two daughters. A nasty head wound at Omdurman in September. Isn't healing entirely. But he's doing well. And that's Mr Lighthorn.' They paused near a much younger man, with some sort of raised cage holding up the blankets, covering his lower limbs. 'Lost a leg in the same battle. And a little gangrene on the other. But we think we've saved it. We have the doctors in from the Army Hospital at Aldershot – and we employ others from Harley Street.'

They walked up towards the other end of the room.

'Gangrene?' Frances asked.

'Yes – the wound untended. Necrosis. The flesh decomposes, right down to the bone, goes green and putrid. You usually have to amputate.' Ruth was brisk, matter of fact, looking at Frances out of the corner of her eye as she tried to subdue a small grimace. 'Was that what may have been "meant" – what drew you in here, do you think?' she asked her a little sharply. 'A feeling for all that – for service, for nursing?'

'Oh, no. I know nothing about it – nothing at all. As I say, it was the music . . .'

'I simply wondered. Because the music is only the icing here, the officers just wounded men. And some young women are attracted by the idea . . .' She hesitated. 'Of such service – but not by the facts of it, when they see them.'

'Yes, I'm sure.' But Frances was not certain of what she was sure of at all. They came to the end of the room, by the big double doors leading out on to the gloomy landing. She felt the moment had come for her to leave, there was nothing more to be said. But Ruth Wechsberg, interpreting her feelings, had indeed more to say. 'Well, Miss Cordiner, I'm certainly not a *clairvoyante*, but something tells me you came in here because you've found yourself at a loose end in London – on your own, over from Ireland, you say?' She looked at her with an easy, entirely unpatronizing regard. 'I've absolutely no wish to pry or presume, but I wonder if that's really what brought you in here – simply a need to talk to someone? If so, I'd be delighted if you took tea with me, after I've seen to the visitors.'

Frances nodded, her face breaking into a smile, a fuller smile than she remembered offering for many months. 'Of course, but I don't want to delay or inconvenience you—'

'You don't,' Ruth Wechsberg replied very promptly. 'I

said I would be delighted. And I can assure you of one thing – I always mean what I say.'

When Frances returned, in high good humour, to Wilton Place, she found Eileen, red-eyed and moping, sitting in the basement kitchen over a plate of bread and dripping which she had obviously been consoling herself with.

'Eileen, what's wrong? You don't have to eat that, you know—'

'Well, I *do*, Miss – sure, wasn't it always what we had at home?' Eileen got up and went towards the range, wiping her lips, bosom heaving with emotion.

'Eileen, Eileen dearest – what *is* the matter?' Frances moved to comfort the girl, who was beginning to cry silently now, pretending to occupy herself over the range so that a tear fell on the hot plate, briefly sizzling.

'It's just I miss home. And – and I've heard no word at all from my friend . . .' She sobbed openly then, head bowed, her back turned to Frances who at once went over and put an arm round her.

'Your friend?'

'It's Pat Kennedy, Miss,' she burst out.

'I see. Of course.' Frances understood. She had been aware of this *tendresse*, on Eileen's part at least – Eileen had clearly hinted at it last spring – but, not wishing to pry or embarrass the girl, Frances had never pursued the matter with her. 'And you've written to him?' she asked her now.

'Indeed I have – three times!'

'Oh dear – men can be so insensitive. But it's as much my fault, for taking you away. Eileen—' She turned the girl round, offering her a handkerchief. 'Eileen, you can easily go home, you know, if you want.'

Eileen looked affronted suddenly, annoyed. 'Sure and I don't want to go home – amn't I good and happy here? And I get on grand with Mrs Moxon in the mornings – and there's Mary Lynch from Galway down the street that I walk out with . . .'

'Yes, you told me. You've seemed happy—'

'Indeed I am, sure – in this grand place. And isn't it a wonderful opportunity and experience altogether? – if only I was hearing from him,' she added, the sobs coming back into her voice, 'and knowing he was all right.'

'I'm sure he is.'

'Well, he mightn't be, d'ye see?' Eileen looked at her in a strange way, a frightened look.

'I'll tell you what,' Frances said quickly. 'I'll write home this very night – I should have done before – and I'll ask my father about Pat. Ask him to tell me how he is – and tell him to write to you. Tactfully, of course.'

'Tactfully?' Eileen asked, perking up a bit.

'I mean I won't make a thing of it.'

'That'd be grand, then.' Eileen moved towards the big deal table.

'That's been my problem, too,' Frances called after her, watching the girl starting to pick at the bread and dripping again. 'Not hearing from Summer Hill. And that's my fault too. I see it now, I was too proud to write home.'

Eileen turned. 'Yes, Miss. I suppose you were – though it was the right thing you did, opening the house up that way and putting the air through it. But I wasn't too proud to write,' she added. 'And I should have been.'

'No, you were quite right. And I've been wrong. Pride is such a stupid thing. If you really love something – a person or a place – you lose pride. You have to.'

Frances saw now what had been wrong in her life since she had left Summer Hill: she had refused to admit how much she had missed the place – and Eileen had vividly reminded her of this blindness. She had been proud, arrogant, angry – believing these sentiments entirely appropriate to her condition of exile. Yet they had been mere substitutes for happiness, which she had encouraged vehemently the more to avoid the fact of her great unhappiness. Now, as a result of her teatime conversation with Ruth Wechsberg, she was at ease for the first time since she had left home and so no longer needed to be proud.

'Listen!' she said with the excitement of this realization, going over to Eileen. 'Forget the bread and dripping.

There's that delicious fruit cake we had yesterday. Let's finish it, gorge on it, with strong tea. A little party! – like we used to have in the kitchen at home with Mrs Molloy – and I'll tell you what happened to me this afternoon.'

Eileen was surprised, the dimple sinking in her chin as she smiled for the first time. 'What happened, Miss? Do tell us! You met someone nice – a man?'

'Yes. But a woman, Eileen, not a man. Enough of men – for the moment.' She started to root vigorously about the cupboards and shelves, opening tins, looking for the fruit cake, while Eileen put the kettle on the hob, where it started to sing at once, before she closed the basement shutters against the November night; the two women, happy together, preparing the room for their cosy tea, a homecoming tea, in the mind at least, as they forgot their exile.

Frances wrote to her parents that night before dinner.

'Dear Mama and Papa, I realize now that I was hasty and insensitive in my behaviour to you both at Summer Hill. I do apologize. I have been unhappy since I left but am no longer so, and thus can see my behaviour in a more objective light – and so make apologies for it. But I am happy now, for today I have met a remarkable woman, Miss Ruth Wechsberg . . .'

She paused, looking into the glowing coals of her bedroom fire, remembering once more the conversation that afternoon during tea with Ruth Wechsberg – tea served from the finest bone china in her little drawing room looking back over the mews in Grosvenor Crescent, where she had told her all about herself, her family problems, her reasons for being in London.

It had been an easy confession. Ruth Wechsberg had not in any way encouraged or invited these confidences. She had seemed, in her easy detachment, rather to accept such intimacies as a perfectly normal conversational topic, part of any civilized exchange; she was not in the least surprised or censorious. Other people avoided reality in polite chat about the weather and the crops; Ruth Wechsberg looked on true feeling as the only proper basis for conversation, so that Frances, in talking to her, did not sense for a moment that she was being presumptuous or was divulging any unworthy secrets, freely unburdening herself to her.

'And I have to admit, too,' Frances had said to her later, 'that I noticed you in the Park several weeks ago – you and your sister. And I followed her back this afternoon, before I heard the music.'

'Why? Why was that?'

'Intrigued. And time on my hands, I suppose.'

Ruth had looked at her sharply, summing her up. 'Good observation – and good hands,' she remarked. 'I noticed your fine hands and your eyes at once, when we met.'

Frances remembered how she had held her hand, a fraction longer than necessary, at that meeting. 'And you know,' Ruth had continued, leaning forward, adding more hot water to the silver teapot, 'those are the two most important qualities in the sort of work we do here: careful observation of the patients, and above all feeling for them – with your hands, your mind. The rest can be taught. But not those two gifts. And I think you have them already.'

'Thank you.' Frances had taken these remarks as no more than a social compliment.

'Of course, there is more to nursing – a lot more: the detail, the strict *facts* – timetables, long hours, discipline, all the scientific elements. And this can be irksome – and some of the facts are downright unpleasant. Gangrene for example – or dressing a fresh amputation . . .'

'Yes, I'm sure. The blood and such.'

'The stump shivers, my dear,' she had said, offering her another cup of tea.

'Does it?' Frances had asked, with more curiosity than distaste in her voice, and Ruth had nodded, noting this response favourably.

'But, as I say,' she went on, 'in nursing, it's the need for sensitive enquiry that is paramount: keeping your eyes and ears open, *feeling* things. And I was much struck by your obvious gifts here – when you told me that something had beckoned you into the house, more than simple curiosity.'

'Yes, it was a sense – do you know? – of *déjà vu* as I stood out there on the pavement, that I'd stood in front of this house before at some point.'

'But was it not some other hidden need that gave you that feeling? – a need to justify, to *do* something with your curiosity?'

'Yes, perhaps it was. For I have felt just that: the need to do something with my life.' It had begun to dawn on Frances what lay behind Ruth's comments here.

'Well, then,' Ruth said, a small note of triumph in her voice, 'would you like to learn about nursing here? I believe you might take to it very well. And I believe, too – though as I've said I'm no *clairvoyante*, much more a rationalist – that that is what may have been "meant" by your walking in here today. As simple as that!'

'Could I?' Frances had been genuinely astonished. 'It had never crossed my mind – I assure you.'

'Oh, and I believe you, Frances. One thing I do know, in my own case, is that nursing never crossed my mind either, until quite suddenly I had to deal with my mother, several years ago. I realized then that I should have been doing it from the very beginning, that I had a gift, a love for it – to serve them, the patients. So, you see, I believe you completely. That's the strange thing, isn't it? – how we often don't see what's meant for us. We have to "walk by faith and not by sight" as the Testament has it. The faith came so late for me. But perhaps not for you.'

'I'd love to – I'd love to try it,' Frances had said with shy enthusiasm, a small pit of excitement opening in her stomach.

Now, paraphrasing this conversation, as she had to Eileen, she wrote it down for her mother and father. And, that evening at supper, she elaborated on it once more for Dermot.

'Do you know, I think I have heard of her,' he said. 'A rich woman, Jewish, a nursing home for officers – how very surprising. But do you really think . . . it's *you*, Frances?'

It was. Frances took to the business of nursing almost at once. Though she soon realized that it was the absorbing company and agreeable circumstances that eased her passage here. At the same time she did not bridle at the strict disciplines – arriving sharp at 8.30 each morning, staying until 6.30 or later in the evening, with one hour off for lunch and one day off a week. This surprised her – as it did Ruth – that, having been waited upon all her life, she should so readily accept these long hours of waiting upon others.

Ruth remarked on this one day. 'I imagine, for all that you've told me of your life at home in Ireland, it's perhaps been a matter of replacing one ordered life by another. You must have a need of that.'

'I think I do.'

'It surprised me a little – the one thing that worried me in your work here, for you seem to be, how shall I put it? – impulsive, volatile by nature.'

'Yes, that as well . . .'

'An interesting mix.'

'You mean perhaps – a dangerous one?'

'No – difficult, if you like. A warring nature! But then our bodies rebel. And we are coming more and more to cure that. And I believe that in time we may be able to do the same for problems of the mind. I have long been interested in the psychological aspect of medicine: nervous complaints, neurasthenia, dreams, nightmares. There is a doctor in Vienna at present, a Dr Freud, whose papers on the subject I have been reading with great interest. But enough of that – for the moment we must deal with the obvious ills, and I hope I can help you there.'

So it was Ruth, when they met together in her little drawing room, who outlined the ethics and theory of nursing. 'To care and to cure,' she said. 'There is the whole basis – to nourish, in short. You cannot be a distant figure to these patients. They need you, not as the healthy do, but because they are unwell. And this makes them very different people. You will see men here at their worst – mentally as well as physically in the raw: difficult, demanding, ungrateful – sometimes cruelly so. For they are entirely dependent, helpless, which is what brings out these unhappy traits. And they are dependent on *you*, without wanting to be, which produces this impatience and arrogance – so that you will find yourself retreating from them initially, in your mind at least. But it's precisely your mind, as much as your hands, that they require. So you must cultivate a genuine sociability with them. Be patient, good-humoured – most important that.' Ruth smiled. 'Remember to smile, even in the worst circumstances. A smile can cure as much as anything.'

'I believe I can smile.'

'I'm sure you can – and that can be the greatest tonic. The other gifts, as I've said, you have: observation and touch. But you must develop them, rigorously. *Watch* the patients – there is the real learning. See how they sleep; note any increased restlessness, a difference in breathing patterns. Watch for changes in their colouring, the lips, the ear lobes. Listen to their mildest complaints: why does someone seem to have a headache over one eye in the morning, over the other in the afternoon? Your prompt response to such changes could prove vital – literally. Hence the importance of what may seem irksome or repetitive detail in your work: the adoption of strict cleanliness, method, rule, the exact amount and timing in the administration of medicines. You see, these men must be able to depend on you *entirely* – very much part of their cure, their mental well-being. So you cannot afford . . . to be casual in any way, do you see?'

Frances looked at her pointedly. 'Am I?'

'No,' Ruth replied firmly, yet with an expression that still seemed to doubt something. 'No, not casual. But headstrong, perhaps, as I've said. Reliability is the basis of every other gift in nursing. A patient, you see – he feels his body has betrayed him, become corrupt. So he looks for absolute fidelity, incorruptibility, in you.'

'Which makes it a vocation.'

'Exactly – which is what makes it difficult. It is no mere laying on of hands. One must believe, you see . . .'

'I think I do. I do want to be of some service to somebody.'

Ruth looked at her carefully. 'Yes, I can see that, from all you've told me – your break with your fiancé, your brother's death, your disagreements with your mother, the fracas of your last day at Summer Hill. You've so wanted to serve your house, and have been bitterly disappointed. But I wonder – I hope you'll forgive me: one cannot serve imperiously.'

Frances saw how well Ruth understood her, the contradictions in her nature. 'Yes,' she admitted. 'I do see that.'

'Well, there perhaps is your problem: whether you can resolve such contradictions – whether you will *want* to, which is more to the point, for such disagreements within oneself may seem the very stuff of life. But a divided nature, permanently unreconciled, can become an illness. There is that whole other world of mind, beyond body, which we know almost nothing about. But forgive me again – we must deal with the facts here, not the secrets.'

It was Ruth's younger sister, Agnes, who was responsible for the practicalities of Frances's initial training – Agnes a reduced image of her elder sister in every way: small, seemingly frosty and certainly tongue-tied, who, though she was in charge of most of the actual day-to-day nursing at Grosvenor Crescent, took a back seat in every other way. She was not in the least unkind or dismissive with Frances. But she gave, nonetheless, in her preoccupied reserve, an impression of not really being in touch with her. Agnes lived in her elegant sister's shadow and it was never apparent whether she had chosen or suffered this position.

'The bed,' she told her bluntly as they stood together in an empty room not yet made over as a ward. Then she itemized the coverings, picking them up from a pile. 'Under-mackintosh, sheets, blankets, pillows, cases.'

Then, without another word, she made the bed up, and stripped it, before indicating that Frances should copy her. Afterwards they continued the training with a jointed mannequin which Agnes put on the mackintosh sheet, demonstrating a bed bath with it, how to move the patient and administer a bed pan – the whole performance conducted almost soundlessly.

'Here is a typical dressing tray,' Agnes said when they had moved into the nurses' room, next to the long salon, with its medicines and other stores. 'Cotton swabs, gauze, bandages, lint, carbolic, iodine, boiled water, safety pins, scissors, tweezers.' But she said nothing more of their purposes before taking the tray out to the ward where she proceeded to dress Lieutenant Lighthorn's amputated stump. This, since the wound was dry and almost healed, Frances found a relatively easy exercise when she came to repeat it: certainly the stump no longer shivered. Dressing his other leg, though, was something of a shock. The wound, running right down the side of the calf, had been deep and left untended for several days in the burning African bush. It had since been sewn together and there was nothing putrid about it. But the general appearance was still grim: a veined purplish colour, the emaciated flesh hillocky and strangely flaky so that small lumps of it came away like bits of old Stilton cheese.

'How nice to see a fresh face,' Lighthorn said easily while the dressing was going on, looking at Frances in her smart new uniform – starched cap, high collar and white apron with a red cross emblazoned over her chest – Frances, with a very wary face leaning over the man's smashed lower body. 'I'm William – Billy if you like.' He offered her a quizzical half-smile.

'My name is Frances – Frances Cordiner.' She glanced at him quickly.

'Yes, I know. Saw you the other day, listening to the music. Thought you were someone's sister – we all thought so.' He looked round at the others in the long room. 'But then found you weren't – all sorry about that! So it's a pretty nice surprise to find you're going to be here all the time.' His smile broadened. He's flirting with me already, Frances thought.

And so he was. And, soon enough, most of the other men followed his lead, made happier thereby, and Frances thrived on this without taking advantage of it. For she found as the days passed a stronger excitement in the work – a sense, almost, of intoxication: she was needed here, often and obviously, without equivocation. She was a life-line, literally, in helping these once vigorous men regain what had been paramount in their lives: their strength and mobility. The fact thrilled her.

And as she learnt, and she learnt quickly, she found another charm in the work. She was able, when alone in the ward and if only to some small extent, to take control, to organize, plan, even dictate. She was in charge. And she saw then how much she had craved this very thing in Summer Hill. Of course it was exactly that inperious feeling which Ruth had warned her against. But she justified the feeling, and its expression then, by reminding herself how the men, in their debility, needed just such control. And they did – soon coming to appreciate her little firmnesses and dictates.

But there was a further and even greater instinctive pleasure which she found in something which she had at first dreaded. She discovered an impersonal joy in handling the men's bodies. Their torn limbs, emaciated torsos – at first she had touched these with fear and embarrassment. But soon, to her great surprise, she found a solace in it, as the men did. This strange pleasure came, she thought, from seeing for the first time the whole body, beneath the head, behind the clothes, and realizing how each part was so wonderfully linked, dependent upon another – how life lay not only in a smile, in the eyes or voice, but in every minute part of the entire envelope and its contents, from toe to scalp. The whole fabric, intimately displayed, amazed and humbled her. Though broken, cut, bruised, cauterized – these bodies seemed all the more precious, vibrant mysteries coursing beneath the flesh. So that when she touched the limbs they no longer seemed mere anonymous appendages to the face but were equally imbued with the miraculous expression of life itself. A toe, she came to feel, contained as much emotion as a heart.

She said as much one evening at dinner with Dermot and Mortimer, who had come back early from the House.

'A toe – smiling? I wouldn't have seen it that way,' Mortimer commented drily.

'Well, it's just that every pore of skin . . . says something.' Frances put her head on one side, looking into the candlelight. 'I can't really explain it.'

'Oh, you have – you've put it very well,' Dermot said. 'A big toe smiling. I like that idea!' He looked at her. 'Listen, you have the day off tomorrow. And I have to go down to Salisbury Plain first thing – watch a new field gun being tested, send a report on it out to Army Command in the Cape. Would you like to come with me? We could take lunch somewhere afterwards, have a look at the countryside.'

'I'd love to.' Frances nodded happily. 'Though I don't know about the gun,' she added as a sudden after-thought.

'No, indeed,' Mortimer broke in. 'I should think not – seeing the results of such infernal weapons each day!'

'My dear Papa,' Dermot responded with a smile, 'your Home Rulers and their Fenian friends are not averse to using them either.'

'Quite different. They do not use field guns—'

'They would if they had them—'

'Besides, as you know, I have no truck with those violent Home Rulers – am concerned only to prosper the right of a nation to choose its own destiny, by peaceful means. The will of the people, dear boy! When will you realize that no gun, in the end, can ever resist that?'

The point was not taken by Dermot. But the two men still managed to exchange smiles before Dermot added, 'A gun, as I see it, is there to defend that very will, Papa, not suppress it. I think we disagree about the Irish destiny there. But never mind, Frances can lurk behind Stonehenge with cotton-wool in her ears – that can be her destiny tomorrow. But you will come, won't you?'

He looked at her, suddenly anxious, and she nodded. She wanted to come, not to see the horrid field gun but to be free and out of town for the day with Dermot.

5

They looked out at the bare trees and frosty fields, alone in the warm compartment, the land falling away beyond the downs, approaching Salisbury Plain, so that soon the view was one of shallow, rolling hills, without hedges or other boundaries, only a few tracks and coppices to break the monotony of the chilly morning scene. Dermot, immaculate in his Captain's uniform and long brown boots, sat opposite her, his back to the engine, so that Frances saw all that was coming in sight and he could only gaze at its swift disappearance. He let his pipe die and picked up *The Times*. Frances, head against the window, scanned the land ahead attentively, as if expecting something.

'Nothing much to see,' Dermot remarked from behind the paper.

'The spire – Salisbury Cathedral.'

'Hardly near it yet.'

'Did you know? – it's almost 400 feet high and without any proper foundations. No one quite understands how it's stood up all this time.'

'Faith, I should imagine.'

'Are you that sort of person – religious, I mean?'

'No. I think not.'

'Not very?'

'No, I meant not at all. You either are or you aren't. It's fraudulent to sit on the fence. Having it both ways. What about you?' He put the paper down, lit his pipe again, then shook the box of Swan Vestas vigorously, like a rattle.

'You're blunt, aren't you?'

'Like you – saying what you mean, meaning what you say.'

'I don't quite know about religion. I like the *idea* of it . . .'

'Then you're not. It's a faith or nothing. You can't have it as an idea to play around with – that's a philosophy. Now, I like that – systems of thought. Much more in my line.'

'You were so much better educated. Women aren't. I wish I had been – those fearful governesses at home and that awful dame school in Dublin.'

'You shouldn't regret it. You have something else – tremendous intuition. I wish I had that.'

'In battle, you mean? – for killing people, knowing what the other side is going to do.'

'You *are* sharp this morning—'

'Just saying what I mean—'

'Well, your latter point, yes. But I wish I knew more about what ordinary people were thinking, day to day.'

'The whole mysterious business of the mind that Ruth Wechsberg's been telling me about. She talks about that – what she calls illnesses there, dreams, things that happen to you as a child that can affect your whole life. I don't understand her – how people can become quite different, in their behaviour, because of unconscious things, that happened long before. And how you can unearth the real problems of their lives by talking to them, hearing about their dreams and so on. Do you follow it?'

'No. But it sounds fascinating.'

'It is. What makes me so want to annoy and get the better of Mama, for example?'

Dermot shrugged. 'Your nature, obviously.'

'Yes, but why wasn't that in Henry's nature, or Eustace's? Same blood. Why only me? And you, Dermot,' she went on enthusiastically, carried along simply by a spirit of pure scientific enquiry. 'Why are you different, from other men?'

He was taken aback. 'I don't know. I've never considered why,' he said at last, lighting his pipe quickly, rattling the box of matches once more. Then he leant forward, craning his neck round, peering out of the window. 'Look! That's it – the cathedral spire. Nearly there.'

But Frances, still absorbed by science, was not so taken with this vision of faith when it appeared, much more curious to know – since he must have considered this very question – why Dermot had lied about it.

Dermot meanwhile, getting his army greatcoat and attaché case down from the rack, considered Frances's sharpness and regretted that he had ever spoken to her of this aberration in his personality.

An army staff wagon met them at the station, taking them to the firing range, north of Salisbury on the Devizes road, where they turned off up a track towards the Artillery Ordnance Depot, surrounded by a screen of trees in the lee of the hill.

'You may have to wait at the depot,' Dermot told her, when they arrived at the first of the low brick buildings, a great red flag raised above it. 'I'll ask the Colonel if you can watch.'

It was nearly eleven o'clock, the sun finally piercing through the mists that lay over the higher ground here, dissolving the white cover, pools of blue appearing in the sky. The frosty gravel crunched beneath Dermot's boots as he walked away towards the guardhouse. Soldiers moved briskly to and fro, tending gun carriages, loading ammunition wagons; grooms placated restless horses between the shafts, champing at the bit, the warm breath from their nostrils running in bright plumes into the chilly air. There was a sense of impending sunny adventure in the morning – and Frances, released from the confines and disciplines of Grosvenor Crescent, suddenly wanted to be part of it, not to stay at the Depot. The idea of rash, violent action excited her, a girl playing truant from school among rough boys whose company had been strictly forbidden.

Dermot returned. Permission had been granted. 'But you must keep well back and stay in the wagon all the time,' he said as the two of them, accompanied by their driver, a staff sergeant, left the compound and drove up the hill.

On the far side, looking north over a vast expanse of empty land, a group of officers and men stood in the strengthening sun around two field guns, another red flag above them, a flash of colour set against a sky that was almost clear now, a wash of pale blue running into a milky horizon. A series of large white targets, crossed with black lines, had been placed at varying distances from the guns, disappearing out into the plain. Dermot joined the other officers, leaving Frances in the wagon with the sergeant, an affable local man, getting on in years, who was happy to entertain and instruct this attractive young visitor, producing field glasses, offering them to her.

'Four different targets you see, Miss – the first at a thousand feet, then every 500 feet after. Though it's not the range they're bothered with today. It's a new breech block or some such – so they say. Though I'd be surprised if it were any better than the last guns we tried up here. Can't beat the old ways, I say.'

The guns started to fire then, in tandem, quickly, one after the other, recoiling on their wheels, little gasps of white smoke emerging from the open breech as the men reloaded, stood away, and fired again. There was a splendid rhythm and speed to the business, the gleaming barrels spitting like provoked animals. But Frances was surprised at the lack of noise. The guns, from where she sat above them, seemed like toys, cap guns, harmless. She remarked on this.

'Ah,' the sergeant told her, brushing his extravagant moustaches, 'not at the receiving end, though – I can vouch for that. But there's no charge in these shells today, you see, Miss, when they hit the target.'

'They don't seem to be doing that, though,' Frances put the field glasses down.

'Well, they're only concerned with the speed of firing, Miss, not the aim.'

Frances watched Dermot standing among the other

officers – motionless, intent, ramrod-straight, with their braided caps, swagger sticks and red flashes on their tunic collars. It all seemed very unreal, the sun burning out the last of the mists now, warming the tingling air, so that away to the north, swivelling the glasses round, she suddenly made out the great boulders of Stonehenge on the horizon. They're all playing at soldiers, she felt then. Yet she had seen the results of their games at Grosvenor Crescent. It made no sense. Was this what Dermot was going to spend his life doing? Such quick intelligence and sympathy in the man – how could he find reward in these childish games? She turned to the sergeant during a lull in the firing. 'What's it like – being a soldier?'

'Never thought about it, Miss. Never been anything else, leastways.'

The same answer Dermot had given her in the train. They did not really think or feel, these soldiers. That was how they could maim and kill people so easily. But Dermot certainly thought and felt. There was the contradiction and it annoyed her that he should fail to see this. Watching the guns as they started up again, she suddenly wanted to alter his life for him.

'Oh, I loved the colour and excitement of it all,' she said later as they walked around Stonehenge, the sergeant waiting for them in the wagon. 'Liked all that – the little puffs of smoke, gleaming brass, red flags and the frosty blue air – all pretty as a picture. But just as you asked me about nursing – is it really *you*, Dermot? I kept asking myself that as I watched – toy soldiers, that you get over in the nursery.'

They stood beside one of the great monoliths, the slanting sun casting a long shadow of the stone across the grass. 'Oh, I love it all,' Dermot replied simply, turning away, dropping so obvious a topic.

'Yes, but—' Frances continued forcefully.

'Like you love Summer Hill. Same feeling – the army is a whole life for me: mentally, physically, the companionship. That's what you like at home, isn't it? – complete satisfaction all in one thing.'

137

'Yes, but I don't have to kill people for my satisfaction there.'

He raised his eyebrows. 'I wonder. Your actions against your Mama – that's a sort of mental killing between you both, isn't it?'

'I've left all that, though.'

'Perforce. Be fair, Frances: you've left it because you had to and you haven't forgotten it. You contemplate a return to the fray! And yours, if I may say so, is a hopeless cause.'

She fingered the huge slab beside her. It was cold and damp. She walked out into the sun, lifting her face to it, warming herself, before turning to him. 'Very well then, I've been dissuaded from it—'

'But you haven't! Rather you want to dissuade me, in my army career. That's what's interesting. You have a wonderful need to interfere and try and change people's lives, Frances – with Henry, your mother and now me.' He laughed, not at all cruel in his insights.

'Well, I'm sorry. It's not done with malice.'

'I'm sure it isn't. But it's brick walling, as my father told you. You haven't seen that – that it's really impossible to change the way people are, their natures. You've not seen that immutable plan in the battle.'

'But I don't believe that. People *can* change!'

Dermot shook his head. 'I wish I could save you from the defeats in trying.' He watched her walk away, crunching over the still-frosty grass.

'Oh, but you can, dear Dermot!' Her mood changed completely now – provocative, flirtatious, as she did a little dance back towards him, taking him by the arm, drawing him out into the sun. 'You *can* save me from all sorts of defeats.' She opened her eyes wide, finding his, staring into them, before kissing him briefly on the cheek. 'You can save me with lunch at least. I'm famished. Aren't you?'

He took her arm and they walked away from the great grey circle of stone. He no longer regretted anything he had said to this bright woman, regretting only his nature that forbade him a closer contact with her warmth and vivacity. A longing for her came over him then which, for those moments at least, did not appear hopeless. People could change, she was sure. Perhaps she was right and he ought to believe her, he thought, turning his back on the immutable stone.

They sat in wooden booths over a late lunch in the Bear Hotel at Salisbury, a stone-flagged saloon near a big log fire – a half-timbered chop house in this quarter of the inn, with sporting prints and flintlocks covering the bent and twisted walls. Frances attacked her mutton cutlets, dabbing them with onion sauce. Dermot quaffed a pewter tankard of ale and mopped his brow. Wafts of gravy and burning meat came from the swinging kitchen door behind them. There was a touch of manure in the air as well – local squires and farmers in town for the day, stamping their rough boots, together with a few legal men in frock coats, portly gluttons all, gossiping, arguing the toss everywhere around them.

'We could have eaten in the dining room,' Dermot remarked.

'Nicer here, among the men. I can't bear the cold frou-frou air of provincial hotel dining rooms – anxious maids in pinnies threatening you with *petits pois* and *blancmange*. Can I try your ale?'

He pushed the tankard across. 'I can get you some—'

'See if I like it first.'

She did and he called the pot boy over. 'Lucky Miss Wechsberg's not here to see you,' he told her when the second tankard arrived and she had sucked the froth from it, the foamy beads giving her a brief moustache.

'It's my day off.' She was happily impudent. 'Miss Wechsberg has days off, too. I wonder what she does with them. It's strange she's not married – so elegant and gifted. A little governessy. But men like that, too, don't they?'

Dermot smiled. 'Like you, Frances. A little governessy.' He cut some fat from the mutton. A big tabby cat, wide-eyed and anxious, looked up at them intently from the flagstones. Frances reached across, took the fat from his plate and gave it to the cat.

'Pussy, pussy,' she said. 'I like it here. Yes, governessy . . .' She sat back, considering this appellation. 'It's just that I don't like footlers, can't-make-up-their-mind people – people who won't *respond*.' She stared at him, half-smile, half-glare.

'A little uncharitable?'

'Nonsense! We all have tongues in our head. It's just cowardice, mostly, when people stay mum. *Je Responderay* – "I will reply" – there was a girl at the dame school, one of the Willoughby-Hughes girls; that was their family motto and I've often thought about it, so inappropriate for she was a poor silent creature. Wished it were my motto: "I will answer" – for who and what I am. Well, of course, most people do nothing of the sort – no answer in them at all, no echo, like talking to a log, and so no conversation, no sharing, no truth. Even with highly intelligent people, Dermot – sometimes there's no answer, to the real things.' She provoked him gently.

But he refused to be baited, saying finally and rather formally, 'That's all very well, Frances. But there are some things better hid.' He resumed his meal, looking down intently at his plate.

'I'm sorry.' She leant across and touched his arm. 'You know, I thought nothing wrong of your loving Henry – really not, nothing shaming there, so I don't understand? . . .'

'My reluctance in the matter? But you don't know the world, Frances. They are most reluctant about such things.'

'I don't care about the world! It's the same thing, isn't it? – loving a man or woman – same thing at heart, same feeling.' Warmed by the fire and the ale, she pursued her theme. 'So, if you can love one, that surely doesn't prevent you loving the other.'

'Not for you perhaps. But, well, I've tried the other. And it didn't really work.' He looked at Frances, this candid woman across the plain table, so warm in everything – remembering her face offered to the sun that morning, now flushed and excited by the heat of the room. She lived in warmth and truth, taking certainty from these fires. And he realized then, with Henry's death, how very cold and lost he was in his own life. 'Well, you may be right,' he said. 'Who knows?'

'She probably wasn't your sort, or you didn't appeal to her,' Frances said off-handedly, resuming her meal. 'But I love you, Dermot,' she added, in the casual tones of someone remarking on the weather.

It was a strange courtship. Frances made the running – while he, in response, took a pace forward, then one back. For her the frustration – for him temptation. For he was tempted. But he could not call it love, there was the problem. It was everything else – affection, admiration, a lighter heart whenever she appeared in the room or street. But it was not that head-over-heels involvement, that overwhelming need, which he had felt before, with men. And despite their other great truth sharings he could not tell her this. But she persevered. Though here again she would not admit to him any such effort in the affair, nor the sudden storms in her heart which overcame her in the following weeks as she grew more attached to him. She kept mum on these things, like an angler tempting a trout from a deep pool, experiencing the truth now of what he had told her – how some things were better hid. The process was a strain on her real nature. She wanted Dermot but had to forbid herself any real moves towards this end, withholding herself from him, while he moved in and out of her orbit with wary fascination. In short it was an unsatisfactory business for both of them – a fact which they equally denied to each other, thus feeding a predicament which might have continued indefinitely but for a fortuitous intervention a week later.

Eileen, alone in the house with Frances, opened the door to the stranger one early evening – the stooping, wizened old beggar man, fearfully whiskered in a battered bowler and torn greatcoat tied with string, a rusty campaign medal pinned to his lapel, with a hooked nose and aggressive, staring eyes, a Fagin in the lamplight.

'God bless ye, Miss,' the old horror said with an Irish brogue, a smell of strong spirits on his breath. 'Amn't I travelling the streets since the dawn of day, an oul' sodjer, down on me luck. We'ed ye ever have a few coppers for a cuppa tay – or a pair of boots or iny small thing at all in that line.'

He had put his foot on the threshold. But Eileen held the door against him. 'Well, I don't know now. I'll ask the young lady—'

'Ah ye'd take pity on a pour soul like me. Sure and don't I hear your voice – from the oul' counthry like meself. What part are ye from at all?'

'I'm – I'm from Kilkenny.'

'Sure an' don't I know it well!' He raised his voice now, a nasal enthusiastic whine, pushing further in towards her. 'A grand place altogether – the Marble City, know it well. Sure and if that's the case ye'd have a sup of whiskey for me then, and I travellin' the cold streets since the dawn o' day—'

'Well, I don't know about that,' Eileen said firmly, trying to close the door on him. But he had his foot in the jamb now, whining at her still, but in a more aggressive tone.

'Ah, just a sup, Miss – take pity on an oul' man. A drop of the crathur – and may the blessed Virgin and all the saints and angels . . .' He pushed right past her now.

'I'll get the police – I'll call the constable!' Eileen turned back to the stairs then. 'Miss Frances – Miss Frances! Come down quick!'

The beggar, in the hall now, turned into the dining room where he went straight to the sideboard, picked up the sherry decanter and started to swig at it in long draughts, the drink splashing over his chin and neck. Then, just as Frances and Eileen appeared in the doorway and greatly encouraged by the alcohol, he started a little jig, hopping from one foot to the other round the Chippendale table, holding the decanter, starting to sing an Irish ballad in a cracked and raucous voice. '"And on *next* Sunday morn-ning, I'll meet her, *meet* her, meet her – next

Sun-day morn-ning, I'll meet her . . . and I am the *best* of them all!"' he sang out before stumbling and falling heavily on the floor, a bundle of flying rags and boots, the bowler spinning into the grate.

'Get up at once – you brute!' Frances shouted. 'What are you doing here? Eileen – see if you can find a constable.'

The man rose shakily to his feet. 'Arrah now and you wouldn't run in an oul' sodjer,' he whined again drunkenly, touching his campaign medal. 'Look – the Crimea, Miss. And didn't I get a bullet in me back out there from one of those Turkey fellows.' He made a shaky attempt to stand to attention, raising a hand in a wobbly salute, before embarking on 'The Minstrel Boy' in a heavily slurred voice: '"The Minstrel Boy to-o the war-r-r-s is gone . . ."' He piped out a few lines of the song before forgetting it, with a vacant look, spittle running down his chin. Then, pulling himself together again, he started on a stentorian rendering of 'God Save the Queen'.

Frances was enraged. 'You must leave at once. Eileen, fetch a constable!'

'Ah, an angry wumman,' the beggar opined with a crooked smile. 'Nuttin' lovelier.' He leered at her, stumbling towards the sherry decanter on the table. 'Now why don't you and I sit down here and take our eaase over a glass or two. And cripes,' he added, picking up the decanter, appraising the sherry, 'isn't this the finest stuff? A man'd be lacking that and he walking the cold streets since the dawn o' day—'

'Give it me, you wretch! The police—' Frances, trying to retrieve the decanter, started to wrestle with him over the table.

'Oh and thim's fightin' words,' he purred. 'A tough little vixen – nothin' nicer . . .'

The two of them swayed about the room then, each clinging to the decanter. 'Be God, ye can dance too – we'll take a spin surely before we take a sup.' He started to hum a waltz, clasping Frances firmly by the arms, swaying round the floor together. Finally the old reprobate let her go, laughing uproariously.

'My, you do dance superbly,' he said in a completely changed, a most cultured accent. He pulled at his bird's nest whiskers, his hooked nose and tattered grey hair. They all came away in his hands before he wiped his face with a handkerchief and the features of quite a different man clearly emerged.

'Humphrey!' Frances shouted. 'You shocker! – you beast! You had me . . .' She was speechless. It was Humphrey Saunders, her mother's old friend, who had brought the Spanish dancers to Summer Hill – boisterous in quite a different way now, the suave man-of-the-world again, entirely taken with his latest practical joke.

'Ah yes, I had you there – both of you!' He looked at Eileen standing open-mouthed at the doorway. He took off his shabby greatcoat and filthy scarf, found his bowler in the grate and dusted it. 'It's quite extraordinary, isn't it! – what a few old clothes, a different costume, will do. Change the world with a change of clothes, couldn't you? I heard you were over in London, Frances – Mortimer was in touch with me the other day and I thought I'd come round, little surprise, variety the spice of life and what have you. You've rather fallen out with your Mama, I understand?'

'Somewhat, yes.' Frances had regained some of her composure now. Eileen left the room and Humphrey sank into a chair.

'Exhausting business – this acting.' He drew a long breath. 'Sorry to hear about your mother. Never mind – a charming but difficult woman, not unlike you: bound to clash.'

'Am I difficult?'

'Oh yes.' He started to take his frightful old boots off. 'Part of the charm. Like her – when she was young.'

'You knew her well then, didn't you?'

'I was in love with your beautiful Mama – more than thirty years ago, before she met Desmond.'

'Did she marry the wrong man, do you think?' Frances asked pertly.

'No. She would have tried to have her own way with

whoever she married. Very forceful character.' He bent down, rubbing his toes. 'These old boots, real shockers. Wore them last for *East Lynne* at the Metropolitan, Edgware Road – played a very good drunk there, too.'

'You're a wonderful actor, there's no doubt.'

'Ah yes.' He looked up with a judicious smile. 'That's why your Mama didn't finally take to me, I believe. She realized I would always be able to act my way out of her clutches when we married, if I felt like it.'

'Couldn't pin you down.'

'Exactly.'

'But she's quite an actress, too, at heart.'

'Indeed she is – and that was another problem: too much alike in that way, both treading the boards at the same time, you might say, the two of us acting up to each other like one o'clock – to get what we wanted.'

'What did she want?'

Humphrey looked at her in surprise, putting a tongue in his cheek, playing the old roué now. 'My dear, what do you think? What does she want of everyone?'

'Their unswerving obedience.'

'You have it,' he exclaimed. 'You have it!'

'To her every whim?'

'Exactly!' he said joyously.

'So much better – if we could be real to each other, say what we mean.'

'Ah, but would it? Miss out on all the fun then! The cut and thrust, dear Frances – what would life be without it? How very dull, if we were real to each other all the time. And then again, perforce – since most of us have no roles handed out to us – we have to choose, have to create one. Perfectly obvious: all the world's a stage and so on. Quite true.'

'And you – what have you chosen?'

He sighed. 'Something different every day, so that I hardly know who I am. The penalty – for so much enjoyment. But I wouldn't have had it otherwise. Acting has got me what I wanted, a means to an end.'

'What end?'

'*Living!* I'm alive, dear girl! A change of scene, a new backcloth, a dash of limelight, a different costume – and I'm *free*. I told you – a dirty beard and an old wig and the world is yours for an hour or two. You saw how it was just now, didn't you?'

Frances nodded. She had indeed seen how it was. And later, over a spirited supper with Humphrey when the other men returned, looking across at Dermot, she pondered the idea of invention and deception in her life. Dermot had praised her candid nature. And she herself, quite apart from the duty she felt towards the truth, believed this might be part of her charm. But perhaps she was wrong – in so far as Dermot was concerned at least. Perhaps the impasse in their relationship was due simply to her being too truthful, too literal, with him. Perhaps, as Humphrey had just done, she should surprise, astonish him in some way.

The fog thickened as she walked down Regent Street on her next day off, closing in over the upper storeys of the great stores, so that only their bright windows, filled with enticing displays like miniature stage sets, gleamed clearly through the afternoon murk. Laden with boxes and parcels, people staggered, pushed and collided on the pavement, stampeding about in the yellow gloom. Other sounds were hidden – disembodied voices, footsteps, horses' feet and the cries of provoked cabbies, echoing invisibly up and down the street. The fog, and the hide-and-seek it imposed, thrilled Frances – this barely controlled pandemonium, figures appearing and disappearing like excited ghosts through the swirling cotton-wool.

She joined a crowd looking at some of the new clockwork trains in a big toyshop window. A frock-coated assistant wound a green and gold engine up behind the display, before placing it on a circular rail and setting it off in front of a line of tin carriages. She thought of Dermot during the train journey back from Salisbury when she had fallen asleep on his shoulder. But something more than that unconscious intimacy was needed, now.

In a window of Liberty's further down a puppet display was in progress behind a highly coloured proscenium, the eighteenth-century figures, men and women in various fancy dress, being manipulated on thread through a courtly dance against a Versailles backdrop.

She had been looking, in fact, for some small Christmas gifts – some clothes for herself too, perhaps, though she had little money in hand. Her allowance had indeed been cut off; she had not even had a reply to her letter home. And she was angry when she thought of this now – all her old pride and arrogance returning. Mortimer had advanced her £50 and Ruth Wechsberg had insisted that she take a nominal wage at least during her training. But what did this amount to, in this opulent street? – a mere pinprick of money. Confronted by these extravagant displays and expensive gifts, she wished she was really rich. Money was power – and, surrounded by these wealthy crowds laden with gaily ribboned boxes, she wanted that now – unbridled power, all her nursing precepts of self-sacrifice forgotten.

She looked back at the courtly puppets again, moving jerkily to and fro in their fancy dress ball. An idea occurred to her then – a plan which found its form a few minutes later when, crossing Piccadilly and going into Leicester Square, she saw the splendid uniform in the brightly lit window of Nathan's theatrical costumiers: a lovely scarlet Dragoon's tunic, double-breasted, brass-buttoned, swirls of braid on the cuffs, wide shimmering green lapels, dark narrow trousers with red piping beneath.

Frances promptly entered the costumiers and hired the uniform. 'The Rosscommon Dragoons,' the man told her. 'A defunct Irish regiment, I understand' – which delighted Frances all the more, seeing something additionally meant now in her scheme.

The uniform needed taking in here and there and the trousers were too long. But she and Eileen made alterations to it that evening, so that in the end it fitted very well. But it came with a heavy high-peaked officer's cap. She tried this on, sitting down in front of the mirror – took it off, then put it on again.

'You look a scream, either way!' Eileen told her.

'I feel like a lighthouse.'

They giggled. Frances stood up, put her hands in the trouser pockets and strutted round the bedroom. 'Funny having pockets,' she said. 'Should have some money to jangle in them.'

'Funny being a man at all, Miss, isn't it?'

'Yes.'

'What a lark! But what's it all *for*, Miss? Do tell!'

'A surprise. A secret!' she said in considerable excitement.

But the real surprise – the tragedy – was that Dermot, when she went down to the drawing room before dinner dressed as a Rosscommon Dragoon, was not at all amused by her transformation. For several moments, when she entered the room and he first saw her by the doorway, he was obviously taken in by this vision of a slim, dark-haired soldier and his face showed a bright surprise. But, when Frances came forward into the light and he recognized her, his expression clouded; he was annoyed.

'Frances – how could you?'

'You don't like it?'

He had stood up eagerly at first, but now he paced the room nervously, shaking his match box. 'Frances, Frances – I like you as a *woman*, not as a man. What could you have been thinking of?'

'Just a joke,' she said limply. What had she been thinking of? She was not sure now. She had not analysed her scheme completely. It had just been a vague 'plan' – the uniform in the bright window promising her something out of the fog, Humphrey's success in the same manner, the idea of changing one's life, Dermot's life, just an idea, an adventure, a means to an end. But she had never thought it through, to this end.

Dermot cleared his throat. 'A joke? Oh, Frances, you didn't really think, did you? . . .'

'Think what?' she asked rather arrogantly now.

'Think that that would . . . attract me?'

'No, of course not! Just saw it in a window this

afternoon – thought it would be a funny thing, like Humphrey in his old beggar's outfit. Spice of life and all that . . .' But she found she could not maintain her conceit or composure now, bursting into tears, rushing from the room. She had fallen in love with a man who could only love other men, who could not be changed. And she suffered the agony then of her exposure, wearing her heart on the sleeve of this stupid uniform – suffering, as she tore the hated clothes off in her bedroom, one more defeat.

Frances, having failed at adventure and deception, returned to the literal and prosaic in her life. Dermot's subsequent apologies were profuse and genuine. They were soon friends again. But there was no longer a feeling of impending intimacy between them. That was over. Touching his hand, lips brushing his cheek, head on his shoulder – all the preludes to love were gone. She saw how they could never become lovers.

Dermot, in her most secret thoughts, had offered her a future, a way out: they might have married, lived in Ireland – lived at Summer Hill, even . . . Yes, that fantasy, too, had seemed momentarily possible. Now all this bright invention had betrayed her, and she was hardened by it, sensing, for the first time, how real emotion, towards people, was an idiocy which would get her nowhere in life, something which would always be spurned or wasted. Only objects maintained fidelity, returned it – a place, a landscape, a house.

Her thoughts returned to Summer Hill. There was a world which would not betray her. Christmas was approaching. She would return for the holiday, whether her parents wished it or not. Besides, there was Eileen to think of; she, too, would want to go home for the Christmas season. She had kept in polite touch with Eustace, at Aldershot with his regiment, and now she wrote to him again, telling him of her plans. He replied, agreeing with her in an entirely vague and non-committal way. She spoke to Ruth Wechsberg, who freely offered her the time off, and to Mortimer who equally encouraged her, as did Dermot.

Everyone was on Frances's side. But she felt somehow powerless and unconfident about this homecoming. 'A return to the fray,' Dermot had described her earlier ambitions at Summer Hill. Yet she longed for security and peace there now – not war. Dermot might have offered her this in himself – or at least been a vital support, a means to that end at Summer Hill. But she could not now expect such intimate help from him. Dermot was a friend. Everyone was a friend. None of them really understood the heart of things in her life – her longing for a house, for a hill in summer – so that she gave up thinking she would ever find a true ally in that cause.

6

The front door bell at Grosvenor Crescent had rung, pulled vigorously several times, breaking the somnolence of the dark December evening. Frances had heard voices in the hall – gruff male laughter, then Ruth's voice and some lively ensuing chatter before heavy footsteps climbed the Florentine staircase, followed by the rich aroma of a cigar, drifting into the nurses' room where Frances was preparing a dressing tray. She had started a week of night duty in the ward that evening, under Agnes's direction. Now she turned to her questioningly.

'Who? . . .'

Agnes looked up knowingly, smoothed her hair, then stroked the side of her nose, as if prettying herself in a mirror. But she said nothing.

'I wonder who it can be?' Frances persisted. 'Visiting just before supper.'

But the footsteps had gone now, disappearing into the back of the house where Ruth had her quarters, her little drawing and dining room: a private guest had arrived, not a visitor to the ward, so that Frances dropped her enquiry and went out to dress Lieutenant Lighthorn's stump. He too had heard the vigorous bell, smelt the rich cigar.

'Thought we were about to see my papa,' he told Frances. 'He puffs at those grand weeds. But Sister Ruth told him very firmly to desist last time he was here.'

'No. A private guest. They went back to Sister Ruth's rooms.'

'A *man* though,' Lighthorn said impishly. She dabbed away some flaky skin with spirit lotion, then ran the clean bandage round the stump. 'Sister Frances—' he went on confidently.

'Not Sister yet.'

'Well, Miss Frances – may I ask you? – do you have a friend, a particular friend?'

'No,' she said firmly.

He sighed. 'Oh, if I only had my legs again, you would have. I wonder who Sister Ruth's particular friend is?'

'He's been here before, you mean?' Frances could not contain her curiosity.

'Oh yes. That same rich cigar, jolly laughter. Every week or so, in the evenings. You've not been here. We've all wondered.'

'Well, I'm sure Sister Ruth does have some male friends, you know,' Frances said off-handedly, finally pinning the bandage, then patting the mummified stump. 'There you are. You'll be quite ready for your supper now.'

'Yes, but *who*?' he asked with mischief, eyes rolling in mock agony. His enforced idleness and lack of mobility among these women had greatly promoted the subaltern's amorous thoughts, a lascivious curiosity, a taste for liaisons – real or imagined. Marooned in bed he lived vicariously – just as Frances did, equally curious now. In their separate despairs, they both longed for answers, access into the secrets of other people's happy lives.

Their curiosity was unexpectedly satisfied – an hour after supper in the ward: an answer introduced by the same rich cigar aroma, followed by a bearded, balding head emerging from a swirl of blue smoke, the beaming figure coming clear, like sun through the fog, as the substantial figure paused resolutely in the doorway, a Holbein grandee, portly and middle-aged, whose evening clothes cut with superb tact did much to disguise both facts.

'Now, sir, if you'll forgive me, but I really must insist – I must ask you not to smoke in the ward.' Ruth, in a restrained grey silk evening dress, was tactful but no less firm than usual.

'Ah, such a taskmistress! My dear woman.' The neatly badger-bearded man turned and admired her. 'Irish stew, rice pudding – and now no smokes! What a regimen you impose. An evening with you is stricter than a month at Bad Homburg! But as you will – noblesse oblige!' He stubbed the cigar out in an ashtray by the door, then continued the banter. 'As you will indeed – any-thing which may allow me acc-ess to your holy of holies: I am to see it all at last. I have been much in-ter-ested, my dear Ruth, in your ac-tivities – which you have de-nied me!'

He clearly spaced and hit each syllable in longer words, a curious hesitancy which might have disguised a stutter. Yet there was nothing delayed in his general conversational approach. Rolling his r's, he attacked his sentences with a genial and energetic relish, just as he walked down the centre of the ward now – quickly, precisely, despite his considerable bulk – a store of energy and impatience behind the neat steps, someone who knew where he was going, the hooded, blue-grey eyes seeing and appraising everything with equal confidence and enjoyment; a protuberant lower lip moving, tongue flickering, as if testing the air like a food for all its possible surprises.

Frances watched the commanding figure and immediately felt, despite his imperious airs, that here was really a child in a man's clothes. It was her clear impression: a child got up in fancy dress, beard, cigar and tails, who roamed through the rooms of life, as he had come into the ward just then, seeing each room as another and more wonderful nursery.

The visitor stopped finally at Lighthorn's bed. The officer sat up now, both arms rigid by his side, giving him much-needed support in his surprise. 'His Royal Highness,' Ruth presented her dinner guest, 'the Prince of Wales. And this is Miss Frances Cordiner, who is helping us, learning her duties.'

Frances curtsied, a short brief genuflection, the starch in her apron crackling as she bent and straightened. But then to her surprise the Prince offered her his own large square hand. She had done less than glance at him, just an unfocused run over his features, and would not have dared look him straight in the eye unless, as he did then, he had not held on to her fingers, and continued to hold them for what seemed an eternity, so that Frances, fearing her responsibility for some frightful social gaffe, had suddenly stared at the Prince, holding him eye to eye as if pleading for mercy.

'Learning her duties. I say!'

'Yes, she has just started – on night duty.'

'Night duty, of course.' He considered the idea vaguely, preoccupied by some quite different thought, reluctantly letting her hand go at last, his earlier smile gone, but staring back at her now.

'My dear,' Ruth Wechsberg said to her next morning, 'the Prince of Wales has asked that we both take dinner with him – at Marlborough House.'

'Oh – how very kind.'

'Yes. But I fear not.' Ruth turned away, starting to smooth the covers on the one easy chair, set by the fire, in her otherwise spartan little drawing room – the very chair which the Prince himself had occupied the previous evening, Frances thought; a vague odour of cigar smoke still hung in the air. 'I have made it clear to the Prince,' Ruth continued, 'that I prefer not to venture on his territory. His Marlborough House set . . . are not mine.'

Frances wondered, since Ruth had apparently declined the invitation, why she had brought the subject up at all. It was a question, given their open relationship, that she would normally have asked. But that morning there was a slight *frisson*, a distance between them. However, disguised as advice, the answer was forthcoming. 'I tell you this, Frances, because the Prince is a wilful man, rarely crossed in his social ambitions. He will certainly attempt to make direct contact with you himself.'

'Oh? Will he?' Frances's innocence was well feigned. But Ruth was not taken in. She sighed, opening the window on a dull foggy morning. A damp air crept into the room, a chilly displeasure from the world.

'Yes, my dear, he will.' She sighed once more. It was not like her, repeating a mannerism in this way – she who, in usual times, was so sure of herself. 'He was, apparently, considerably taken by you,' she went on. 'And so I must warn you – since I know him well – that he has a penchant for young unmarried women, a tendency to take them up – and drop them. You would not be the first or the last among his current "virgin band" to suffer in this way. I regard his behaviour as reprehensible, to a degree, and have told him so. I know the risks, in your case—'

'But, Ruth, the risks – I barely spoke to the Prince.'

'It was enough – not what you said but, for him, what you appeared to be. And what you must not be – a mere plaything, to be taken up like his games of baccarat, then dropped for one of whist or bridge. It is his way and I must protect you from it.'

Frances wondered, if this was his way with women, how Ruth, with her sensible disciplines and prohibitions, had ever come to play a part in the Prince's irresponsible life. Again, she longed to ask her before the answer struck her with some force: it had been apparent in all that Ruth had said of the Prince. Her role in his life was one of nanny, a most elegantly attractive one no doubt, but nanny none the less. With Ruth, Frances thought, in that same easy chair by the fire, the Prince could pour his heart out, take succour, or touch faith by making confession for all his misdemeanours in the great world outside this nursery – which was her drawing room. Here, for an evening, the naughty child became the good child, taking his milk and biscuits without tears before bedtime.

Ruth's part in the Prince's life was obvious – as clear as lines written for two protagonists in a drama. And Ruth knew both parts by heart, just as she knew the briefer and less happy roles which lay in store for subsidiary characters, other women who could only achieve mere walk-on roles in the play, to be unceremoniously dumped after the first act. Ruth had cast Frances in just such a part. But Frances was determined on something better.

'Of course,' Frances said, 'I take your point. I understand you perfectly,' she added meekly. But she smiled at her then, the complicit smile of someone who had understood everything that Ruth had *not* said, who had read between the lines of her words and sensed a starring role there. If Ruth was nanny to the Prince, Frances's smile said, and other women mere playthings, then she might offer him something else, neither mutton stew nor caviare, but a dish more to his taste than either.

A chilly pall descended on the room now, the cold of charity. Frances left politely, closing the door behind her, shutting the chill out, leaving the odour of dead cigars, quickening her step along the warm corridor, moving into life once more, mimicking the Prince's energetic progress through the ward, trailing, pursuing, sniffing at the hems of power – certain, though nothing had yet happened to warrant it, that she was moving towards a happy destiny.

She wondered at this confidence, since all her certainties in love were gone. Why did she feel so sure? Perhaps because she felt intuitively that, in this instance, she would not have to put herself at risk or wear her heart upon her sleeve. She felt certain of that from the way the Prince had looked at her – a look that every woman understands.

She had not long to wait for confirmation of her feelings. An anonymous messenger, dressed like a clerk, arrived two days later at Wilton Place: a plain envelope, with a card inside, die-stamped The Marlborough Club, Pall Mall, S.W. 'Dear Miss Cordiner, I much enjoyed our meeting. Would you do me the honour of dining with some friends and myself this Friday coming at nine, 55

Eaton Square? I would send a carriage for you at a quarter to – and can, I hope, look forward to your company. Edward, Wales.'

She saw at once something not only informal but clandestine in the invitation. She was being asked unchaperoned to some anonymous house. An assumption about her morals had already been made by the Prince – a risqué assumption. Yet the Prince, in so clearly and permanently identifying himself in the invitation, had put himself equally at risk. He trusted her. And she was charmed by it all – it was just as she would have had it. The joint risks implied in the note confirmed a fellow feeling – they were conspirators together. And conspiracy demanded secrecy. So she told Mortimer and Dermot that an invitation had come from Miss Wechsberg, for that Friday evening, that they were to dine in town together, with friends. To Eileen she decided to tell the same thing, though she hated any deception with her, when for so long they had been deceivers together. But such was the sympathy between them that Eileen came to suspect something quite out of the usual was at hand.

She had prepared Frances's one good evening costume – the midnight blue silk dress, ruched in narrow green panels, smoothing it down on the hanger before taking a hot iron from the grate to secure the folds. 'Just a dinner party?' she asked. 'But a *special* one?'

'Not really. Just some friends of Miss Wechsberg's.' As she lied she suddenly hated the lie. She felt no need to boast. But she saw the deceit not only as a disloyalty towards Eileen, but the beginning of a whole future of lies, to everyone, a programme which ran entirely against the grain of her nature – she who had made truth one of her hallmarks. She saw, too, how this deception, if she had to maintain it with everyone, would isolate her, would somehow condemn her in advance as a mere plaything of the Prince's. So, for her own peace of mind, there had to be one other who shared the secret – a life raft if the boat sank, a confidante with whom, from the beginning, she would have kept faith if all were lost.

'Just friends of Sister Ruth's?' Eileen asked, ironing the dress now. 'But not all nurses – men as well?'

Frances, in her petticoats, looked into the mirror, wondering about her hair. It had grown out again now, and she would leave it so, unfashionably tossed. 'No, men as well,' she said. 'A man, at least – a friend of Sister Ruth's. The Prince of Wales has asked me to dinner.'

Eileen went on ironing for a moment, then stopped. 'The Prince of who?'

'Wales.'

'You don't mean . . . that old bearded fellow? You're pulling me leg.'

'I *do* mean that old bearded fellow.'

'You're joking – he's old enough to be your father.'

'My grandfather even. But why not?'

'He's married – he's going to be King. You couldn't be . . .'

'What?'

'Going out with him.'

'Well, I *am*. And that's why you mustn't speak a word of it, not to *anybody*, promise?'

Eileen, astonished, picked the iron off the silk before it singed. 'I promise. Oh, Miss Frances – what a lark! Like a fairy tale!'

Frances turned and looked at Eileen with surprise. This was a point which had not crossed her mind at all.

She had already decided exactly the advantages she sought from her meeting with the Prince: power – the power she would derive, if she found favour there, from an alliance with this most powerful figure. It was as simple as that. Any other benefits would be entirely subsidiary. But it was not the power of money or gifts, no material thing she sought – least of all was it a fairy tale she wished to be part of. She looked, simply, for the support of such a name in her campaign for a house in another country.

Besides the Prince, there were two other couples and a further man in the light-panelled drawing room in Eaton

Square when she was shown in. The Prince advanced energetically, making introductions.

'Miss Jenni Stonor; Sir Seymour Fortescue; Miss Isabelle Marshall-Hall; Major Clarke . . . And, last but not least, Major Augustus Lumley, my mother's Master of Ceremonies – so that I may say you are in entirely appropriate hands, Miss Cordiner!'

Frances barely noticed their features as she was introduced but understood at once that none of the men present was here with his own wife. The two young women were something of her own age, others in the Prince's virgin band no doubt. Miss Stonor was dark and pretty with a hint of plumpness; Miss Marshall-Hall, refined and delicate, was excruciatingly thin, with a wasp waist exaggerated to the point of deformity. Both were superbly dressed and coiffed, leaving Frances feeling frumpish. Yet she did not worry for long, for it was soon clear that her own particular wild dark beauty had made a strong impression all round.

The mood of the party was informal, without being in any way *louche* – the guests unconstrained in their movements and chatter, no hint of stuffy formality, nor yet of licence. For a moment, though, the Prince engaged elsewhere, Frances had no one to speak to, gazing instead at an equestrian picture above the mantelpiece. But the Prince turned then and, seeing her interest, spoke to her with sudden enthusiasm.

'You like it? I thought you might. You are from Ireland, of course. You will appreciate such things. One of mine. From Marlborough House. Stubbs. "The Jockey on Turf". First-rate man – only painter I can abide. First-rate, don't you think? Look here—' He approached the painting, pointing at the exactly rendered faces, the minute features of the jockey and groom lost against a large landscape of hills and puffy clouds. 'Actual people – *real* people, you understand, not just in-vented. That is what I so admire – see the scowls on their faces!'

'It is a fine picture,' Frances said simply, for it was. It

reminded her of Summer Hill. And suddenly she felt the wound of homesickness, a great emptiness, a misery with London. 'There!' she said before she could stop herself, pointing to the beeches in the picture, eyes alight. 'That beech wood, we have one just like it, on Cooper's hill at home – I used to love it – a secret grove with the wind in the trees!'

'Good! Very good!' he exclaimed. 'I see I have an ally here. I have yet to persuade some of my friends – of the excellence of this man Stubbs. But come, we are not at the Royal Academy – I'm pleased to say. Let me offer you some re-fresh-ment.'

The Prince, wonderfully genial and at ease now as a result of this fortuitous coming together over the picture, led her towards a sideboard where he poured them both glasses of dry champagne. 'You must tell me about yourself,' he said. 'My dear friend Ruth has told me a little. But . . .' He paused, the hooded eyes narrowing in a smile. 'It was very little. She was not actively disposed that we should meet.'

'No.'

'She does not trust me – entirely. But one must be one's own man, do you not think?'

'Indeed. And I am most honoured by your invitation.'

'You did not tell her of it then?'

'No.'

'You would have been quite free to do so. She is a dear friend.'

'And to me – which is why I would not wish to upset her.'

'Exactly.' The Prince nodded his wholehearted agreement and Frances, taking encouragement from this, found more of her voice.

'Nor did I tell my cousins, with whom I am staying.'

'Indeed?' The Prince was surprised at this instance of discretion. 'You have reached your ma-jority, I understand. You may dine with whom you choose.'

'Hardly, sir.'

'In private, I mean.'

'That, surely, would be the ultimate breach of convention, sir.'

The Prince suddenly took the point. 'I see, I see. Quite so.'

Could he really have been unaware of these social conventions, Frances wondered. He could not. Was he then simply being forgetful, flustered? There was certainly no irony in his voice. He was preoccupied, Frances decided – a preoccupation, it seemed, with her, for he had barely ceased to gaze at her since her entry.

'I told my maid,' Frances said uppishly. 'That was all.'

The Prince smiled hugely. 'You trust her?'

'More than anyone. We trust each other completely.'

This particular confidence appealed to the Prince. 'Good – how very good! I wish I were such a hero to my valet. But come. We talk too much of meeting, when we are well met already, are we not?'

Frances paused for several seconds, then gave him the slightest nod of her head. He offered her his arm in return. 'Let us to dinner, then. Miss Rosa Lewis from the Cavendish Hotel has prepared something simple.'

Dinner was served in a comfortable, though not opulent dining room, the men's white shirts gleaming in the candlelight, white carnations or gardenias in their buttonholes, Miss Marshall-Hall with orchids in her corsage. Frances sat at the Prince's right hand. The food was not at all simple. It was elaborate and extensive beyond anything Frances had ever experienced. Baked truffles in warm napkins were served first, followed by silver salvers of oysters on ice, which the Prince swallowed at a rush, between mouthfuls of brown bread and butter – like a famished chop house diner, in a manner that astonished Frances who had never seen oysters so dispatched, at such speed or in so cavalier a manner. There was caviare then, with plover's eggs and ortolans in aspic, followed by sole poached in chablis, garnished with prawns. Boned snipe came next, stuffed with a forcemeat of truffles in a madeira sauce; then quail packed with foie gras, followed by the only simple dish of the meal – individual crowns of lamb served with redcurrant jelly, accompanied by cauliflower and celery. Finally came a rum-flavoured chocolate mousse and a raspberry ice cream laced with kirsch. Apart from a Château Lafite with the snipe and the lamb they drank champagne throughout the meal, Duminy *Extra Sec*.

The Prince's appetite and attack remained undiminished to the end of the dinner. Indeed such was his interest in the food that, apart from the short intervals between courses, he barely spoke to Frances. It was clear, in fact, that he wished for no real interruption in his *dégustation*, appearing quite happy to listen to the others round the table, who fed him anecdotes and gossip as he fed himself.

It was clear, too, even when they all adjourned to the drawing room (there was to be no post-prandial division of the sexes, Frances was pleased to realize), that the Prince was no great conversationalist. He preferred the role of benevolent listener and his interjections were mainly in the form of repeated questions – 'Who was it?' and 'Why?' and 'How come?' He lit a vast and pungent Corona y Corona and took his coffee with a chasse-café of cognac, as the other men did, for no other spirits or port were served. Stories were swapped, sporting or military anecdotes, and as if on cue the Prince was tempted to embark on some of his own jokes, well-worn ones apparently, which were received none the less with appropriate silence, then uproarious, if slightly forced, laughter. One story, concerning the Shah of Persia's visit to Buckingham Palace, in which the savage infidel had mistaken the lavatory bowl for a wash basin, went on for ever.

He was an indifferent raconteur, Frances thought – ponderous in emphasis, lost in his introductory scene-setting, repetitive, quite without the light touch required in such jovial banter. His friends indulged him carefully. Were he not Prince of Wales, Frances thought, he would have been dismissed as a crashing bore in any company.

She found it all quite unexpectedly pathetic – this Prince wallowing among his toadies – she who, from Irish dinner parties, was used to such real wit and unafraid debate among guests with the sharpest minds. The Prince's mental equipment and agility, by comparison, seemed those of a dullard; his jokes were like lead, his table manners and gargantuan appetite bizarre – a man like a great sleepy bear, who only really seemed to come alive over his food. Being honest, she could only describe the Prince as a vulgarian.

And yet, when he looked at her, raised those sharply arched eyebrows above the hooded, blue-grey orbs, she saw quite a different man in that kindly gaze – someone almost shy, meek, lost: the gaze of a confused child. This was the hidden quality which attracted her. There was something else in his heart, which explained his frustrated nervous energy – a sadness behind the façade of bonhomie. So that Frances, sensing and sympathizing with this other man she saw in him, thought she might respond to it, search out that real spirit and release it.

He fed himself so, she thought, to satisfy an immaterial hunger. He was a man of questions which had always been misunderstood. She would understand, and respond. 'Je Responderay'. Frog Prince – she would transform the beast – a touch, a kiss – which would return to him his true form.

'So,' he said, when they came to talk, sitting a little aside from the company, 'you wish to become a nurse?'

'I think so, sir.'

'You are not sure?'

'I may not have the application, the patience.'

'Ruth speaks very highly . . .' He drew on his cigar, looking at her through rings of smoke.

'I am more concerned . . .' She started enthusiastically before letting her hand fall, turning away listlessly. Then, resuming control, she leant forward intently towards him, blinking rapidly. 'I have had problems at home in Ireland,' she said finally. 'Things I should like put right before I consider any other future.'

'Problems? Your mother, Lady Cordiner, is old Basil Halevy's daughter, is she not?' Frances nodded. 'I met him once or twice – and remember more of his reputation certainly: he was a sound and most successful man. So I take it the problem is not one of . . . subsistence?'

'No. No, indeed. Rather of temperament – between my mother and myself. We do not see eye to eye, to say the least. She is a woman of some authority – indeed overwhelmingly so. We – I particularly – find her shadow constricting.'

The Prince, listening attentively, seemed to catch an echo here of something he well understood. 'I see, I see – quite so. I have had some such similar problems in my own circle.' He smiled diffidently.

'But Mama and I have *quite* fallen out. In fact, I have been forbidden the house, our house at Summer Hill.' She laughed at this, as though it had been a minor deprivation, the result of a mere whim of her mother's. But then she changed tack, becoming serious once more. 'And since I love the place dearly – there is the problem.'

Without dwelling on any one incident, nor yet treating the case too lightly, she explained matters further – her break with her fiancé, the death of her elder brother – adding detail to the row with her mother, how she had broken the mourning and rung the bells throughout the house – finally returning to her 'banishment' as she put it, a light reference to it again, the rash dictate of an unhappy woman.

The Prince absorbed her story with increasing interest and sympathy, with few interjections. Yet when she finished Frances was rather disappointed that he simply said, 'I see, I see indeed. Quite so.' He paused for some time, stroking his greying beard, pouting his lower lip, licking it pensively. Then, as if making up his mind about something and sure of her confidence, he spoke with a husky warmth. 'I am dis-tinctly inter-ested. Your history so resembles my own. I, too, was to have married someone much to my mother's taste, but not to mine – lost a father and a brother – and quite like you have suffered the whims and dictates of a dear good mother who, like your own, took to a life of mourning, without respite or con-sid-er-ation that others, at least, must go on living.' He nodded his head several times, putting down his cigar, smiling slowly. 'I wish only that I might have had the courage to ring all the bells at Windsor! I have had to be satisfied . . . with less public manifestations of myself!' He glanced round the little drawing room.

'Indeed, sir.' Frances smiled at him in return. But she said no more.

'I have wished, too,' the Prince continued, warming to his theme, 'always for some *rapprochement* with my mother – in our differences. Apart from my feelings there, it is so obviously my duty, as it must be yours. I quite see that. In what way, if I may ask, do you intend proceeding to that end?'

'I have written to my parents, some six weeks ago, offering apologies for my behaviour. But they have not replied.'

'Indeed. That is dis-con-certing. I believe though, if I may offer you my own experience in these matters, that you must come face to face with them, with your mother.' He smiled again, with irony now. 'I have found that the actual *appearance* – though it may not be wished – of the penitent prodigal, has much to recommend it! A *mauvais quart d'heure* perhaps. But there is no better way to be forgiven, with a loved one, than that they *see* how one has relented. Letters are a poor substitute.'

'Indeed. One can so dissemble there.'

'But you have not done that?'

'No, I have offered my heartfelt apologies. They have gone entirely unregarded. So that I fear there may now be no reconciliation.'

'My dear,' he said rousing himself now, speaking with brio, 'I have thought just the same myself in the past in my own case – that there could be no real coming together. And I have proved it otherwise. Perhaps, if you will allow me, I may help you in the matter.'

'Sir, it is unnecessary. You are called by so many much more important things—'

'Miss Cordiner,' he smiled a little sadly, reaching out and touching her hand briefly, 'I have been called, for so many years now, on only the *least* important things, I may assure you! What more important than that you should find your home again? You would do me honour.'

'Well, Lumley, what do you say? What do you think of her?' the Prince asked later, speaking to the former House-hold Cavalry Major, the Queen's Master of Ceremonies, whose task at Court was to decide who was socially accept-able and who was not, and who did the same for the Prince less formally – a man thus much feared in every fashion-able circle, who could make or break a person's social ambitions with a turn of his head. More commonly, as a code between the Prince and himself, the words 'Rose' or 'Cabbage' were designated as indicators of acceptability.

Lumley, a small silver-haired man, stiffly military but with clever, darting eyes, stroked his formidable mous-taches. 'A rose, I should say, sir.'

'Good – good.'

'Though I wonder if not . . . too wild a rose.'

'I saw nothing of that – a *most* tactful young woman.' The Prince gave, as an example, her discretion over his invitation.

'But it is there in the eyes, sir. And you will know how she is Irish—'

'Only half so – old Basil Halevy's granddaughter: she is half-Jewish.'

'Worse still – a most *provocative* mix, if I may say so, sir. By all accounts there is a headstrongness there. I am reminded of Charles Beresford, all that trouble—'

'She has nothing to do with that intemperate Waterford clan.'

'None the less, there is a distinct air of having her own way.'

'A taking from her mother perhaps, but diluted. She has much grace.'

Lumley pursed his lips judiciously. 'More, she has astonishing beauty . . .' He paused, doubting something now.

'Yes?'

'But she has an equal sharpness of mind. I have rarely encountered so great a mix of beauty and brains.'

'You fear that?'

'I am certainly forewarned by such – if you wish to have your way there.'

The Prince considered this idea. 'I had not intended that, in the manner you suppose,' he said stiffly.

'I am anxious, too,' Lumley went on tactfully, 'that with such intelligence she may be put to schemes. A woman of such mental equipment, not yet married, tends to scheme in some other way. I would fear that.'

'She and her fiancé – Lord Norton's son – they broke their engagement. There is nothing untoward there.'

'I am not surprised. The son is much the pale shadow – no match for her.'

'Besides, she asked for nothing – no hint. It was I who offered her my support.'

Major Lumley became agitated at this news. 'Of what kind, if I may ask, sir?'

'I offered help – mediation – in effecting a *rapprochement* between her and Lady Cordiner, her mother. They have fallen out badly.'

'I see. You do not then propose any . . . any informal liaison, which I understood was your thought in inviting her here this evening?'

'No. Not necessarily. Certainly not. I should like to give her my public support.'

'Without her having a chaperone – and I understood Miss Wechsberg has refused that role – how would you intend proceeding in such an open course?'

'She shall have a suitable chaperone, Lumley. We – you – shall see to it. You will arrange that.'

Lumley was much put out. 'But who, sir? Had you someone in mind? It is not so easy, to simply pick the girl a duenna – out of a hat, so to speak.'

'Not out of a *hat*, Lumley. You will consider the matter most carefully.' The Prince prepared to leave.

'There is one other matter, sir, in any future you contemplate here. Her cousin, Mortimer Cordiner, with whom she presently resides, is a most vociferous Home Rule M.P. in the House. It would be as well to bear that in mind. Your support for Miss Cordiner should not be misinterpreted as any support for his policies.'

'Why should it be? Distant cousins merely. And you assured me that, in Ireland, her own immediate family were impeccable, socially and in their politics.'

'Indeed, sir. It is just that, again, I suspect schemes.'

'*Schemes*, Lumley?' The Prince raised his voice. 'That she has a mind of her own must imply schemes?' he bellowed.

'I have found it so, sir.'

'Fiddlesticks, Lumley. She is a breath of fresh air in that respect. Her only scheme is to make amends at home. She has suffered much loss. She is in distress. I cannot turn my back on her.'

The Prince turned his back on Lumley instead. As he left, Lumley marvelled once again at the Prince's eager self-deception, his foolhardiness. He could never refuse the role of knight errant in a manoeuvre which, Lumley thought, had a distinctly less honourable end in view. He was besotted with the girl. She would already be well aware of this. Therefore she would have schemes. Lumley had seen it all before – particularly in the case of another Frances, the Prince's Darling Daisy, now the Countess of Warwick – an affair between them that had started in just the same manner, the Prince taking her side as a damsel in distress in the matter of her affair with Lord Charles Beresford. That had been a fracas with a distinctly Irish side to it, resulting in no end of upset, every kind of social awkwardness and upheaval. And Lumley, to his intense embarrassment, had been much involved, in a business that had reflected badly on everyone, himself included. So he looked now with horror on the Prince's demand that he act as go-between – worse, as a sort of maiden aunt – in procuring a chaperone for this girl. He was sure that in so doing he would be aiding and abetting another act of sheer folly on the Prince's part.

*

Returning home that evening Frances rightly thought that things could not have gone better. She had first of all avoided any indelicate end to the evening – which she was aware, given the circumstances of meeting in this anonymous house in Eaton Square, might have been among the Prince's intentions. Further, she had not openly advanced her plans in any way; the Prince had done all that for her. Only one thing gave her pause for doubt – she liked the man, liked him quite aside from her schemes, quite beyond any idea of flirtation with him. It was a deeper thing. There was a hidden store of real sympathy, affection, a great kindness in the Prince, which worldly appetites and demands had overlaid, she felt. She had glimpsed this from the beginning and he had truly confirmed it now, offering her a sight of this other man, a vision of himself not as Prince but as fallible human, much aware of common hurt, broken familial bonds, all domestic heartbreak, which he had experienced himself, with a grief-maddened, autocratic mother like her own, so that, once he had become aware that they shared these experiences, he had dropped any idea of her as plaything, she thought, and taken to her almost as an equal – two people who understood the pain of family exile.

Eileen had waited up for her. 'Well? Tell us – tell us, do!' She could not restrain the pitch of excitement in her voice.

'Not so loud, Eileen.' Eileen helped her off with her dress.

'Did you, did he – did you *meet* him even?'

'Yes. Yes, he was most kind.'

'*Kind?* Was that all? Wasn't there dancing and things?'

'No – nor midnight chimes, a silver slipper or a pumpkin coach!' Frances turned and smiled at Eileen's disappointment.

'Oh dear . . .'

'It was all much better than that, Eileen. It was *real*.'

'I don't follow? Wasn't there music and . . . and laughing and all *that*?'

'No. We just talked, he and I.'

'But, Miss, you could talk *any* time. But, with a Prince, surely don't you do *other* things?'

'No. The talk was everything.'

'Sure, you'd do better at a crossroads *celidhe* beyant Cloone. It must have been a dull evening. Was there *nothing* else?' she asked desperately.

Frances ruffled her curls, thinking. She was sad now for a moment. 'There was everything else. But we haven't come to it yet.'

Eileen shook her head in bewilderment. 'You're a quare one and no mistake.'

The following morning Frances left earlier than usual for Grosvenor Crescent, in order to avoid facing Dermot or Mortimer with any account of her dinner party. She needed more time to think about her response there.

The Prince had, of course, asked that they meet again – but in a general way, without specifying a place or time, or in what manner she was to appear with him, formally or informally again. She had tactfully alluded to these imprecisions, the general difficulties inherent in both their positions over any future meeting. But the Prince, very much the Sir Galahad, had assured her that matters would be arranged in an entirely appropriate form, that he would be in touch with her. Her impatience lay only in that soon, with Christmas only three weeks away, she would have to leave for Ireland. Mortimer and Dermot were due to sail for Dublin in two weeks' time: she and Eileen would naturally expect to travel with them, if they were going.

But she had told the Prince of these plans, in an offhand way, shuddering briefly at the prospect of a worse than chilly reception at Summer Hill. This unfeigned shudder, these heartfelt words, had rallied the Prince to an increased sympathy and identification with her cause. The joust was in train; his standard, he clearly implied, was at her disposal; she had but to attach her colours to his lance – which she did, on leaving, by shaking his hand and holding it thereafter for considerably longer than convention required, just as he had done with her on their first encounter. He would propose another meeting soon after Christmas no doubt, she thought. Meanwhile she would simply have to wait.

Augustus Lumley reported to the Prince several days later – meeting in his over-furnished, darkly-cluttered study at Marlborough House. The Prince, his long-haired fox terrier Caesar on a tiger skin by the fire, was seated at his small desk, a desk overcome with a confusion of papers and knick-knacks – among which silver-framed photographs of his wife, Princess Alexandra, and his children were the only things clearly to be displayed.

As Lumley entered, the dog Caesar growled, took to his feet and thence, in furious yapping bounds, to Lumley's feet, worrying at his boots and trouser turn-ups, getting his teeth into the cloth, so that Lumley was forced to kick out, swinging the dog round briefly in the air like a conker on a string before the snarling animal released its grip and started instead to bark furiously, head lowered, certain that this rabbit, without further close encounter, could be worried to death.

The Prince, much amused, did nothing to restrain the dog. 'Sir,' Lumley cried. 'Ask the beast to heel!' It was not the first time he, or others in the Prince's retinue, had been so attacked. Though Lumley believed that, in his own case, the Prince was always particularly lax in restraining the brute.

'Caesar!' the Prince eventually bellowed. 'Caesar – come here. You naughty, *naughty* dog.' The dog returned to his master, tail wagging, entirely undismayed, as the Prince himself appeared to be. He was that morning in any case in a particularly genial mood – and the dog's antics had merely sharpened his pleasure. The Prince had been doing what he liked best – surveying and pondering an immense list of intended Christmas presents, to his family, courtiers, staff and friends, both at Marlborough House and at Sandringham, a list which his private secretary had prepared and left with him earlier that day. Now, with Lumley's arrival and Caesar's performance making a very suitable entr'acte to his morning, he dropped these enjoyable considerations and looked at the Master of Ceremonies with a beady eye.

'Well, Lumley, what have you come up with?'

'Sir, in the matter of your Boxing Day shoot at Sandringham, I have to report that Sir Archibald MacIntosh, much the cabbage in any case, is also a most unreliable shot.'

The Prince let him finish, drumming his fingers the while with increasing tempo on the desk. '*Yes*, Lumley.' He spoke with heavy emphasis. 'We shall take due precautions. But I spoke of the *other* matter – of Miss Cordiner.'

Lumley bit his lip. 'Sir, I cannot report any real success there. Lady Filmer, who seemed a possibility, is not the age she was. Nor the Dowager Duchess of Manchester, another possibility. Miss de Vere Trumpington, a distinct possibility, has taken to her bed following a contretemps with her horse – a parting of the ways over a ditch with the Quorn. Then I had thought of the Countess of Berwick—'

'I know you have *thought*, Lumley – it is not beyond you. But who have you come *up* with?'

Lumley, exasperated now, came up with the truth. 'Sir, I must be honest: I have it on the best authority that there is *no* one suitable for such a commission. The matter is altogether too delicate – fraught with difficulty and risk – for anyone in your circle or at court to put themselves in jeopardy over it. Miss Cordiner, for them, is a quite unknown quantity. And it is this factor, as I have said to you myself, that entirely restrains them – as, if I may say so, it should equally restrain your Royal Highness.'

The Prince sighed, stood up, lit a cigar by the fireplace, looked at Landseer's dreamy oval portrait of his mother, with himself and the Princess Royal as children, over the mantelpiece. Then, after a long and ominous pause, he rounded on Lumley – not losing his temper, as Lumley had half-expected, but worse in that he spoke to him slowly, with heavy sarcasm, pitying condescension, spacing his syllables and rolling his r's more than was his custom. 'The Queen's Master of Ceremonies,' he said, 'who can-not ar-r-ange a social matter entirely right and proper and above board; that a young woman most em-in-ently bred, of grace and in-tell-ectual distinction, the daughter of one of my Irish earls—'

'Her father is a mere baronet, sir—'

'Don't *in-ter-rupt*, Lumley! – Such a long-established baronetcy outruns most earldoms, as far as I am concerned – a Master of Ceremonies who cannot arrange ac-cess of such a person to Court – Lumley, you are failing at your job. Do you hear? Do you?' The Prince's voice, like an approaching avalanche, had become louder, more threat-ening as he spoke, so that Lumley knew that he must forestall him somehow if he was not now to be engulfed in a whirlwind of rage.

'Sir,' he put in, an idea striking him, coming to his rescue at the last moment. 'If I might make so bold—'

'Dispense with the preambles, Lumley: pray *make* bold.'

'I take your point, sir. And mine is this: if it is all to be so much above board with Miss Cordiner, and she is in such palpable need of familial support, I wonder if you might not, with the best advantage, welcome her as a guest in your *own* home at Sandringham for Christmas – where you and Her Royal Highness might, with all due propriety, act *in loco parentis* as it were to the poor girl. In this manner no chaperone would be required: Her Royal Highness would naturally fill that role. And I am sure,' he added unctuously, 'that you could well persuade the Princess of this, given her boundless sympathies – and of course the pitiable circumstances of the young woman.'

Lumley waited anxiously for a response as the Prince walked to and fro between the velveteen sofa and the fire-place. Finally the Prince spoke. 'Capital, Lumley, capital. I shall speak to Alix this very morning. I wonder I didn't think of the idea myself. I am obliged to you. Oh, and I think in that other matter of Sir Archibald MacIntosh – we may dispense with his company altogether on the Boxing Day shoot. I have no wish to suffer the random inattentions of a Glasgow grocer in the line. Besides, I shall have so many more attractive guests to attend to over the season.' He smiled broadly. Lumley reciprocated with a small courtly bow. 'As your Royal Highness *desires*,' he said, moving backwards, before the Prince turned on him once more.

'And, Lumley, a little less of this Royal Highnessing, if you please. You and I have no need to stand on *such* ceremony, in private at least. We are old friends, are we not? – been through many a little scrap together.' The Prince drew on his cigar, appraised Lumley in a knowing fashion – with a slow smile, perhaps even the hint of a wink.

'Indeed, sir – quite so, quite so.'

'See him out then, Caesar! See him out!' The Prince nudged the sleeping fox terrier on the tiger skin. Dreaming of other quarry, the dog, waking with a start, followed his master's directions, running full tilt for Lumley's trousers again as the man turned to make a hasty exit.

Lumley heard the Prince's roars of laughter as he passed down the corridor. He was pleased with the way things had gone, but still anxious. His desperate suggestion, given the renowned good nature and impulsive kindness of the Princess, was quite likely to be accepted by her. But if, subsequently, matters degenerated in the relationship between the Prince and Miss Cordiner – and he expected they would – the Prince would be the first to remember that it was he, Lumley, who had first suggested the idea. He, and not Miss Cordiner, would then be accused of scheming.

That afternoon, having spoken to his wife, the Prince returned to his study. At his desk he took the stopper from one of several tubes set in a frame, blew into the orifice vigorously, waiting an instant before shouting down it. 'Fortescue, I have some im-portant e-men-dations to your list of Christmas guests at Sandringham: delete MacIntosh – insert Miss Frances Cordiner. Have an invitation made out straight away and sent round to her address – 17 Wilton Place. Yes. What? No, she is not to be ac-companied by anyone. She is to be the guest of the Princess and myself: a *family* guest. Good, Fortescue – and I shall be obliged if you will see to it *at once*.'

He returned the stopper, leant back and surveyed the many photographs in front of him, finally picking up the largest of the silver frames, an early court photograph of Alix taken just after their marriage – wide-eyed, girlish, coolly beautiful. 'Yes, indeed,' he murmured to himself. 'You – above all . . .'

He set the photograph down rather sadly before reaching for some notepaper, beginning a short letter which would accompany the formal invitation to Frances. 'Dear Miss Cordiner,' he began. 'It would give the Princess and myself much pleasure . . .' He paused. Would it? Yes, but not of the sort which perhaps he had originally in mind. There was a quite different essence in this girl – not just something to play with, to touch, fondle, make love to, but something more interesting, more exciting even.

Frances brought out a tenderness in him, a compassion that he had only felt before for Alix, his wife. It was uncanny, since the two women were not alike in any way – one classic, regal, considered, statuesque; the other a mix of sharp child and wild gypsy. But the emotions that Frances drew from him were just those that Alix had once inspired. Her loss of home drew his sympathy more than anything. He himself as a child and young man – shunted endlessly between Windsor, Buckingham Palace, Osborne and Balmoral – knew this feeling of homelessness all too well. Frances, by her account and his own intuition, had suffered in much the same way. Thinking thus, with some rage now, of his own suppressed youth, he was determined to give Frances's life back to her before it was too late – offer her, in the first instance, the sanctuary of his own home. He remembered her face, of course, as well – that lovely astonished look when they had first met. All in all the whole thing struck him as a most worthy – and appealing – crusade.

Caesar slept on the tiger skin. The light outside died over Pall Mall. The red coals in the fire, unattended for nearly an hour, turned to ash. The Prince left his desk and stretched himself out on the velveteen sofa. For the first time in years he felt a distinct lack of appetite, of nervous energy – no need to ring for the footman, to see to the fire, to order a lobster tea, or send for Fortescue about the Christmas guest and present lists, or make last-minute rearrangements over his plans for that evening. For the first time in years, thinking of Frances – content with mere *thoughts*, he reminded himself with astonishment – he was no longer bored. He dozed off then, his breath slowing, becoming one with Caesar's, the sleep of the just.

The atmosphere next morning at Wilton Place on the other hand, after the Prince's invitation had arrived in the first post, was electrifying. Frances could no longer dissemble. She met Dermot at breakfast, handing him the Prince's letter and invitation without comment. Dermot glanced at them, read carefully, then threw both aside.

'One of your pranks, Frances. Or someone else's prank. Dear Humphrey Saunders at work again, no doubt.'

'No. It's true. I met the Prince at Ruth's on Monday evening last week. They're great friends. And it was he who asked me to dinner last Friday, not Ruth. I lied – I'm sorry. I wasn't sure of things then.'

Dermot considered the matter. Then he said, 'It's hardly credible.'

'No. But it is.'

Dermot looked at the invitation again, then held the letter up to the light. 'It has the watermarked arms – the ostrich feathers and "Ich Dien". "I serve" – but how will it serve you, Frances?'

'I want to change my life, do I not?'

'Nobody ever really does.'

'This might.'

'For the worse.'

'Why? Don't tell me – I know: his reputation with women is not altogether savoury . . .'

'To put it mildly—'

'But—'

'But how *could* you, Frances? – accept such an invitation on your own, unchaperoned. It's simply not done—'

'It *is* done. I've done it myself already, and nothing untoward happened. Besides I've been asked by the Princess, his wife, as well – to their *home*, Dermot, not to some lewd house of assignation. So of course I shall accept.'

Dermot looked at her, a touch of envy, sadness in his expression. He was losing her. So that Frances, seeing his feelings, jumped up impulsively, rounded the table and shook him by the shoulders, taking his hand.

'Dermot, it's not a sad thing! I wouldn't do it if it were. It – it will bring me home one day, don't you see? Won't take me away, from you and Mortimer and all the family. It will bring me *back* to you all. In Ireland.'

'So that's the plan, is it?' He looked at her calmly. 'It's really Summer Hill again, behind it all.'

'Yes. The Prince offered to help me make things up at home. That's the whole point. To be friends again with Mama – what you said I should do. Well, don't you see? – Mama would just *love* the Prince . . .'

'Yes, I do see. But what will you have to give in return?'

'Oh, Dermot, it's not like that!'

'I should be very surprised if it weren't – in the end.'

'You'll *be* surprised then – because it won't!'

An hour later Frances had a rather similar conversation with Ruth Wechsberg – though much more chilly in form for most of its duration. But towards the end Ruth seemed to relent, becoming less severe in her strictures. Indeed, she was almost apologetic.

'I'm sorry,' she said, 'I have not been entirely open with you either. I, too, have received a communication from the Prince this morning.' She moved to her little Sheraton bureau, picking up an envelope there. 'A letter in which he explains his and the Princess of Wales's position in your regard. And I must say it corresponds almost exactly with your own account of the matter. He also . . .' She paused, waving the notepaper in her hand, fanning herself with it excitedly. 'He has also offered – has *asked* indeed, that he become patron of the nursing home here, and has enclosed a cheque for one thousand pounds with a promise that he will enlist further financial support from his friends in the same cause.'

Holding the letter and cheque, she turned to Frances. 'I've not told you, nor anyone else either – but without this unexpected donation we should have had to close the nursing home here in the New Year.' She smiled then. 'I believe I may have you to thank for this as much as anyone.' She walked over to Frances then, taking her hand. 'Dear Frances, all I hope is that you . . . will be careful. A life like yours is very precious. The Prince may appreciate this now. But he is a child at heart – of whims and toys.'

The implication was obvious. Frances would, in the end, be a mere caprice of the Prince's. But then, Frances thought, the banker's draft from Coutts for £1,000 which Ruth held in her hand was no doubt a product of the same childish fancy. Whims were not necessarily unproductive.

7

Ruth, as thanks for Frances's part in saving the nursing home, made her a gift of £50 for Christmas. 'Besides, you will need some new dresses and costumes at Sandringham – indoors and out. Gloves, scarves and hats. Boots, shoes and slippers! Why not?'

'No, you are too—'

Ruth had looked at her severely, the governess in her eyes again. 'If a thing is worth doing, then it *must* be done properly.' And Frances, overcome by this generosity and by Ruth's stringent stipulation, had been frightened suddenly, realizing for the first time all the many implications and pitfalls of this visit. Now she was really broaching an unknown world among Royalty, the cream of the land no doubt. She could not play the flirtatious *ingénue* now, the wild Irish girl or the pretty nurse. She would have to draw on other, more subtle, strengths. There were serious social responsibilities ahead of her, and Ruth must have sensed the fears she had about this.

'It shall be done properly,' she went on in a softer voice, 'because you must have every confidence in yourself. And you must not therefore, for any reason, find yourself at a disadvantage with the Prince and his company. Or, put another way, you must not allow *him* to take advantage of *you*. That, as you know, has been my fear. He should not for a moment be allowed to think of you as being in the "poor relation" department for example – or be given any excuse for indulging an unreal or exaggerated sympathy for you. In character you are more than his equal – and you must dress accordingly!'

With which Frances, much heartened, had gone out to Woolland's and Harrods in Knightsbridge and purchased a new wardrobe: a long white organdie evening dress, with tartan lines over silk, black plastrons on the front, black kilting, piping and cuffs; another dress in red velvet with turned-back white lace, with an under-dress in ruched green silk; a third in maroon voile with a white collar and cuffs and a pleated satin front. For outdoors she already had her Russian hat with the ankle-length, sable-trimmed coat, its rows of Hussar buttons down the front. She supplemented this now with a blue dress in light serge with a mauve waistband, rosettes and a Zouave jacket – and another in brown cloth, a long jacket in brown corduroy velvet with mussel-shell buttons and a velvet hat trimmed with ostrich feathers, together with several pale tea-gowns, assorted silk blouses, gloves, shoes, slippers and a new pair of black lace-up bootees.

When the purchases were delivered she brought them up to her bedroom, with Eileen taking the costumes out from their tissue-papered boxes.

'Oh my,' Eileen said with excitement, holding up the white organdie and tartan ball gown. 'You're going to look a wonder in this, Miss Frances!'

'Am I?'

'Can't fail to!'

Frances saw the longing in the girl's eyes then. There were several other boxes, not yet opened, by the door. Frances went and picked the first of them up. 'And these are for you, Eileen, a Christmas present.'

'Oh, Miss, you needn't—'

'Of course I need. Go on – look at them, if they're all right!'

Eileen opened the first of the boxes, then the second. Inside were four plainer, though none the less smart and attractive, dresses together with various accessories. Eileen held one of the costumes up admiringly.

'I know your size,' Frances told her. 'So they should fit. But if you don't like the style or the colour we can go round and change them first thing tomorrow.'

'No, no – they're lovely. Lovely.'

'Take them with you to Ireland – and I have some small things for your parents.'

Eileen looked undecided, glancing over at Frances's new clothes laid out on the bed.

'What's the matter?'

'Just – I envy you.' Eileen picked up her dresses a little sadly, folding them, putting them back in their fine tissue paper nests.

'You mean?' Frances looked at her in surprise. The girl had a moist glaze in her eyes now. 'Oh, Eileen, you mean – you'd like to come with me?' Frances moved towards her, Eileen nodding her head dumbly, biting her lip. Frances suddenly embraced her – the two women murmuring together.

'Oh, I wish you would, Eileen – I feel so excited, but a little afraid—'

'I would – I really would *love* to come with you.'

'Well, you shall. I told you, wherever I go, you can come.'

Frances's emotion comprised as much guilt as it did joy, for she had bought Eileen's new outfits with the secret thought that, when she saw them, together with Frances's own exciting costumes, she would be tempted to forgo her

Christmas holiday in Ireland with her family and come with her to Sandringham.

Dermot and Mortimer, prior to taking the Irish Mail that evening from Euston, saw the two women off at King's Cross, in a private compartment on the train for Wolverton in Norfolk. The four of them stood on the platform for a few minutes, among the Christmas bustle, the women's trunks, bags and hat boxes surrounding them, before porters removed most of them to the guard's van. Frances wore her sable-trimmed coat and muff and her Russian hat against the cold. As the engines sighed and roared all round them, spumes of cotton-wool rising to the glass roof high above, Frances fidgeted; Eileen seemed much calmer.

'Well, au revoir,' Mortimer said, clapping his gloved hands, whiskers bristling, smiling kindly. 'The great adventure! What a family we are. I spend my life trying to release my country from the Imperial yoke – and here you are putting your neck right into the heart of it, with Dermot supporting you with his new field guns. What about you, Eileen – what do you feel about it?'

Eileen was flustered suddenly. 'Oh, sir, I just like being with Miss Frances . . .'

'I really can't win, can I?' Mortimer reflected.

Frances was moved by his isolation from them all. 'Oh, you will, Mortimer,' she told him impulsively. 'You will win in the end – I know you will!' She didn't really know what she was saying at all, offering mere consolatory words to her cousin.

'Oh, yes, I know that, dear Frances – we all have to be free in the end. But will I be there to see it? Perhaps you might speed things up a little, put a good word in for us Home Rulers with the Prince!'

'Yes, of course.' She paused, then added ironically, 'If I ever have the chance.'

'You will, you will.' Dermot nodded his head sagely, as if he foresaw Frances's future in exact detail.

Dermot kissed her goodbye. 'It's extraordinary,' he told

her. 'In three months you've lost one house – and gained another. But *what* a house!'

She looked at him sharply then. 'There's only one house for me, Dermot, you know that.'

'Yes,' he sighed. 'I was hoping you might be able to forget that now.'

A few hours later, met at Wolverton in a Royal carriage by a coachman and groom, they were driving through the vast wrought-iron gates of Sandringham, moving through a flat, sparsely wooded parkland, towards an equally large, rather ugly, red-bricked, bow-windowed Victorian house, set on a slight rise in the distance, surrounded by scrubby trees. A piercing east wind rattled the carriage glass, sweeping across the desolate land from the North Sea. The two women looked straight ahead, dumbly, nervously. Frances thought desperately about what she might do or say on her arrival, what active measures she might take to promote the success of her visit – after all, since she suspected she might be here largely as part of some unrealized intention of the Prince's, she wondered what shape this might take.

At Sandringham it was the Prince's inordinate superstitiousness which, like the Stubbs painting in Eaton Square, formed another of these fortuitous links between them. The Prince, escorting Lady Filmer to her place at the first evening's dinner, noticed how two knives in her elaborate cutlery service were very nearly crossed. His poise was quite shattered. A footman was summoned and reprimanded. Some fuss was made of it all, to the discomfiture and embarrassment of the other guests.

But later, speaking to the Prince in the big hall-saloon after dinner, Frances sympathized, even tactfully commended his behaviour. 'At home in Ireland,' she said, 'my father has regard for much the same omens.'

'Indeed, I am pleased to hear it. I am thought a great ninny in my superstitious feelings on the matter.'

'Not at all—'

'You feel the same?'

'I am Irish.'

'Thirteen at table and all that?'

'Most especially. Indeed at home in Summer Hill, not so long ago, as a surety of luck an empty place was always laid at dinner for the unexpected guest – some wandering storyteller or minstrel.'

'Excellent – capital! I wonder if I may institute the same procedure here. But I fear I should be worse mocked!'

The next morning, when she met the Prince in the oak-panelled hall after breakfast, he gave her, surreptitiously, a tiny ivory elephant attached by a short chain to a gold ring. 'One of my little mascots,' he told her. 'I was given it in India, in '75. I have rather a collection, over my bedstead. But keep it to yourself – my valet thinks me much the peasant in harbouring such charms.'

Though at first she refused, taken aback by the importance of the gift, she finally accepted it, putting the ring over her finger so that, when she closed her hand, the little elephant was then completely hidden in her palm.

'Exactly the way!' the Prince commended her. 'One mustn't expose one's luck – to every rough wind. And now, my dear, what have you to do today?'

Frances thought the Prince almost rashly attentive. It was not until some time later that she discovered he asked every apparently unoccupied guest the same question, so that the experienced visitor, set on doing nothing, must needs have an immediate plan or excuse to offer – a pressing trip to the library for a book or to the gun room to inspect the Prince's collection of firearms. But on that morning Frances had no plan or ready excuses.

'I shall be busy for the moment – I should like to show you round the estate later,' he said. 'But Alix – she told me herself just now upstairs – she would be much pleased with your company.' Frances was aghast. She had barely spoken more than a few words with the Princess, and that in company. Now she was to face her alone. But there was no mistaking the tones of Royal command in the Prince's voice. A footman brought her upstairs to the Princess's suite of rooms on the first floor, knocking most firmly on the outer door. A maid of the bedchamber opened it, taking Frances across a drawing room, before admitting her to a small boudoir beyond, then leaving her.

At first Frances seemed to have entered an antique shop, art gallery and photographer's display room all in one. Barely a foot of the walls or floor had been left as free space. A vast clutter of ornaments, prints, pictures, photographs, and winter house plants had been set up everywhere, on a dozen occasional tables, glass-fronted display cases, wall-brackets and shelves. A wrong step would send one crashing into a huge aspidistra, set by a portfolio screen filled with Christmas cards; another would certainly result in an earthquake among the hinged silver and tortoiseshell photographs, twenty of them crushed onto a small Benares brass table. A fierce-looking white parrot sat on a perch in the middle of the room.

Frances stood petrified among this jungle of knick-knacks, as the bird inspected her malevolently. A bright morning light streamed in from the one window, blinding her, just as the stacks of furniture and screens obscured her view. Apart from the parrot, the room seemed unoccupied. Finally, almost hidden by a Chinese screen near the small fireplace at the far side of the boudoir, she saw the silk-covered knees, the disembodied hands at some needlepoint, of the seated Princess.

Frances moved towards the window so that she might become visible to her Royal Highness, seeing herself reflected for a moment in the large gilt mirror over the mantelpiece – a terrified spectacle. But the Princess, in an exquisite primrose silk morning dress with high lace collar tightly drawn round her neck, still did not see her, intent on her needlepoint.

'Your Royal Highness . . .' Frances curtsied. But still nothing from the elegantly upright figure. Frances coughed. 'Your Royal *Highness*.'

The Princess looked up, alert now in the eyes at least, offering a most gracious smile. 'Ah, my dear, you've come. So good of you, so nice. Please, please – do take a seat.' She gestured to a spindly gilt chair, which Frances, trembling, drew up beside her. 'That's right – next to me – here!' Her accent retained all the heavier hints of her Danish background. But its tone was wonderfully light, bell-like, full of melody. There was a great repose and refinement about her – the features delicate, beautifully moulded – mouth, high curled crown of hair and small ears all perfect. Though in her mid-fifties, she was still astonishingly thin and well-preserved – looking almost half her age.

'First, are you comfortable, my dear? – the bed not too hard? I have been worried by the mattresses lately. We shall really have to renew some, if not all of them. We've had them since we took the place, over thirty years ago now . . .' She chatted on about the mattresses, the household linens, the general accoutrements of Frances's bedroom, without pause for several minutes, so that all Frances could do was nod her head agreeably. 'You must tell me if you find *anything* uncomfortable or amiss.'

'No. Not at all—'

'I should be most put out to think that you were in any way incommoded.'

'No, I am *most* comfortable—'

'Given the state of some of the beds and mattresses here, I have found the tale of the Princess and the pea often all too appropriate! And the damp, to boot – some of the guttering – we had a fire here some years ago. The repairs afterwards were not what they might have been. On the other hand our new bathing rooms are really rather satisfying . . .'

She wandered on incessantly, through a maze of domestic rigmarole, before embarking on further serpentine résumés, of a familial and dynastic nature. At the end of half an hour the Princess put aside her needlepoint, seeming to indicate that the meeting was over. She stood up and with her slight limp made stately progress towards the window, looking out on the empty flower-beds, the intricate diamonds and circles of low box hedges. The sun had gone in. The Princess shivered a fraction.

'Well, my dear, the main thing is that you stay warm, wrap up well. You must rest and be comfortable here.

Recover yourself. Nothing strenuous. Consider yourself quite at home here for Christmas. I really do feel for you in your predicaments – and what can I say but that . . . well, that time heals all wounds?'

She offered Frances another of her lovely smiles – so truly sympathetic, tender even, that Frances was genuinely touched as she curtsied before leaving.

Later that morning the Princess spoke of Frances to Lady Melbury, one of her current ladies-in-waiting. 'The poor dear girl,' she commented. 'Most charming. But nothing to say for herself, quite desolate, the pinched face – and looked so *cold*. I was most concerned for her comfort, most touched by her. And quite without guile – I cannot think where that gossip came from. She is a mere child, a babe-in-the-wood. Not the Prince's sort at *all*. Just a kindness on his part – the dear good man.'

Lady Melbury, who had observed Frances with some care since her arrival and noticed, too, several of the Prince's attentive gestures towards her, was less convinced. On the other hand she knew the Prince well enough to doubt that he would bring such a young woman into the bosom of his home if his motives were merely predatory. With all her experience of the Prince's circle, and his liaisons among them, this was one conjunction that she could not fathom. However, she was prepared to give both parties the benefit of her doubts – especially since this charity seemed so to appeal to the Princess, while the Prince himself, she had seen, had been in particularly good humour ever since Frances's arrival.

A babe-in-the-wood? Perhaps that was the key to it, Lady Melbury thought. This girl, with her childish vivacity and wild young looks, reminded the royal couple of their own daughters, similarly untutored and unruly, who had long since left the family nest. It was not only a kindness on their part to have the girl here, she thought – it was their own youthful happy family life revived.

In her bedroom before luncheon, with just time for the letter to reach Summer Hill before Christmas, Frances wrote to her parents, addressing herself to the pale blue notepaper, die-stamped simply 'Sandringham House, Norfolk'.

'I am sad,' she wrote, 'that you have not seen fit to reply to my earlier letter to you both. I cannot think that my previous behaviour, though it may still warrant your disapproval, should also result in your continued silence. However that may be, and though I much wished to spend this Christmas season with you at home – and send you all my best wishes for the season – I have accepted a most kind invitation from their Royal Highnesses the Prince and Princess of Wales, to spend Christmas with them here at Sandringham.

'Mortimer or Dermot, as I have asked them, will I hope already have told you of all this. I am very happy here. The Prince and Princess both have been most kind and attentive. I expect to return to Wilton Place after the holiday and to continue my nursing with Miss Wechsberg at Grosvenor Crescent. My life, it seems, will continue in England for the moment. But I would most sincerely ask you to remember that my *home* is at Summer Hill and that I very much hope that I may see you both there at some point in the New Year. Again, every good Xmas wish, Frances.'

She had thought, perhaps, to have ended with something on the lines of 'Your obedient daughter' – to have offered more fulsome apologies. But, no, the balance was just right; it was not to be too conciliatory a letter, nor yet too provocative. Its purpose was simply to intimate clearly – and the Sandringham heading to the notepaper would do most of that – that in her concerns with her mother she now worked from a position of strength.

It was a large house party at Sandringham, with guests from the most unexpected and varied backgrounds, Frances soon realized: all of them pleasant and civil, all either very rich or equally aristocratic, with a few, such as the Duke of Sutherland, both rich beyond the dreams of avarice and of the most august lineage. One or two others, among them the Bishop of Peterborough and Colonel Higgins – a Catholic, she understood – brought no inherited title or wealth with them but simply an ecclesiastical position or a particular intimacy with the Prince – as did Henry Chaplin, one of the Prince's oldest and closest friends from his Oxford days, who though poor in his own right had made great amends by marrying the old Duke of Sutherland's daughter, Lady Florence Leveson-Gower.

Mr Chaplin, sitting near the Prince at luncheon, had regaled the company at that end of the long table with amusing, highly melodramatic accounts of his expeditions among the warring Blackfoot Indians in the Rocky Mountains thirty years before.

'"Indian country," my guide told me enthusiastically, pointing to one branch of the fork in the track. "*Must* we go that way?" I enquired, finally persuading him that discretion was the better part of valour . . .'

Besides these guests, and the Royal couple's immediate retinue of staff taken from Marlborough House – the Prince's secretary and some half a dozen others – there were several Jews, including Sir Anthony de Rothschild and his daughter; an Italian Countess, originally English, with her daughter, once a Catholic, but now reformed; Lady Filmer, Lady Melbury, the Duchess of Berwick; Lords Cadogan, Carrington and Houghton with their wives, together with a set of younger peers with their ladies.

Nearly all of these guests had been forcibly conducted about the model estate after lunch on the second day by the Prince, most anxiously proud of his horticultural and landscape gardening achievements in this – as Lady Macclesfield had rightly observed – rather featureless and desolate spot. After the Princess had fed the horses lumps of apple and sugar in the stable yard, and then retired, the Prince led the party off, a most vigorous major-domo, on a long and tiring walk in the chilly wind. They visited, in turn, the kitchen gardens, the hothouses – for all too brief a period – the Italian and alpine gardens, the lavender walk, the small zoo, the joss-house, the kennels where the

Princess's dogs were kept and the pet cemetery where they would be buried. A collection of eminently alive pugs, beagles, basset hounds, chows, terriers, Eskimo sledge-dogs and French bull-dogs accompanied them, digging in the cemetery among the bones of their forebears.

On their return to the house, in an even keener wind, chilling them to the marrow, the Bishop of Peterborough remarked to Frances how he fancied in this 'vigorous marine atmosphere, with its stunted firs and splendid Scandinavian sunsets' that he was visiting 'Dukes and Princes of the Baltic, Regents of the midnight sun' – a description which Frances thought quite excessive, though she admired it for its diplomacy, as the Bishop himself must have done, for a few minutes later she heard him repeat the encomium in exactly the same words to the Prince.

The house, when she toured it, was much like the Princess's boudoir, crammed with furniture in not the best taste. Hunting trophies, together with paintings of yachts, highland cattle and stags at bay contested the space on every wall with weapons, ancient and modern – crossed cutlasses, dirks, pikes, ceremonial swords, muskets and rifles; while at each corner and along every corridor coverts of potted plants and regiments of cold statuary lay in wait for the unwary: grim Roman worthies staring out from between the heavy fronds of fern or aspidistra – almost as unnerving to Frances as the stuffed baboon inside the front door, its paws outstretched to receive visiting cards.

The huge house, indeed, with its endless poky rooms upstairs, large spaces on the ground floor, its permanently stationed or often moving footmen, pages and maids, its many guests ambling along the corridors, or darting purposefully through doorways if the Prince was about – the house had the air of a busy and very grand railway terminal, where the aristocratic passengers were much intent on their own pressing journeys, or on avoiding the over-vigilant station-master, so that Frances did not feel set apart or taken undue notice of.

Indeed, since the Bishop of Peterborough had taken

something of a fancy to her and they were sometimes seen together, she was thought by some to be his niece or daughter – and by others, more correctly, knowing of the Princess's interest in her, to be the victim of some family tragedy in Ireland, now an unofficial ward of the Royal couple. Though in truth, given the air of bustle and festivity in the house, no one – other than the Prince and his wife – was much concerned about Frances at all.

Tea was taken promptly at five o'clock every day in the entrance hall – an elaborate meal ranging from cold lobster and oyster patties to hot scones filled with clotted cream and raspberry jam – the men in short dark jackets, the ladies in elaborate and flowing tea-gowns, Gottlieb's orchestra in attendance, an unlikely mix of Teutonic and Italian players who fiddled their way through *The Gipsy Baron* and *Die Fledermaus* while the company gorged and chattered under the warm electric lights.

As far as the Prince was concerned, at least, it was a particularly festive tea on the second afternoon in that the first of his several practical jokes proved a resounding success when the Bishop of Peterborough, induced to accept a mince pie by his host, found it filled with Colman's mustard – to his real discomfort and the company's less than genuine amusement. If the Bishop himself was considered fair game for such rough jests what worse might they expect in their own cases?

The atmosphere, though apparently so informal, was trying in such ways. There were severe pitfalls lying in wait for the incautious guest, most particularly in the matter of dress, where the Prince could not bear to see a decoration wrongly worn – or any item, even a button, misplaced. Both the Duchess of Berwick and the Prince's medical friend, Sir Felix Semon, took the whip of a royal reprimand that evening at the formal dinner.

'The Star of the Victorian Order, Sir Felix, is *usually* worn on the *left* breast,' the poor doctor was told with biting sarcasm, while the Duchess, who had appeared splendidly crowned with a diamond crescent instead of the prescribed tiara, was similarly, if more tactfully, rebuked. Frances – the daughter of a mere baronet, in her simple but finely cut organdie and tartan dress, lovely chiselled features and with only her blue amethyst pendant as jewellery – was beyond reproach. She had had, too, the most careful attentions, in her coiffure and wardrobe, from Eileen, happily ensconced now in the small dressing room next to Frances's bedroom. So that the Prince, at one end of the dinner table, often glanced at Frances, their eyes meeting for a second, before he returned unwillingly to his more immediate concerns.

After dinner, before the party and card games – general post, whist, bridge, carpet bowls and later baccarat – the Prince spoke to Frances in the hall.

'How do you find it all, my dear?'

'Splendid! I am *most* enjoying my visit.'

'I am sorry I have not more time for you myself.' He lit a cigar. 'The general *demands*,' he went on, sighing, gesturing round at the other guests assembling at the card tables set out everywhere now. 'And tomorrow I must spend most of the day with Alix preparing the Christmas presents. Indeed, I am *overcome* with pleasant demands . . .'

'I perfectly understand. I am more than happy—'

'The Bishop – he does not weary you, I trust?'

'Not the least . . .'

The Prince smiled wryly. 'You are being diplomatic. I will admit, confidentially, that he rather wearies me. I fear, for his Christmas sermon, that he will outrun the prescribed ten minutes.'

'Oh, I shall look *forward* to it!' She smiled brightly back at him – and something stirred in the Prince's eyes then, a conflict of appreciation, a mix of tenderness and desire.

On Christmas Eve, after tea, when the Royal couple were to dispense their presents, tension among the company approached one of several climaxes over the holiday season – particularly since, together with other officials of the Court retinue, and according to invariable custom at Sandringham, everyone was forced to line up in the corridor outside the ballroom before being called in one at a time to receive the Royal bounty.

This quite unaccustomed waiting game, this standing about cheek by jowl, for these august, normally well-separated and restless people, led to some indecorous coughing, scuffling and whispering in the corridor – a generally nervy champing at the bit, made none the easier by some facetious remark from one of the younger guests to the effect that he was completely out of brass ink-stands and hoped now for a suitable replacement.

Nor did it help matters when, in the crush and obstructed by the bulk of the Italian countess, Sir Felix Semon inadvertently trod on one of the Princess's pug dogs, causing the beast little pain but great annoyance, so that it promptly bit the ankle of Henry Chaplin, who at once, and with entirely feigned emphasis, took up similar moan.

All in all it was a most trying experience, not eased by the final entrance to the ballroom where, when Frances's turn came, she was confronted by a vast empty space of floor with a long trestle table at one end – the Royal couple, standing at either side of a great line of wrapped gifts, seeming to stare at her ogreishly over the great distance.

Approaching them, she received two beautifully wrapped packages, one of awkward bulk, the other very neat and small. Taking the gifts she blushed, muttered profuse thanks, curtsied and was about to depart when she realized she had committed a great gaffe. There was more to come.

'Wait, my dear!' the Princess said, the Prince concurring, before they both embarked on a lengthy and comprehensive description of the hidden objects.

'You will find this patent sulphur dispenser,' the Princess said, '*most* convenient for your bedside. It but needs to be lit beneath – the little spirit lamp is included – to produce the most *efficacious* fumes, for any chestiness, bronchitis or such—'

'The little lapel watch,' the Prince interrupted his wife, 'is the *best* of timekeepers, I am assured – I should have given it to you, Alix – and further has a most ringing and melodious chime on the hour, if needs be.'

The Prince beamed, blossomed. He was so genuinely and naïvely pleased. It was clear that nothing gave him so much pleasure as this distribution of largesse – so that Frances, saddened at first that the whole element of surprise in these gifts had been denied her, consoled herself with his joy.

'And you will find it a suitably jewelled timepiece as well—'

'You must beware, however, not to leave the spirit lamp burning—'

'I had the watch from Hunt and Roskill—'

'And, above all, not *all* night, you would be quite fumigated—'

'Made by a Russian émigré there, from Monsieur Fabergé's workshops in St Petersburg . . .'

Frances stood there, sweating, gasping alternately to each of them 'Thank you – thank you, so much, so much.' There was nothing else she could say and it was a stupendous relief in the end to make a final curtsy and leave.

That same Christmas Eve, in the last post delivered from Cloone to Summer Hill, Frances's letter from Sandringham arrived with Lady Cordiner – brought to her boudoir by Flood the butler among a pile of other Christmas mail. She recognized her daughter's hand on the envelope, then the postmark 'Sandringham' – and her heart fluttered dangerously. But perhaps there was some mistake. Other people had country homes in the Sandringham area, friends of this Ruth Wechsberg perhaps . . . But now, opening and reading the letter, she could no longer doubt her daughter's actions, her social success. Frances had reached a pinnacle which she had been denied. The news cut her to the quick.

Lady Cordiner had – or so she thought – not been at all well in the months since Henry's death, spending much of each day in bed or at least in her bedroom. But now, fingering the letter, she felt positively ill – giddy, faint –

and worse, there was a sharp pain in her side, as if part of her body had been cut away from her, her actual physical presence diminished. She had thought at first that this Sandringham news was a mere tease, a ploy of Frances's – that in fact her daughter would be spending Christmas with Ruth Wechsberg. Now she would have completely to rearrange her views.

She stood up and walked slowly over to the window. It was already twilight – the trees in the river gorge just a grey pall against the dark sky beyond. Tea would be served in half an hour. Sir Desmond and Eustace would be there, together with Bunty and Austin Cordiner, their two boys and Isabelle – and, distant cousins of hers, the elderly Samuel and Martha Bischoffsheim over from Brighton, staying for the season. Company impended. Was she to speak of all this – how her daughter was spending Christmas with the Prince and Princess of Wales – with the heir to the throne, a man who very soon, and it could not now be long delayed, would be the King Emperor?

Then, thinking of this imminent elevation, she was suddenly struck by an obvious answer to the whole matter. Yes, now that she was calmer, she saw it all: one did not hide one's light under a bushel in such matters. That Frances was at Sandringham for Christmas was an honour: it reflected very well on her daughter. It could no doubt be made to reflect even better on her, Lady Cordiner thought.

At tea, beaming, she announced to the company, 'I am really *so* pleased. We have had news of Frances at last – you know how I've been so worried about her. But now we hear – she is spending Christmas with their Royal Highnesses the Prince and Princess of Wales!'

Lady Cordiner glanced round the company regally. But there was no response other than a stunned silence.

'Oh, good,' Sir Desmond finally said, at a loss for further words.

'At Sandringham?' Eustace asked in an off-hand way, as if his sister went there quite often for Christmas. His mother nodded.

'Well, good for her,' Austin Cordiner said. 'I didn't

know she was a friend of theirs.' He, too, seemed to regard the matter as not unusual.

'Oh, yes,' Lady Cordiner said lightly. 'But I didn't want to speak of it, until I knew the details.'

Bunty, so surprised at this news that she had been unable to comment on it at all, finally laughed – a little uncontrollable titter in the silent room.

'I fail to see the humour in it,' Lady Cordiner addressed her severely.

Bunty regained her composure. 'No. It's just so unexpected – such a *pleasure* for her,' she added, looking at Lady Cordiner pointedly. Bunty had gathered strength from this news – strength in her own battles with Lady Cordiner, knowing now how this malicious woman whom she so disliked had been outdone in her own vast social ambitions by her daughter. '*Such* a pleasure,' Bunty continued. 'Surely a cause for celebration?' she asked finally.

'Yes, indeed!' Sir Desmond broke the silence then. 'We shall have champagne for supper.' He was heartened by his wife's sudden re-emergence as a happy woman – forceful once more, seemingly in charge again after months of gloom in the household. Yet he knew of old how in this mood his wife would soon start to execute 'plans' – how such good humour in her always presaged plans, schemes . . . And this made him uneasy.

'Champagne for dinner? – certainly not,' Lady Cordiner said. 'We are still in mourning, you must remember, for poor dear Henry . . .'

Lady Cordiner had plans indeed. But they did not include any such open celebration of her daughter's social success. Her plan was that she alone of the company, in due course, would celebrate this distinction, by sharing in it, by using it towards her own advancement.

It would need careful planning, of course, she thought later that evening – subtle handling in every way, most obviously with her daughter. How strange it was, Lady Cordiner reflected, that Frances had so played into her hands in this way: this disobedient, ungrateful girl who all unknowing had offered her access now to that social pinnacle. A friend of the Royal couple indeed! How little, in her selfish naïvety, did Frances realize what a prize she had put within her reach.

On Christmas morning in the Sandringham church, the Prince, as was his habit, propped his half-hunter watch up on the pew in front of him – his traditional reminder to the local vicar not to outrun the allotted ten minutes in his sermon. However, on this occasion, it was the Bishop of Peterborough who was giving the address. And, although the Prince had previously spoken to him jocularly about 'not outstaying his welcome' in the matter, the Bishop had taken this literally as a joke, or had at least come quite to disregard the warning, warbling on now for ten, fifteen, then nearly twenty minutes.

'. . . and I thought to myself,' he intoned lugubriously and unctuously, 'coming here to Sandringham, to this vigorous marine atmosphere, with its stunted firs and splendid Scandinavian sunsets, that I was visiting Dukes and Princes of the Baltic, Regents of the midnight sun; that – as in St Matthew's gospel – "I was a stranger here and you made me welcome". And then I reflected how, finally, it was that King of Kings, the Lord God himself, who had made us all welcome in this lovely place . . . '

A fierce wind, whipping off the marshes from the Urals, rattled the church windows. The Prince, further annoyed by this suggestion of *lèse-majesté*, could no longer contain himself. He picked up his watch, fiddled with it, put it to his ear, then held it up high, as if to inspect its face, right in front of the Bishop, who paused only for a second before continuing his theme, his view of the testaments as a kind of Almanack de Gotha, in which the Prince, though not paramount, nonetheless occupied a position in direct succession, close to God. 'Yes, indeed, and I thought that even Moses on the mountain top, even Solomon in all his glory . . . '

It was at that moment that Frances's watch, which she wore on her lapel, broke out with its surprisingly loud chimes, starting with an introductory tinkle, then beginning to strike twelve times, the hour of midday. Before going to church she had failed to secure the little catch which silenced the chiming mechanism. And now she fiddled furiously with the timepiece, quite unable to stop it, the melodious notes spreading through the silent church.

The Bishop stopped in his tracks. Others in the congregation stared at her with scorn or embarrassment, seated as she was at one end of the pew behind the Royal couple. But the Prince turned to her and offered her one of his kindest, most heartfelt smiles. The Bishop ceased his long-windedness very shortly afterwards.

Outside, after the service, the Prince took her aside for a moment. 'My dear,' he said, with a twinkly smile, 'you did us all the *greatest* favour. I must have your company more often!'

After Christmas Frances and Eileen returned to Wilton Place, Frances resuming her work at the nursing home. Mortimer and Dermot came back from Ireland, both of them, to various blunt or discreet degree, agog to hear news of her visit to Sandringham. She told them the truth, entirely openly – how much she had enjoyed herself.

Subsequently, in the following months, she and the Prince met again, formally and informally, at Marlborough House and Eaton Square. Yet their need was more to talk than to flirt on these occasions. They talked of horses, of bloodstock in Ireland, of racing at the Curragh, the Prince reminiscing on boisterous times he had spent there as a young army officer forty years before. They spoke of such and such a play, and of real drama seen at the theatre when Frances accompanied the Prince and his party to the Haymarket or Drury Lane, or to a screened box at Evans' Music Hall at Covent Garden. And they spoke alone sometimes at Eaton Square in the evening – of Frances's future, the Prince's concerns, of less indulgent things.

Their relationship grew on such conversations, Frances searching out that secret man behind the façade of forced bonhomie and uneasy practical jokes, so that gradually, with her, the Prince relaxed, became less fraught and nervous, releasing his truer nature. He responded to her, as she had hoped, in many more agile ways, becoming less heavy-handed – in his jokes, his manner, conversation, when he ceased his chaffing, along with most of his huge cigars and gargantuan meals. Under her influence he became a lighter man in every way. Alone with her, or together in company, he no longer merely interjected abrupt questions; he contributed to, shared in the conversation. Frances, with her bright sympathy and intelligence, gave him real speech, where before he had done little more than offer vague comments and platitudes.

'Je Responderay' – that was the secret she had released in him, she thought, as she saw him respond – drawing thoughts, words, from the Prince that he did not know he possessed. He was not a block of wood – there were all sorts of echoes there now, as he sloughed off the carapace of toad in her attentive light and found his true form. The Prince in return offered her support and consolation in her exile.

But their relationship was not only a matter of such shared personal sympathies. The Prince found he could talk to her of public and political matters of the day, among them the ever-present Irish question.

'I should like to travel there more often,' he told her. 'I was most happy, years ago at the Curragh, and with the Irish people generally. But I am entirely discouraged – if not actually forbidden – in my visiting the country, by Mama and the Cabinet. It is thought I might put my foot in it, upset things, negotiations – whereas it is my view that, in any case, the Crown should be presented in Ireland in a more human manner, that bridges might at least be mended, if not crossed in that way.'

'I should very much have thought so.'

'Your cousin, though, Mortimer Cordiner, to judge from *The Times*' parliamentary reports, does not see it in the same way?'

'No. But he is quite committed to the opposite view

– a complete break between the two countries, without compromise.'

'I fear that will always remain the problem with the Irish – their inability to compromise, as we usually must in the long run.'

'Indeed, for we are both English and Irish in Ireland – and even with Home Rule we would still have to share that rule, in some measure. And I believe we would very likely make a mess of sharing anything. We are – each side – so stuck in our ways.'

Frances, with her sharp thoughts and her beauty, was, for the Prince, an idealized version of any one of his own three daughters – Louise, Victoria and Maud – with whom, though he loved them all dearly, he had never been able to have such conversations. And the only thing that gave the Prince pause in his relationship with Frances was the feeling of disloyalty he had in being able so to take up with her in a way he had never managed with them. In talking with Frances, the Prince achieved a ready equality, a close and easy understanding. And it was this verbal intimacy with the Prince which Frances came to hide from her friends and relations, for this between them she came to hold sacrosanct. Her friends could think what they wished of her association with him, think the worst if they wanted. What they would not know was how easily and calmly she got on with this man. That was the secret – the two of them were involved not only in rounds of pleasure, but rounds of the mind.

Their serious rapport gained momentum with the arrival of Lady Cordiner's letter later in the new year. Frances had met the Prince that evening alone, at his invitation, in Eaton Place, and had shown him the letter.

My dear,
We were so glad to receive your note and to hear that you were happy at last in England. Of course, you have been most fortunate in your social life and it is a great honour indeed that their Royal Highnesses should have so kindly taken you up in this way. I can only hope that you thoroughly appreciate your good fortune and are suitably grateful.

Of course you are forgiven for your earlier behaviour here – and your *home* is, indeed, here at Summer Hill. You must remember that, previously, I never *denied* you this home, merely pointed out to you that you should not, given your virtues (and, indeed, your faults!), think of burying yourself here indefinitely – that you should go out into the world, as you have at last done, and find your happy place there. And I am *most* pleased with that. Your present patronage is a rare gift – I hope you will not misuse it. And I hope we may see something of you and your company at Summer Hill in the not too distant future. Your father joins me in sending every good wish.

Your loving Mama.

'Well,' the Prince said. 'It seems you have effected a *rapprochement*!'

'It is you who have done that – not I.'

'How so?'

'As my mother suggests – by your patronage, by my staying at Sandringham.'

'Then I am more than pleased!'

They sat at either side of the fire in the small drawing room. Now the Prince stood up, lit a last Abdullah cigarette before dinner, warming the backs of his legs against the bright coals.

'She would not have forgiven me on my own.'

'Perhaps not. But then what are friends for? I think you may regard the problem as solved.' He looked down at Frances, saw a sadness in her face, and realized then how his last words had an unintended ring of finality about them – as if, in having so helped her, their association had no further meaning, so that he said to her now, by way of indicating a future between them, 'And, my dear, I wanted to tell you how there are *other* futures too for you now. You must start to be happy again, in other ways. As your mother rightly says, you must find your happy place in the world.'

'Yes, of course.'

'She is – your mother – perhaps a wiser woman than you realize, or will allow yourself to realize. You have been too close in your wars with her. And she with you. You each fail to see the other's virtues. I have found that myself, so often, in the old days, with my own dear Mama.'

'That is possible – indeed.'

'I am *sure* it is.'

'It's just that I fear she is forgiving me purely because of you – and the Princess – and not for myself.'

'Well, let her do so. It is a beginning. We may cement the relationship in the future – you and I and with Alix herself, indeed. As I said last time we met – I should much like to visit Ireland again, an unofficial visit. And perhaps I might then meet your mother. To tell the truth—' He looked carefully at Frances. 'There is something intriguing about her: the mother of such a daughter!'

'I would not ask that. You have done enough already, Edward.'

'In fact, I have done nothing, as yet. We have hardly begun, you and I.' His eyes twinkled as he raised his glass and she joined him in a toast to this.

But to what exactly, she wondered?

8

The frost was sharp, but the sun shone from a cloudless pale blue sky. The chill air streamed over her face, biting into her eyes, so that tears blew across her cheeks as the motor bumped down the Brighton road at more than twenty miles an hour. It was the most exciting experience that Frances had ever had.

Covered by a great fur rug, she sat high up on the button-leather seat at the back, the Prince on one side, his equerry, Sir Seymour Fortescue, on the other – with the dog Caesar, nose into the wind like a look-out, on the front seat, next to Henry Stamper, the Prince's motor mechanic in his leather gaiters, knickerbockers and peaked cap. Stamper bent over the wheel now, seeming to coax the motor forward, like a horse, to ever greater speeds.

The claret-coloured De Dion Bouton had just been delivered to the Prince from France. And he was determined, that fine frosty morning in January, to put it through its paces at once, asking Frances and his equerry to accompany him.

The Prince steadied himself – and his excitement – hand grasping the rail above the side-door, as the motor lurched repeatedly, hitting a succession of potholes on the old coach road. They were in the country now, on a long straight stretch, so that they could see the carriages and farm carts way ahead of them. Stamper furiously pumped the rubber ball of the klaxon at these distant obstructions – the sounds, like a flock of startled geese, piercing the cold air, echoing down the straight road, so that other travellers, long before the Prince's motor came near, had made for the ditch, stopping in alarm, the horses rearing, drivers cursing, as the De Dion Bouton sped past in a great swish of air, a clatter of machinery and a fiendish dragon's breath from the exhaust pipe.

'Sir! – it is most illegal,' Sir Seymour shouted across to the Prince. 'You must ask Stamper to slacken pace—'

'Nonsense, Fortescue! We shall drive the motor to its limit. And here is the only stretch of road where we may do so with impunity!' The Prince leant forward now, eyes glazed, staring ahead, just like Stamper, the two of them egging the motor on. 'Are we approaching thirty miles per hour yet, Stamper?' the Prince demanded, shouting over the roar of the engine.

'Not yet, sir—'

'But we are not permitted to do more than twelve miles per hour, I believe,' Fortescue interjected, highly alarmed now.

'An entirely unnecessary law, Fortescue. In France it is *quite* different. On, Stamper, on!'

'But we are not *in* France, sir—'

'Soon will be, at this rate—'

The motor hit another pothole, throwing them all to one side, the Prince hitting Frances's shoulder, the dog Caesar toppling over into Stamper's lap, starting to bark loudly as Stamper, watching the little dial in front, finally achieved the desired speed.

'Now, sir, we have it! Thirty miles per hour. We have it!'

'Well done, Stamper – well done! A fine run, a really fine run!' The Prince was beside himself, in ecstasy as they pulled into the side of the road, stopping by a farm gate. They got out to stretch their legs and to embark on a hamper of game pie and anchovy sandwiches with a flask of brandy, while Stamper opened the bonnet, attending to the steaming engine.

'That really was . . . terribly exciting!' Frances said to the Prince, her face, which had been blue with cold, now turning red as she wiped the tears from her eyes, gasping with pleasure, sipping the brandy, exhilarated, as they both were, by their sensational pace through the tingling cold sunny morning.

'Indeed,' the Prince agreed. 'Nothing finer – the coming age, the age of the motor! What do you think, Fortescue?'

Fortescue, wiping his nose, could not restrain his aggravation. 'I must be honest, sir – I find it an entirely disagreeable conveyance: shaky, windy and smelly to boot – not to mention the danger to life and limb.'

'My dear fellow, they said just that of the railway – and look what has happened there! We must move with the times, Fortescue. No denying progress.'

'Perhaps not all progress is to be equally welcomed, sir. Besides, if I may say so, it seems a most undignified method of transportation for – for someone in your position.'

'But I am *one* with the age, Fortescue!' The Prince, in high good humour, lectured his equerry now. 'As I *should* be in my position, with such new developments. Remember, Fortescue, we are approaching a new century.' He looked at Frances. 'Youth at the helm and so on – and I consider I should not be left on the shelf in such matters. I forecast a time, quite soon, when this very road will be *buzzing* with such motor vehicles, up and down, without let or hindrance. I am *impatient* for it all!'

'Indeed, sir. I cannot say I share your agitation.'

'Ah, Fortescue.' The Prince drained his glass. 'You are not young at heart! Come, my dear.' He took Frances's arm. 'Let us return to our speed-fest. Stamper? How is the engine? Suitably fed and watered?'

'Yes, sir.'

'Let us climb aboard then. I have an appointment with the Colonial Secretary at Marlborough House – these intemperate Boers again. Caesar?' He called for his dog, still in the field, scouring the hedgerows. 'Caesar! – come here, at once.' They called the dog fruitlessly for several minutes before it finally returned. The Prince shook his finger at it. 'You naughty, *naughty* dog! Denying me the Colonial Secretary,' he said slowly, while Caesar looked up at him very cheerfully, wagging his tail.

A few minutes later they were on their way back to London, the Prince taking Frances's hand under the rug when they lurched into another pothole – and keeping it there afterwards, as the wind rushed over their faces and tears glazed their excited eyes once more.

The Prince was increasingly taken with Frances, until suddenly she became indispensable to him. He was in love with her – and told her as much one evening in March as they dined alone in Eaton Place.

'Yes,' he told her, 'from the first moment I saw you, that evening at Grosvenor Crescent – quite changed my life.'

'Surely not, Edward—'

'Yes, yes – it was a *coup de foudre*, my dearest. It was your nose that so took my attention.'

'My nose? But it is my worst feature.'

'My dear, it is sheer elegance: that straight sweep from brow to lip with barely a conjunction. It was your nose,' he teased her gently now, 'which you dislike, that I loved at once. Something quite unique. Indeed, it has been well said that if Cleopatra's nose had been shorter the whole world would have been different!'

Frances on the other hand believed that something less

apparent and more designing in her nature had brought about her present position with the Prince. He loved what he saw of her, not what he knew about her or of her designs – while she was more flattered and intrigued than in love with him.

And yet these differences of belief, in what constituted the play between them, made their relationship all the more compelling, led them forward, ever deeper. It gave an exciting, provocative tension to their association – the Prince always taken by what he saw as Frances's mystery, while she was more tempted by what she wanted, and what was so very obvious in him: his forthright power.

It was these cross purposes which led, among other things, to the success of their liaison – in which Frances was bound to withhold the truth, and the Prince, stimulated by this discretion, felt equally obliged to protect or broach it, according to his mood. They were held together by his ignorance of the real situation and her knowledge of it, by his innocence and her deceit, by his obvious and her ulterior motives. In these respects their ploys and ambitions were, indeed, the unadmitted commonplaces of most affairs.

Yet, reflecting an equal commonplace – as a repeated theme barely noticed in this conflicting orchestration – there was, as they both came to recognize, a quieter passage of music through their partnership, the delicate chords of real need and affection. Despite their best efforts at deceiving themselves or each other in the grand manner, they grew together in quite mundane ways. They did so not through any *coup de foudre*, but through often uneventful meetings and habit. And it was this easy regular exposure with the Prince, when they could talk so readily, that allowed Frances one day to realize she loved him. It was speech that brought her love, when she finally spoke the truth.

They had shared a bottle of Duminy *Extra Sec* before dinner one spring evening at Eaton Square. The plane trees in the square had just come into leaf, a late sun was slanting into the drawing room, the window was half-open, bringing a balmy soft air from the city, the sound of carriages, the easy clip-clop of horses' feet coming down Sloane Street. Summer was just an inch away.

'Well, my dear Frances, what of the future?' the Prince had said to her brightly, raising his glass expectantly.

'I am to take the first of my nursing examinations next week.'

'I think perhaps I meant your future – with people. You do not, surely, expect simply to nurse all your life?'

'I had not really thought.' Her eye fell on the Stubbs painting above the mantelpiece. She saw the little beech grove on the hill behind the stallion – so like the grove in Cooper's Wood above Summer Hill. Yes, that was what she was thinking about. That was her future. But she could not start to explain all this again to the Prince.

The Prince walked to the window, gazing out pensively. Now he returned. 'Yes, with people.' He resumed his theme. 'I am curious, for example, given your recent social connections – so many suitable young men – that you have not taken up with any of them. Several, I know – young Wilson for example, Lord Beecher's son – have been more than taken with you!'

'I have not been of similar mind, Edward.' She looked at him openly, spoke without any dissembling. In his company and among his sophisticated friends, she had matured in the past six months – become a woman, far more assured, confident of herself and her relationships. Yet she lied about one thing to the Prince, about what remained most real in her life, what she could not achieve: she wanted her home, and that was why she had wanted him. 'No,' she went on, 'I was not taken by young Wilson, or any of them for that matter. Suitable perhaps, but so gauche!'

'Indeed – and I am grateful for that.' The Prince smiled. 'But still, if I may state the obvious, you are not the spinster type, the maiden aunt. You must expect at some point—'

'A good marriage?'

The Prince nodded. 'It is *most* likely.'

'I am happy as I am. You speak as my mother does, as though marriage were a bounden duty.'

'Not a duty alone – a pleasure, I hope.'

'Yes. But as yet – I have still my mother, my home, to consider.'

'You have made things up there. Surely that is no longer a problem.'

'I have not yet returned there, faced them all – as I remember you said I should.'

'Nothing now prevents you – after your examinations.'

Frances finished her glass in one gulp – stood up impatiently, nervously. It was her turn to walk to the window.

'What is it that still so worries you at home?' The Prince was anxious himself now.

Frances turned decisively. 'Not things there so much, as here, with you: with things . . . I have not told you.' She looked at him with some agitation.

'My dear, you may entirely confide in me.'

'That is my problem – that I have not done so.' She paused, biting her lip. 'I have used you,' she went on quickly, 'used you to effect my reconciliation at home, Edward.' She turned away, in dismay at her admission.

The Prince was relieved. He laughed. 'Is that all? But Frances, it was I who offered to mediate, not you who asked me. How have you used me?'

'I have not been true with you. It was my purpose from the beginning – to enlist your support against my mother. I did not tell you so.'

'But the matter with your mother,' he said. 'That was settled months ago! – in January, when you received her letter, when she forgave you. And you and I have continued to meet since. You have . . . wished to see me?' The Prince, not put out in the least by her admissions, was simply perplexed.

'Yes, I have.'

'Well, then,' he said in an easier tone. 'And we have got on well, have we not?'

'Yes, indeed.'

'So you are not using me in that respect, I can assure you! Your company has been a continual delight,' he added with feeling. 'You have quite taken me out of my old self.'

He approached her, as if to take her hand. But she drew back, annoyed that the Prince should forgive or misunderstand her so readily. Did he not realize her deceit?

'Edward, do you not *see?*' she asked, a bitter frustration rising in her voice, 'that although I have so enjoyed myself with you, none the less my original intention, as regards my mother—'

'Of *course* I see,' the Prince interrupted, rounding on her, angry himself now. 'But you have exaggerated the whole issue, in your usual impetuous manner. I am not such a fool that I do not see how originally, with me, you sought only my support with your mother. But since then we have discovered . . . quite other things to concern us, have we not?' He offered a hesitant smile.

'Yes, but—'

'Well, then,' he was suddenly decisive, 'if that be so, let us drop your Mama for the moment. The matter is done with, except in so far that I am curious that you should bring it up all over again. Why does it so absorb you? She, your home, everything that is behind you – when the *future* beckons, or should do so.' Frances did not, could not, answer. Now the Prince, his anger gone, took her hand. 'Why is it that you so hark back to things when you have the whole world in front of you?'

'I . . .'

'Come, you may tell me. I shall not be surprised or—'

'I have wished my mother dead, Edward!' Frances finally burst out, speaking with great vehemence, a long pent-up emotion. 'Wished her dead, yes, for the way she treated all of us at home – bullying and driving us out of her life, literally in the case of my dear brother Henry. And when he died I vowed to make up for his life, the life he might have had at Summer Hill – by living there *myself*. Do you see?'

'I can't say—'

'I *want* that house, Edward, more than anything else in the world.'

'I don't see how. Your father is very much alive, I understand. And you have told me of your other brother Eustace, who will now inherit it.'

Frances nearly stamped her foot in frustration. '*Exactly!* So now you understand my feelings – that I cannot have the place.'

The Prince was taken aback at this outburst, not knowing how to cope with it. Here was one desire of hers which, given the laws of primogeniture, he could never satisfy. But he rallied quickly.

'Not the house, perhaps – but you can have so much else.'

'What I may have will not be *there*, though.'

'Surely, my dear one, it is simply a matter of your being *between* lives which makes you uneasy – your youth and your future. When you have properly found the latter you will not so crave the other. You will see it all very differently once you have your *own* house – and family, when that is secure.'

'I could have had that already – with Lord Norton's son.'

'But you told me you did not care for him, which was why you broke the match. And there is nothing amiss in that. You will find someone else—'

'I don't *want* to find someone else!' She turned away.

'You will, my dearest – in time, in time.' He took her by the shoulders, gently turning her, then kissing her on the cheek.

'My dear Edward,' she told him slowly and clearly, drawing away from him, but keeping her hands on his shoulders. 'With you, I don't need anyone else – you have so understood.'

'I fear not, in that I cannot see how you may have the house—'

'But that I so *want* it – and you have not mocked me for that.'

The Prince sighed. 'Not mocked you – indeed, I could never do that. But I fear I cannot help you. For women – well, to put it mildly, the laws do not favour them in such matters. Such inheritance descends in the male line – your brother, his children. And if not him, for any reason, then I imagine you have uncles and their male progeny who would expect to inherit. I cannot see how . . .?' He shook his head in bewilderment.

'Yes, indeed, I know – my uncle Austin and his little prim mouse of a wife Bunty and their two milksop boys – there are all of them. Yet they have no *right* to the place!'

'Perhaps not. But your brother Eustace certainly does.'

'He is a tidy little military man, a captain – your own Royal Rifles – presently at Aldershot, entirely bound up in his army career: shortsighted in his ideas generally, literal, mundane to a degree. He has no real love for the place. He has made his career, his life, over here. He looks on home – looks on Ireland – as something second best. When he inherits, at worst, he may close the place down, or sell it up. At best, if he lives there, it will become a dingy mausoleum, a barn, empty of everything – of *life* – just filled with him and his military cronies and their silly wives and children. You've no idea! – how dull and terrible it will all become. At least my mother – well, she gives a sparkle to it, or she did. Yet there could be so much more there, so *much* more! The whole place could breathe, be so wonderfully exciting and happy.'

She paused. Tears had come in her eyes as she spoke. The Prince had listened attentively. He lit a cigarette now, one of his oval Sullivan Egyptians which, in Frances's company, he had taken to instead of his huge Coronas. 'I see,' he said. 'I think I do see. Your view of home is so much mine of Buckingham Palace, Windsor Castle, Osborne, and the rest: all of them mausoleums, for many years now, where nothing has been changed a jot since father's death nearly forty years ago. And I have felt just the same – what a waste it is, how much I should like to change things, breathe a new wind into everything, into *my* inheritance: make it live, just as you say of your own home – make it a happy, not a mournful thing. I am so much of the same mind . . .'

'You, at least, will have that opportunity.'

'I sometimes wonder. I am nearly sixty. My mother, old as she is, retains an iron will and an excellent constitution. She may outlive me.' The Prince was both ironic and sad at this thought, drawing on the cigarette.

'I'm sure not—'

'Oh, just like you,' he interrupted her now, speaking with some of Frances's earlier vehemence, 'I should so like to get my hands on this Royal inheritance! Yes, I long to be King!' he exclaimed, like a boy looking into a shop window full of toys. 'I have been so frustrated, for many years – treated like a child by everyone, forbidden access to state papers, having to *beg* for information from my few personal friends in the Cabinet. You have no idea how this mistrust, this *waiting*, has drained me – made me short-tempered, bitter. I do so understand your feelings there, with your own mother – wanting to change things, longing for the time, for action, fearing it may never come.'

'It *will* come, dear Edward – I am sure . . .'

'We are so alike, with our Mamas, and in our homes – in wanting some action, are we not?' He had walked over to the window again while speaking. Now he returned, pouring himself and Frances the last of the champagne. They drained their glasses in silence, looking at each other.

'Action,' Frances said at last, almost whispering. 'Action, yes . . .' She set her glass down, moved towards him, like a sleepwalker, putting her arms out, embracing him quickly.

And suddenly they had started to make love – there and then, standing up, before supper, in the little panelled drawing room with its window half-open on the spring evening, quite unable to resist or to control themselves, reaching for each other's bodies, touching, caressing, undressing – Frances pulling up her dress and petticoats, discarding her underclothes, suddenly feeling her sex alive when the Prince touched her, falling with her onto the sofa, skirts above her waist now, her stockings down, twisting about in little dizzy spasms as he went on caressing her, between her thighs, high up, higher and higher, so that her legs opened as he fed himself on her, pushing her clothes right up above her hip bones, above the navel so that he could explore it with his tongue, and it was this that offered Frances a forecast of pure ecstasy, making her whole body shake, so that after a few minutes she almost shouted with urgency. 'Edward, yes, please, *please!*'

He moved into her then, gently at first, and slow, then less gently, when it began to hurt, when she thought she would scream with pleasure and pain, when something was stretching and stinging inside her, until suddenly the pressure and pain vanished and he reached up far inside her in one fell swoop, while she lay motionless for a while, before starting to share in his movements, easing herself further down, raising her thighs, so that against his force she could offer her own in return, a gradually rising counterpoint, a seesaw of pleasure – where soon, such was the fluid ease and rhythm of things, that he left her body almost entirely before pushing straight up inside her again, in one long thrust, right into her belly it seemed – rising, rising for minutes on end in a delirious crescendo that suddenly exploded between them as pieces of her body seemed to disintegrate in pleasure.

'Oh, my darling, my darling!' Her head swam. She felt herself sinking through the cushions, falling, observing herself, outside her body, in a long free-floating fall, a dizzy spinning that lasted and lasted, which had no time to it, until finally she was conscious again, in the real world, felt warm and tingling, and immeasurably different – confident, so alive and lighthearted in a way she had never been. 'My darling,' she said once more, in quiet surprise now, shaking her head in wonder, like a traveller returned from a miraculous voyage, glimpsing the infinite, for whom nothing now on earth could ever be the same again.

They lay there for several minutes, youth and age, innocence and experience mingled now, both of them speechless, bewildered by their success. The Prince rose at last. But Frances stayed, letting the soft breeze from the window play over her thighs, arching her head back on the cushions, unwilling to break the spell. She glanced at the Stubbs painting once more, seeing the airy beech grove on the hill. She thought of home again. But now she saw Summer Hill and its lands as something almost within her grasp. With the lovely confidence she felt, the warm sense of relief still coursing through her body, anything was possible. She no longer had to lie to the Prince. They were one together – they understood, they loved, they wanted each other. Her deceit, the tensions she had felt with him, these were over, replaced now only by another and delicious tension she felt rising in her – of suddenly wanting him once more, there and then.

'Edward?' she asked him smiling quizzically. 'Come to me again . . .'

'My dearest, hardly now—'

'But you *will*?' She sat up quickly. 'We will, won't we?'

He nodded, a little sadly, with a tired smile.

But at supper he had regained his attack, vigorous once more, seeking out all sorts of other excitements between them.

'My dear,' he told her over the first course, 'I have been thinking: if we are to see each other happily in the future – we must lay the ghost of your mother. We must make things up entirely there. Return home after your examinations, speak to her; ask her if she would do me the honour, with you, of coming with me to Marienbad this summer.'

'To Marienbad?'

'Yes, a most attractive little spa in Bohemia. I have been there once before. And given the present delicate situation between this country and Germany – the intemperate, warlike struttings of my nephew the Kaiser – I have decided not to patronize Bad Homburg any more for my annual

Kur. I shall go to Marienbad instead – I have an excellent relationship with the old Emperor Franz Josef. And if you can persuade your Mama to join my party – well then, we may kill two birds: I may truly effect a lasting reconciliation between you and her, while enjoying your company openly at the same time. What do you say?'

Frances looked at him uncertainly. 'I . . .'

'It is what you want, is it not? She to be friends with you – and I to be . . .' He left the definition open, hanging on the air.

'Yes, yes – I do! It's just . . .'

'What then?' He had stopped eating entirely, quite unaware of his food now.

'I had not expected it – the offer. But yes, of course! I will ask her.'

What Frances, in truth, had not expected was how her plans that the Prince might somehow meet her mother should so readily fall into place, without her instigating them.

But why did she wish the Prince to meet her mother? What could that achieve, which his patronage and their friendship had not already achieved at Summer Hill? And why satisfy her mother's rampant social ambitions in any case? She did not really want to please her, after all – she recognized that – nor even impress her. She had no wish to flaunt the closeness of her royal connection, far from it: it was a private thing, a secret which she wished least of all to share with her mother.

Yet something spurred her towards the idea of their meeting – an intuition, like that of a gambler in possession of extraordinary cards who none the less senses that he may have to play out the whole hand, down to the last ace, in order to win.

Frances wrote to her mother the next day, asking if she might come home next month, saying that she had exciting news for them both – relating to the Prince of Wales. Lady Cordiner offered her a most heartfelt welcome by return of post.

*

At the beginning of June, when Frances and Eileen came back to Summer Hill, high summer was already bursting over the valley. An unusually clement spring had brought everything on early, the white candelabra drooping on the chestnuts, the beech and oak almost in full leaf – a day of warm wind that stroked the grass in long swaths of changing green and sent the clouds scudding over Mount Brandon, hiding the sun intermittently before it emerged again, a sudden limelight on the valley, rising quickly up the higher land, a spreading flood of gold against the blue.

Molloy himself, in his best head coachman's uniform and braided top hat, had met them with a groom at Thomastown station. And, instead of the little waggonette and the old cob that had taken them away eight months before, they came home now in the freshly painted grey landau, with the hood down, pulled by two smart grey mares, the polished horse-brasses and black leather gleaming in the light.

Frances smelt a drift of turf smoke from one of the estate cottage chimneys on the way up the hill from Cloone: a dry, brackish, sweet-and-sour breath on the wind. She could never define it, isolate any single ingredient – a hint of straw, grass, Irish earth and water: all Ireland, which she had so missed, in one smouldering bit of bog – a smell of slow warmth and quiet and security, that tugged at her soul, saying, 'Home, you are coming home.'

They had turned into the long drive at the top of the hill and now they trotted briskly through the tussocky demesne dotted with grazing cattle, up the rise to the brow of the hill until suddenly the long east flank of the house came in sight, a flash of pale limestone through the trees. The tall sash windows sparkled in the noon sun, the rooks cawed clamorously, blown about in gusty swerves and spirals above the flock of chimneys. And at that moment, hearing the harsh melody, Frances could not restrain herself.

'The rooks—' The words caught in her throat. 'I've never heard them so loud.'

'Indeed,' Eileen said. 'Sure they're sweeping them out of them chimneys be the looks of it, that's why.'

They saw the men on the roof then, with chimney brushes and ropes, and heard the dogs barking as they drove round the pleasure gardens to the south front of the house. Monster and Sergeant, the two terriers, rushed forward kicking up the gravel behind them, yapping furiously, as the landau drew up by the porch, the hall door open where Lady Cordiner, composed but somehow less formidable now in Frances's eyes, was on the steps to meet them. Frances jumped out of the carriage and ran towards her.

'Mama!'

'My dearest!' They embraced quickly, spontaneously. And Frances forgot all her old enmities and had the illusion of peace with her mother in this homecoming.

Sir Desmond came on to the porch then, blinking behind his spectacles in the bright light, his short beard teased by the wind, and the dogs, in a tizzy of confusion at this important arrival, leapt up against his knees instead of welcoming Frances and Eileen.

'Down, Sergeant! Down, Monster!' her father roared. It had always been his welcome, Frances remembered: the dogs to be subdued first before the guests could be greeted, as he greeted his daughter vaguely now.

'Papa! – you are here . . .' Frances grasped his hand, feeling the warmth of tears pricking her eyes.

'Where else, my dear?'

'Fiddling with your aeronautical machines, I'd thought.'

Frances wanted to hug him. But she had never done that, and could not now, and already he was moving away from her, taking a back seat.

Pat Kennedy, the under-butler, emerged from the porch with a footman to take the luggage. Eileen stood by the landau, gathering up some hat boxes. She glanced up as he arrived, looking at him calmly, distantly.

'Well, indeed.' His voice was low and sardonic. 'So you're back at last.'

'Indeed, and why wouldn't I be?'

'Too grand now for the likes of us, I'll be bound – and you hobnobbing with Royalty.' He lugged a trunk from the front seat.

'Certainly, and wasn't it a grand thing altogether – the best of times we had, down there in Sandringham.'

'You should be ashamed of yourself – that blackguard with the beard, that Prince of Wales—'

''Tis you who should be ashamed, Pat Kennedy, and you never sending me word at all – all the time I was away.' Eileen stumped off with the hat boxes, leaving him there, deflated, petulant.

'And Aunt Emily?' Frances asked. 'How is she? *Where* is she?'

'Upstairs – of course,' her father said offhandedly. 'On some drawing scheme of hers.'

'Oh, Papa, why doesn't she come down – and greet people?'

Her father shrugged his shoulders. And Frances was suddenly downcast, her happy mood broken, reminded now of all the strictures and impositions in the house – the hatreds, secrets, closed rooms. She rushed upstairs to see Aunt Emily, running to the end of the landing, only to find her bedroom door locked. Pat Kennedy had come up the stairs behind her, helping with the luggage. 'The key – the stupid key, Pat. You have it?' He reached into his pocket, giving it to her. 'It's absolute *nonsense*,' she told him. 'Locking the door on her in this way – we must stop it!'

'Yes, Miss Frances.' He paused. 'Only we had a spot of trouble with Miss Emily, do you see – she ran away a few weeks ago. Her Ladyship insisted afterwards that the door be kept locked again—'

'Ran away?'

'To Waterford, Miss. She got one of the new grooms to drive her to the train. And she was on the boat then, for England, when they got her off it, just before it sailed.'

'I see.'

Pat looked at her superciliously, so that Frances returned his look, encouraged at the same time to take up a point with him there and then which she had thought to speak to him about later, if at all. 'Oh, and Pat, while you're here, I might as well mention it: you never wrote to Eileen, all the time she was away. Now I don't wish to pry – it's entirely your own business – except to say she was most unhappy about it. A little unfeeling of you, surely?' She looked at him coldly.

'Well, yes, Miss – but it is my business.' He was equally cold.

'I only mention it since, as you know, I am so very fond of Eileen.'

'I know, Miss Frances – taking her to Sandry'ham and all.' It was obvious from his tone that he saw this as no favour whatsoever.

'Yes, well, I want her to be happy, that's all.'

'I'm sure she was, Miss.' He was so sardonic that Frances was tempted to reprimand him. But she refrained. 'Well, I just think you might have been more considerate, Pat.' She turned towards her aunt's bedroom door.

'Oh, and Miss,' Pat called out, so that she turned again, hearing him speak in a much quieter voice. 'Another thing, since we're here, I have to tell you. The men this morning – they were sweeping the chimneys, in your bedroom, too.'

He looked at her as if she knew the possible implications of this – and she did. Her heart thumped. 'Yes?'

'They found some stuff hidden in the flue, there's a sort of a ledge there above the grate – little bits and pieces, silver boxes, wine glasses,' he said pointedly. 'And them glass weights with the flowers trapped inside of them that her Ladyship keeps in the drawing room . . .'

'And?'

'The men told me about it – I was up there at the time seeing to Miss Emily. I took charge of the stuff, cleaned the soot off it, and left it all back in your wardrobe.'

'Did you tell my mother?'

'No,' he said wisely. 'I wouldn't want to do that now, would I, Miss? – and get Eileen Donaghy into trouble.' He let his eyes rest on Frances's for several seconds before turning abruptly and walking away, while Frances stayed, covered in shame and embarrassment – caught out, a hostage now to one of the servants, who must know all about her previous thieving escapades with Eileen.

All that other earlier life of hers at Summer Hill – her troubled adolescence as she saw it now, of stealing things – came back to her. She was disgusted, now that she saw herself as a grown woman, to think of the frivolous, dishonest, unhappy girl she had once been. So that, when she unlocked the door and went into her aunt's room, she was almost in tears of rage and frustration.

Aunt Emily, as usual, was completely absorbed in a drawing. She did not look up. But she was aware all the same of Frances's upset.

'So, back again – and unhappy already.'

'I'm so annoyed with myself, Aunt—'

'And so you should be, coming back here, when you were well off where you were.' Her voice was not quite so fierce and scatty as usual; the slight brogue had a kindness in it, an understanding. Yet she remained head down over her work.

'I'm not upset about my coming home. Just annoyed – to find your door locked and all that nonsense again.'

'Ah, that's not what troubles you at all.' Her aunt leant forward, running a fine-pointed watercolour brush along a line. 'And that shouldn't worry you in any case. Fact of the matter is I can get out of here whenever I want – Pat Kennedy and I are the best of friends, we have all sorts of little arrangements.' She leant back from her work at last.

'May I look?'

'Why not? It's for you, in the first place.'

Frances bent over her shoulder. The drawing, full of baroque detail and delicate colour, was a wicked, indeed an indecent pastiche of the Cinderella tale: it showed a gilded pumpkin coach waiting below the steps of a great palace, with Frances disappearing into it, her sequined ball gown all torn and dishevelled, one of her breasts partly visible, with a silver slipper left on the top step, a regal figure emerging in the foreground to pick it up – the Prince of the story, but elderly and rather gross – and in this case very like the Prince of Wales, a coronet askew on his head, in a similar state of undress, hitching up his trousers as he ran.

'Aunt!' Frances exclaimed, her earlier shame quite forgotten. 'It's disgusting. And absolutely nothing like the truth!'

'Excuse yourself, girl. We all know – you're the Prince's mistress.'

'Certainly not!'

'Don't deny it – to me at any rate. And I must say you've done very well for yourself. So why come back here?' Her aunt looked up at her. 'With the world at your feet? That was stupid.'

'It's not at my feet. And I'm only a friend of the Prince's.'

'He has no women *friends* – they're all mistresses, sooner or later. So excuse yourself – you don't have to pull the wool over my eyes. I know what's what these days – here, take a look at this, if you think I haven't my wits about me.'

She opened a drawer beneath her in the table. Inside was one of Lady Cordiner's richest and most attractive paperweights, a posy of dog roses embedded in the crystal. Aunt Emily smirked with pleasure.

'What *have* you been doing, Aunt?'

'Took a fancy to it,' Aunt Emily said shortly. 'And why not? Gives me an interest – when I go downstairs. Oh, I get out and about these days you know. Pat Kennedy and me, I told you – we have nice little arrangements over it.'

Aunt Emily returned to her drawing, chuckling, altogether the happy child now, so that Frances suddenly felt herself to be the older woman. And as such, feeling her maturity, her now well-established balance, she was appalled once more at the prohibitions of Summer Hill, the madness, malice, cruelty and insensitivity that reigned here, introduced and sustained by her mother, which had led to all this eccentric behaviour, her own and Aunt

Emily's, not to mention her father's crackpot inventions in the yard with his aerial machines. She would stand it no longer.

'Aunt, it's nonsense – your taking that paperweight.'

Her aunt looked up at her slyly. 'Is it indeed? Speak for yourself, girl – it was *you* who gave me the idea. Oh, don't think I don't know: all the little tricks you and Eileen Donaghy got up to in the old days here. I'm just carrying on the tradition!'

Frances was dumbfounded. 'Who told you?'

'Ah, I have my secrets, too.'

'Pat Kennedy told you.'

Her aunt looked at her blandly. 'Perhaps I guessed. Since it wasn't me in those days, it can only have been you. We're alike after all, aren't we? – in our little tricks with your Mama!'

'The point is, Aunt,' Frances spoke to her very firmly like a governess, 'we don't *have* to go on with them. We can just behave in perfectly ordinary ways here—'

Aunt Emily broke in with a great guffaw. 'Oh, that's a good one, very good—' She spluttered, nearly choking with mirth, before recovering. 'You're out of your mind, girl, if you think that,' she continued now with great acerbity. 'It's only the little tricks that keep you sane here.' She turned back to her drawing. 'I have a few other small items in mind downstairs,' she said in a considered, choosy voice, before taking up her brush and adding a gilt flourish to the pumpkin coach.

Frances was appalled as much as amused. 'Oh, Aunt – I do so wish it wasn't all like this.' After her experience in London she was able to confirm now how far the house had deviated, was void of sensible life, where everything that meant anything to its inhabitants – apart from her mother – was unbalanced, underhand, conducted in secret or out in the yard. Though she had changed, things were just the same at Summer Hill – people made to cringe and steal and hide in the big house, scratching and burrowing about insanely: her mother, as ever, a Gorgon – trapping them all in this bizarre cave.

After lunch Frances spoke to her mother of the Prince's Marienbad suggestion, alone over coffee in the drawing room, her father having disappeared as usual to his study.

'Well,' Lady Cordiner said pleasantly when she heard the news, her usually creased and severe face clearing with a smile. 'And whose idea was it? – tell me, really.' She looked at Frances, her smile changing from the pleasant to the patronizing, intent on dominating her daughter once more, as she had in the past – the wise, all-knowing, authoritative Mama.

'His – it was the Prince's idea entirely, Mama,' Frances replied with even more authority, determined from the start not to let her mother outface her.

'I am uncertain of your relationship with him, you see,' Lady Cordiner temporized.

'I am simply a friend, a good friend – through Miss Wechsberg, as I told you: a friend to them both, the Princess as well.'

'Why should I be asked, though?'

'Papa, too, if he cares—'

'Oh, I doubt that,' Lady Cordiner said at once.

'Well, then, you and I,' Frances continued pleasantly, playing her mother like a fish. 'It would be a happy change for us both in any case – taking the *Kur* at Marienbad!'

'I should miss the Dublin Horse Show . . .'

'I think not. The Prince will be in Scotland for the opening of the grouse season on the 12th. He would not leave for Marienbad until mid-August.'

'You are well-informed,' Lady Cordiner said somewhat acidly.

'Of course – he has told me.'

Her mother sipped her coffee, silent for a long moment. 'Still,' she said at last, 'I remain unclear as to the *purpose* of the visit.'

'No more than that you should meet. You are my family after all. The Prince, and Princess Alix too – they take a distinct interest in me, my background, naturally.'

'Naturally.' Lady Cordiner echoed the thought suspiciously. She did not trust her daughter an inch. And, though she longed to meet the Prince, she sensed some trap in the whole idea. She had no idea what it might be.

'Well, let us consider it,' Lady Cordiner went on, temporizing once more, hoping that in the course of Frances's stay she would identify what made her uneasy in the invitation: Frances would let something drop – or perhaps she would discover it for herself. So that meanwhile, Lady Cordiner decided, she would keep a particularly sharp eye on her daughter.

This was no easy matter, for at once, immediately after coffee, Frances changed into an old riding jacket and set off – first round the house and then, with a mare, about the estate, revisiting all the rooms, the attics, galloping the woods and fields, until late in the afternoon – journeys, taking her well out of her mother's way, which she kept up almost every day of her short visit.

She took to the house and grounds and all her secret haunts there, thirstily, a traveller returned from a desert, making the world of Summer Hill hers again, marking the place – the walls, the lawn, the river walk, the airy beech grove on Cooper's Hill, all the lands running to the mountains – like an animal re-establishing bounds to its territory.

She knelt by the slow, clear stream which joined the big river at the southern boundary of the estate, seeing her reflection there, a woman who had once been a child dabbling in these same shallows, before she bent down, putting her arm through the mirror, drawing sprigs of watercress from the beds and nibbling them.

Later, returning to the house, she ran her hand over the letters carved in the bark of the big maple by the croquet lawn, where she and her brothers had cut their initials years before, growth almost entirely obscuring the incisions now.

In the drowsy afternoons she sometimes went up into the long attic above the old nurseries, gazing at the portraits of her Cordiner ancestors and the fine Irish

Georgian furniture which her mother had discarded here from the rooms downstairs. In one dusty corner, behind a pile of cabin trunks labelled 'P & O' and 'Port Said', she found a tea-chest filled with playthings she had used as a child – her Caldicott and Kate Greenaway picture books, a small doll's kitchen stove complete with miniature tin kettles, pots and pans. Beneath these she discovered her old nursery music box in a walnut case, a Xylophone, with one of the toothed metal discs still in place. She wound it up, amazed at the sudden sharp memory it brought, a return to the nursery, as the tinkling, bell-like melody emerged – 'The Dashing White Sergeant'.

The toys, like the lovely Irish Sheraton and Chippendale furniture and the portraits of her ancestors, had become irrelevant, lost up here in the attic. But they were not, Frances knew. It was just these qualities of gaiety and play, of a graceful past, which belonged to the rooms downstairs, which she longed to bring back here.

In default of this, at one end of the attic, Frances cleared a space under the skylights and set it up as a happy, hidden room for herself – an oval table and chairs in the middle, with the portraits set round it against the eaves and the music box on an inlaid bureau beside her. And here Frances sat in her ideal home, writing to the Prince, listening to the tinkly music, suspended above the real house like a bird of prey waiting its chance to fall from the sky like a stone.

At night, often going to her room early, she lay on the bedspread, stomach down, looking out on the long summer twilight, southwards, far down the valley, to where the forest at the very end of the estate, rising up on both sides of the river, made a dark V shape against the pink-blue sky: the woods of childhood, she thought, thinking of her years in this same room as a girl, when she had left the nursery, and had stayed awake on just such summer evenings, waiting to see the first star. And so she did now on her return, watching the sky slowly fill with glimmering silver dots, until at last she brought her oil lamp in from the landing, to read for the third or fourth time that day the Prince's latest letter to her.

Marlborough Club
Pall Mall SW

My dear one,

Today we attended the Derby meeting and I write to you now, in quite a hurry – forgive me – just prior to our annual Derby dinner here. I do wish you could have been with us all this afternoon. The racing was admirable, even tho' neither of my fillies took a place. I was given a tip however on a smallish grey in the 4.30 – the unfancied 'La Gioconda' – which (surprisingly for I never fancy greys on short runs) came home in the last furlong, and I collected something of a handsome sum thereby!

It was all most enjoyable – but that you were not there. You are sorely missed, in *every* way. However, from your last letter I see you may expect to return at the beginning of July. I await the day eagerly. May you be here to join our party at Cowes? You are missing the season – unclouded but for the wretched news from South Africa. I fear now that there cannot but be serious trouble with these intemperate Transvaalers before the year is out.

On the other hand it is so wise of you to repair any remaining damage at home and I am so pleased to hear of your success there. I do hope we may all meet together at Marienbad.

My darling one – in my thoughts most often,

E.

Lady Cordiner meanwhile watched and waited, as did Frances. She did not press the Prince's invitation, merely let the idea lie fallow, waiting to bloom. She felt almost certain that her mother – left to her own imaginings and unable to restrain herself – would bring the topic up again, as she did a week later, taking tea in the porch, putting down *The Times* in which, as was her habit, she had been reading the City and financial news. In this instance, though, she had obviously been looking at the sporting page as well.

'I note the Prince of Wales was off racing again yesterday,' she said drily. 'Seems to do nothing but.'

'Yes,' Frances replied nonchalantly, feeding a biscuit to one of the terriers. 'It is his passion.'

'One of them.'

By way of comment Frances merely smiled at her mother. 'Of course if I don't go to Marienbad,' her mother continued lightly, 'you will not be able to travel there yourself – alone. The Princess does not accompany him to these watering places. You would be without a chaperone,' she added with a note of triumph, sensing a victory with her daughter.

But Frances had anticipated just such a move. 'Of course not, Mama – I could not go alone.'

'Which is the only reason you require my presence – it is all most clear – merely that you may enjoy yourself.'

Frances was treading thin ice. What her mother had said was perfectly true. The Princess did not go on these annual visits to the European spas. And without her presence Frances could no longer be seen as *en famille* with the Royal couple. But she staked the game with her mother on the mere possession of these Royal cards which, though she might not play them to the full, she could let drop – apparently unwittingly, innocently, temptingly.

'Mama,' she said, turning to her confidingly, with an air of suppressed brio and disingenuous verity, 'do come! It was the Prince alone who asked – not I who suggested it. And we should *both* so enjoy ourselves. You have no idea – he is *such* good company, so kind, considerate and amusing. His equerry, too, Sir Seymour Fortescue – a little dry, but witty in his own way. He plays a fine hand at bridge. And the Prince's secretary, Francis Knollys – his golf and croquet are really most bizarre!'

'You have done these things with them all?'

'But of course, Mama! I have been at Sandringham several times, and often at Marlborough House,' Frances said wide-eyed.

Lady Cordiner could bear this documentation of her daughter's social success no longer. The bait had been dangled before her eyes long enough. She snapped at it.

'Very well then, if you really—' She stopped herself. 'If the Prince wishes it, how can one refuse?'

'Indeed, one might well see it that way,' Frances replied humorously. 'A Royal command!'

Thus both women took a victory in the matter – Lady Cordiner by allowing that it was her duty to comply, while Frances won through the pure pleasure of besting her mother.

Frances rose early, watching from first light onwards – the strange procession of pilgrims making for the waters, emerging from guest houses, villas, grand hotels and from out of the pine-clad hills that lay all around the little Bohemian spa – congregating in successive groups on the paved promenade that led to the Kreuzbrunnen, the main spring at Marienbad, the holy of holies, under the rotunda at the end of the long colonnade.

They arrived soon after dawn, out of the side-streets, from up and down the hill, strolling players making an entrance on to this gradually brightening, sun-streaked stage, supplicants shuffling along, before reaching out eagerly for their cups at the marble fountain, filling them, returning down the promenade, sipping the water in rapt devotion, celebrating a holy rite.

First, in the half-light, like wood-demons from the forest, came groups of Russian and Polish Jews in black kaftans, their faces gaunt and wasted with expressions of extreme melancholy. Afterwards the monks from the Abbey of Tepl processed in long white robes, gliding ghosts in the pink light, kindly but aloof figures, for the town was theirs after all, its lands and precious waters.

Then came the less important foreign visitors – minor nobility, retired generals, insignificant ambassadors and super annuated politicians with their overdressed wives. When they had taken their cups and moved into the wings of the colonnade, the stage was free for several minutes, scanned only by an advance guard for the new arrivals – secretaries, valets and ladies-in-waiting – who, like scene-shifters, had come to see the promenade clear for their masters and mistresses, the *crème de la crème* of European society, who shortly made their entry, full of pomp and circumstance: a few kings, from Bulgaria and Portugal; princes and princesses from several other minor dynasties; archdukes, dukes and duchesses from the Habsburg Court, a whole cousinage of the Tsar's from St Petersburg; upper crust English aristocracy, exotic maharajahs and maharanees, mysterious Jewish financiers – all of whom commandeered the stage now, in a secretly expectant mood.

Finally, towards eight o'clock, as it seemed a climax to the overture, a portly, bearded man in a dark blue linen jacket, perfectly creased white trousers and a grey felt hat walked briskly on to the scene, accompanied by his secretary and an equerry – a simply dressed figure, travelling incognito as the Duke of Lancaster, yet whom everyone knew to be the Prince of Wales.

As if on cue the real performance began then, the frockcoated orchestra under the colonnade tuning up on many violins, before breaking into the 'Imperial Polka', when the glittering company filed towards the healing spring, stepping gaily out to the rhythm of the music.

It was mid-morning, almost a week after Frances, with Eileen and Lady Cordiner, had arrived at Marienbad. They sat with the Prince on the wide first-floor balcony outside his apartments in the palatial Hotel Weimar, overlooking the little town and the forested hills beyond.

'Ah, Lady Cordiner, you are right!' The Prince raised his coffee cup appraisingly. 'How much better than the waters indeed! No one makes coffee better than the Viennese. My valet Midinger is from that city – I have him make it specially for me. I fear, though, with all this cream on top, we must drink it secretly. My good physician here, Dr Ott, must not know of it!'

'Indeed.' Lady Cordiner nodded in happy agreement. 'I believe, though, that one may overdo the *Kur*, your Royal Highness.'

'True. And some do so, I believe. But I am not numbered among them!' The Prince beamed. He sat very upright on a small gilt chair that seemed impossibly frail under his weight. The weather was warm, even close. He eased his collar a fraction, his hands perspiring.

'Of course, these physicians here,' Lady Cordiner went on amiably, but with a clear hint of teasing authority in her voice, 'I believe they are misguided. They imagine that a single month of self-denial can make up for eleven of self-indulgence. Whereas, it were better the other way about: to live reasonably and rationally for eleven months and "let oneself go" for the twelfth!'

'Wise counsel, Lady Cordiner.' The Prince agreed. 'I am of a mind that these physicians here – they are not adept in the art of living.'

'Oh, they don't know the first thing about it.' Lady Cordiner spoke dismissively. She was happy now, having won the earlier conversational point with the Prince, thoroughly to confirm his subsequent remarks.

Though of course their tastes in the art of living were very different, Frances thought then – yet how well they got on together. They were alike, of course, in their need to dominate, to win – in their sure possession, appreciation and use of power: a characteristic which they could admire in each other without penalty for they shared no social history, had no bones to pick there.

Lady Cordiner, released from the dictatorial poisons which Summer Hill had instilled in her, unbent in the balmy summer air, the fragrance of pine and fir from the hills, the meticulous service at the Hotel Weimar, the aura of social distinction and luxury that lay over everything she touched or looked at – so very different from the rude, rough airs of the Irish and County Kilkenny.

At Marienbad, without responsibilities, free of the bossy round that governed her life at home, her other sophisticated character bloomed. Her wit was no longer frustrated or malicious but used in the cause now of a long-dormant attribute, an informed and cultured mind. An almost youthful, elegant dash – overlaid by years of provincial Irish life – returned to her. She became the person she could once have been, had she not married someone so emotionally bland and socially withdrawn as Sir Desmond. Lacking satisfaction there, her husband's house and lands, and her own money, had come to absorb her love, perverting it.

But now, basking on this longed-for pinnacle of social success, her forgotten better nature was resurgent. Here she found her true station in life, which she was well equipped to maintain – better than most of the Prince's friends indeed, for with her quick Jewish wit and intelligence allied to her sense of occasion and eye for the main chance she outdid them in her social skills.

Lady Cordiner soon emerged as one of the great social successes of the season at Marienbad. The Prince took to her with enthusiasm, while she knew exactly how to handle him, so that the Prince, in turn, assured of her good will, was able to pursue his dalliance with Frances openly – and privately.

Of course, Lady Cordiner's great social acuity was just the factor which soon alerted her to the real nature of the Prince's association with her daughter. And here she was in a quandary. She could not but disapprove of it. On the other hand she saw clearly that her own burgeoning friendship with the Prince depended upon the continuation of her daughter's liaison.

She touched obliquely on the matter one afternoon with Frances, in the drawing room of their suite at the Weimar.

'Of course, my dear, I am quite aware now . . . of the *real* nature of the Prince's interest in you. How it is between you both,' she added distastefully.

'Yes, Mama,' Frances replied coldly, eyes alight. There was no point in denying it any longer. Indeed, now that her mother was aware of the truth, Frances was pleased to confirm it. It was another – and in this case resounding – victory for her, in the several she had recently gained over her mother.

'Of course, a quite passing concern,' Lady Cordiner continued dismissively. 'And it matters not one whit in itself – as long as there is no talk of it, no hint of scandal. You are clear about that, I hope?'

Frances smiled, equally dismissive. 'Oh yes, Mama. We are both aware of *that*.'

And now Frances knew why she had wanted her mother to meet the Prince – why she wished the meeting a success, as it had been. At last, she thought, she could identify the winning card she held. If anything were to go wrong in her affair with the Prince, if any 'hint of scandal' did seem about to emerge, she would have a tremendous lever then against her mother, who would, Frances knew, do anything to maintain her own association with the Prince and his circle. In short, the card she had identified was one of 'scandal', which she could, if the need arose, blackmail her mother with.

They shared an extensive suite at the Weimar, on the second floor, just above the Prince's rooms. And it was an easy matter, when her mother was taking her siesta or late at night when she had retired to her own bedroom, for Frances to walk down the service stairs at the side of the hotel and enter the Prince's rooms by way of his dining room door at the end of the corridor. Further along, at the entrance to the main salon, the Prince's detectives, either Mr Quinn from Scotland Yard, or Paoli, the Corsican, were always stationed. But they had been well briefed: Frances could come and go as she pleased. And that afternoon, after their conversation about the Marienbad physicians, the Prince said to her, 'My dear, your mother is admirable; she is most witty and informed. I cannot think how you ever came to fall out with her.'

'I may tell you, Edward, she is quite different at home.'

She did not wish to pursue the matter. It was enough that both got on so well together. To change the topic she came to him now, touching his collar, settling it, where it had come slightly adrift.

'My fourth collar today,' the Prince remarked. 'It is too hot, too close altogether. Though at home there is a heatwave.' He gestured to the big red dispatch box that had been brought up from the Legation in Vienna, containing various state papers and the last three editions of

The Times. 'Worse than here, if anything. They have seen nothing like it for years.'

The Prince went over to the dispatch box. He was preoccupied with something, drumming his fingers on the table now as he bent over it. Frances followed him.

'What is it?'

'Nothing . . .'

'Edward, I *am* interested . . . in other things.'

'The fool Chamberlain – and Milner, too,' the Prince burst out suddenly. 'They are pushing us into a war in the Cape Colony – and I can do nothing about it. I have had news today from one of my friends in the Cabinet – they have put us in an impossible position. Already they have purchased hundreds of mules, sent out a dozen staff officers and millions of rounds of small arms ammunition – to provoke the Boers on the Transvaal frontier. The jingo element has entirely taken control at home. And today I learn they have forced General Butler to resign, the Officer Commanding in the Cape, the only voice of reason out there. The Boers have been put into a corner. They can do nothing but fight now. And they will – they are well prepared for it. Yet we are quite unprepared, we have no real troops, no army in the Cape to fight them with. It will lead to disaster – and all quite uncalled for.'

'I thought the Boers . . . were bad?'

'My dear, not *bad*! Uncouth, devious, arrogant, no doubt. But then they have an understandable pride in themselves and their lands they have carved out on the high veldt there. And we have done nothing but undermine that pride, aggravating them quite unnecessarily for years with our sabre-rattling, so that they *must* fight – yet they are not worth the fighting.' The Prince shook his head. 'There is no real *casus belli*. Whereas there is always a cause for peace – I see that as my life's work, indeed.'

'I agree so much.' Frances stood behind him as he returned the papers to the dispatch box. 'You remember my cousin – Captain Dermot Cordiner? He is attached to Milner's staff at the War Office. I imagine, from what you say, he will shortly be leaving for the Cape.'

The Prince nodded. 'Of course. It may be even he, indeed, at the War Office, who had the purchasing of those mules!'

'I have told him – how against his army career I was, for someone of such intelligence, sensitivity.'

The Prince smiled in agreement. 'I am reminded of the staff officer I met, returned from Omdurman with half his head blown away, put out to grass at the War Office as a result. "Oh, I am quite pleased," he told me, "for I shall not need my brains there." In positions where it matters, they are mostly a shortsighted and incompetent lot – and all entirely without finesse. I fear the very worst.'

Frances moved round the salon fiddling with things, while the Prince lay down on the chaise-longue, taking up *The Times*. 'My brother Eustace, with the King's Rifles,' she said. 'No doubt he would be going too?'

'When it comes, everyone will have to be sent – a vast land. They will need several armies to contain the Boers, let alone defeat them.' He returned to the racing news in the paper.

'And I?' Frances spoke more urgently now. But the Prince did not respond. 'If there is war I shall go, too – as a nurse – I have passed my first exams. They will need nurses.'

The Prince looked up, paying attention now, concerned. 'I could not bear to . . . I would miss you,' he said quite openly, looking across the room to where Frances was fingering the handle of his carriage clock on the ornate mantelpiece.

'But, Edward, I must do something with my life.'

She gazed at the clock face, watching the tiny second hand tick by, suddenly feeling her own life ebbing away with it. She had achieved so much in the past year, in work and love. So often the clock had stopped for her – at the nursing home in Grosvenor Crescent – thrilled by the vital needs she found she could supply there; at Sandringham with the Prince, at Eaton Place making love with him.

But now, with his talk of war, she sensed impending change for her as well. Happy in his affection, their need for each other, she knew none the less that she could not remain a fixed object in his life. She had achieved her ambition with the Prince, with him and with her mother. Now she would have to go on to something else: fill her life with something fresh, stop the clocks in some new adventure.

'Of course you must do something – I see that,' the Prince admitted despondently. 'Though I wish now—' He laughed half-heartedly. 'I rather wish now that you *had* taken up with young Wilson, who so admired you.'

'Why so?'

'Why, for entirely selfish reasons: you might be married to him soon. And, since he has no concern with the army, that would keep you in London, away from any war – where I could at least *see* you.'

Frances was moved by this admission, coming to him on the chaise-longue, kneeling beside him. 'My dearest dear.' She took his hand, shaking her head, looking at him; he had turned away now, rather ashamed of what he had just said. 'Edward, I cannot take to people I do not love.'

'Of course not, simply a jest—'

'*We* take together in that way – you and I,' she said evenly. 'So I cannot consider others at the same time – I have no need to.'

'Yes, and it surprises me.' The Prince turned to her now, ruffling her dark curls for an instant. 'Most touches me – your single-mindedness.'

'Oh, I know – so unlike you!' Frances lightened the exchange, prodding him delicately in the ribs. 'You and that pretty Frau Pistl for example, who runs the shop in the Colonnade, selling those frightful Styrian hats – your little attentions there, they have not escaped me!'

'My dear, it was nothing—'

'Of course not. But you *are* flirtatious, Edward!'

'I have been – but so much less so of late. And it is obvious why . . .'

'Thank you – and it is the same with me. I had much the same inclinations, before we met. But they don't touch me now.'

'They will, for you *do* have your own life – and I must encourage it. But South Africa . . .' He frowned.

'It may never happen.'

'Be assured—'

'If it does, I will go – and come back. And there is still now.' She pressed his hand. They no longer had to speak.

The carriage clock chimed, the half-hour after three. A close, hot air ran off the hills, through the open windows, stirring the lace curtains. The town, shut down for the afternoon, embalmed the visitors in sleep.

Getting up, undoing the tightly clasped belt round her waist as she moved across the salon, Frances went through the small anteroom and into the Prince's bedroom, where she undressed completely, lying naked on the white counterpane of the huge bed, leaning back, playing with the Prince's little charms, the silver lizard and other lucky mascots that dangled from the brass bedpost.

The Prince joined her. She rose suddenly while he undressed, stripping the counterpane and the top sheet clear away, and they lay there on the velvet-smooth, cooler sheet beneath, slowly discovering each other again, ever more adventurous explorers through the baking afternoon.

She lay around, beside, on top of him – more skilled now, more loving, in her lovemaking: pushing down on him, rising back, arched above him, rotating in little spasms while he touched her breasts – before she fell on him again, nurturing an ecstasy, letting it become a fever in the warm room, so that eventually, with the heat, exertion, excitement, she could bear the restraint no longer, falling over him finally, pressing down, letting him come far inside her, when for one last moment everything was withheld, unmoving, balancing on a precipice, before her whole body shuddered, seemed to levitate, and she felt herself soaring away in the air in a long arc, melting then, falling, dazed with joy for minutes afterwards.

They slept for half an hour, until a distant rumble of thunder woke them. And half an hour later, just as the glittering company was sitting down to tea on the long terrace of the Bellevue Café opposite, the hot muggy afternoon was suddenly split by a huge clap of thunder, followed by successive fierce cannonades, echoing down from the hills above the Abbey, like a brutal artillery barrage against the town.

In another few minutes the swirling, plum-bruised skies opened in sheets of rain, deluging the women in their frilly lace and silk tea-gowns, and sending the orchestra scurrying with their tubas and French horns. The rain, in glittering great rods, made sudden pools in the empty tea-cups, set the icing running on the rich cakes, flooded the cutlery, and doused the spirit lamps under the silver teapots.

The customers panicked now – the men clearing the tables, china crashing to the ground, as they pulled the linen table cloths to shroud the women, attempting to herd them out to their carriages, brandishing walking sticks and shouting at the coachmen beneath the terrace. It was a rout. People fell in the aisles or down the steps, the women, clad like nuns in the great cloths, tripping over themselves.

In five minutes what had been a most elegant company, preening themselves, about to enjoy the *café-concert*, had become a bedraggled, vicious horde of animals intent only on survival, pushing and shoving each other without mercy, rampaging for shelter as the thunder crashed and forks of lightning streaked above them, the rain falling in steaming curtains, drumming like an advancing army.

Frances, with just a towel round her waist, watched amazed from behind the lace curtains at this frenzied, cowardly stampede. The Prince came up and stood by her shoulder.

'Just look at them!' she said. 'Wild animals. The Boers are not alone in their uncouth arrogance.'

'A little harsh?' He offered the comment half-heartedly.

'Their manners are only skin deep, Edward, whatever you may say – look at them!'

She smiled, pleased at their discomfiture. They deserved it. There was something over-refined, etiolated, about this society, these people. They had no fibre, no purpose. A rain shower was sufficient to scatter them – this quite insubstantial pageant. Frances suddenly despised them all.

But it hardly mattered. Summer was ending. The season at Marienbad was almost over in any case – the pleasant walks along the winding paths among the hills, the golf, the croquet, the *café-concerts*: all the endless privileged dalliances throughout the warm days – it was all done with and Frances was glad.

Ten minutes later, when she had dressed, she looked out of the window again. The storm had rolled by, all the muggy heat gone, leaving the air deliciously fresh and cool. The debris of upset chairs and tables and crockery made the terrace of the Bellevue seem like a battlefield now, the waiters picking their way over it disconsolately. Frances breathed a great sigh of relief.

9

Dawn came to the vast flat land – first a gleam above the Drakensberg Mountains to the east, then quick flames spreading up into the violet gloom, saffron and milky gold, before the sun was suddenly there, a half-orb of fire snuffing out all the western stars, melting the wispy clouds, the hills black against the horizon now, throwing long shadows as the beams dipped onto the plain.

The train, which had stopped overnight at Frere station, pushed its way into the dazzling shafts of light, fountains of white smoke mushrooming up into the keen morning air. It was the second week of December – unseasonable weather: the rains had come and gone before their time. And for more than two days – its passengers alternately chilled and roasted – the train had wound slowly up from Durban, through Natal, approaching the veldt, making for Chieveley Camp where General Sir Redvers Buller's army was gathering itself, waiting on reinforcements from the coast, before attempting to relieve the besieged British garrison at Ladysmith, twenty miles north across the Tugela river.

The Boer commando detachment – some seventy men

with their horses – had camped behind the kopje half a mile away, looking down over the railway, waiting to ambush the next troop train. Now their leader, the bushy-bearded veldt-cornet, lying on the brow of the hill, saw the necklace of carriages crawl out of the darkness and into the sun-streaked valley beneath them.

He tensed, waiting to give the signal to attack. But taking up his field glasses he saw the red crosses painted on all the carriages: an empty hospital train. He relaxed, disappointed. The other men in the lea of the kopje dismounted, standing easy with their Mauser rifles.

'Not for us.' The veldt-cornet spoke to them in Cape Dutch. 'Only for them. They'll need it.' He turned to the verkenner, the scout attached to their small group. 'Ride up to the main commando at Blaauwkrans nek – tell the veldt-cornet there, just a hospital train: no ambush. We'll have to let it through.' He turned to a companion then. 'It's a pity. We have had such good attacks on those armoured trains. Last month at Chieveley, what a rout . . .'

His friend agreed. 'We will have no more, I think. After Chieveley, they will bring no more armoured trains up here.'

The two men nodded, smiling, watching the verkenner as he galloped furiously away down the other side of the kopje.

'They have no mobility, these British troops,' the veldt-cornet remarked, looking at the fast-disappearing rider. 'As slow about the place as my old grandmother. Sitting ducks.'

Frances dozed on the bottom bunk next to the window in the carriage of the No. 2 Field Hospital train. She had shivered in the cold, falling in and out of sleep all night while they were stopped at Frere station, lying fully dressed in her crumpled uniform. But now the first bright slants of sun woke her, seeming to offer some warmth. As she looked out of the window, shading her eyes against the great orange rising over the hills to the east, she felt vaguely sick in the stomach. It was the food or the country – or both. There was a vast emptiness and silence in these high table lands which oppressed her, even with the lovely sunrise: an unfathomable, uninhabited plain; yellow-grey, streaked with green here and there, like a scaly beast, broken only by the purple wart of a distant kopje, sprouts of bush and prickly pear: hot, dry, stony, sandy, desolate.

Her older companion, Sister Mary Turner, a big, spiteful, florid-faced woman from Dulwich, with arms like legs of mutton, sat on the bunk opposite, fiddling with a paste brooch at her throat, the small stone at the centre glittering now in the sunlight. Her fiancé had bought it for her at Gamage's on their last day out together before her departure for the Cape.

She and Frances were the only women on the train. The rest of the staff – the twelve Royal Army Medical Corps orderlies and the two Surgeon-Majors, Dodds and Brazier-Creagh – had their quarters in the last carriage next to the Surgery and Dispensary.

'We can't be far now,' Sister Turner said flatly, as if they were on an omnibus between Dulwich and Trafalgar Square. She opened a Fry's chocolate tin beside her and ate most of what was left, masticating, chomping it vigorously with her great jaws. Then she offered the box to Frances. Only one small piece remained.

'No thank you.' Frances picked up the Sherlock Holmes stories she had been reading – the only possible literature she had found during her month at the main base hospital in Capetown.

Sister Turner devoured the last piece of chocolate herself, watching Frances covertly through her spectacles. She did not care for this woman who had travelled out with her on the boat from Southampton nearly two months before – the freshly converted hospital ship *The Princess of Wales*, originally a pleasure steamer for which the Princess herself had largely paid, and raised a subscription.

Sister Turner did not like Frances because she feared her, both for her class and even more for the influence she must have in first being allowed out to the Cape without being properly qualified, and then being permitted to take the boat on to Durban and travel up to the front line field hospital at Chieveley.

Sister Turner had heard rumours – on the boat and at the base hospital: Frances Cordiner was in the special charge of Surgeon-Major Brazier-Creagh; she was a friend, perhaps even a mistress, of the Prince of Wales.

It was disgraceful, Sister Turner thought. Miss Cordiner should never have been allowed to leave Capetown, let alone come on to Durban and up to the front. Though she had to admit there might have been some small excuse for this. She herself might not have been going to Chieveley but for the virulent outbreaks of enteric fever which had struck down many of the male orderlies, so that a number of nurses at the base hospital at Wynberg just outside Capetown had been drafted in at the last minute to replace them.

All the same, it was not right – a woman like that, hardly nursing for more than a year and far too refined: she would be of little use in the face of any real trouble, when it came, as Sister Turner hoped it would. She thrived on her work – the more blood and gore the better. She remembered the men back at Wynberg after the battle of Elandslaagte some weeks before – fearful wounds, shot to pieces many of them. She had really thrown her weight into seeing them fit and well again. It was simply bad luck that, even with her care, so many had lapsed in the end – hauled out to the cemetery or shipped back home as senseless mental cases.

War was a funny business. She had seen something of it, serving in a hospital in Cairo after the battle of Omdurman. But one thing she was sure of: to be any good at fighting, or helping afterwards, you had to relish it. And Frances Cordiner certainly did not look the type. Sister Turner peered into the chocolate tin, hoping to find a last remnant.

'It can't be good for you,' Frances said suddenly, looking up from her book. 'All that chocolate, first thing in the morning.' Her own stomach churned again at the very thought of it.

Sister Turner wanted to reprimand her for this cheek. But she hesitated. She had noticed Brazier-Creagh's regard for Miss Cordiner – an interest beyond the merely professional, she thought. The man was a frightful womanizer, of course. She had worked under him before at Omdurman – as quick with women as he was with the knife. But for her own advancement she did not want to openly antagonize either of them just now. Besides, she and Miss Cordiner were not strictly on duty yet. So, saying nothing, she simply glowered at Frances through her gold-rimmed spectacles. She would take revenge later.

They left the train at Chieveley station, moving northwest across the blazing veldt in two mule-drawn ambulance wagons with their stores and medical supplies, making towards the hundreds of khaki tents a mile away, set out in expanding squares and parallel lines over a vast area on slightly rising ground, looking down on the Tugela river valley two miles away to the north, with a ridge of steep, flat-topped hills towering up immediately beyond the snaking water course. Ladysmith lay behind these formidable barriers.

The heat was intense. So were the swarms of flies beneath the canopy. Frances had stopped sweating long before, her skin dry and abrasive as sandpaper, tasting only the caked saliva now in her mouth as she watched the grey pall of dust rising everywhere above the camp, broken here and there with vicious little sandy whirlpools, whipped up by a baking wind, spinning into the lead-blue dome above.

She heard the dull sound of some big guns then, firing way over to the west beyond the camp – sullen, echoing reports every few minutes.

'What is it? Have they started fighting already?' she asked Brazier-Creagh who was sitting just ahead of her in the front of the wagon.

'No. But they must be about to start, by the sound of it. Those are the big naval guns they took up from the coast – bombarding the Boer entrenchments – there, on those hills.' He pointed to the slopes beyond the river.

'Where? I can't see anything.'

'Just the problem. The Boers are well-hidden. Our guns will do little damage, if any.'

As they drove into the camp, troops were moving to and fro everywhere – collecting mail from home, making for the mess tents, and the water barrels. Some officers and men from a field battery were limbering up ammunition wagons to their twelve-pounders; another group of Kaffirs tried to manhandle an ox team back towards one of the guns, the unhappy beasts doing nothing but swivel round hopelessly in clouds of dust.

Further on a line of tethered cavalry horses, tormented by the flies, foraged restlessly under long khaki sheets. A war-balloon was being made ready, while a civilian technician, kneeling on the ground beside it, adjusted the telegraphic apparatus that it would carry aloft over the battle field. Despite the heat the men were out and about everywhere – a tense but happy expectancy in the air, sharpened every few minutes by the sound of the big guns as they barked imperiously, their great shells whistling over the camp.

A loud, discordant, clanging chime rang out the midday hour as they moved through the centre of the camp towards the field hospital. Frances watched a trooper with an old sword as he struck the empty artillery shell, suspended from a sort of gibbet outside the Army Command Headquarters tent.

'Every convenience, you see,' Brazier-Creagh remarked drily, consulting his own fob-watch. 'Except they're about two minutes slow.'

Brazier-Creagh was a precise little man: heavily side-whiskered, balding, contained, neat – but explosive; either very taciturn or, when he did speak, often alarmingly voluble. He was like a ferret with his quick eyes, his stillness and sudden incisive movements – unpredictable and dangerous, Frances thought, as she gazed at the endless conical tents shimmering in the heat.

'A real army,' she remarked.

'More than enough – for us,' Brazier-Creagh replied. 'But almost certainly too few – for the Boers.' He looked out over the camp, shading his eyes. 'Must be 20,000 men here – fifteen infantry battalions at least, not to mention the artillery companies and the cavalry – the Royal Dragoons and the 13th Hussars.'

'My cousin's with the Hussars – his old regiment, he rejoined them in order to get out here.'

'Oh, is he? I thought that was your brother.'

'No. He's with the King's Rifles.'

'Well, they've been up here some time.'

'I've not seen either of them, since I came out.'

'Quite a little family reunion for you then. If you can find them – in all this.'

Brazier-Creagh looked at her quickly, a smile passing across his face, gone in an instant. He liked this attractive young woman. There was no difficulty about that, of course. And he admired her for her courage. At least, he hoped that was what it was. Certainly he had not understood her vehement insistence, when she had spoke to him in Capetown, that she accompany him and the hospital train up to the front. At first he had refused her request. His tactful but none the less firm instruction in London from the Prince of Wales's physician, Dr Makins, had been to see that she was cared for suitably, whenever it was in his power to do so: Miss Cordiner was a very special friend of the Prince of Wales, Dr Makins had intimated.

Brazier-Creagh had told Frances of these instructions in Capetown, when she had become agitated, pointing out to him that, if this was the case, his ridiculous commission would be best implemented by her travelling with him on the hospital train. And he had seen the sense of this. But was she one of those romantic, fluttery women, camp followers, in love with brave officers and the glory of war, never having seen it? He prayed not. He had a horror of such women, though he had seduced them often enough. He had half-asked her about this during their interview in Capetown and now he thought to broach the topic again.

But just then, coming to the dozen bell tents and marquees of the field hospital on the far side of the Camp, they saw the medical orderlies, accompanied by a small honour guard, taking two shrouded bodies out into the veldt on stretchers – a burial party, getting the corpses underground as soon as possible in the fierce heat.

The ambulance wagon stopped, allowing the flies to redouble their attack under the burning canvas. Brazier-Creagh took off his solar topi as the burial party passed in front of them.

'Enteric fever again, I'll be bound. Take more than the Boers will in the end.'

'We brought up plenty of alum on the train,' Frances commented.

'Too late. They should have filtered the water through it from the start on these up-country marches.' The wagon moved forward again. 'So you see . . . Miss Cordiner.' He spoke to himself as much as to Frances.

'Yes.'

'You see.' He turned to her abruptly, a frustrated annoyance flooding his face. 'I've wondered why you want to – you don't admire all this, do you?' He waved his hand round the camp, at the burial party walking through the spinning dust devils out across the veldt towards the makeshift cemetery, where already well over a score of earthen mounds, miniature kopjes in neat lines, rose out of the flat, sizzling emptiness.

'No. I hate it.'

'Why, then? . . .' Frances was silent. 'Have you some love of suffering, some romantic notion about war?' he asked her harshly, his voice rising, his little white-ish eyes drilling into her. 'Why come up here, when you could have stayed in Capetown? No need to come up here, was there?'

'No.' Frances was terrified by the surgeon's sudden anger – terrified, shaking and tortured by the flies now in

the confined space. 'But yes, I do know – I want to nurse.'
Yet the response was half-hearted.

Brazier-Creagh nodded ironically several times. 'Well,
we can't complain about that, can we?'

Frances was suddenly angry herself now. 'Why complain at all?' she answered back sharply. 'I'm here.'

'Because I'm not certain I believe you.' He looked at
her closely. 'You don't know what you've let yourself in
for.'

'I've seen bad wounds before – amputations, gangrene
– men back from Omdurman in London. And tended
them.'

Brazier-Creagh cackled drily. 'In *London*,' he said. They
drove on. Frances jumped at the sound of the rifle volleys
over the graves, after they'd lowered the two men into the
shallow soil.

'They do bury them quickly,' she remarked conver-
sationally, trying to lower the tension between them.

'The lucky ones,' Brazier-Creagh replied.

That afternoon Frances walked round the camp, searching for Eustace and Dermot. It was not easy. There was a
huge area to cover, the heat was worse for the wind had
died, and the men who noticed her did so with mocking
or lecherous surprise. One of the medical orderlies had
told her that Eustace's regiment, the 3rd King's Royal
Rifles, was part of Major-General Lyttelton's brigade,
stationed at the centre, and on the northern edge of the
camp. But when she arrived at this section she found nothing but a line of empty tents. A slovenly field cook told
her that the King's Rifles had been sent out that afternoon,
back towards Chieveley station, crossing the railway there
on a reconnaissance in force: a Boer commando group had
been seen in the hills beyond.

'And the cavalry?' Frances asked.

The cook opened another tin of filthy-looking meat and
vegetable stew – 'knock-me-down' stew, with a fearful
smell, yellow-streaked like dog's vomit – pouring the mess
into a great pan. Frances felt faint, turning away before
he replied.

'Ah, Miss, the cavalry – it's over there.' He licked his fingers, pointing eastwards. 'And there.' He gestured towards the west.

'The Hussars?'

'Don't know, Miss.' He looked at her sullenly.

Moving away, she was soon lost again in this city of tents. She walked east, towards where she had seen the horses that morning. In an open space she came on some officers and civilians standing in a semi-circle, watching something intently. Pushing into the edge of the group she saw another civilian in puttees and a solar topi standing half-way up a tall laddered platform, tending a great black box on top with the words 'Biograph Company' stencilled in white letters.

'What – what is it?' she asked one of the civilians standing next to her, a great, swarthy, bear-like man, roguishly bearded, in a slouch leather hat. He looked like a Boer farmer.

'It's a bioscope – one of these new machines – for taking photographs. But running photographs. They move.' He spoke with an American accent.

'They *what*?'

'Yes,' he said coolly, turning and looking at her appraisingly, drawing on a cheroot. 'They aim to show the war back home with it – on a white sheet – as if you were there, or here, I mean. Great new American invention. I'm Clement Springfield, of the *New York Post*. You nursing up here? Didn't know they'd brought any women up to the front line.'

'Yes. Enteric fever took so many of the male orderlies. I'm looking for the Hussars. I wonder if you know where they're camped?'

Springfield looked at her with distinct interest now, sensing a good news item here. 'Yes, I do. They're part of Dundonald's Mounted Brigade, far side of the camp, to the east, right at the edge. Let me show you.'

'Thank you. But I'll find my own way.'

'Oh, go on, be a sport – I know exactly where they are.'

Frances walked away. But the man followed. 'You'll only get lost – I'll show you,' he shouted, before joining her.

Lord Dundonald had attended a battle briefing that afternoon – he and the other four Brigade commanders – with General Buller in his Army Headquarters marquee. Now, back in his own tent, he had called together the senior cavalry officers of his brigade – from the Royal Dragoons, the Hussars and from the three locally assembled South African mounted regiments. It was time to outline the plan of attack.

He stood at the centre of the big bell tent at a trestle table, a map of the area in front of him, the men grouped round, including Captain Dermot Cordiner – aide-de-camp now to Colonel Baxter, officer commanding the 13th Hussars.

'It's tomorrow then,' Dundonald told the officers. 'The four infantry brigades will move off an hour before first light, Hart and Hildyard's brigades will aim to cross the river here – and here.' He pointed to the two fords, above and below the railway bridge at the village of Colenso. 'Lyttelton and Barton's two brigades will follow on, left and right of the centre – here – ready to give support to either of the advance brigades. We're on the extreme right of the line – here, facing Hlangwane Hill, on this side of the river, just where it takes that big bend north. That hill is our objective, with the 7th Field Battery behind us, softening them up before we attack. We have to take that hill, outflank the Boers on the right, and enfilade their lines from it. If we don't, they can play havoc with our infantry.'

'All looks simple enough,' Colonel Baxter said enthusiastically. 'They've been flattening that hill – and the others – all day with the big naval guns. Can't be anyone left up there.'

'Yes – we saw a lot of Boers this morning, scuttling away from their entrenchments,' another officer remarked.

'I'm sure of it,' Colonel Baxter confirmed. 'They're falling back, all of them. They don't intend holding the line at the Tugela river at all.' Colonel Baxter was very cock-a-hoop.

Lord Dundonald – a canny, mistrustful Northern Irishman – was less confident. 'We should not be sure of that at all, Colonel. Though you certainly share Buller's optimism,' he added drily, eyeing the man carefully. 'The point is, these maps of the area are almost useless and our scouts have barely been over the river, let alone up in any of the hills. We've no idea how many men they may have up there – ten, twenty, could be thirty thousand. And all the time in the world to have got themselves well dug in.'

'But one of our scouts actually stood on the far side of the railway bridge this morning – not a sight or sound of any of them.'

'Colonel, these men are defending, not attacking. Would you give your positions away in such circumstances?'

'But we *saw* many of them running away – they're just a lot of farmers anyway.'

Lord Dundonald sighed. 'Farmers are sly people, Colonel Baxter – especially these ones. A ruse, a trick!' His voice rose in irony. 'There could be many more waiting for us than the few we saw running away.' The officers looked at Dundonald doubtfully, thinking him far too careful an old party, disappointed that he should so prick their optimism. 'As far as I'm concerned,' he continued brusquely, 'we are to assume that Hlangwane Hill is defended in force, and act accordingly. There will be no unnecessary heroics – the infantry will supply that, no doubt.'

Just then there was a commotion outside the tent, the sentry shouting, the sound of another raised voice.

'Good God, it's that frightful Yankee journalist again.' Dundonald looked up. 'Been pestering me for days.'

Colonel Baxter, taking the initiative, turned to Dermot standing behind him. 'Captain Cordiner, go out – see the bloody man off, will you?'

'On the other hand . . .' Lord Dundonald said, almost to himself, suddenly thinking of something.

Dermot pushed his way through the tent flap. The sentry was still remonstrating with Springfield. And Frances was standing behind him, anxious and embarrassed.

'Frances!' Dermot exclaimed. But she put a finger to her lips, gesturing hopelessly. Dermot turned to Springfield instead. 'Lord Dundonald cannot speak to you.'

'He *said* he would. And this young woman wants him—'

'I'm afraid not. You must leave—'

'But he did say he would, I promise you.' Springfield was aggrieved, apparently telling the truth.

At that moment Dundonald himself pushed his way through the tent flap behind them. He was almost genial. 'Yes, indeed, Springfield,' he told the man. 'I may speak to you afterwards. But first I want you to speak to us.'

'I don't follow?'

'Come on, old man.' Dundonald took him by the arm. 'You've been over there recently, haven't you? At Ladysmith – and Colenso as well, I'm sure.'

'Oh, that was some time ago.' Springfield was rattled.

'No – it was *very* recently, I think. I want you to come inside and give my men a briefing – on the Boer strength over there. Come on, old man.' He took him firmly by the arm and led him inside the tent, leaving Frances and Dermot outside.

'Is he a spy?' Frances asked, astonished.

'No. Just he speaks Dutch. And some of the foreign journalists here have been covering both sides.'

'What a funny way . . . to fight a war! He *could* be a spy.'

'Never mind – you're here. I never thought you'd get out to the Cape, after I left, let alone up here. I'd no idea! But I'll have to get back inside. Where are you?'

'Right the far side—'

'At the field hospital? . . . I'll come round this evening, after the mess supper.'

'I have to find Eustace—'

'I'll help you – later.'

'But why on earth *did* you come up here?'

Frances walked with Dermot through the long moonlit alleys between the tents, the camp and the plain behind, flooded with a chill silver air, so that both of them wore their capes.

'Well, I told you – I couldn't find you, or Eustace, anywhere in Capetown. That was one reason – you were both up here!' She turned, smiling at him, his thin face and crinkly hair visible now as they moved out of the shadow of a tent.

'But, Frances, we're attacking at first light tomorrow—'

'Are we? Brazier-Creagh thought that too!'

Dermot saw her eyes glisten in the moonlight. He could not understand her enthusiasm. 'Frances, you won't be safe.'

'Nonsense – it's my job.'

They came suddenly on a group of men, smoking, bending over a small fire at the back of a tent. Seeing Dermot's cavalry mess uniform they hurriedly stamped the fire out.

'Don't be bloody stupid,' Dermot told them.

'Sorry, sir. Just it's . . . cold.' A young trooper had stood up, saluting.

'Stand easy. Get some rest, for God's sake. You'll need it.'

He walked on with Frances, moving out to the very edge of the camp where the plain ran away seemingly for ever to the west, the moonlight falling on the sandy soil, touching it everywhere like a hoar frost.

'Only thing really worries me,' she said, 'I can't find Eustace. He's been out all afternoon, chasing some Boers beyond Chieveley station.'

'I've seen him – yesterday. He must be back by now. I'll take you round there. But, Frances—' He stopped, taking her by the arm. 'You know, neither Eustace nor I may get out of here alive. And if you're in one of the forward dressing stations . . .'

'I hope I am!'

'But why? – when you could have stayed safely in Capetown?'

'Oh, Dermot.' She glared at him petulantly. 'I'm not going to hide from anything, *ever*.'

Dermot shook his head. 'Strange, when you seemed to have everything going so well for you in London – making things up with your Mama on that trip to Marienbad. And with your friend the Prince of Wales, too. And now you want to risk all that – you, who said you hated everything to do with the army – telling *me* to leave it!'

'Yes, and I still say that. But I couldn't just sit in London when everyone else was coming out here. I have to *move* in my life – forward – don't you see that?'

'Move towards what, though? Bravery? You have that already. You don't have to prove it.'

'Towards you, perhaps? You still don't realize? . . .'

She looked at him quizzically, sadly, her lips trembling a moment in the cold. He ran his finger down her cheek suddenly. 'I only wish I could do something about that.' He turned away quickly and they walked back towards the sleeping camp.

Frances did not see Eustace that night. Stopping at the field hospital on their way across to his station, Sister Turner met her at the flap of one of the fever tents.

'Oh, Miss Cordiner – I wondered where you'd got to. There's a man dying here, enteric fever. I want you to see to him.'

'But, Sister, could you find someone else – *please?* I've been desperately looking for my brother all day. He'll be back by now. We were just going to go and see him—'

'Miss Cordiner,' Sister Turner spoke with harsh cynicism. 'Your brother is alive. There is a man *dying* in there – and no one else available. I'm afraid not.'

'But, Sister—' Frances pleaded strenuously.

'Miss Cordiner, I shouldn't have to repeat myself.' She held the tent flap open, looking coldly at Dermot.

'I'm sorry,' Dermot said. 'I'll go and tell him – how you couldn't come.'

'Will you? And give him my love and tell him I'll see him tomorrow.' She reached up quickly and kissed Dermot. 'And you too,' she added vehemently.

*

An hour before sunrise the infantry moved off in huge shadowy masses, down the long slope towards the river – the dense columns gradually dividing, opening out into skirmishing order as the day began to break, radiantly clear and fine, over the distant ridges of the Drakensberg.

At first light the naval 12-pounders opened fire at Fort Wylie, the nearest of the hills, 4,000 yards away across the river – pouring in a terrific storm of shells and shrapnel.

The impatient, bristling Colonel Long, commanding the 14th and 66th Field Batteries, took up the bombardment with his 15-pounders. To the right, on the extreme edge of the line, Lord Dundonald, mounted on a black charger, held his cavalry regiments back, allowing the 7th Field Battery to pulverize the Boer entrenchments on Hlangwane Hill ahead of him. Dermot had his frisky horse beside Colonel Baxter's, at the head of the Hussars. He tightened the strap of his pith helmet, checked the lanyard attached to his revolver, eased his sword a fraction in its scabbard beside him. There was no more he could do in a material way to prepare himself for his first battle: only his nerves to control now, as he watched the shells burst in a line half-way up the hill.

'Bloody range must be wrong,' the Colonel remarked after ten minutes of fierce bombardment, putting down his field glasses. 'Can't see anyone moving up there at all. Or else, just as I thought, there *is* no one there.' He picked up his glasses again. There was absolutely no sign of life from the long, indistinct line of Boer entrenchments, flickering in the heat-mist under the rising sun. He swivelled his glasses round towards the other hills on the left. 'Same thing. Whole place is deserted, not a sound or sight of them anywhere. They've all run – overnight.' Then he spotted something right on top of the ridge, but still well within the range of the guns. 'My God! – I wouldn't have credited it – a group of Boers and some of their women, standing there, just watching us! – like a bloody tennis match.'

At the back, and at the centre of the line, Eustace led his platoon down the slope, behind the other men in

Lyttelton's brigade, dispersing gradually to the right, until they moved along beside the railway track, making for the ford just above Colenso railway bridge. To the right, and behind his platoon, Colonel Long's guns were firing rapidly – almost too close for comfort, Eustace thought, more annoyed than ever now that he had been placed at the back of the line here, with his own guns seeming to threaten him and little chance of being anywhere near first in for a crack at the Boers.

Springfield, considering his options, had finally decided to break loose from the other journalists and watch the battle from a point as close to the Tugela river as he could safely reach; that was where the real fighting would be, he was sure.

To this end, he followed General Hart's infantry brigade at the extreme left of the line, placing himself beyond them in open country, as a sort of outrider, hugging cover whenever he could beneath the bank of a small stream running north, which he knew must join the Tugela a mile ahead. He could then move down the big river, hidden in the thick scrub which covered its banks, towards the battle.

He checked his supply of cheroots, his field glasses, water bottle and the Colt .45 hidden in his waistband, before pulling down his slouch hat against the brightening sun and moving off.

'God,' he thought, 'another blistering day.' He watched Hart's infantry now as they made towards the Tugela, marching down the slope in rigid formation, battle lines precisely drawn, as if on parade on a vast barracks square: all of them sitting ducks. And ducks didn't like the heat either, he remembered.

Brazier-Creagh had given directions to his staff first thing that morning. 'Half an hour after the main advance, we'll be taking No. 3 hospital train down the track – to here.' He pointed to a spot on the map about a mile from the river. 'We then disperse the six field dressing stations we have on board, three to the left of the track, three to the right, moving them as close to the river as we can get them. The No. 1 train will follow us, with the ambulance wagons, setting up the reserve dressing stations behind us.'

He had turned then to the eighty or so turbanned Indian stretcher-bearers who had joined their hospital train, speaking to their headman. 'You people will divide half and half, either side of the railway. The same with the male orderlies.' He turned to these men, considerably increased in force now. Then he spoke to Sister Turner and Frances. 'You both will stay on the train – prepare the operating tables, chloroform drips and so on, for the serious cases we'll hope to get up to you. And keep the train doors open, the bunks ready, for the other wounded.' He looked at Frances then. 'And I don't want either of you to leave the train – that clear?'

Now, an hour later, Frances looked out of the dispensary window as the train nosed slowly down the slope behind the advancing army – the massed lines of grey khaki, spread out below her for over a mile along the valley, a great blanket, the four brigades, each marching to a different rhythm, rising and falling in slow waves across the wide front, rifles angled forward, bayonets glinting. They moved with sure step and wonderful confidence towards the hills where nothing stirred except the sudden greenish blooms of smoke from the big naval lyddite shells as they exploded, mysterious ugly blossoms flowering everywhere all along the hills.

The sun was well up now in a brilliant blue sky, hidden at times by great towers of puffy clouds, illuminating this military panorama with gorgeous colours, ever-changing shafts of light and shade, as the army moved forward in perfect formations, pieces in a vast soldier set. Frances saw the beauty of it all – against her will. She clutched the lucky mascot in her apron pocket, the little ivory elephant the Prince had given her at Sandringham.

She thought of him, and all the endearing – even daring – letters he had written her since she had come out to the Cape. She remembered the anger in them, too, against Chamberlain and Lord Landsdowne and Sir Alfred Milner whose foolhardy machinations had made the war inevitable and taken her away from him. She missed the Prince now, for his indiscreet love, for his peaceful intent. And yet she was excited by this coming adventure in a war he had failed to prevent.

An hour after the bombardment had started – and though he had been ordered to keep his field batteries under cover of Barton's brigade – the impetuous Colonel Long, with his artillery in the centre, determined to bring his guns closer in towards the river, where they could operate with better effect, clearly believing that the enemy had retreated everywhere under the heavy British fire. Certainly they had seen no sign of life on the hills, except a few more Boers retreating, and not a single shot had been fired in return.

He gave the order that his twelve field guns, and the six big naval guns under Lieutenant James, should now move forward to a point barely 800 yards from the river and only 1,200 yards from the Boer entrenchments at Fort Wylie on a hill just beyond.

'But, sir,' an artillery captain entreated him, 'they may still be there, hidden in force – in that scrub by the river, or up on the hill! Simply a ruse—'

'Nonsense, Captain Jennings.'

'Sir, in that forward position we shall be nearly half a mile ahead of Hildyard's brigade, without any infantry or other cover.'

The Colonel turned on him. 'Forward, Captain. There's no one there – lily-livered lot of bloody farmers. We're not of the same mould, I hope? On, I say! Get the guns limbered up, the teams together. On, on!'

Ten minutes later the two field batteries galloped forward, outstripping their infantry escort almost immediately – Lieutenant James's naval battery following more slowly with their ox teams. Their progress was quite unimpeded as they made right down the slope, getting well ahead of their line, approaching a point about 1,000 yards away from the river.

There was an absolute silence from the hill straight ahead of them now. Nothing moved in the burning sun. Captain Jennings thought the Colonel must be right. The Boers had fled. Yet something made him uneasy. He had noticed the white-painted boulders here and there as they had galloped down the slope. Painted — but why? Then it suddenly struck him: of course, they were range-markers. But the British hadn't painted them — the stones were all on this side of the Tugela, right in the line of the British infantry advance. The Boers must have set out these artillery range points, some time before. He thought no more about it, though. He did not dare think about it.

Just then a single shot rang out from somewhere above Colenso village, and instantly both scrub-lined banks of the river, and the hills beyond, broke into flame with a fearful crackling and roaring, mixed with the rhythmic heavy hammering of the Boer one-pounder Maxim automatic guns.

A piercing deluge of shells from rifle, cannon and machine gun descended on Colonel Long's artillery. The British gunners faced it calmly, as if still on parade — unlimbering the ammunition wagons, picking up the range and opening fire on Fort Wylie without undue haste. But already, within a few minutes of returning the fire, two of their twelve guns, together with most of their crews, had been hit and put out of action.

Behind them, Lieutenant James's naval guns with their ox teams had been lumbering down the hill. The Boers had seen the danger here straight away, directing their fire willy-nilly among the ox-teams and their Kaffir drivers, so that the animals were killed or stampeded in a minute. The sailors managed to drag most of their guns back to a position well in the rear of Colonel Long's artillery, and from here they gave all the aid they could in beating down the fire from Fort Wylie, the hill one continuous cloud of smoke now from the bursting shells.

But the Boer gunners, deep behind their earthworks, seemed immune from the British fire. With their quick-firing Maxims, at this short range, they were able to pour a rain of destruction over Colonel Long's two batteries, completely exposed now in the open space before Colenso. They were in a quite hopeless position: it was a massacre. Within twenty minutes most of their horses and two-thirds of their men, including Captain Jennings and Colonel Long himself, had fallen dead or wounded.

Help was sent for. But none came, the few survivors round the guns held down now by a mercilessly accurate rifle fire. Colonel Long, shot through the arm and liver, was urged to abandon the guns and retreat. 'Abandon, be damned,' he shouted. 'We never abandon guns!'

Yet the fury of the enemy's fire eventually drove them back several hundred yards to the shelter of a dry water course, a *donga*, where they remained, emerging whenever they could, in a lull of firing, to take up their guns again. But it was useless. Each little detachment that ran forward was cut to pieces by the furious Boer fire, so that in the end only one of the twelve guns was left operating, with only two gunners to man it.

The first one bent down to the breech, was hit, and fell over the muzzle. His companion, the last survivor, turned and, disdaining flight, walked slowly back to the *donga* in the rear until he, too, was taken, transfixed with a piece of shrapnel, stumbling forward, struggling along on his knees for a moment, before he fell spreadeagled across an anthill. It was the end of the 14th Field Battery. Colonel Long, delirious now and bleeding profusely, lay propped up on the lip of the *donga*. 'Ah, my gunners! My gunners are splendid. Look at them!' But barely a single gunner of his remained alive.

Springfield, nearing the Tugela with Hart's brigade on the left marching in close order, watched with his field glasses the shell and shrapnel pour into the men. He was not surprised – he had warned Dundonald, at least, of the Boer forces in the hills. But he was amazed at Hart's temerity and foolishness – in allowing his men to go forward in such close order here. The Boers had two huge 45-pounder guns, he knew, on Groblers Kloof and Red Hill just behind Colenso. And now he saw the terrible effect as these shells burst among the closed ranks.

When the smoke cleared each time, not two or three but upwards of a dozen men had simply been cut out of the line, half of them disintegrating, becoming invisible, so that very soon the brigade companies behind had to be deployed, moving forward in steady order, still advancing towards the ford above the railway bridge. But now, breaking ranks, they ran desperately, the men falling singly instead in a hail of Boer Mauser fire.

Eustace's platoon, which had started at the back of Lyttelton's brigade, found they were nearing the front of the line, as the infantry ahead, breaking ranks under the withering fire, fell everywhere. And soon they found themselves right at the head of the line, great gaps in it everywhere now, leaving a wash behind of dead or wounded men, shells still falling all round them. It was literally do or die now, Eustace realized.

'Break!' he shouted to his men. 'And run – run *forward* out of their range, quick as you can – it's our only chance, make for the ford.' Taking his service revolver out, he and the remains of his platoon sprinted ahead, given some cover by a *donga* at first, but finding themselves in the open country as they neared the scrubby bushes hiding the river bank. But now he realized the Boers were hidden there as well, peppering them with a hail of Mauser fire as they ran across the open ground, bullets whining round their ears.

He turned briefly in his crazy run, hearing the strangely mild exclamations from one of his men right behind him.

'Damn it, bloody thing . . .' He watched the trooper, apparently quite unharmed, simply staggering a little as if from a blow of a fist. The man recovered and ran on for several paces. Then suddenly he tipped forward, crumbling at the knees, like an infant stumbling on a garden path, all the life gone out of him.

On the right, Dundonald's cavalry attack on Hlangwane Hill had at first gone forward successfully and almost without incident. But now the three South African regiments of Light Horse, first in the line and breasting the middle slopes of the hill, had suddenly met with an impossible fusillade coming from the summit – Maxims, cannon and rifle. The horses, already at an angle on the slope, were hit time and again, so that they reared up and spun back all too easily, throwing their riders, before beasts and men rolled down the hill as so much dead weight.

Dermot, still at the bottom of the slope with the Hussars and the Dragoons, tried to move forward now, up a dry gully, pressing the attack in place of the Light Horse. But with the Boer fire, and the riderless horses retreating in panic down the same gully, it was almost impossible for any of them to move forwards. They were trapped in a great mêlée of rearing, stampeding beasts beneath the hill, the animals charging in circles as the men attempted to force them upwards – meanwhile making a perfect target for the indiscriminate Boer artillery fire. The shells burst among the cavalry then like great dollops of puffy cream, smothering, obliterating the animals and riders at random.

Dermot watched in astonishment as a single horse galloped past him: the rider was firmly fixed in his deep cavalry saddle, the reins tossed loose with the horse's mane, both the officer's hands clenched against its flanks – but his head cut clean off at the shoulders.

Eustace, driven now to such a pitch of heady exhilaration that he was quite unaware of the carnage and bullets all round him, reached the scrub by the river, the first in Buller's army to do so, half of his platoon still behind him. They shot and carved a path through the bush. But the Boers had left this section of the river and the way was clear ahead, down the bank to the mud-coloured water, only a few feet deep, Eustace estimated.

He jumped, followed by his men, all of them plunging boldly in. But the Boers had dammed the river somewhere lower down and in place of three or four feet there was eight or ten now of swirling water. The men, with their heavy equipment, sank like stones. Eustace felt the long gash opening in his thigh, the prongs of submerged barbed wire ripping down his leg as he pushed wildly out for the far bank. Several of his men, unable to swim, remained under water or were swept downstream, struggling desperately, heads bobbing in and out of the sun-flecked surface, crying out, gasping for life.

Only Eustace, his Colour-Sergeant, the bugler boy and three other of his men reached the far side, to clamber up the steep bank. But here, on reaching the top, they met with murderous rifle fire from a small Boer force behind an African kraal a few hundred yards directly ahead of them.

Again, inspired by their success, there was no question of retreat. The bugler boy sounded the attack. The Colour-Sergeant came abreast of Eustace, shouting, 'Let's make a name for ourselves and die!' – as the six men left the cover of the river bank, setting out at a rush for the kraal.

Springfield, outstripping Hart's decimated infantry and reaching the Tugela some time ahead of them, had made a comparatively easy passage down the river, under cover of the bush. Now he had reached a point a little above where Eustace and his men had just crossed the stream. Hidden in the bushes, he saw them stumble up the other bank, meet the bullets; he heard the bugle, and then – unbelieving – watched them disappear somewhere ahead into the hail of fire. He jumped into the stream himself then, swimming quickly across, anxious to witness the result of this mad action.

Eustace barely felt the pain of the long gash down his leg as he tore zig-zag across the stony ground. And he felt almost nothing either when the hard, slim Mauser bullet pierced him, just inside his shoulder-blade, half-way in his mad dash for the kraal. The bullet went clean through him, in a straight trajectory, causing little damage. But immediately afterwards, tumbling in the air, the lead struck one of the men behind in the chest, opening a great gaping wound there, killing him in his tracks.

Two more of his platoon fell a few seconds later. Then the bugler boy was hit, in both legs, it seemed, for he crumpled up completely, only his head and torso writhing about on the open ground. Approaching the kraal now,

Eustace saw one of the Boers kneeling inside the low entrance, and another behind the hut. He fired his revolver as he ran, but wildly and without effect.

Then he heard the rifle shots behind him – the rapid fire of a Lee-Metford. The Boer at the doorway dropped – and the man behind the hut, just aiming to shoot, fell immediately afterwards. Eustace turned in his sprint. Only one of his men was still running with him, and he was not using his rifle at that point. Then Eustace saw the other man, in civilian clothes and a slouch hat, on the lip of the river bank, using an abandoned rifle with deadly effect.

Arriving at the kraal, firing his revolver at will through the low entrance, Eustace found the Boer inside there dead; two others behind the hut had been killed and two more, who had been with them there, were now running away across the veldt, full tilt, towards Colenso village. Eustace fired after them until his revolver was empty.

He had taken the positon. But it was a hollow victory. He saw now that he was the only one of his platoon to have arrived at the kraal. His Colour-Sergeant, and the other men following, were all lying dead or wounded out in the veldt behind him. Eustace turned away for a moment, reloading his revolver, considering the position.

He never heard the Boer come up behind him – clutching him with both arms round the neck suddenly, tightening the grip viciously, strangling him. He tried to throw the man off, stooping down, writhing about. But the wounds gave him no strength in one arm and little purchase on the ground with his legs, so that he was hopeless in the grip of his assailant, some big Boer farmer, twice his size and strength.

He felt the man's arms round his windpipe, the breath being driven out of him, choking, gasping, fainting. His head was jerked up into the brilliant sun, blinding him, his last look at the world, he thought.

Suddenly the Boer's arms disappeared, tugged violently away from his neck, so that Eustace found himself free. He turned and saw how the big Boer, with his beard and crossed bandoliers and slouch hat, was in the grip now of an even larger man with a similar beard and hat. It was the civilian who had been firing from the Tugela a few minutes before. The two men struggled, arms clasped around each other's bodies like Chinese wrestlers, grunting, moving in slow circles, scratching the dust with their big boots, the sweat streaming down their grimy faces.

Eustace, still faint and for a moment gathering his strength, watched the contest as the men swayed about above him, both caught in a fierce, vice-like grip. But gradually the civilian got the upper hand, squeezing the man ever tighter in a great bear grip, bending him backwards at the same time, so that finally the Boer fell on the ground, the civilian astride him now, his legs pinning the other man's arms to his sides, as he brought his own hands up to the Boer's face, putting his thumbs in the man's deep-set eyes, pressing sharply, pressing, pressing – so that Eustace had to turn away. When he did glance back half a minute later the Boer's face was just a bloody football, both eyeballs removed, lying out like marbles on his cheeks.

Eustace turned away again. The wounded men in his platoon, out on the open veldt between the kraal and the river – the Colour-Sergeant, the bugler boy and two others still alive, he saw – had all come under heavy shell fire now from a Boer position somewhere in Colenso village, a quarter of a mile north of the kraal. The kraal itself, with its bush and thorn walls, offered no real protection. The only thing was to try to get his wounded men back to the cover of the Tugela river bank a few hundred yards away.

Eustace immediately ran back into the fire, zig-zagging again towards his Colour-Sergeant who was lying about fifty yards from the kraal.

'Get the boy first!' the Colour-Sergeant moaned. He had been shot somewhere in the stomach, and was using both arms to hold his guts in. Eustace bent down, picking the Sergeant up with his one good arm, and together they both set off like men in a three-legged race back to the river. They made it.

Meanwhile the civilian, taking one of the abandoned Mausers at the kraal, had opened fire on the Boer position in Colenso, giving Eustace cover as he left the Tugela again, ran out, picked up the bugler boy bodily and brought him back.

Twice more he managed to do the same thing with the other two wounded men, his strength failing now as he dragged the last one back, so that he stumbled and fell with his load, within twenty yards of the river bank. Then the shell exploded just beside him. His wounded comrade, protected by Eustace's body when they had fallen, was able to crawl on to the safety of the river. But Eustace lay where he was, quite still, hit by the shrapnel, a great jagged piece of metal sticking out from his side, plugging the flow there. He was bleeding profusely now from other smaller pieces of steel that had pierced his temple. He felt no pain at all from these new wounds. He was beyond pain.

The civilian sprinted back across the veldt, picked Eustace up and holding the small plump body in his arms ran on to the cover of the river bank.

Most of the forward dressing stations had come under fire throughout the morning and now four of the surgeons, including Brazier-Creagh, had returned to the No. 2 hospital train and were operating in the relative safety of the surgery there – the most serious cases being brought up the slope to them in ambulance wagons.

The train windows were closed against the dust and flies, so that at midday the heat was intense, the air filled with the sweet reek of chloroform and fresh blood, as the wounded men were brought on to the four operating tables, two in the surgery itself and two other makeshift tables set up in the carriage next door.

Frances was working in the carriage with Brazier-Creagh, holding the chloroform pad over each patient as they came on to the table, making sure the man could still breathe, while the Surgeon-Major, braces hanging down, only a vest on above his trousers, wielded his knife beside her.

Frances had seen operations in London: a slow, meticulous process. She had never thought it possible to work with the speed and precision which Brazier-Creagh showed now on these terrible wounds, as he began the debridement on each patient – removing all the dead or damaged tissue round the wound in great cutting swaths of his scalpel, scything whole chunks of skin and muscle away. It had to be done this way, Frances knew, to prevent subsequent infection or gangrene in the dead muscle. But seeing the brutal process in action for the first time, she was none the less astonished at Brazier-Creagh's apparent butchery.

'Put the bloody drip pad closer, woman!' he suddenly shouted at her. 'He's moving – can't you see? Don't look at me – look at *him*,' he roared at her above the shell fire as he cut away at the man's thigh.

He turned then to a medical orderly behind him, using a syringe, tending an unconscious figure who had just arrived in the carriage, lying out on one of the bunks. 'He's going, that man – I can see from here: shock and blood loss. Stop playing about with three- or four-drop strychnine doses. Give him eight or ten – it's his only chance.'

Frances followed the surgeon's gaze for a moment, looking at the young officer who had just been brought in, most of his uniform stripped away, lying almost naked, covered in grime and dirt, a great piece of shrapnel sticking from his side, blood seeping everywhere from other wounds in his temple, his shoulder and one of his legs.

There was something familiar about the ruined figure, she thought – in the plump, blood-soaked cheeks, the line of nose, the matted curly hair: something familiar indeed. It was Eustace, her brother, next in line for Brazier-Creagh's attentions.

Frances nearly fainted. But she made a supreme effort, pulling herself together, saying nothing. Her hand began to shake, though, the chloroform pad dancing over the patient's face beneath her.

'Hold the pad still, woman!' Brazier-Creagh said. 'I'm

almost done here. Have to get that other chap on the table as soon as possible.'

Brazier-Creagh ran his eye over Eustace's wounds when the orderlies had moved him onto the table. He mopped his brow. 'A fresh pad, Miss Cordiner – though I fancy he's too far gone to feel anything anyway. And swabs,' he went on. 'As many as you have – he's lost a lot of blood.' He turned to a male orderly. 'Intravenous infusion of saline here – quick, man! – or he'll haemorrhage to death.'

The orderly brought a large syringe, while Frances set about her business. If anyone could save Eustace this man could, she thought. She swabbed the blood away from her brother's face, laying the pad gently over his nose, while Brazier-Creagh immediately set to work removing some of the shrapnel splinters from around Eustace's ear. But soon afterwards he remarked, 'Too serious – nothing I can do up here. Brain surgery, if he ever gets to a base hospital.'

He transferred his attentions to Eustace's shoulder. 'Smashed shoulder-blade – I think.' He humphed, pausing in his work, seeming undecided for the first time that morning. Then he looked at the jagged piece of shrapnel, three or four inches of it sticking out from Eustace's side just below his rib-cage. 'Can't remove that – bleed to death at once. Patch up the shoulder and leg, maybe.' He considered the long gash in Eustace's leg, then looked back at the mess round his head. 'Hardly worth it – poor blighter would be better off dead.'

Then Frances spoke to him. 'Sir, he's my brother – Eustace, the one I told you about, in the King's Rifles.'

Brazier-Creagh looked up at her calmly, licking his dry lips an instant. 'I'm sorry. But it wouldn't matter if he was the King of England – there's little we can do for him. Real wound is in the head, and we can't begin to deal with that here.'

'But –?' Frances, almost at the end of her tether now, began to plead with the surgeon, looking him straight in the eye.

'Miss Cordiner, with a head wound like that, it's a miracle they even got him up here alive. The shrapnel has pierced the cranium in half a dozen places – not to mention the other wounds. Even if we could operate immediately, in ideal conditions, chances almost certainly are that he'd die. Far too much blood lost, and shock – he'd die if I started any serious operation now. I'll clean the wounds, give him some more strychnine, saline, then put him aside, see what happens.'

He looked at Frances. He had noticed, while he was speaking, how she had left the chloroform pad rather too firmly over the man's nose and mouth. He did not remark on it, starting work again, swabbing the wounds, dressing them. But half-way through he stopped, putting a hand on Eustace's chest.

'Strychnine!' he shouted to the orderly. 'Saline, too.' A few minutes later he raised one of Eustace's eyelids. 'It's no use, I'm afraid. He's gone. I'm very sorry, but it was quite hopeless, from the start.'

Frances looked at him across the bloodied remains of her brother. She was numb, feeling nothing, except that she was swaying, falling . . . Then she fainted. The orderly caught her, just after she had fallen, hitting her head on the side of the bunk.

Poor bloody woman, Brazier-Creagh thought. Her brother would never have lived, of course: might have survived another half-hour or so, at most, if she had not inadvertently suffocated him with the chloroform pad. And the best thing, too – put him out of his misery.

Sister Turner, working with happy vigour at the other operating table in the carriage, saw Frances fall. Silly woman, she thought, pleased to confirm what she had suspected all along: women like that were no use when the going got really rough.

By three o'clock that afternoon, the guns of Colonel Long's two field batteries had been entirely abandoned, while the repeated cavalry assaults on Hlangwane Hill had equally failed. Without almost half their artillery, and lacking this vital hill where they could have turned the Boer flank and enfiladed their positions above Colenso, the battle could never have been won by Buller's army. And now the Boers, seeing their clear advantage, began to win it convincingly for themselves, renewing their heavy fire all along the line, so that the British troops fell further back everywhere.

Yet again, just as in their initial attack, they did so as if on parade – moving in perfect order, slowly, steadily, all the correct intervals between them, officers taking a measured step behind each company. So that again they made an easy target for the Boer Maxims and cannon, and many more were lost on the retreat, killed or wounded – those others left there to endure terrible agony, without water, under the scorching sun.

By five o'clock when the sun dipped at last, and the sky turned pink and violet, the Boer fire slackened and died away: no British troops remained within range to fire at. Only the many hundreds of dead and maimed offered a target now on the slopes leading down to the river, fallen in clusters, like obscene statuary, round the abandoned guns, or isolated in death, lone figures dotted about the veldt, some stretched out quite comfortably, it seemed, as if they had been sunbathing, while others lay in positions of fierce torture, their bodies grilled by a stronger fire.

A sour smell of flame and cordite hung in the air. Soon the battlefield was nearly silent in the waning light, but for the odd sharp cries of the wounded, like bird shrieks, that echoed up the valley as the sun finally disappeared, drawing a curtain over the calamity, sheer catastrophe, this humiliating British defeat.

'Well, do you have any news?' Frances asked urgently, later that night, when Brazier-Creagh came to see her in a curtained-off partition in one of the hospital tents.

'Yes, one of my orderlies spoke to an adjutant in the Hussars. Your cousin is safe. His horse was shot from under him. But he was unscathed, apart from a few cuts and bruises.'

'Thank God! Oh, thank goodness . . .' Frances spoke passionately, leaning up a moment in the bunk. She had barely recovered from her fall, was still in a state of shock, beginning to shiver in the chill night air, so that, while he was examining her, Brazier-Creagh ordered more blankets brought. She was a brave woman certainly – and her brother braver still: news had spread round the camp, how Lieutenant Cordiner, storming the kraal in a hail of fire, had taken the most advanced position of the day, only falling back to save the injured in his platoon, being mortally wounded then himself.

Finishing his examination Brazier-Creagh drew the blankets up, pulling them round Frances's chin. He looked at her for several moments, hiding his surprise, uncertain now as to what he should say. He temporized.

'By all accounts your brother – he distinguished himself, most admirably.' Frances said nothing, looking up into the tent roof. 'And I must apologize to you, for my earlier doubts about your abilities: you, too, especially – given the personal circumstances – behaved with very great courage.'

'I didn't – just fainted. Oh, God, how *awful* . . .' She turned away, lips beginning to chatter. 'And my brother, too, just when we were dealing with him.'

Brazier-Creagh, who had been unsure of his approach, now drew himself together. 'Miss Cordiner, I have to tell you, you fainted because you are pregnant – as much as anything else.'

Frances turned to him. There was little surprise in her dulled eyes as she looked up. 'I thought something must be amiss,' she said simply.

Her cousin, Brazier-Creagh thought: this cavalry officer, of course. That was why she had so wanted to come up here, to be near him – why she was so concerned for his safety. A distant cousin – they were lovers: that was why she had used all her royal influence in London, to join him. It all made sense now and he had been wrong in thinking the girl was one of the Prince of Wales's mistresses. Poor woman. Still, she was alive, as her lover was – and so was the child, he had confirmed – among so many dead and maimed.

'Well, we can all forget Ladysmith for the time being,

Miss Cordiner. And it's back to Capetown and home to England for you. I'll have you go out on the train tomorrow morning first thing.'

When he had left, Frances lay awake for a long time in the dark, listening to the cries, the agony of the wounded men in the other part of the tent, some of them obviously living their last hours. It gave her the only hope she could muster just then. She was alive. But how wrong she had been about her brother – about that sallow, plump youth, set in his dull army career. Her brother had turned out to be the bravest of the brave. She cried with guilt and grief. And yet, despite the depths she sank to that night, there was something she could go on towards now with hope: she carried it inside her. A new life had been confirmed, would emerge from the deaths all round her: something had been rescued from all this appalling and unnecessary carnage. The Prince, surely, would see the virtue of that. She clutched his little lucky ivory mascot, pressing it to her stomach.

Next morning Dermot came to the camp hospital, his arm in a sling, as the wounded were being moved into ambulance wagons before taking them down to the waiting train. Frances was gathering her things in the tent, but they had a little time together, since Sister Turner, hearing of Eustace's bravery, had ceased to harry her.

'I heard the news, about Eustace. It's terrible.' Dermot had a cut just beneath the chin, a field dressing round it now, like a helmet strap, so that he spoke with some difficulty.

'Yes – and I never *saw* him before he went out – and I feel so guilty, so awful.'

'You tried, though. And I did manage to see him – and he was perfectly happy and understood. He was very proud – that you'd come up all this way to the front, joining us.'

'But I was so *wrong* about him, Dermot – thinking him just a dull mousy army man, no real spirit. So wrong.'

'Yes. But so was I – all those juvenile practical jokes he used to play, apple pie beds and so on. I was quite wrong about him, too. So you're not alone there. He was very brave. He'll almost certainly be recommended for a Victoria Cross, I hear.'

'What good will that do him? – or us?'

'Your mother and father. It will be some recompense for them, at least.'

'Dermot, there is no reward – it's all just a terrible needless slaughter, without any sense.' She finished packing her case. 'I'll have to go now, help with the men. I'll be going back to Capetown with them.' She looked up at Dermot quickly. 'And then home.'

'Home – to Summer Hill?'

'Yes, I suppose so. You see I'm going to have a child, Dermot, a baby.' She looked at him as calmly as she could.

'Frances,' was all he could mumble through his bandages.

'Yes. But don't worry, it's the only thing I've got to be pleased about.'

'But Frances, whose? . . .'

'His. Who else?' She looked at him, a look that became a glare, then changed again, a mix of tenderness and annoyance. 'Not yours – I'm afraid.' She kissed him quickly on his bandages, before moving away towards the ambulance wagon. But he followed her, taking her by the shoulder.

'If I can do anything, anything at all – you could say the child was mine, if it would help.'

She turned to him. 'Thank you. But the only thing for you to do is not to die out here – dearest Dermot.'

She moved away through the straggling lines of men, the walking wounded on crutches, the many more being taken on stretchers towards the wagons, another gorgeously fine day rising all round the stricken camp, a vast blue sky with puffy white clouds towering away to the west. Dermot watched her go, cursing himself once more for his disability with this woman, with all women, wishing he could have been her lover and the father of the child to come.

*

Lady Cordiner glanced at the small leather case again, examining the dull brown gunmetal cross and the wide maroon ribbon nestling on a bed of fine white satin. The medal looked so unbright, she thought, so unprepossessing an object to represent such bravery.

Then she read the copperplate citation that had come with this posthumous Victoria Cross for her son: '. . . who on the 15th December 1899 showed conspicuous gallantry at the Battle of Colenso, in being first to cross the Tugela River under heavy fire with some of his company, then taking the most advanced position of the day, and who afterwards, ever mindful of his wounded comrades, returned under equally heavy fire to rescue them: all enterprises carried out successfully and without thought for his own safety, where finally he gave his own life for his men . . . actions far above and beyond the call of duty . . . the greatest courage and self-sacrifice, in the very highest traditions of the army . . .'

Lady Cordiner's eyes clouded over. She could read no more. Instead, she turned angrily to Frances, who was standing by the window of her boudoir at Summer Hill. It was late January, the afternoon of a wet midwinter day, the trees bare and windswept across the valley, the rain falling steadily.

'Well, at least my dear son has gone on – with honour.' Lady Cordiner spoke with bitter sarcasm. 'Whereas you, Frances, can live with nothing but dishonour now. For yourself, of course. But just as much for us, your family. Words fail me.' But they did not. Lady Cordiner rushed on with a torrent of invective. 'That you should have been so reckless, so concerned only for your own sluttish pleasure, so *selfish*, so unthinking – for us, your family, and the dishonour you now bring us.'

Frances looked at her mother calmly. 'Mama, it was not I alone, you know.'

'How dare you! To drag his Royal Highness down into the gutter with you – you little hussy!'

'What nonsense. I did no such thing. Both of us, we loved—'

'Don't besmirch the name of love – with your gross behaviour,' her mother stormed at her.

'Mama, you have quite lost control.'

'Not I, but you – and you shall pay for it! I have only one thing to say: you must leave, as far away as possible – and have your child, out of sight, out of mind – leave as soon as possible. I have considered it already. There is only one possibility – your father's old friends, the Grants, in the West Indian colonies. He is a planter there of some sort, in one of the smaller islands, which could not be more remote, I understand. We shall pay, of course. But you will go there, and stay there. I shall write to them today.'

Frances was astonished. 'The West Indies?' She approached her mother now, fiercely. 'Mama, I may tell you, I refuse to be exiled a second time, to some island. This is my home. I shall stay *here*. Or return to London.'

Lady Cordiner smirked at her suddenly. 'You will not remain here, I can assure you of that. And if you return to London, well, you can no longer work in your condition – and we will not supply a penny to support you there. Unless you imagine the Prince will support you?' She looked at Frances, a clear hint of triumph in her eyes. 'He has offered that?'

'No. I should not ask it.'

'But you have told him . . . of the impending event?'

'Yes.'

'And his reply?'

'He has not replied . . . as yet.'

Lady Cordiner's triumph was complete now. 'Nor will he. He will naturally cease to have anything to do with you. Can you think that he would? – heir to the throne, soon to be King Emperor – that he would associate himself with your scandal, by admitting or continuing the relationship, or by supporting you in any way.'

'It is his child, as well as mine!'

'Perhaps. But are you so naïve as to think he will ever admit it, in *any* way?'

'Not openly, but privately—'

'In no way, *ever*, I can assure you. I warned you in Marienbad – one breath of scandal, let alone *this*, and it is quite finished between you. You are, besides, as good as dead in society, in London or in Ireland. You have only one course left open: you must disappear, abandon the world.' Lady Cordiner, once again invoking all her Old Testament demons, spoke with disgusted finality.

Frances laughed. But it was an uncontrolled reponse. She was losing her grip, forced to admit the plausibility of her mother's argument: it seemed as if the Prince had indeed cast her aside. Though she knew well enough what really angered her mother: the end of her own great social ambitions, so successfully prospered since her meeting with the Prince at Marienbad, if this news got about. However, Frances rallied quickly.

'I may leave for a while, Mama . . . abandon the world, as you put it. But I assure you of one thing, I shall abandon nothing – *nothing* of this house!'

She looked at her mother with stinging contempt, then let her eyes stray to the walls, the ceiling, so that her fierce gaze seemed to penetrate right through the whole house, possessing all the rooms, landings, attics, outhouses – and beyond that the whole landscape of Summer Hill.

book two

I

'See! This water is fresh – the other salt!' Frances Fraser explained the phenomenon to her eight-year-old daughter Henrietta and her friend Robert Grant, almost a year older, as the two children sat in the shallow freshwater stream under the palms.

Henrietta suddenly launched herself forward in the current, her bottom sliding deliciously over the sandbank, soon caught by the flow, rushing now towards the sea. Robert followed her. The stream narrowed into a turbulent gully a few yards ahead and once the water took hold of them the children were wonderfully propelled in a cloud of spray out to where the waves roared up to the top of the beach and the two waters met. Henrietta cupped her hands in the sea.

'No! Don't drink it.' But she had and was spluttering now.

'Why is one water salt and the other isn't?' Henrietta demanded. But before her mother could reply the thin, dark-haired, freckle-faced girl had stood up in the sea, shouting petulantly, 'I like the *other* water.' She refused to play with Robert then, running back to the sandy freshwater pool in the stream. Robert stayed where he was among the thrashing waves, preferring them, thinking Henrietta a coward.

'She's just frightened. Hetty is a cowardy cow,' Robert told his mother Mildred, as she dried him later, putting his sun-hat back on, which he hated. Henrietta meanwhile was being fussed over and scolded by her own mother, some distance away by the fire and the picnic table, where Josephine, Robert's creole nanny, was bending down, her great bottom in the air, blowing the sticks alight, with a large black kettle over them. Two of the men from the Fraser estate, Jules the Sailor and Slinky, one of the odd-job boys, were lying out on the deck of the small steam launch, pulled up on the shingle further down the beach.

'No, she's not a coward,' Mildred told her son. 'Hetty just likes fresh water, that's all. People like different things.'

Robert looked over at the picnic table where Mr Fraser had lit one of his small cigars, puffing it, before raising his rum glass again and drinking. Robert was curious. Nobody drank rum in the afternoons, he knew, especially not at a picnic. There was something wrong with Hetty's father. He said so little, sitting there in his white duck suit and dark tie, just drinking, barely ever talking to them. And there was something wrong with Mrs Fraser, too, Hetty's mother. They were both sad, Robert thought – but in different ways. Mr Fraser was grim and silent. With Mrs Fraser – well, whatever it was, it made her angry. She was quite often angry, and very suddenly, over nothing, when she bunched her fingers in and out in a funny way. Robert blotted the hot sun out, burying his face in his mother's neck and arms as she dried his back.

'*Why* are people different, Mama? And why is some water salt and other water isn't?' He mumbled the words quietly into his mother's hot-smelling, frilly white blouse so that Hetty would not hear anything.

'People have to be different. And I don't honestly know about salt and fresh water. It just is. Your father would know.'

'I don't like Hetty – she's annoying. I wish we didn't have to come all the way over this side of the island for holidays. There's no one here and the water's cold.'

'Try and like her, darling. She's really very nice. A little highly strung – and wilful,' she added, looking over to where Hetty was wriggling frantically in her mother's arms. 'She likes you – I'm sure she does. And we can't just not like people because they are different from us.'

'Yes, but *why* is she different from us? I'm much browner – she has freckly spots on her face and her whitey skin.' Robert was frustrated now. He started to struggle, hating his sun-hat and being dried. 'And why hasn't she got a *real* father?' He finally released himself from his mother's arms and looked at her in triumph.

'Robert! What do you mean?' Mildred looked at her son, alarmed. 'Of *course* she has a real father: Bruce – Mr Fraser – over there.'

'That's not what Josephine says. I've heard her talking – round the back of the kitchens at the Hall. She said Mr Fraser wasn't Hetty's *real* father!'

'That's not true, Robert. You mustn't spread lies like that – you're not to talk of it ever again, do you hear? *Ever.*'

'Well, anyway, he doesn't seem like her father – away all the time. He's never here.'

'He's very busy – with his family plantations in Barbados,' Mildred lied.

'Like Papa? Does he work at lime trees and go down to the factory every day?'

'No. They don't grow limes in Barbados. Only here – in Domenica.'

'Is that why Mrs Fraser is so angry? – because Mr Fraser isn't here. And, when he is here, he just sits by himself, drinking all that rum?'

'Robert, you're *not* to talk of it.' Mildred raised her voice a fraction, looking round her cautiously. 'And you must be kind to Hetty.' She lowered her voice, smoothing her son's damp dark hair. 'Because her father isn't often here, she needs *more* kindness – do you see?'

'No. Not really.'

Robert noticed his mother's reproachful look. Or was she just being sad again, he wondered? She sometimes looked that way. But she was never angry. And at least he knew why she was sad, because he was sad himself for the same reason. His father was really an inventor, not a planter. But his inventions usually didn't work, over in their own house, Lime Hill, above Roseau, far away on the other side of the island where everyone lived and the sea was always warm. His father Bertie was always playing with strange grown-up things, just like toys. 'But they're not playthings, you see,' his mother had told him wearily. 'They're real.' But they mostly broke down. Like the funny new machine he'd built in the yard of Lime Hill for squeezing limes, from bits of a washing mangle with chains attached to the pedals of a bicycle – a lovely black brand-new bicycle which had come all the way out on the boat from England, which he hadn't bought to ride, but just to nail down and fix up to the stupid rollers and things in the yard. His father never came on holiday with them over to this side of the island. He had to stay at home – waiting for things from England. Robert could see him now, down on the busy jetty at Roseau, watching the boys load boxes and big crates and things from England, putting them onto the mule cart and dragging them up into the hills.

His father was always looking out to sea, with the long brass telescope, from the terrace at Lime Hill, waiting for the ships, expecting things with a sad face – which often didn't come, and, when they did, he messed them all up so that they didn't work. That was why his mother was sad and spent holidays over on this side of the island – keeping Mrs Fraser company, she said. But he knew the real reason.

His mother turned the brim of his horrid sun-hat down then. He turned it up again. His mother sighed. 'Well, you must just try and be nice to Hetty. People have to *try*, you know, dearest.'

'But she won't play pirates with me, or anything. She just cuddles and cries with Elly. And last night – she hurt me.'

'What?'

'She said there was a big frog, a *crapaud*, in my bed – and Elly didn't scold her, when there wasn't.'

'That's just teasing, not hurting, darling. She teases. We all do sometimes.'

'But she *always* teases me, Mama, so it *does* hurt.'

'Well, you'll just have to try – you are nearly a year older, you know – have to be a rather grown-up boy now and try and understand her.'

'Yes, I suppose so.' Robert so wanted to be older and wiser then. 'It's really because of her father, isn't it? – because he's never here. I know it's that, because last Christmas, when we were over here, she wrote to him, instead of Father Christmas, asking him for things. And I told her she wouldn't get anything, because he never sends her anything, not even on her birthday. And Hetty pushed me then and cried.'

'Robert, you shouldn't – you mustn't say things like that to Hetty.'

'I was only telling her the truth. You said I should always tell the truth.'

'Not when it hurts people.'

They had their picnic tea soon after. Robert did not like it very much. There was a plum cake that was very hard and black on top and all dry and crumbly and not nice inside, because it had come all the way from England. Most things that came from England were nice, he thought. But not this cake. He wished they could bring snow from England – and fog. Fog was thick, like pea soup, his father had told him. But he had never had pea soup either. And never seen snow, of course. Snow was like white rain, his mother had said, even better, like sugar flakes that melted on your tongue, coming out of the sky and covering the whole earth in a great white cold blanket. Could that really be true? It made him tingle with excitement just to think about it.

Later in the afternoon, when Josephine had packed up the picnic things, they all walked down the beach to the steam launch, which Jules and Slinky had pulled up into the shallow waves, turning it about so that the stern and the little ladder there faced inwards, and they all climbed aboard, getting their feet wet. But nobody minded, except Mr Fraser who missed his footing, stumbled about in the shallows and made a fuss about spoiling his smart white suit.

Robert sat next to Big Jules at the tiller in the back, while Slinky stoked the boiler ahead of them. The others sat on either side of the cockpit as they moved out into the surge of Atlantic waves, rounding the headland. This was one thing Robert really liked about coming to Fraser Hall – these lovely bouncy, dippy trips in the steam launch, through these big white-crested waves which they never had on the other, Caribbean, side of the island. Here, with the spray in his eyes, he could really pretend he was a pirate – Captain Morgan with all his treasure – making for the secret cove just below the great white house on the cliff in St David's Bay on the other side of the headland.

Fraser Hall, with its windswept stockade of magnificent Emperor palms, stood on the short cliff, the coral stone façade dazzling white in the sun, patterned with rippling light and shadow, reflecting the endless sea glitter beneath, so that the house seemed alive, appeared to sway and dance, agitated by the prism of colours slanting off the water.

Below it the sea moved in deep swells and crashing breakers, a huge leonine presence, throwing itself on the rocks, exploding in crystal drifts of sunlit spume, retreating in a fizzy turmoil of blue and green, renewing itself further out in menacing rollers of deep purple. But the house mocked the great waves – and the wild land behind it, a startling conceit on this deserted coast, a white vision rearing up from the aquamarine ocean set against a backdrop of jade-green mountains: a large four-square two-storeyed villa somewhat in the French manner – for the buildings here had maintained that character in an island that had belonged to France less than a hundred years before – with a mansard roof, green louvred storm shutters and metal canopies over the windows – a dozen hooded eyes that gazed dismissively out over the vast Atlantic rollers.

The coral stone had been shipped from Barbados twenty years before, by Bruce Fraser's father when he had first decided to develop this almost uninhabited Atlantic side of Domenica as an agricultural estate: an eccentric, expensive gesture on a volcanic island where nearly all the other plantation houses were set on stilts or ballast brick, built of wood, with shingle or tin roofs.

But then old Alisdair Fraser, though Scottish, never did things by halves. He was cannily extravagant and expansive, which thrust no doubt lay behind the fortune he had inherited and increased from his family's sugar plantations in Barbados. Besides, in the matter of any building in these parts, he rightly feared hurricanes. And so Fraser Hall had been built to survive the worst whirlwind, as it always had, where other houses on the island every five years or so, had lost their roofs and worse, the vicious scything windspouts taking everything away with them: life and limb, wood and tin – everything; lock, stock and barrel.

The sole concession to the elements in the house was the wide veranda with its graceful stone arches, which had been set around two sides at the back, facing inland out of the wind – and the gales when they came with their raging breakers. The veranda, covered in bougainvillaea and hibiscus, with its chairs and chintz sofas, gave out on to a large, sheltered lawn, brilliant green, enclosed by Emperor palms: coarse-grassed, with a mango grove at one end, a lovely casuarina tree with a swing in the middle, and filled with clumps of exotic shrubs and flowers – orchids, anturiums, heliconias – which bloomed fiercely the year round.

Beyond the lawn, to either side, up and down the narrow coastal strip, the land had been cleared years ago for the sugar and citrus plantations. But now, long-neglected, more wild and overgrown each year, the estate was falling into livid decay, a rash of bright weeds rising among the overblown lime and grapefruit trees. The sugar cane had not prospered. The citrus had got withertip, and Alisdair Fraser, cutting his losses, had returned to concentrate on his surer profits in Barbados, leaving the house, its dilapidated estate, and a sizeable income besides, as a marriage gift to his dissolute younger son Bruce – on condition that he never set foot in Barbados again.

Due west of the terrace, less than a mile inland, the great saw-toothed mountains of the island rose everywhere, range after higher range, in ever-deepening perspective, forest-clad, in a variety of astonishing shapes and colours, forming a gaudy green chiaroscuro backdrop to the white house. Green of every shade: jade, moss, yellow, olive, tweed-dark and black green – the steep tropical rain forests running up into cloudy peaks before diving into fathomless dim ravines beyond. Here lay almost uninhabited, impenetrable territory, occupied only by the Caribs, last remnants of the fierce cannibal tribe who had once dominated all these windward islands.

To the left of the high bluff on which the house was set, down a gentler slope, the Belle Fille river ran towards the bay, where, before it reached the sea, water was taken from it along a stone aqueduct towards the old sugar mill with its tall brick chimney, barely used now, except to extract enough cane juice for the boiling coppers to produce a strong rum, once famous throughout the island, but now only produced for domestic consumption.

Beyond the factory, a mile north along the bay, lay the small settlement of Castle Bruce: a few tin shacks, a general store run by a Syrian, and the Catholic church, the parish administered by Father Bertin, a French priest from the Holy Ghost order in Guadeloupe, the next island to the north.

Immediately below the house, down a winding cliff path, lay the sheltered cove with a jetty where the boats were moored – the steam launch *Sisserou*, an unseaworthy sloop *Arethusa*, and two dinghies. Once a fortnight the mail packet, from the capital Roseau, dropped anchor here with supplies, newspapers and letters. The packet was the one link Fraser Hall had with the outside world. Only half a dozen other plantation houses lay on this rugged windward side of the island, and the first two of these were ten miles north and south of Castle Bruce, at Marigot and Rosalie – neighbours in a sense, but never visited now by the inhabitants of the Hall. Roseau, the capital, with its semblance of civilization, lay two days' journey right round the island by boat. Apart from the few dirt tracks leading out of Roseau, there were no roads on Domenica – and Fraser Hall ruled quite alone on this section of it: isolated, magnificent, secret.

'I don't really care whether you come or go, after your usual behaviour – this afternoon,' Frances told her husband that evening at dinner, as they sat at opposite ends of the long lamp-lit dining table. Mildred had retired early, pleading a sick headache. Frances picked at her dolphin steak. Bruce Fraser had not yet touched the claret decanter, still drinking rum. The high-ceilinged room was hot and humid in this summer season before the August storms. Beyond the open louvred shutters lay the arched veranda and beyond that fireflies danced over the dark lawn, while other insects, despite the muslin netting over the jalousy windows, crowded round the yellow globe of the oil lamp, feinting, buzzing, dying with little spits and pops above the glass chimney. There was an oppressive, sweet-and-sour air in the heavy, dark-furnished room – a mix of paraffin oil, rum and mildew.

'I shall "come", if you put it like that. It is my house, after all,' he said petulantly.

'As you wish. You do me no favour, one way or the other.'

'I did, though – remember that!'

'How could I forget it.' Frances laughed icily.

'We were not so distant then.'

'No. Nor did you spend your time drinking – or months away in the fleshpots of Spanish Town, Jamaica.'

Bruce Fraser sighed, allowing himself a wan smile. Again, he was dressed immaculately – dark dinner jacket, boiled white shirt, black tie, dancing pumps, gold cufflinks that gleamed in the yellow light. This sartorial propriety only served to accentuate his covert drunkenness. He was held up, held firm within the walls of his stiff clothes, so that it was all the more apparent how he trembled and swayed inside them, his brown eyes unsteady beams atop a dark lighthouse. Though only in his early thirties his cheeks were puffy and blotched, enlarging an already heavy face, still handsome in its way, but with a childish cast to it now, as if the drink had taken him back to a sort of infancy, this rum-formed baby fat spreading about his jowls and chin.

'You were pleased to take my name – and money, once,' he said reasonably. 'Yet since then . . . you deny me –

everything. One may drink because of it,' he added shortly, looking down the table, trying to clear his eyes, focus them on her.

'You drank before I met you . . .'

'You have only yourself to blame, then, for marrying me.' He leant forward sharply, the better to insinuate his attack. 'But of course you were not concerned with my morals, my drinking then, not with blame of any sort – merely that you should give your child a father. I see that now, of course. It was your plan from the start – which I failed to see then. Well, she has a father, in name at least – so you may rest content. And I may drink.' He raised his rum glass to her in an ironic salute. Then, puzzled suddenly, he set the glass down. 'Yet it wasn't always so.' He spoke more to himself, than to Frances. 'You saw something in me once.'

Indeed, that was true, Frances thought. Bruce had been witty years before, when they had first met in Roseau, up with the Grants at Lime Hill, only a week after she and Eileen had arrived from England: witty, confident, warm. But she had not seen then how these qualities had largely been the product of his tippling. She bunched her fingers together now, making fists over the elaborate settings of glowing silver cutlery.

'You were a different person then,' she lied to him, for he had not been. She had just failed to recognize his real nature where, under the rum-based bonhomie, he was weak, undecided – and violent, too, because of these defects. Yet he was, and remained, intelligent. She recognized that in his reply.

'I was no different then – drank less perhaps. You want to see me as different now, because you won't admit that it is *you* who have changed, getting all that you wanted – a name, house, money, possessions, a father to your child. You came here an outcast, with nothing but that child in your belly. I offered you everything – I had everything. Now it's the other way around. You've won and I've lost. That's all there is to it.'

He opened the claret decanter then. Frances did not

reply. She closed up absolutely – as she always did when her husband confronted her with these drunken truths.

Upstairs, in the children's bedroom at the end of the corridor looking over the outhouses, the kitchens and servants' quarters, Eileen read the poem from the *Irish Fireside and Homestead* magazine, which arrived for her every month from Ireland, Robert and Henrietta in their beds to either side, Eileen on the rocking chair between them.

'"Come away O human child!
  to the waters and the wild,
  With a faery, hand in hand,
  For the world's more full of weeping
  Than you can understand."

'There,' she said when she'd finished the poem. 'That's grand, isn't it? All the way from Ireland!'

'Are the fairies there real?' Henrietta asked.

'And why wouldn't they be?'

'Like Josephine's and cook's zombies and werewolves – down behind the kitchens?'

'Yes, but the fairies in Ireland are *much* nicer and kinder. Josephine's are real divils!' Eileen shuddered.

'Where is Island?' Robert asked.

'*Ir*eland. Though it's an island too. But much bigger than this one. Where I come from – and Mrs Fraser as well. And Hetty in a way, though she's not been there yet.'

'Snow and fog – do they have that there?'

'Yes – sometimes. But not very much.'

'They have it in England, a *lot* of it,' Robert said proudly. 'I'm English. They have real pea-soupers there, in London.'

He turned to look at Henrietta. 'See, you're just from *Ir*eland, just a little island.'

'England's only an island as well,' Eileen told him, getting up, tucking him under his single sheet, closing the mosquito canopy over him.

'See!' Henrietta shouted over to him. 'You're only from

an island as well – and I don't want to see snow anyway – or pea-soupers, so there! I don't want everything all white and cold. I want it all cosy-warm. Don't I, Elly?' she added, thumb in her mouth, looking up with frail hope, as Eileen came across to her.

'Yes, Mavourneen, of course you do. And you are.'

She settled Hetty down and cuddled her for a minute, her heart going out to this expectant, delicate-featured child with her long strands of wavy dark hair and great blue eyes. A child of such mixtures, so rude one minute, shy the next, you never knew where you were with her – such sudden tantrums and quiet, long silences, eyes gazing nowhere, as if she had gone into another world. Yes, a child touched in a way, Eileen thought, just like the one in the poem. A changeling maybe, that the fairies would take if they were back home. And, God love her, why wouldn't she be like that? – out here in this God-forsaken place with so much to put up with: her mother on edge most of the time, neglecting her, and her father at the rum bottle whenever he appeared. Not her real father, of course. She had always known who that was – the King of England. Hetty was her little princess.

'Now lie down and go to sleep, the two of ye,' she told them. 'And no chitter-chatter, or I'll have Josephine with her divils up the stairs at ye!'

Eileen took the lamp, leaving a night-light burning on a stool by the half-open door leading to the dark landing. Outside the wind had dropped and the croak of frogs everywhere on the lawn rose clearly up into the nursery out of the velvet night.

Robert sighed and bit his lips. Even before Hetty had pretended to put the great *crapaud* in his bed he'd been frightened of the frogs, but couldn't admit it. The huge frogs were everywhere on the island, quite harmless – they ate them even, though he didn't. Mountain chicken they called them. But he had nightmares about them now.

'Hear the froggies, can you?' Hetty whispered over to him.

'No.'

'Yes, you can. They don't hurt, you know. Here, I've got something for you, if you're frightened.'

'I'm *not* frightened.'

'I sometimes am – cook's werewolves and zombies.'

Hetty pushed the mosquito netting aside and tiptoed across to Robert's bed. She held a reel of button thread, taken from Mildred's sewing basket that afternoon. 'Here, you hold one end,' she told Robert. 'And I hold the other. And if we're frightened in the night we can just pull on it.'

She gave Robert one end, returning to her own bed, playing out the cotton-reel behind her.

'That's a stupid idea,' Robert mumbled.

'No, it's not. You'll see!'

In her own bed now, she pulled the thread, gently, reassuringly, several times. After a long moment, grudgingly, Robert pulled it back. They drifted to sleep, the thread still in their hands.

Sometime after dinner, when Frances had gone to her bedroom, Bruce, glass in hand, moved into the hall and started playing the collection of mildewed hurdy-gurdies, barrel organs and pianolas that his father had collected and brought to the house in the years when he had stayed there. Bruce was swaying now as he set them all off in a twanging cacophony of discordant sound: 'Down at the Old Bull and Bush', 'The Blue Danube', 'Pale Hands I Loved'.

Letting the instruments stammer on alone then, moving to the centre of the hall by the mahogany staircase, he danced with himself, swirling around in his stiff evening clothes and pumps – swooping and floundering as he tried to egg on an imaginary partner to ever greater efforts. The machines gradually wound down; the music stopped. He made for the rum bottle again in the dining room, drank the rest of it, then went upstairs, entering Frances's bedroom where she was well awake.

'Let me – sleep here – with you.'

'No – in no circumstances—' He stumbled, falling

through the mosquito netting over the big bed. 'No, you drunken oaf. No, *never*!'

'Ah, please,' he whined. 'It would make it, us – everything so much better.'

He reached forward, lying on his stomach, pawing at her, his sweaty hands sliding over, but failing to grip, her almost equally damp skin. Then, angry suddenly and violent, he tried to force himself on her, clawing up over the sheet, flailing his hands about in the netting. Rising to his knees as he approached her, he stripped the sheet away in one wild movement where she lay before him now in a thin cotton nightdress.

He tried to rape her, pulling at her shoulders, ripping the fine material there, exposing her breasts, tugging the dress down below her midriff. But, before he could do more, Frances leapt from the bed.

She fought him then, nightdress gone, a naked virago, in a tremendous battle up and down the bedroom, as if her life depended on it – as it might have done: a vicious, silent bout which had the air of some condemned sport, the room a gladiators' pit or a cock-fighting pen now, the two of them circling each other, black and white figures, Frances's bare limbs and moist ivory skin shining in the lamplight, confronting this enraged stage-door Johnny in his dark dress suit.

She did not have his strength, but he was drunk and slipshod – while her fury, her terror and horror of the man, released a tremendous energy in her, a long pent-up frustration as she parried his blows, dodged round chairs, lunged at him with a brass candlestick, as he tried to corner her. Finally, seeming to have trapped her, he crouched in front of her, about to spring. She thumped the candlestick down on him. But it glanced off his shoulder – and then he was on to her, only inches between their sweating faces, pinioning her arms to the wall. She bit him deeply on the neck and he yelled out and she escaped into the room again.

Rounding the bed he caught her before she reached the door, dragging her back, clasping her in both arms, lifting her bodily towards the bed. But he stumbled then and they both fell, wrestling over and over on the floor, where, with his weight, it seemed he must finally get the better of her, pinning her arms down now, straddling her.

Looking up at him, she appeared to relax, letting her body go limp. She even smiled a fraction. He moved onto her. Then, at the last moment, she brought her leg up sharply into his groin – a vicious blow with her kneecap – so that he screamed again, doubled up, rolling away from her, writhing in agony.

Frances was on her feet in a flash, opening the door, running down the landing to Eileen's room at the far end, where Eileen, disturbed by the general commotion, was already standing by the doorway. She took Frances inside, locking them in. Frances's skin was bruised, grazed – and coursing with sweat. But there were no tears. She was simply furious.

'What happened—'

'What do you think?'

'No – no.'

'Except that it didn't happen. But I'll kill him all the same. I'll *kill* him.'

'No, be calm—'

'What else, Elly? What else can I do?' she asked venomously.

'Nothing. Wait till morning. Stay here with me.'

At the other end of the dark landing the children stood peeking out from the half-open doorway of their bedroom. Henrietta had heard the shouts and seen her mother, a shadowy naked figure running down the landing. She put her thumb in her mouth now, sucking vigorously, wide-eyed. Then she saw her father leave the bedroom, bent over, groaning as he made for the staircase. What had happened? He must have eaten something nasty – that was it. She hoped he had. She hated him. Robert stood beside her. 'I don't like it at all,' he said. 'The frogs – and now this. I don't like it – even with the thread.'

'We could run away.' Henrietta turned to him.

'Where?'

'The mountains. Slinky said he'd show us.'

'No. The Caribs live up there. They eat people.'

'Not now, silly – Mama said.'

'Still—'

'Anyway, Slinky is nearly a Carib. He knows them. We'd be quite safe.'

'We'll see.'

'He must have eaten something very bad,' Hetty said as they went back to their beds.

'Yes. One of those awful frogs, I expect. Serves him right.'

They set the thread up between them again, pulling at it several times before they finally slept once more.

Bruce Fraser left on the packet next day, without speaking to her – and thank God, Frances thought. He would be away for months now, in Jamaica, where he shared a house with some army cronies, or in Fort de France, south in Martinique, where he had a Creole mistress – or back in Europe even, in Paris or Piccadilly. She never knew where. They never corresponded. The old belt-and-braces Scotsman, McTear, who lived by the sugar mill, ran what was left to run of the estate. Bruce came and went as the mood – and his considerable fortune – took him. He would be here again in the winter, no doubt, with his friends from Jamaica, for the shooting – the annual drive on the sheer-sided plateau in the mountains behind the house where Alisdair Fraser had imported some bison and deer from America years before. And the two cougars, which had been heard but not seen since. Meanwhile she had six months' peace and freedom before he returned. Time to think, to plan. But to plan what? How to escape from him? Escape where?

Out on the veranda, she took another crystallized fruit – a Carlsbad plum – from the half-empty box beside her, munched it, biting into its deep sticky juices appraisingly: the last box, but she had ordered another dozen from the Army and Navy Stores in London. So what if she had put on a good deal of weight? – if these sweet sticky fruits and other bonbons had become an irresistible obsession with her in these last years? *Tant pis*. Who would notice her weight out here anyway? It was her one luxury and she needed it more than ever that afternoon.

She lay in the creaking canvas hammock looking out at the great green mountains, another day of humid sunshine, lowering clouds rolling in from the Atlantic, listening to the waves, a faint but ever-present roar on the other side of the house. She had come to love this windward side of the island, where so few people either lived, or fancied living – the several hundred colonial administrators, businessmen and planters with their families who clustered about Roseau. They rarely ventured windward across the island, for it was a quite different world here, a different climate divided by the great mist-topped mountains, looking east towards Europe, sometimes almost European in its weather: a world of cloud-coloured sunrise, moist daybreak, and vivid fresh, rain-damp mornings, sudden downpours alternating with long fierce bouts of sunshine throughout the day. If you looked seaward and forgot the rampant green vegetation – well, one might almost have been in Ireland, on that headland in Kerry, nudging out into the warm Gulf Stream, which she had visited as a child from Summer Hill, where there were even a few palm trees, tropical plants . . .

Yes, this windy, sea-spumed, rocky coast reminded Frances a little of Ireland, where she wanted to be – whereas the leeward side of Domenica, when she was there, did nothing but suggest a permanent exile for her: a kingdom of torpid afternoons and calm sunsets, ever-clear skies and glittering smooth Caribbean waters, a crystal sea, pellucid lagoons – where coloured fish spun and dived languidly. She had come to resent all the lax, unrelentingly tropical beauty there – as if the drowsy, balmy climate over that part of the island might weaken her resolve, disarm her, relax her fierce purpose, which was to return home. So she saw herself, remembering her mother's Spanish phrase *sol y sombra*, as a woman in shadow here, as the sun sank early below the mountains – but temporary shadow, dispelled very early each morning by glorious windswept, spume-drifting day.

These incandescent sunrises – seen from her bedroom window before she went riding along the dew-soaked overgrown tracks across the citrus fields – seemed to offer her sure promise of a change in her life, a place in the sun without shadow, one day, somehow. So, as often before in her life, she saw herself in only temporary eclipse. Meanwhile she thrived on this wild coast, drew strength from its bracing winds, bitter storms and fierce sun – which so exactly reflected the imbalance and vehemence of her own nature now: the anger, the wilful overstatement and exaggeration of the exile.

She moved in the hammock, easing the bruise on her back, looking over at Mildred: Mildred, rather prim and correct, sitting in a high-backed chair near by, sewing the torn collar on one of Robert's sailor suits. Noticing Frances's gaze, and seeing again the other livid bruise on her cheek, Mildred looked down, embarrassed, concentrating once more on her work. 'He won't need the suit till he's back in Roseau next term. But how he does go through his clothes! I suppose you'll be sending Hetty over to the nuns, too,' she added without looking up.

'Yes. No. I don't know.'

'But, Frances, she can't go on running wild over here, just with you and Elly and the priest teaching her – have to have some real lessons. Robert, as well. He'll have to go to school in England soon.' Mildred looked up, touching the mousy curls on the crown of her head, scratching the scalp there, delicately, surreptitiously.

'I want us both to go *home*, not settle here – you know that, Milly,' she told her impatiently. Mildred was kind but poor, Frances thought: fatally put upon by her decent, but impossibly vague husband. She was too yielding, afraid even to think of her best interests there. Though five years older than her, Mildred, with her thin cheeks, watery blue eyes and small mouth, had the air of a simple, uncertain child. She had never criticized Frances for her indiscretions; she had seemed simply unaware of them, as if she really believed babies came from storks or from beneath gooseberry bushes.

Of course Mildred, though she knew of the inappropriate pregnancy, had not witnessed or known any details of Henrietta's birth. No one on the island had. She and Bruce had been married in Jamaica, where he was serving with a West Indian regiment, and they had left at once for an extended honeymoon, lasting nearly six months, in America, where Henrietta had been born in the large apartment they had rented in New York, a house looking over the Hudson on Riverside Drive. And Milly had never since commented on these tactful evasions.

Yes, Frances thought, she had always been kind and considerate in her way, ever since she and Eileen had first arrived on the island. But it was an infuriatingly vague, and therefore an unhelpful, understanding which she had offered, so that the idea of having to live permanently in that indeterminate, discreet atmosphere, where nothing seemed entirely understood or meant, where not even birth seemed important, had appalled Frances.

And so, all the more, she had taken to Bruce – seeing, beyond the man, to the freedom of this big house where she could be her own mistress. Yes, she had rushed into the marriage, for that among the other reasons her husband had mentioned the previous night. It had all been a calculated act of desperation, and she had since paid the price for it with her husband. Yet the house remained at least where, when he was away, she controlled her own destiny. And that had been worth the price. Yet she could not live here for ever – not for a moment.

'We must go *home*, at some point, Milly. You do see that.'

'Indeed, the way he treats you . . .' Mildred paused. Then, with a rare tremor of emotion in her bland voice, she said, 'It cannot be *safe* for you here alone with him, Frances. But how may you return? Apart from Bruce, your mother remains adamant, I imagine?'

'I imagine – we never correspond. But these things are sent to try us, Milly. There will be a way. It will happen.'

'But, meanwhile, why not come back with us to Roseau? To Lime Hill – there is more than enough room. Hetty would have Robert and the other girls at school. I cannot think how you *survive* out here alone – just you and the girl.'

'Oh, I have my riding, my walks – the dispensary in the village every morning. And what I can do to keep the house and estate up – with old McTear: a dour fish. But at least we see eye to eye. And there's Father Bertin – my English conversation lessons with him. Not the greatest company – lacks response – but a decent enough young man. And I have Elly – and my letters, books, newspapers from home.'

The letters, Frances thought: yes, they were her real lifeline – the correspondence she maintained with Dermot and with Ruth Wechsberg at Grosvenor Crescent, still running the nursing home. Apart from her mother and Eileen only these two others knew the real paternity of her child – and so, with them, she could be entirely open, about the past, present, future.

So she waited on the jetty eagerly each fortnight for the mail packet – to send out her own letters, taking in those others which meant so much to her. One letter, of course, had never come – from the Prince, now King Edward VII: no whisper of a message, though she had written to him again from New York after Hetty's birth. Silence – as if they had never met, loved, so needed each other: a complete, dead-making silence which had amazed her before the anger had come, a black hatred for him, as for her mother, who had so casually forecast just such a result.

Ruth Wechsberg had explained his behaviour with more tact – but none the less as something which Frances ought to have seen as inevitable: of course, the Prince had behaved like a child. But he had become at that point the King Emperor, as well as a child, and it was simply these combined factors which had prevented him making any acknowledgement of her plight, of his paternity. Surely Frances could appreciate that? Frances had been unable to. As Prince he had managed everything to his – and her

– advantage. As King, with all the more power, he had betrayed her. It was as simple as that.

His courtiers – Lumley, Knollys and the others – would have insisted on an absolute break and denial, of course, Frances knew that. But Edward himself, remembering their trust together, should certainly have responded. She had wanted nothing material of him, she had made that clear – nothing but a simple acknowledgement of, and hope for, their child. Failing in this, he had denied his own blood – and that was what she would not forgive him for. Blood transcended everything, she felt – even royal dynasties. She had written as much to Ruth, only to have the reply that unfortunately it was precisely this dynastic element in the matter that had sealed Edward's mouth, and would do so, for ever.

But Frances still refused to accept the situation. Instead, she fanned the flames – was pleased to let this betrayal come to obsess her. During these eight years on the island she increasingly brooded on the injustice of her fate, encouraged the running sore, tore the scab off each morning, so that it had become a great wound. She thrived on exaggerating her plight – at the hands of the Prince, her mother, her husband Bruce. She saw herself as a martyr and was happy to feed the urge she now felt for pain – a pain that could only be truly satisfied by revenge.

This seemed to her an entirely natural response. She was not aware that, in pursuing these thoughts so exclusively, her character had changed much for the worse. She was no longer outgoing; her happy, voracious taste for life had almost entirely disappeared. She stopped no clocks now, for she held no bright deeds before her. Time out here, in this rampant green world, enfolded her, immobile, with only one real, if unconscious, aim in mind – to punish others as she had been punished.

Indeed, without her being aware of this either, Frances had taken on all the dark aspects of the island – the malignity, sickness, horror, that lay behind the drowsy beauty – creeping up about her, stifling her, like the vines and lianas over the proud trees. For there was that, too, in

Domenica – a haunting sense of menace and evil: in the ever-present mildew, the grotesque phallic-shaped flowers, the huge black copulating toads, the vicious undertow of tides, the Boiling Lake, the Valley of Desolation, the great Devil Mountain. All the vivid, sun-drenched richness here concealed a suppurating decay – and Frances was part of this secret dissolution on the island.

So, in the intervals of nurturing this prized and pure obsession, she sought release only in mundane detail, in hawk-eyed, bullying attentions about the house and estate. She constantly reprimanded the servants, chivvied the cook, complained of the laundry, checked the larders each day against the food consumed – while her exchanges with McTear were not always carried on eye to eye, but in sharp argument. Her conversation lessons with poor Father Bertin were conducted very much *de haut en bas*, and she ran her village dispensary with a hard hand.

Yet to Frances these character changes, when she recognized them at all, were entirely justified. They were part of a higher purpose, foundations to a holy cause; she had purged herself of happiness and pleasure, living in a searing fire now, and thus all the more certain of resurrection. So taken was she by these grim defects, that she never saw how she had assumed what she most scorned: all the worst characteristics of her mother.

She fingered the Carlsbad plums – ate two of them in quick succession, then looked at Mildred: poor Mildred, she thought, accepting her fate, settling for so much less.

'A plum, Milly?' She offered her the last in the box.

'No, my dear, not now.' Mildred looked at her kindly – withholding the reproof she felt. How the poor woman fed herself, she thought, between meals, with these great sticky fruits. Quite shocking really, and what a bad example to the children. But then Frances had always been so wilful and unrealistic – and so unbalanced generally now. It was a charity to be here, to keep her company, to see she came to no harm. She hoped all the more she could persuade her to return to Roseau with her in September, at the end of the holidays.

A mournful horn, a single drawn-out funereal note, sounded then – slowly, faintly repeated on the wind coming from the bay: a conch shell. Some Caribs returning in their canoes from a fishing expedition, advertising their arrival. Mildred felt a shiver of unease creep up over the back of her neck, a cold *frisson* of fear in the humid afternoon. The Caribs had been tamed long ago, so it was said, and none of them lived now on the leeward side of the island. They had all been moved to a reserve, on the windward side, up in the mountains beyond Castle Bruce, four years ago. But Mildred feared them somehow all the more for that – in that they were hidden now, all together in one group, free to plot any sort of mischief, inaccessible in the vast jungle above them, whence she felt they might emerge one day in force, to rape and pillage or, worse, devour one – for that had been their speciality.

'Those Caribs,' she said to Frances. 'They make me uneasy. You really shouldn't stay here alone.'

'Nonsense, Milly. Unless aggravated, they're quite harmless. Lying in their hammocks smoking that weed, fishing, a little brandy-smuggling, from the French islands: that's all they're up to now – and their snakeskin and basketwork. Quite wonderful. Look at your own sewing basket there, those lovely diamond patterns!'

Mildred looked doubtfully at the snake-skinned basket by her feet, then moved her ankles away sharply. Frances ate the last of the Carlsbad plums.

The children, with Slinky, were at the end of the lawn where he was scything the long grass beyond the mango trees with a cutlass. He paused, suddenly, in his work. Something rustled in the undergrowth of fern and columbine.

'Voyé,' he said, a sly smile spreading over his copper-coloured, slightly Carib-featured face. 'Someone là.' He spoke a rough mix of English and the island patois.

'A *crapaud*?' Hetty asked. Robert retreated a fraction. For answer Slinky put his hand into the greenery and pulled out a large snapping land crab, a vivid orangey-pink colour, holding it judiciously by the back of the shell.

'My!' Hetty beamed, coming up to examine it more closely.

'Vou' mange ça.' Slinky looked appraisingly at the vicious animal.

'It's horrible.' Robert turned away. 'Come on, Hetty – Elly promised to take us to the Emerald Pool this afternoon.'

They left Slinky, running across the lawn towards the outhouses and kitchens to one side of it. Josephine was there, inside the smoky kitchen, talking to Annie, the cook and obeah woman, and Jules the sailor. Cook was at the table, making a paste of bread and water, flattening it out. Beside her, in an open matchbox, Hetty saw the large spider, a furry beast, quite motionless. Annie picked the insect up then, delicately, sitting it on the dough, doubling it over with equal care so as not to kill the spider, making a sandwich of it – and giving the snack to big Jules who ate it down in one mouthful.

Robert looked on horrified. Hetty had seen it all before. Jules was very pleased with himself. 'Dat much good – très bon.' He stretched. 'Ma poor bones – they al' stiffy and crackling from too much sea,' he said, smiling hugely.

'Big Jules – he got the akeanpain,' Josephine said.

'And Slinky caught a great, *great* crab,' Hetty shouted. 'Out in the ditch beyond the mango trees.'

'Good for he,' Josephine said. 'He eat him très bon and fast. Je'spare he don' get that one anaconde là, but.'

Big Jules laughed, white teeth glittering now, as he digested his medicine. He shook, his great dark muscles dancing beneath the old loose blue, brass-buttoned navy waistcoat, which was all he wore above his trousers. 'Slinky,' he said, 'he want no anaconde woun' all roun' lui.'

'There's *no* snakes out there,' Robert said firmly, hoping the wish would stand for the fact. 'Only in the mountains. Where's Elly? She's promised to take us to the Emerald pool.'

'Voyé!' Jules bent down to Robert conspiratorially.

'When you get to Emerpool – you take that big gommier tree là, you know him by water?' Robert nodded. 'You cut skin off him, petit peu, and you come back and give it here to Josephine. She wan' that one petit peu skin of that tree!' He stood up, laughing uproariously. Josephine scolded him good-naturedly, flapping her arms about over his head. 'Diable homme!' she shouted. 'J'n' veux pas le gommier – pas tou'!' She scolded him some more, chasing him round the kitchen, before the children left.

'What's special about the skin of the gommier tree?' Robert asked Eileen as they walked away beyond the lawn, across a ruined citrus field, towards the forested hills and the Emerald pool half a mile away.

'Who was talking about it?'

'Big Jules – he said I should get some for Josephine.'

'Nothing. Just a charm. One of their medicines.' Eileen hid her embarrassment. The *gommier* bark, in fact, stewed up, was one of their strongest love potions.

'Like the spiders they eat – Jules was having a spider,' Hetty said easily. 'They eat all *sorts* of strange things over here to make them better, you see,' Hetty told Robert wisely.

She picked up a little hard green lime from an old tree as they passed – sticking her nails into it, scoring the skin deeply, putting it to her face immediately, the sharp tart smell fizzing up her nose. She loved this limey essence of the island, loved all this windward part of it with its wild greenery, towering rain forests, mountains, birds, animals; the wonderfully coloured Sisserou parrot, the tiny humming birds, just like dragonflies, stabbing their rapier beaks into the sweet orchids, the rare *siffleur montagne* with its half-dozen sadly repeated flute-like notes; the possums, land crabs, frogs – even the great cockroaches that crackled across the floor or buzzed over the evening lamps.

She knew every hidden track and grove and stream between the estate and the hills, running wild in this arcadia, touched with dazzling, rain-filtered light – rainbows arching out, one after the other, over each mist-topped hill, a lost world at the end of the wide Sargasso

Sea: the ripe fruit dropping everywhere about the estate – coconuts, breadfruit, bananas, mango, papaya, grapefruit, oranges, limes – fallen in the long grass, where she could slake thirst or hunger; the servants round the cook-house in the short twilight at Hallowe'en or Christmas, murmuring of zombies, soucriants and loups-garoux – the mysteries then as she looked out into the shadowy night, velvet-blue, soft, with muted calls and little stirrings.

This was Henrietta's world, which enveloped her, an ever-renewed wonder that took her heart each morning, day long, until she snuggled up with Eileen after sunset. She never wanted to go back to Roseau – or go to England or Ireland for that matter, wherever they were, with all that silly snow and pea-soupers.

They walked now, beyond the estate, up rising ground into the hills, along a moss-slippy forest path towards the Emerald pool. The temperature dropped quickly after they entered the forest – becoming mould-damp beneath the vast, vine-clad trees. Finally, hidden at the bottom of the winding path, lay the pool, crystal-green, with a sheer fall of water from a gash in the cliff fifty feet above it, the rock bowl beneath shrouded by overhanging branches, huge trees, the mammoth-buttressed *châtaignier* tree and the *gommier*, a wonderfully smooth grey, pillar-like hardwood rising a hundred feet. Beneath these primeval giants, in the filtered sunlight, climbing plants pushed and clung everywhere – lianas, vines, growing up from a carpet of silver and gold ferns, gold-dusted on the underside, leaving a meticulously detailed imprint on your hand when you grasped them.

Henrietta adored this secret bathing place – the 'Shamelady' tendrils in the moss, withdrawing, seeming to die when you touched them; the tiny mushrooms, which she cupped in her hands, seeing them glow luminously in the dark; the razor grass which guarded the approaches: this no-one-else-in-the-world place, even the air a scented green, she thought.

The children frolicked in the pool, drumming their feet in the water from smooth dark boulders, slipping down into the creamy green foam, splashing in the shallows. Eileen, on the rim of the pool, sat in a brilliant shaft of sunlight, watching them: Hetty, tall for her age, but skinny, with far more of her mother's features than her father's – the raven-dark, gold-tinted hair falling away in straggling ringlets to either side of a high brow, a very straight nose between the perfectly oval blue eyes, the mouth shaped in an equally perfect cupid's bow, a doll's chin jutting out, before receding delicately to the long neck. Yes, like a china doll, Eileen thought, with that pale skin that had never browned or taken on the olive shades from her mother.

Yet in every other way, outside these perfect frail features, she was so far from any cosy repose – the character of a wilful tomboy, forever moving, pushing, dancing about, all a restless twitter, like a bird. All this – and then the sudden silences, striking her down, after some rebuff or rebuke or without reason, when the thumb-sucking started and the deep blank gaze into nowhere. And when you spoke to her then – at best the stammered, strangled response, unable to get a word out properly.

Robert, against this seesaw of busy tirades or silences, kept a ready balance with Hetty most of the time, unmoved by her violent swings of behaviour: a steady boy, slow to anger, Eileen knew – tall for his age, dark, lank hair, mild-eyed, careful, considerate, an ordinary boy. Hetty was lucky to have him as a companion. Most other children would never have put up with her.

She watched them playing tag now in the water – Hetty pushing and feinting about expertly, teasing, even bullying Robert in the game, despite her being a year younger. Robert was stronger. But he did not use the advantage, Eileen saw – allowing her to get the better of him.

'Stop it, Hetty!' Eileen shouted. 'Don't pull his hair like that – that's not tag.' The two of them were locked together, struggling in the middle of the pool.

'Stop it!'

They did – when Robert, using his superior strength at

last, simply pushed Hetty over backwards, and she went under, coming up choking, crying.

Eileen waded in, carrying her out of the pool. 'I told you, Hetty, *not* to go on teasing him – serves you right. You must listen to me.'

'Won't!' Hetty screamed between her sobs. 'Won't ever! He's just *rude*,' she screamed.

'It's you who are rude, my girl. Pulling his hair like that – the very idea! Why can't you behave yourself, just for once?' Eileen was angry.

Hetty went all quiet then, apart from an odd choked whimper, sucking her thumb, looking up at Eileen with doleful, tear-filled eyes, an unbearably sad expression, so that Eileen took her in her arms for a moment. 'Now, Hetty, don't – please – go all like that. *Please.*'

'C-c-can't help,' she stammered, before burying herself in Eileen's arms.

High above them, in the deep clotted undergrowth over the waterfall, the young, half-naked Carib gazed down at them through the leaves, puzzled at all this strange behaviour beneath him. His skin was a light shining bronze, minutely beaded with spume-mist from the falls, the hair straight and jet-black, cut in a perfect fringe across his high forehead, a dark curtain over the Mongolian features, wide cheek-bones, slanting almond eyes. He stood there, unblinking, dead still yet intensely alert – the face of an Inca god, a gold disc staring out of the greenery.

He had been lying in wait for the anaconda for several hours. He knew it was there, somewhere about the pool. He had seen it, stalked it down here, all morning. And now these white people had come to disturb it, before time, before twilight when it would come out to feed by the pool. He was annoyed, fingering the cutlass at his side. It was a fine snake, almost as long as his father's fishing dug-out – therefore old and bad-tempered. But he would have it.

Then, in the sloping undergrowth on the far side of the pool, he saw a slow rippling movement, following a line, as if the ferns had been caught in a breeze. A few moments later, the big, questing wedge head came in sight, followed by the great olive-green length of the anaconda with its double line of black spots: the snake was easing down towards the water where the little boy was still playing.

Running and sliding now, half-way down the side of the gorge, the Carib heard the screams. By the time he reached the pool the snake was already in the water, making purposefully for the boy, who had slipped in his attempts to escape it, now on his feet again, but with the anaconda still closing on him.

The Carib dived at it, going straight for the head, grasping it there with both hands, squeezing behind its now-distended jaws, wrenching it away, grappling with it, arching its head up, as the coils, thick as a fat thigh, began to encircle him, its tail thrashing about in fountains of spray.

The reptile tightened its grip, flailing round the Carib's legs like a rope, so that he lost balance, swayed and fell, wrestling with the snake in a fierce battle, turning over and over in a turmoil of foam, snake and man wedded together in one pulsing body – two skins, bronze and green, merging, flashing, fighting for their lives, in the sunlight.

The Carib disappeared underwater altogether, the anaconda in its true element now, crushing, squeezing. And, though the man rose a few moments later, he was half-trussed now, up to his waist, in its glistening, pumping coils, taut string tightening over a parcel.

Robert had escaped unharmed to the other bank – part of a huddled, screaming group there. The Carib meanwhile, his arms still free, had managed to struggle with his great burden to the far side of the pool where he had left his cutlass. Picking it up he started to slash repeatedly at the snake, opening livid gashes in the coils about his thighs and feet. The anaconda relaxed its grip a fraction, blood beginning to colour the water as the young man cut away at his bonds, chunks of skin and flesh flying out like chips from a tree.

But, even so wounded, the snake fought on viciously,

continuing to wind its upper coils round his chest. Finally, its body severed almost completely half-way along its length, the snake, losing its anchor, fell away from him. The Carib, covered in blood, some from his own self-inflicted wounds, shouted exultantly. Eileen and the two children fled.

The atmosphere was exhaustingly humid and still on the veranda. The breeze had died entirely in the twilight, and a great blanket of bruised grey cloud had come to hover over the house. 'There's no question,' Mildred told Frances. 'You – we – we cannot stay here. We must leave, all of us, at once – all far too dangerous. Robert is quite devastated, the shock—'

'No, I'm not, Mama.'

Robert, in fact, after his initial terror, had come to reflect on the afternoon's adventure with growing pride: he had escaped the great serpent – why, he had very nearly fought and grappled with it himself. Hetty had been full of praise for him.

'It was *wonderful*,' she told her mother happily. 'The brave Carib, saving our lives—'

'That's just it,' Mildred put in, greatly agitated. 'Think what might have happened!'

'Indeed.' Frances was actually quite relaxed over the matter. 'I only wish we could thank him for his bravery.' She turned to Mildred. 'We shall stay here. You, of course, must do as you think best. Though I wonder if you're not making a little too much of it all? And, remember, it's August, start of the bad weather: hurricane season, storms and gales at least. You and Robert might run far more risk on the boat back to Roseau.'

'Frances!' Mildred summoned up a quite unusual firmness in her attitude now. 'We shall leave on the next packet. And you should come with us.'

Almost as soon as she had finished speaking they heard the first of the thunder, a long gathering rumble out over the bay, which soon moved over the house, in crackling explosions with spits of blue lightning. Afterwards the rain came in solid curtains and during the night a fierce wind, which lasted for days, the sea rising in vast breakers, dashing up over the cliff beneath the house, rattling the storm shutters, the Hall tight shut now all round against the searing gales. The packet from Roseau was inevitably cancelled and everyone stayed indoors for the next two weeks.

Hetty looked at her mother, across the table from her, explaining Consequences. They were playing with Robert and Mildred.

'I do the head,' her mother spoke dictatorially. 'Then fold the paper over – so – then pass on for you to do the neck, a funny neck, then Mildred does the body—'

'Yes, Mama – I *do* see how.'

Her mother frowned at this interruption, bunched her fingers up. Mama was so bossy, Hetty thought. She pushed the lock of dangling hair from her eye, for the umpteenth time.

'You really must wear that hair-clip, Hetty,' her mother said. 'Told you a dozen times – you'll get a squint.'

'Don't want a hair-clip.'

'Eileen will have to sugar your hair again, then – and you won't like that.'

Hetty glowered at her mother. No, Elly wouldn't. Several times, for 'occasions' – the last had been for the funeral of the estate foreman's wife at the Catholic church – Eileen, on her Mama's instructions, had soaked all the wavy frizzle from her hair with a sticky mix of sugar and water, flattening it, letting it dry out in a hard shell: horrible. Why was her mother so beastly – and why did she have such difficult, long, wavy dark hair anyway?

'I'm tired of my hair,' Hetty said, most petulantly. 'Why don't I have easy straight short hair – like you and Papa? Then I'd never have to have beastly clips or sugar in it!'

Her mother did not reply, looked down at her bit of paper, bunching her fingers again.

When Hetty's turn came she drew, as her neck, the long spotted neck of a giraffe – so long that it went right down to the bottom of the paper and they had to start the game all over again.

'You are *difficult*, Hetty,' her mother said aggressively.

'But you said to draw a *funny* neck.' Hetty was genuinely surprised at there being any fault in her contribution. She thought: I don't like these games with the grown-ups – I prefer to play with Robert. After his courage in the pool with the great serpent she had come to like Robert. With all his fuss over that frog business in his bed, she had thought him a cissy. But he wasn't. Yes, he was more fun now. She really liked him – quite a lot.

'"Oh, soldier, soldier, won't you marry me
  With your musket, fife and drum!"'

Hetty sang out the first part of the game, which Aunt Mildred was teaching them. Then Robert sang his bit.

'"Oh, no! sweet maid, I cannot marry thee
  For I've got no hat to put on."'

Then Hetty came in again.

'"So up she went to her Grandmother's chest
  And she fetched him a hat of the very, very best,
  And the soldier put it on."'

'Now, Hetty,' Mildred said, 'you go out and get a hat for Robert – any hat will do: there's lots in the back hall.'

Hetty left the drawing room. She thought she was going to like this game, for she knew where there were some real army hats, and a lot of other army things, belonging to her father, in the cloakroom beneath the big staircase. She opened the door, smelling a damp mildewy smell, peering into the dark. But soon she found just what she wanted: a tall furry hat with a funny cockade, a red coat with lovely goldy things on the shoulders and a pair of great big black shiny boots. She took the hat out and brought it to Robert.

'Splendid!' Mildred said. 'Where did you get it?'

'In the cloakroom.' She put it on Robert, where it dropped right down over his eyes. But he looked lovely.

Hetty cooed with pleasure. 'Go on, Robert – sing the next bits – you need coats and boots and things now.'

'Can't – you have to sing your bit first.'

'"Oh soldier, soldier, won't you marry me
With your musket, fife and drum?"'

'"Oh, no sweet maid, I cannot marry thee
For I've got no coat to put on . . ."'

Hetty left again, bringing back the gold-braided scarlet tunic – and then the tall cavalry boots, until Robert was staggering round the room, the great boots almost up to his waist, arms half-way down the sleeves of the tunic – laughing fit to burst, Aunt Milly as well. Then her mother suddenly came into the room.

'Hetty! – what on earth's going on?' She looked at Robert, gallivanting around like a scarecrow. Her mother was angry.

'We're dressing Robert up – Aunt Mildred's teaching us the game – "Oh, soldier, soldier, won't you marry me?"'

Hetty looked up at her mother, surprised. She was very angry now.

'Who said you could? You're not to dress up in – in those army things. I forbid you – never – they're your father's, he'd be simply horrified.'

Her mother was flustered as well as angry, Mildred saw. 'I'm sorry, Frances,' she broke in. 'My fault – I'd no idea . . .' And nor she had, for she knew that Bruce could not care less about these old clothes of his, could not care less about anything in Fraser Hall.

Frances relented slightly then. 'No, I'm sorry.' She paused then, at a loss. 'It's just – I'm so much against – army things, especially for children.'

Hetty was upset. The game had to end, just when she was loving it, everyone loving it. Why *was* her mother such a spoilsport?

Mildred spoke to Frances later when they were alone. 'I'd really no idea,' she apologized again. 'Those old army things . . .'

'It's just I don't like them dressing up that way. So much against anything to do with war, the Boer war, you remember – I was there.'

She lied to Mildred convincingly. The pain had come back to her sharply, of course, the moment she had seen Robert dressed up, playing the soldier in the red tunic – so like the Dragoon's tunic she had once worn to capture Dermot's love. Frances hated her past then, all the failures there – and that failure, perhaps, more than any: if only she had been able to marry Dermot, none of this, nothing of it – this exile, this unruly child, this awful betrayal by the Prince – *none* of it would have occurred. How she hated herself, once more, for allowing it all to happen.

'I'm sorry – about the Boer war,' Mildred said. 'I'd quite forgotten. Your brother . . . Of course, I should have realized.'

'Never mind,' Frances said, still rather sharp, hearing the wind batter at the storm shutters. 'It's all a war really, isn't it? These things are sent to try us.'

She repeated the cliché, not in any stoic Christian tone – much more that of an Amazon about to do battle.

'Read us that fairy poem again,' Hetty said to Eileen that night, the two children tucked up in bed, listening to the wind whistle and moan outside.

'That's cissy,' Robert snorted.

'No, it's not—'

'Read us that story about the battle, Elly – the one you read the other night – that Finn man, who was he?'

'Fionn McCool, the great Irish warrior – picked up a clod of earth big as a whole county in the north, and threw it south, where it's a mountain now—'

'That's it!'

'I'll read both to ye – there, how's that?'

Elly got out the Irish *Homestead and Fireside* magazine again and read the tale of Fionn, one of his great exploits from the Gaelic sagas. Then she read the poem.

" "Where the wandering water gushes
From the hills above Glen-Car,
In pools among the rushes
That scarce could bathe a star,
We seek for slumbering trout
And whispering in their ears
Give them unquiet dreams;
Leaning softly out
From ferns that drop their tears
Over the young streams.
Come away, O human child
To the waters and the wild
With a faery, hand in hand,
For the world's more full of weeping
     than you can understand.' "

Hetty was not asleep, or near it, when Eileen came to
give her a goodnight kiss. She was almost agitated. 'What
ails ye, girl?' Eileen leant over her.

'The words,' she said. 'I don't know – not like ordinary
words, are they? All slippy and slidy and smooth!' Hetty
beamed, alive to something.

'Indeed, sure, isn't that the whole idea of it, girl? That's
poetry!'

2

At Christmas the weather was at its best – warm days, a
calmer sea, the leaves on the palms around Fraser Hall
idly flapping in the brilliant light. The flower beds on the
lawn bloomed with amaryllis, and were edged with great
sun-struck clumps of silver fern and pink and mauve columbine. And what was left to the fruit from the wrecked
citrus fields about the estate fell on the ground now, abandoned, over-ripe, soon rotten.

Flooding showers still came. But they fell from isolated, beleaguered clouds, running helter-skelter across the vast blue sky, pushed on by the fiery warmth of sun and wind, so that they dropped their load quickly, with a sudden drumming hiss, on the hot foliage, before disappearing over the mountains in drifting rainbows.

Henrietta itched and fidgeted in her stiff white blouse, long skirt, black stockings, black buttoned boots and wide-brimmed white hat with elastic under the chin – hating these special clothes, even though it was a special day. She sat on the veranda steps – neatly, quietly reading her book, as instructed by her mother, lying out behind her in the hammock. Hetty turned every few minutes, glancing covertly at her. At last her mother fell asleep.

Hetty stole away then, tip-toeing at first, before running down to the end of the lawn and hiding in the mango grove. She picked a fruit – ripe, deep red and yellow, small, round, very sweet and juicy as she sank her teeth into it. But the smell was even better than the taste, she thought, putting the warm skin, the freshly dripping bite, to her nose: a yellowy smooth sweet smell, like the colour somehow, but with another air to it, a deeper touch of something much stronger, the perfume of roses: yes, some of the garden roses – the ones her mother called Albertine, by the veranda – had the same overpowering, mysterious smell.

Taking the half-eaten fruit, she danced across the lawn, stopping, dipping her nose into various flowers as she went – roses, orchids, heliconias – comparing the flavours, darting from one to the next, savouring each bloom, feeding on it, like a humming bird. But soon, sated and confused by the different odours, she ran on round the house to her look-out point, a flat raised rock on the cliff above the cove, a crow's nest giving out over the bay, where she could wait for the packet steamer.

The breeze tipped and flapped at the brim of her hat, the elastic pinching her chin. Taking it off, she let her hair free, blowing out suddenly behind her, the long dark curls cutting sharply back over her brow, singing in her ears, as she gazed over the deep purple ocean with its dazzling whitecaps.

Free. She always felt a surging ecstasy, here on this rock, the waves moving towards her, rolling in, one after the other in endless succession, mesmerizing her, so that after a minute or two, as she gazed steadily at the same point out to sea, she felt as if she were moving, herself, floating away from the island, a strange sinking feeling in her stomach – as though she was swinging above the ocean on the bowsprit of a huge ship.

There was no sign of the packet yet, so she finished the mango and started to count off on her fingers the various exciting, favourite smells in her life. 'Well, there's lime,' she said. 'That's the first. Then mango and cook's ginger cake and those white roses by the veranda . . .' Then the other smells, she thought, quite different, strange – in the tin-roofed church at Castle Bruce where she went every Sunday with Elly.

There was that sort of flower pot on chains that Father Bertin swung about, which smoked and steamed and smelled delicious, a dry nose-tickling burny smell. That was exciting and so was Father Bertin in his green robe and white nightgown thing, his back turned to everyone, raising a silver cup and speaking to God in a funny language – and the little bell that one of the village boys rang every now and then, standing beside Father Bertin, dressed in another shorter white nightgown – and more than anything the statue of a young woman to one side of the table up there, almost a girl, dressed in a very grand gold and blue nightgown, who looked out at everyone with a terribly sad face. All that was very exciting – and strange because she never took any part in it, was cut off from it all.

Father Bertin and the boy were doing something frightfully important up at the table there, and she wished she was part of it all – the funny language, the little bell ringing, the tickly smell and the silences. But she wasn't. She was all kept out of it, and never went near the high table like the others did, sipping wine and eating little biscuity things. It wasn't her church, her mother had told her – that was why she couldn't ever join in on the game. She only went there with Elly because her church didn't exist in Castle Bruce. But she didn't want her church anyway. She longed to be part of Elly's church, to know what was going on up there at the table.

They were praying and offering things to God, of course – she'd been told that. But where was he? Elly had told her he was up in the sky, invisible, very far away. But she thought he must be sitting on the rafters, just above them – as he would have to be somewhere quite close to hear the prayers. And it was strange that people, everyone around her, took so much notice of someone they couldn't see at all. It was certainly some kind of game which these grown-ups played – a game to please God. God liked these games, though it was funny that he didn't seem to play at all in return – just sat on the rafters, invisible.

Some of the estate people and servants at the Hall didn't like God – Cook and Big Jules for example. They had a wicked God and played different games with him, and that was all very bad and secret, Elly had told her – because they were praying to the *devil*, not God at all. And Hetty knew how true this was. She had seen them playing with their strange church things behind the kitchens, beyond the laundry, only a week before, with Cook and Big Jules and some of the others, when they had killed the chicken – broken its legs and wings and then torn its neck off and the blood had spilled out all over the place. Horrible. That was a terrible game to play, but she hadn't told anyone about it, because she shouldn't have been hiding in the bushes in the first place, watching it all.

Well, that was the devil, of course. That was why it was all so horrible, and the church in Castle Bruce so nice, with the burny smell and the little bells and the lovely sad girl dressed all in blue and gold. That was all nice because it was God and it was good. And the other game with the chicken and the blood was bad. It was very simple – she could see that. The only trouble was that Cook and Big Jules were very kind to her and she had lots of fun with them. So why did they do such bad things playing with the devil?

She heard the ship's siren then, several long hoots, from out in the bay. The packet was arriving from Roseau, the last before Christmas: everyone was coming for the holidays – Aunt Mildred, Uncle Bertie, Robert, even her father with his army friends. Christmas was in three days' time – presents, tinsel, carols, crackers, and other good things, plum pudding, mincemeat pies and the big Christmas cake with icy snow on top, all the way from England. Henrietta ran back into the house, joining her mother and Elly and some of the boys, before they all made their way down the winding path to the cove and on to the jetty.

The packet was just dropping anchor beyond the cove, Big Jules and Slinky already out there, idling by with the steam launch, waiting to take the passengers and provisions off. Hetty jumped up and down, skidding on the wooden jetty with excitement.

'Keep still, child,' Elly told her. 'You'll fall in.'

'Can't wait. Look! – look at all those funny boxes and things.'

She had already seen her father, with his two friends, climbing down into the launch, carrying long leather cases over their shoulders. The Grants were already in the launch.

'And look – there's Robert!' Hetty waved at him, but he did not notice her in all the commotion.

'Yes, and you just behave with him this time, my girl. Remember what I said—'

'Oh, I'll behave – with all those presents from Father Christmas, Elly. What do you think he's got?'

'Wait and see.'

'He doesn't come down the chimney here, does he? Because we don't have any chimneys. He must come here by boat – must be on the packet there, somewhere hidden, mustn't he? We won't see him though, will we?'

'Quite right – hidden on the boat.'

'But he can't be *really* hidden, because someone would

see him, in his red coat and beard. So he must be invisible – like God.'

'That's right, girl. Invisible. But he comes all the same – you'll see!'

Invisible, Hetty thought – what an annoying word. Why couldn't you *see* things and people that were most important? Why couldn't you *see* a smell? All you had was words to tell you about them, and that wasn't the same thing at all. Words didn't actually give you the smell of the roses or the limes – except perhaps the poetry and the stories Elly read from her Irish book. That was funny – you felt something, you could almost smell things, from those kinds of words.

'Well? – what have you been doing out here?' Robert spoke in a distant, superior voice.

'Oh, the usual things.'

'I've been moved up to the fourth form at school in Roseau. We've been playing cricket this term. And I'm going to England next year – to a much bigger and better school, where I'll *sleep*, a *boarding* school!'

'Oh.'

'Lots of hard work and learning, my father says,' Robert declared with relish.

Hetty sat on her bed, fiddling with the mosquito netting, looking across at Robert arranging his things very neatly on his own bed: school books, exercise books, a wooden pencil box that he had brought with him. Hetty, seeing all this evidence of 'learning' and 'hard work', was a little in awe of him suddenly. Her own lessons, with her mother and Elly and Father Bertin, didn't seem half so grand. She had no pencil box.

'Why don't *you* go to school?' Robert took out a compass and a pair of dividers from the box, inspecting them carefully. 'You ought to. Everyone does.'

'Mama teaches me—'

'That's not *school*.'

'No. But there isn't a real school here – just for the villagers – so I can't.'

'My mother says you ought to be in Roseau with the nuns there.'

'Don't want to go to the nuns.' Hetty stood up. 'I have much better things over here.' She went to her chest of drawers and took out a collection of brilliant blue and green parrot feathers. 'Look! Slinky got them for me, in the mountains – from a real Sisserou parrot. The Caribs wear them in their noses and ears when they have a feast!'

'It's horrid – to kill parrots.' Robert looked at the feathers dismissively.

'And I've got this.' Hetty went back to the chest and pulled a Carib basket from beneath it, bringing it over to Robert, opening it carefully. Inside, on a bedding of stones, was a small iguana, beady-eyed, motionless, very dragon-like. 'A baby one. Lost its mother. I found it in the ditch beyond the lawn.'

Robert inspected it, from a distance. 'I don't like it,' he said finally, turning away.

'You're not frightened any more, are you – of froggies and things?'

'Course not.' He picked up a book he had brought with him. 'Just I'm busy with other things now, cricket – and trains and things.' He opened the book – *The Boy's Book of Railways* with a coloured picture of a steam engine on the front.

'Trains?' Henrietta said, rather bemused. 'Where you sit down in armchairs and get pulled along by a great smoky thing?'

'Of *course*, stupid. They don't have them here on any of these tiny little islands. But they're all *over* England. I'll be going on a train to my boarding school when I go home, Mama said. A *big* school.'

Hetty was annoyed. Robert had gone all grown up. He wouldn't want to play with her any more now – with all his talk about learning and cricket and trains. He wasn't the least interested in her parrot feathers or the little dragon. How could *she* be grown up? You had to go to the nuns in Roseau to be grown up, and then to a grand school in England and travel on trains and have a big pencil box.

But she wasn't going to these places and didn't have any pencil boxes or even proper exercise books.

Then she thought, well, I have those picture postcards that Mama's friend Miss Wechsberg and her cousin Dermot sometimes sent her, from all sorts of exciting places in England – photographs of places called Canterbury and Stratford-upon-Avon – and the huge hotel building in somewhere called Brighton.

She took the little collection of postcards from her drawer, showing them to Robert. 'See!' she said, rather huffily, 'I'll be going to all *these* grand places soon, on the train as well, when *I* go to England.' She pointed to the huge building, the hotel on the seafront in Brighton. 'I shall be going to school *there*,' she said stiffly. 'And that's the church I'll be going to, with *hundreds* of nuns inside.' She showed him the picture of Canterbury Cathedral; 'So, you see, I'll be doing much grander things than you very soon.'

Robert glanced at the postcards, bemused himself now. 'Well,' he said, putting them down. 'So what? Everyone goes to big churches and schools – in *England*.'

He believed her! She never thought he would – but he had. She'd told some really whopping lies and he'd believed them all! How terrible of her – but wasn't it funny when you made something up like that and people believed you? Just with words! You could change things exactly the way you wanted them, when they weren't really like that at all. You could be grown up in a moment with words, be anything you liked with them. That was very exciting. It was lying, of course. But what did that matter if it made you feel better – made you feel grown up and happy?

All the same she had qualms then and thought she ought to say something truthful. 'And anyway,' she said, 'when we go back home, Mama and Elly and me, we'll be living in a *much* bigger house than yours at Lime Hill or any of these ones: our *real* home, in Ireland – Mama's told me and shown me pictures of it – as big as Buckingham Palace!'

Robert laughed at her then, nastily. 'Well *that's* not

true,' he said. 'That's a lie! Your home is here – and you haven't got anywhere else.'

'It *is* true – we have!' Hetty raised her voice in desperation. 'Mama's told me, *promise* we have.'

'Rubbish.'

Hetty turned away, shocked and surprised. She started to suck her thumb. She wasn't going to cry, because it *was* true about Summer Hill, the huge house in Ireland. She *had* seen the pictures of it. Her mother had often talked about it, promising her – how one day they would be going back there. Funny, she thought, that people believed your lies but didn't when you told the truth.

Christmas approached with all its traditional local excitements. The strolling Creole carol singers, from Petit Soufriere in the south of the island, came up to the Hall on Christmas Eve, a dozen of them standing on the hot lawn with their banjos, fiddles and a wailing accordion. The women danced, clapping, singing in a wild syncopated rhythm, Africa revived across the ocean now, dressed in bright cotton prints – brilliant blues, red, yellows – with cockaded head scarves, while the men brought a similar frenzy to their instruments. The assembled company at the Hall watched from the veranda, the two children sitting in front of the steps, as the gaudy, loud-mouthed women, in the vivid patois of these Sewinal songs, rent the drowsy afternoon apart.

Sé pas dòt ki konmpè micho ki di
Sen Jozef papa Bon Dyé
Nou ka swété tout moun
An bon nwèl . . .

The voices swelled in unison, then fell away softly, almost to a whisper; then started up again in a burst – a sudden splatter of words, each hit harder than the last, running away from the music in a crescendo. Henrietta was entranced by it all: being black was warm and happy, she thought – white was cold and sad. She wished she was black.

Afterwards the players were given coffee and rum outside the kitchen quarters, with a hot broth and smoked wild meat, agouti and manicou, to go with it. And later, after dark in the flare-lit space beyond the laundry, there was more dancing and singing with the Hall servants and estate workers, going on far into the night.

At dinner the company heard the wild music, the songs, coming to them clearly on the still air.

'What *do* they sing about? It can hardly be Christian,' Mildred said, a note of unease in her voice, as the noise increased momentarily.

'Oh, yes – it *is* Christian,' Frances told her promptly. 'Those devils – "Diablotin" – they're singing about now: they believe they were all cast out when Christ was born and have been roaming about ever since, looking for somewhere to hide, which is why the locals have to band together now, to stop them getting into their houses. They're defending themselves from the devils with those songs – very Christian!'

Bruce, at the top of the table, looked at her derisively. 'You read far too much into these nigger songs. They have no real truck with Christianity – just to please us – and get their feasting and drinking here afterwards.'

'Not true!' Frances glared at him from the other end of the table. 'You ought to see them at church here – absolutely believing.'

'Just the Catholic mumbo-jumbo – that's what gets them: the Latin and the incense and communion and so on: like a black mass to them. That's why they take to it – and much more because they get baptismal presents for every child. Why, a lot of them move their children from parish to parish here, just to get the presents. But what can you expect from niggers?'

He drank deeply, smiling at his bachelor army friends, Algy Hermon and Roland Stockton. The two men, both a little younger than Bruce, returned the smile nervously. Algy, the taller one, prematurely balding, stroked his moustache carefully, seeming to think of a response. Roland, a nondescript, chubby little man, cleared his throat, as if about to speak. But nothing emerged from either of them.

Frances found both men dull and uncongenial to a degree. But their presence at the Hall occupied her husband, kept him away from her, and that suited her perfectly. Her husband led them by the nose, she could see that: they were in awe of him – his wealth, his possessions, his sophisticated airs. They came here only for the shooting, the annual Boxing Day drive up on the plateau, and thankfully would be gone soon afterwards, along with Bruce.

But meanwhile she was not going to let his last remarks pass. She was not to be so exposed, put down in public without a rebuttal; nor would she accept his dismissive references to the negroes. For all their faults, they were a subject people, just like the Irish: the British had made them so. And ever since her break with the Prince – the so-called 'King Emperor' now – she had taken violently against his empire and everything to do with it, infused with a nascent republican spirit.

'"Niggers"?' she said tartly, her voice rising. 'They are black because they are African, brought over here as slaves, by you people the British. And you simply dismiss them as niggers!'

'I do, for that is what they are – a heathen horde.' Bruce was getting drunk. 'Though we do our best for them.'

'What nonsense! You have done nothing but disinherit and enslave them, take them from their country, their homes – just as you've done with us, the Irish.'

'Hardly in your case, my dear,' he said sarcastically. 'It was not we – the British – who brought you here. A mere family matter, I believe.'

Frances was furious. A *frisson* of embarrassment had come over the dinner table. But she persisted – in angrily identifying now, as she had increasingly done during her exile, with both the negroes and the native Irish. 'My case has nothing to do with it. But with the others – they will rule themselves one day!'

'Ah, we have a "Home Ruler" here, I see. Not surprising, I suppose, given your cousin Mortimer Cordiner – up to the same mischief at Westminster! Well, so be it. Except it won't be. A pipe dream,' he added lightly, laughing easily, breaking the tension, so that the company laughed with him.

'The King,' Bruce said to them all then, suddenly raising his glass, getting up, the others joining him, chairs squeaking back on the floor.

Frances could have killed him: not because he knew the King was Hetty's father – he did not; but because he was forcing her now to honour a man whom she loathed beyond all men. Well, she wouldn't. She remained firmly in her seat. The others looked at her expectantly, glasses poised, waiting for her to rise. Instead, when she did rise, she turned on them and walked smartly out of the room.

'The poor woman,' Mildred murmured to her husband afterwards. 'Quite unhinged. As if the dear King were to blame for her problems.'

Bruce and the others had come back late after their Boxing Day shoot and Frances had not seen them that evening. But, the next morning, she sensed that something had gone wrong up on the plateau. The men had taken Slinky with them and a dozen others from the estate as beaters – and Slinky had not appeared for work in the garden that day. Frances went and spoke to Cook, finding her in an agitated state, fidgeting about the kitchen.

'What's happened, Annie – and where's Slinky?'

'Ah, Madame – Sinky, him not bon – he got the akeanpane au'joudi.' Cook rolled her eyes. Frances saw she was very upset about something.

'Not well? And you – what's the matter with you, Annie?'

'Madame, Sinky lui say to you—'

'No, *you* say to me!'

'There is one bad thing up on *morne* last jour.' Cook turned away, head in air, aghast at something.

'What bad thing up on the mountain?'

'The Carib peoples – Sinky lui say deu' shootin' là. Deu' morts.'

'Two *dead*?'

Cook nodded her head. 'Bang-bang an' they lie down and no get up encor.'

Frances left at once, confronting Bruce and his two friends in the dining room where they had just come down for a late breakfast.

'What nonsense,' Bruce told her. '*One* Carib and he certainly isn't dead! Slinky and Cook – exaggerating as usual.' He laughed nervously. The others joined him, picking at their grapefruit.

'One Carib? – well, what happened?'

'Just winged him in the arm – perfectly all right. We were driving a thick covert, full of bushes, by the stream up there. And these two Caribs – well, they were hidden in the bush, and one of them, like a bloody fool, started to move out of the bushes when they heard us, and I winged him. But he's perfectly fine – bandaged him up and gave him some money and he went home pleased as punch.'

Algy and Roland, albeit rather shamefacedly, concurred in this, so that Frances thought to believe them. It was true, after all – the locals, and especially Slinky, did tend to exaggerate things.

She began to think otherwise, though, when she went to look for Slinky down in the labour lines by the old sugar factory, and found he was not there. His room was empty. He had disappeared. She went on and found McTear, standing by the big entrance doors to the factory, the space deserted behind him and the man himself in a considerable state of dour agitation.

'What's happened? Where's Slinky? And all your men?'

'I was just coming up to the Hall to see ye, Mrs Fraser.' He spoke sharply. 'There's no men about,' he went on in his gruff Scots accent. 'They're all afeared – after what Mr Fraser and his party done yisterday up in yon hills—'

'What—'

'Shootin' yon Carib fella. They're all afeared now. And I dinna blame them. There'll be trouble.'

Frances was incredulous. 'But I've just been speaking

to Mr Fraser. He told me the Carib was only wounded, just grazed, that he went home—'

'He's no telling the truth then, Mrs Fraser. I talked wi' most of my men this morning, the ones beatin' up there yisterday, and they all say the same thing: the first Carib was shot dead – and the other behind him as well as far as I can tell.'

'I don't believe—'

'Why do ye think all the men have disappeared – only for that? Them Caribs are quiet enough – don't I know it meself these twenty years out here. But if ye cross thim, if ye *kill* thim, they'll take to the rum and the weed – and there'll be ructions.'

'What do you mean?'

McTear humphed. 'More than likely they'll be at us, that's wha' I mean.'

'*Attack* us?'

'That's what I hear – that's why the men ran.'

'But we'll have to get the police at once—'

'Indeed, old Sergeant Alwin and his two dozy men at Castle Bruce: a lot of use—'

'I mean at Roseau.'

'There's no packet for three days, Mrs Fraser – we're on our own out here till then.'

'Send the steam launch, then – get Big Jules.'

'I canna do that, Mrs Fraser, till the launch is repaired: remember, the boiler is out, since before the holiday.'

'So what can we do?'

'That's what I was just coming up to tell ye: git ready for them, Mrs Fraser, if they do come – that's all a body can do. And in the meantime meself and Big Jules will get on with repairing the launch.'

Frances returned to the Hall. She walked up to the head of the dining table where her husband was still at breakfast, pushing the plate of ham and eggs away from him, sending the lot spinning to the floor. Then, in her fury, she stood back and spat at him.

'You liar, you swine!' she told him, trembling. 'You killed one of those Caribs. I've just seen McTear – he says they may take revenge. You fool – you fools!' She turned and swept out of the room.

Bruce considered the matter. 'I'll go and see the old sergeant at Castle Bruce,' he told Algy. 'I can easily square him.'

The two men looked very ill at ease now. 'We'll have to get to Roseau as soon as possible, Bruce, tell them at police headquarters. It can't be a question of squaring anyone now,' Algy said carefully.

Bruce could no longer bluff his way out of it. 'Of course,' he said amiably. 'Well, we'll do that. But let's not lose our heads, shall we? Remember, it was an *accident*.'

Mildred turned white when Frances told her the news. She was in the drawing room, dallying with a novel, her husband Bertie at one of the open windows, looking out absentmindedly over the bay.

'What?' He turned, only half-hearing the story. 'The Caribs on the warpath, are they? I'd like to see that – hasn't been any of that for years. Caught brandy-smuggling again, have they?' Frances explained the situation once more for him. 'Oh, I *see*: Bruce shot them, did he? How very careless.' He spoke as if Bruce had done no more than poke them inadvertently with an umbrella. Bertie, an awkward, bumpy figure, much older than his nervous wife, rather frail and ageing, with deep-set sea-blue eyes and a careless beard, wore a permanently disengaged expression – always thinking of something else; his mind, like his body, spinning off at tangents. 'So what will they do now?' he asked vaguely, in his rather high-pitched sing-song colonial accent. 'War canoes? – they used to have splendid forty-foot war canoes.' He turned, picked up the field glasses kept by the window, and focused them out over the bay.

'Oh, don't be *stupid*, Bertie,' Mildred yelped at him. 'Not out there! They live up in the reservation, *behind* us, up in the hills. That's where they'll come from.'

'They probably – they won't do anything to us at all,'

Frances reassured her. 'Nothing to worry about. It's just that—'

'We shall all of us have to get away at once,' Mildred interrupted her, already in a panic. 'The steam launch, Bertie!' She stood up. 'The children. Where's Robert? We must all get away.'

'That's what I was just about to say,' Frances put in. 'The launch is out of action – being repaired. McTear and Jules are working on it now—'

'No *launch*? Oh, no! . . .' Mildred started to blub quietly then, shaking all over in little convulsions, seeming to shiver in the hot morning.

'My dear.' Bertie came over, consoling her. 'You mustn't take on so. It's nothing.'

'*Nothing?*' Milly was horrified. 'But they are *cannibals*, Bertie! How can you say it's nothing? We shall all be devoured.'

'Dearest.' He put his hand on her shoulder. 'The Caribs have not eaten in years – people, that is. Not in centuries. And this is the *twentieth* century – a Crown colony, magistrates, police . . .' He babbled on. 'And, besides, they eat only – only yams, breadfruit, bananas, a little maize . . .' He tripped on invitingly through a strictly vegetarian menu. 'There is no likelihood of their wanting to eat *us*,' he ended, like a butcher dismissing a very coarse cut.

'None at all, Milly!' Frances smiled quickly. 'There's nothing to worry about. Just that McTear said, well, that we should take precautions.'

'Precautions?' Milly wailed. 'We must do battle with them?'

'Of course not. Just . . .' Frances herself wasn't quite certain of what precautions might be in order. 'Just – we must all keep our heads and be alert – until we can get the launch going. Meanwhile, I'll look after everything.'

And so she did – going straightaway to speak to Bruce, out on the veranda now, smoking with his friends. She confronted them all with cold efficiency, like a sergeant-major. 'The men have nearly all disappeared,' she told them. 'McTear is trying to get the launch going. But until he does, and we can get to Roseau, you three stay out here on the veranda, in case they get drunk up in the hills and decide to do something stupid—'

'They won't,' Bruce told her brusquely. 'You're talking rubbish—'

'Don't *talk* to me! Just do as I say – stay here, outside with your wretched guns, if needs be – have them ready in any case.'

'What nonsense – against a few savages? They wouldn't dare!'

She glared at him. 'I prefer to believe McTear in the matter. Just *do* as I say!' she shouted.

Frances went off to find Elly and the children then. They were upstairs in their bedroom. Robert was playing with a new train set and Hetty reading her Christmas present from the Grants – *The Red Fairy Book*, engrossed in the tale of 'The Princess Mayblossom'. Elly was tidying their clothes in the wardrobe. Frances gave them the news tactfully. Only Elly was disturbed.

'Mother of God, what's Mr Bruce gone and done now—'

Frances, a finger to her lips, stopped her. 'Now, children,' she told them. 'You must not, on *any* account, leave the house. Elly, you'll stay with them, up here, all the time.'

'Will they fight us soon?' Hetty asked brightly. 'Before lunch, I mean. 'Cos I want to play outside with my new kite after lunch.'

Frances was surprised; she had mentioned nothing about any fight or attack. 'Yes, I'm sure you can play with your kite – very soon.'

Robert left his train set and was thinking about something. 'I have my new bow and arrow present,' he said pensively. 'That'll be useful now.'

Frances left them then, going down the hill and along the river to the factory. McTear was there, with the old police sergeant and Father Bertin. McTear was bolting and locking the big doors when she arrived.

'Keep them away from the rum at least,' McTear told

her. The sergeant, in his pith helmet and red-piped trousers, bowed shortly to Frances. Father Bertin, the breeze flapping his soutane, said, 'Goo' marnin', Mrs Fraser.' Talking more to McTear than to Frances over the years, he had taken on a Scots intonation in his meagre English.

Frances barely acknowledged his greeting. 'You're locking up, McTear?'

'Aye. It's best. I'll join ye in the Hall, if ye've no objection.'

'And the launch?' Frances asked him, looking over his shoulder, up at the headland to her right above the cove. 'I see you've got steam up again.' They all turned to look at the plume of dark smoke rising above the rocks.

'I'll be damned,' McTear was astonished. 'I was there not fifteen minutes ago an' the boiler was nowhere near ready.'

'Well, it's burning up well now,' Frances said. 'We should be able to get off to Roseau at once.'

'That's no the bloody boiler, Mrs Fraser! That must be the launch itself.' McTear was moving off, up to the headland, before he had finished speaking, the others chasing after him.

The steam launch was in flames, burning fiercely at the jetty, when they got down there, Big Jules standing helplessly nearby. In his hand was a long hardwood arrow, the metal head sheathed with a ball of smouldering cotton. Three or four similar arrows, they could see now, were embedded among the flames along the cockpit and foredeck of the now fiercely burning launch. Big Jules gestured up to the other side of the cove, to the scrub on the lip of the cliff above them.

'They was là, Madame! Trois, quatre, cinq of them. And I can do no thing 'bout it – 'cept sauvez me!'

McTear took the arrow from him, looking at it closely. Beneath the smouldering cotton a thin strand of red-daubed vine had been twined round the stem. He rubbed his finger over it, the colour staining his skin. 'Fresh,' he remarked easily. 'That's the war paint – the *roucou* dye they use.' Then he sniffed the cotton sheath. 'Brandy – they'll have plenty of that, and drinking it, too.' He held up the arrow, shaking it rather merrily. 'That's the old way with them – tho' it'll ha' little effect on the slates or the coral stone. But that's what they must have in mind: firing the Hall.'

Frances was appalled at this news. She had not thought the Caribs would take any really violent action against them. 'You – you think they intend something serious?'

McTear glanced at the flaming launch, nodding. 'And nay just the Hall, Mrs Fraser. They want us as well – burning yon boat there so we canna get away . . .' He smiled, very matter of fact about the whole business. 'I'll get me shotgun – and join you at the Hall.'

'Mais, c'est vraiment sérieux,' Father Bertin said, rubbing his thin hands together nervously. McTear nodded again.

'Indeed, Father – "an eye for an eye, a tooth for a tooth" – that's the way they see it! They're no Christian up there in yon hills, ye know!' He turned to the sergeant then. 'You go back to the village – see if ye can get any sort of a boat at all – and get someone off to Roseau, soon as you can. Right? Then bring yourself and the two constables and any kinda weapons you've got up to the Hall. Right?' He put his arm on the sergeant's shoulder, enjoying his role as commander, which he had taken over from Frances.

'Yes, sah!' Sergeant Alwin, half terrified, half enjoying the excitement, set off running, the other three following him quickly up the winding cliff path.

They barricaded themselves into the Hall, bringing beds, mattresses and heavy furniture out, piling them all up between the pillars of the veranda, making a first line of defence here, where the men could bring their guns to bear, poking through the obstacles, giving a clear line of fire over the wide lawn, and beyond that to the mango grove and the ditch which led out to the scrubby citrus fields.

Bruce and his friends had their Winchester sporting

rifles and plenty of ammunition, McTear had his 12-bore shotgun, and the sergeant had brought a Webley .45 service revolver which, though not part of his official equipment, he had conveniently unearthed somewhere back at Castle Bruce. He had only six cartridges for it, though. The two young constables with him had ancient cutlasses, jagged and rusty, relics from the Napoleonic wars about the islands, which they carried awkwardly like umbrellas, while Big Jules, with only his brass-buttoned navy-blue waistcoat on over his naked torso, had two cutlasses, along with a red bandanna round his head, which gave him an entirely piratical air.

Bertie had no weapon, nor could he have used one in any case. He stayed indoors with Father Bertin, with the women and children and the remnants of the servants, all of them camped behind further barricades in the hall, for the house, given its very sturdy construction, had no hurricane cellar.

McTear, again, took charge – some fierce old Scottish border spirit happily renewed in him, moving his great bulk around decisively, beard bristling, giving directions right and left, easily usurping any authority Bruce might have offered: organizing pails of water against fire, sending one of the constables up with the field glasses on to the roof as look-out, telling Cook to get a strong broth ready and plenty of food in from the kitchens, advising Frances where to set up a first aid post, just inside the dining room door.

'You don't have to tell me, McTear. I did all this before – in the South African war,' she told him testily, and he left her then, returning to the veranda.

'What do you expect, McTear?' Bruce asked him. 'They're not likely to run straight into all these guns are they? – knowing we have them.'

'With enough brandy and that strong *tafia* weed they smoke they could do anything, Mr Fraser – believe you me.'

'In broad daylight? But they'd be massacred, coming straight across the open lawn at us.'

'The *night* – they may well come after dark. That's the danger.'

'But they've no proper guns anyway.'

'They have a few muskets. And those arrows: they can hit a sixpence at fifty yards.'

'We can do better than that.' Bruce patted his rifle. 'Can't we?' Algy and Roland nodded. But they were not so confident. The three men had taken up positions next to each other along the centre of the wide veranda, McTear and the sergeant to one side of them, Big Jules and the second constable on the other, each archway thus well defended.

Bruce turned and drank a noggin of rum. He had a bottle with him, along with his ammunition, on the table. 'Can't be any match for us. Besides, I don't believe they'll attack at all. Just trying to get us into a funk, burning the launch.'

'Don't be too sure,' McTear said. 'It's my hope they'll come in daylight – we can mebbe handle them then. But, after dark, it'd be a different matter.'

'We'll get them anyway, whatever way they come.' Bruce drained his glass. Dutch courage, McTear thought.

He looked up at the mountains then, a darkening green silhouette now as the afternoon light began to dip down behind them. In another hour the sun would have disappeared entirely beneath the peaks and half an hour after that it would be pitch black. If the Caribs had any sense, he thought, they'd attack then, after sunset. He prayed they'd have drunk and smoked enough already to lose all sense – and come for them in daylight.

They waited then, at their fire posts, listlessly fidgeting, through the hot afternoon, gazing out at the vivid, flower-filled lawn with its darting humming birds and butterflies, the placid grove of mangoes beyond. The ring of Emperor palms stirred gently now and then in a faint sea breeze, their great leaves grating together, like sandpaper, in the silence. The sun beat down on them, and after some hours came to slant directly into their eyes, almost blinding the men as they scanned the lawn for any sign of movement.

McTear cursed the strong light, listening intently now for any change in the bird call, since he could no longer see properly into the glare. He had made no allowance for this vast spotlight of sun, which so impaired their vision now, putting them almost as much at a disadvantage as if they had been in the dark.

Still, he thought, another fifteen minutes and the sun would have dropped behind the hills, and there'd be a further half-hour's perfectly reasonable light after that. He put his shotgun down, taking a handkerchief out to wipe the sweat from his brow and eyes. He'd have to see to the lamps soon – they weren't going to come now: they'd attack after dark. He stood up, head and shoulders rising a little above the parapet of sofas and mattresses, turning towards the doorway behind him.

But before he had moved a yard the long arrow struck him fiercely in the right shoulder blade. It was followed by a flock of arrows, interspersed with the heavy thud of musket fire – and then the sharp repeated cracks of the sporting rifles, bolts moving rapidly to and fro, as the men returned the fire, aiming wildly round the edge of the lawn and the ditch a hundred yards ahead of them.

The Caribs, stalking unseen through the overgrown citrus fields, and still invisible, had taken up positions all around them, hidden in the cover of the ditch, the mango grove and behind the great boles of the Emperor palms. Now they raked the veranda at leisure with their muskets and arrows, the defenders barely able to see to aim their guns in the brilliant slanting light.

McTear had stumbled forward through the veranda doors into the dining room, almost falling on Frances by the long table where she had set up her first aid equipment. The arrow, hitting him squarely on the bone, had sheared away to the right then, tearing the flesh in a great gash right down to his armpit. Frances cut his braces and tore at his collarless shirt, removing the arrow. McTear, conscious but in great pain, groaned deeply. 'As long as – as there's no of that *machineeel* poison on it.' Blood spread down his back as he lay face down on the pine floor.

'No – I don't think so. It's quite clean, the arrow.' Frances dabbed and swabbed away at the gash, deftly, quickly, putting a field dressing over it, then a bandage.

McTear sat up, trying to move his arm, while she made a sling for him. 'It's gone,' he said. 'I canna move it.'

Frances, settling the sling, left him then, going into the hall, clambering over the barricades, to where the children and the others were crouching around and beneath the great mahogany staircase. Bertie and Father Bertin were doing their best to comfort Mildred and the servants – all these women, hearing the cannonades, in a great state of fear. Only Elly, with Robert and Henrietta, appeared reasonably calm. They were sitting on the staircase, Elly with her arms about them both, Hetty sucking her thumb, Robert clutching the tin engine from his train set. They were calm enough – Elly was calming them. But they were all very frightened, Frances could see.

'Don't worry,' she said. 'It'll be quite all right. You'll see.'

She comforted them herself then. But suddenly, a hot flush of fear coming over her, Frances realized that it might not be all right at all. McTear, who had been leading and encouraging them all, was wounded, out of action certainly, a gun less on the stockade. And the Caribs, without McTear and worked up into a frenzy with drink and *tafia*, might well manage to storm the house now and that could be the end of everyone. They wouldn't be eaten – oh, no, the Caribs didn't eat people nowadays – they'd simply all be massacred, hacked to pieces by their cutlasses.

Frances turned back then, thinking of this awful fate, a savage anger rising in her – against her husband who had so jeopardized all their lives, against the Caribs perforce, simply because she knew now they meant to murder them, and saw how they might well succeed. It was against all her principles – this warfare she hated: but she would fight them herself. There was no alternative.

Outside the firing had continued, ineffectually, from

both sides. But after five minutes the Caribs dispensed with their musket fire and there was a complete silence from the ring of trees. The men waited nervously, Bruce once more taking to the rum bottle.

Then, in the failing light, they saw the little spouts of fire rising here and there all round the semicircle of trees, followed almost immediately by a whooshing sound as the arrows with their flaming cotton balls sped through the air, a volley in long smoking arcs, striking home into the mattresses and furniture, soon igniting them. But still their assailants remained invisible.

McTear, out on the veranda again, his right arm useless, saw the flames rising from the stockade. 'The pails – get the water pails!' he shouted. Frances, in her bloodstained muslin dress, had just come out on to the veranda. McTear gestured to the line of water buckets. But she did not hear him, or pretended not to. Instead she picked up his shotgun, and cartridge bandolier, took them to the fire port he had been using, and started shooting there herself, then broke the breech smartly, inserting two new cartridges.

'It's nay use, I tell ye!' McTear shouted at her. 'Unless ye git the fire out.' The flames had begun to catch well now, a dense, smoky pall rising from the obstacles, which made it difficult for anyone to see out, let alone aim with any accuracy. And quite apart from that, McTear saw, the flames would soon engulf them, turning inwards, choking them, when this front line could no longer be held.

'Ye'll all ha' to go back!' he shouted again. 'Behind the saloon windows.'

This was their second line of defence, in the dining room, behind the half-dozen jalousy windows. A few minutes later, the stockade burning fiercely now, they retreated into the house, taking up fresh positions, watching the leaping flames all along the veranda. But at least, meanwhile, this fiery barrier would prevent the Caribs making a run at them. They had time to regroup.

'When yon fire dies and the light goes behind them

hills,' McTear told them, 'they'll surely come then. Here, gi' me that revolver, Alwin.' He spoke to the sergeant. 'That's all I can use now. You and the boys – you take the cutlasses. Jules, give the boy one of yours. You dinna need two o' them.'

McTear walked along the dining room then, through the acrid drift of smoke, checking the positions at the windows. Bruce, half-drunk and in a high state of excitement, said, 'When we get to *see* the bloody niggers! – they won't stand a chance.' He slapped his rifle.

But they did not get to see them. As soon as the flames began to subside on the stockade, the Caribs, still hidden, let off another volley of burning arrows, aimed at the jalousy windows this time, half of them finding their mark, sailing into the louvred wooden shutters, setting them alight, so that soon the dining room was full of smoke and the men were forced to push out the burning shutters with their rifle butts.

Only then, in the waning firelight, the windows nude, the stockades burnt down and part of the dining room itself now on fire, did the Caribs attack. They rose up all round from the cover of the trees – short, dark, largely naked, war-painted figures, whooping and shouting, red and white circles and lines drawn round their bodies, their hair tied in knots above the crowns of their heads, brandishing muskets, maces, adzes and cutlasses. They started to run across the lawn – not at any great pace, but zigzagging across the anthurium and orchid beds, so that the men found it difficult to maintain any sure aim.

In their first volley only a few of the twenty or so Caribs fell. The second volley was no more effective. A dozen Caribs were half-way across the lawn now. McTear, with only six cartridges for the revolver, held his fire. He would need those for close quarters. Meanwhile Frances, repeatedly shooting and reloading, blasted away with the shotgun. Two of the leading Caribs stumbled and fell. But half a dozen others, right behind, were almost up to the veranda now, about to jump over the burning debris, flailing around wildly with their assorted weapons.

It was close combat now, as the leading Carib, flourishing a great mace, leaping over the flames, made for the doorway, burst it open with one blow and landed in the room. McTear shot him at almost point-blank range. But there were two more behind – and two others storming the empty windows at the far end, inside now, turning, coming straight for them.

It was time for the cutlasses, Big Jules decided, running forward to meet these two assailants, laying about him – while McTear stood up to the others, in at the doorway now, trying to pick them off. Bruce and the other two with their rifles, had no chance of using them in the cramped, enclosed space. Frances had retreated behind the big table at the far end of the saloon with the shotgun.

A furious mêlée ensued, hand-to-hand fighting about the room, cutlasses, maces and rifle butts flailing. One of the constables was cut down, cleanly, like a stick of sugar cane. The other, pursued by a Carib, tried to flee. Bruce, Algy and Roland – with only their rifle butts now, swinging them round their heads – were being gradually forced back. One of the Caribs cornered Bruce, edging him towards the far wall.

Driven wild by the drink he had consumed throughout the afternoon, he fought the man savagely, but it was clear he would be no match for him. Algy and Roland, still engaged with the Caribs by the doorway, were unable to help. Then the shotgun went off, from the far side of the dining room table – two crashing reports.

The Carib, cutlass raised, about to end matters with Bruce, suddenly jolted away, as if pushed by a huge invisible hand, sprawling several yards from him on the floor, lying there motionless. But Bruce had fallen too, much more slowly, gently, his back sliding down the wall, knees buckling, before he pitched outwards, his skull cracking with a thump on the coral flagstones.

The other two Caribs by the door, seeing their leader dead, fled out into the twilight; the battle was over, the flames in the dining room, running along the wainscoting behind a burning chair, illuminated a Pyrrhic victory.

Frances, unblinking, her face strangely lit in the flickering yellow light, dropped the shotgun on the table.

She made no move towards her husband. It was all too clear – everyone could see it: he was dead. In the sudden silence they heard the women wailing in the hall, the children crying. Of course, McTear thought, she had tried to save her husband, not kill him. That was perfectly obvious. That would be his version of events anyway. Otherwise, with Mrs Fraser put away for murder and the estate sold up, he would be out of a job . . .

'It was an accident – the whole thing: all a dreadful accident.'

Frances's aggressive tones to the chief inspector from Roseau quite belied her apologetic, explanatory words. McCracken – a dry and cleverly evasive northern Irishman who knew all about the Frasers, and the chilly relationship between them – had arrived on a Revenue launch that morning from the capital, some days after the battle, with a posse of armed policemen, who had at once set off in hopeless pursuit of the Caribs back into the mountains. Bruce had already been buried, with the young constable, in the little Catholic cemetery at Castle Bruce, while the eight Caribs who had died had been set in ground just outside it and three others, wounded, sent to the dispensary. Now, in the front drawing room, with McTear and Bruce's two friends, McCracken conducted his preliminary enquiry.

'An accident indeed,' McTear vigorously confirmed Frances's words. 'Yon Carib, he had the cutlass right up – above Mr Fraser. He would have had no chance . . .'

'Who would have had no chance, Mr McTear – the Carib or Mr Fraser?' McCracken asked studiously.

'Why, Mr Fraser of course.' McTear pretended to be mystified by McCracken's question.

'Of course,' McCracken said with the faintest hint of a smile. 'All most unfortunate – and you have my deepest sympathy there, Mrs Fraser, in your loss.' He looked across at her blandly, licking dry lips for an instant like a lizard in the heat of the shuttered room. 'And I'm sure the court of enquiry will fairly set aside the circumstances of your husband's death – as quite unpremeditated manslaughter. Except . . .' He paused, consulting some papers. 'I have the evidence from the sergeant here – Sergeant Alwin – that you fired off *both* barrels of the shotgun, Mrs Fraser, when one might have been thought sufficient?' He glanced at her coolly again, removing his half-moon spectacles.

Frances was outraged. 'In the heat of the moment, Inspector – in the literal heat of the moment, for the dining room was ablaze – I had no idea of *how* many barrels I was firing off. I was intent only – on firing!'

'To save him, to save your husband. Of course. I ask, just to remind myself – of how things were.'

'Inspector,' Frances told him, openly aggressive now. 'It was a matter of kill or be killed. You can have no idea of the situation here: there were children and helpless women in the next room, twenty or so Caribs out to murder us, the veranda, the dining room, in flames. We were all of us about to be—'

'Of course, I see that – as you say: a matter of kill or be killed, Mrs Fraser. And, as I said, you have my deepest sympathy in . . . your loss.' He looked at her, the eyes very penetrating, but the face empty, expressing nothing. What did he mean, she wondered? What was he getting at, with all these ambivalent questions and condolences?

'I'm afraid I don't follow you, Inspector,' she said very coldly.

And she did not. It was a genuine incomprehension. As with her long exile, being the instrument of Bruce's death had greatly changed her: it had blinded her to any doubts whatsoever about her action. Faced with a choice of guilt or complete self-justification in the matter, she had taken the latter course, quite blocking out of her mind that she might have intentionally killed him, by firing both barrels. That was impossible, she had assured herself: despite people's worst faults, one didn't *kill* them. The idea was preposterous. She had, as she had explained, fired in the heat of the moment, quite unaware of how many barrels had been dispatched. That was perfectly obvious. McTear had already confirmed the point. Bruce's death had been a piece of sheer bad luck, a subsidiary incident, dependent on the much more urgent imperatives of the moment – which had been to save him, to save themselves, the women and children. Bruce had simply been a casualty of war.

'I was merely confirming your points, Mrs Fraser,' McCracken said easily. 'I'm very sorry . . . for your trouble.' He used the Irish form of condolence – knowing Mrs Fraser shared his own nationality. But, in turn, his eyes quite belied the words: they were knowing, lightly ironic.

As McCracken had forecast, the subsequent court of inquiry at Roseau cleared Frances entirely – and her husband – of any criminal actions in the whole business. While the Caribs – insofar as they could be, hidden again in their mountain vastness – were variously punished: several were executed, others sentenced to penal servitude in Jamaica, the Carib kingship abolished, their royal mace removed to Government House at Roseau, and their ten shilling a month grant-in-aid from Westminster discontinued.

Frances meanwhile was confirmed in a new role – as owner of Fraser Hall and estate, and inheritor, since Bruce had made no will, of all his other financial assets: a considerable sum, approaching £30,000. But something much more important had also been confirmed in her now – a taste for victory through physical action, through forcibly, violently asserting herself, which she had not done before.

She related these new ambitions to herself, to women generally, to subjugated races and nations – but also, and more importantly, to Summer Hill. Here was a final, long-dormant cause which attracted her new uncompromising feelings: by indulging these qualities further, she thought, she might regain her home.

So that, far from being appalled by her battle with the Caribs or by her responsibility for her husband's death, these violent events liberated Frances. Since she could not admit her guilt in Bruce's end, she obliterated her crime there by giving herself no pause to think about it, by maintaining, even increasing, her aggressive stance. Attack became her entire defence, both as a frenetic means of suppressing her guilt and as a way of life, of achieving future goals.

In short, she gave herself over entirely to the idea that the end justified the means – an equation which her earlier better nature would have led her to dismiss. She was liberated indeed.

3

Sir Desmond Cordiner, to his bitter regret, was not the first man to achieve powered flight. In 1903 the Wright brothers pre-empted him there – and by 1905 they had developed a safely manoeuvrable flying machine, which could do figure eights, fly half an hour for up to thirty miles or more. The American government, blind to the importance of the Wrights' achievement, saw no reason to encourage these two bicycle-manufacturers, while officials in Europe, where aviators had never managed more than short hops in straight flight, were in a much stronger position to condemn them as naïve maniacs and their machines as mere toys.

Only Sir Desmond, J. W. Dunne, his rival at the Balloon School in Farnborough S. F. Cody, Louis Blériot and a few other intrepid individuals persevered, knowing better. Sir Desmond himself had been one among these 'straight hoppers' for several years, without ever managing more than low flights of a few hundred yards above the meadow across the river from Summer Hill.

However, in the summer of 1908, when the Wright brothers arrived in France with their demonstration flights in a passenger-carrying machine, this general lack of interest vanished overnight. Flying machines became all the rage. Sir Desmond, attending these astonishing demonstrations at Le Mans, had met the Wright brothers, carefully inspected their machine and had taken several glorious, stomach-turning trips with them as a passenger.

Their 'Flyer', like his own machine, was a biplane. And indeed, at a casual glance, they seemed to resemble each other in many other ways: the two broad, superimposed, linen-covered wings giving them the shape of an elongated box kite – engines amidship, the controlling planes jutting out fore and aft. But on closer inspection, as Sir Desmond saw, there were vital differences: the Wrights' more powerful aluminium 30-horsepower engine, ingeniously water-cooled, was a lightweight which did not overheat; the crucial elevator which they had mounted forward of the wings, instead of behind – and above all the fact that the 'Flyer' had intentionally been built to an unstable design. The wing-tips, via a series of pulleys and wires, had been made to warp in flight, thus providing essential lateral control, so making the machine very much safer and more manoeuvrable than any European model. It was the lack of this warping factor in Sir Desmond's aeroplane, built to a rigid design, which had never allowed him to do more than swoop and fall alarmingly in a more or less straight line, a few dozen feet above the meadows at Summer Hill.

But now, armed with this new knowledge, Sir Desmond returned home, re-designing his own machine in the following months, so that by late in the year 1908, having introduced warp control, a more powerful 'Antoinette' 50-horsepower engine, and re-positioned his elevator forward, he was impatient – more than impatient – to get his new machine into the air.

The weather over Christmas was entirely against him: cold, windswept, rainy – conditions likely to last well into the new year, everyone thought. However, in February a calm spell arrived, a false spring, a succession of mild fine days with a light southerly breeze, conditions which seemed set fair for a week. And the ground, the short-cropped grass in the long meadow, soon dried out, leaving a firm, even surface. Sir Desmond could not resist the temptation.

At first, in the early days of that week, he simply made trial runs – taxiing his new machine, which he had christened *Zephyr*, up and down the meadow, taking off on a dozen occasions, rising fifty feet or so, and travelling easily for several hundred yards, before descending. With his new warp control, forward elevators and increased power, he seemed to have achieved almost perfect stability and manoeuvrability now. It but remained to get properly airborne above the trees at the end of the meadow, so that then, with sufficient height, he could turn *Zephyr*, make a few circuits and land again. If the weather held, he would do so next morning.

Daybreak, when he went down to the meadow before breakfast, confirmed his best hopes. The ground remained hard, the wind in the south, blowing straight up the valley, which would give him all the lift he needed in taking off – and the sky was almost cloudless, a pale blue, rising in a great dome over the bare trees by the river, where the birds, deceived by the weather, took voice in the warm sun.

'I'll take her up,' Sir Desmond said to Lady Cordiner after breakfast. 'Take her up today!'

'But we have our important lunch party today!' she reminded him vehemently. 'Have you forgotten? The Aberdeens and the Wandesfordes. You cannot appear with your overalls – drenched in castor oil, stinking of benzine!'

'Oh, I shall be back long before that. Plenty of time to clean up. Have no fear.'

'But is it wise in any case – your flying so early in the year?' she asked him then, though there was no real concern in her voice since, for her, his passion for these aerial toys had never been wise. The whole thing was an aberration, she had always thought, one more flaw in the Cordiner make-up.

'My dear, if not now – when? I am getting no younger.'

'To the contrary, I believe in the whole matter that you have entered a second childhood.'

She did not smile in saying this, which might have offered Sir Desmond some encouragement, some hope in his enterprise; that was not her way with her husband. It had not been for many years. None the less, he maintained his enthusiastic approach with her.

'You will not come down with me then – to the meadow?'

She shook her head. 'The fumes, the noise of your machine – they give me a headache. In your success, which you so expect, I may surely see you from here, rising above the trees, in all your glory.' She smiled a fraction now, but with sarcasm not favour.

Sir Desmond was still not disheartened. 'You will come out on the porch then? Good. I shall hope to fly right over you, over the house.'

Lady Cordiner was aghast. 'Not over the stables, I trust. You would stampede the horses.'

'No. Straight across the pleasure garden: I shall pass *directly* over the centre, the old astrolabe.'

She looked at him mockingly. 'I very much doubt it – that you could achieve any such exactitude in that foolish string and canvas contraption of yours! Why, it can barely leave the meadow . . . The idea that it could rise directly above us, up here: ludicrous!'

'You will see! You will see, my dear – how wrong you are,' he told her brightly. In fact he was hurt, even angry. But he hid it, as he had for years, putting up once more with his wife's sarcasm and disbelief in his flying abilities. She was arrogant and heartless, he knew. But she was not a fool. Could she be so entirely unaware of the vast potential and importance of these new flying machines, which would soon enable whole numbers of people to travel regularly from city to city, indeed from one country to another – machines which would liberate mankind, make them as birds, which would annihilate all distance and inconvenience in travel?

Yes, she was blind to all this. Well, he would show

her – and the Viceroy Lord Aberdeen and the wealthy Wandesfordes, too, as an added bonus – by undeniable example, that very morning, how wrong she was, how his life had not been wasted with 'foolish string and canvas contraptions' but in pursuit of a dream which, albeit late, he would finally achieve himself, participating in the reality of flight which would soon change everyone's lives, the world over. He would take *Zephyr*, with all the precision of a ship's navigator, directly over the great astrolabe in the centre of the pleasure gardens: the old astrolabe – so appropriate a goal – a device once used to measure the height of the stars, which would now meet, soaring above it, a new machine which could actually take men into the heavens.

Sir Desmond, with his leather helmet, goggles and his thick blue dungarees, left the house shortly afterwards – driving down to the meadow with Dick Gregory, his chief mechanic, and the two terriers, Ginger and Billy (direct descendants of the old dogs Sergeant and Monster), yapping excitedly in the back seat of the open Daimler.

Lady Cordiner meanwhile went to her office-boudoir to see the housekeeper, Mrs Martin, giving her instructions for the day – and more importantly for the lunch party that afternoon. Lord Aberdeen, the Viceroy, and his wife, were stopping off *en route* for the Devonshires at Lismore; while the Wandesfordes, coal barons from Castlecomer, who were joining them, were friends of all concerned. Nothing must go wrong. So that, when she had finished her domestic business, Lady Cordiner advised Mrs Martin of Sir Desmond's plans. 'The Master is making one of his aerial voyages this morning. He believes he will actually fly up here – directly over the house. And, though I very much doubt he will succeed in this, you will warn the servants: the noise may surprise them. I want no breakages or any other unseemly behaviour – and they must keep away from the windows. The guests are expected at midday.'

Mrs Martin duly warned the household staff, with the result that most of them straight away became excited, broke things and took to the windows, lurking expectantly behind the curtains for the rest of the morning.

They brought the *Zephyr* out from the barn which Sir Desmond had extended as a workshop and hangar at one end of the long meadow – pulling it gently on its two landing skids and central wheel, through the dark doorway, out into the sparkling morning light. It seemed a cumbersome affair – this clumsy kite, elevator and rudder projecting awkwardly fore and aft, the body filled with a confusion of wooden struts, pulleys, criss-crossed wires and chains. It had the air of something fated to stay on earth, a da Vinci doodle rashly translated into physical shape.

And yet, as the sun glinted on the aluminium four-in-line engine, dazzling the primrose-yellow canvas, the breeze trembling the wings, the machine appeared pregnant with a beauty, a power, a purpose, which, though not evident in the design, somehow lurked in it: a glimmer of future life.

They took photographs of the company in front of the machine: Sir Desmond in his flying suit, a terrier in each arm, together with Dick Gregory, the other two mechanics and several of the local villagers from Cloone who had turned up to gawk – though there were not many of these since Sir Desmond's limited swoops and falls along the meadow had become a commonplace in recent years. The terriers, true to the tradition of their bellicose parents, started a fight in Sir Desmond's arms almost at once, so that he rapidly dispensed with them, before attending to the machine, walking round and checking it.

There was a fault in the pitch control wire; it was slack, allowing the forward elevator too much play. And the same problem was found with the back rudder. It took them an hour or more to make suitable adjustments, so that it was not until nearly midday that they were ready to take *Zephyr* up, and Sir Desmond, quite forgetting his august guests and the lunch party, finally climbed into the wicker seat in front, sandwiched between the two wings. He ran over the controls for the last time, the levers to either side of his seat, one for pitch, the other for roll: both were in perfect order now.

Meanwhile Dick Gregory had primed the engine, checked the oil and the small petrol reservoir, before going forward to swing one of the propellers.

'Ready?' he called out.

Sir Desmond confirmed that his engine cut-out was just in the advance position.

'Contact!' he shouted back.

Martin spun the wooden blade and the motor sprang to life, an easy throb, *Zephyr* vibrating steadily now as the two six-foot, scimitar-shaped propellers rotated evenly, already tempting the machine forward. Finally, ensuring that the vital oil flow was satisfactory – the drips of yellow castor already spinning out in misty spirals behind him – Sir Desmond pushed the ignition lever to 'Advance', the engine roared and *Zephyr* moved sharply forward, hesitating for an instant before it turned into the wind and started to rush along the grass, the two terriers barking furiously, pursuing the machine hopelessly down the bright meadow.

As it gathered speed, the wings juddered alarmingly, the tail plane swinging to and fro, the whole machine bumping and slewing about for long agonizing seconds: the earth would not release it.

But suddenly the magic came, lifting it off the grass, transforming the machine, as it lost its shadow life, and *Zephyr* was born, free of all its agony, its ponderous weight. Now, without any awkwardness, it climbed gradually into its true element, a primrose bird against the blue, quite sure of itself, easily clearing the trees at the far end of the meadow.

Gaining height then, rising some hundreds of feet above the winding river, Sir Desmond flew down the great wooded valley. After a minute he put *Zephyr* into a first turn, a delicate mix of rudder and warp, going left. The port wings dipped, the controls responding perfectly, as he moved gradually round by 180 degrees.

He flew back up the valley then, towards the barn and

the men beneath, waving at them vigorously for a moment, gaining height now for another turn, to starboard this time, which would take him back along the same course. And, again, it was all perfect – a lovely gravity-defying turn, giving him a delicious shiver in the stomach, and then an extraordinary sense of buoyancy as the machine took height again on the straight.

Three or four hundred feet beneath him, he saw the glinting river, the long bridge at Cloone, the salmon traps, the little village square and the church spire brilliantly outlined in the midday light – things which he had known and looked on all his life at Summer Hill but which now appeared in such a totally different configuration and perspective that they seemed objects in a dream, recognizable, yet unrecognizable, familiar, entirely new. Away to his right, almost exactly on a level with him now, lay the house of Summer Hill, rising up out of the bare trees, the sun shimmering on the blue limestone.

As he soared above all this topography of his life, the machine riding the waves of balmy air, the wind streaming through his beard, flapping his collar, tickling his neck, the long-lost exhilaration of childhood returned to him, when everything in the world was quite new, as it was now: a feeling without memory, where all hurt and disappointment were obliterated, where there was only limitless joy.

He had been born again, with *Zephyr*. Here I am, he thought, where I ought to be. Now, at last, he understood the world unfolding beneath him. All partial vision gone, the river valley and the hills struck him as a map of Eden. He saw the master plan: *this* was how it was – no other way but this. Happy at last.

He turned again towards the end of the valley, making several more trips up and down, gaining height all the while, so that finally he was well above Summer Hill. Then he noticed the two large motor cars drawing up in front of the house. The lunch party, of course: he had quite forgotten it. The Aberdeens and the Wandesfordes had arrived. And then, he remembered, he had promised his wife: he would fly directly over the house, and at just the right moment, too, now that the illustrious guests had arrived. Lady Cordiner would cease to scoff – all of them would see just what these flying machines were capable of. He turned *Zephyr*, high over the river, flying above the ruins of his ancestor's castle on the steep side of the valley, heading straight for the garden terrace and the great astrolabe, seeing the dark-dressed, frock-coated figures emerging from the vehicles, half a dozen people already looking upward.

'My word!' said Lord Aberdeen. 'I had no idea we were to be regaled with an aeronautical display!

'I do apologize,' Lady Cordiner told him on the steps of the porch, hiding her outrage. 'I had no idea myself. My husband – Sir Desmond – he should have finished long ago – here to greet you all. I had no idea—'

'Not at all, Lady Cordiner, make no apologies – I am most intrigued!'

The company moved from the porch steps out on to the middle of the gravel surround for a better view of *Zephyr*, a yellow smudge against the blue, growing bigger, the throb of the engine increasing, as it drew near the house.

'What a brave fellow!' Mr Wandesforde remarked, agog with enthusiasm. 'I do so admire him. I had no idea these . . . these machines could actually achieve *real* flight. Quite splendid – I must have one myself. At once, do you hear, Molly?' He turned to his wife. 'We shall have one at once.'

'Dearest, they cannot be safe,' she responded with some agitation as the machine approached them.

'Nonsense – look at Sir Desmond: safe as houses up there!'

At almost every window of Summer Hill now the servants were gathered – chamber, still room, scullery, laundry and dairy maids, cooks and grooms, stewards, butlers, under-butlers and footmen: the whole vast household eyes out on stalks as the primrose machine approached.

'Holy Mother of God!' Bridey, one of the scullery maids exclaimed. 'The Masther's comin' straight for us!'

And, indeed, this was so. Nothing had gone wrong with *Zephyr*. Simply, in Sir Desmond keeping it up too long, extending his trip to fly over the house, it had run out of its small supply of benzine. The engine stopped suddenly, just over the astrolabe. The machine glided on for a few seconds, clearing the parapet of the house, before it dived steeply, crashing into the flat roof of Summer Hill with a terrible rending and splintering.

The company on the gravel, craning their heads round, saw the machine disappear over the parapet, then heard the commotion as several chimney stacks were demolished, high above them.

'My word,' Lord Aberdeen said again, puzzled. 'I had no idea . . . that that was how they landed. Home for luncheon – how droll!'

'You idiot,' his wife advised him in a strong whisper. 'He cannot have intended it – unless he is made of iron.'

Lady Aberdeen was right. Sir Desmond had not intended this and had been made of flesh and bone.

Some few weeks later, Frances, down on the jetty beneath Fraser Hall, waited impatiently for the fortnightly steam packet with the mail and provisions. Instead, before anything else was unloaded, she saw two men disembark and get into the steam launch, followed by a number of crates and boxes, some of them evidently with very fragile contents, since they were lowered to an accompaniment of strident directions and imprecations from the taller of the two strangers, a handsome bear-like man in a leather jerkin, jodhpurs and army boots. His bearded companion – a much smaller figure in grubby linen tropicals, his servant or assistant to judge by the sound of things – finally stowed all their luggage in the cockpit, together with the mail, and Big Jules turned the launch towards the jetty. Frances shaded her eyes against the sun, not recognizing either of them, curious.

'Hallo there!' The big, tousle-haired man in his late thirties, a dead cheroot in his mouth, leapt with great agility on to the jetty before the launch had been moored, coming towards Frances with easy, indeed over-familiar purpose, offering his hand. 'I'm Clem Springfield – sorry I couldn't get word to you in advance – only arrived on the island three days ago.'

Frances looked at him, surprised, withholding her hand, saying nothing.

'Clement Springfield – of the *New York Post*.' He repeated the name, adding his employer, as if he expected Frances to know both. And then, having gazed at each other for long seconds, they both did know something – they were not certain what – of each other.

'Why?. . .' Springfield screwed up his bright brown eyes in a quizzical smile. 'Why, we *have* met, somewhere before – haven't we? Somewhere . . .' He turned away momentarily, clicking his fingers, concentrating. 'Why, yes!' He looked back at her, with a happy smile of recognition. 'You're the nurse I met out in South Africa, at Colenso. The war . . . your brother. Yes, your brother Lieutenant . . . Cordiner. Yes, that's it! I carried him back from the Boer lines – and met you before that, took you to Dundonald's tent! Remember?'

And Frances did remember now, softening, offering her hand. 'Yes, of course – we did meet. And they told me afterwards, how you'd carried my brother back across the river to the dressing station. How extraordinary! But you had a huge beard then and a slouch hat and you looked like a Boer, Mr Springfield!'

'Clem – call me Clem. I knew we'd met before. Couldn't forget – all that dark hair, the face!' He took her hand appraisingly. Then he turned, lighting his cheroot, before introducing her to his companion. 'And this is Oscar Stein, my picture photographer. Oscar, meet – Mrs Bruce Fraser, isn't it?'

'Yes – Mrs *Frances* Fraser,' she replied correcting the American, happy – in her new liberation – to point out her status as a widow. Then she greeted the curly-haired, busy little man who had been supervising the unloading from the launch.

'I'm very sorry to hear about your husband, Mrs Fraser.

They told me in Roseau – and of course we read about it in New York. You have all my sympathy there.'

She believed him; he meant it. Perhaps it was his refreshing American accent that lent credence to his words, she thought – the easy, out-going tones, the generally open and confident bearing: so unlike the pompously cagey attitudes of the British on the islands.

'Yes, well, it was all a fearful business. But really I have nothing more to say about it, if that was—'

'Oh, not at all, Mrs Fraser. As I said, we heard all about the Carib attack in New York. We came here to get a feature story on them and a few pictures. Not to interview you,' he added, lying, but with such smiling conviction that Frances believed him once more.

'I see. But I doubt you'll get near any of them now – they've apparently left the reserve and gone to ground, somewhere way up there in the mountains.' She gestured to the great wall of green, towering inland, just visible above the cove.

'Oh, we'll find a way, Mrs Fraser. We have ways. The paper is very keen to get a story on them – cannibal tribe and so on!'

'But that's not true, Mr Springfield – an entirely peaceable tribe, unless goaded.'

He looked at her sympathetically, drawing on his cheroot. 'Yes, I heard about that: how your husband shot – had an accident with one or two of them. Great tragedy. All the same, there's a story my editor wants there, but from the anthropological point of view: mysterious lost tribe from the rain forests, a sort of Conan Doyle "lost world" up there, I understand. Your husband imported a lot of wild animals—'

'My husband's *father*—'

'Yes, of course – buffalo, deer, cougars. You can see the sort of thing I have in mind – obvious attractions. But nothing to do with you, Mrs Fraser.'

'I'd rather you didn't all the same. There have been enough problems already.'

'Mrs Fraser, I really don't want to impose,' he said

nicely. 'But we've both come a long way.' He looked at Oscar, sweating in his subfusc suit, manhandling the trunks and boxes on to the jetty. 'We have a job to do, a living to earn – and my editor was particularly keen that I should come out here, do the story. And of course I'd no idea that I'd meet you here. Old friends – in a way.'

He smiled disarmingly, the earlier sympathy still in his eyes. And that was true, Frances thought – they had met and, much more than that, he had risked his life in trying to save her brother at Colenso. She could hardly, in the circumstances, refuse to help him.

'Very well then, as long as you see my own position in the matter—'

'Nothing to worry about there, Mrs Fraser. The *Post* has a reputation for discretion,' he lied once more. 'You can rely on me.'

He smiled again, almost over-familiar, coming towards her, a great bulk of a man, hand outstretched, as if he expected to take her arm and lead her up the cliff path straightaway. Frances withdrew a fraction, but he touched her arm all the same, resting his hand there a second. 'Don't worry. It's just the Caribs we're interested in – nothing about you, I assure you.'

Their eyes met – cornflower-blue and dark brown, unblinking for a long moment in the bright sun. And something vaguely electric passed between them, a flicker of mutual attraction, which Frances dismissed at once. All men, as she saw it now, were her enemies. They were violent, insensitive, deceitful. They had betrayed her time and again. And here was a man who, in his throbbing, easy confidence, seemed quite capable of the same sins, of following in that tradition. Yet she could not deny that he had considerable charm, seemed honest, and was certainly brave. She would bear with him.

'Well, then, perhaps you'd care to stay with us for a few days? McTear, our estate manager here, may have some ideas.' She had turned away while speaking, but now she faced him again suddenly. 'But where *had* you intended to stay over here?'

'Oh, we have tents and supplies, Mrs Fraser – in those cases. And I'd intended hiring porters.'

'You've certainly brought enough equipment with you.' Frances looked at the baggage piling up on the jetty.

'Well, there are the big plate cameras, you see, that's the main thing – and a dark room tent and chemicals for developing the pictures. All quite elaborate. The *Post* prides itself on its pictures, you see, Mrs Fraser – Oscar here, a great photographer. I just supply the captions,' he added deprecatingly, crinkling up his eyes again in a smile, letting a whiff of smoke curl from his lips. Frances watched the misty blue spirals rise over his face, up into his tousled hair, as if mesmerized. 'But that's no matter,' he continued. 'I haven't thanked you—'

'For what, Mr Springfield?' Frances was lost.

'Why . . . why for your offer of hospitality, of course. Most appreciate it!'

'Oh, that – yes, of course.' Frances came back into the world. 'You're welcome, Mr Springfield.' She smiled at him, a free and open smile such as she had not given a man in years. But then, thinking she had gone too far, she added, 'You – and Mr Stein.' She looked over Springfield's shoulder to where the little man, with Jules and Slinky, had finally established a base camp on the jetty. They left shortly after for the Hall, walking up the cliff path together, the other men stumbling behind them, carrying Springfield's equipment, the provisions and the mail.

Having settled them both in, showing them their bedrooms, Frances brought the mail to her bureau in the drawing room. There was a letter from Ruth Wechsberg – and another from her cousin Dermot Cordiner. She recognized his handwriting at once, assuming it was his reply to her own letter – letters to him, his father Mortimer and to Ruth – telling them all of the Carib attack and Bruce's death.

She opened it and was surprised to see that it had been written from Summer Hill. The contents of the letter – nothing to do with her own, which he could not have received – were more startling still.

'My dearest Frances,

Forgive me – a harbinger of bad tidings. I write to tell you that your father has died. Poor man, he met with a flying accident, just three days ago, while taking his machine over Summer Hill – colliding with the roof there for some reason – killed instantly, the doctor says.

We both, Papa and I, were over in Dublin at the time and came down at once, of course, and I write this the morning after the funeral at Cloone.

Anyway, I know it will be a great shock to you – and Papa and I want to send you every sympathy. I know you were never very close to your Papa. None the less, these things cut deeply. And Mortimer and I (his letter is enclosed) particularly wanted to write to you at once, since your mother, I'm afraid, refuses to send you any word of this – continuing her foolish policy of having nothing whatsoever to do with you. Papa and I spoke to her this morning. She remains adamant in regard to you. And it really is a sad business – that she should continue so to behave in this bitter, unforgiving manner, especially in the present circumstances, which might have been expected to bring you together.

However, there is little to be done about it as far as I can see. And worse, as I must tell you, she sees you as permanently outcast. My Papa took pains to speak to her on this very point, suggesting that it was time for her to forgive and forget – and that she should consider, at least, the idea of your returning to Summer Hill now, with Hetty.

After all, as Papa tactfully reminded her, you are their one surviving child. And with your father's death Mortimer now assumed that you would inherit Summer Hill. At this surmise, however, your mother became most vindictively roused, telling us something we were both quite unaware of – and you will be too, I imagine: that Sir Desmond, in the event of his pre-deceasing her, had made over the house and estate to your mother quite some years ago – after Henry and Eustace died – to use during her lifetime, and with the absolute discretion to dispose of it afterwards as she sees fit.

The place has not therefore, as we expected, either been left to you or entailed to your uncle Austin – which was the other expected eventuality. However, your mother then went on to say that this latter course was the one she intended taking now: Summer Hill would be left to Austin and Bunty, and she had informed them of this while they were down there for the funeral.

Now I know your views on Austin and Bunty. He is a decent innocuous man. But she is something quite else – grasping, small-minded, pretentious, I'm afraid – not at all the sort to take over Summer Hill. And besides, if they did, they would still have their own substantial house and estate in Queen's county, while you would have nothing.

It is all most unjust of your mother – and we feel she cuts you out in this way largely out of spite, for we all know how little regard she has for Austin, much less for Bunty. However, there it is and you should know the situation. We both think you should return here and see what could be done – perhaps you might talk her out of this course? But perhaps in any case you should come to London first and talk to Papa? I think you should do that.

In haste, ever most affectionately,
Dermot.'

Frances was outraged. She had recognized the possibility that her father, if he died before her mother and did not leave Summer Hill to her, might entail it to Austin and Bunty. But that her mother should inherit it, in the first place, without any strings attached, had not occurred to Frances. The house and estate had been restored with her mother's money, of course. And Lady Cordiner, ever the schemer, had ensured her pound of flesh in return. What a fiend she was – and Dermot was right: she had obviously manipulated Sir Desmond, gaining this control over Summer Hill, just so that she might disinherit her, if the opportunity arose. It had, indeed, been pure spite, guile, enmity. And Frances, in return and tenfold, felt the same acid emotions rising in her once more against her mother. Her father's death, by comparison, upset her much less. It was this impending loss of Summer Hill that cut her to the quick.

Her whole life – at home and in exile – had gravitated about this house, which she so loved, which she thought

– somehow, one day – she might possess. And now, finally, irrevocably, it was slipping from her grasp – to be given over to the banal ministrations of her uncle Austin and, worse, to the frightful Bunty.

She rose from her desk, paced the room a minute, then went to the window, opening the louvred shutters, looking out at the dark spume of smoke from the disappearing packet steamer. Yes, she could return to Europe, speak to Dermot and Mortimer – and see her mother. But to what avail? Her mother would not change her mind. She could not force or cajole her – she was certain of that. Was there any other way of saving the situation?

She returned to her desk, opening the letter from Ruth Wechsberg. And there, a few minutes later, in the last paragraph, she thought she recognized something – a ploy, a lever, a desperate move which she might make. Ruth, who had received the news of Bruce's death, had replied with her sympathy, adding later, 'I wish I were with you, to *speak* these words, rather than having to put them in a letter, which I feel is so distant a means of communicating, at least for me, who am not good at them. All one can really say of letters is that, in default of the person, they are lasting evidence of feeling, of my feelings for you in your many hardships . . .'

It was the idea of letters as 'lasting evidence' that struck Frances then: letters, thinking of her father's will, almost as legal documents. And from there it was an easy step: letters . . . the Prince's letters, some dozens of them that he had written to her during their love affair.

These, too, were 'lasting evidence' of that affair – and, more importantly, of the Prince's amorous and political indiscretions in conducting it. There was the lever. Of course! And here, she thought, if needs be – right here in Fraser Hall at that moment – was the means of activating it: the journalist Clement Springfield.

She picked up the month-old copy of the *New York Post* which he had given her on arrival at the house, reading the huge headline – '200,000 DEAD IN ITALIAN 'QUAKE' – turning pages then to look at the accompanying photographs of the catastrophe, completely devastated buildings in Calabria and Sicily. Well, she had material just as explosive.

She took a key, opening a pigeonhole drawer in the back of the desk, taking out the cache of old letters from the Prince, together with the other once-loved mementoes which he had given her – the little gold-ringed ivory elephant charm, the chiming watch from Hunt and Roskill, some elaborately decorated menus from Sandringham and the Weimar Hotel in Marienbad.

She had not looked at these things in years. Now she skimmed quickly through a few of the letters, noting some of the phrases: 'My dear one, my dearest . . .' 'Of course, Milner and Chamberlain have both behaved outrageously . . .' 'My lovely girl, in *every* way – I so think of you out there at the war, fear for you, wish you were back close to me. Oh, what I should have missed had I never met you! Sad . . .'

Frances, just for an instant, was filled with happiness in re-reading these endearments, feeling again the joy of their relationship, the trust and the love. But in a moment these memories sickened her, made her shudder with embarrassment and anger, giving her almost a physical shock, as if some lecherous old man was pawing her at that very moment with these words. She threw the letters down, where they landed among the opened pages of the *New York Post*. She almost laughed aloud, seeing the lethal combination at once.

Why had she not thought of using these letters in this manner before? Simply, she supposed, that she had so entirely put the Prince from her mind, despising him. And then again the idea of such blackmail would have been abhorrent to her. But it was not now: she saw it as her only chance. It was not the King Emperor she wished to blackmail, of course. It was her mother.

It would need careful handling, she realized. She would return and confront her mother with the letters – threaten to publish them if she did not change her will in her favour. Meanwhile she would say nothing on the matter to Springfield – merely sound him out, perhaps hint that she had some interesting 'memoirs' to offer. There would be no harm in that. Springfield, after all, would know nothing of her past, least of all of her relationship with the Prince of Wales. There was a knock on the door then. She quickly hid the letters, closing the newspaper pages over them. It was Eileen. 'Those visitors,' she said. 'Cook wants to know if they've to eat with you – or on their own?'

'Oh dear, do they look that common?'

'Cook must have thought so.'

'True, they are just newspaper men. But they can eat with me.' Frances smiled regally: newspaper men indeed, but they might well have their uses.

Upstairs, as soon as Frances had left them, Springfield came into Stein's bedroom in a high state of excitement. Stein, exhausted from his efforts with the baggage and mistrusting the mosquito-canopied bed, lay prostrate on the bare wooden floor.

'Oscar, you bum – get up! I have news for you.'

Oscar groaned. 'I ain't goin' *no* place, Clem – doin' nothin'. I'm *eggs*-hausted.'

'You don't have to go any place – just listen!' Springfield knelt down beside him. 'That Fraser woman, know who she is?'

'No. Yes – you have to interview her, get the news on what she was up to with her husband: "She shot him" – page one – stop the presses – shut up – le' me be.'

'No, you fool. I mean who she *was*! A much bigger story.'

'Who was she, then?' Stein cupped his hands behind his head and looked up at the ceiling blankly. 'The King of Spain's daughter?'

'No – the King of England's mistress, even better. Or used to be. Same woman – I had it all in South Africa, from one of the other nurses there.'

'So what? That's not the story we came out here for.'

'No. This is a bigger story! *Much* bigger.'

*

Frances waited several days before the opportunity occurred of broaching her topic – days in which the two men unpacked their equipment, tested the camera, talked to McTear and made short and unsuccessful forays into the hills looking for the Caribs.

Then one morning Springfield brought her out to the dark room tent which Stein had set up on the lawn, showing her the equipment there, which Stein was working on just then, developing some plates which he had exposed the previous day. The interior, with its single red lantern, was suffocating, stinking of chemicals, and Frances was pleased to leave the enclosed space, walking back towards the house with Springfield.

'Interesting work, no doubt,' she told him, watching the humming birds hover over the great flowers.

'Mine or his?'

'Both. My elder brother always had a plate camera with him on his travels, just like you. And your writing, of course! I remember my brother reading Stanley's books on Africa with such interest: finding Livingstone and going down the Congo – fascinating. A fascinating profession. I've kept a journal myself over the years,' she added offhandedly.

Springfield showed a quick interest – which he failed to hide. 'Have you, Mrs Fraser? That should be quite something – given your experiences!' He looked at her pointedly as they arrived on the veranda steps – rather too pointedly, Frances thought.

'Oh, just thoughts – about the war in South Africa, for example. Nothing much.' She underplayed her literary endeavours.

'Of course. But there's your recent adventures on the island here – even better! The Carib attack. And your husband . . .'

'That's of no interest,' she told him brusquely.

'And of course you're a friend of the King – the King of England,' Springfield continued easily. 'Knew him when he was Prince of Wales. That must have been quite something.'

Some of McTear's men were repairing the veranda shutters after the fire, hammering about near them, so that at first Frances thought she had misheard him.

'I'm sorry?' She looked at Springfield, half-astonished, then entirely so, realizing she had not misheard him. But she hid her surprise. 'I'm afraid I . . . I don't follow you,' she said calmly.

'Well, you must remember the Sister – out there at Colenso, that other nurse you worked with – what was her name? She told me about your being a friend of his. I don't want to pry, of course – but that must have been a very interesting experience, Mrs Fraser. That's all I was thinking, a matter of some public interest . . .'

'Not really, I'm afraid.' Frances, regaining control with an effort, smiled deprecatingly. 'I only knew the Prince very slightly, before the South African war. He was a friend of the woman whose nursing home I worked at in London. I met him there once or twice, that's all.'

'All the same, you've led an extraordinary life – for a woman. Had you thought to publish anything on it? Write your memoirs? My newspaper would certainly be very interested.'

They had moved indoors now, away from the noise on the veranda, walking through into the cool of the hall.

'No, I'd not thought of that, Mr Springfield. Besides, I can't really write.'

'I'd be pleased to help you there, Mrs Fraser. Put your experiences down for you.'

'Most kind,' she told him distantly. 'But really I have nothing to say – for the moment. And now, if you'll excuse me, I have some letters to write.'

Closeted in the drawing room at her desk, Frances tried to compose herself. She remained astonished. How much did Springfield really know about her relationship with the Prince? No more than the little he'd said? – mere gossip, simply, from that spiteful, ignorant, chocolate-gorging Sister Turner, who had picked up some rumour of her royal association from Brazier-Creagh? It could not have been more than that, she decided. And it hardly mattered in any case. Such ancient gossip could not be made to mean anything now, years later. And Springfield could have no other firm evidence to go on, which might make trouble for her.

In fact, he had simply made things easier, if and when she wished to use him; he had agreed in advance to take her 'memoirs' – even help her to write them. She now had another genuine lever with her mother – an offer, in effect, from the *New York Post* to publish this scandal which, when word of it got abroad, would ruin Lady Cordiner's life, set all her social success at naught. Though, of course, it would never come to that. When her mother saw the letters, realized their explosive nature, she would capitulate. So there was really no problem with Springfield. He would never get to see these 'memoirs', let alone publish them.

Springfield, in his greed for a sensational story, made the best of the way their conversation had gone when he spoke to Stein in the dark room tent later, telling him what had passed between them.

'So what?' Stein said. 'So, she was a girlfriend of the old guy. But he had *hundreds* of girls – well known – always the Lothario. No story there – forget it.' Stein held up a plate of the Emerald pool, gazing at it intently against the red lantern.

'I don't know – there's something special here. I can feel it. Those rumours in Roseau, remember? That she did her husband in, on purpose. And that child of hers, with the awful stammer – that it wasn't Mr Fraser's child at all. Remember?'

Stein nodded mechanically. 'Yes, yes, I remember.'

'Well, you know something? I think the King might have been that girl's father. The dates fit – roughly. She must be nine or ten years old – just when Mrs Fraser knew him, before she went out to South Africa. And another thing, Oscar: why would a woman like that – rich aristocrat, so well-connected at home – come out and bury herself in a dump like this? Unless maybe to get away from the scandal of having an illegitimate child back home?'

'Why wouldn't she come out here? A vacation. And then she met Fraser, with this great house, and married him – and stayed here, naturally. That makes sense.'

'Not entirely. She didn't get on with him at all—'

'That happens *plenty*, Clem. Nothing unusual there. I tell you – you're going up a dead end. Let's find these savages, take a few pictures of 'em and get the hell outa here.'

But Springfield was not persuaded. 'Yes, it's that girl, you know,' he said pensively. 'I'd lay money on it. Why, the kid even looks something like the King – those big blue eyes and the high brow—'

'And the beard and the big cigar – Clem, you're outta your mind. Come on, let's do some serious *work*.'

Springfield, with nothing more to go on, might have left it at that – but for Frances's carelessness and the lucky chance he had in benefiting from it that afternoon. In the drawing room, taking coffee with Frances after lunch, he saw the copy of the *Post* which he had given her, lying on top of some other magazines and papers on a small occasional table beside her.

He picked it up casually, remarking on the headline, the frightful earthquake in Italy a month before. 'Terrible business,' he added, as a vague afterthought.

'Indeed.' Frances spoke from over by the window, her back towards him. 'I'm surprised you didn't go straight out there yourself, instead of coming here.'

'Oh, we have several people in Italy already, Mrs Fraser. No need for me.'

He continued to turn the pages over idly, flicking through the paper. And then the letter fell out, landing in his lap: 'Marlborough House, SW. My dearest one, how I have missed you, without any news, and fear for you in that dreadful war. I do so wish you could return, be near me once more. I miss you – in every way – and long to do again all the things we did . . .'

Springfield restrained himself admirably. He pocketed the letter quickly, while Frances was still at the window, continuing to glance through the paper. Frances turned to him then, seeing him reading.

'Ah, rummaging through your old work, are you?' She remarked on the article by Springfield in the paper which she had read that morning herself. 'Your account of floundering about in those hot baths at Saratoga Springs sounded . . . fascinating!' She looked at him almost suggestively, eyes narrowing in a smile.

'Oh, that was nothing, Mrs Fraser. I can do much better than that – I assure you! Let me show you some other things I've done.' He stood up. 'I've got some cuttings upstairs.'

'Oh, don't bother.'

'No bother. I'd like to.'

He left the drawing room, still holding the copy of the *Post*. Upstairs he read through the Prince's letter carefully. There was no doubt about it. They had been much more than mere acquaintances. Mrs Fraser had been his mistress. And the child? Well, he was probably right, it was theirs. But he needed more information – if he could get it, which seemed unlikely. He was in a quandary. Finally, getting out some of his old cuttings, he went downstairs again, deciding he had nothing to lose by simply putting his cards on the table.

'Mrs Fraser,' he told her, holding up the letter. 'Upstairs – this letter fell out of the paper. I think it must be yours.'

He handed it over. She glanced at it – managing with equal skill to restrain herself, showing no concern. 'Oh, how careless of me.' She put it down on the desk. 'I must have left it inside when I was looking at your article this morning. Now what are your plans for this afternoon, Mr Springfield?'

'Mrs Fraser, I'm afraid my journalist's curiosity got the better of me. I read that letter.'

She turned to him coolly. 'How very ill-mannered of you – people's private correspondence. Still, as you say, it's to be expected – from a journalist.'

'Sheer chance it fell out of the paper. I apologize. I really didn't want to pry.'

He spoke meekly, and apparently truthfully. Like Frances, he had the charm to lie with absolute conviction.

Frances meanwhile was preparing her own lies, her next move: yes, she would humour him – or better still, now that the cat was out of the bag, she would manipulate, control, trap him in return.

'Well, so you've read it!' She laughed easily, with a sigh of relief, as if pleased that he should have discovered her secret, which now allowed an openness between them. 'But it's of no real importance. It all happened a long time ago, over and done with. Though naturally . . .' She looked at him steadily, with an expression of conniving intimacy. 'It's not for public consumption. I can rely on your discretion there – of course.'

'Of course – absolutely.' There was silence then. They had both produced their lies now. Yet neither really believed the other, and each knew that. The room was hot and still, the louvred shutters spreading bars of bright light over the floor and the heavy furniture.

They looked at each other amiably – an agreement, an understanding reached between them, an apparent trust formed. There was a distinct hint of conspiratorial mischief in Frances's face now, a knowing smile, which Springfield responded to in kind. They were suddenly enjoying each other's lies, excited by their mutual deceits, and the burgeoning conspiracy it suggested.

'On the other hand . . .' Springfield said, returning her gaze. He paused.

'What?' Frances moved towards him, stopping just a few feet away. 'On the other hand *what*, Mr Springfield!' She ran a hand quickly through her dark curls, looking up at him coquettishly.

'Well, it is an extraordinary story,' he went on, shaking his head in genuine astonishment now, sensing something even more unexpected in Frances's expression and approach to him.

'What? – that the Prince was my lover?' she said provocatively. 'Why should that surprise you?' She narrowed her eyes in a canny flirtatious smile, opening her lips a fraction, a wonderful demon rising in her, sure of her power over him, taking a vast pleasure in it. She had not so tempted a man like this in years, and the pleasure was all the greater since, whereas before, with the Prince, she had done this with love, now she offered herself to Springfield out of pure physical hunger, mixed with derision, spite, hatred. It was a new and exceedingly satisfying feeling, for she controlled him now, and so she let him take her, partly in pleasure, partly as a poisonous flower tempts an insect to destruction.

And he took the bait greedily, falling into her, over her, trying to kiss her – one cheek, then the other, searching out her lips as she twisted to and fro, avoiding that contact, letting him crush her instead, feeling his mouth on her neck, tongue exploring her ear, her head arched backwards by the force of his body against hers, feeling him rising against her thighs – and feeling her own mounting excitement, too, so that she made no resistance as he started to fumble at the buttons of her fine muslin blouse, picking at them, unable to undo them.

Frustrated eventually, she stepped away from him, flushed and impatient, looking at him with a vehement mix of desire and an enmity which he did not recognize.

'Lock the door,' she told him breathlessly. He left her, fumbling with the key there as well, so that by the time he returned she had taken the blouse off herself, together with the silk half-bodice beneath, and was standing there, naked to the waist. Then, impatient to be freer still – of the rest of her clothes and his bungling attentions – she was already picking at the hooks and eyes at the side of her starched linen skirt, turning her head round, one arm squeezed tightly round her breast, as she fiddled with the clips.

'Let me,' he said easily. He prised her arm gently away, so that her breasts were open to him now, offering him the dark, tumescent areolea, which he kissed as he undid the last of the catches, stooping, running his hand down her midriff, pulling her skirt down at the same time.

And then Frances, again pre-empting him – her passion rising, in desperate hurry now – did the rest for him, pulling away from him, stepping out of her slip and camiknickers, before going over to the long sofa, naked. He followed her, hurriedly undressing as he went.

She lay down on her back, looking up at him as he came towards her, quite startled by his size, in every way – his taut sex, vast, curving in a great arc, as he knelt between her thighs and she grasped and stroked the extraordinary instrument which he offered to her.

And then marvelling, and marvellously excited, she quite forgot how she despised this man and, sitting up quickly, arching her back forward, she bent down into him and took it in her lips, letting it run into her mouth, realizing what a small fraction of it she could contain. It had been years since she had last made love. And, just as she had so completely repressed all desire during that time, so now, going to the other extreme, she threw all caution and propriety to the winds.

She mouthed and fingered him wildly, with an excitement that was all the greater since he was nothing but an object for her, whom she cared nothing for, whom she hated. There was only his body and she exulted in that alone and all its possibilities, pushing her mouth right down, feeling him in her throat.

Then, wilfully, she pulled away from him and lay back, put her hands at her hips, pushing herself up there, offering him her own sex. And when she first felt him she thought she might choke or scream, a great surge of expectancy coursing through her. It was a sheer physical joy, quite divorced from any emotion, which she could not have thought possible; smooth, liquid, intense.

He moved forward then, holding himself over her, bracing his arms, to either side of her head, his body suspended high above her, quite motionless as, lower down, he began to glide and explore between her thighs. She could feel his sex, moist-topped, teasing, pushing, retreating, sliding up in front, then behind, intentionally missing the mark, she thought, so that she gasped in frustration, opening herself to him, arms writhing behind her neck, head twisting about in a delicious agony. So that when he did finally come into her, pushing gently, she gasped again, then held her breath, unbelieving, waiting.

But he suddenly stopped, stayed there at the just-opened door, so that she shivered, anticipating the pain. And then she felt what she could not believe, what she thought she could not contain, as he quietly moved forward again, fraction by fraction, and there was no pain – just an endless smooth sliding movement, a widening and a deepening, right down, until he seemed to come to the end of her. And, when he had, she gripped him, contracting her muscles, tightening all round him, so that, when he started to move again, the joy was intense as she enclosed him, the whole deep length of him, she thought. But it was not so. There was more, and more to spare, so that she realized she could never have him all, even when, eventually, frenzied now, they charged right into each other, time and again, and he finally flowed into her and she responded, in spasm after ringing spasm, one exploding firework igniting the next, seemingly without end. Frances had never experienced such a thing, never believed it possible: this cataract, these successive bursts of pleasure, exploding one after the other deep inside her.

4

Springfield was pleased with his performance, believing that it had given him a power over Frances more important than the sexual: that he could now, presuming on their intimacy, the more readily persuade her to indulge the full story of her affair with the Prince. Frances was pleased, too, in that, knowing he would make just such a presumption, she could forestall him, yet at the same time learn what he knew and intended in advance.

What she had not expected was that he would so soon, so brashly, take up the running and try and push her on the matter. And it was in this crass hurrying that Springfield, quite unaware of the vital plan Frances had with her mother, made a serious mistake. For of course if anything were made public of her affair with the Prince, before Frances had the opportunity of showing the letters to Lady Cordiner, there would then be no lever in them and her last chance of rescuing Summer Hill for herself would have disappeared.

So it was that Frances, when Springfield started to push her, reacted with violent alarm. And, since she could not delay his ambitions by explaining her real plans for the letters, it was then that she first realized that she might have to consider some other means of ensuring his silence.

Springfield had taken up the subject very soon after their bout on the sofa – that same evening after dinner, when Stein had gone to his room and they were both on the veranda, lying back in the cushioned steamer chairs, taking coffee, looking out on the dark lawn with its polka dots of dancing fireflies.

'Well, Frances! . . .' He stared knowingly across at her in the lamplight, drawing on a cheroot, his previous confidence strengthened now by an air of sexual dominance which infuriated Frances.

None the less, flickering her eyelids, she maintained something of her earlier flirtatious attitude. 'Well – what?' She picked out a Carlsbad plum.

'Well, it was wonderful,' he told her frankly and simply. They had not been alone with each other since their coupling. Frances responded with a minute nod. Springfield sat up then, leaning over enthusiastically. 'Really – wonderful . . .' He admired her, undressing her with his eyes, hoping to confirm how they had both caught sex like an infection, a raging fever, which they must now inevitably continue to suffer: sex – which would guarantee his own professional future, so that he spoke now with exactly that advantage in mind. 'But the future,' he went on in the same caressing, yet slightly overbearing voice. 'I can really help you there.'

'I don't see—'

'Well, with your husband gone, you can't just bury yourself here for the rest of your life, can you? Come back with me to New York!'

'What on earth for?'

'Why, we could do things together, go places. And those letters,' he added as an apparent afterthought. 'Your memoirs – I could fix those up for you. They'd be worth a fortune, you know – start a whole new life in America. Why don't you?'

Frances had reacted to his sly enthusiasm with a first real spasm of alarm – knowing exactly what lay behind it: not her, but her 'memoirs'. 'I don't know that I want to live in America – Clement,' she added nicely.

'Well, not for ever maybe. But, Frances – look at the *opportunities*! Your story, you and the Prince – why, it's worth fifty, a hundred thousand dollars, I tell you.'

'*Is* it?' she asked innocently, yet with a suitable hint of greed, hoping to encourage him in further disclosures.

'Why yes, and maybe more. You must have dozens of those letters?'

She did not reply. But she smiled broadly now, as if agreeing with him silently, prodding him to other surmises.

Springfield took the bait – and then a most dangerous plunge. 'And little Henrietta,' he said, confidently playing what he thought to be his ace. 'She's his child, isn't she? Why, that alone makes it all – really so much better. She is, isn't she?'

Springfield looked across at her intently, hoping to discern the answer in her eyes, if not in her voice. Frances was astonished, raging inwardly at this loathsome man – for his greed and his insights. Yet again she said nothing – while again repeating her look of implicit confirmation.

'I knew it!' he said triumphantly. 'So you see – I see it all. We've no need to beat about the bush any more. We can set your story up together – right away and publish it. We have it all in front of us – a future!'

What Springfield could not have seen then was that, in

so displaying his dangerous intuitions and his grasping ambition to capitalize on them as soon as possible, he might not have a future at all.

Yet Frances initially had to play for time. 'All right,' she assented. 'It's a possibility – we'll consider it. But meanwhile tell no one: not anybody, not even your friend Stein. Fair?'

'Fair enough. The fewer the better – for the moment!'

They exchanged a final knowing smile, as a seal on their present silent collusion and future co-operation, and Frances had gained a respite in the game.

But her quandary remained – and she saw how deep it was. Even if she offered him no future help, Springfield already knew enough of her affair with the Prince to embroider or invent the rest, in anything he might publish – as he surely would, whether she co-operated with him or not. And once he left the island, if she did not accompany him, she would have no further control over his designs. And, of course, she had no intention of going anywhere with him. If this was the equation – and she saw no other – then there was only one answer to it: he must not leave Domenica. That answer was very simple. But it immediately produced a much more difficult problem: how could he be prevented from leaving the island?

There was a truly delicate point. And Frances considered it in that exact manner, without any malice aforethought, wondering if he might meet with some accident, out boating or in pursuit of the Caribs . . . God knows, she thought, the island, with its violent and unpredictable natural elements, was a dangerous enough place . . . Yet she was forced to admit that even she could not expect to bend the natural order to suit her own immediate purposes here.

In the event Springfield himself offered a possible answer to her problem when he told her next morning of his plan to make a long trek, in pursuit of the Caribs, up into the mountains in the heart of the island.

'You see, they're nowhere in their reserve right now,' he told her. 'From all the evidence, they've scattered – here and there.' He pointed to the map he was showing her. 'Up round this Trois Pitons mountain apparently – and beyond: this Valley of Desolation and the Boiling Lake.'

Frances suddenly paid attention. 'Yes, no doubt they have. You should look for them there, why not? Around that valley – and the Boiling Lake. Fascinating places in any case. We visited them, soon after we were married. Terrify—' She stopped herself. 'Unbelievable!'

Frances, indeed, had stood amazed – and fearful – on the high rock above the sulphurous lake eight years before, and shuddered at its boiling horrors, just a false step away, gurgling and erupting some hundreds of feet beneath her. The journey itself had been dangerous enough – along knife-edged ridges with sheer falls to either side, across crevices on makeshift rope bridges: a journey up through the fetid rain forest and along the treacherously slippy paths over the corrugated volcanic peaks, where one of their porters, taken by a loose stone on the narrow ridge-way, had tumbled to his death, smashed on the rocks far below. Springfield, she thought, might just meet with something of the same fate. It was certainly not a journey she ever wished to repeat herself.

'Right then!' Springfield beamed powerfully. 'We'll start tomorrow.'

'You and Mr Stein.'

He turned to her quickly, something very sly in his smile. 'Why, no – all three of us, of course.'

'But, Clement, I can't come.'

'But you must, Frances. Show us the way – you've been there before. Besides, I'll need you along with me – we can talk over our plans for your "memoirs".'

Springfield, overnight, had considered his relationship with Frances and had decided he did not trust her. He thought he had seen through her amiable consent to his publishing plans. She had been too quick in agreeing with him, had simply been toying with him for some reason – and he thought now he knew why. Quite ignorant of her assets until he had unearthed and valued them for her, she would now, if left alone, simply take the first opportunity of quitting the island and placing her memoirs elsewhere. She was just that sort, he had seen it from the start – calculating, devious, dangerous. He would keep a strict eye on her, keep her with him at all times.

Frances, on the other hand, confronted by this *force majeure*, decided not to contest it. She would make the trip again. Indeed, by accompanying him, she saw how, in some as yet quite undetermined manner, she might turn Springfield's invitation not to his, but to her own, advantage.

They set out at first light across the citrus fields, before rising gently up into the hills, soon entering the cavernous rain forests. It was a full day's journey to the Lake. They rode three scraggy ponies to begin with – two mules behind carrying tents and provisions and Stein's plate camera, with Big Jules in charge of half a dozen armed porters conscripted from the estate.

But by mid-morning, making a base camp at the foot of the Trois Pitons mountain, they were forced to abandon the mules and ponies, taking to their feet up into much denser rain forest. Here, as they scaled the lower mountain slopes at an angle of forty-five degrees, there was nothing but a narrow, muddy, undergrowth-tangled path to move on, interspersed with log steps, ladder-like, rising almost vertically.

Later the going became even more exhausting since soon, emerging from the tree line, they found themselves on the loose-stoned mountain ridges. On this section, struggling upwards for half an hour, then forced to descend for the same length of time, they moved forward in such an up and down manner for several hours, apparently rising no higher. Finally, however, coming to the top of a ridge, they saw how far in fact they had climbed – for there, miles below them to the west, they could just make out the tiny white speck of Fraser Hall and the sea beyond.

But now there were other problems. They were on the knife-edged ridgeway skirting the summit of Trois Pitons, which led round the mountain to the Valley of Desolation and the Boiling Lake beyond – a twisting track no more than a yard wide in some places, where the crest dropped sheer away on either side, hundreds of feet into deep, tree-filled valleys beneath.

Ahead of them, higher peaks loomed, covered in swirling mists, rain clouds sweeping in over the top of them. And soon the storms had engulfed the party, drenching them, buffeting them, as they crouched on the tiny path, clinging on while the rain swept over them. Then, just as suddenly, the clouds and mist disappeared and a brilliant sun emerged, drying them, allowing them to proceed, as the party took a second wind, rounding the mountain shoulder eventually, getting right into the heart of the island. Now the travel became easier as they descended a great boulder-strewn slope towards the Valley of Desolation below.

And so it was. Here all the lush vegetation of the island disappeared completely, replaced by jagged bleached white stones, flaky or pumice-like, with hot streams oozing slowly through these outcrops; everywhere sulphur geysers sighed and hissed, slowly erupting with a noisome, choking smell of rotten eggs. Nothing moved or lived here, a true slough of despond, a world's end.

Eventually, crossing this nightmare landscape and rising up the other side, they reached the top of a plateau, a smooth square of rock, with damp mists and a choking steam vapour swirling all about them. They could see nothing, wrapped and sweating profusely in these stinking folds of warm cotton wool.

'So?' Springfield said. 'All that – just for this? There's nothing to see.' He looked at Frances, standing in her filthy, mud-spattered jodhpurs beside him, throwing down her pith helmet, mopping her face.

'So – you wanted to come.'

Stein joined them, with Big Jules and the porters carrying his plate camera. 'Nothing to see – and not a sign of any Caribs either. Crazy.'

Stein wandered away from the group, towards the swirling vapour. 'You no go too much that way, sah!' Big Jules called out.

Stein turned, puzzled. 'But there's nothing there, is there?'

'You see – if it clear comes.'

A minute later, in a change of wind, it did – all the smoky vapours suddenly dispersing. Everyone stepped back quickly; Frances, suddenly alarmed, kneeling down for safety.

They had, they saw now, been standing near the edge of a vast cauldron of rock, with a lake at the bottom of it, a quarter of a mile in diameter: a lead-grey expanse of thick, porridge-like water – all bubbling, boiling steadily, rising and spattering, fuming with clouds of steam. It was an awesome sight, an Old Testament vision, symbol of Jehovah's wrath, the very mouth of hell where the damned would fall and boil for eternity. Everyone stepped even further back from the sheer edge.

'Sweet Jesus,' Springfield said simply. Stein, unpacking his big camera, prepared to photograph it. Frances, still crouching, sweating in the sticky, oppressive air, listened to the awful gurgles, invisible to her now, beyond the edge of the rock.

'Has anyone ever fallen in?' Springfield asked Big Jules.

'Yes – one homme! He once do that – boiled too hot très tôt!'

'What? – he fell right over, here?'

Big Jules nodded.

'How hot is it, do you think?' Springfield turned to Stein then, fiddling with his camera.

'What d'ya mean – how hot? You can see: it's *boiling*, isn't it? You wanna test it or sometin?' Springfield considered the matter.

Then, without warning, in another change of wind, they were suddenly enveloped in the sickly vapours, which turned off the lake and swirled around them. Frances, still sitting on her haunches, could barely see her hand in front of her face. But she saw her opportunity. Or, rather, she considered it: the problem was, if she were to stand up and make any movement, she ran the risk of falling over the edge herself . . .

'All of you – stay where you are! Don't move an inch!'

She heard Springfield's voice. Before the mists had closed in, he had been standing some half a dozen yards away from her. But now his words came from a closer point. Springfield, at least, disobeying his own instructions, was moving. Indeed, she could hear his footsteps on the rock – treading softly, coming straight towards her. And then, as the vapour cleared for an instant, looking up she saw him looming above her, making for her, reaching out his arms.

She half-rose to her feet, hoping to avoid him, scuttling away sideways like a crab from the edge. Then the fog closed round the eerie face and he was gone and she thought she had escaped him – until she suddenly felt a hand grasping her shirt collar, behind the neck, dragging her to her feet.

'Oh, no – not so fast!' She heard the soft voice out of the mist as he yanked her face round – then saw his great bulk towering above her, a look of ominous malice in his ghostly features. 'You think I don't know why you came all this way with me? – when you were terrified of the place: look at you now! – on your knees with fear. You never wanted to come – except maybe you thought you could ditch me here, push me over the edge or some such. That's why you came. Well, I'm going to keep you *right* with me, Frances!' He tightened his grip behind her neck.

'Where the hell are you, Clem?' It was Stein, calling out urgently from some distance away.

'I'm fine, Oscar. Just stay put,' he shouted back. 'I'm with Mrs Fraser – looking after her. Seeing she comes to no harm.'

Frances struggled a moment, but it was useless. 'You're talking nonsense,' she told him sharply.

'Am I?' He lowered his voice, full of icy sarcasm now. 'You killed your husband – so everyone says. So why not me, if you got the chance? I know too much, don't I? I saw it all afterwards, thinking about it. You agreed to everything far too easily, didn't you? You don't really want your "memoirs" published at all – or not by *me*, leastways.

And all that flirting – and romping on the divan – that was some other game you were playing. Took me for a complete fool, didn't you?' He wrung her collar, like a tourniquet, closer round her neck.

'I *do* want them published, I will—' she gasped out, ashamed by her fear, which made her furious.

'Why, you little—' He tightened his grip.

'You can have the letters!'

His face emerged suddenly from the fog, then disappeared again. 'Oh, I can, can I?'

'Yes, yes – you can have them!' She hardly realized what she was saying, sensing only her violent fury, caught by the neck, dangling like a cat, in the grip of this horrifying man.

'So, maybe I don't need you at all then?' He jerked her forwards, towards the edge of the chasm, so that she cried out then.

'Help! Help me – Jules, Mr Stein—'

'You all good an' safe là, Madame?' Big Jules called back.

'She's fine, Jules. Just slipped. But I've got her safely now. Don't any of you move – I've got her quite safely.'

In fact, without his noticing it in the thick fog, he no longer had her safely at all. In gripping her collar so firmly – pulling at it, some of the buttons snapping – the blouse had eased its way out from her waistband and begun to ride up her midriff.

Frances saw her chance. In an instant, bending down and straightening out both arms, she pulled herself violently away from him. And, though he hung on to her viciously, the blouse tore away, sliding over her head, and she was free. A second afterwards she lunged forwards into the choking mists, arms still outstretched, her hands meeting him full on his chest, pushing him violently, so that he overbalanced and fell away from her, disappearing into the swirling grey pall, launched out into space over the edge of the rock, without a sound as he fell into the boiling, gurgling depths far beneath.

Frances knew at once that he had gone over the precipice. It was only ten minutes later, when the mists cleared again, and the others had searched for Springfield everywhere on the high plateau and the rocks behind it, that they, too, realized he had gone this way.

Frances crouched down again then, kneeling, covering herself, half-naked, her body glistening with warm beads of vapour – the smudged, sweaty marks of his hands about her neck. She swayed to and fro gently, crying, gulping back sobs, as if in a state of shock. But they were happy tears – tears of relief and joy. Beyond her, on the lip of the chasm, lay the torn remains of her blouse. Stein reached for it gingerly, brought it back and considered it. The implication appeared obvious to him. But he turned to Frances for confirmation.

'What in hell happened? Did he . . .? Was he trying to . . .?'

Frances nodded. 'Yes, he tried to take me – he had me by the collar, just tore the blouse straight off, then fell back . . .'

'The crazy fool.' Stein turned away, gazing over the precipice where the wind, changing once more, had cleared the air above the lake, the sullen grey waves and eddies visible again, burbling and spitting. There was not the slightest sign of Springfield, swallowed up and drawn down into the seething depths of the cauldron. 'The crazy fool,' Stein said again to himself. 'As if he hadn't had enough women in his life already.'

An accident – everyone agreed to that. It was obvious: Springfield had slipped, lost his footing in the mists. And Stein, with Frances, was happy to say nothing of how, before he went, Springfield had ripped her blouse off, trying to molest her. So Frances conveniently came to believe this was the entire cause of his death: that Springfield had spun out into space simply as a result of hanging onto her blouse, like an anchor, which, when it had come adrift, had catapulted him over the edge. She saw her own part in his death as quite secondary, so that she readily forgot about it. It was unimportant – Springfield was gone.

The island, with its unpredictable natural hazards and elements, was indeed a dangerous place.

Leaving Hetty and Eileen with the Grants in their house on the hills above Roseau, she took the packet for Jamaica a week later – and then the Royal Mail Steamship *Orion* from Kingston to Liverpool. And with her she took the Prince's letters.

Ten days later, crossing direct from Liverpool to Dublin, she arrived without warning at Summer Hill, taking old Newman's hackney trap from Thomastown station, trotting up the long drive, the trees in the demesne still bare, the land cold and uninviting.

But the great house when she saw it at the top of the rise – with its long façade of tall windows reflecting the soft spring light – seemed to her full of warm promise. Sheltered by its necklace of old trees, it ran along just below the crest of the hill, formidable and serene as ever – surveying, dominating the valley, all unsuspecting, as Frances approached it, an army of one, about to ambush it. It lay there for her, waiting to be taken, the ultimate prize of her life.

Disturbed by the trap, the rooks threw themselves into the pearl-grey sky – wheeling in great cawing flocks above the chimney stacks: the sound of Summer Hill, so that Frances knew she had come home – to this house that would be hers. She would make sure of that this time. Surviving every setback in the long years of exile, she was more than hardened by adversity now: she was light-headed, intoxicated with confidence. After all she had suffered, her mother would no longer prove any match for her.

'Yes, Mama – *publish* the Prince's letters, in full, in America. I have already hinted of it to the press there: they will be snapped up. That is my intention, if you deny me the house.'

'Really, you are pathetic – of unsound mind. You should seek medical treatment.'

Lady Cordiner, to begin with, had been sardonically dismissive – dealing, as she thought initially, with a dazed and damaged child who offered no threat. She remained unconcerned, sitting quietly at the desk in her boudoir. 'Your proposals – your threats – can have no source other than in some acute mental derangement.' She turned then, raised her pince-nez, inspecting Frances as though studying some medical curiosity.

'I should say the same of you, Mama – with your monstrous behaviour over the years.' Frances spoke with equal sober irony. 'But we must face facts here: we are neither of us the slightest bit weak in the head. Just the opposite. We both weigh things most carefully, mean exactly what we say – as I mean what I have just told you. Every word of it.'

'Then you are criminally insane – and may expect soon to be confined in an institution for such people.' Lady Cordiner dropped her pince-nez. 'Now, if you will please leave. I, at least, have many real and pressing concerns.' She resumed her correspondence.

Frances noticed the array of black-bordered condolence cards on the mantelpiece: from the Aberdeens, the Ormondes, the Devonshires – with a similar collection of mournful letters lying on top of her desk: society everywhere offering sympathy in Sir Desmond's demise, letters which Lady Cordiner was still acknowledging over a month after his death.

Frances, deciding it was time to engage her mother more actively, saw her opportunity here. She picked up the card from the Viceroy, Lord Aberdeen, and his wife, headed by a gilt crown surmounting the simple copperplate legend 'Dublin Castle', and held it out to Lady Cordiner like a writ.

'I have to tell you,' she said much less blandly, a cold command in her voice, 'if you refuse to take any note of the Prince's letters, how all your treasured associations here, at the Castle' – she tapped the card – 'with the King's meddlesome Viceroy, and with all your other aristocratic friends, will cease immediately. If these letters from the

King are published you will be *dead* socially. Quite dead. You have only to read them, just one, to see what I mean.'

Lady Cordiner, unable to resist this bait now and feeling a secret alarm for the first time, rose from her desk, drew herself up on her small feet with immense scorn. 'You threaten me!'

'I do, believe me—'

'But it is *you* who are, and will remain, the complete social pariah. Not I. You have quite lost your senses. As if I should want to see those letters! – or be reminded in any way of your squalid *affaire*, which remains utterly repugnant to me.'

But Frances, in so graphically offering this threat of social extinction, and thus getting her mother to her feet, knew she had struck a most raw nerve. She returned to the theme and proceeded to open the wound, picking up the other cards on the mantelpiece. 'The Ormondes, the Waterfords, the Devonshires, Clanricardes, de Vescis . . .' She shuffled through the black-bordered missives, offering each one up as a harbinger of quite another doom for her mother. 'You will never show your face again – at the Castle, Curraghmore, Mount Juliet, Jenkinstown . . . No more Court levées, society luncheons, dinners, *soirées musicales* or tennis parties on the lawn. They will all be forbidden you! Every one . . .'

Frances, her voice cruel with opulent suggestiveness, and reversing the earlier roles – playing nanny to a recalcitrant child now – taunted her mother with this horrifying vision, this exile from Eden. 'Why, given the quite misguided royalist sentiment generally here in this county, most of the local tradesmen will boycott you. You will lose all face – even with your grocer and coal merchant!'

Lady Cordiner, like a rabbit smelling the ferret for the first time, became roused now, genuinely alarmed. She decided to retreat – in strength. Her satin widow's weeds rustling over the floor, she opened the door and moved briskly out into the heavily draped drawing room which, together with the rest of the house, was still festooned in black crêpe and other grim evidence of her traditionally exaggerated mourning.

Frances, seeing this exit, the predatory animal now sensing blood, took a first point in the contest: she had goaded her prey from its secure lair. She would pursue the attack – from room to room throughout the house if needs be: follow her mother to the kill. She left the boudoir swiftly, snapping at her mother's heels, as it were.

Lady Cordiner, hearing her steps so close behind, turned half-way across the drawing room and rounded on her, renewing her own response, which was to counterattack, choosing this as her best means of defence, pince-nez dancing over her bosom, her face colouring, voice rising, as the whole pace of their exchange increased subtly.

'You will desist from following me!' She almost shouted, thus confirming that battle was joined, that she was no longer dealing with a harmless idiot, and so Frances won another advantage: she had at last forced her mother to admit the reality of her threat. 'I have no wish to see your sluttish correspondence,' Lady Cordiner continued. 'Or you, which is more to the point. How dare you come here! You are not wanted. I have not the slightest intention of collaborating in your evil schemes – nor the least interest in you or your bastard child. And that you should so presume this house as yours and attempt to blackmail me in the matter – well, it is simply laughable, insane! You will leave at once – now, today, this instant. I shall have you forcibly ejected.'

While her mother stormed on, Frances had been slowly and menacingly approaching her, so that now only a few feet separated the two women. Finally they met eye to eye, in silence, as Lady Cordiner's tirade eventually died.

'Do you think I care in the slightest what you think of me? Or Henrietta – or my actions?' Frances said evenly, but weighing each word with ominous intent. 'The issue is quite other: what will you think – and *do* – when these are published?' She brought out one of the Prince's letters which she had been carrying with her, dangling it provocatively beneath her mother's nose.

379

Lady Cordiner snatched the letter and tore it into shreds. 'There! – that's what I think of your letters. And let that be an end to it. Now you must leave.'

Frances smiled with happy condescension. 'You have simply destroyed a copy of the letter, Mama – not the original. You cannot think me so foolish as to—'

'Wicked, not foolish. Your idiocy is something entirely malign.' Lady Cordiner pushed her aside then, making for the bell pull by the fireplace, tugging it vigorously.

'If you wish to conduct our business in front of the servants, I am *quite* willing,' Frances taunted her once more.

Her mother turned, her great dark eyes ablaze now beneath a cowl of starkly greying hair. 'We have *no* business to discuss.'

'Oh, but we have! Your future – and mine: this house.'

Frances looked round the shrouded drawing room – and beyond that, her eyes lifting, she seemed to stare through the walls, the ceiling, her gaze roaming and encapsulating the whole vast building and estate beyond.

The two women glared savagely at each other, both openly acknowledging the real nature of their battle now. The issue, which had been avoided or denied between them until then, was at last brutally clear: the prize they fought for was not the Viceroy's or society's good opinion, but the house itself – the ultimate resource, the fountainhead of both their lives. Victory lay in its simple possession – and whoever lost would lose everything. Now, both recognizing this, their battle became the more desperate – no longer concerned with mere social, but with literal, survival.

A footman had arrived in the room and Lady Cordiner, unwilling to take up her daughter's challenge in front of him, pushed past her, past the servant, leaving the drawing room, almost running now.

Frances, matching her pace, pursued her into the hall. 'If you refuse to discuss it – so much the worse for you,' she called to her across the echoing, pillared space.

There was silence, before the grandfather clock chimed

the hour of noon – twelve imperious, doom-touched notes – as her mother, undecided for a moment, hovered at the foot of the great staircase. Two housemaids, polishing the landing balustrade high above them, observed her down the stairwell. Lady Cordiner, seeing her way blocked there, herself turned sharply, making for the privacy of the dining room. Frances tracked her quickly once more, the pace increasing as the two women scurried across the wide hall.

Her mother, she thought, was mistaken in seeking this as a sanctuary, for the dining room, apart from a passage-way leading to the pantries and the kitchens, had only one entrance – and Frances shut this now, closing on Lady Cordiner again as she made for the green baize servants' door at the other end of the room. 'Of course! – we may continue our conversation in front of Mrs Molloy and all the kitchen maids!' she shouted after her.

Lady Cordiner, ever aware of the domestic proprieties, hesitated again and turned. A small, frail figure now, she felt a spasm of fear as she watched her daughter take up a commanding position at the other end of the long table – a fear which, though she remained outwardly calm, prompted her to move and take up refuge by the great Victorian Gothic sideboard with its collection of silver-topped meat dishes and carving implements. She glanced at the bone-handled cutlery here, drawing confidence from the sharp instruments, before turning and facing her daughter.

'I must tell you,' she said, puffing herself up, renewing the attack, taking further strength from the vast piece of furniture which formed a rampart behind her. 'If you continue to follow and badger me in this matter, I shall take steps – forcible steps . . .' Her voice rose in angry tremolos, her lower lip trembling.

But Frances mocked her. 'I am not afraid of you, Mama – never have been. Which, of course, is what you cannot bear in me. I alone, among all the family, you were unable to hurt or dominate in your long reign of terror here. Though you tried hard enough—'

'What ravings!'

'With that swing on the maple over the croquet court. Remember? Knowing, as a child, how much I loved it, you had it cut down—'

'You were not a child then – merely a spiteful, difficult, ungrateful young woman—'

'And before that, my dappled grey pony you sold—'

'You were too grown for it—'

'And the dances you forbade me at Kilkenny Castle—'

'You were not asked, far too young.'

'I was a young woman then, you have just said.'

'Yes, a thieving young woman, stealing my little *objets d'art* all over the house: nothing but a common thief!'

Frances paused, disturbed by this reminder, and her mother, sensing the advantage, counterattacked vigorously. 'Do you think I would give this house over to such a person? Why, you would have the place cleared with the auctioneers within a month!' Lady Cordiner, pressing her attack, advanced a few feet towards Frances. 'You,' she said with deep scorn, 'you are no fit person to run a hovel, let alone a great house and estate like this. You have not the slightest household knowledge, nor business acumen. And, besides, have you not thought? – without me, there would not be a penny to *run* the place! The estate was near bankruptcy when I married your father: all the capital in it now is mine – which, of course, is why he left it to me to dispose of at my discretion. And be assured – that discretion will never favour you! So you see, quite apart from me, your plan to take over Summer Hill is entirely illusory: you would not have a penny to maintain it.'

'I am not concerned with your money. You forget, I have been left rather well off myself: enough, certainly, to continue things appropriately here – if not in the vulgar, ostentatious manner you have always promoted in the house.'

Lady Cordiner, badly pricked by this comment, was furious. 'You – you despicable little hussy. You harlot!'

Frances laughed. Yet she, too, was almost losing control, speaking with stark emotion now. 'Harlot? – there is life to that, at least. You have always been death to this place: a *monster* of cruelty, selfishness – to all of us. The others have gone now, and you had so much to do with their going. But you will not get rid of me so easily.'

'You venomous little . . . bitch!'

Their engagement had reached a climax – the two women revelling in their mutual hatred, sustained by an oxygen of pure joy in expressing it, taking an almost delirious pleasure in the wounds they caused, in the other's pain – concentrating all their years of enmity in this final confrontation: feeding their malice, letting it bloom and grow as an evil flower, adorning it with every lethal barb. They were, for long moments then – quite forgetting the real cause of their battle – both wonderfully fulfilled and happy.

It was Frances, taking a grip on herself, who brought things down to earth. She sighed, unwilling to relinquish the heady joy of this character assassination, then said, 'This takes us nowhere. Let us concentrate on the real issues. Blackmail? You may regard it as such – but that is irrelevant. The letters? You refuse to look at them. Very well then, you should simply take my word for it: they are revealing and indiscreet to a degree – there is no doubt of that. The Prince is now the King Emperor. Their publication would cause a major constitutional and political scandal – perhaps even his abdication. I should not be affected. I have no connection with society here – I should simply return to Domenica, or go to America and start a new life. You, on the other hand, will hardly be able to show your face again in public, let alone in society—'

'You would not do such a thing?' Lady Cordiner cried out, seeming to command Frances, unaware of the alarm in her voice, or how her questioning words contradicted her imperious intent. 'The disgrace—'

'Exactly! But it would fall entirely on you, not me—'

'And the whole family.' Lady Cordiner glanced at the Cordiner ancestral portraits hanging round the dining room walls, Frances following her gaze.

'Indeed. I realize that. But then that is the whole

point of my business here: exactly that – the family! And its preservation. My father, my two brothers, are all dead. Hetty and I are now the family, *my* family, not yours – and so my wish to inherit what rightfully belongs to me and ensure the continuation of the line, the house itself. And you deny me that right, my birth-right—'

'I deny it to a slattern, to a vile blackmailing hussy.'

'That, too, is quite irrelevant. We talk of blood, not character, here, Mama: *my* blood, and therefore my house and Hetty's, not yours, or Austin's and Bunty's. It's all quite simple. There is nothing improper in my demand. I am merely forced, given your spiteful, wicked intransigence, to consider extreme measures in obtaining satisfaction.' Frances left the table and approached her mother slowly. 'And, believe me, I will take those measures – be in no doubt of that. I have nothing to lose. You have everything: your whole life here – and everywhere else for that matter.'

Lady Cordiner considered things. She still refused to believe that Frances would take the action she had promised. She decided to call her bluff. 'Very well then,' she told her grandly. 'Do what you will with your squalid letters. Publish them! You do not intimidate me. I shall not be blackmailed – I shall take the consequences.' She glared arrogantly at her daughter, who remained silent for a long moment, so that Lady Cordiner, for the first time, sensed the possibility of victory.

But Frances had prepared herself for just such a response from her mother. 'Very well, then – I shall take the mail boat for London this evening. The letters will be in the hands of the *New York Post*'s American correspondent there by this time tomorrow.' She turned abruptly, opened the door, leaving it wide open as she marched with ringing steps across the hall. Lady Cordiner remained, motionless at the end of the long table, fingering her pince-nez – suddenly aware how isolated and vulnerable she was, alone in the great room, surrounded only by the dismissive faces in the Cordiner family portraits, staring down all round her, seeming to laugh or glower at her: as an interloper finally repulsed.

Then, after half a minute, she started to scream.

Her face convulsed. She bit her lips. She yelled. She threw a pettish fit, which rapidly became real as she added to the invention – embroidering it, feeding, stoking it, with every sort of real and imagined persecution: fanning the flames of her outrage and defeat, so that very soon she was possessed by a genuine mania, gripped by an over-whelming, teeth-grinding energy, in which all her malice and repressed unhappiness was translated into vicious physical action.

She threw herself across the heavily draped dining table, clutching at the dark serge there – tugging, pulling the cloth towards her, so that the two candelabra at the centre crashed to the floor, and she with them, ending up half-covered in the material, writhing about, folding herself in it, then rolling out of it.

She stood up, her pince-nez broken, hair dishevelled and started to sway about the room, resuming her piercing wails and shrieks as she moved towards the sideboard. She picked up one of the long carving knives.

Frances had returned to the room, followed almost immediately by Pat Kennedy, now head butler at Summer Hill, and by one of the footmen. Grouped together at the doorway, they watched amazed as Lady Cordiner flourished the knife.

From the other entrance – the green baize door leading to the kitchens – Mrs Molloy and two kitchen maids had emerged timidly – looking on with fear and astonishment as Lady Cordiner moved towards Frances. She had stopped her screaming now. Instead she had a much more direct and obvious intent – to attack her daughter.

'You!' she shouted. 'This time – too far! A thorn in my side – too long, too long!' She advanced, holding the knife awkwardly, clutching it downwards in her fist, like a dagger.

'Stand back, Miss Frances!' Pat Kennedy warned, taking up one of the heavy dining room chairs and using it as a protective screen, prodding the air with it like a bull fighter with a cape, as Lady Cordiner moved inexorably forward. 'Michael!' he shouted to the footman. 'The table cloth – get hold of it, get behind her Ladyship – quick, man!'

The footman, circling round the other side of the long table, picked up the vast serge cloth, and attempted to manipulate it as a sort of net to trap this wild woman. But the material was far too cumbersome. Instead it enveloped him completely, blinding him as he staggered forward with it, nearly tripping in its folds.

Pat Kennedy meanwhile, advancing slowly with the chair, hoped to pin Lady Cordiner between its legs against the sideboard or the wall.

Frances suddenly smiled. Her victory was nearly complete. The situation was comic. She touched Pat Kennedy's arm, pushing him gently aside. 'Let her be,' she told him. 'Let her face me.'

'But, Miss Frances—'

'No – it is all quite undignified. Put the chair down, Pat. It's all an act – can't you see? She is simply pretending.'

Pat Kennedy set the chair down and Frances moved in front of him, to stand facing her mother. There was complete silence in the big room.

'Mama, you know well – this is no answer.' She spoke firmly to her mother, but softly, a sad nanny to her once more. 'Hand me the knife.'

In these last moments of the contest Frances never let her gaze stray a fraction from her mother's eyes – holding her fixedly, hypnotically, letting her own sense of superior power and impending victory pour into the other woman, willing her to hand over the knife.

But her mother, having gone thus far, was determined on one last flourish. Turning quickly to the wall behind her, and using the knife as a flailing scythe, she proceeded to cut and slash at the Cordiner family portraits, reaching for the first one, the canvas ripping as Sir William Cordiner took the brunt of her attack.

'There!' she cried as she criss-crossed the elegant

Georgian painting, shredding the bewigged and dignified old face. 'I think *that* of you and your family! That I should ever have become involved with them. Take them! Take everything to do with your wretched family.'

She slashed again, cutting deep down Sir William's blue and gold-braided tunic, then running a line round his wrist, so that his tattered remains fell from the frame. 'I want *nothing* to do with you or them – or with anything else in this vile, ignorant, godforsaken country. Good riddance to you and your feckless, spendthrift family – whom *I* saved, *my* family, with our money. Without me this place would have gone years ago.'

She paused in her mayhem, turning to Frances. 'Well, you can have the house now. I will leave. But remember one thing: you will have it without a penny of mine. And remember something else – the house remains in *my* possession. I may dispose of it as I want – now or when I am gone. And you will not have it, nor your child, nor any other Cordiner. I spit on you – I spit on your family!'

She turned back then and had moved on to the next portrait with the knife, before Pat Kennedy, with the footman, managed to overpower her – though she struggled to the end, falling over and twisting her leg painfully before she surrendered.

Frances took her victory gracelessly. 'Get a chair. Carry her up to her bedroom and stay there until the doctor arrives.' She spoke to Mrs Martin, the housekeeper – commanding her, already assuming the role of mistress in Summer Hill.

Lady Cordiner, slumped in one of the long chairs from the porch, a liveried footman at either end, was manoeuvred out of the room with ignominious ceremony – Frances observing the little ambulance procession with unconcealed satisfaction.

Later, when old Mitchell, the family doctor, had visited, he came downstairs. Frances interviewed him in the drawing room.

'Your mother,' he began diffidently, in his soft, slight Cork brogue, 'she appears . . . she's very disturbed.'

'I am not surprised. She has behaved most foolishly – dangerously.'

'But, apart from the leg, nothing really wrong with her.'

'She is mad, Dr Mitchell.'

'Ah, now, I wouldn't go that far, no. But I've given her a sedative – Frances.' He tried to get on more familiar terms with this cold and harsh woman. 'But I wonder – if you mightn't go a bit easier with her, making things up in some way? She's taken a lot of bad knocks recently.'

'Doctor!' Frances was impatient now, bunching her fingers together, making fists of them. 'She attacked me, intent to murder me – with a knife!'

'Ah yes, well . . .' He hesitated. 'A formidable and difficult old lady, I'll grant you that. But she . . . she meant no harm.'

'Meant no harm? She might have killed us all, besides destroying half the dining room! She has obviously lost her wits completely – is a danger to herself and others. She must have treatment, be confined somewhere. She cannot be left alone for an instant.' Frances harangued the man now.

'Oh no, dear me, no – I don't think it's anywhere near as serious as that. A few days, a week's rest upstairs here and she'll be right as rain. And perhaps . . .' He took out his pipe, tapping the bowl easily. 'Maybe you could spend a bit of time up in Dublin meanwhile.' He smiled, hoping to initiate a mild conspiracy between them. 'You know what I mean. Take the pressure off her, allow her to recover.'

Frances rounded on him. 'Dr Mitchell, you don't understand. It is my *mother* who will be leaving here – not I.'

'No.' He was startled. 'No, I don't think I follow you there.'

'Yes, indeed. She is leaving Summer Hill – permanently. She confirmed as much, in front of witnesses.'

'Ah, now!' The doctor was almost jocular in his alarm. 'I'm sure she didn't mean a word of it.' He laughed uneasily. 'Not a word of it! Give her a week or two by herself and she'll be right as rain—'

'But *I* mean that she leaves here – and will ensure she does.'

'But, Frances—' Dr Mitchell was thoroughly put about now.

'There is no point in discussing it. Did you imagine that I returned home – all this way from the West Indies – merely to temporize with my mother once more? We have come to an agreement: she has disowned me, this house, all the Cordiners – in front of everybody. Therefore it's all perfectly clear: I, as rightful heir, now assume control of Summer Hill.'

The doctor puzzled over this legalistic statement for a moment. 'Forgive me, but I understood – your father and I were very old friends – that Sir Desmond had left the house and estate to your mother, to use during her lifetime and to dispose of afterwards at her discretion. Has she left you the house formally then?'

'No, not formally.'

'Then – forgive me again – I don't quite see the grounds you have? . . .'

'That will be a matter for the solicitors. But there are obvious grounds already: "unsound mind", Dr Mitchell.'

'Ah, now, Frances, that's going a bit too far altogether. As her physician I couldn't really support you in that theory. Simply a temporary lapse. As I said, she'll be right as rain in a week or so. You'll see!'

'I have no wish to see, Dr Mitchell – nor to seek your advice or support in the matter. Lady Cordiner will leave here at the soonest opportunity. You may depend on it.'

The doctor departed shortly afterwards. And Frances, alone in the great room, the light waning beyond the shrouded windows, considered her position. Of course, the doctor was right: her grounds were insecure. He had, in fact, simply confirmed the flaw in her victory, the real threat in her mother's last words to her. She might possess the house for the moment. But it was a quite impermanent possession. Lady Cordiner, legally, still retained absolute and final control of its destiny.

As well, given the possible stipulations in her father's

will, Lady Cordiner might – when she regained her senses and with a good lawyer – have her evicted from Summer Hill, almost at once or at some point in the future when, with the King dead, his letters would no longer form the threat to Lady Cordiner which they did at present.

Thinking of all this, Frances realized how precarious her position was. She had merely won a battle, not the war. She must, she saw, take steps at once to secure the position. Before her mother left Summer Hill, she would have to change her will – would, of course, have to be forced to do so. Frances considered possible means to this end.

She would have to confront her mother again in any case – make out a codicil for her to sign, there and then. Going into Lady Cordiner's boudoir, Frances set to work immediately, preparing just such a document in which, apart from her mother's possessions and capital, all of Summer Hill and its estate were to be left to her, and any previous legacy made of the property be revoked.

That same evening she took the document upstairs. Her mother, sullen-faced, in a night cap and heavily shawled, lay propped up in the great four-poster bed, the curtains drawn, a lamp burning on a table, another by her bedside. Bridey, her maid, was sitting nearby. There was a fuggy air of sal volatile and paraffin in the room.

'Bridey, if you will leave us please. I shall stay here for the moment.'

Her mother barely noticed her, glancing in her direction then turning away. Frances presented her with the codicil. 'Mama, you will please read – and sign – this.' The old lady did nothing, continuing to gaze sideways at the lamp, allowing the paper to fall unregarded on the counterpane. 'It sets out the new arrangements over the house – a codicil to your will.'

Lady Cordiner made no response whatsoever, maintaining her steady gaze at the red lampshade, as if at some nirvana, the rays of light casting an orange glow over her sour features. Frances became impatient. 'It will do you no good – this dog-in-the-manger attitude. I have prepared a perfectly fair document, in which you retain all your possessions and capital here, but where I become the legal owner of the house, now and in the future. I have no intention of allowing you to hold a sword of Damocles over me in the matter. You will sign this – or else, as I promised yesterday, I will publish those letters, without hesitation.'

Lady Cordiner finally turned and looked at Frances. She laughed drily. She cackled. She spluttered and coughed in her glee. But still, as she ignored the paper on her bed, there was no word from her. Frances played another card.

'Of course, if you refuse to sign – and quite apart from the Prince's letters – you will lose all control of the house in any case. Your behaviour this morning, in front of everyone, makes that perfectly obvious: unsound mind – a danger to yourself and everyone else. You will be confined in an institution in Dublin. I shall see to it. I have already spoken to Dr Mitchell.'

Lady Cordiner laughed again – a full, entirely sane laugh, followed by a most satisfied smile. The siege appeared to have failed – and her mother revelled in the victory, relishing it now in continued silence.

Frances stood by the bed, considering the impasse for a moment. Then, deciding upon something, she moved abruptly to the door, locked it, turned and confronted her mother.

'Very well then, if you refuse to sign, we shall neither of us have the house.'

She walked swiftly forward to the mahogany drum table in the centre of the room, lifted the globe from the second lamp there, turned the wick down, extinguished the flame, removed the glass funnel and then unscrewed the cap from the oil reservoir.

Holding the pedestal, she approached her mother, then tipped the lamp over, letting the oil fall on the carpet, making a circle with the paraffin right round the great bed. She spoke calmly as she went.

'You still have a chance to sign – or see this house burnt.'

Now at last, understanding how Frances's intention was that she, as well as the house, should burn, her mother spoke. 'Don't be stupid! What folly are you up to?' She struggled to get out of bed. But her twisted leg prevented her. 'How dare you!' she shouted impotently. 'You will ruin the carpet. Bridey?' she shouted, floundering about. 'Bridey!'

'Bridey has gone down to the kitchen for her supper. No one will hear you.'

Lady Cordiner stretched an arm out then, reaching for the long tasselled bell rope hanging above her bedside table. Frances removed it, pulling the cord right away from her and tucking the end behind a picture on the wall. Then she moved back to the table, picking up a box of matches, rattling them ominously.

'You wouldn't dare!' her mother advised her scornfully.

'I would – I *will*.'

Lady Cordiner, though still in control of herself, was alarmed now. 'Why, you think to murder me! – you imagine you would get away with that?' she scoffed.

'Not at all, Mama. Simply the house will burn down around you. An accident, with the lamp here. You were trying to leave your bed, it fell on the floor. With your leg you were unable to reach the door. I shall have left the room by then. I shall try and save you, of course. We shall all try and save you. But we will be too late.'

Frances struck a match then, allowing it to flare brightly. Then she blew it out. 'Well, what do you say?'

Her mother struggled up in the bed once more, but again could not summon the strength to leave it. 'I forbid you!' she shouted.

'You are quite past forbidding me anything. If you value your life, you have only one course of action open: sign that document – and I shall then have your signature witnessed.'

Calling her daughter's bluff once more, Lady Cordiner still resisted. 'No – never!'

Frances moved forward calmly, bent down, lit a second match and set it to the trail of oil on the carpet. It took several moments to catch and then only slowly. But soon, gathering appetite, the flame licked along the path, running like a fuse, turning the corners of the bed neatly and speeding up the far side, so that within a minute Lady Cordiner and the great four-poster were held in a circle of hungry fire.

Frances calmly watched the flames rise, seeing her mother's agonized features now beyond the smoky pall – the great eyes wide, her face alive with impotent fear. Lady Cordiner screamed. But, with wafts of acrid smoke blowing towards her, the screams soon stopped and she began to cough and choke.

Then, and only then, did she capitulate. 'Yes!' she cried out finally. 'Yes!'

Frances seized the big water jug from its bowl on the wash-stand, doused the flames with it, before stamping them out all round the bed. Then, retrieving the codicil from a fold in the eiderdown, she took it to her mother, together with a pen she had brought upstairs with her.

'You will live to regret this,' her mother told her bitterly, as she signed. 'Every single thing you have done here today. I promise you that.'

Frances, taking the document, leant forward then, peering coldly into her mother's eyes, shaking her head slowly. 'You obstinate old woman,' she told her quietly. 'Will you never learn? It was the way you always *threatened* us in the old days – even by your simple presence – that made us hate you. And *still* you do it!'

Lady Cordiner seemed about to embark on another tirade. 'I shall inform the police – how you extorted this signature from me, attempted to murder me.'

'After your insane performance in the dining room today, they will not believe you. Besides, remember the Prince's letters. If you attempt to make any more trouble, I will have them published. As I've said, the scandal will not affect me. I have no wish to hobnob with society here – just the opposite: I want the British Crown out of Ireland, as soon as possible. That lackey the Viceroy, people like you and all your cronies – all the years of misrule: you in this house and the others up at Dublin Castle. Your time is over in Ireland. So why jeopardize your future in

England? – where I imagine you will now return. A house in London or Brighton? A pleasant retirement . . . Why not? You have many friends over there already. But there is no doubt they would all cut you dead if one word of this royal scandal emerged. So my advice to you is that you say nothing of all this' – she glanced round the smoky room – '*ever*. If you hold to that, I shall do likewise: no mention that the King is Henrietta's father, ever, not even to Hetty herself. Your social prospects will remain intact thereby. But if you think to prolong this battle – in *any* way, now or in the future – you will condemn yourself to a lonely and miserable old age.'

Lady Cordiner, still brooding and malevolent, said nothing. But it was clear from her silence, from the look of resignation in her tired, bloodshot eyes, that she was considering her assent to all this, that she thought – soberly now – to cut her losses, be done with the whole affair, and leave Ireland for just such a pleasant retirement.

Frances, in any case, took her silence for agreement, turning then, unhitching the bell pull from the picture and tugging at it vigorously. Then she went over and unlocked the bedroom door before facing her mother once more.

'So! We have an agreement – at last . . .'

Her mother still could not bring herself to say yes. But for Frances the message was now entirely clear: Summer Hill was hers. All the years of thwarted desire and waiting were over. She had come into her inheritance at last. And it was like a marriage for her just then, standing at the threshold by the doorway, a bride at the altar of the house; she would now enter it – all the other rooms, from attics to cellars and the land about – possessing it, being possessed by it; now and always, hers.

'*Mine*,' Frances said simply, opening the bedroom door wide, letting the air into the smoky room, going across and opening the window then, so that a soft evening breeze filled the murky space, a mix of turf smoke and sweet wind running off the moist river valley: renewed life, fresh life, a hint of all the different life to come to this beautiful house which for so long had remained sealed and dumb, asleep, caught in the briar-like toils spun by the old witch who lay defeated in the great bed now. Frances, at last penetrating the evil thorns, had broken the spell, would now – just as she had promised so long ago – kiss Summer Hill back to life.

Two thousand miles away, in the humid air lying just above the warm waters of the Caribbean, another less benevolent wind was taking shape.

At first there seemed little to it. The over-heated air, spiralling lazily upwards, cooled and condensed rapidly, so that, high over the ocean, clouds formed and some rain fell.

But soon more and warmer air, great swaths of it, was sucked into the updraught, reinforcing and enlarging it, creating vicious eddies and a sudden drop in the air pressure. The phenomenon, like an evil genie released from a bottle, took a first hesitant shape – an uncertain brew of wind, heat, motion and energy – until all these forces coalesced, sustaining, provoking each other furiously, rising up and darkening the whole atmosphere, where the cloudy commotion showed its true colours as a hurricane.

The funnel of air became a whirling cauldron, filled with sea birds trapped in the eerie calm at the centre, widening out and spiralling up, fed by violent winds now, forming waterspouts over the tossing ocean: a billowing monster, erupting, climbing, an implacable engine of destruction which finally – establishing itself as an immense black pillar over the ocean, surrounded by a coliseum of clouds – moved towards the first of the Caribbean islands, Domenica, which lay directly in its path.

The sea in the bay beyond Roseau became strangely quiet, the air unnaturally calm. The waves changed their pattern, retreating from the shoreline, and then lapping on the shingle beaches only three or four times a minute now, as if fatally weakened by some great force pulling them in the opposite direction far out to sea.

In the hall of the tin-roofed Carnegie Library on the sea-front the barometer fell astonishingly. But Miss Oliphant, the librarian, chatting softly of the new Galsworthy novel to Mildred Grant by her desk, failed to notice it.

At Fort Young, behind the bandstand in Marine Gardens, the sentry on duty between the two great cannon felt his ears pop, but took no account of it. He yawned and swallowed several times, wiped the sweat from his brow, and remained surprised only by the complete silence in the air, even when he had cleared his ears. He looked over the parapet, noticing how the waves had receded, far below their usual level, half-way down the moist shingle, exposing a collection of old boots and beer bottles. But it was his first tour in the West Indies and he thought little of it.

Further along the seafront though, at the bar of the Club by the Botanical Gardens, just before lunch, one of the older members, gulping the last of his whisky, remarked to Bertie Grant how he tasted blood in his mouth and Bertie commented how his eardrums had begun to sing. At the same moment the two men, both old-timers on the island, realized the cause of their discomfiture – and joined by the other members, all making for the terrace, they saw the first of the great waves, riding ahead of the storm, travelling in a wide semicircle round the small bay, heading straight towards them. And, beyond the wave, they saw the huge swirling bar of cloud, rapidly obscuring all the light, a heavy black wall closing in upon them like a curtain of doom.

The first wave sank half a dozen small boats and demolished part of the wooden jetty down by the port at the end of Main Street: a small wave. The others, roaring in behind it, were five and ten yards high, vast hills of tidal water. They crashed all along the shore line, destroying the rest of the jetty, capsizing a big sloop moored there, wrecking the terrace and seafront windows of the Carnegie Library, and riding in colossal drifts of spume right up to the top of the ramparts of Fort Young.

Then, the great funnelling cloud closing on the little town, the rain came in vicious squalls, the water falling with the force of hailstones – to be followed at last by the demon king in the storm: an unbelievably venomous wind, that hit Roseau like thunder, a successive slapping of vast hands which altered everything, where the earlier waves and the rain had been mere pinpricks; a circling, thrusting, implacable, devious wind – lifting the roofs, seeking out and laying bare every secret place, toying with everything before destroying it.

Establishing itself with a noise like the manic rattle of hundreds of engines rushing through a tunnel, the wind began to suck the town up, a famished beast leaving the barren ocean, feeding voraciously now for the first time on dry land – gorging, making a single mouthful of whole warehouses, villas, the Anglican church on the hill.

The hurricane, settling to its meal, and having strolled before, now started to gallop through the streets, swallowing everything. Houses were picked up, suspended in mid-air, inspected for a moment, then digested, disintegrating, the bones spat out hundreds of yards away.

The church spire disappeared like an arrow northwards, shooting out over the bay. The great *châtaignier* tree in the Botanical Gardens keeled over, all its roots free above the ground, before it rolled down the emerald lawn, pulverizing the shrubs and flower borders, and killing a number of unfortunate people unable to escape its path.

Then, as the eye of the hurricane passed directly over the town, in the airless heart of the storm, the pressure fell to zero and there was a sinister calm in which another sort of destruction bloomed. The better stone houses, with firm walls, windows and foundations, built to resist just such a wind, seemed to explode.

The walls and glazing of the telegraph office in Brunswick Street, unable to cope with the enormous difference in air pressure, simply burst apart like rotten fruit. The chickens in the compound behind the post office in Hanover Street, caught in the same airless funnel, expanded like balloons before detonating – the air sealed in the quills of their feathers released now like machine gun shots.

At its circumference – in the whirling circle of sharp rock, shingle, brick, pieces of wood and mud – people were caught up: beheaded, torn apart, maimed, carried aloft; stripped of their clothing before being thrown out of the murderous carousel, naked, encrusted with sticky dirt – riddled, as if by gun-fire, with stones, nails, splinters.

In the Carnegie Library, Mildred Grant, with Miss Oliphant and a few others caught there, all took shelter between the interior walls of Miss Oliphant's small office, huddling between stacks of new books and fresh copies of the *Sphere* and *Illustrated London News*. But, when the wind got beneath the eaves of the corrugated roof, gripping it boldly from one end and tearing it back like the lid of a sardine tin, they found themselves crammed together like fish, taking the brunt of the weather on their heads.

Mildred never saw the great iron rafter which, released from one side of the roof, fell towards her, spearing her from behind, striking her in the back, beneath the neat bun in her wispy hair. Miss Oliphant screamed, seeing her friend impaled, like a butterfly in a collection case, secured by a pin.

At the Club they tried forcibly to restrain Bertie Grant from leaving the building, where those members who had not escaped immediately were now taking shelter in the cellar stores beneath the bar.

'Don't be a damn fool, man! Milly will be perfectly safe – the library is well made of stone. Stay where you are!'

But, his absentmindedness forgotten and overcome by a sort of guilty panic, Bertie insisted, struggling free and running up the cellar steps.

Behind the bar, bottles shook and broke – while in the dining room next door plates and cutlery flew off the tables, taken by a fierce wind from the broken windows, as if the whole Club was a ship at sea about to founder.

Bertie ran out into the choking, dust-filled air of the Botanical Gardens. The *châtaignier* tree had rolled down the lawn, coming to a stop near the gates. Beyond them he saw the roof ripped off the library. He quickened his pace. He ran with wonderful speed, taken by the wind pushing him forwards, the long jacket tails of his white tropical suit swirling above his head. But the tree completely barred his exit from the gardens. Beneath it, as he approached, he saw the body of one of the Club staff, the Goanese cook, just the legs sticking out, the rest of the man invisible.

Deciding to conquer the obstacle, and sheltered against the bole of the tree for a moment now, he scrambled up on to its trunk – the wind helping him again, like a comrade. But, once he was on top of the smooth bole, crouching, beginning to stand, quite clear of any shelter and taking the full force of the storm, the wind behind turned traitor and in a sudden burst of energy picked him up like a doll.

Caught by the terrible wind, he sailed straight off the tree trunk, white tails flying, arms outstretched, a dozen feet off the ground, like a bizarre angel – out over the wall, high across the road and into Marine Gardens, where only a bandstand pillar prevented him from disappearing out to sea.

He lay there, half-naked, eyes and nostrils filled with mud, impaled everywhere with sharp debris – spread-eagled on the bandstand platform, where still the wind nudged and pushed him, sliding him across the tiles, moving his broken limbs about as if there was still some life in him.

The hurricane, continuing its feast, contented itself with the rich pickings of the town, avoiding the interior, moving slowly north now along the coast towards the top of the island.

High up, four miles away in the hills above Roseau in the Grants' house at Lime Hill, Hetty with Robert, Eileen and the other servants watched the hurricane move over the town far beneath them – a great tormented cloud, obscuring everything, raging along; at Lime Hill, though the air was dark and turbulent, they had been barely touched by the storm.

'Isn't it *exciting*!' Hetty exclaimed, the wind running in her dark hair, looking over the scene from the long veranda of the house.

Eileen said nothing. The other servants were equally grim-faced.

'I hope Mama and Papa are all right, though,' Robert said, less happily. 'I so wanted her back. I've all my things to get ready, haven't I, Eileen? – for school in England. All my packing!' He turned to Hetty joyously then. 'Packing! – so yah-boo and sucks to you! *I'm* going to *school* in *England*!' he chanted. 'Mama's coming with me the day after tomorrow – and you'll be just left here on your own.'

Hetty glowered at him. 'Oh, no, I won't. *My* Mama is going to take me to Ireland soon. She's over there now seeing to it – isn't she, Elly? We're all going back – to live there in my *real* home. A much bigger place than this. And far better than your old school in England. Isn't that true, Elly? Elly's been there before – she knows all about it. It's wonderful, isn't it, Elly? As big as Buckingham Palace. So sucks to you, you stupid little brat of a colonial boy!'

The two children nearly came to blows before Eileen separated them, taking them both smartly indoors, as the storm raged on, moving away up the coast.

'I'll have no more of it,' she told them sharply. 'This fighting and squabbling. You two are going to behave yourselves and get along together – as long as I'm around and wherever you are. Yes, get along together – that's the ticket!'

She kept them apart, holding their collars, like two fighting cocks, as the children continued to look daggers at each other.

book three

I

Hidden behind the curtains and sitting quite still on the window seat, alone in the great hall at Summer Hill, Hetty saw the big rat. Shiny-grey, glistening-eyed, with a long, long tail, it emerged from somewhere behind the tall stairway, frisked its whiskers an instant, seemed to gaze at her, quite unafraid, then came clear out into the open – stopping, sniffing the air, before lolloping over to the big wickerwood basket on the far side by the hall door, where it disappeared.

'Mr Rat!' Hetty said to herself in approving wonder. It wasn't half as big or wild as the rats in Domenica: a friendly Irish rat. Perhaps she might make a friend of it. She badly missed her pet iguana.

Then she heard the green baize door behind the staircase opening softly, and soft footfalls as Pat Kennedy, with the funny curls over his brow – 'kiss curls' Elly called them mockingly – came into the hall, in his dark tailcoat and trousers. Pat was the butler here – whatever that meant. He was the head servant anyway, she knew that. He put his hand in his trouser pocket now, moving quickly across the hall, glancing up the stairway, then to either side, as he neared the basket of logs. Bending down then, he sprinkled a handful of yellow corn all around the bottom of the basket, before returning, just as silently, the way he had come.

Hetty smiled. A nice man! He'd been leaving food out for Mr Rat! And sure enough, a minute later, the same great rat emerged to feed greedily on the corn. Hetty was spellbound, watching it eat – thinking of Pat's kindness: at least there was one nice man in this huge frightening house.

The rat disappeared and Hetty, emerging from behind the curtains, drew up the long hem of her muslin dress, turned and, kneeling on the window seat now, noticed the tiny pane of coloured glass in the bottom corner of the tall window. It was a picture of some great bird with its wings spread out – like one of the frigate birds in Domenica, sitting on top of a strange tin hat, with something written beneath it in funny wiggly letters: 'Audaces Fortuna Juvat'.

She mouthed the words to herself. What could they mean? It wasn't English anyway, not even the strange sort of English most people spoke here in Ireland. But the bird was interesting, with its great beak facing sideways and fierce yellow eye which gleamed brightly in the cloudy autumn sunlight from beyond the window. She thought of the frigate birds – endlessly, lazily sweeping over the bay at Fraser Hall against the huge, always sunny blue sky. Big Jules had told her they were the spirits of dead sailors drowned at sea, looking for their old homes, their wives, families and friends. And, thinking of this and of Big Jules and Cook and Slinky the garden boy, Hetty was suddenly terribly homesick again.

She sucked her thumb fiercely, digging the other thumbnail into the little, perfectly round lime fruit which she carried about with her everywhere now, ever since she had arrived at Summer Hill a month before; then put the fruit to her nose, loving the prickly sweet and sour smell of her old home, a smell that was dying now, the skin pricked nervously all over with her nails since she had left Domenica and come to this strange, cold place.

Outside, in the racing clouds and sunshine, she saw the quick shadows running over the squares and terraces and diamond-shaped flower beds of the 'Pleasure Garden' as they called it. Though she could see no pleasure in it. She wasn't allowed to play anywhere there, among the rose bushes, the tiny little hedges, the shiny red gravel paths and the stone steps – so many stone steps – going up to a big tree whose leaves were turning a bright yellow. Next to the tree she saw the flat bit of very short grass with white hoops and a coloured pole scattered about it – a game the grown-ups played here, Elly had told her, called 'crocket'.

Beyond this was another piece of grass, the 'tennis

court', with a sort of droopy fishing net spread across it. That sounded great fun, though no one had played either of these games since she'd arrived, because there weren't any family grown-ups in the house now, only her mother and the funny, straggly-haired woman, her great-aunt Emily, who wandered about the house and gardens all the time, singing nursery rhymes and laughing to herself.

Elly had told her that her great-aunt Emily was 'touched'. Touched? Who had touched her to make her like this? Elly couldn't tell her. God had touched her, Hetty supposed, and made her silly like this. But how silly of him.

Anyway, great-aunt Emily never played at these outdoor games, she simply drew and painted all the time in a big white drawing book like a child; nor did her mother, far too busy changing and 'planning' things about the house. And Robert, of course, couldn't play at all now, upstairs in bed coughing all day and night, with Elly looking after him for the past week.

She had been on her own most of the time ever since she'd arrived, hiding, running around, exploring. Anyway, these outdoor games were soon going to be put away for the winter, Elly had told her before she'd disappeared into Robert's bedroom: the 'winter', when the ice and the cold and the snow came, though it was only the start of 'autumn' now. There were four of these funny 'seasons' here, when there had only been one in Domenica.

In autumn here the leaves turned yellow and red, when they had been green before. That was what autumn was, Elly had said happily: when the fruit was ripe and the corn gathered in and squirrels and people stored everything away for the winter. They'd be cutting and threshing the corn any day now – a big steam engine was coming to do that, Elly told her, which she hadn't understood ('The same great engine that took us down from Dublin?' 'No.'). And, as for the autumn fruit at Summer Hill, well, she hadn't known what to make of that either: all the trees in the great walled vegetable garden and orchard behind it.

The fruit was extraordinary here, like nothing she'd ever

seen in Domenica – small, all funny shapes and colours. It had looked poisonous to her: apples, pears, quinces, plums, damsons, medlars, they were called – and grapes in the vine house.

At first she hadn't even touched any of it, until one hot afternoon an old gardener man, a kind man really, called Martin, with a moustache, had told her in his strange Irish voice that all the fruit here was 'the best of eating'. Then he'd shown her a special tree in a walled-off corner of the vegetable garden with tiny round apples on it, light yellow, with a faint crimson blush: crab apples, Martin called them, eating one himself, before giving her one.

The taste was strange, not entirely nice; sour, pricking her tongue, but then a small strange sweetness. The tree, Martin had told her, was the 'childer's tree'. It had been planted a long time ago, by her grandfather when he was young – 'God rest his soul,' he'd said, before crossing himself in that funny way that Elly did – 'And then it was for your mother here after him, when she was a child, and her two brothers, God rest their souls as well.'

'Why should God have to rest their souls?' she'd asked him then and he'd looked at her in a sad way and said, 'An' sure aren't they all dead and gone from here.' He sighed, polishing another of the little rosy apples. 'An' they all eating in their time from this tree – an' that's why it's called the childer's tree, an' you the only child left in the family now.' She'd been frightened then. 'We-we-were they killed by these apples?' and she'd tried to spit the last mouthful out.

'Ah, sure, not at all, at all. 'Twasn't thim apples that took thim. Thim's special little apples – the Apples of Life we call thim here in Ireland, growing wild all over the place, and a great cure for the ague or a cold or iny kind of chestiness.'

'Magic apples?' Hetty had asked him. 'Like the ones in my *Red Fairy Tale* book?'

'Indeed – indeed you're right. That's what they are – ye could well say: magic apples!' And they'd held the happy secret between them then, in the hot, high-walled space in the corner of the garden. 'No, indeed,' Martin had said sadly, ''Twasn't thim apples that took thim – 'twas God took thim, all in his own good time.'

Hetty thought about this now, kneeling on the window seat of the hall: the magic apples and God taking people like this in Ireland in his 'own good time'. Well, it wasn't a good time over here at all that God was managing. At home in Domenica the fruit and the weather had been pretty much the same all the year round. But here God changed the wind and sun, the heat and cold, every few months. He killed people to 'rest their souls' – hadn't they been able to have a good sleep in their own beds when they were tired? – and he 'touched' other people and made them silly, and he fiddled about with the sun all the time. Why couldn't he leave well alone, as he did in Domenica? – apart from the hurricanes.

But of course, she realized, like everyone else she had seen in England and Ireland since she'd arrived, God was *extremely busy* over in this part of the world, always doing things, mile-a-minute as the trains went, an interfering old busybody. She decided she didn't like God in Ireland. He was a much better person in Domenica.

She heard her mother's voice then, coming from the drawing room behind her – loud words, speaking to Mr O'Donovan, the tall, white-haired, bushy-bearded man in a stiff black suit who was the head man outside the house, who ran everything in the yard and farm. The 'Steward' he was called – he did the same things as nice old Mr McTear did at Fraser Hall, but he wasn't at all as friendly. Mr O'Donovan looked rather like God, Hetty thought – or the one they had over here anyway. He was always frightfully busy. The voices were coming toward her, and she hid behind the long dark window curtains again.

Ever since she'd arrived she'd taken to hiding from her Mama, since whenever they did meet, and with Elly hidden away with Robert who had an 'infectious disease', Mama had found nasty things for her to do, or told her to stay in her room, when what she had wanted to do was roam the house, discovering things. Because, one good thing at least, unlike Fraser Hall, there were so *many* absolutely wonderful places to hide, in this huge dark house: endless rooms and landings everywhere and all filled with cubby-holes, nooks and crannies – and with great dark furniture and long curtains and heavily draped tables, which she could hide behind or beneath, all cosy and warm, for the cold here was *terrible*, even though it wasn't yet winter, when it got *worse*.

'So that's settled then, O'Donovan,' she heard her mother say as they came into the hall. 'I shall need half a dozen of the yard and farm men in here for the next few weeks – to clear out all this frightful furniture, curtains, pictures and things. Store it, sell it, burn it – anything. And then help me get all the good old furniture down from the attics. I shall clear the house out by degrees, then redecorate the whole place – white and blue limewash for the most part, so we shall need the painters in then, ladders and so on.'

'Yes, Mrs Fraser.' The man spoke rather crossly as the two of them stood in the hall. But her mother's voice sounded even more cross.

'And these gloomy Roman busts everywhere in the hall, O'Donovan – I shall want them all removed – and replaced, in those niches there, with the two original statues, "Cupid" and "Psyche".'

'Statues, ma'am?'

'Yes, the two here originally: classical Greek, in white marble.'

'I don't know, Mrs Fraser – not in my time.'

'But of *course*, O'Donovan, they were here in the old days, before my mother took over. They must be somewhere about. I think I remember seeing them up in that garden store beyond the vine house: two white marble statues. Two young people, O'Donovan – naked, you know.'

'Two . . . young people. Yes, Mrs Fraser. I'll see if I can find them. I'll . . . I'll ask Appleton to go through the garden outhouses.'

'And don't forget the tennis court – I want to get that in hand straight away: don't want it any more – want it planted out in some fashion, young willow saplings, I'd thought. I want to make a willow or rock garden out of it with a waterfall.'

'I don't know if it's quite the season, ma'am, for planting out saplings—'

'Talk to Appleton about it, get the ground prepared anyway – I want *rid* of that tennis court, that's the main thing.'

'Yes, ma'am.'

'Oh, and O'Donovan, what about all these rats? There seems a plague of them – Mrs Martin has told me. In the kitchens, cellars – and I've even seen them here in the hall.'

'In the yard as well, ma'am.'

'How do you account for them? – is someone *feeding* them?'

'Can't account for them, ma'am – not this early in the year. Unless it's the wet summer maybe. They've come in to feed early about the house. I'll put poison down – and we'll have the terriers at them.'

'Whatever, O'Donovan. Get rid of them. Can't have a lot of *rats* about the place.'

'No, Mrs Fraser. I'll see to it.'

O'Donovan left the hall and Hetty, still crushed in behind the long window drapes, heard the motor car drive up outside on the gravel surround. Peeping through the curtain, she saw the terrifying spluttering machine come to a halt in front of the porch. It was the old doctor. He had come every day, once or twice a day, ever since Robert had started coughing. Hetty stayed where she was as the man walked up the steps and into the hall.

'Ah, Dr Mitchell.'

'And how is the young man today?'

'No better. I'm worried.'

'Poor chap, he's taken a lot of knocks recently, what with his parents going in the hurricane like that – and generally run down. The whooping cough gets a real grip then. You're keeping the little lass well away from him, I hope?'

'Of *course*, Dr Mitchell – I was a nurse myself, you know.'

Her mother's voice sounded very rude. They went upstairs then and Hetty emerged from her hiding place, outraged. What a *frightful* busybody her mother was. Mr Rat was to be poisoned or gobbled up by the nasty, bitey little terriers – the tennis court, where she had hoped to play with Robert, made into a stupid wood of some sort, and, worst of all, all the nice old dark furniture and curtains which she could hide behind taken out of the house and *burnt*! What a *terribly* stupid thing to do. It was 'criminal', that's what it was, like Elly said about some *very* stupid things people did.

Could she rescue some of the furniture, take it, hide it, before it all went? Yes, perhaps she could, and find some secret place to keep it, just for herself. She moved off at once, starting her explorations again, going down the dark, warm-woody-smelling passageway behind the great staircase and into a murky, book-lined room with a huge desk in the middle. It was her grandfather's study, she knew. He'd fallen off the roof of the house in a flying machine, which was something like a motor car with wings, Elly had told her. But that was impossible, motor cars couldn't fly. So mustn't he have been 'taken by God' and been flying up to him in the first place, she'd asked Elly? But no: he'd just had an 'accident'. It didn't make sense.

Then she saw a toy of this flying machine on a table by the window. She gazed at it, most curiously. So it had been real – a motor car with wings! An insect of a sort she had never seen in Domenica, like a tiny bean with red spots dotted all over it, was asleep on the toy. She touched it very delicately and it flew away suddenly, making her jump. Only birds and insects and things could fly. No wonder her grandfather had gone up to God, thinking he could fly. What a stupid thing to do. People really were very stupid over here in Ireland. And she knew why: like God, they were always so *busy*. Well, she wouldn't be. She determined then and there not *ever* to be busy. It killed you.

Going on then into the billiard room further along the passageway she saw the great table with funny net pockets all round – another grown-ups' game, for *men* only, Elly had said. What *could* they do here? She set her lime fruit on the green cloth and pushed it around, trying to get it into one of the pockets. But it wouldn't. It squiggled all over the place. Only men played this game, so she supposed that was why she couldn't. And there weren't any men in the house now. Though there had been a lot once – her grandfather and her two uncles. But they had gone up to God as well, resting their souls.

She hated this God more and more. But she feared him just as much. Was he going to take Robert away, too? How *awful* if he did. She could play with Robert, at least. Sometimes, even, she quite liked him. And she really *did* like him now, because . . . because, well, she'd been bad to him often enough in Domenica, and on the boat over, and perhaps this busybody God was going to punish her for that now by taking him away.

'Oh, please God,' she said out loud suddenly, firmly, not pleading, 'please don't take Robert away from us. Please don't make him rest his soul. Let him rest nicely, just here, and get better in his own cosy-warm bed.' She could hear Robert coughing now, faint awful whoopy-whoopy coughs, somewhere above her. 'Please God,' she said, remembering the crab apples. 'I'll give him some of those magic apples. Shall I?' But there was silence. Then she made a great effort and a great promise: 'God, if you don't take him away, I won't *ever* think you are an awful busybody again. I promise, never ever.'

She went back into the hall then, running upstairs and round the first floor balustrade into the upper hall, where two landings on either side ran back into the depths of the gloomy house. Hesitating – and very daring, for she had been strictly forbidden this floor and these landings by her mother, even before Robert had been moved down to one of the grown-up bedrooms – she chose the right-hand corridor which she thought must lead to Robert's bedroom, tip-toeing along it in the gloom.

But half-way down, hearing footsteps coming up the servants' stairs at the far end, she ducked behind a heavy chest of drawers. Peering out she saw one of the kitchen maids carrying a tray, turning away from the end of the landing and going back somewhere further into the end of the house. Where was she going – with a tray and food? It could only be for Robert. That's where he was, right at the back of the house somewhere.

Hetty silently followed the maid, the woman in her starched white apron and cap just visible in the shadows before she disappeared up some stone steps, leaving this first floor for some quite different part of the house. Running now behind her, Hetty was just in time to see the maid at the top of the flight of steps unlocking a heavy door there, leaving it open, and going on into another much narrower corridor with funny small diamond-shaped windows on one side looking over the yard.

Half-way down the maid stopped again, unlocking a second door, going inside with the tray, before the door was closed sharply. So this was where they'd hidden Robert, Hetty thought, with his 'infectious disease' – as far away as possible from everyone else in the house. Poor Robert. But at least she knew where he was now. She could come and see him, somehow, and give him one of the magic apples. She moved closer to the door then, listening at the keyhole. She was surprised for at first she heard nothing, no coughing, no sound at all.

But then there was a sudden terrible noise and Hetty drew back from the keyhole in surprised horror: it was an old woman's voice, witch-like, screechy, stopping and starting, wailing; then *laughing*. There were no words in the voice, just this crying out, these angry shrieks. Then she heard the maid say something – 'Now, don't take on so, your Ladyship. I've got some nice tea and biscuits . . .'

But by then Hetty was running back down the corridor – it wasn't Robert at all. Someone else, someone she'd never heard of, was living in this mysterious room at the back of the house. Someone locked up all the time, so they must be *very* bad.

She ran down the stone steps, back into the long corridor of the main house and out into the upper hall again. Robert must be somewhere here – she'd taken the wrong landing. So now she chose the one on the left, tip-toeing down it, passing all the great bedroom doors – until she heard Robert coughing: at last – she'd found out where he was and, seeing a great china bowl, she squeezed in behind it and settled down to wait. Her mother and the doctor must be inside with him. She would see exactly which room he was in when they came out.

She heard a rustling noise behind her, a scratching somewhere on the floor further up the landing. Mr Rat again, she wondered? Or a Mrs Rat? Then a window rattled suddenly somewhere – a vicious rattle-rattle – before a door opened ahead of her and she heard Robert coughing clearly now and voices on the landing, her mother and the doctor, and there was a funny smell in the air now. A burnt, sweetish, nasty smell.

'Yes, keep the fumigations going. And the glycerine. And keep him quiet and the room dark as possible. There's little else . . .'

'The poor mite,' her mother said. 'It's painful to see him. Horrid.'

'Doing all that can be done – if he gets through the night.'

Hetty grimaced, a sick feeling coming into her tummy. The smell was awful, a rotting smell. It was the smell of death. That's what happened to people, how they died – they started to rot away. It was death coming to Robert and not getting through the night and this cruel God lurking somewhere, everywhere here, on the landing, waiting to take people up into the sky to their awful rest. It was terrible – unless she could save Robert with one of those magic apples. But it was all the worse now, with that screechy old woman's voice in one room and death rattling at the door of another and she was suddenly too frightened of everything.

When her mother and the doctor had gone downstairs, Hetty ran helter-skelter, as if pursued by this vengeful God, down the landing and up the back-stairs to the top floor of the house, where her bedroom was, a room which she had been given temporarily, which had once been her uncle's room, Elly had told her – her soldier uncle who had been killed by 'bores' in South Africa. Inside, safe at last, she slammed the door very hard, and stood there panting.

Then, unbelievably, the door of the huge tall cupboard next to her started to swing open slowly and she shrieked – shrieked and shrieked.

There was a *man* inside it – a fat great red-coated man with a gold belt and black trousers. And no *head*. Still screaming she ran from the room.

'Ah, now, don't take on so – it's all right now – what ails ye at all, girl?' Mrs Molloy stroked Hetty's hair, holding her in her arms, comforting her in the big kitchen.

'A-a-a. A gre-gre . . .' She couldn't get the words out. Words hardly ever came properly now, ever since she'd been at Summer Hill. And Hetty cried in fear and frustration, great blubby, thick-throated tears.

'What was it? What was it at all – tell me.' Mrs Molloy took her to a cupboard and gave her a ginger biscuit. 'Tell me now, what ails ye?'

'Me-my-be-*bed*room. A me-me-*man*!'

Mrs Molloy turned to Biddy, one of the kitchen maids. 'Go up to her room, Biddy, and see what she's on about at all.'

'Yes! Ina-ina-re-re-red coat!'

Mrs Molloy sighed, shook her head, then stroked the girl's glossy-dark curls, while Hetty looked up at her pleadingly, thumb in mouth, her great blackberry eyes glistening with tears. 'Now, you come along with me, girl, and help me make this greengage jam.'

She led Hetty over to the big range where a cauldron of sugared fruit was boiling away furiously. 'Now ye sit there.' She drew up a high kitchen stool for her. 'We'll be taking the fruit off in a moment, bottling it. And, when it cools a bit, ye can taste it. It's grand stuff.'

Hetty, up on the high stool now, hands on knees, leant forward and watched the fruit bubbling and spitting. There was a wonderful warm sugary smell. Biddy returned from upstairs then. 'Ah, and sure there was nothing in the room at all. The cupboard door was open, with one of Masther Eustace's oul' army uniforms standing up in it. Nothing at all.'

Mrs Molloy explained this to Hetty. 'So you see, it was just your uncle's old army clothes hanging up there in the press.'

Hetty's face clouded again at this news. 'Bu-bu-but there wa-was no *head*?'

'No, well, you see . . .' Mrs Molloy decided to distract her again. 'Come on now and we'll bottle the jam,' she said. And she took her over to the long kitchen table, where soon Hetty became entirely absorbed, watching Mrs Molloy and Biddy and Sally, the other kitchen maid, putting the jam into tall jars, with a ladle through a funnel.

This was good fun, Hetty thought – especially when Mrs Molloy gave her a big spoon and her own jam-jar and told her to fill it up. The greeny-yellow mix slithered down the glass. The green was lighter and cloudier than the lime-green of the fruit in her pocket, Hetty thought. It was 'greengage' green. That was a nice colour, a nice sound. Mrs Molloy showed her one of the greengages, from a chip basket on the window-sill.

'There, that's the fruit itself now. Lovely and sweet – the best of all the plums. Try one!'

Hetty looked up at this big kind fat woman in the long white apron. Then, trusting her, she took out her own little crinkled, pinched lime fruit.

'C-c-c could you ma-ma-make g-g-*jam* with this?'

Mrs Molloy inspected the fruit with great interest. 'Indeed ye could! It's a little lime. I've not seen one in a while. Ye hardly ever get thim over here. But it's a kind of marmalade ye'd make with it and ye'd need a lot of thim. But it'd be *very* tasty!'

Hetty was pleased with this information. She smiled. 'It's fra-fra-from home,' she said. 'My home – in Dom-Dom-Domenica.' And suddenly she was crying again, couldn't stop herself. She longed for that other home now, her *real* home, that warm, sunny, friendly place, with Slinky and Big Jules and the frigate birds in the great blue sky and the Emerald pool and the long grassy walks through the old lime groves into the wild forest and the glittering white coral house and green shutters, with Cook, that other cook, and her slices of ginger cake.

Mrs Molloy left the jam-bottling and comforted her again. 'Ah, now, don't cry. *This* is your home now – and, sure, ye'll get to like it, ye will—'

'I won't – I hate it, *hate* it!' In her anger and agony of homesickness then, Hetty's stammer quite disappeared.

But again Mrs Molloy managed to distract her. 'Come on then, alanah, we'll have no more tears. Ye've got your own jam-pot now, so you'll have to write a label for it, won't you?' Hetty looked at her doubtfully. Mrs Molloy picked up a label and a dip pen. 'Ye can write, can't ye?' she asked brightly, and Hetty, affronted at this, nodded vigorously. She *could* write – that was one thing she could do. 'Oh, yes,' she said, her tears drying. 'I can write *much* better than Robert.'

'Well, here ye are then, you copy this.' And Mrs Molloy wrote out in capitals 'GREENGAGE – SEPT 1909. Miss Henrietta's Jam'. And Hetty copied it slowly and carefully and very nicely, before glueing the label and sticking it on her own jar.

'Now, there ye are – your very own jam and ye've made it all yourself!' Mrs Molloy held the warm jar up to the light, and Hetty saw all the mottled yellowy-green colours – and she loved it, quite forgetting her homesickness and the headless man. She'd *made* this jam – well, nearly made it. It was hers and she had a wonderfully warm feeling inside her then, which she wanted to speak about, but couldn't, the words trapped again.

When Hetty had left the kitchen, Biddy turned to Mrs

Molloy. 'Well, an' there's a strange one and no mistake – and she not able to get a word out edgeways, suckin' her thumb and those eyes as big as saucers out on stalks lookin' at ye all the time. Wouldn't ye pity her altogether?'

Mrs Molloy didn't agree. 'Well, now, isn't it a great thing not to be chatterin' all the time, like ye be doin', Biddy Walsh. And they do say, when ye can't talk at all like that, it's because ye have too full a heart.'

'I-ma-ma-I-ma-made some g-g-*jam*!' Hetty told her mother proudly in her little study room next to the drawing room that evening, when she had come down to see her before her nursery supper – as she had been instructed to do, every evening at six o'clock.

She sat on the edge of a big high-backed chair now, all neat and tidy, hair combed, curls forced together with two blue ribbons, in a horrid navy-blue, lace-trimmed velvet dress, long white socks and shiny black, sharply buttoned, very pinching dancing shoes. Molly had done all this, helped her into these frightfully tight and uncomfy hot clothes – Molly, her great-aunt Emily's old maid who was looking after her now while Elly was busy with Robert in his sick room. But it was her mother who had insisted upon it, and now Hetty sat there nervously, smoothing her hands over the sticky velvet, trying not to look at her mother sitting at the desk by the window, reading papers, pen in hand.

Finally Frances looked at her daughter. 'Yes, Henrietta,' she said vaguely. Then she suddenly turned to her. '*Jam*, Henrietta. It's not a difficult word. "J" – there is no "G" in it. Try again.'

'G-g-g-g-*jam* . . .'

Silence. 'I can't understand it,' her mother finally said, looking at her crossly. 'You were never so bad with your words at Fraser Hall. You really must make an effort to speak properly. It's *most* unbecoming, to stutter and stammer like that.'

'Yes, Me-Me-Mama.' Hetty froze completely then. She had wanted to ask her mother about Robert – and even more about the strange, screechy-voiced old woman in the back of the house. But she didn't dare now.

'Still . . .' Her mother surveyed her distantly. 'When we're more settled here, you'll have to make a real effort. And no doubt this Miss Goulden will make you speak properly.' She held up a letter. 'She's coming next week, from Limerick. The highest recommendations. She is to be your governess – for you. And Robert.'

'Ge-ge-*gover*less!'

'Gover*ness*.' Her mother corrected her sharply, standing up now, bunching her fingers, cracking the joints in her annoyed way. 'She's going to *teach* you – French and sums and things. Teach you all *sorts* of lessons,' she added.

Hetty swallowed nervously. 'Ke-ke-*can* I have a pe-pe-*pen*cil box then?'

'A pencil box?' Her mother was surprised.

'Yes, for my pe-pe-pens and pe-pe-pencils. Like Robert has, for his le-le-lessons.'

Her mother shook her head indignantly. 'You shall have a pencil box when you stop that frightful stammering,' she told her even more sharply.

Robert's cough got worse that night. Hetty heard him whooping away long after her supper in the nursery. And lurking at the head of the servants' stairs later she heard the doctor again and whispered conversations on the landing below, people coming and going. Robert was dying, God was taking him away. Only the crab apples – the apples of life – would save him now.

Hetty had a store of them in her bedroom, and she bit into one then, as if to give her strength for what she had to do. Molly, who slept in the next room on the nursery landing, would be easy enough to avoid. She snored when she slept. But what about the others, when she went down-stairs? In fairy stories they did magic things so easily. But this was real.

Molly had tucked her into bed, leaving just the dumpy little wax nightlight burning by the door. Then, hours and hours later, it seemed, she heard her going to bed – and, soon after, she was snoring. It was time.

Holding the nightlight in one hand, and a few of the apples gathered up in the hem of her nightdress in the other, she made her way slowly down the servants' stairs, then turned into the dark first floor landing. She waited at the corner, listening. There was just Robert's coughing every so often, no other sound. It must be the very *middle* of the night. She tip-toed quickly along towards Robert's door, then paused at it undecided for a moment. Both her hands were full – she couldn't open it. Kneeling then, putting down the nightlight, she was just about to rise when she heard a rustling rushing noise like the wind coming down the landing towards her, the nightlight flame suddenly dancing.

She had no time to escape. It was her mother, towering above her, her face twisted with anger in the flickering yellow shadows, as she bent down, taking her by the collar of her nightdress.

'You little wretch!' The apples spilled from the hem of her nightdress, as her mother pulled her all the way down the landing to the upper hall. Then she slapped her face. 'What *do* you think you're doing? – at this hour of the night? Waking poor Robert – with those apples everywhere.' She shook her then, in the faint light. 'How *dare* you try and disturb him. And it's you then, who've been feeding these beastly rats everywhere, leaving apples out for them. You little mischief-making wretch!' She shook her violently again.

Hetty was terrified. 'No, Mama! I wa t-t-t-*try*ing to help him ge-get better, with those me-me-*magic* apples—'

'What nonsense! You will go straight to your bed now and I'll have Molly sleep with you in future, with the door locked! Don't you know Robert is *very* ill – and here you are trying to wake him up or poison him with those stupid apples.'

Her mother dragged her upstairs, woke Molly, and made a terrible fuss over the whole thing. And, when Hetty was back in bed, she thought how much she really *hated* her mother. It was *she* who was trying to kill Robert, by not letting him have the magic apples. And she whispered to herself, 'Please God – I *will* get those apples to him. We'll find some way of getting the apples to him, won't we? Promise?'

The next morning Hetty thought she saw a way. Her great-aunt Emily was out with her drawing book, up on the high bank beyond the big yellow-leafed tree – a lovely breezy sunny day. Her aunt had a floppy straw hat on, tied over the top and under her throat with a spotted scarf, and was wearing a funny long green corduroy coat. She was humming, singing something as Hetty stole up to her.

Hetty stood beside her. She wasn't frightened of great-aunt Emily at all – didn't even stammer very much with her. She was really like a child herself. The only thing was she never spoke a lot – and when she did it was in a terrible hurry. Hetty stood there now for a minute watching her draw.

'Great-aunt Emily?' she said at last.

No reply. Aunt Emily had a small paint brush in one hand and a big dabby paint box and several little water jars in front of her attached to the wooden stand. She was doing a coloured picture of the tennis court below her and the house beyond. The only very funny thing was that she'd made the tennis court full of people playing and other people in grand frilly long dresses having tea from silver teapots on the bank. And there *weren't* any people there at all. Of course, she *was* 'touched'. Surely she could see there was no one there at all?

'Great-aunt Emily?' she asked again.

'Yes, yes, child, in a minute – when I've got this dress right.'

'But Aunt Emily,' Hetty couldn't restrain herself. 'There *aren't* any people on the tennis court.'

Aunt Emily turned on her then, peering at her haughtily down her very long thin straight nose, two dark little eyes, like mice eyes, on either side. 'Excuse yourself, girl! The lawn is full of people. Just because *you* can't see them, doesn't mean they're not there. You can be sure of it – if I *put* them there – they *are* there.'

Hetty looked at the lawn and tennis court very carefully then, shading her eyes. It must be some kind of magic. Perhaps the people were there after all. 'I'm s-s-sorry,' she said.

'Oh, they're there all right, girl – don't worry about that. But your mother in her great foolishness is having the whole court grubbed up, so I'm remembering it before she does.'

'Yes, wh-wh-why is she doing that?'

'Ah, some other foolishness on the court here years and years ago, before you were born. With *men*.' Her aunt made a sour face then. 'She was jilted on it, that's why.'

'Jilted?' It sounded like falling off a horse. 'Di-di-did she fall down or som-som-something?'

Her aunt smiled. 'You could say that, yes – she took a bad fall! And all her own fault, for I'd warned her of it, having to do with *men*. Told her that, but she took no notice. And now look where they've got her!' Her aunt cackled then.

'I wanted to play tennis here, with Robert. And that's what I wa-wa-wanted to ask you aba-about.' She looked up at her aunt hopefully.

'Robert, yes. There were ructions, I heard, last night. What were you up to?' Aunt Emily had returned to her drawing.

'I wa-wa-was trying to give him awa-awa-one of these.' She produced one of the apples, holding it up. 'They're magic, you see! Old Martin the gardener said: apples of life, he said. But me-me-Mama stopped me. C-c-could *you* bring it him?'

Aunt Emily turned and looked at the tiny apple intently, but said nothing, so that Hetty thought she was going to scoff at her.

'Quite right, girl – magic apples. Wonder they didn't think of them before. My friend Pat goes up to his room now and then. I'll give it to him – and *he'll* give it to

Robert.' She took the apple and put it on the ledge by the paint box.

'Oh, thank you, *thank you!* P-p-Pat the butler, you mean? He *is* a nice man. I saw him—' But she stopped. Pat had been feeding Mr Rat. And that, according to her mother, was very wrong. But why, since Pat was so nice, was he doing something so wrong? It didn't make sense. But then great-aunt Emily's drawing didn't make sense either, and she was *very* nice. So it was all quite clear: good people did these strange things, but they had to do them in secret, like she had tried to do with the apples, because it was her *mother* who was *bad* and tried to stop them all the time.

That was how it was. So she was one of the nice, good people really, trying to help, like Pat and Aunt Emily. And they would all just have to go on doing things in secret, and tell no one about it. That was the answer. It was just like in the fairy stories –'The Two Ugly Sisters' and 'Little Red Riding Hood' – which were always full of bad, wicked people like her mother, and nice good secret people who were unhappy – but happy in the end. Well, she was one of these, just like Cinderella who became a princess – and she would go on doing these secret things, because they were right. It was just like Aunt Emily had said about her drawing. You could put people on the paper even if they weren't there! That was all part of the magic thing about good people.

Hetty felt very much better as she went back to the house. Now she knew she was right about things, she would start at once – rescuing those nice old bits and pieces of furniture and curtains and things.

All that day and the next, whenever she had the opportunity or when the yard men, in to clear the house, were taking their dinner, Hetty chose what she fancied and could carry of the dark furniture and drapes. She took a stool, a small, straight-backed chair, several nice little pictures of donkeys and sheep and things, a funny glass dome with pretend flowers inside and – greatest prize of all – a whole pile of dark curtains left in the upper hall over lunchtime. She hid them all in her nursery bedroom at first. And then, in the days that followed, bit by bit, she took them out to the very secret place she had found, away deep in the woods to the south of the house, high on the ridge above the valley where, some time before, she had discovered a sort of hole in the hill, spread over with rotten branches and laurel and tangly briars. Here, burrowing into this undergrowth, and clearing the old sticks away, she made a space for the furniture on the mossy ground, a house in the woods, hanging the big curtains over it, then hiding that with other sticks and leaves and bits of moss. By the end of the week she had made herself a cosy and warm secret hiding place, dark inside but with two half-burnt candles she had taken, and a gap in the curtains giving out to the light when she wanted. And by the end of that same week – since Pat must have got the magic apple to him – Robert was over the worst and getting better. All her magic things had worked!

She lit one of the candles then in the secret place, like she'd seen them do in the church in Domenica, and put it in front of one of the pictures her mother had so disliked, a picture of a bearded man on a donkey – and she said, 'Thank you, God, for not taking Robert away to rest his soul. I won't *ever* think you're awful again – like I promised.' She paused. Then she added – she couldn't not really, could she? – 'But you do see, don't you? – the magic apple I gave him, that must have made it a lot easier for you.'

Hetty watched the threshing in the high field beyond the yard where the hay barns and corn lofts were. There was a huge black steam engine there, a thundering smoky thing, with a great wheel going round and a long belt driving another machine, into which the men were feeding stooks of corn, and the grain and the straw were separated.

The outer yard was crammed with people – extra men from the village and old women helping and others boiling up endless kettles of tea over a fire to one side. Bits of chaff flew in the wind and stuck in Hetty's eyes and it was very hot and noisy, but exciting.

When they stopped for their dinner at midday, Hetty saw a strange one-armed man, in a tattered black coat tied with string, and all his face eaten away in a terrible way. He sat at the long trestle table and some of the women brought their tea mugs to him – drinking them or swirling them round at first, then emptying them, when the man looked inside them, telling them something afterwards. Hetty was fascinated. She stole up to the trestle table to get a closer look.

'Ah, now,' she heard the awful eaten-away-face man say to one of the women, 'I see a dark stranger for ye here, from somewhere beyant . . .' He looked into the big mug again carefully. 'In America, it is – and ye'll meet him out dancin' . . .'

The woman laughed loudly, the others joining her. Then everyone stopped laughing and there was silence. They had noticed Hetty standing behind them. Their faces turned to her – funny, hot, big red faces, looking at her intently, so that she felt shy, but could not move.

'Ah, sure, an' isn't it the young Missy of the house come to see us!' one of the jollier old women said. 'Come on, alanah, and have yer fortune told – Snipe here will tell ye yer future!' Hetty did not move. But the old woman was beckoning to her in a friendly way. Telling your future? Hetty thought. Another sort of magic. She was tempted.

'Come on, indeed,' the eaten-away-face man said. 'Give her a bit of tay there, and lit her run it round the mug.'

An old woman poured some tea into a mug and handed it to Hetty. 'Turn it round there a bit and throw it out,' she said to her. And Hetty, now within the group, did as she was bid, leaving a lot of thick tea-leaves in the bottom. The man they called Snipe took the mug from her and looked into it deeply, turning it this way and that, eyeing it carefully down his nose – which wasn't there, just two holes, so that Hetty couldn't look at him.

'Be'gob,' the man said at last. 'And isn't this the quarest lay of leaves I iver saw.' He looked up at Hetty then, peering at her closely, then back inside the mug. 'Ah, an' sure it couldn't be,' he said at last. The women began to look worried. What was it? Hetty thought. Didn't she have a future?

'Ah, 'tis a great future altogether,' he said and everyone looked relieved. 'Away in the big world ye'll be – and doin' every sort of thing, all sorts of handiwork. But here's the ting . . .' He looked doubtful again. 'There's a man here behind you – well, he's rich – 'deed he's so rich ye wouldn't be talking about it, owns half the world, and he'll look after you.' The man looked back in the mug again. 'But here's the ting I can't follow – an' this man a king or a prince of some sort.'

The old women were mockingly pleased. 'Will she marry him then, Snipe? Is that it?'

'No,' said Snipe. 'It's not so much the marrying, but sure don't she belong to him now in some kind of a way. In the leaves there – clear as day.'

The women laughed. 'Ah, sure, Snipe, and haven't you got it wrong this time!' they cackled.

'I have *not*. Clear as day,' Snipe said again, aggrieved now. 'An' she a princess herself already.'

At news of this, the jolly women were hushed, turning to Hetty, gazing at her, with Snipe – his face a frightening staring mask. Everyone was all serious now and Hetty didn't understand this magic. A secret princess – a fairy story, like 'Cinderella'? She backed away slowly then. And the crush of people who had gathered round the table from about the yard moved aside to let her pass, staring at her, wondering, not smiling any more, as if they were frightened of her. Hetty moved through the crowd slowly at first – then, frightened herself, as they opened out leaving a wide gap, she started to run.

2

In the next year Summer Hill and its inhabitants were variously transformed. Frances, replacing Lady Cordiner – who had suffered a mild stroke and was now confined as an invalid to the Victorian back wing of the house – became every bit as dictatorial, but with quite different aims. The rooms of the house, painted in glittering blues and whites and filled with all the old Irish Georgian furnishings and silver, were restored to their original, elegant, eighteenth-century condition. Much of the heavy Victorian furniture and all the other dowdy knick-knacks of the period, were disposed of; the rest went to fill out Lady Cordiner's quarters, where she lived as a confused and bitter recluse surrounded by these dark remnants of her past existence.

To the embarrassment of Mrs Martin, the Presbyterian housekeeper, and the other servants, the delicate marble nudes of Cupid and Psyche returned to their niches in the great hall. Outside, the tennis court was grubbed up, made over as a rock and willow garden; soon an artificial waterfall flowed through a limestone grotto – for ever and completely erasing the memory of Frances's indignity here, at the hands of Lord Norton's son during the tennis party over a decade before.

As well as Lady Cordiner's quarters, some few other parts of the house and outbuildings remained locked, untouched, forbidden: Sir Desmond Cordiner's workshops in the yard, filled now with the scattered debris of his aerial ambitions, and his son Henry's rooms in the old nurseries along the top floor, where he had worked so intently with Dermot on their collection of tropical butterflies and exotic stuffed animals.

Lady Cordiner had kept these latter rooms as an inviolate memorial to her favourite son. And Frances did the same. She was quite unaware that Robert, after his recovery the previous autumn, had found a way into Henry's shrouded rooms, from the children's schoolroom window nearby, moving out along the sloping lead guttering that ran down to the roof balustrade, forcing the catch on Henry's window through a broken pane.

And it was here – in these stuffy workrooms with their dead bluebottles and spiders left untouched since the day of Henry's death, still with his Lepidoptera notes open on the work bench, a great Amazonian Swallowtail half-pinned into the display case – that Robert, and Hetty on his invitation, retreated to escape the stresses and strains of life which, under Frances's ruthless hand, soon enveloped the entire household.

They sat there one afternoon, in the spring of the following year, when their spiteful governess, Miss Goulden, had taken the train to Kilkenny on her day off – Hetty sitting in Henry's shabby chintz chair by the grate, where the old dead coals and ash still lay, Robert standing at the work bench by the window, peering down a microscope.

'Wha-wha-what would we do, if w-w-we didn't have here?' Hetty sighed, rubbing her eyes, for, though it wasn't warm up here, she was sleepy. It was the bottle that Robert had made her smell – 'Ether' it had said on the label. It was for killing insects, he'd told her.

'If *I* hadn't discovered the place,' Robert said proprietorially. 'You have your *own* secret place in the woods.'

'Yes, but it's been winter and far too wet and cold out there. I can go again soon, though, and you can come – and share it.' That was a whole long lot of words, Hetty thought, without a single stammer. Robert was the only person she could really manage that with. Funny. She wanted to be nice to Robert – he had no parents. But it was difficult. He was difficult.

'I prefer it here anyway,' he said abruptly. 'Much more to do. All these stuffed animals and butterflies and things. And *guns*.' He glanced over at Henry's Winchester sporting rifle, still lying, disassembled in bits and pieces, on another table. 'I'll learn how to put that gun together soon – and there's lots and lots of other things here I haven't even *begun* to discover.'

'They'll kill us if they find out.'

'They *won't* – unless you squeal.'

'*I* w-w-won't squeal!'

'Don't talk so loudly.'

Hetty's clothes began to chafe her again. She stood up, hopping about, scratching her legs. Robert turned to her. 'Don't make a *noise!*'

'These horrid Irish clothes.'

'Yes. They *are* horrid.'

On the insistence of her mother, Hetty wore a pleated Celtic tartan skirt now, held together at the side by a big Tara brooch, with a coarse, white woollen pullover whose oily wool tickled her neck. 'Just like all those stupid Irish words that beardy O'Grady man from Kilkenny teaches us,' she said now. 'I *hate* it – can't d-d-do it, at all. What's the use of it? No one *speaks* Irish here. So *why?* Can you do it, Robert?'

Robert, engrossed in the microscope, did not reply. Hetty, as she usually did when she got to these secret rooms, suddenly pulled off the rough jersey, unpinned and stepped out of the tartan skirt, and stood in her knickers and long vest. Then she tiptoed towards Robert who was trying to focus the microscope.

'Can *you* do the Irish, Robert?'

'No. Just pretend I can.'

'But he *knows* you're pre-pre-pretending.'

'I'm not Irish anyway. I don't have to learn the stupid language. You are, though.'

'No, I'm not!'

'Yes, you are – just like your Mama – and she's learning Irish from O'Grady as well. You're *both* really Irish, so now you have to learn everything about the place – those stupid clothes and the words and everything.'

'But Ireland is supposed to be just like England – Elly said so.'

'Well, it's not really. It's quite different. They all want to be properly Irish here now, or something – and they're fighting and rowing about it, have been for years, and that's why she has all those funny people down here, from

428

Dublin, and that beardy O'Grady from Kilkenny – they all secretly want to fight the English as well.'

'Actually old beardy is quite nice. A bit of a fibber, though. He read me a book of Irish fairy tales – which *he* said were all real: about a huge man called Cuckoo Cullen who could pick up whole *mountains* and throw them about.'

'Yes, but they're all doing something very wrong – and if the police knew about it they wouldn't like it and there'd be *awful* trouble, with guns and things. I *know*.'

'How do you know?'

'I heard Mrs Martin talking about it.'

'Well, I just don't like the horrid clothes – and those Irish words. Even the alphabet is all different.'

Robert was not listening. Then, looking up from the microscope, he said more or less to himself: 'They want to fight, you see, fight the English – with *guns*.' He looked over at the bits and pieces of Henry's rifle. 'If I could put that together again, we could fight back, like in Domenica . . .'

'But that would be *awful*!'

'Yes. But we may have to—'

'But the Irish aren't like the Caribs. They don't eat people – and they're *white*, not black.'

'Doesn't matter – they want to do just like the Caribs – take over the house here and the land. They're annoyed, you see. Mrs Martin said. I heard her talking to old Mr Flood, who lives in the yard. Those two aren't like the other servants here, you know. They're like the English, like us. They go to our church. They're Protestant.'

'But if we're all Protestant, like the English, why is Mama trying to make us all Irish, with these awful clothes and words and things?' Hetty tried to engage Robert's attention, but he had returned to the microscope.

'*Why*, Robert?' she pleaded.

'I don't know,' he said at last. 'Your Mama's mad, I suppose. Like your Grandmama is, locked up in the back of the house – *and* your Aunt Emily. Everyone's mad in Ireland – that's what Mrs Martin said to old Flood.' He left the microscope then. 'We'd better get back. I have my piano lesson with Miss Moffatt.'

He left the work bench and went towards a big covered tea-chest standing in a corner beyond the grate. 'Come over here,' he called to Hetty. 'Come and see this.' Hetty beside him now, he lifted the lid. And suddenly he drew out a long necklace of whitened bones, the linked vertebrae of a snake, and rattled them fiercely in Hetty's face. She shrieked.

'You idiot!' he whispered angrily. 'Only a dead snake.'

'You *hated* snakes, at home on the island. Remember the one at the Emerald pool?'

'Yes, well, but I'm not frightened of them any more – *am* I?' he added, even more angrily, rattling the bones again. 'Not frightened of anything here, in this stupid place.'

But he looked sadly at her then, Hetty thought. It was so difficult to be nice to him. And when she was, like saying he could share her secret house in the woods, he was nasty back to her. And all just because his parents were dead. Well, so was *her* father, and she didn't make such a fuss about that. But at least she had Elly.

She spoke to Elly later that afternoon, in the school-room, while Robert was having his piano lesson.

'Why is Robert having all these piano lessons? He doesn't really like it anyway – and he's no good at it.'

'Your mother wants him to have every advantage. He's lost everything, you see, parents and all. And she's become "responsible" for him now. She's his guardian.'

'Yes, well, why didn't Mama ask me if I wa-wa-wanted to learn the per-per-piano? She's *my* Mama, isn't she?'

'Yes, but, sure, you didn't really show any interest—'

'She never *asked* me – never asks me anything! She just dotes around Robert all the time. And Robert is nasty to me – even when I'm nice as pe-pe-pie to him.'

'Well, we all have to be kind to him, don't you see—'

'But *my* Papa is dead, too – the Caribs killed him!'

Elly, knowing the truth, became slightly tense. 'I know that, Hetty darlin'.' She reached across the table and ruffled the girl's curls for an instant. 'But at least you have your own mother.'

'I wish I didn't.' Hetty opened the book of Irish fairy tales that Mr O'Grady had given her, looking at the pictures of Cuckoo Cullen ripping up the great mountain with all the strange squiggly alphabet beneath. 'All Mama wants me to do is learn this stupid thing. And wear these awful clothes. I do so wish I could go back to my corduroy dresses and comfy things.'

'She wants you to be *Irish*,' Elly said, trying to hide the doubt in her voice. 'You *are* Irish, when you come down to it, after all. You're going to *live* here. This is your home now, your own house.'

'No, I'm not Irish! And I *hate* it here, hate it. And I want to be *English*.'

What she really wanted was to be loved, Elly thought. And indeed it was a cruel thing, how her own mother – when she wasn't chiding her in that high screechy voice she'd taken to now – neglected her, devoting what little time she had to spare from her devilish Fenian activities to young Robert.

Hetty turned and gazed out from the high schoolroom window, then across the woody valley to the green hills and blue mountains away on the skyline. England was over there, beyond those mountains – she knew that from the map on the schoolroom wall. And she turned to Elly with tears of hurt anger and frustration in her eyes, pointing back out of the window. 'That's where I'm going to live, Elly, in England. There's the great King over there and he owns half the world, as well as Ireland, Miss Goulden said so in lessons. And they live properly in England, don't have to learn Irish or wear stupid itchy clothes. So that's where *I'm* going . . .' She paused in her tirade. 'Besides,' she went on, picking up courage, daring now to tell Elly what she had never told her before. 'I don't really belong here. I'm a secret Pr-Pr-Princess!'

Elly was astonished. 'Who-who said? Who told you that?' she asked, her round dimpled cheeks colouring.

'Snipe – you know him, that funny man with no face,

last year at the threshing when he told people's fortunes in mugs of tea. And sometimes he comes here with Mr Hennessy's van.'

'Ah, now, don't you be believing him—'

'But he *said* I was. He knows all about what's going to happen to people in the future.'

'Ah, he'd tell ye any kind of nonsense—'

'But he did, he *did*! And I *don't* have to like Robert, when he's nasty to me and has piano lessons all the time and no one asks me if *I'd* like to learn the piano.'

In the event Hetty did learn the piano, first assaulting the instrument in the playroom alone one day, out of sheer spite, before something gradually took her in the sound of the keys – especially the shiny black ones – and she started to tinker with them more gently, creating a crude music, returning and developing this on subsequent days, when Elly was there, so that eventually Elly, sensing this musical gift, persuaded Frances that Hetty should take lessons too – which she did, from Mr Beckett, the organist at the local parish church in Cloone. And soon, under his sensitive tutelage, developing real gifts, Hetty became much more proficient than Robert.

However, that afternoon with Elly, she ran from the room, just to show how annoyed she was about things in general. Though in fact she really left because she wanted to get to the yard as soon as possible.

The horses were going to be shod, when they came in from work, and she ran downstairs and outside to watch. She wanted to see that nice stable boy, too, who helped the blacksmith. Mickey Joe, he was called. He smoked cigarettes – and he'd promised to let her try a few puffs next time they met.

Elly sat at the schoolroom table after Hetty had left. 'God save us,' she said to herself. 'What'll be the end of it all, I *don't* know.'

The rats had continued their depredations about the house all that winter. Neither the poison O'Donovan had laid, nor the sporadic but vicious attentions of the two terriers, had made much difference to the burgeoning population of these voracious beasts that had come to infest the place.

Frances had seen the remnants of corn along skirting boards and in the hall, confirming that someone in the household must be feeding them – trying to sabotage her work, her whole new life, as she felt it to be, at Summer Hill.

But it was not Henrietta. Frances had established that. In the same manner she had assured herself that Aunt Emily had no hand in the matter. And as for the servants – why should they encourage the beasts? They were terrified of them.

Frances was mystified – and much put out. It seemed a thing of great ill omen that her rule in Summer Hill should so begin and continue with this plague. It was an affront to all her cleansing ambitions, to her transforming the house, turning it on its axis, away from everything English – which she had come to loathe and despise – and towards all things Celtic. And these rats had sullied her dream in this renaissance.

By a process of elimination then she reduced the suspects to one of the men, or boys, in the household. And in turn, watching them, she thought she must discount Robert, and Carty Mike the garden boy who brought in the vegetables, as well as the two new footmen, Brian and Billy Walsh, and the under butler, Willy Phelan, whose father had just died and would thus never risk his job in such a manner.

This really only left the saturnine Pat Kennedy, a man whom she had long mistrusted, and – unique to Summer Hill – to some extent feared. Yet she had not replaced him as head butler. She told herself there were perfectly good reasons for this – he was most competent, meticulous indeed, at his job. But she wished none the less, that she could get rid of him, find some excuse – and perhaps this rat business might serve – for Pat Kennedy knew far too much about her, about her thefts with Elly in the house years before, when he had found the stolen baccarat paperweights in the chimney flue of her bedroom, and had mocked her with this knowledge on her return from London. He had, of course, as well, behaved badly towards Elly at that time, coldly withdrawing his attentions.

So she determined to stalk him. And when, in the next few weeks, this bore no fruit, she decided to search his room, in the servants' wing overlooking the yard. An opportunity arose the following Sunday morning, when most of the servants had gone to early mass at Cloone. And it was then that Frances went into the back of the house and opened his bedroom door.

It was the same bedroom, she realized, in which, years before, she had gone to see the Spanish dancing girls – and had met their guitar-playing leader Rodrigo instead, when he had so suddenly and expertly embraced and touched her. And the memory of this, together with the vague odours of Pat Kennedy's habitation here – a smell of brilliantine and sweaty linen – excited her now for an instant, reviving the animal instincts which she had so suppressed towards men in the last ten years.

Quickly, in something of a fever, she searched the place – opening drawers in the small dressing table, pulling the mattress up, looking in his boots, finally going through his wardrobe. And it was here, in the pocket of a dark winter overcoat, that she felt the awkward object, before drawing out the revolver.

Astonished but then fearful, thinking she heard a faint rustle of something outside, she rammed the revolver back inside the coat. But the noise ceased and Frances went hurriedly through the other pockets – of his day-time livery, then his evening tail-coat, and here, in one of the pockets, she was rewarded, drawing out half a dozen grains of corn.

So, Pat Kennedy fed the rats! She had thought as much. But what of the gun? What could be his need, his intention here? She didn't stop to think now, leaving the room and quickly returning along the landing. In the urgency of her flight she quite failed to notice Hetty, crouching behind a pyramid of red fire buckets along one wall – Hetty who had followed her that morning, watching her go into Pat's room, equally intent on her own surveillances about the house. And now Hetty was outraged. Her mother, with Pat at church, was trying to trap him in some way – because nice Pat had been feeding nice Mr Rat. Well, there was only one thing to be done . . .

Pat, sorting the silver later that day in his butler's pantry, leant down towards Hetty, not certain that he had heard her right the first time, the kiss curls neatly poised on his brow, the dark still eyes gazing at her kindly, but intently.

'What is it, little one? I didn't hear . . .'

'My Me-Me-Mama, she w-w-went to your re-re-room this morning – because you w-w-were feeding Mr Rat. She awa-awa-wants to catch you!'

Pat bent down on his haunches so that he was on a level with Hetty. Then he broadened his smile. 'Ah, no, sure an' doesn't she check the servants' rooms like that oftentimes, Miss Hetty, just like her old mother used to. She was just inspecting.' He patted her cheek.

'I see. Be-be-but you *do* feed Mr Rat. I've seen you. And that wa-wa-was kind, and I wa-wa-wanted to help, so you we-wouldn't be trapped.'

'And you have helped, little one, you have. But it's nothing. She wasn't up to any harm, your mother. Nothing to worry about.'

'But – but you we-won't tell her I told you?'

He held her by both shoulders now. 'Never, *never*,' he said. 'It's a secret between us – just us two – entirely.'

Frances confronted Pat Kennedy next morning in her mother's old office-boudoir, which she had since redecorated in her own purer taste: free of all its previous clutter, with a light wallpaper and a handsome Irish Sheraton desk in the window, where she sat now, her back to the light.

'No point in beating about the bush,' she told him quickly and coldly. 'Why have you been feeding the rats? – encouraging them into the house, ever since I arrived back here.' She gazed at him steadily.

'The rats, ma'am?'

'Yes, the rats, Pat Kennedy. No point in denying it.' There was silence – thirty seconds, a minute. Pat seemed never likely to reply and faced with this unexpected response Frances was at a loss, then suddenly angry. 'If you can offer no good reason – and what one could there be? – I take your silence as an admission of guilt. You must leave the household at once.'

'Very well, ma'am.' Pat Kennedy spoke at last, with utter calm, and turned to go, at which Frances was even more put out.

'Wait!' she called to him. 'I want to know *why*? Have you some hatred of me, that you wish to despoil the house in this way? You object to the changes I have made here?'

At the door now, Pat turned back to her, still speaking calmly, but with a harder, more ominous tone. 'I object to all your sort in Ireland, Mrs Fraser. You English, you landlords here, who've taken everything from us Irish, for centuries.'

Frances suddenly relaxed, even offered him the hint of a smile. 'So *that's* it! Well, I may tell you, you may rest assured – I thought you would have noticed it already – I am *entirely* of your opinion. I am equally against everything English myself, which is part of the change here. I wish the house, indeed the whole country, back in all its old Irish ways.' Frances's voice was touched with passion now. 'I abhor the English treatment of Ireland and am anxious to do everything I can, in a constitutional way, to end their occupation here. Have you not noticed? – my friend from Kilkenny, Mr Standish O'Grady? He has always been of that mind and written much about it. And, from Dublin, Mr Redmond, leader of our Home Rule party at Westminster – and my cousin, Mortimer Cordiner, an MP in the same party. You have seen them all down here, have you not? You must realize I share, am entirely committed to, their aims. And so to yours.'

Pat Kennedy had returned half-way across the room, more relaxed now, but still with an icy tone in his voice. 'Yes, ma'am, I have noticed these visitors – and know who they are. But if you hope for change through them – or even through Arthur Griffith's Sinn Feiners – you're wasting your time.'

'Why so?'

'We've tried for years, Mrs Fraser, to get our independence through London, in Westminster. But, with Parnell gone, that was the end of that way. Parnell had the following and the power, at home and in London – he might well have won our freedom, constitutionally. But Mr Redmond never will, nor Mr Griffith. And the British know that. They'll stay on here as long as they want now, any old excuse. They'll only be persuaded to leave Ireland by . . . by other means.'

Frances knew what he meant. Of course she did: she had found his revolver. He was not one with Redmond's constitutional Home Rulers. He supported the shadowy and illegal Irish Republican Brotherhood and their secret army, dedicated to overthrowing the British by violence and revolution. But of this she could not speak to him. She must temporize for the moment.

'Well, you may be right – that is another and wider issue. But, for the moment, you and I, have we an understanding? – that I am not a rackrent landlord here; that I wish, like you, for an end to British rule everywhere in Ireland?'

'Yes, ma'am. We have that understanding.'

Frances stood up, relieved, believing she had settled her differences with Pat; that now she had an ally, not an enemy, in the man. 'So, if we see eye to eye in the matter, I shall hope for your support in my political and other endeavours at Summer Hill, not your hindrance. Do I have your word on that, too?'

'Yes, ma'am.'

'Good. We must not be divided in our cause, Pat. That way the British will certainly maintain their stranglehold here – indefinitely.'

'Yes, ma'am.' He turned to go.

'Oh, and what of the rats? – You're feeding them, Mr Kennedy,' she called lightly to him.

He turned again – for the first time smiling a fraction.

'Ah, that was just out of the softness of my heart, ma'am.'

He bowed briefly before leaving the room. But there was nothing of the servant in his gesture, Frances thought – more as if, at least her equal, he had just been paying court to her. And this disturbed Frances, just as his revolver had done. For she had to acknowledge then the hidden violence in her own temperament which she had repressed these last months in her happy repossession of the house . . . had to admit how violence had so well served her own purposes in Domenica and in regaining Summer Hill. Perhaps Pat Kennedy was right in his beliefs there – perhaps, for Ireland to be free, it would have to come to revolvers in the end.

In the drawing room of the square, lime-washed Georgian house at Wellfield, some sixty miles north in Queen's County, Bunty Cordiner once more took up the issue of Summer Hill with her gentle, myopic husband Austin, Sir Desmond's younger brother – flourishing that week's *Irish Tatler* in his face.

'You see! – your niece's ridiculous renovations at Summer Hill have even found their way into the *Tatler*! It is too much, too *much*!' Bosom heaving, Bunty's tiny body shook with anger as she stomped about the room, while her husband – fallen asleep some minutes before by the fire over the latest cattle prices in the *Irish Times* – tried to pacify her.

'My dear, we are not responsible for the decorations there—'

'But we *would* have been,' she rounded viciously on him, 'had you shown an ounce of will in the matter. Lady Cordiner, remember – she left the house and the whole estate to *us*. Told us so, the very day after your brother's funeral—'

'Dearest, we have been through that a hundred times: she *changed* her will – not unknown – indeed a far too common occurrence in this country.'

'Yes, for that little hussy – that *harlot* – Frances!'

'I hardly think . . . She *is* her daughter, my dear.'

'Lady Cordiner loathed and despised her. She would never normally have made a will in her favour, least of all disinherited us, if Frances had not brought pressure to bear. Yes, blackmailed her in some manner. I'm convinced of it.'

'Blackmail – so you have said, often enough. But how so? How so?' Austin, as always, to avoid open warfare, tried to reason with his wife; his logic only served to infuriate her all the more.

'The daughter!' Bunty roared at him. 'Henrietta – there was the lever. I believe she is not legitimate!' she added, playing this trump card for the first time.

Austin showed vague but genuine astonishment. 'But, my dear, she must be – the daughter of that Fraser chap, the no-good sugar planter—'

'I doubt it.'

'And besides, if Henrietta were illegitimate . . . all the more reason for Lady Cordiner's not passing the house on to Frances. You cannot be right. It is an unjust surmise.'

'In any case, I am convinced that Henrietta is the key to the whole matter.'

'I should say something rather less dramatic, Bunty dear: you forget . . . the forceful character of Frances and the advice we know my cousins gave her at the time: Mortimer and Dermot – *they* persuaded her, to make things up with Sarah, to maintain the direct family line. She is her daughter after all.'

'You know perfectly well your sister-in-law never took *any*one's advice. And she *despised* Frances. And now, by all accounts, she is locked up, held prisoner, at Summer Hill – supposedly demented, insane! Can you really think that her personality should have undergone such a complete change without some extraordinary reason, pressure, *blackmail*?'

'Granted, dear. But the reasons are surely much more obvious – the successive tragedies she underwent, the death of her two sons, my nephews; then her husband, hardly in his mid-sixties . . . the long estrangement with Frances. It all unhinged her. And I am not surprised!

Imagine your own feelings, dearest, had you suffered the same torments and bereavements in our family?'

Bunty turned away. She was not capable of imagining such feelings. She could think only how she had been dispossessed of the great house – and the role she had long imagined for herself there, as gracious hostess to the county. And her bitterness was sustained by an avaricious fire, a constant sense of indignity and injustice, nibbling away at her soul – that this prize, actually in her hands at one point, had so unaccountably been snatched away from her. And so she had spent the intervening months pondering how she could reverse Lady Cordiner's decision, working on various theories, pursuing them secretly, seeking a way in which she could unmask both Frances and her daughter, prove her theories correct, and thus in some manner regain the glory she had lost. Now she turned to Austin, wishing to offer him a hint of her success in this direction.

'I can only imagine one thing – and I have told you it: we have been quite improperly deprived of our rights. And I shall prove this. I have my ways, in Summer Hill itself!'

'In Summer Hill? But you have not been there—'

'No. But through a quite astonishing piece of good luck I have a friend there now, in the heart of the enemy's camp. I shall prove my point!'

Austin was somewhat shocked. 'My dear, you should do nothing rash—'

'*Rash?* Rash to regain what is rightfully ours? It is no more than common sense,' she added. 'A commodity you are not overburdened with, Austin,' she told him, before leaving the room abruptly. Austin had long been embarrassed by his wife. But there was absolutely nothing he could do about it – he had realized that for almost as long.

The following winter Robert and Henrietta, becoming known about the neighbourhood and with Frances's Home Rule sympathies still largely unrecognized by the other county families, were asked to various children's parties. Greatest of these, traditionally, was the juvenile fancy dress ball held every Christmas at Curraghmore, Lord Waterford's family seat.

Frances, given her feelings about the Anglo-Irish aristocracy, did not accompany the children. In the charge of Miss Goulden, with Elly in attendance, they all took an early train to Waterford and travelled thence, in the dim winter afternoon, in several coaches, sent to meet them and other guests at the station.

Hetty and Robert changed into their costumes in one of the bedrooms made over for this purpose, on a landing directly above the great baronial hall: Robert in Lincoln green, a tasselled costume and peaked hat, with leather boots and a bow and arrow, as Robin Hood; Hetty, barefoot, in a loose-fitting, belted dress of the same material, as Maid Marian. Despite the big coal fire in the bedroom she shivered.

'I hate it – I've hardly any ke-clothes on.'

'Should have thought of that when you tried it on at home.' Elly tossed her hair. 'At least you don't have to have ribbons – just out of the great greenwood you are!'

'I've no real arrows in my quiver,' Robert complained. 'Only pretend. It's all too stupid.'

He twanged his bow several times, loosing off imaginary arrows at the Boothby-Smyth twins, Michael and Johnny. They were going as Tweedledum and Tweedledee, wearing cramped school blazers and corduroy knickerbockers, in yellow-striped waistcoats and similarly patterned caps, both with cushions stuffed into their trousers, fattening them out. How stupid they looked, Robert thought. They were his age and had been sent over to play at Summer Hill several times. He disliked them both, a feeling entirely reciprocated. He loosed off a last arrow in their direction – and Tweedledum stuck his tongue out at him in return.

Beyond these two, hogging the warmth of the fire, Hetty saw Priscilla Armitage, being titivated by her fusspot of a nanny, Miss Biggs. Priscilla was a tallish girl, normally with long blonde ringlets. But now she was dressed as a miniature Marie-Antoinette, her hair replaced by an elaborate powdered wig: a spiteful, haughty girl, Hetty thought her, on the few times that Priscilla had come over to play with her. And Hetty was pleased at her obvious discomfiture.

Later, downstairs in one of the long dark corridors that led into the great hall, and before the main events of the afternoon got underway, the children mixed awkwardly in the lamplit shadows, variously disguised, uncertain who was who. But Robert, when he came downstairs with Hetty, recognized the two Tweedles with Marie-Antoinette readily enough: beside a big oak chest where a bran tub waited, they were all three standing together – sniggering at them.

'You couldn't shoot a thing with that stupid little bow and arrow,' Tweedledum mocked Robert as he passed. And Priscilla Armitage laughed outright at Hetty. 'O-o-o-ps! Just look!' She smirked at her. 'Adam and Eve – with no proper clothes on. Straight out of the trees, from the jungles you came from. No proper clo-o-thes!' she sang out, rustling her voluminous, beribboned satin dress and shaking a tortoiseshell fan just beneath a large beauty spot painted beside her priggish chin.

Robert might have walked on. But Hetty stopped, turned back. 'You look like a huge stupid doll in that dress,' she told Priscilla smartly. 'And that wig is like a tea cosy with flour all over it.'

'It's *not* flour! It's just like the French aristocrats had, Mama told me – and it's her best gardenia face powder – so *there*, you stupid little girl.'

Robert had joined Hetty, adding his own riposte now. 'You get your head chopped off anyway,' he told Priscilla. 'All the rich French people did then. Read it in my history book – and *good* riddance to you.'

Tweedledee advanced on Robert, trying to pull the bow away. 'Suppose you think it's all *very* clever coming like that,' he told him. ''Cos you think you're such a famous hunter and shooter – all those fibs and lies you told us about your shooting cannibals and savages on that island you say you lived—'

'Didn't lie – it's true! They did attack us.'

'Like Robinson Crusoe, I suppose, you little liar! Isn't he, Michael?' Tweedledee turned to his brother. 'Just a little fibber, like that big snake you said attacked you and how the savage cut it all up into little pieces—'

'It *did*—'

'Don't even *talk* to them,' Priscilla interrupted grandly, fluttering her fan even more vigorously. 'They're both little savages themselves. Why, they haven't even got proper fathers and mothers – Mama said so. Have you, Robin Hood? *Have* you? No – just two silly little babes in the wood! That's what you should have come—'

Hetty went for Priscilla before she had finished the sentence, grappling with her, sending her wig askew, just as Miss Goulden, arriving on the scene, intervened.

'What *do* you think you're both doing?' She dragged Hetty and Robert away, back down the corridor, to a cloakroom at the far end.

'They were being horrible to us! – saying we were liars and savages and had no proper parents,' Hetty said to her, flustered, but still angry though not crying. Miss Goulden, in a severe grey woollen dress, was an emaciated woman of dyspeptic temper – her mouth a thin, shuttered line beneath hair-sprouting nostrils and bitter eyes, with coarse yellowish hair tightly wrenched back in a hair-pinned bun. But she suddenly softened her approach now, bending down to Hetty.

'Well, that was *quite* wrong of them, my dear.' Closer now, she peered at Hetty, forming a smile through her gold-rimmed spectacles. 'Why, of *course* you both had proper parents, didn't you? But poor Robert's – they went in that nasty hurricane. And your own dear Papa, those fearful savages—'

'He *wasn't* my own dear Papa,' Hetty interjected. 'I *hated* him – always fighting with Mama and drinking rum all day. He wasn't *my* dear Papa at all.' And now tears at last came welling into Hetty's eyes. And Miss Goulden, made more curious by this last revelation, but mistaking Hetty's meaning, leant even closer to her, became even nicer in an oily way.

'My dear, you must not say such things! He *was* your Papa, Mr Fraser. Why, who else could have been?' Then, unable to restrain herself, she added the sudden earnest enquiry: 'Was there someone else?'

Hetty looked at her blankly: this frightening-faced woman with her hairy nose, bearing down on her, asking these strange questions.

'Tell me, girl, tell me what you mean – had you some *other* dear Papa on the island then? Tell me!' Her voice had hardened and she nearly shook Hetty now.

'No, no!' Hetty was confused. What did Miss Goulden mean – 'some other Papa'? There had only been Mr Fraser, that horrid, sweaty man in a white suit, drinking rum, even on the beach at her birthday party.

Miss Goulden, letting her go, was disappointed. But she had hit on something here, she felt. She would, given time, quarry it further. In due course, she would have something to tell Mrs Austin Cordiner, at Wellfield – Bunty Cordiner, such a sensible woman, for whom she had worked many years ago, over a holiday season with Mrs Cordiner's own children in Clifden, Co. Galway – and whom, quite by chance, she had met again, just prior to taking up her post as governess at Summer Hill; met at the Royal Dublin Society's tearooms in Ballsbridge – an afternoon a year before, when Mrs Austin Cordiner, hearing of her new position had, in a most tactful way, explained her own interests in Summer Hill and asked her help, making various and potentially advantageous proposals . . .

Hetty and Robert hated the party – the more so, since Priscilla won second prize in the girls' fancy dress, and neither of them came anywhere, while their turn at the bran tub unearthed no more than an Irish clay pipe for Hetty and a pack of playing cards, with dull views of Killarney on the back, for Robert. Even the conjuror failed to amuse them: a pallid shadow of the voodoo ceremonies both children had witnessed in Domenica, with his babble of brogue-ish talk, coloured handkerchiefs and white rabbits.

'Just stupid rabbits!' Robert said scathingly to Hetty. 'I'd like to shoot them.'

'Yes, it's all quite stupid – you can see, he has them somewhere up his sleeve.'

Only the magic lantern show, given to round off the proceedings, changed their dire opinion of the party. This, at least, Domenica had not offered them. They had never seen such a thing before – the vivid coloured pictures, of Ali Baba and the Forty Thieves, of Little Red Riding Hood, coming one after the other, shining on a white sheet, sent from the other end of the great hall through a dazzling cone of light from a smoking machine. It was all sheer enchantment, especially for Hetty, sitting next to Robert in the darkness.

'How is it *done*?' she whispered to him, grasping his hand involuntarily in her rapture.

'Oh, it's just bright lamplight, magnified through a glass eye – like they have in microscopes,' he told her prosaically.

'Yes, but the pictures, the story, all the *colours* – how can they get over to the sheet?'

'Just told you.'

Hetty did not really believe him. 'No, it *is* magic,' she told him. And yet she wondered. He might be right. He was so good at history and microscopes and things. She looked across at him now, his nose and his Robin Hood hat outlined against the streak of dazzling light. He looked rather handsome. But then she heard him sniffling faintly. Why was he crying? She leant over. 'What's wrong? You're crying . . .'

'No, I'm not.'

'Don't cry—'

'Shush!' someone said.

At the station in Waterford, as they waited for the train back to Thomastown and while the two women were out of earshot, Hetty said to Robert, 'Well, you *didn't* look stupid as Robin Hood. So you needn't be sad. And you really know a lot more than those other awful Irish boys – about microscopes and those rich French ladies and things.' He'd walked away then, towards the slot machine offering penny bars of Fry's chocolate. 'And anyway,' she went on, following him, 'they don't know *anything* and we did *much* more be-be-braver and exciting things on the island, and we were both good and rude to them – *and* I nearly tipped Priscilla's horrid we-we-wig off, so we won't play with any of them ever again, we-will we?'

'No. We won't.' He turned to her. 'Yes, you were good and rude to her,' he said ruefully, admiring her. 'Wish I'd done the same to those fat Tweedles. But look,' he said, in a low voice, glancing up the platform. 'I've got a penny – stand in front, so the others don't see.' He put the penny in the machine then and they shared the chocolate bar quickly and secretly. And later on the train home, both exhausted by the festivities, they fell asleep, leaning against each other, in the corner of the compartment.

But Hetty's peace with Robert did not last. There was too much submerged hurt in both their lives for that. What was unexplained or unhappy in Hetty's past was more than equalled by the stark tragedy in Robert's. And, since Frances was no mother to Hetty, they were both really orphans – though loath to admit it; both searching for some vital contact, trying to establish roots. And to this process, this search for a confiding heart, a sure and certain corner-stone in their lives, they brought an unconscious ruth-lessness, with its by-products of mutual anger and antagonism, which at times flooded from the well of their discontent, poisoning their relationship, so that for every happy truce they made between themselves, as bonded allies against the cruelty of others in this cold new world, they found afterwards some hot *casus belli*.

Their knowledge of each other's unhappiness, their parentless state, both repelled and drew them together. They clung to, yet hated, each other, by turns, in equal measure. Thus, their engagements were the more bitter across the traditional battlegrounds of childhood. And in this see-saw of war and peace they ran the gamut between the roles they took and swapped about: mistress and master alternately, to the other's slave – coming, in the process, to know every weakness, where they could most wound by subtle probes or open frontal assaults.

For Hetty, her strength was in her growing, if sporadic, confidence and hauteur – a mind like her features: sharp, adventurous, daringly cut; an outdoor, wind-blown face in one way, poised, controlled, the bright dark eyes full of determination, a will to power. Conversely, with her pale skin, the cheeks touched with high colour, her small, delicate ears, equally sculpted nose and thin, reedy limbs, she had the air of a frail indoor flower. There was a contradictory mix of the Valkyrie and Botticelli maiden in Hetty's looks and bearing – repeated in her mind, for the confidence she often showed there was only skin-deep, her stammer continuing evidence of her limitations, the vocal tip of an iceberg standing for so much repressed fear and uncertainty beneath.

And here, in this stammer, was a weakness which Robert, when cornered or upset by something in himself, would viciously exploit – and tragically, for with him alone Hetty had come to make her words flow, whereas with everyone else speech was a hair-raising, often tear-filled business, the words spilling forth at first bright, intricate thoughts and phrases, avalanche-fashion; only for the whole creation to be suddenly toppled as she fought for breath, failing to achieve the vital word which was the keystone of her offering.

One day – out of nothing, in what seemed so peaceful a site, in the brick-domed dovecote beyond the upper pleasure garden, the birds fluttering in and out from the circle of sunlight far above them – they found a war which, for a time, drove them far apart. They had brought corn to lay for the birds – and Hetty, for some ten minutes, had been trying to tempt one of them, her special dove Matilda, to perch on her arm, an endeavour which came to bore and tire Robert, so that, impatient, he turned away, before noticing the two terriers who had run up to the iron-barred entrance to the dovecote.

'Don't let them in!' Hetty whispered urgently to him

as, just at that moment, the dove came at last to perch on her forearm. But in a fit of pique Robert did just that, the dogs jumping and barking furiously about inside, so that all the birds took fright, with a loud clapping of wings and dancing feathers, as they flew upwards, crowding through the dome hole into the light.

Hetty was outraged. 'You *stupid* little brute! – you did it on purpose! What for? – just when I had Matilda on my arm. You stupid wretched little colonial boy – ignorant horrible *beast*!' She stormed at him.

But Robert was quite unrepentant. 'Tired and bored with all this – feeding the stupid birds. You said we'd go to the river—'

'I won't now! Just as I was getting Matilda used to it all – and she'll *never* come again now, and I'll never pe-pe-play any more with you, you little fe-fe-fool!'

'You're the fool, much more – speaking and spluttering all the time – can't even *speak* properly, so why should I do things with you, when you can't even tell me things straight? You can't speak to *anyone*, you little spluttering girl . . .'

They were close, glaring at each other, Hetty's face red with anger and hurt now. 'I—' she started. 'I ke-ke-ke-*can* sp-sp-*speak*, perfectly well!'

Robert laughed outright then. 'You little liar – look at you, you can't as-pe, as-pe, as-speak *at all*!' He mimicked her cruelly, so that she burst into tears then, running from the dovecote, running, running, to the secret house where Robert had not yet been, in the heart of the woods.

Dermot Cordiner, now a major with the 13th Hussars, took part of his leave away from England that spring, by more or less inviting himself to Summer Hill. Frances, though she had remained in vague contact, had not encouraged him in any such visit. More than ever now she frowned on his army career, his implicit purpose there in maintaining the Empire. Nor had she forgotten her love for, and failure with, him, years before in London. Only he, of course, with Elly, Ruth Wechsberg and her mother, knew the real identity of Henrietta's father. And such knowledge angered Frances now, as did any revived memory of her disastrous *affaire* with the King Emperor.

On the other hand, Dermot was her cousin, and she owed him a considerable debt through his having warned her, in Domenica, of her mother's intentions over Summer Hill. Without his early letter then she might not have had the house at all, so that she could hardly deny him it now.

In any case, she thought, he is simply coming for a holiday; he could form no permanent threat or irk to her. And no doubt, too, he would be interested to see in what splendid manner she had achieved all her old ambitions with Summer Hill – how she had, as she had so long ago promised him, returned there, laid seige to the place and emerged victorious. Dermot, who had always doubted her in this! Well, he would see for himself now, how much a woman of her word she was. Thinking thus, she actually came to look forward to his visit, as a successful commander might, finally offering an allied but disbelieving general a view of the spoils. In fact, for his own part, Dermot's visit was motivated by quite other considerations which, tactfully, he made her aware of soon after his arrival.

But not tactfully enough. As they walked through the beech hedge maze beyond the upper pleasure gardens, on a rain-cleared, bright spring morning, some days after his arrival, Frances rounded on him.

'Dermot, I know what you hint at: you have had it from your father on his visits here – and it is unjust: that I unduly dominate here, that I have neglected Hetty!'

'I said, rather, that your *political* activities seem to have come to dominate your life, dear Frances – as they have my father's, which I've told him many's the time is to his detriment—'

'But that *is* my life now, as it is your father's, which you will not accept: Irish freedom – just as your life, in the British army, is one of *preventing* such freedoms everywhere!'

'We need not argue that. We have done so, often before – to no avail!' He smiled then. His thin, ascetic features had become even more pronounced with age. His frizzy, straw-coloured hair, parted severely down the middle, had whitened over his temples now, which together with his strangely hooded eyes, whose lids had come more to droop over either side, hiding the edges of his pupils, gave him rather the air of a young sage. Yet his neat waxy moustache, generally severe trim and ramrod bearing proclaimed him an active, military sage, which he was – so successful in his career that, not yet thirty-five, he was the youngest major in his regiment. Then, as one briefly repulsed and regrouping, he took another line in his attack.

'What I meant was that . . . it seems to me, with all your other great gifts, your beauty, you are wasting them in these political bitternesses. Or at least,' he temporized, 'denying so much else that is just as worthwhile in your temperament?' He looked at her searchingly, as they paused, undecided, at a junction in the maze.

'You mean, simply, that I have become a termagant, in my attitude, my views?' She looked at him steadily then, with some venom, entirely confirming his views.

'You have tended—'

'You have forgotten, perhaps, the things that may have driven me to this position?'

'No. You have had more to contend with, in what you hint at, than almost anyone else I know. But I can remember another woman . . .' he added vaguely.

'Yes,' Frances burst out. 'And remember, too, how you turned that woman down!' She walked away quickly, blindly, further into the maze.

Joining her at once, Dermot took her arm. 'I could not – I was not the man you thought me—'

'Doubtless!'

'I cannot so change my basic temper – as you have since done, my dear Frances. That is more a comment than a criticism. You have come to let hatred overwhelm you—'

She turned on him sharply again. 'Indeed! – for it was the one feeling I have been consistently faced with in my own life: that and betrayal. And one cannot remain untouched and unchanged by such experiences. One *changes*, don't you see? – returns like with like.'

'Yes, perhaps – I do see that. But surely, now that you have achieved everything you wanted here . . .' He looked round at the dense, overhanging hedges of the maze. 'Surely now you may be less insistent, more easy-hearted? What of all the laughter you intended bringing to Summer Hill? And what of Hetty?'

They had reached an impasse in the beech puzzle. Frances turned abruptly, back to the hedge, cornered in several ways now. 'My dear Dermot,' she retaliated by avoiding his questions. 'Despite their provocative nature, I take your comments . . . in the best spirit. I realize, too, your concern for my well-being – you have always shown me that, and I am grateful to you. But you do not see,' she burst out loudly again, 'how life does not suddenly cease to offer its challenges – and I have another and greater one now: the freedom of my country. And there, equally, one must remain hard.' On this decisive note she stopped suddenly, her hair feathering about in the windy spring sunshine.

'I do see that, which is what troubles me.'

'You would do no less in your own career, if offered a good war, would you?'

'There is little chance of that! We seem in the midst of another long peace.'

'Well, here in Ireland we are *not* so peacefully situated! There's the difference.'

Dermot looked around him, considering the impasse, both literal and conversational, to which they had come. 'We seem to be lost,' he said, the kind, hooded eyes narrowing even further in a placatory smile.

'Not so,' Frances answered brightly. 'I know my way here!' And she strode forward, more purposefully than ever, seeking the real exit to the maze. Dermot sadly watched her go. She believed she had won everything, he thought – yet the truth of the matter was that she had been thoroughly defeated.

*

Hetty, unhappy generally and particularly embittered by her last fracas with Robert, retreated more and more into her secret den in the woods. And Dermot's arrival did nothing to improve her sullen temper; indeed, he exacerbated it – some boring army man, a distant cousin, and worse, a friend of her mother's. But, worst of all, such a *great* friend of Robert's now: Robert, who had taken to him immediately, badgering him and playing with him at every opportunity, the day long, talking about guns and things. Hetty – loath to admit it – suffered agonies of jealousy, hatred, frustration then. Why could she not be part of all this exciting male world? – do, and talk about, daring things, fiddle with guns? She felt more than ever outcast, and came deeply to resent Dermot.

Dermot on the other hand made every effort to befriend her, but with no success, until one afternoon, finding himself obscured by the artificial waterfall in the grotto and seeing Hetty stalk secretively down the great monkey puzzle avenue and into the woods to the south of the house, he decided to track her, see where she went and perhaps, in some manner, get on easier terms with her.

But, on this occasion, Hetty's fieldcraft outdid Dermot's. She soon realized he was following her and, a plan forming in her mind, decided to lead him on. Instead of making for her secret house she twisted and turned among the woods, leading Dermot into the thickest, most briary parts, chuckling at his discomfiture, before she left the trees altogether, cutting across the pasture, straight down the valley, into the steep forested ramparts there, finally coming out on the river bank.

Some way behind her, tattered and torn, Dermot felt as if he were pursuing the White Rabbit in *Alice in Wonderland*. He thought he had lost her until, emerging near the river himself, he saw the flash of her primrose dress, some way down the bank, as she made for the octagonal stone boathouse.

Just below the boathouse, he knew, the river narrowed in a gorge and with the spring rains the current here, full of vicious swirling eddies, would be flowing fast. Surely, he hoped – surely she was not taking one of the Summer Hill boats out, alone on the river, at this moment?

Which is exactly what Hetty did. Dermot started to run. But, before he reached the boathouse, Hetty had emerged in one of the light dinghies at the other side. She held an oar in one hand, the other not yet properly set in its rowlock, as she swayed about, standing amidships, so that, before she even got set to row, the boat had nosed into the middle of the current, and she was being swept downstream.

'Hetty!' he roared after her, seeing her trying to head the boat into the stream. She might have seen him as he stood on the jetty. But she did not hear him, the dark flood waters rushing by now, sucking at the banks, the boat a swirling leaf, uncontrolled, disappearing rapidly round the river bend.

Jumping into a second boat, Dermot pursued her. Cutting fast out into midstream and rowing furiously, he soon narrowed the distance between them, and rounding the bend he saw her then, some distance away. She was no longer trying to fight the current, simply gripping on to the sides of the boat, both the oars gone, quite powerless.

Dermot redoubled his energies – for he knew, too, of the further and greater danger here: the big weir by the mill further downstream which would whisk her down its steep, torrential slope onto the sharp, half-submerged stones beneath.

Yet when he rounded a further bend, with the brink of the roaring weir in sight now, Dermot suddenly saw Hetty reach into the bottom of the boat, pick out the two oars, put them expertly into the rowlocks, before pulling the boat away from the V of the weir, aiming for the mill race bank near by. So that it was Dermot, astonished by this turnabout and not quite looking where he was going, who found himself caught in the vortex of the powerful current and, unable to pull his boat aside, disappeared over the edge into the raging torrent.

In the event, and because of the high water generally, he sluiced safely down the weir, the dinghy riding high in the white water, over the hidden rocks at the bottom. He only lost one oar in the process, before managing to pull the boat in to the bank a little downstream.

Hetty, her boat moored upstream at the entrance to the mill race and standing on the bank there now, was enchanted by her ruse. Dermot, when he eventually joined her, sopping wet, was less pleased. But he had decided, in the cause of gaining her friendship, to make very light of his experience.

'My! – you *did* row then,' he gasped, taking off his squelching boots.

'Of *course* I can re-re-row. Learnt all about that from Big Jules in Domenica, in *much* re-re-rougher water.'

'But you didn't have any oars, when I saw you going down. I was worried.'

'Just drifting,' she said very casually.

He looked at her quizzically. 'Indeed . . . But are you allowed to take the boat out . . . on your own?'

'No. Just because you were fe-fe-following me.'

'So! You planned that I should go to a watery grave – down there!' He looked at the rushing white water below the weir.

'Oh, no!' she answered sweetly.

You little liar, he thought. Yet he had to admire her courage and skills in the whole deceit. Just the same sort of wilful, daring, rather spiteful gifts as her mother: a regal disregard for others. And, thinking of this word, he wondered if she had inherited these arrogant traits more from her Royal father?

It was difficult to think of Hetty in that way, and he had to remind himself, with some astonishment, gazing at this unhappy, frail, stammering little girl, lovely but unloved, that he was looking at the King of England's daughter who, if fate had played a different card, he would never have come within a mile of, let alone finding himself at her mercy, here in the middle of Ireland. A granddaughter of Victoria, that so formal and correct old Queen, Dermot considered – and, beyond that, part of a wandering line that led, none the less, back to the great Tudor and Plantagenet monarchs. It was a strange thought.

He took off his wet Norfolk jacket, letting it dry in the sun as he sat in the carpet of kingcups. Hetty crouched nearby, then knelt in the yellow blooms, glad that he was not angry, but still wary of him.

Dermot gazed across at her as he pulled off his socks, still with a look of wonder in his wry, hooded eyes. 'You're a clever girl – no doubt!' He smiled faintly, shaking his head.

'Yes,' she said bluntly.

'You spend so much time on your own,' Dermot went on. 'I was curious – to see what you do here.'

'Oh, just like I did in De-De-Domenica. Exploring, de-doing exciting things,' she boasted.

'Indeed.' He got his pipe out and tried to light it, with no success.

'In Domenica I did *lots* of strange things, really strange, up in the hills, with ke-ke-cannibals and snakes and things. Here it's all very de-de-dull. No snakes at all in Ireland,' she added offhandedly.

'Yes, I expect it is rather dull by comparison.' Then he picked one of the kingcups by his side, fingering it vaguely. 'Except there *are* interesting things here, if you look closely. Know what this is?'

'Oh, that's just a stupid little Irish fe-fe-flower. We had *real* flowers at Fraser Hall in the garden, orchids and great red poker flowers which the humming birds dipped their beaks into. Those fe-flowers are nothing.'

'Yes, but what's this one called?'

'It's a primrose or something stupid.'

'It's a kingcup. Marsh marigold,' he told her easily. '*Caltha palustris* . . .' He murmured the Latin name to himself.

'Nothing exciting about *that*,' she told him scornfully.

'Nice to know the names, though. Part of the buttercup family.' He stood up then. 'But look – over there.' He pointed towards a muddy pool nearby, an overflow from the mill race. 'Now, that *is* an exciting flower,' he turned to Hetty who had followed him. 'Greater Spearwort, greatest and noblest of the Spearwort family. Grows up to three foot high in the summer, with flowers twice as big as the ordinary meadow buttercups.'

He bent down, inspecting the flower, before something else caught his eye. 'And look here,' he went on, groping in the water. 'A *real* rarity!' Quite forgetting Hetty then in his excitement, he dredged up a very dull-looking clump of spiky, fleshy, upright tendrils. 'The water soldier! Extraordinary! *Stratiotes aloides*.'

Hetty, attracted by his excitement, followed his gaze, though seeing nothing the least special in what he so praised. 'My goodness! I've not seen that in a long while.' Dermot fingered the slimy growth delicately. 'A perennial – grows all the year round: extraordinary plant – lives underwater, like now, then rises to blossom in midsummer before sinking to the bottom again. It's a *very* strange, rare wild flower, Hetty, I can tell you! Find it in East Anglia usually, no idea it was over here.'

'You do know a lot about flowers.' Hetty began to admire this excited, friendly man, who played about in ponds finding strange things, sharing them with her.

Dermot stood up. 'Yes, your uncle and I, years ago, we did a lot of travelling, looking for rare flowers – insects and animals and things. I know a little about it all. But he was a great botanist and zoologist.'

'A "zoologist"?'

'An animal man, interested in animals – wild animals especially.'

'Snakes and things?'

'Yes.'

'Uncle Henry was killed by a snake, wasn't he? Elly said.'

Dermot's face clouded. 'Yes, he was.'

'So was Robert nearly. But there are no snakes in Ireland – Elly said Saint P-P-Patrick kicked them all out. So how was he killed by one here?'

'He collected them . . .'

'That was clever of him.'

'Was it?'

'Yes,' Hetty rushed on. 'I *like* snakes. But Robert doesn't. He's very scared of them. And frogs, when we lived in D-D-Domenica, the croaky kind, croaked all night. He was t-t-*terrified* of them.'

'Was he?'

'Yes, but I wasn't frightened at all. Not frightened of things like *that* . . .'

They wandered off down the bank then, to retrieve their boats, Hetty talking to Dermot nineteen to the dozen, telling him everything now, whatever floated to mind, a friendship budding between them – the little girl in the primrose dress, the man with his pipe and lugubrious Norfolk jacket – as they swished through the yellow kingcups.

Before the end of Dermot's leave that spring they had become firm friends, together walking the land and the woods, where he taught her to recognize all the wild things in this temperate landscape: the flowers, birds and animals which before she had despised as pale shadows of their tropical equivalents. He showed how to wait for otters, hidden by the riverbank, in the lengthening twilight; pointed out the secret pattern in the evening stars – the flight of geese in the early-morning sky, the different sorts of birdsong clamorous at dawn in the rising spring.

For the first time since she had come to Ireland, Dermot made her feel at home in the country. He brought her into life, gave her a feel for masculine pleasures, so that a deep and silent understanding grew between them, which others could not know, and they came to feel they were like one another, in a world quite different from them. There was some magic in their rapport which startled Dermot, displeased Frances and Robert, and which for Hetty was a balm. Here, at last, was a keystone in her life, a father.

Dermot recognized this, too, and so found it all the more ironic, that morning towards the middle of May, when news came of King Edward's death. The household would normally have gone into brief mourning. Not so, of course, in this instance. Frances gave strict orders that no such respects should be paid.

She would have gone shopping extravagantly, as a celebration, in Kilkenny, but for the fact she knew all the shops would be closed there for the day. Instead, she took her horse out alone for most of the morning, riding wildly over the land, and spent the afternoon closeted in her office. Here, unable to resist the temptation, she unearthed the King's letters from the locked deed box – the jewelled Fabergé brooch-watch, the little ivory elephant, the elaborate coloured menus from Sandringham and all the other mementoes.

She was tempted to destroy everything, there and then. Something stopped her – not sentiment, certainly. Perhaps hatred? Surely, she thought, one could hold on to such things as a spur to hatred as much as love, as a way of keeping that feeling evergreen?

Hetty, disturbed that day by the doom and flurry and tense atmosphere about the house, asked Elly what had happened. Elly tried to control herself, but tears grew in her eyes.

'The King is dead,' she said at last.

'Oh, well, he's nothing to do with us, is he? Here, I mean. So why is everyone so funny and upset?'

Elly turned away then, unable to face the girl, letting out a great hubbub of tears.

Later Hetty talked to Dermot, out by the artificial waterfall on the old tennis court.

'Everyone's all awfully cryey and sad today! Did you know? – the King is dead!' she told him brightly.

'Yes,' he replied evenly, looking at her delicate, wide-eyed features, her dark curls set against the blowy sky. 'He was quite an old man. Everyone, everything, dies—'

'Oh, I know that,' she put in. '*I'm* not unhappy. But all the others are – in an *awful* tizzy, Elly crying her eyes out. But you're not, are you – unhappy, I mean?'

'Well, I am . . . a little,' he told her honestly. 'He was my king.'

'But *I* needn't be, need I?'

'No. No, you needn't be.' He turned away, hating the lie then, for the death of anyone's father was the sorest thing, even if they had no knowledge of him, no inkling of his blood in theirs.

'Anyway,' Hetty said, 'he *was* rather a fat, ugly old man with a great beard, wasn't he? I've seen pictures of him! It doesn't really matter, does it?'

'Well, yes, it does. He has family, you know —'

'Are they all fat and beardy like him, too?'

'No.' Dermot turned back, running his finger quickly down her straight nose. 'No, some of them are *very* beautiful. Like you.'

3

When Dermot left a few days later, Hetty was inconsolable. Elly tried to help. 'That present he gave you – a sort of diary, was it? Well, why not write in it? – all the nice things you did with him!'

'Don't want to write in it – not the same as his being here.'

'Or pictures then. Your Aunt Emily does lovely pictures in that kind of book. Why don't you go and see her?'

'Can't draw.'

None the less later she went to see Aunt Emily, taking Dermot's present with her, with its lovely marble-patterned covers – knocking on the door of her room in the west wing of the house, with its funny paintings all over the walls. Aunt Emily never allowed anyone else of the family into the room, but she did not object to Hetty.

'It's me!' she called out.

Inside Aunt Emily, busy at her work table, was concentrating on a watercolour in a book much like Hetty's. Hetty stood behind her for a moment, looking at the picture: a lot of fierce black crows, in the middle of a field, devouring a young rabbit, the red blood and guts of the poor animal spilled out all over the place, a frightful mess on the green grass. Hetty was horrified.

'That's *awfully* nasty, Aunt Emily!'

'Excuse yourself, girl!' She did not turn round. 'That's how things are: red in tooth and claw. Didn't you know that?' She turned now to look at Hetty, her bright little blue eyes beaming under a fuzz of greying hair.

'Yes, everything dies, I know that – Dermot told me.' She brightened then at the thought of him. 'Look! He gave me this lovely book.' She held it out hesitantly. 'But wha-wha-what shall I do with it?'

Aunt Emily inspected the book carefully. 'A fine little sketch-book, Combridge's best – and nicely bound.' She fingered the book acquisitively.

'But I can't draw, like you. And I don't want to mess it all up with writing.'

'Tell you what then,' Aunt Emily said sharply. 'I'll give you half a crown for it – then you can buy something you really want.'

But Hetty took the book back then, holding it firmly into her stomach. 'Oh no, I couldn't – Dermot gave it me.'

Aunt Emily considered the implication of this rebuff. 'Ah dear me, so you've taken to him – that's the problem, is it?' Hetty mumbled something incoherent, fidgeting. 'Tell you what then,' Aunt Emily sped on, 'I'll draw pictures on one page and you write on the opposite one.'

Hetty was mystified. 'Wha-wha-what shall I write?'

'Excuse yourself – the *words* of course. We'll make a story book out of it.'

'But wha-what story – I don't know any stories.'

'You will soon enough, girl – stories are always easy to do, once you get a good idea for the beginning. That's the only difficult part. We'll make one up.'

She took the book back, set it on her work table, opening the first page. 'Now then, what'll it be?' She smiled at Hetty mischievously.

'I . . . I don't know!' Hetty felt a tingle of excitement at this proffered mystery.

'Think of something, girl!' But already, with a soft pencil, Aunt Emily had started to draw rapidly on the right-hand page – the figure of a man with frizzy, neatly parted hair and a small moustache, droopy eyelids, wearing a Norfolk jacket.

And now Hetty beamed hugely at her in return. 'It's Dermot! But what's he *doing*?' she enquired as Aunt Emily quickly filled in the rest of the body, the limbs, the man in gaiters and big country walking boots.

'Ah, that's for you to decide! That's the story . . .'

Hetty looked at the developing figure: the man was dancing, hopping up and down, but quite alone in a room which, as Aunt Emily filled out the background, turned out to be very grand, with cherubs on the ceiling and a chandelier hanging in the middle, a ballroom.

'He's dancing a jig!' Hetty said, laughing.

'And so he is – an Irish jig.' Aunt Emily was drawing furiously now, setting an Irish jaunting car, with a fat pony in the shafts, incongruously parked at the big double doors to the ballroom, the pony wearing a straw hat, ears poking through, head on one side, gazing at the dancing man quizzically.

'But what's the pony doing there – and the funny trap?'

'No idea – that's for you to decide. And it's a jaunting car, not a trap.'

'Shall I be on it then?' Hetty asked tentatively.

'Why not, if you'd like to be – anything's possible.' And Aunt Emily drew a little girl, like Hetty, setting her up in the driver's seat holding the reins. 'That's it now, d'you see? There's your story – there's these two people, in a magic jaunting car, takes them anywhere they want, all over the world, they only have to wish for it. And that's the adventure. Here they are at the beginning of it, at this grand ball—'

'But there aren't any other people—'

'Not yet there aren't! But you can have anything and everything you want in a story. You only have to say the word!'

'Just like that?'

'Of course! Isn't that the whole point of it, when you make up something? It's not a *dull* business, like real life, you know.'

'We can call it "The Magic Jaunting Car" then, couldn't we?'

'Indeed, a grand title!' Aunt Emily returned to the drawing, adding other figures to the dance, stuffy dowagers in elaborate ball-gowns and outraged, blustery old men in tail-coats. 'So we'll have them here at this great ball to start with—'

'Except all those other smart people wouldn't like them there, would they? The man in his clumpy boots and that old pony and trap!'

'Indeed, you're right – they wouldn't like it at all – those sort of people never like anything interesting. So we'll have this grand old fool of a woman kick them out of the place!' She drew a most haughty party, with a pince-nez, very like old Lady Cordiner, remonstrating with the man in the Norfolk jacket. 'And *that'll* start them out on their adventures, just the two of them – and the pony with the straw bonnet. What'll we call the pony? That's important.'

Hetty smiled, completely drawn into the developing fantasy now. 'We'll call him – we'll call him "Awful". He does look rather naughty and awful, doesn't he?'

'"Awful" it is then.' Aunt Emily continued to draw, filling in the detail, Hetty close beside her, spellbound at these ready inventions of her aunt's – a story about Dermot and herself, which somehow returned him to her, so that he was almost there, in the room, doing things with her again: all their real adventures of the past weeks renewed and continued in these magic ones. Through the story she was living with him again. It was quite extraordinary she felt, that a story – just some pictures and writing, really – could bring a person back like that, make everything good and well again, make you excited and happy, just as you had been with that person. There was magic in stories, of course, like all the ones in her *Red Fairy Book* – she knew that. But she hadn't quite seen that you could make the magic up, yourself – that things you made up like this, in a book, could take away the hurt outside, in real life.

She looked at Aunt Emily in admiration. 'I wish *I* could do it all, like you. You *are* clever.'

'And you *can*, girl!' Aunt Emily turned over the page then. 'So what's their next adventure?'

Hetty considered the matter. 'Well . . . Well, if it's a *magic* jaunting car, it could go out on the sea, couldn't it?'

'Indeed—'

'To some island, with palm trees and strange things . . .'

'And gobbly beasts . . . But they'll have to go down-river to the sea first—'

'Or on the railway, couldn't they? That'd be rather fun!'

'*Exactly!*' Aunt Emily proceeded to put the jaunting car on the tracks, next to the platform of a country station, much like the local one at Thomastown.

'And the ticket man can make a fuss about that!'

'Just as they always do . . .'

For the next few weeks Hetty went to her great-aunt's room almost every afternoon, working on the story of 'The Magic Jaunting Car' – creating, following the adventures of the little girl and the man in the Norfolk jacket, as they went down the railway to the sea, then across to the ocean isle where the Gobblies and the Marsh Mallows lived: strange beasts – the first with too many heads, so that they did not know which mouth to feed, where or what to look at, venturing forth only by day; the others, frightening, blobbish watery animals, with only one eye, coming out only at night from stagnant, noisome pools. So that quite soon the book was half-filled, the story going like one o'clock.

And, as the days progressed, in her intense identification with the hero, Hetty came to see this man, befriending the Gobblies, doing battle with the evil Marsh Mallows, as her special protector – and more than that she came quite clearly to believe that this man, in reality, was the father she had never had: this figure here imagined, yet equally real, whom she knew to be living somewhere beyond the blue mountains in England.

Here was someone, as his life was renewed each day in the blank pages, through the character of the little girl, in whom she could confide, discuss and plan things: a knight in shining armour, just like the picture in her King Arthur book, though his chain-mail was a Norfolk jacket. But he was exactly the same sort of person as King Arthur, Lancelot and the others – fighting for the good against the bad. That was just it – that was the great thing about him: he could kill the evil, the hurt and the pain.

And so Hetty could as easily remove him from the story, whenever she wanted, and set him up in her mind as a foil against her own unhappy predicaments at Summer Hill. Here, too, the man came to bear her standard, against the wiles of Miss Goulden, Robert's tantrums, her mother's dismissive coldness.

Dermot was the answer, the missing piece in the puzzle of her life. Why, of course, Hetty confirmed the thought: that was it! *He* was her 'real dear Papa' – the man Miss Goulden had asked such strange questions about at the fancy dress party; not the awful Mr Fraser, but Dermot, her mother's old friend.

And with this thought, finally worked out and established in her mind, Hetty, that summer, became much more confident and happy – as well as insolent and audacious. It was so obvious, after all, she thought: that was why he had been so kind to her, had paid her all those attentions, sent postcards now of the horses changing guard in London – *he* was her real dear Papa!

She kept the thought to herself, though, nursing the happy secret, all that summer, until, with the onset of autumn, the children came to play indoors again – in the schoolroom with Elly and sometimes downstairs with Frances and Aunt Emily: card games of Rummy, Beggar My Neighbour, Old Maid, as well as charades and dumb crambo.

Because of her stammer, and since there were no words in this latter drama of acting out some well-known title –

of a fairy story, a song, a famous poem – and no doubt, too, because of the histrionic Cordiner gifts in her blood, Hetty, under the particular tutelage of Aunt Emily, soon showed a ready ability in the mime.

One early evening, at a rare Summer Hill children's party, Hetty – when her turn came in the dumb crambo and on Aunt Emily's suggestion – chose to enact 'The Lady of Shalott' – playing the lovelorn maiden, standing, as if in her high tower, on a stool in the middle of the drawing room. She gazed into an imaginary hand mirror, combing her hair the while, turning the mirror then, so as to reflect the view from a window, of some longed-for vision. The other children, with the grown-ups, grouped round the fireplace, hazarded various guesses.

'Helen of Troy?'

'Penelope?'

'Berenice – and her burning hair?'

Some further mythic beauties were invoked, with no success, until the impatient, frustrated, jealous Robert burst out, 'I know! – she's just playing herself, waiting for Dermot!' He turned to a companion then, sniggering, 'She thinks Cousin Dermot's her Papa!'

But nearly everyone heard him – including Hetty, who coloured quickly, quite losing touch with her act. She walked up to Robert. 'No, I wasn't! I was doing "The Lady of Shalott", you stupid, stupid brute!' She was furious now, agonized by this public embarrassment, starting to grapple with Robert, so that they had to be separated.

Later she spoke to Aunt Emily in her room. 'How did Robert *know* about Dermot? I never told him anything, or about our story book. And *you* didn't tell him, did you?'

'Of course not, girl.' Aunt Emily was brusquely matter of fact. 'Never tell men *anything* – never trust them, you see.'

'So how did he—'

'Oh, they suspect everything. They're clever that way – always poking their noses in.'

'I'll never speak to him again!'

'Oh, you will, girl, you will . . .'

And she did, for the following day, prompted by Elly, Robert came and said he was sorry. Hetty had been in the schoolroom, Miss Goulden on her afternoon off. 'I'm *not* speaking to you,' she told him.

Robert went over to the fire. He had hidden some chestnuts in the warm ash beneath the grate. Now he raked them out with a poker, fingering them quickly, before offering one to Hetty. 'They're *quite* nice,' he said uncertainly.

'Go away! I don't want your nasty chestnuts. They're horrid – like you.'

'I didn't mean it,' he said rather sourly, but genuinely apologetic. Hetty had gone to the window then, looking out at the steady rain, a dim, cold autumn afternoon. 'I miss Uncle Dermot too,' Robert went on. 'Those guns and things. He was great fun.'

Hetty turned, looking at him grudgingly. 'Why did you think,' she spoke at last, 'that he was my Papa?'

Robert peeled the crackly skin from a chestnut, ate a bit, but did not go on with it. 'Dunno, really. We never liked your real Papa in Fraser Hall, did we? And fat old Josephine there, she said once he wasn't your real Papa, so I thought . . .'

'Well?'

'I thought perhaps Uncle Dermot might be him, always being so nice to you.'

'But he was just as nice to you as well.'

'But I *know* my Papa is dead.'

Robert gazed into the fire and Hetty relented a fraction. 'Wonder why Josephine said that?' She walked over to him then, thinking hard. They both crouched down by the fire, picking at the chestnuts, gazing meditatively into the embers.

'Oh, she was always gossiping and chattering away, old Josy. Probably wasn't true. Why wouldn't Mr Fraser have been your Papa?'

'He was so *nasty*, that's why.'

'Still, he must have been. That's how people *are* fathers,

as soon as they marry the mothers. They have to do that first, then they have babies. Elly said so.'

'No, you don't! Animals don't marry – my pet rabbits and things. They just get on top of each other to have babies. Seen them. And Mickey Joe in the stables told me horses do it in just the same way – the men horses with *lots* of other horses, and they're not married *at all*.'

'That's animals, though. People aren't the same. They have to be married first, in church, before they can do it. So Mr Fraser *must* have been your Papa.'

Hetty was not convinced. Nor, indeed, was Robert. But he wanted to humour Hetty, reassure her. 'Anyway,' she said now, 'I don't want him to be my Papa. I hated him.'

'Well, you have to have *someone* as a Papa, don't you? – else you wouldn't *be* here. But it can't be Uncle Dermot, can it?'

'Why not?'

' 'Cos he's a relation. And you can't marry relations.'

'Only a cousin.'

'Same thing though: can't be a relation *and* be your Papa.'

Hetty was confused. 'Oh, what does it matter, *anyhow*,' she said angrily, though her anger was no longer directed at Robert, but at this still-unhappy, unresolved mystery. 'Here, I've got some more baccy from Mickey Joe.' She got up then and went to the hole in the wainscoting where she kept her clay pipe hidden – the one from the fancy dress the year before. She got it out. 'Goolley's gone to Kilkenny. Let's smoke a bit.'

Lighting a spill from the fire she started to puff at the coarse-cut plug tobacco that Mickey Joe had cut up and prepared for her, before passing the pipe over to Robert. He took a puff, just to show willing, hiding his distaste, then handed it back. He could not understand why it did not make *her* feel sick as well.

But it was quite a mystery, he felt, about her Papa. Hetty didn't have a father, he was dead, killed by the Caribs, everyone knew that. Yet she thought, and some other people did as well, that there *was* someone else, a real father, still alive. And that made Hetty unhappy, which was why she was so prickly and difficult. Robert wished he could help her about it, find this other man somehow, whoever he was. And he was sorry he'd been so bad to Hetty then. He liked her a lot really, as they knelt there now, cosy by the fire, eating the chestnuts as the rain drizzled outside.

'I tell you what,' he said then, by way of cementing this new truce between them. 'I've found another secret thing, now they've moved the hay all out of the stable yard: up in the loft there, at the end, there's a crack in the floor, just above where old Flood used to live, where Pat Kennedy lives now. I'll show it to you.'

'All right,' she said. ''Cept he hasn't gone to live there yet.'

'No. He's just been putting his furniture and things in, since Flood died. But it's still quite interesting.'

Robert took her out there the following afternoon, climbing a ladder from the stables, up into the old hay loft, then tip-toeing right along to the end in the dark, until they got to the space above the rooms once occupied by the old butler. Kneeling on the rafters, Robert showed her the crack in the plaster and lath beneath them. Hetty gazed down into the room beneath. 'It's empty,' she whispered to him. 'Just a lot of old boxes and blankets and things. And a bed.'

'It must be old Flood's bedroom. Pat's moving in there.'

'Yes. But Pat's nice. We shouldn't look – his going to bed and everything.'

'No. 'Course not. Just wanted to show it to you.'

And they left it at that.

But this illicit view of Pat's room remained an unmentioned temptation to both of them: a forbidden gratification of which they could avail themselves, as revenge against the various indignities and prohibitions they suffered in the household. The crack in the ceiling was like a hidden tin of jam tarts, awaiting their pleasure, offering a sure solace against the trials and tribulations of their life at Summer Hill.

And these remained – in the shape of Miss Goulden or in Frances's spite, her Celtic fantasies, which she continued to impose on her daughter, so that it was not long before Hetty, finding herself alone in the stable yard one afternoon, with Robert at his piano lessons, decided to go up in the loft herself – just to take a quick peep, she thought, into the room below.

She heard voices drifting up to her, before she even looked through the crack. And when she did so she was astonished to see her mother there, in the one easy chair, with Pat Kennedy and another fair-haired man in a check suit with a floppy cap on his knee, both sitting less easily near by. What was her mother doing here, in Pat's new rooms? – and what were they all on about? Hetty couldn't make head or tail of it.

Frances gazed intently at the small, clever-faced young man with the tam-o'-shanter cap. With his fashionably sporty tweed suit, serious pale blue eyes and spectacles, there was something both academic and racy about him: a mix of intellect and fun. She liked the look of this unusual Irishman, whose background or profession she could not begin to place.

'Honoured as I am, Mr . . .?'

'Mr Murphy,' Peadar O'Hegarty lied promptly.

'Honoured as I am, Mr Murphy – I don't quite understand why you've come all this way with your suggestion. You surely know nothing about me . . .'

O'Hegarty shifted the cap carefully from one knee to the other. 'Believe me, Mrs Fraser,' he said pleasantly in a soft Dublin accent, 'I would not have come all this way if we didn't know a good deal about you already. We have gone into your character and activities carefully enough.' He glanced over at Pat Kennedy. 'Indeed, we have first-hand evidence of it. And, besides, there's a deal of quite public evidence – your work with the Fianna youth movement. And with Miss Gonne's Daughters of Ireland, so particularly dedicated to Irish liberty—'

'But just as much to obtaining equal rights for women,' Frances put in sharply.

'Indeed, indeed—' O'Hegarty started to placate her.

'Which is why I remain surprised that you should propose me for membership of your organization, the Irish Republican *Brother*hood.'

'One need not take the gender there quite literally, Mrs Fraser. You are a good friend of several other women patriots – Miss Gonne, for example . . .'

'Yes, and she is not, so far as I am aware, a member of your . . . your society,' she answered stiffly.

O'Hegarty smiled weakly. 'If she were, and you were not, you would never know it, Mrs Fraser. Naturally, we are a secret organization, bound by the strictest oath.'

'Indeed! So it would seem that, in presenting yourself here and taking my involvement for granted, you have rather offered hostages to fortune in the matter.' She glared at him then, a proud, rather mad look in her burning eyes.

'Not so, Mrs Fraser, not so. As I said, we have, some time ago, established the most comprehensive *bona fides* as to your character and beliefs. So that we have felt certain, in advance, that we could rely on your co-operation – you and Mr Kennedy here – in creating a more active branch of our organization in south Kilkenny. We are anxious now to revive the movement in every way we can – younger blood, new people.'

Frances seemed to understand and agree with all this, nodding as he spoke. Yet once more she temporized. 'In my position here at Summer Hill, not to mention my background and religion, I would seem a most unlikely choice!'

'Indeed – and all the better. Because we're not limited by sect or class in the IRB, Mrs Fraser. Oh, no indeed! Not at all! We look only for dedicated people, be they from cottage or castle, who are prepared to *fight* . . .' he paused, 'when the time comes, in the common name of Irish men . . . and women. And you would not be the first member of the English landlord class here to belong to the movement.'

'I, and my family, have always been *Irish*, Mr Murphy, not English,' she corrected him acidly. But she was none the less taken by the man's measured use of words, the air of steely purpose behind the mild accents and manner: attracted by his power, too, for she suspected he must, in coming all this way and making such a direct approach to her, be one of the leaders of the IRB. Yet still she delayed her open acceptance. 'I have had my doubts – about the use of force in winning our freedom.'

'We know you have – and close contacts as well with Mr Redmond and his Home Rule party at Westminster. But it is equally true, is it not, that latterly you have had something of a falling out with them? – indeed, that you have largely relinquished such doubts?' He looked over at Pat Kennedy again.

'Yes, I think it is,' she admitted.

'Besides,' O'Hegarty continued, 'you have just the sort of experience we need – more military than political or parliamentary, if I may say so!' He smiled again, a wan smile, putting his hand in his pocket as he spoke, taking out some pages from an old newspaper, unfolding them, glancing down. 'You were a nurse in the South African war, commended at the battle of Colenso. And later . . .' He turned a page. 'Later you handled firearms – evidently with some skill – when you lived – yes, in the West Indies . . .'

She saw what he had been reading: pages from the *New York Post*, the article describing her early career, her part in the vicious battle against the Caribs in Domenica, and the subsequent unfortunate death of one of their special reporters there at the Boiling Lake.

'It seems you are not unacquainted with violent methods, Mrs Fraser,' O'Hegarty said sweetly.

'Where on earth did you get that?'

'As I said, we make the fullest enquiries – our people in New York . . . Will you accept?'

Frances nodded. 'Yes . . . yes, I will.'

'We can have the oath-taking straight away then.'

All three of them stood. And Frances felt a tingling thrill then, coursing down her spine. She was about to be formally accepted into an organization which would license her violent nature. No longer an outsider, a pariah between two camps, she was soon to be part of the secret spirit of the times in Ireland, joining the ranks of a hidden army with whom at some point in the future – and the day could not long be delayed – she could righteously take up arms against all that she hated – King, Empire, everything that had betrayed her. In short – though this she could not admit to herself for a moment – she would, in a moment or two, receive a commission in personal vengeance.

Hetty, still gazing through the crack, heard the strange words float up to her. 'In the presence of God, I, Frances Fraser, do solemnly swear that I will do my utmost to establish the National independence of Ireland . . . bear true allegiance to the supreme Council of the Irish Republican Brotherhood . . . implicitly obeying the Constitution . . . and all my superior officers . . . that I will preserve inviolate all the secrets of the organization.'

What were they doing now, Hetty wondered? Swearing to keep secrets, in some secret game, Hetty could see that: just like children played. But they were all grown-ups.

Her mother must be mad, as Robert had said. Would she tell him about it? Or Elly? No. There was something dangerous about this game. It was *very* secret. She should never have known about it. Perhaps they'd even kill her if they found out.

She waited, frightened in the dark loft, until they had all left the room below. Here was another mystery, a danger, a further source of unhappiness, Hetty felt – one more horrid secret hanging in the air of Summer Hill. A week later, towards Hallowe'en, another experience added to Hetty's sense of hidden disruption in the great house. She had come to know, long before, that it was her grandmother who lived in the back wing of the house. But she had never seen her. Her mother had told her that she was a 'permanent invalid', a 'recluse'. Elly, Robert and some of the servants had been more blunt: old Lady Cordiner was mad, dotty, touched, dangerous even. She could not be let out of her rooms, must be hidden, forgotten – that was what had to be done with mad people in a family: there was something disgraceful and embarrassing about them.

But Hetty had never quite accepted this view of her grandmother. Indeed, she felt for her in a way – all locked up like an animal in a cage, never seeing the light of day. And besides, with her sharp curiosity, she *wanted* to see her, so that she lurked from time to time, hidden near the stone steps by the great locked door that led into her Grandmama's quarters, hoping for a glimpse of her, a sight of *something*.

What did a mad person look like? Like the face on the hollowed-out turnip masks they were making now with Elly for Hallowe'en? – a candle inside, and a ghostly yellow light coming from the slitty eyes and toothy mouth? Oh, how horrible! Or did a mad person look even *worse*?

She asked Robert, as they looked at a finished turnip in the playroom.

'Oh, a *really* mad person would look much worse,' he advised her distantly.

'Like Grandmama?'

He turned away. 'I should think she would look *terrible* . . .'

'Will you? – shall we? Shall we try and see her. Will you come?'

'We're not allowed. It's all locked,' Robert said, taking up a fresh turnip. Going all goody-goody and grown up, Hetty thought.

'But I think I *know* a way – of seeing her, without being seen,' she told him then.

'How?'

'Just like we saw into Pat's rooms. There must be a loft or an attic above Grandmama's rooms.'

'There isn't. Just the roof.'

'Yes, but there must be some sort of *space* there, which we could get into and cut a hole and look down.'

Robert showed no enthusiasm for the idea. But Hetty, the next day, made various investigations, exploring the aerial geography of that part of the house. And by the following day she had found a way in. It had meant climbing out on to the balustraded roof of the main house, walking back its whole length, then down some steep slates – to a valley of leaded guttering which joined the gable end of the roof on the new back wing.

And in this gable end was a small door. The rest was fairly easy. She took a candle and a sharp-pointed kitchen knife with her, treading very gently over the rafters, until she came to a position half-way down the dark space, beneath which she judged her Grandmama's rooms to be. Like the stable loft there was lath and plaster here, but it was tougher, and it was some time, prodding very carefully, before she could make any opening. And, when she did so and looked down, she was disappointed. It was just an empty, a spare, room.

But the following afternoon she tried further along – and here she was rewarded. After the same careful excavations in the plaster, kneeling on the rafters and putting her eye right down to the florin-sized hole, she saw something quite strange and frightening.

The long space beneath seemed like a dining room. But, though it was bright outside, all the windows were heavily curtained, the room lit by a number of candles, an oil lamp and the dancing flames of some logs in a vast fireplace, so that it was filled with eerie shapes and shadows. The dark-panelled walls were covered with dozens of small grimy pictures, stuck about like postage stamps. A great canopied four-poster bed lay at one end, heavy furniture everywhere, with a long dining table down the middle and narrow high-backed chairs running along either side. The table was laid from end to end with rubbish, Hetty thought, until her eyes became accustomed to the flickering light.

Then she managed to pick out some of the objects: crystal balls, paperweights, dozens of heavy-framed photographs, small stuffed animals, sheathed swords, braided military tunics, bear-skin hats and a hundred other vague things, covered in cobwebs and dust.

Hetty, peering down into this cave, was not to know how old Lady Cordiner, before her intended departure for England and the various subsequent strokes which had finally left her immobile and speechless, had removed herself together with most of her possessions and many of the Victorian knick-knacks in the house – to this long room in the Gothic wing at the back, having her great bed set up there as well; insisting afterwards, when she had to remain there, that all this heavy decor, these family photographs and mementoes of Henry and Eustace, should be left untouched, so that she could survey these emblems of her once-proud sovereignty at Summer Hill from her high bed, gorging on these props of her autocratic rule, now falling apart, decaying with the years, become ideal scaffolding for spiders' webs, and bedding for mice.

Hetty saw all this, but couldn't see her Grandmother. Where was she? She couldn't see her, in fact, for the hole she had made lay almost directly above the canopy of the four-poster where Lady Cordiner now dozed. The room seemed deserted.

But a few minutes later one of the maids – old Molly it was – brought in another oil lamp, set it on a table and prepared to take a seat near by. 'There you are, your Ladyship – a little more light. How are you feeling at all today?' But Molly turned away as she spoke, as if expecting no reply to her question. And indeed there was none – absolute silence from the bed.

Hetty was frustrated. Her Grandmama was there all right, but she would get no glimpse of her at this rate. She was about to give up her vigil when the bedroom door opened again and her mother, carrying a carpet bag, came into the circle of lamplight.

'It's all right, Molly, I'll see to her, stay with her for a while, read to her.'

Old Molly left. Her mother had a book under her arm. But, as soon as the maid disappeared, she put it aside, unopened. Instead, from the bag, she drew out one of the hollow turnip heads which they had been making in the playroom for the past week and placed it on her mother's bedside table. She lit a candle then, before taking the top off the turnip and placing the light inside, adjusting the terrifying mask so that it faced directly towards the head of the four-poster. Then, turning back, she lowered the wick of the oil lamp. The room was plunged in shadow and the turnip head shone more brightly, emitting a jaundiced light from the slitty eyes and mouth.

'I thought you'd like it,' her mother said then, in a pleasant voice, lifting her head in a conquering fashion. 'It's Hallowe'en, you know, tonight.'

She took a seat near by, so that Hetty could just see the expression on her face. It was happy, as her voice had been, and yet there was something terribly cruel in it – and Hetty was frightened herself now. What was the point of all this? Grown-ups didn't play with these Hallowe'en turnips. They were for children. And why, above all, was there no sound, no voice, from her Grandmama in the great bed? She must be alive there, mustn't she? – so why didn't she speak? And she must be frightened, too. Was that why her Grandmama didn't speak – *because* she was so frightened?

Hetty found no answer to this, for afterwards she did not speak of the incident. Who could she speak to? Who could possibly know why her mother had been playing with the horrible turnip head, offering it to the old lady in this way, with such a gloating face?

On the other hand Miss Goulden, a week later when she met Bunty Cordiner in the tea room of Wynn's Hotel in Dublin, had plenty to say. Bunty, cup raised to her disappointed lips, looked at her askance over the sugared buns.

'You say the girl *admitted* that her cousin Dermot was her father?'

'No, the boy Robert said so – he lived with them on the island.'

'Fancy . . .' Bunty considered the matter.

'Indeed, he was quite clear about it. And Henrietta was

much upset – attacked him! Attacked him physically.'

'Just as I thought – she is not legitimate!'

Yet Bunty knew she was little further ahead in her ambitions. She had seen long before that, in order to regain the house, she would have legally to contest Lady Cordiner's change of will – prove her new will to Frances invalid. The fact of an illegitimate child in the family would not alone suffice to this end. She would have to prove, as she herself had long suspected, that Lady Cordiner had made the new will under duress, or while of unsound mind. And here, more crucially, was where she needed the hard evidence: from one of the servants present at the time of Frances's sudden and unexpected return to Summer Hill – or from the local doctor who attended Lady Cordiner, old Dr Mitchell. He, the family doctor for many years, would be unlikely to collaborate. But one of the servants? There was more ready material here.

In a roundabout way she put these thoughts to Miss Goulden, asking her opinion of likely recruits in this cause.

'Oh, the servants were all there – when Lady Cordiner took her violent turn in the dining room, telling Frances she could have Summer Hill and slashing the family portraits—'

'Yes, but what *induced* her to say she could have the house, so that she took to her bed subsequently and changed her will?'

'Ah, that I don't know. As you know there was a fire, the day following, in Lady Cordiner's bedroom, while she lay there injured – might have been burnt alive by all accounts, before Mrs Fraser rescued her. A bedside lamp spilled . . .'

'Mrs Fraser may have tipped the lamp over herself,' Bunty said acidly. 'Were there no servants present?'

'Yes, I believe her maid Molly was there, some time before, but had left for her supper.'

'Left Lady Cordiner *alone*?'

'As far as I know—'

'And not *told* to leave, by Mrs Fraser?'

'That is possible.'

'I wonder if you might make some discreet enquiries of the maid?'

Miss Goulden became nervous, fearing for her position at Summer Hill. 'I doubt if, in my making such enquiries, one could rely on *her* discretion in the matter.'

'I see . . .' Bunty was disappointed.

'I wonder, rather, if you might find some lever in the company Mrs Fraser now keeps?' Miss Goulden said brightly, hoping to rescue something in her commission.

'The company of those dreadful Home Rulers you mean?'

'No, indeed, *very* much worse than that.' Miss Goulden's lips curled in embarrassed disapproval. 'How shall I put it? She is . . . most unsuitably involved with the butler there, Pat Kennedy. I have heard them conversing, closeted in her boudoir.'

'What were they saying?'

'I didn't hear exactly. But I remarked on the excessive duration of his visits there. And, more to the point,' she leant forward eagerly over the seed cake, 'a week ago I saw her emerge from his rooms in the stable yard!'

Bunty was avid now. 'You are *sure?*'

'I am in no doubt,' she said primly.

'The little hussy, the harlot!' Bunty could not restrain her voice, embarrassing some prim women at a nearby table. Yet, despite her agitation, she could not see how this new disclosure would further her purposes either. Frances's current behaviour, no matter how flagrant, was not proof that Lady Cordiner had been of unsound mind, or that her daughter had blackmailed her.

There, of course, was the key to it – Bunty Cordiner was convinced: blackmail. But how? What had been the instrument here? Bunty had long felt this to have been Henrietta in some way – that Frances had threatened her mother with social disgrace by exposing the girl's illegitimacy. But, even if Dermot Cordiner was the father, such exposure would hardly have been sufficient threat for the old lady to have made over the whole place to her daughter whom she despised.

Where was the key to it all?

'If only I could speak to Lady Cordiner *herself*,' she told Miss Goulden vehemently. 'There I would have an ally, I am sure! – and a ready answer to the whole matter.'

Miss Goulden looked crestfallen. 'I am afraid you would be disappointed. In the months since I spoke to you last, Lady Cordiner's condition has deteriorated. She has had another "turn" – her heart. She cannot, as I understand it, speak at all now . . .'

Bunty Cordiner, appalled at this news, was suddenly speechless herself.

Despite all these manipulations, seen and unseen – and with Hetty's consequent fears, sulks and tantrums – her life at Summer Hill for the next few years was by no means uniformly unhappy. Though she was never at ease in the house itself, there were the great gifts in the landscape which she came to love – in the estate, the forests, the river valley, the hills and blue mountains beyond. Here, from the windows of Summer Hill, Hetty grew up with a view of Arcady – and, in the huge green world outside, where she spent so much more time alone, she became almost a recluse.

Dermot, every year in the spring and usually at Christmas with his father, took part of his leave at Summer Hill: Hetty's friendship with him and their growing correspondence when he was away, flourished – so that, at home or abroad, Dermot became one certainty in her life. And there were others.

With Great-Aunt Emily, though 'The Magic Jaunting Car' book had long since been completed, Hetty developed all sorts of close, sometimes bizarre associations. As she became older herself, Hetty came more and more to see her aunt as a child, but adored her no less for that. For the childishness there, she realized, was part of her aunt's magic, a gift which set her quite apart from everyone else in the household, a shield against the world, behind which another and much more interesting reality existed: a life of the mind in which the world could be quite differently ordered and put to rights. In this way, as Elly remarked, her aunt had a 'mind of her own' – a condition which Hetty soon came to emulate. And, besides, Aunt Emily was not all child. She was full of so much, and most surprising, grown-up comment and information, too.

And so, in these years, it was largely from her aunt, and not through Miss Goulden or her mother, that Hetty took her theories of the world. A distorted vision perhaps, but there was a decisiveness, a wit and passion in her aunt's strange angles on life which appealed to Hetty. Talking to her aunt always excited and surprised her. She felt her brain bulging with contradictory impressions – of the world, of men and women, of what all these were *really* like. Aunt Emily seemed to see *through* everything – that was the exciting thing. Her magic gave her a key to everything, which no other person, except Dermot in quite a different way, possessed. Aunt Emily, in a few moments with her words or drawings, could turn life into a balm or thrilling adventure, when life in fact at that point was full of grey, unhappy things.

With Elly, Hetty found a more conventional solace – and in Robert she had a difficult but invigorating playmate. As he grew – and despite, or more because of, their disagreements and armed truces – she came to respect his steady firmness, the good sense which lay behind his sudden acts of unreason and temper. Robert in these years regained most of the nature he had lost with the sudden death of his parents: a balance, already almost academic in its niceties, a mind where intellect and his voracious reading formed a growing bastion against all that was difficult or hurtful in his life. He was someone, Hetty came to see, who could not be bullied indefinitely or in any way finally put down. And though, with her own essentially autocratic nature, her sporadic vindictiveness and passionate rages, she resented her inability to dominate him, she had to admit that this final layer of steel in Robert made him a worthy opponent.

Only with her mother did Hetty fail to make any connections. Their relationship became increasingly bitter – for

Hetty felt deceived by her always, cheated, lied to. And of course, in truth, this was just the case. Frances, so long indulging her disappointments and with the advent now of her militant political activities, was entirely unaware of how this core of bitterness in her soul had quite eroded her intelligence. She remained clever and spirited now only in her ability to hurt people: a tragedy which Hetty could not see, but which she suffered none the less.

It irked Hetty, too, that only towards Robert did her mother show any semblance of concern or affection. She had heard, or overheard, her mother praise his steady virtues, his boyish good looks – and indeed often suffered quite open and detrimental comparisons with her mother here. Was she not then good-looking? She could not be – and the thought hurt her deeply.

In fact, at thirteen, Hetty, without her mother being able to admit it, had developed in ways which were quite different from, and far outshone, mere good looks. There were in her all the lineaments of a distinctive beauty, the promise of something quite beyond the conventions.

As her features and bearing began to take a final shape and balance – waist narrowing, lengthening thighs, budding breasts – it was clear that the eventual form here would be original . . . and sensational.

No, she was not good-looking. All the qualities in her face now – the risen cheek-bones, perfectly straight nose, the fierce glinting eyes, the long delicately bowed lips, pointed chin, the unruly cascade of silky dark curls running down either side to the jaw – all were coagulating into a beauty which was both arrogant and divine: the flesh machined so finely, yet overlooked by these bold blue eyes. There was a radiance, a startling, almost harsh elegance blooming here; a sudden flush of insolence or rage which could as soon change and soften into lines of humility and grace.

Chameleon in her looks, which so quickly reflected the see-saw in her heart, tortured by her inarticulacy and by the strength of her emotions, she ran between extremes with such mobility and variety of expression that overall the face was difficult to define, other than by the emotions it presented. At few points was there something static to take hold of and identify her by – only a succession of faces, which could enchant or sadden or terrify the onlooker.

Though as dark-haired as her mother, Hetty would be taller and less plump than her – and without that olive-ivory tinge to her skin, which was a very faint, almost translucent pink. Frances's slightly gypsy looks had been refined here – lengthened, teased out, and re-set in a classic mould. And yet that mould was broken, too, and re-cast again in one more exclusive still – by her eyes, which were her most captivating feature: the mix of Cordiner Wedgwood and pale Hanoverian blue, set in great oval saucers, topped by long scimitar-shaped eyebrows, beneath this framing cowl of black hair: so surprising a colour combination of light and dark, where the expected tinges and mixes had never been arrived at, leaving instead these brilliant contrasts of blue and black and pink.

As she stood on its threshold, life, with its larger battles, had not yet engaged Hetty. But what she presented to it already, in her beauty and sharp will, suggested a lively campaign, one in which she would give no ground, where victory of some sort – as it had been for her mother – would always be of paramount importance.

Unlike her mother, though, these dominant qualities were tempered by artistry, by all sorts of fears and sensitivities, betrayed by her stammer which she never quite threw off. And these fierce qualities, which had their virtues too, she tried to hide, as the shadow side of a coin – not knowing then how, in so vehemently pursuing all her choices, she would eventually have to pay on both sides.

But at thirteen, as old as the century, Hetty's first real battleground was chosen for her. Her mother, having arranged for Robert to board at a Protestant boys' college outside Dublin, but with her horror of anything English for Hetty, sent her to a convent school in France.

4

The two girls, in their uniform of starched white linen skirts and severe cambric blouses, had stopped among the tall trees in the beech alley behind the château leading to the chapel. Hetty was beginning to have second thoughts about their plan.

'Oh, come on!' Léonie whispered hotly. 'It's not as if it was a *real* saint's bone – only a bit of rabbit or something.'

'Still . . .'

'And we're not even Catholic *anyway* – don't have to believe in all that mumbo-jumbo, like the other girls.' Léonie swivelled round, stamping her foot, making a little dance on the mossy grass, the thick carpet of bluebells and wood anemones beneath the trees. 'We're only here for the "ed-u-kay-shun" anyway,' Léonie drawled the word out, exaggerating her slight American accent, laughing quickly.

A breeze stirred the scented spring afternoon. It was the middle of Hetty's second term at the Couvent du Sacré-Coeur; the nuns had inherited the vast, rather ugly, red-and-white-bricked Château de Héricourt, on the edge of a village some miles south of Bayeux, in the middle of the lush Normandy countryside.

Hetty had not been there as long as Léonie, and though, in their growing friendship and various escapades, she had rarely been less daring than her, in this instance she felt a stab of real cowardice: the relic above the altar in its gold-and-red-enamelled box – a finger bone from the hand of Saint Matilda, it was said – was so *very* holy . . .

'There'll be real trouble, if we're caught.' Hetty voiced her doubts again.

'We *won't* be caught.'

Hetty gazed – fear overcome by admiration – at this deep-eyed gamine, a year older than her but several inches smaller, the breeze scattering her fluffy dark brown hair, swishing it across her slightly aquiline nose, where it snagged in her long eyelashes. Nearly fifteen, though Léonie was small, she had the body of an older girl, well-developed, rather chunky, full of sharp angles – in a firm jaw line and a jutting chin beneath a generous mouth filled with perfectly formed, very white square teeth; a waist that already narrowed dramatically, prominent hip bones, a flat behind, strong legs that kicked the linen skirt about restlessly. And she accentuated these aggressive yet sensuous attributes now, returning Hetty's gaze, hand on hip, chin up, lips ajar, looking at her provocatively from the depths of her grey-green eyes.

Léonie's expression, always direct and searching, often reflected the excitement of some difficult decision being weighed in her mind, usually a straight choice between good and bad, when she seemed to savour the thrill of delaying an answer, the more to enjoy the illicit act itself. And Hetty had been attracted by this air of repressed audacity and knowing ardour ever since she had arrived at the Convent the previous autumn, taking the next cubicle to hers in the junior dormitory.

It was a Saturday afternoon, their free hours, during which the thirty or so other girls were dutifully sewing, reading Racine in the great first floor *salon*, or out walking in the grounds in pairs, for they were never allowed to go alone.

'Look, it's quite simple,' Léonie insisted. 'We just go in and sit down and pray and pretend to be holy and then, if the coast is really clear, we flit up, open the box and take a look.'

'What if the box is locked?'

'Then it's *locked*, you ninny!'

Léonie tugged her towards the chapel. This small building, with its blue-and-gilt baroque interior, was empty, and all went according to plan – except that when Léonie tried to open the good enamel reliquary it was, indeed, locked.

'Shame,' she whispered, tugging once more at the lid. Hetty tried then, and to their astonishment it opened easily. Inside, attached by a gold thread to a velvet cushion, was a tiny sliver of grey bone. They both gazed at it in awe. Then Léonie looked at Hetty. 'How on earth were you able to open it – and I couldn't?'

'Don't know.'

Léonie closed the box, then tried to open it herself once more. The lid would not budge. 'A miracle,' she said shortly.

'Come on,' Hetty whispered urgently. 'Let's leave before someone comes.'

The girls ran out into the late sunshine – breathless and flushed with the success of their endeavour, rushing over the deep carpet of bluebells beyond the chapel.

The convent – which some few parents mistakenly saw simply as a finishing school, so that their girls were not admitted or soon left – had, as its real attraction, a reputation for academic excellence. And it was for this reason that Benjamin Straus, a marine lawyer in his mid-forties and graduate of Columbia Law School in New York, had sent his only daughter Léonie there. He was determined that she should have the best schooling available then for girls in France, no matter that it was not Jewish. He held that faith only very lightly now in any case, as did his wife Effi, a dark-haired girl from Brooklyn, whom he had met sixteen years before, married in a month, and taken back with him to France.

The Strauses had a small town house in Paris – where Hetty had stayed with them for a few days before Christmas – in the *seizième*, one of the last of the eighteenth-century village houses still there in Passy, shadowed and surrounded now by heavy *belle époque* apartment buildings.

American Marine Salvage and Insurance, the company of which Benjamin Straus was overseas director, had their European head office in Paris, with a branch at Le Havre, not far from the château convent. And this had been another reason for sending Léonie there. Benjamin loved his daughter and, as often as the discipline there allowed, came to visit her on his business trips to the port.

Unorthodox both in his faith and temperament, Ben

Straus was a brisk and genial man of the world. His views were liberal and advanced – traits which his daughter seemed about to inherit in abundance. They were both originals – in their fiery confidence, happy intellect, sharp intuitions. And Straus's business acumen was perhaps sharper still. Through private investments he had made money – and enjoyed spending it, particularly on young women, and especially on his daughter and her new Irish friend, Hetty. He had a taste for beautiful things – one which he hoped to indulge the following day that spring, at the Hôtel Lion d'Or in Bayeux, where he had arranged lunch for the two girls.

The Mother Superior, Mother Agnes, had granted permission – a little unwillingly. But Mr Straus's air of reliability and charm during earlier visits to the convent, and his equally reassuring letter in this instance, had prevailed over the Mother Superior, with the proviso that he should accompany the girls to and from Bayeux.

All went according to plan. Benjamin, in a creamy grey homburg, white spats and with a silver-topped cane, with his chauffeur in the huge Peugeot cabriolet he had just purchased, picked the girls up at the gates of the château – both dressed in their Sunday best: long white, fluttery, layered muslin skirts, fine cotton embroidered blouses and straw bonnets – and within the hour they were driving into the cobbled courtyard of the Lion d'Or, where shortly afterwards, taking lunch at a large round table, decorated with little vases of wild spring flowers, they studied the simple *carte du jour*.

As an apéritif they sipped glasses from a half-bottle of Roederer brut. The girls, agog, savoured the warm smells from the kitchen and watched the bubbles break and rise, the champagne sparkling in the bright sunlight slanting through the half-open window.

'Papa, we finally got to take a look at that old relic,' Léonie told her father, from whom she had few, if any, secrets. 'It *was* a bit of old rabbit bone, I'm sure. But the strange thing was – *I* couldn't open the gold box, but Hetty could!'

Mr Straus looked at Hetty, then raised his glass to her. 'Well, that figures – it's the Irish in her. All sorts of magic there.'

Hetty blushed. Léonie interjected boisterously: 'But, Papa, *we* have magic, too. You always said so: the Jews!'

'So we have! We're both of us – the Jews and the Irish – the Magic People. But Hetty must have even more of it.' He looked at his daughter again, with a kindly, quizzical surmise. 'After all, Hetty's Irish *and* Jewish, isn't she?'

They ate simply but well – a moist *terrine*, fresh *crevettes* with mayonnaise, the local *truite aux amandes*, fruit and cheese, and a light Vouvray to go with it all, a lunch which, for Hetty, vibrated with every sort of pleasure, happiness: the slightly tart smell of the pale wine, the burnt-sweet taste of crackly almonds, the faint perfume of lilac from a tree in the courtyard just outside the window, garlic and piquant lemon in the air, warmth and satisfaction emanating from the other guests – all this, with the wine, seemed to lift Hetty several inches above her chair, gave her a cloudy sensation of ecstasy, the feeling of being in a dream which was yet entirely real, so that life at that moment was better than in her wildest fancies.

The chatter between the loquacious Strauses was nearly continuous and Hetty was quite content to bask in such happy surroundings. Benjamin spoke of Paris, the gossip among his French friends and the American community there – of the theatre and café life, which Hetty had only briefly sampled in her few days with the family before Christmas. They had all gone to the Cirque d'Hiver and a performance of Racine's *Andromaque* at the Comédie Française, and dined at Fouquet's in the Champs-Elysées. It was a life and a city which Hetty had loved, but which existed for her now only as a memorable taste. Mr Straus drew her into the conversation; they had been talking of the future.

'And what would you like to do there, Henrietta?'

'Oh, I'd like to live in Pa-Pa-Paris!' she said at once.

'Well, so you shall – why not? I wanted just the same thing. And look – there I am!'

'But you have a b-b-business.'

'A good wife, too!'

'I mean, I don't have a business . . .'

'Why, you *can*—'

'Or a husband,' Léonie interjected.

'Indeed,' her father confirmed the point. 'Or a good husband, which is more to the point.'

Hetty looked uncertain.

'I want to be a singer – at the Opera! That's right, isn't it, Papa?' Léonie ran on.

'If you work hard at it, why not?'

'Yes, Léonie sings so well.' Hetty spoke out now, her stammer lost for a moment. 'The "Ave Maria" in the chapel choir. But my voice goes all cracked on the high notes.'

'Well, something else then,' Mr Straus said. 'There's plenty of go in your family, as I understand it. And that's the great thing in life, isn't it, girls? – a bit of get up and go!' He lit a cigar. 'So what do you say? I don't much fancy another look at that old Norman tapestry here. Had enough of conquerors. What if we take the auto to the seaside for the afternoon?'

Which they did, driving north-east to Cabourg, running on the beach there and walking along the promenade among the fashionably dressed crowds with their tiny parasols and vast picture hats, before taking tea in the palm court of the Grand Hotel. And all this, too, was a wonder to Hetty: the promise of a sort of freedom she had never known in her isolated life in Ireland, a freedom linked to other people's adventures. She sensed she was not alone in her desires – that her wild thoughts of future success, of love and adventure, were not unique to her, but shared, with Léonie, Léonie's father, and surely all the other people on the promenade and in the palm court, with their top hats, sticks and feather boas.

Hetty relished life that day. She was loath to return to the convent, where all such life was prohibited, hedged about with so many petty rules, made to be broken. A few weeks later, Hetty and Léonie agreed on a plan. And, this time, they intended they should be caught – taking their weekly bath, in the two screened tubs, without wearing the required cotton bathing shifts. The two girls sat there, in the hot water, naked, splashing about in the soap suds, making a great noise. So that it was not long before Sister Thérèse, their dormitory monitor, arrived on the scene. A diminutive martinet with a brassy Alsace accent, she was horrified.

'Your shifts! Where are your shifts?' she shouted at them, waving her arms through the wafts of steam. The girls grinned at her.

'I can't wash properly in a shift,' Léonie told her promptly, washing herself with exaggerated movements, raising one arm, then the other, in a suggestive ballet, an olive-skinned odalisque, massaging her rib-cage, her neat breasts.

'It's *dirty*, washing in a shift,' Hetty added, soaping herself with similarly provocative vigour.

Sister Thérèse nearly exploded.

But, the next morning, Mother Superior took a quieter, insidious, much more Jesuitical line.

'You say you cannot *wash* properly in your shifts?' She sat behind an ornate Louis Quinze bureau in her study, an incongruously plain crucifix on the heavy fleur de lys wallpaper behind her.

'Yes – just that.'

Mother Agnes sighed. 'That may or may not be so,' she said icily. 'But honesty should compel you to admit that you *also* bathed in such a manner simply to break the regulations and provoke Sister Thérèse – for the *joy* of so doing. Both of you are sufficiently intelligent to distinguish between these quite separate reasons: it is *good* that you should want to wash properly; not good that you should wilfully disobey our rules here.'

'Are the rules more important then than our washing properly?' Léonie asked innocently.

'The two issues are not comparable in the manner you suggest.' Mother Agnes, a tall, grim-faced woman, stood up, clasping her hands, going over to the window. She turned then, with a look of fierce reason in her eyes. 'You must obey the rules *and* wash properly. That is the sequence – and the whole point of law: that it stands *a priori* – you know what that means? – as a first cause, in front of, before, everything else. Therefore you may wash only within the context of the law here. Is that not perfectly clear?'

Mother Agnes returned to her bureau, and took up a quill pen, prior to setting out their punishment.

'But, M-M-Mother Agnes, that's not fair,' Hetty tried to forestall her now, breathlessly, pleading her case with a great, but entirely assumed innocence in her wide eyes. 'We w-w-*were* just wanting to wash properly, not just to be bad.'

'Now you lie, girl, and compound the offence.'

'How do you know I'm l-l-lying?' she stammered.

'I know,' the old woman said deeply. 'And, what's more, *you* know you are. Useless to pretend otherwise.' She shook her head. 'You see, Henrietta, *I* know you, your every temptation, every sin – almost as God knows them – everything . . . Remember, when you think to perpetrate these sins again – remember what His Son Jesus Christ said: "Behold, I am with you always – even unto the end of the world." You can never escape that final retribution.'

Mother Agnes passed sentence then, confirming it as she spoke in the big leather-bound punishment book. 'You will walk the grounds, commencing this Saturday, every Saturday in free time, from now until the end of term. And of course there will be no more exeats.' She closed the book with a decisive thump. Then she gazed at the two girls, before adding as her lugubrious peroration: 'And your shifts – you will remember your shifts . . .'

'Well, at least she didn't chuck us out.' Léonie picked a kingcup on the first of their punishment walks that same afternoon, munched the stalk an instant before throwing it in the fast-flowing chalk stream. Kneeling down, Hetty gazed at her reflection in the water.

'No. She wouldn't have expelled us.' Hetty stared down into the green shallows. 'She's too clever for that: prefers to make us feel really guilty.'

'Well, I don't . . . I just think she's an old cow.'

'A clever old cow, thought. We *did* do it to annoy—'

'*And* to wash properly—'

'But we *wanted* to be caught.'

'Of course, to make a point, how stupid it all is. Why should we hide everything? Like the other girls – always hiding things and sniggering and keeping little secret bits of mirror in their cupboards—'

'And writing secret *billets-doux* – to imaginary *beaux*, getting old Michel to post them in the village. *We* don't have to do that.' The girls chuckled. 'The men we write to are *real*!' Hetty said, thinking of Dermot, and they chuckled again.

The two girls lay on their stomachs, gazing at their reflections in the water.

'You can see yourself here at least,' Hetty said. 'So stupid, not being allowed to have any mirrors anywhere in the château.'

'All part of the "context of the law".' Léonie leant out, dipping her arm in the water, wondering if she could tickle the brown trout that wavered in the stream some yards upstream. 'Oh, the *agony* of it all,' she suddenly moaned, her voice full of mock drama. 'Are we really going to spend years and years here, being pestered by Sister Thérèse and Mother Superior? Tell me, Hetty, can we *bear* it?'

'I can – if you can.' Hetty lay on her back now, looking up at the blue arc of sky. Then, she put her hand out, vaguely pawing the air before, like a butterfly net trapping an insect, she let it fall over Léonie's mouth. '*We* can bear it . . .'

'Um-m-m-m.' Léonie's lips fed an instant on Hetty's gentle fingers.

Mother Superior might have known better. Her punishment cemented a friendship which, in the giddy reverses of such adolescent associations, might otherwise have waned or lapsed entirely – a friendship in any case which, had the old woman known more of the human heart, she would surely have thought unsuitable from the beginning. As it was, in commanding these long walks together, she bound the girls to pleasure, not to penance.

Perhaps since on the surface they were so unalike – the tall, stammering, gauche but haughty Irish girl and this compact, sweet-sly European – Mother Superior believed them to be quite incompatible as real friends, and therefore no threat to each other. But of course it was just these wide differences in their character which drew them together – this very factor which, like a lit taper held above a jar of pure oxygen, made their friendship dangerously inflammable.

'I do wish I had someone to write to – properly, I mean – like you do.' Léonie was chattering away the following Saturday, a colder day, with grey rain clouds scudding above the poplars, so that the girls wore mufflers with their green serge topcoats, together with tall lace-up boots as protection against the muddy paths.

'But you *do* have – your uncle Eli in New York who sends you those amazing presents, those real Indian beads and things.'

'Not the same . . . as Dermot, in the *army* and everything. That's exciting. You're so lucky! He's so handsome!' Léonie faced Hetty as they neared one of the trout traps. 'Show me that photograph again – do! The one of him on that great horse in his uniform.'

'It's hidden in my cupboard.'

'No, it's not – you keep it under your vest!'

'No, I don't! Anyway, you can see him properly – this summer, when you come to stay in Ireland. I've written to Mama . . .' Hetty's face clouded then.

'But you haven't heard from her, have you?'

'She hardly ever writes.'

'But Dermot does!'

They had come to the trout trap now, a little tributary, with a metal grille at either end, running out and back from the main stream, where half a dozen fish languished, gills palpitating, heads against the flow of the green-dark water.

'Yes, you'll like Dermot,' Hetty went on. 'He's such tremendous fun.' But she turned to Léonie then, biting her lip, a doubt in her eyes. She did not want Léonie to like him *too* much.

'What's the matter?'

'Nothing. And there's Robert, too,' Hetty ran on, changing the topic, thinking to introduce an alternative male friend for Léonie. 'You'll see him, he's nice. He'll be back from school in Dublin.'

'Robert, your brother . . .?'

'No, not really – remember, I told you: his parents were killed in a hurricane. We were just brought up together.'

'Oh yes – Robert.' But Léonie did not seem very interested in Robert, and it was she who changed the subject. 'Shall we let the fish out?'

'Or fish *for* them – wouldn't that be more fun?'

'What with?'

'A bent pin – I've got one – and our boot-laces. And a worm.'

They found a worm, took off their boots, undid all the laces, and Hetty unfastened a safety pin which had been holding up her skirt, so that it collapsed about her ankles. Then they roared with laughter, dancing about the trout trap, terrifying the fish.

Later, Hetty found a small snail on the path, with a wonderfully coloured shell, striped in brilliant green and yellow bands. She gently picked it up, setting it on her hand; after a minute or two, the snail, which had retreated inside its house, re-emerged. Léonie thought it gruesome.

'It's just a beautiful little snail,' Hetty told her. 'Here, you hold it.'

Léonie grimaced, backing away. 'It's all slimy, though – horrible!'

'No, it's not, it's sweet.'

'Put it on your head, then, if it's so sweet. I dare you!'

Hetty did just that, holding the snail there until it

seemed to take root, a brightly coloured emblem like a third eye in the middle of her forehead.

Léonie watched the performance with disgust. But she was impressed. And now she was ashamed at her cowardice.

'All right,' she said finally, steeling herself. 'Do it to me.'

Hetty walked slowly forward. Léonie, her back against the trunk of a tree, stood quite still with her eyes closed, unresisting, as Hetty transferred the snail, placing it delicately on Léonie's brow. The moment she felt its cold touch – she shivered violently, as if about to suffer a delicious agony.

'There!' Hetty said, when the snail had once more taken up residence. 'See, I told you, it's nothing.' Léonie opened her eyes a fraction, squinting upwards, unable to see the snail, but still fearful. 'You did it!' Hetty ran on, excited, happy. 'You did it!'

Léonie smiled briefly then, keeping her head absolutely still. 'Yes,' she said limply, 'I did it . . .'

Afterwards they walked on, arm in arm, true companions now, as if, in this mutual contact with the snail, they had finally put the seal on their friendship.

Back at Summer Hill, Frances's life had gone from bad to worse. Her militant republican career – all she really lived for now – had suffered various setbacks. Like Hetty, she had been kicking at the traces. But for Frances there was no release in any tender friendship, only an increasing bitterness that she could not now, literally, take up arms against the British.

With the surprising advent of Asquith's Liberal Home Rule Bill in 1912, popular support for Arthur Griffith's Sinn Fein Abstentionist Party in Ireland fell away dramatically. And worse, as far as Frances and the other members of the secret Irish Republican Brotherhood were concerned, there was now almost no public support in Ireland for revolution or violence of any sort.

As a result of Asquith's bill, Redmond's old Irish Home

Rule Party was once more everywhere in the ascendant, both in Ireland and at Westminster. In return for supporting the Liberal Party in the House of Commons, Redmond had extracted this bill from Asquith and had thus seemed to guarantee Home Rule for Ireland within a year or two – an entirely peaceful transfer of power from London to Dublin. And so all Frances's dreams of violent glory had been set at nothing; Pat Kennedy's too. After centuries of bloodshed the physical force movement in Ireland was now obsolete. The country would achieve its liberty constitutionally, without Pat Kennedy's revolver or Frances's equally vigorous help – and Frances took this setback badly, as a vampire denied blood, kicking her heels about Summer Hill, working off her ire by bullying everyone more than ever.

So that, by the early summer of 1914, when Hetty and Léonie travelled to Summer Hill, they found Frances in a particularly fierce and unresponsive mood. Often she was away, at clandestine meetings in Dublin or Belfast, with her fellow conspirators in the IRB – O'Hegarty, Eoin MacNeill, Padraic Pearse – among whom she found more congenial company, as they pondered their lost revolution. Thus the two girls, since Miss Goulden had long since departed, had the house much to themselves, until Dermot arrived for his annual visit, coming down on the train with Robert, home from school in Dublin, in the middle of June – a month that started with rain, but soon turned brilliantly fine and hot, the flaming cloudless weather lasting day after day, seemingly set fair for the rest of the summer.

Frances was away for the day when Dermot and Robert arrived, so Dermot immediately took the three young people out salmon fishing, wading into the stream with his rod, while Robert and the girls watched from upstream near the boathouse, where a picnic tea awaited them.

The two girls, leaving Robert on the bank with the big salmon net, returned to the boathouse to prepare the tea, setting plates out and putting the kettle to boil on the small grate at the back of the stone building. They were in shadow now, but it was hot, especially when the dry tinder took fire under the kettle and the flames leapt up. Outside, beyond the jetty, the river glittered fiercely in the sun. Léonie ran a hand over her brow, as the sweat trickled down her cheeks. Then she laughed.

'All this making *tea* you do over here – seem to live on it in Ireland.' She drew away from the fire, flapping her hands.

'Well?' Hetty asked with excited impatience. 'Wha-wha-what do you think of him?'

'Oh, he's nice. Quiet, but very nice. How long has he been at school in Dublin?'

Hetty was astonished, annoyed. 'I meant *Dermot*, you ninny! Not Robert.'

'Oh.' Léonie pulled herself together. 'Well, he's very nice as well. But I *knew* that.'

They went out on to the jetty then, shading their eyes against the glare, gazing downstream at Dermot. But Léonie's eyes soon strayed towards Robert: slim, but much taller now and no longer a boy, handsome in a sharply chiselled, rather farouche way, with a shank of thick dark hair running sideways across his head; an isolated but composed figure as he stood on the bank, quite still, holding the salmon net, a sentinel with a spear in the dazzling sunlight.

'Tea's ready!' Hetty sang out to Dermot, longing to set him down at the little bench in the boathouse, minister to him, generally show him off to Léonie. But, when he did come to tea, he seemed preoccupied, taking little notice of Hetty.

'Will you take Léonie and me – and Robert,' she added as a rather unwilling afterthought, 'out in the trap this evening? We could go over to Brandon, climb the mountain . . .?'

'I'd like to, perhaps tomorrow—'

'Or the otters? Come out and see if we can see them this evening?'

'I'm a little tired, Hetty . . .'

Hetty was crestfallen.

496

In fact Dermot wanted to speak to Frances – when she got back from Dublin that evening, the next morning, as soon as possible in any case: more anxious to do this than to entertain Hetty and her new friend. The business with Frances was far more urgent, he was sure.

He had heard from his father, who had seen and been in touch with Frances regularly during the past year, heard how very difficult she had become. Violent, insensate – these were some of the words his father had used of her. He feared for her sanity. And then there was an entirely certain matter to take up with her: the deplorable incident with Appleton, the English head gardener, who had done so much for the place under Lady Cordiner's earlier directions. Frances had apparently insisted that he undo all his work in the neat pleasure gardens, changing the formal patterns there, demanding a bosky wildness everywhere – and, when the man had demurred, she had struck him in the face and given him immediate notice. It was obvious – Frances was close to some sort of nervous breakdown. So that Dermot, remembering their old intimacies, saw that he must help her if he could, make one last effort to try to ease her many disappointments, set her to rights.

He took his opportunity the following morning, first indulging in pleasantries with her in the porch after breakfast before following her into her boudoir. She showed surprise at this invasion: surprise and then, as he had expected and prepared himself for, scalding anger at his presumption.

'We have had this quite pointless conversation before, as I remember,' she told him in her harsh voice. 'Let me repeat myself: I do *not* require you to come here, to my house, and tell me how to run it – or my life!'

Dermot had taken up position by the door, in case she thought to bolt, for he had decided now that, if it came to it, nothing could be lost in his taking a very firm line with this dangerously intemperate woman.

He gazed at her then, standing against the bright summer light, a vase of huge white peonies on her Sheraton desk. At nearly forty, apart from a few greying hairs, she had not lost her dark beauty: the almost ruler-straight nose, great blackberry eyes, wide proud mouth, the olive-skinned gypsy looks. The beauty was still there, but appeared now only as a lovely and vague illustration seen through tracing paper, as if each of these original designs had been overlaid with cruel alterations: the lips pouted in permanent disapproval, curling down at either side, the chin puckered like folds on a toby jug, the eyes soured with long antagonisms – and her once sweet voice screeched now as she bunched and cracked her finger joints like angry castanets. The gypsy had become a witch.

The transformation was piteous. And Dermot, remembering the other lovely woman, wished desperately to change the whole mould here, wave a magic wand and return Frances to her better nature.

'Frances, dear Frances,' he began, 'that is *not* what I am doing here, believe me—'

'What else—'

'Please don't *interrupt!*' he told her firmly, showing steel. 'You know perfectly well – things have reached a bad pass down here. We must try and do something about it.' She attempted to interrupt again. 'No, hear me out – first this business with Appleton. You put the matter in my father's hands, his Dublin legal office, and he has asked me to speak to you.' He took a document from his pocket. 'Appleton's solicitors have filed suit with the courts here, for assault and improper dismissal. The case comes up in Waterford next month—'

'Indeed! And we will win it. The man was outrageously impertinent, refused to obey instructions.'

'That may well be so. But in your physical assault he has a more serious case against you and it could well go his way. He has witnesses to the event—'

'It will be up to your father's office to see that it does *not* go his way, else I shall take other legal counsel.'

'My dear Frances, that's not really the point – you know it well. We must speak of other things, come to the root of the matter – of what so worries and upsets you. Already you have seriously jeopardized your life here at Summer

Hill. You are, I know, losing staff, in the household and on the estate. And other local people will not work for you – soon the whole place will become unmanageable, the farm bankrupt. If matters continue this way you will destroy your inheritance here – and I only speak to you in this way to prevent that happening. The house here is as dear to me as it is to you. Do you not see all this?'

Frances had stared at him unbelievingly as he spoke, speechless with anger, merely waiting for him to finish before answering him viciously. Yet, when he did stop, she said nothing.

Instead, she walked quickly across the room, raised her arm, and aimed a blow to Dermot's cheek. But Dermot, just as quickly, snatched her arm, held it tightly, bent it back, forcing it down as she resisted fiercely.

'Traitor!' she screamed at him, raising her other arm, until he grasped that, too, holding both as if in a vice, so that they swayed about the room together, locked in a grim dance.

'Traitor! Bully! You interfering great bully!' She continued her tirade.

'No,' he told her urgently, his gentle voice quite at odds with his physical dominance. 'I have *not* betrayed you – others have, but not I. I have always been true to you, told the truth, about myself and about you. If you could only *see* that!'

She continued the struggle, more fiercely still – and still he would not let her go. So that eventually, in this violent proximity, something cracked in Frances – and the end of the contest was just as dramatic as its beginning. Suddenly she quite ceased the struggle and fell into Dermot's arms with an almost equal violence, sobbing on his shoulder.

Embarrassed by this sudden emotional volte-face, Dermot none the less took every advantage of it. He consoled her, patting her on the back, while at the same time gently trying to ease his way out of her embrace. 'Now tell me,' he said, 'what is it, tell me, that makes you so unhappy, so many years after . . . all those earlier sorrows?'

She continued weeping on his shoulder. Then suddenly she drew away from him, still holding his shoulders, but shaking them now. 'What do you *think* is the matter – if not all those "earlier sorrows" as you politely put them?'

'Dearest, it was all so long ago—'

'Does that alter it, the pain?'

'But the Prince is dead and gone these many—'

She shook him again. 'You can't be so naïve! Not so much him, but *you* – you, Dermot.' She turned away then, taking out a handkerchief, mopping her eyes. 'Don't you see? It all went wrong for me *then*, before him, with *you*. I loved you – oh, more than *any*one, ever.' Crushed by so much emotion, she went over to the window.

'I wish I could make it up to you,' he said, rooted to the spot, gazing at her blankly. 'I wished it then – I wish it now. But . . .' He did not go on, fearing another outburst from her.

'But you can't.' She said the words for him, bitterly.

She had altered in the last few minutes – regaining, as if from the warm impact of his body, something of her old self, the bright, happy woman she had once been. And Dermot feared now, in her last acid words, that, unless he made some positive gesture, she would relapse once more into her bitter life.

So he came across to her then, and gave himself to her, in so far as he could, taking her chastely in his arms and holding her there.

'You have me – at least in every other way,' he told her. 'Cannot you see that – feel it?'

'Indeed . . .' She smiled for an instant, looking over his shoulder. 'There is the whole problem.' And Dermot saw then, felt the emotion intensely, how he alone had it in his power to make this woman happy and change her life, take her away from all this emotional and political frustration. But he feared to implement the power, for he knew, because of his real nature, how he could not truly satisfy her. And she knew it, too, without either of them having to express the fact. None the less Dermot recognized the crucial watershed at which they had both arrived, which he had contrived, which it was his responsibility to resolve in some fashion. And he knew, too, how one false word or move on his part at this point would ruin everything.

So he said, 'If you could bear with me – with my nature – we might marry?'

He so accentuated the doubt in this proposal that at first Frances responded in kind, simply shaking her head in disbelief. 'Do you mean it?' she said at last, her face still frozen in surprise.

'Why, yes.'

'A marriage of convenience . . .' She turned away, sad, dismissive.

'No, a marriage of . . . whatever we made it.' He was almost annoyed suddenly, anxious to contradict her.

Her face relaxed then as she laughed abruptly, turning back to him. 'I could bear with your nature, Dermot. The doubt is – could you bear with mine?'

'Yes,' he said with real enthusiasm now. 'The wonderful nature you had, and have only . . . mislaid.'

'No,' she said wanly. 'I have since changed completely in other ways—'

'Oh, if you mean your Home Rule enthusiasms! But why should I object to that now? Asquith's bill will go through before the end of the year and Ireland will be free. There is no problem there, surely? You will have won your cause without violence and there'll be a happy end to it – for both of us.'

'Well, let us think about your suggestion, shall we?'

There was silence. One of the huge peony petals fell limply to the floor and, outside, a cloud raced across the sun, darkening the room for a moment. Then she moved towards him and kissed him briefly, but with a long-forgotten tenderness.

Frances was truly happy for the first time in years. Her foul humours dissolved. She began to take a relaxed and kindly interest in people and in her surroundings. In short, she mellowed in the warmth of Dermot's affection – all of which, as a quite expected consequence, enraged Hetty.

She no longer had Dermot to herself – sharing with him only a small part of the fun and adventure she had expected. In this sudden turn-about she felt betrayed by him – and worse was the fact that he should neglect her for her mother, whom she hated.

So that when, partly on Dermot's suggestion, Frances tried to make things up with her daughter, Hetty violently rejected these peace overtures. They talked together one morning on the porch.

'I have tried to explain,' Frances still spoke formally, but not coldly. 'There have been such difficulties from the beginning – your father's death, all the problems with your Grandmama when we came here: I have not given you the attention I should have.'

Hetty fidgeted by the high-backed wicker chair, anxious to join Léonie and Robert playing croquet on the upper lawn. 'Yes,' she scowled. 'So – now you have explained.'

'Hetty, dear, you are so unapproachable: I am *sorry*.'

'But you have *not* explained!' Hetty rounded on her mother. 'My f-f-father, for example. People say – how he is *not* my father—'

'But of course he is!'

'And my Grandmama – why is she locked up?'

'She is . . . unwell.'

'And Dermot!' Hetty burst out, unable to contain herself, shaking with frustrated emotion.

'What of Dermot? He has been a great stay to us both – has he not?'

'Wh-wh-why does he – does he now *haunt* you so?'

'"Haunt" me?' Frances was surprised at the word. But it propelled her into an admission she might not otherwise have made. 'My dear, he does not haunt me. I may tell you now – we hope to marry!' She smiled graciously.

Hetty was thunderstruck. '*Marry* him? But you can't – he's a relation!'

'Only a very distant cousin—'

'But you can't, you can't!' Hetty quite lost control of herself then. 'You *can't* – he's my father!' she shouted, before running away, sobbing, to her bedroom.

Later Frances told Dermot of Hetty's fearful reaction.

'Not unexpected – I so wish she could be told the truth . . .'

'That's out of the question, I'm afraid.' Frances tried to disguise her almost brutal rigidity.

But Hetty's reaction to the news of her mother's impending marriage was openly brutal. That same afternoon, waiting her opportunity, she managed to corner Dermot alone, up by the grotto and the artificial waterfall.

'I *am* sorry, Hetty, that it should so upset you, our marrying—' he told her, before she responded bitterly, 'But you *can't* m-m-marry her – you can't m-marry a desperate Fenian!' She used the word that Elly had often used, covering all violent Irish revolutionaries. 'She's part of a secret group here, against the law! I know it! She and Pat Kennedy – they met a man here, years ago, in Pat's rooms, and they took a secret oath – to fight the British. So how can you m-m-marry someone like that? You in the army and all that? You can't!'

Dermot, thinking she must have invented it all, was not as surprised as Hetty had hoped. 'How do you know this?'

'I *saw* them, from the stable loft above Pat's rooms – all together, when she took the oath. So there!' Hetty was breathless with fury. 'If you m-marry her you will be a traitor yourself.'

She picked a fern, growing out from the rocks in the grotto, and fiddled with it violently.

'But, Hetty,' Dermot said at last, 'Ireland is going to be free in any case now, quite soon. The British are going to give us freedom here, quite legally, so your mother won't have to be involved in any of that sort of thing, any more. Don't you see? – it's all over now – that kind of Irish fighting.'

Hetty was not persuaded by this response, so Dermot took a different line. He turned, leaving the grotto, and gazed down at the house, its bluish limestone and great windows glimmering in the sunlight.

'Hetty, look at the house,' he urged her gently. 'Don't

you want to have it here, keep it – in years to come – as *your* house and home?'

'No. I hate the house,' she told him sullenly. 'Don't like it here in Ireland at all. I like France and Paris m-m-much better. Anyway, what's that to do with me – marrying Mama?'

'Just that I want the house to *be* here – for her and for you later on. And in marrying your Mama I think I can help that happen.'

Hetty was vindictively brusque again. 'You're m-m-marrying her – just to keep the house? That's not a very good reason. Don't you love her? That's why people m-marry, isn't it?'

Dermot found himself in a predicament. So set on the truth in every other way, he could not tell it here – could not begin to explain that he did not love her mother in the expected way, but felt a great tenderness and sympathy for her, a deep affection – and, yes, guilt for all his earlier inabilities and refusals with her. None of this could he tell Hetty, yet he was loath to lie. So he said, 'I love her, like I love you, Hetty. It's more a family love. Can you see that?'

Hetty could not see it. But she was somewhat placated by his answer, which put her, at least, on an equal footing with her mother in his affections, so that she felt emboldened to say, 'In a *family* way?'

'Yes, just that.'

Hetty's eyes were alight with fear and hope now as she rushed on, 'Are you, are you – my f-f-father then? My *real* father?' There was a vast silence, as Dermot fiddled with his pipe and matches. '*Are* you?' she asked despairingly.

'No, Hetty,' he said at last, lighting his pipe. 'No, I'm not. Why should you think that?'

Hetty turned away, close to tears now, crunching up the fern leaf. 'People said – oh, they said it, in Domenica – Robert heard. And that awful Miss Goulden was always asking funny questions . . . And my own Papa, well, *he* was so awful . . .'

'Yes, I see that. But think of it, Hetty – I *will* be your

father, your stepfather at least, when we marry.' He walked back to her, took his pipe from his mouth, and blew a few expert smoke rings into the still summer air, smiled at her, a loving mischief in his eyes, so that he made her smile at last – and they smiled together then, the smoke rings curling round Hetty's ears. 'That's the *great* thing,' he went on, speaking with boundless enthusiasm now, taking her by the shoulder and turning her away from the cold spray of the waterfall, so that they both faced out into the warm sun, looking over the sloping lawns, the glittering house, the lush valley and the purple hump of Mount Brandon beyond. 'The great thing – that we can all be here together: you and I and your Mama, Robert, your friend Léonie! All of us – live here, come here and *do* things together, so much to do! Life can be so happy for all of us, promise you – unimaginably happy. Just look at the house, Hetty! It's full of peace and *promise* now – look at it that way. Isn't it?'

Hetty bit her lip, trying to restrain her tears, as he held her arm tightly. 'Yes,' she spluttered. 'I suppose it is . . .'

She gazed at the house herself then. And indeed, in the light of Dermot's forthright explanations, his renewed affection, in his plans of a future for all of them here, Summer Hill, for the first time, called to Hetty, offering her something. It was no longer a site of unhappiness, of quarrels and long bitterness with her Mama, but a building that had floated clear away from all that dissension, reasserting its ancient truth, showing its long-dormant character, stone and mortar imbued with love now, not hatred. The house touched Hetty then, invisible tendrils reaching out in the hot summer air, embracing her delicately, offering itself to her, as a freehold possession – something of hers, not just her mother's. Yes, in the last of the golden afternoon light, the house *did* promise her something.

The following morning the *Irish Times* carried the bold headline: ARCHDUKE FRANCIS FERDINAND AND CONSORT ASSASSINATED AT SARAJEVO. Some days later Dermot's leave was cancelled – he was recalled to his regiment at Aldershot – and by the end of July Germany had declared war against both Russia and France, with England's declaration of hostilities following a few days later. Peace and promise disappeared everywhere, for everyone, then.

5

Dermot's regiment of Hussars was posted to France almost immediately – among the first of the British Expeditionary Force to land there on the 16th of August, when they were moved straight up to the Belgian front, making a temporary headquarters at the Château de Ghislain on the Mons–Charleroi road. Here, waiting on events in the push towards Mons, and joining up with a squadron of the Royal Irish Dragoons, they bivouacked on the flat farmland beyond the château stables, where many of their horses found ideal quarters.

It was scorchingly hot with an eerie silence, as scouts reported no sign of German troop movements, either around Mons itself, which they held in force, or on the road to Charleroi. The whole flat landscape seemed deserted, unmoving, except for an oven breath which now and then stirred the crimson poppy-heads in the long, gently undulating cornfields to either side of the road.

The war, for Dermot and his men, was somewhere else, or had not yet begun. The two cavalry brigades were stalled and still in the lazy swelter, flies caught in the golden amber of the weather; until the afternoon of the 22nd, when one of the Dragoon scouts rode back furiously into the stable yard, reporting that a troop of Uhlan lancers – some three miles away when he had last seen them, the officer in front casually smoking a cigar – were riding down the road from Mons towards them.

Dermot mustered his brigade with all speed, arranging with his opposite number, Major Bridges of the Irish Dragoons, to turn out at once, taking a course through the fields; they would advance across the corn and hope to surprise the Uhlans on the road in a sudden pincer movement.

In the event their plan did not materialize as expected. The Uhlans, with their own scouts and sensing trouble ahead of them at the château, had chosen a similar plan, leaving the road and dividing their men to either side of it, proceeding through these same cornfields, thus set on a direct collision course with the British. So that Dermot, riding ahead with 'C' squadron up a slight rise, was suddenly confronted by some fifty of the enemy already in battle positions, spread out in line abreast, like medieval cavalry, less than half a mile away across the cornfields, spiked helmets glinting in the afternoon sun, lances angled forward at the ready.

Rapidly Dermot mustered his own men in battle order. '"C" squadron, draw swords, ready to go! Fourth Troop, in the rear to follow up, ready for action! . . .'

His heart fluttered with excitement. His men outnumbered the Uhlans, he thought, and the westering sun shone straight in the enemy's eyes. And, besides these material advantages, he was so confident himself: the Uhlans, he knew, for all their fierce reputation, had never fought in battle before, while he and quite a few of his men had charged and survived at the bloody engagement of Colenso.

For a long moment, as both sides stopped to consider their positions, there was complete silence over the great flat field, broken only by the sudden 'creek-creek' of a corncrake as it flew up into the shimmering air. Then, almost imperceptibly at first, both lines moved forward, very gently increasing pace. Still there was silence, until a strange swishing sound came, gradually rising in volume from everywhere in the field, as hundreds of horses' feet pushed through the dry corn.

Then, quite suddenly, the quiet summer's day changed.

The horses, spurred on, first took to a canter, then rode into full charge at a gallop. The whole earth came alive in a thunderous cacophony of sound – hoof beats, jangling harness metal, vicious shouts from the men, egging each other on or cursing the enemy.

The great war had begun – in a hammering, violent tide of men at arms, sabres drawn, pennanted lances rampant, breastplates gleaming: a vainglorious soldiery, on great black and chestnut chargers galloping across the scarlet-flooded field.

The initial clash was a bloody affair, the Uhlan lances picking off half a dozen of Dermot's squadron in the first affray. But Dermot, ahead of the troop, sword drawn, was lucky. His opposite number in the Uhlan line, a less skilled horseman, lost grip of his reins and allowed his mount to rear up at the last moment. So that Dermot, passing him through the line, was able to swing round quickly and, with one blow, cut the man down from the side, behind his breastplate.

Moving on, he dispatched several more in the same manner, before he stood in his stirrups, marshalling his troops, from a position now some fifty yards behind the Uhlan line. And it was this high stance of command, head and shoulders above the other men, which undid him. Some distance away to the rear, something which Dermot had not noticed, another mounted German troop, supporting the Uhlans, had been concealed below a slope in the land. Unslinging their Mausers now, they looked ahead for likely targets. Dermot, standing in his saddle, formed an ideal mark.

He heard nothing of the rifle crack, felt only the searing force and smash of the bullet as it pitched deep into his back – and felt that only for a split second as he fell unconscious from his horse.

The repercussions of this event in Flanders were unhappy. Partly as a result of losing their commanding officer, the Hussars failed to hold their early advantage in the skirmish and eventually were forced into a hurried withdrawal, leaving their several dead and wounded behind. And subsequently, in the immediate British push for Mons and in their disastrous retreat from the same town, Dermot's body was never found.

Officially he was posted only as missing. But Frances, when she received the news from Dermot's father in Dublin and with her own experience of so many similar deaths at Colenso, read between the lines, believing the worst. And so did Hetty when her mother spoke to her of it.

'We cannot be sure, of course – he may be safe somewhere, or have been taken prisoner. We must hope for the best.'

They had been talking on the porch. It was a mockingly beautiful September day. Hetty left her mother without a word, going to her room where she sobbed uncontrollably.

Without breaking down Frances took the news just as hard. Dermot had offered her a future. When, through Asquith's Home Rule Bill, her own political and military ambitions had come to nothing, this man, once so loved by her, had, quite out of the blue, offered his own love, in a very late return. And it had changed her whole outlook and demeanour, and she recognized this. He had turned her from war towards peace and hope. And now he was gone, in another war, and all that human hope had disappeared with him.

And, when in the following months no news was received of his whereabouts, she had to believe he was dead. So once again, in a final, most awful way, she felt betrayed – by the shabbiest card fate had yet dealt her: a man she had come to love once more, now dead in the cause of an Empire which she despised. She soon returned to all her old bitter ways, but took to them this time with a greatly increased vehemence.

And, in this plunge into vicious despair, the suddenly changed political situation in Ireland helped her in every way. As a result of the outbreak of war, Asquith's Irish Home Rule Bill, which had passed its final stage in the House of Commons and had only to receive the Royal

Assent in September, was suspended, pending cessation of hostilities. Bad as this was, it might not, in itself, have exacerbated matters in Ireland had not John Redmond, leader of the resurgent Home Rule party at Westminster and toadying for British favour, made several disastrous speeches during these months, committing the 180,000-strong Irish Volunteer Army to the British cause, thus appearing a mere recruiting sergeant for the old enemy: a quixotic gesture made without consulting his party and which found almost no support among his countrymen. In any case, as a result of this Home Rule setback and Redmond's naïve misjudgements, the physical force movement in Ireland, long dormant, received a sudden new lease of life.

In September 1914, the Supreme Council of the secret Irish Republican Brotherhood met in Dublin, and decided that a rising against the British should now take place before the end of the war. 'England's difficulty is Ireland's opportunity' was the line taken once again. A Military Council was set up to organize an insurrection as soon as possible. By the end of September Frances, informed of these plans and charged with setting them in motion in south Kilkenny when the time came, was set anew on her violent career. Once more, losing life, Frances had taken to destruction.

For Hetty, the consequences of Dermot's death, though not so openly destructive, warped her soul, blighted her growth. For her, too, there was a terrible sense of betrayal – in losing this father, confidant, friend, and all the future he had promised her. But unlike Frances with her renewed militant outlets – her secret drilling and rifle practice in the deep woods beyond Summer Hill – Hetty had no such ready balm to set on her wounds. Instead, when she returned to the convent that September, there was only Léonie to assuage the bitterness that overwhelmed her.

'You *mustn't* be so down – on and on like this,' Léonie told her firmly one day as they left chapel, where Hetty, head deep in her hands as they prayed, had really been hiding her tears. 'Perhaps he's alive . . .'

'I've prayed for him,' Hetty said softly. Then she repeated herself. 'I've *prayed*!' she almost shouted.

'Of course . . .' Léonie turned away, not wanting Hetty to see how little belief she had in such spiritual levers.

But Hetty sensed her doubts. 'No, it *does* work! Once, years ago, when Robert had terrible whooping cough and was very nearly dying . . . I prayed. And it worked.' Yet she looked at Léonie now, searchingly, as if she might absolutely confirm the efficacy of prayer in this case.

But Léonie could only shake her head. 'They all say the war will be over by Christmas,' she temporized. 'They'll surely find out what's happened – where he is then.'

Some Belgian nuns, sisters in the same order, had arrived the day before and now, refugees at the château convent, walked past them: a sad, grey-faced, unhappy group, hands clasped protectively together below their waists.

Léonie gazed after them. 'How awful! – they say the Germans did really *awful* things to the nuns in Belgium.' Then she realized the tactlessness of her words. 'I'm sorry, Hetty.' She grasped her hand then, massaging it firmly. 'It *will* get better, promise you – I'll make it better for you.' She looked deeply into Hetty's tear-flushed eyes, stroking the soft skin on the inside of her wrist.

That evening in the dormitory, hearing her sporadic, muffled sobs late into the night and risking everything with Sister Thérèse outside in her bed at the end of the central aisle, Léonie climbed up over the wooden partition between their two cubicles, got into Hetty's narrow iron bed and tried to comfort her.

'Léa, what on earth—'

'Shsh!' Léonie whispered, for Hetty had sat up startled, flouncing the bedclothes about, before Léonie pulled them back over them both, putting fingers to Hetty's lips in the darkness.

Hetty's face was damp and slippery with tears. 'You can cry and cry,' Léonie whispered to her then under the sheet. 'And say prayers over and over. But in the end there's just us. We're both here and alive and have each other. That's *real* hope, isn't it?'

'Suppose so . . .' Hetty started to sob again.

'No, Hetty, *don't* – it's *me*.' She moved to her then, clasping her as best she could in the awkward bed. 'I love you, like Dermot does, wherever he is. I really do. And I'm *here*, with you – wherever you are.'

Léonie had leant away as she whispered, but now she returned to Hetty, searching out and finding her face with her fingers again, before caressing her lips, her eyes, cheeks, embracing her long hot body, pressing herself gently against the sweet linen-and-soap smell. '*Please*, you won't cry any more, because you needn't,' Léonie insisted once again. And Hetty, finally sighing, seemed to relax at last, saying nothing, simply reaching her hand up, touching Léonie's fingers as they roved about her face, like a magic wand clearing away her tears and sadness.

'You see?' Léonie said. 'Just with us – it *can* get better . . .'

And, indeed, things did get better – through Hetty's vehement prayers perhaps, and certainly by way of Léonie's tender attentions, that night and later. Shortly after Christmas, which Hetty spent with the Straus family in Paris, word came to Dermot's father in Dublin, via the Red Cross, that Dermot, badly wounded in the affray with the Uhlans, had also been rescued by them – taken back to a German field hospital and thence to a military hospital in Berlin where he had made a good recovery. Now he was a prisoner of war, held at an army barracks among hundreds of other Allied officers near Cologne.

Hetty heard the news from her mother at the start of the spring term, the already opened letter handed to her by Mother Superior. 'I am happy that some, at least, have been saved in this pernicious war,' Mother Agnes told her with as much grace as she could muster. But Hetty, always furious that her letters should be so opened, stamped out of the room without replying.

Outside, Hetty and Léonie danced a little jig – and immediately afterwards, seeking more privacy, putting coats on, and running out into the snow-filled parkland, they hugged each other violently in the icy wind, before sliding over a frozen patch in the big water meadow, their breath like white smoke on the cold air.

'Oh, Léa, it's wonderful!'

'Yes! . . .'

The girls, arms thrashing the air for balance, mufflers flying, waltzed and slid about the ice, before they fell together in a heap, hugging once more as they lay on the cold surface. But Léonie, drawing away and looking at her friend, felt a touch of ice on her heart then – for this man returned to Hetty, at least in spirit, when, for nearly five months, she had been her only love.

The war was not finished by Christmas. With both armies bogged down in the Flanders mud, it had barely begun. While in Ireland, that December and throughout the following year, another war against the British was variously and secretly plotted. Though Patrick Pearse, head of the Military Council of the Irish Republican Brotherhood, asked that summer to give the graveside oration for the old Fenian rebel O'Donovan Rossa, clearly hinted in his peroration at the violence to come: 'The Defenders of this Realm have worked well . . . they think they have pacified Ireland – that they have purchased half of us and intimidated the other half. They think they have foreseen everything, provided against everything. But the fools, the fools, the fools! – they have left us our Fenian dead, and while Ireland holds those graves, Ireland unfree shall never be at peace.'

During the same year Joseph Plunkett, another member of the IRB Military Council, went to Germany on a secret arms mission. In January 1916, James Connolly, leader of the Irish Citizen Army in Dublin, who until then had not in any way supported armed insurrection, now – with the threat of general conscription in Ireland – threw in his lot with Pearse and the IRB. Finally, in March, Pearse received a message from the revolutionary directorate of the Clann na Gael in New York: 'Will send you twenty thousand rifles, ten million rounds of ammunition, to place near Tralee between 22 and 28 April.'

The insurgents – Irish Volunteers and Dublin's Citizen Army now united in one Republican Army, largely under the secret control of the IRB leaders – were ready. The rising was set to begin on Easter Monday in Dublin, the bank holiday, when great numbers would be out of town, at the Fairyhouse races, up in the mountains, or at resorts along the coast.

For Frances the news of Dermot's survival had come too late. Already, in her deeply bitter mood during the autumn and winter of 1914, she had committed herself – body and soul this time – to the cause of renewed violence against the British. Forsaking all her last hopes for personal happiness, she became utterly dedicated, ruthless, ascetic, seeking martyrdom now – driven, with the other leaders of the IRB, to an idea of blood sacrifice on the altar of Ireland's freedom: a holy crusade on behalf of the Gael and all the dead generations gone before in the same cause. And, in this thirst for a cleansing, national bloodletting, personal considerations could be of no account whatsoever. Besides, Dermot, she knew, would never marry her when he discovered her role in all this – as he would, of course, quite soon, when the day of glorious revolution dawned.

So, like a fierce penitent – forsaking every worldly convention and all the comforts of her class – she consecrated herself to this purification by fire, this nobility of death, this halo-bright cause, playing an increasingly important role in the secret revolutionary councils of the IRB and, quite openly, in the Citizen Army, to which she was now attached as a Lieutenant.

She had, of course, from her nursing experience under fire in the South African war, vital skills for the insurgents. These had been immediately recognized, as were her natural organizational ability and blazing dedication – so that late in 1914 her responsibilities in the rising were transferred from Co. Kilkenny to Dublin where she threw herself into a fervour of activity, at the heart of events.

She took charge of the Fianna youth movement, drilling the boy scouts there, with wooden hurley sticks in the Wicklow mountains. She contributed to, and solicited, other funds for the war chest. She arranged – among a few other like-minded Irish Protestants of her class, in possession of suitable yachts – for various successful gun-running expeditions from the Continent; she discussed with Joseph Plunkett, in charge of military strategy, the medical and nursing arrangements for the rising. And she took part in all the sheer drudgery of training as well – fifteen-mile route marches and manoeuvres in every sort of weather.

She relished all the work, even going so far as to design a uniform for herself, a superbly tailored, double-breasted green tunic coat with silver buttons, long skirt and a slouch leather hat, side brim set off by a feather cockade. As final and more compelling additions to this dramatic and glamorous costume, she equipped herself with a Luger automatic and a Mauser rifle. Early in 1916 she was promoted to the rank of Staff Lieutenant within the Military Council, and then, with the rank of Colonel, made deputy to one of the leaders, Commandant Mallin, thus joining the very few people – and as the only woman – privy to all the detailed plans for the rising.

Robert meanwhile continued at his boarding college, St Columba's in the Dublin mountains, while Hetty and Léonie remained at the convent in Normandy – Hetty spending many of her holidays with the Straus family in Paris, so as to avoid the danger of German U-boats in the Channel crossings.

This had been Hetty's intention for Easter 1916. However, at the last moment and without her being able to warn her mother, all these plans were changed. At Verdun that spring the war took a grave turn against the Allies. The French army there, hard pressed within this great fortress for many weeks, seemed likely to collapse at any moment, allowing the Germans a free run through the line to Paris and the rest of France. Many people, who had the opportunity, left the capital. The convent, in the light of these grim facts and worse rumours, closed precipitately, the girls dispersed. It was then that Benjamin Straus, fearing for his daughter if she stayed in Paris, and seeing how both girls could find a safe haven in Ireland at Summer Hill, arranged passage for them with a captain he knew, commanding a neutral American freighter leaving Le Havre for Southampton that Easter weekend.

Neither girl was in the slightest alarmed at the prospect of this adventure. They viewed it with avid excitement – the more so when, allowing for delays in England or Dublin, Mr Straus gave them ten gold sovereigns towards hotels, rail fares, or other unexpected expenses. So it was, after an uneventful journey to Southampton and then to London before taking the Irish Mail to Holyhead, they crossed over to Dublin on Sunday night, on the RMS *Leinster*, arriving in the city early on that Easter Monday.

It was a late Easter that year – the morning fine and bright, already warm, with all the promise of a freak midsummer day. Dublin was pervaded by a holiday calm, as the two girls took a horse cab up from Westland Row station to the Shelbourne Hotel on Stephen's Green.

'We might as well wait here – where we can telegraph Mama and your Papa – and have some breakfast, then get the midday train down to Summer Hill,' Hetty had said to Léonie. And now she bounced up and down on the old leather seat inside the cab, unbuttoning the top of her green convent topcoat.

She was excited, now that their journey – dodging the Channel U-boats – had come to a successful conclusion, though it was not quite over yet. There was still a tempting prospect of metropolitan independence before them – this last morning alone together in Dublin: breakfast at the grandest hotel in town, a quick sprucing up in some spare bedroom there, a stroll on the Green – perhaps a look at the smart shop windows in Grafton Street, even if they could not spend anything there of the sovereigns they had left.

They clip-clopped up through the dark shadows between the buildings to the narrow end of Kildare Street. Then suddenly the whole huge bright space of Stephen's Green opened up before them – tall Georgian buildings all round, bathed in warm sunlight, the cherry blossom and green willow in the big square already bursting or almost in leaf.

The girls were enchanted by this vision. It was a day of wonderful promise, it seemed, so that Hetty suddenly turned and hugged Léonie.

'We're home! – almost home!'

Léonie looked at her friend much more calmly as she drew away from her. 'Yes,' she said simply. And then, gazing at her, some slight sadness in her eyes, she said quietly, 'Oh, I do love it all, you know. You, Hetty – being with you, everything.' And she leant forward then, kissing her quickly in return.

The cab drew up in front of the hotel. Passing between the Nubian maidens holding lamp standards at either side of the monumental porch, they entered the spacious hall, their bags in the grip of two diminutive page-boys in pill-box hats. Inside there was a hint of luxury, but more an air of provincial calm . . . of quiet Irish country house good taste: in the Georgian antiques, mahogany and brass furnishings, in the decent but unshowy hunting pictures and sporting prints, the slightly frayed Aubusson on the floor. Money had been, was being and would be spent here – but no one would ever talk of it.

It was too early for the many guests staying at the hotel for the Fairyhouse races to be up and about. Instead a few tail-coated clerks hovered in the background; a maid in a white pinafore was seen moving for an instant at the top of the broad dark stairway; the slightest hint of fried bacon and freshly ground coffee lay on the air.

The hall porter, genial and discreet in equal measure, looked at them as if their arrival was entirely expected.

'Just breakfast, if you please,' Hetty graciously informed him. 'And if you'd look after our bags meanwhile – we mean to send some telegrams – and hope to catch the midday train for Thomastown. We shall need a cab for Kingsbridge then.'

'Yes, ma'am, of course – that'll all be grand. I'll have a cab ready, and confirm the train. I believe the Waterford train leaves at two o'clock today – the bank holiday. I'll let you know. Can I take your coats?'

He gestured towards a dark recess in the hall, from which a little woman began to emerge. But, before she had moved half-way across the hall, some slight disturbance was heard from the landing at the top of the stairs – voices risen, a man's gruff English voice and another, chirpier and alarmed with a broad Dublin accent; the source of both tongues as yet still hidden. The girls looked up the stairway.

A British army officer, in full field uniform, commenced his descent. His step was steady enough, if slow, as he stuck resolutely to a path down the very middle of the stairs, eschewing all help from either banister. But his eyes, his whole expression, were vague and dreamy, the girls saw, as he came fully into sight half-way down. He had the air of a sleep-walker – long practised in the movement, gazing straight ahead, yet finding each step unerringly – all the more surprising, since he was a very big man, naturally cumbersome, of great girth, barrel chest, strong tree-trunk legs. But his young face was quite at odds with this pugnacious, wrestler's body: wasted, pinched and sensitive, the pale blue eyes shrunk back in their sockets, unseeing, as if they had long before retreated from some blinding hurt – a confusion and shocking disorder apparent everywhere over his wan countenance. As he descended, he repeatedly shook one shoulder, twitching it vehemently, as if trying to shake off some pest, some bird of ill-omen, some nightmare hand that had attached itself to him.

The girls looked at this chilly vision spellbound. Everything had come to a stop in the hall, and there was dead silence now – apart from a vague clink of china in the distant dining room – for what seemed minutes on end.

'Oh, dear God, the Major's got out,' Hetty heard the

porter mutter, before everything started to happen very quickly – and yet in a manner which seemed quite expected, entirely rehearsed.

The Major – resplendent in his full uniform – seeing the two girls, suddenly came to violent life. He skipped down the rest of the stairway in a trice, shouting, 'Mildred! My dear Milly! I knew you'd come!' – making straight for Hetty, running across the hall to her now, arms outstretched, as if to clasp her in a violent embrace.

But before he had gone a yard or more he was set upon, like a circus strong man suddenly infested by dwarfs: two frail clerks, and the page-boys, now joined by others of their kind – all pounced on the man, gripping him at any and every point about his huge body, some going for his legs, others the midriff, the clerks grappling with his great arms, the page-boys jumping up on him from behind, clambering about his broad shoulders, sending his braided officer's cap flying – all of them, faced with his sudden and demonic energy, attempting to bear him down.

It was a difficult task. The man fought like a tiger, swatting at these gadflies, before spinning round like a carousel, his assailants clinging to his arms like conkers at the end of a string, so that half the clerks and page-boys soon found themselves all in a litter, toppled on the floor. But the boys at least, seeming to enjoy the sport, as if it was an accustomed game, part of their job in the hotel, returned with relish to the fray, the marked Dublin accents of all these minders rising now as they set about their task with renewed vigour.

'Git him be t'other lig, Micky Joe!'

'Take his ear, will ya!'

'Oi hav' him be the oxters—'

'Will ya gi' me *leverage* there for the love o' God, Pat – that's *my* arm ye're holdin' . . .'

And then there were strangled interjections in the very different English accent, despair in the officer's voice now. 'Mildred! – Milly! Have them off me – help me!'

With the terrific noise, the hall had been transformed into a prize fight arena. But gradually – a dying leviathan overwhelmed by these pinpricks – the poor proud man sank to the floor. The hall porter had interceded, together with two equally large men in chef's hats from the kitchen, finally subduing the officer, placating him, soothing, almost stroking him – 'There now, Major, calm yerself, ye're all right now' – as they led him gently off into some nether region of the hotel.

Hetty and Léonie meanwhile had retreated, shocked and fascinated in equal measure, before the manager arrived to make pleasant, but not in the least surprised or subservient, excuses – behaving, Hetty thought, as if this was some kind of regular bank holiday treat at the Shelbourne.

'You'll have to excuse the Major,' he told her, quite jauntily. 'It sometimes takes him that way. A very old friend of the hotel's – him and all his family in Ireland. And a very brave man, a real gentleman, quiet as a mouse here in the old days. But it's got to him, you see, this terrible war: entirely shell-shocked, with the French near Verdun. A terrible thing, you wouldn't recognize him. I know you'll understand – in the circumstances.' And then, in just the same pleasant understated tones, he went on, 'Now, if you'll please come with me, I'll show you both to the dining room – famished after your journey, I expect. Or would you like to take a room first? Wash and brush up. We're absolutely chock-a-block for the Fairyhouse races – but I think I can let you use one on the top floor – just for the morning, in the circumstances.'

Then he, too, gestured to the little cloakroom lady who, peeking out to make sure the coast was clear, essayed another light-footed run across the hall, quite unaffected by the furore, taking the girls' coats, before they moved off to the dining room. The hotel regained immediately its air of untroubled calm.

After breakfast the girls repaired to a small, but decent enough room on the very top floor, high up, with a view right over the Green. In an adjacent landing bathroom, they bathed luxuriously in a vast oak-panelled tub, before changing into their proper holiday clothes – high Easter fashions bought just before their departure from Paris – doing their hair and generally titivating themselves for an hour or more.

Later they emerged in the hall again – but transformed, in long, knee-hugging pale lilac skirts, high-throated lace-edged silk blouses, set off by patchwork and velvet, gilt-buttoned waistcoats and, as the *pièces de résistance*, impertinent straw boaters, banded and tailed with flowing red ribbons: two most elegantly beautiful summer girls.

Here, by the telephone switchboard, Hetty made out a telegram to her Mama at Summer Hill . . . and Léonie one to her parents in Paris. The woman took their messages – but after half a dozen attempts she failed to make any connection with the telegraph department at the General Post Office down in the centre of Dublin.

'I'm sorry – a fault on the line. I'll have one of the boys deliver your telegrams there, in person.'

'Oh well,' Hetty said, not surprised; happy, indeed, at this further extension of their freedom. 'The train isn't until two o'clock now anyway. Let's go out – a walk in the Green, shall we . . . then the shops?'

Léonie smiled broadly. 'Yes, let's! Doesn't matter too much about the telegrams – mine will get to Paris later and we'll be seeing your Mama soon enough anyway.'

The band was playing – a medley from *The Yeomen of the Guard* floating over the ornamental lake. The two girls crossed the miniature Bridge of Sighs garlanded in budding willow, and strolled towards the music: the green and gilt bandstand, where, the military bands being away at the war, a small civilian orchestra entertained a mixed audience consisting of a few fashionably dressed promenaders out from the Georgian squares to the east of the Green, staunch *petits bourgeois* from the genteel suburbs, in town for the day, and a number of shoeless ragamuffins escaping the slums behind the College of Surgeons building on the west side of the Green.

The girls stopped, listening to the woodwind and strings – nicely enough played, but not to the taste of a gruff bowler-hatted Dubliner with a big wart on his chin, standing next to them with his prim little wife in a cheap Easter bonnet.

'The military bands were much better. The Royal Munsters now – they had a great band here, every Easter before the war: Pom-titi, Pom-titi, pom-pom-POM! Big drums and all. These creatures – well, a job lot I'd say, from the Rathgar and Rathmines Musical Society . . .'

The man stamped his blackthorn stick on the ground, frustrated at this lack of properly martial music. 'Oh no,' he growled, 'you can't beat the military at this game. The Munsters now, or the old Irish Dragoons. Pom-titi, pom-titi, pom, pom, pom . . .'

He and his wife moved off towards the Grafton Street entrance to the Green, the big mock Arch of Triumph there commemorating Irishmen lost in the Boer War. The two girls took the same direction. 'Might as well take a look at the shop windows at least,' Hetty said. 'It's nearly half past twelve.'

But, before they reached the shops, they were met by a more diverting sight: a group of uniformed boys in green shirts and short grey trousers, with thin neck scarves and high-peaked scout hats, marching two abreast through the Empire-glorifying gates. Serious-faced, set on some high purpose and by chance perfectly in step now with a martial tune from *The Yeomen*, they yet had an air of rural, woodland innocence quite at odds with these sophisticated metropolitan circumstances. The smaller boys had wooden staffs and some had hurley sticks; others bore entrenching equipment, while several of the older, taller boys at the back carried rifles still too big for them.

Once inside the gates, these leprechaun-like figures with their picks and spades and hurley sticks continued their neat march to Sullivan's jaunty rhythms before an order came for them to break ranks, when they took up positions in self-conscious groups by the flowering cherry and forsythia bushes along the railings, at a loss to know what to do next. The ability to stand at ease in the middle of Dublin's most fashionable square, being gawked and laughed at by the slum boys and other caustic bystanders, was not among their accomplishments.

'God save us, Maggie,' the wart-faced man said to his prim wife, 'them's those Fianna scouts – young Sinn Feiners – coming in here for some sort of manoeuvres. Ye'd hardly think they'd lit them in here and they usually at their mischief way up in the mountains . . .'

He stopped then, his attention caught by a further, even more troubling manifestation. Immediately behind the scouts another group – some adult militia, it seemed – had appeared, a hundred or so of them, moving in loose file through the impressive archway: a much more business-like lot in that they all were armed with Mausers or heavy service revolvers, suggesting an army of sorts, a designation which their garb did everything to undermine. They were dressed in a motley assortment of outfits and uniforms: some in dark or heather-green tunic coats, grey serge breeches, or jodhpurs, with slouch leather hats, the brims twisted up at one side, while others sported old British army khaki jackets or trench coats, the tabs and buttons all torn away, and still more were smartly turned out in their Sunday-best dark-blue suits, or in roughest working clothes – collarless striped shirts, baggy trousers, and clumpy boots. It was a raggle-taggle army. But an army it was, with the men – there were women, too – swagged about with crossed cartridge bandoliers, fixing bayonets now to their long-barrelled Mausers, checking their revolvers. Some kind of violent business was obviously meant, but of what kind or to what end was not, as yet, clear.

'Glory be!' The wart-faced man, mopping his brow in the midday heat, was outraged now. 'Ya wouldn't credit it! – littin' them lot of Volunteers and Citizen Army fellows in here. The park keeper'll have somethin' to say on that and no mistake!'

And he was right. A keeper, a tall and haughty fellow in a braided cap and spectacles with a long, sharp-ferruled stick, approached the soldiers now by the archway and started remonstrating with them, shaking his stick, opening his arms out, trying to shoo them out through the great archway like geese.

'Gwan now! I'll not have yees in here!' Hetty heard him call out. 'This is no parade ground – ye'll be outa here this minute or I'll have the constabulary on ye!'

The keeper was speaking to an equally tall man in a slouch hat, apparently the leader of the contingent, who at that moment was sticking up some sort of poster on the side of the gateway. 'Now ye certainly can't put that kinda thing up here!' the keeper yelled at him. 'Rule 4B – ye can see it here for yerself.' He pointed to the notice of park regulations next to the gateway. 'No bill posting – of *iny* sort, kind or description.'

The irate keeper stepped forward, trying to tear the poster from the archway. Then he suddenly disappeared, falling among the group of Volunteers, only to reappear half a minute later, crawling out from between the soldiers' boots, his nose bloodied, spectacles and braided cap gone. But he got to his feet quickly enough and started to blow his whistle repeatedly.

'Clare to God, they'll pay for this,' the warty Dubliner said, as the Volunteers left the archway, the poster securely in place. They were replaced by a small crowd of onlookers, including Hetty and Léonie, who gazed up at the dark, heavy-inked and printed message.

Poblacht na hEireann
The Provisional Government
of the
IRISH REPUBLIC
To the People of Ireland

Irishmen and Irish women. In the name of God and of the dead generations from which she received her old traditions of nationhood, Ireland, through us, summons her children to her flag and strikes for her freedom . . . In every generation the Irish people have asserted their right to national freedom and sovereignty, six times in the past three hundred years they have asserted it in arms . . . We declare the right of the People of Ireland to the ownership of Ireland and to the unfettered control of Irish destinies, to be sovereign and indefensible . . .

The Republic guarantees religious and civil liberties, equal rights and equal opportunities to all its citizens . . .

Signed on behalf of the Provisional Government.

Thomas J. Clarke

Sean MacDiarmada   Thomas MacDonagh
P. H. Pearse   Eamonn Ceannt
James Connolly   Joseph Plunkett

The wart-and-bowler man laughed outright before he had finished reading the text and was soon joined by the other bystanders. 'For the love of God – ye'd hardly credit it! A "Republic" now, are you? – right here in the Green of an Easther's day. A Shangri-la for the takin' – with a few oul rifles and hurleys . . . and they should be out fightin' Kaiser Bill instead of all this malarkey over a "Republic".' But he stopped laughing now and instead scowled at the poster. 'Begod, there'll be hell to pay all the same if they don't stop their messin' and git outa here straight away.' A nervous look came over his swollen, complacent features. Sweating badly now, he glanced around him warily.

'C'mon, Maggie – we'd better git outa here and back to Rathmines before the peelers come.'

'What's it all about?' Hetty asked. But the wart-faced man with his nervous wife had gone, vanished, and Hetty's question was answered instead by an excitable pixie of a fellow, elderly and breathless, who had just joined the group. 'Thim boyhoes the Volunteers,' he yelped. 'Hevn't they gone and taken over the General Post Office, with barricades and bombs and a new flag run up over the top of it! Oh, I tell ye, there'll be no pinshuns given outta there for a while. I tell ye that!' Despite this monetary embargo, the old man was in a state of high good humour. 'Oh, there'll be ructions and no misthake! Ye'll hav' to keep yer hats on now!' And he did a little jig beneath the poster.

Two stern-faced young Volunteer sentries had arrived to move the group on before taking up position by the archway.

'Suppose we'd better get out of the way ourselves – if we're to catch that train,' Hetty said easily. Both girls were no more than amused by all these activities: it was some kind of military exhibition or protest – typical of Irish life. They turned back to the Shelbourne.

It was then that Hetty saw her mother.

She was striding towards them, evidently on the warpath, splendidly attired in a tight-fitting dark-green tunic coat, Sam Browne belt, with a huge Luger pistol, breeches, puttees, and a felt hat, side-brim up, with a bright cock's feather, a beautiful Amazon, lovely but terrifying, issuing orders, to two men at her side.

'. . . yes, and get all the civilians out of the Green *now* – they've had quite enough time to read the proclamation – for we'll have to get the sandbags and barbed wire up straight away at all the gates, and the trenching started . . .'

'Mama!' Hetty shouted while Frances was some little distance away. 'Mama! – what on *earth* are you doing here?'

Her mother, equally startled, came to an abrupt halt, but only for a moment. She looked at her daughter coldly.

'*Doing?*' Her mother answered in her most clipped and arrogant Ascendancy accent, as if she were rebuking a careless servant in her drawing room. 'Why, we are having our rebellion.'

She spoke of this as if it were some long-established, fashionable annual event in the Dublin social calendar, the Vice-regal garden party, perhaps, or the Horse Show or the Curragh races.

'Mama, you cannot be serious—'

A rifle shot rang out then, followed by others, a ragged volley, from the direction of the forsythia bushes. The *Yeomen of the Guard* medley came to a sudden halt. Groups of Volunteers ran past, carrying sandbags and rolls of barbed wire. There was a flurry of activity, shouted commands, as the Fianna scouts and the Volunteers set about creating barricades and manning the defences.

The civilians in the Green had by now all left or been ejected. But Léonie with Hetty – still confronting her mother – were about to be trapped inside.

A flight of mallard, alarmed by the rifle fire which had broken out now all along the Grafton Street corner of the Green, rose from the ornamental lake, circling fast in the blue dome of sky, then making for more placid waters. It was a quarter to one. The revolution had started. And Hetty, looking again at her watch, realized that they were now very likely to miss the two o'clock train.

6

'Mama, you've taken leave of your senses!' Hetty exclaimed, her stammer temporarily lost in her astonishment. 'You can't seriously think to take on all the British army in Dublin with just these few boy scouts and hurley sticks—'

'Nonsense! My boys are brave members of the Irish Republican Army now. And, besides, there are almost no British troops in the city this morning – all out at the Fairyhouse races – which is precisely *why* we are taking them on today. Already, besides the Green here, we have secured half a dozen other vital strongpoints in the city. Everything is going *quite* according to plan!'

'Mama, you must give it up. Come away now, with us. We are at the Shelbourne—'

'Never!' The cock's feather on top of her hat shook violently.

As she spoke, her mother smiled crazily at Hetty. And Hetty suddenly saw in this warlike, deranged performance the essence of her mother, the *raison d'être* for her life – which was death. It was for this ridiculous moment, Hetty felt, that she had suffered all the long years as a child at Summer Hill – the loneliness and neglect, her mother's coldness and anger; her *stupidity*.

Hetty's long hatred of her mother finally exploded. 'Mama, you're a stupid woman! Was it for this – this nonsense – all your beastliness to me at Summer Hill? And can't you see?' She looked round at the Fianna boys stumbling about with heavy sandbags and entrenching tools. 'This is just a game of toy soldiers. But real people will be killed—'

'Indeed, that is exactly our plan: "The heart of a British Tommy at the end of every rifle" – exactly so!'

'That's criminal nonsense! Perfectly innocent people—'

'Have you not read the Proclamation? It is for Ireland and her destiny!'

'It's for nothing of the sort! It's nothing but sheer evil blindness on your part, and your friends – sacrificing these boys and innocent people, against impossible odds. And I *hate* you for it! Stay here then. You'll be killed – and good riddance!'

Her mother shook her head pityingly now. 'You don't understand. But one day you – and the others – you'll see the rightness of our cause, our sacrifice. One day . . .'

For a long instant Hetty stood there, unbelieving but undecided, listening to the increasing rifle fire. Then she tugged at Léonie's arm. 'Come on!' she yelled at her.

The two girls ran together, ran for their lives as they thought – along the gravel paths back towards the Shelbourne. But the exit they needed there was already barricaded and they took another closer by, which gave out across the road to some tall houses with high front door steps much nearer the Grafton Street corner.

Pausing on the pavement, they were just in time to see the reason for the initial fusillade from the Volunteers. A troop of British Lancers, emerging into the Green from a narrow street to their left, and obviously caught quite unawares, had been met by this sudden rifle fire and suffered several casualties. The cavalry had scattered in retreat, galloping back down the narrow street, leaving their wounded behind.

The Volunteers' fire pursued them, then slackened and ceased, so that the two girls, thinking the moment ripe, sprinted out across the road. But, when they were half-way across, a renewed hail of bullets smashed into the windows of the big houses opposite them, so that they fell on to the tramcar tracks. Their straw hats fell off and rolled away, red ribbons spinning over the cobbles into the gutter. They could hear the vicious whirr of bullets, just inches above their heads, it seemed. Hetty reached out, grasping Léonie's arm protectively as they lay there. 'Down! Keep right *down!*' she shrieked.

'I *am* right down, you ninny. *You* keep down!' They pushed their faces ever more firmly into the cobbles, blind and deaf now as the gunfire increased above their heads. Just then, a double-decker tram turned into the Green from Dawson street, and headed straight for them before the driver at the last moment squealed to a halt. The passengers, hearing the commotion all round, disembarked in panic, clattering down the stairs from the open top and, quite disregarding the prostrate girls, ran pell-mell for the shelter offered by the area walls and steps leading up to the houses on the north side of the Green.

Hetty and Léonie, taking advantage of this diversion, picked themselves up, their faces begrimed and their clothes dishevelled, joining the fleeing passengers, finally taking cover beneath the portico of a smart grocer's shop near the corner of Grafton Street.

Here the heavy glass windows had been smashed, either by gunfire or by some of the slum urchins, who, wasting no time over this heaven-sent opportunity, were already shoving through the broken frames, dancing about on the glass inside and helping themselves to the rich provender on display – Parma hams and pots of Gentleman's Relish, jars of calf's foot jelly, bottles of vintage port and claret, chip baskets of dried figs and dates, boxes of Turkish delight and a host of other exotic delicacies.

'Begob, an' they mean business – doin' for thim Lancers like that,' a big red-faced man from the tram opined, before turning in a trice, helping himself to a bottle of vintage Cockburn's and leaping away in the opposite direction.

One of the Lancers' horses, tipped over on its back and propped against the kerb, lay with all four feet up in the air, its rider prostrate in a widening pool of blood nearby, his pennanted lance propped against the horse's belly like a red danger flag denoting some frightful accident.

Two of the barefoot boys, running back to the slums, laden with their booty but seeing the dead Lancer, set down their loot and proceeded to rifle quickly through his pockets.

Almost immediately a shot rang out from the bottom of the narrow street beyond the dead Lancer. And Hetty, peeping out from behind the stone window casement, saw one of the boys topple over, most of his head blown away, as the rest of his meagre body collapsed in a tattered heap. The retreating Lancers, dismounted now and hidden at the bottom of the narrow street, were staging a counter-attack.

But at that point a group of some twenty Volunteers, running out from the Green, commandeered the tram and, under withering fire from the Lancers, drove it down to the Grafton Street corner. Here, they toppled the vehicle over, and it fell with a splintering crash, successfully blocking any advance the Lancers might make up towards the Green.

Taking up positions then, and protected by the tram, the Volunteers renewed their fire, volley after volley, at the remaining Lancers who, surprised again and incurring more wounded in the hail of bullets, made a final retreat, disappearing back towards the centre of the city.

The Green and all its surrounds were firmly in the hands of the rebels. It was half past one. By now, Hetty realized, they had certainly missed their train.

High up, from their top floor bedroom window back in the sanctuary of the Shelbourne, the girls saw the whole drama in the Green develop: the rebels, small figures now, arrayed like set pieces in a game of chess spread out below them in the warm afternoon sunshine – but a game run riot. The whole park was a swarm of little green-clad figures, moving about with apparently manic abandon.

The rifle fire had ceased and in the relative calm the Fianna scouts, Citizen Army and Volunteers were rapidly consolidating their defences, sandbagging every entrance to the Green, setting barbed wire along the top of the railings. Many more were energetically digging trenches.

Hetty could see no rhyme or reason to their efforts, as they struck out in mad criss-crosses, digging hardly more than sunken gulleys – cutting straight across the glowing tulip beds, leaping budding herbaceous borders, doubling back over the central rose arbours, encircling stone monuments to British generals, before coming to abrupt halts: at the ornamental lake, the miniature Bridge of Sighs and the ornate bandstand, now being adapted as a first aid station.

The rebels were as good as moles. Soon a fair part of the Green, its smooth lawns, paths and neatly flowered borders, had the air of a vast bombed pleasure garden, with great swaths and bunches of uprooted plants and shrubs lying atop and around the mounting earthworks.

And though from ground level the insurgents were well protected, by the tall railings and the thick line of trees that circled the green, from any height – and the Green was surrounded by tall buildings – they were quite exposed.

Hetty remarked on this. 'It's mad that they don't see how easily they can be shot at from above!'

The very same thought had occurred to a British officer, in command of a contingent of Sherwood Foresters, hurriedly sent into the city later that afternoon. A section of these troops, moving up Kildare Street, entered the Shelbourne from the back and commandeered the hotel. So that, shortly after four o'clock, the girls' bedroom door suddenly burst open and this same officer confronted them, a very young man in a state of bristling, almost uncontrolled agitation.

'Lieutenant Hardstaff,' he said. 'I'm afraid we must take over your bedroom at once – the rebels in the park – your room has the best vantage point . . .'

Without more ado he gestured behind him and half a

dozen khaki-clad soldiers struggled in behind him, carrying a heavy machine-gun with a tripod and a quantity of
ammunition boxes. Stooping down, and dragging their
gun, they crept over to the window.

Hetty was outraged by the intrusion. 'How d-d-dare you
come in here like this! – with that monstrous great gun!'
She abused the officer roundly. 'B-besides, you can't shoot
it out there – it would be a massacre. There are b-b-boys
out there, tiny boys—'

'They are rebels, Miss – and must take their chances
with the others. They've already killed some of our
Lancers – those "boys" out there.'

He crouched down himself now, stalking towards the
window, supervising the setting up of the machine-gun,
before shouting back, 'You'll have to leave – we have serious business here!' Shaking with martial anticipation, as
if mounting an attack on heavily defended German lines,
Hardstaff was gripped by a fever of derring-do.

The girls tried the room next door. It was not locked.
At the window they saw the Volunteers, unaware of this
threat from above, going quite openly about their defens-
ive business.

'Your mother?' Léonie asked anxiously.

'Exactly! She'll be shot – they all will, with that awful
gun. But I can hardly tell that officer she's my mother,
can I?'

'Not the officer – but we might tell your *mother*, though,'
Léonie thought out loud.

'She doesn't deserve it!'

'Perhaps not – but we can't just stand by and see her
killed – from our bedroom window. Can we? . . .'

'No. Suppose not. But how do we get out into the
Green?'

The girls considered the idea – and the dangers of it. For
a moment all was calm outside, but for several motor-cycle
dispatch riders who came and went with messages for the
rebels, and a few cars, the drivers of which were not yet
aware of the situation. Then, moving easily along the road
beneath them, the girls saw a baker's motor van. It turned

the corner into Kildare Street and they heard it stop somewhere behind the hotel.

'That van – could we drive it?'

'We've driven father's Peugeot, with Albert, in the Bois – we could try it!'

'Come on then! . . .'

The girls, running quickly downstairs, came into the hall, thronged with guests now, and other people, all sheltering in the hotel, peeping gingerly out from the big bow windows of the dining and drawing rooms to either side of the hall. Pushing past the crowd here Hetty and Léonie moved through various green baize doors into the almost deserted kitchens and sculleries at the back.

At the back entrance to the kitchens the baker's man was making his delivery of bread and cakes, handing the big trays to a kitchen boy. The girls hovered, hidden in the background, behind one of the great kitchen ranges.

'Jeez, Mickey,' the delivery man said, 'an' if I'd known that lot were out in the Green I'd niver have come here at all. What's up for the love o' God?'

'Sure and haven't thim rebels gone and taken over the whole Green and the Tommies upstairs with machine-guns! Come on till we take a look? – and all the lads upstairs lookin' outa the windeys inyway.'

The delivery finished, the two of them left the kitchen for the front of the hotel. In a second the girls were out of the back door and sitting up in the seat of the van.

Léonie took the wheel, trying the foot pedals before finding the clutch and ramming the engine into first gear with a fearful grinding noise. She smiled at Hetty. 'Oh my Gawd!' she drawled, crouching down over the half-glass windscreen beneath the open canopy. Then she set the engine roaring, let the clutch in, and the van skidded violently, leaping out of the back area.

She spun the van round into Kildare Street, then turned right into the Green. But, in Léonie's inexpert hands, it swerved suddenly, skidding on the tram tracks as she opened the accelerator lever. She tugged at the wheel desperately, managing to straighten it. Now they were careering towards the Grafton Street corner. Here, sitting on the belly of the dead Lancer's horse, a bottle of looted port in hand, an old shawly woman, well gone with the drink, was singing loudly.

'Boys in Khaki, Boys in Blue,
 Here's the best of Jolly Good Luck to You!'

She brandished the bottle at them as they swerved past.

Rounding the corner at speed, the van was almost out of control as it skittered to and fro over the cobbles past the College of Surgeons.

In front of them, a posse of women rebels, running out from the Green, faced the van, revolvers raised. But the van was on them in a second and they jumped for their lives. Léonie struggled to stop, but could not, the big outside brake lever being too far from her reach.

The van, swaying violently now, made a dash straight for the kerb. It hit the stone bollards and linked chains there, careered off into the road again, and finally came to a halt, nearly driving up the front steps of the Russell Hotel at the south-west corner of the Green.

The rebel women had pursued it – and now, lowering their revolvers, were astonished to see the two girls, lying about drunkenly on the front seat, bruised but otherwise uninjured. Some of the women, opening the back door, proceeded to ransack the van of its remaining bread and cakes. Two others helped the girls out.

'My mother!' Hetty gasped. 'I must speak to her.'

The women thought she must be delirious. 'Your *mother*?'

'Of course! Frances Cordiner.' She spoke imperiously now. 'I must speak to her.'

'So! – you have changed your mind. And how considerate to bring us all those baker's provisions. We shall need every bit of food we can get—'

'I have *not* changed my mind! S-s-simply come to tell you they have set up a great gun in the Shelbourne, and

534

there are probably others. You'll have to leave the park – get all the boys out at least. Any minute now they'll start to fire. Can't you s-see? Have you not seen all the high w-w-windows?'

They had met Frances next to the bandstand, where she had been putting the finishing touches to her field dressing station. From where they stood, behind some tall bushes, all the windows in the Shelbourne were invisible. Her mother, showing no reaction, seemed to think the rest of the Green offered similar cover.

Hetty tugged her arm. 'Come over here – and see – out in the open!' But her mother resisted.

'We have trenches everywhere – do you not see *those*?'

'Mere gulleys.' And Hetty pulled her once more, so that finally she managed to get Frances out into the open where she pointed up to the top floor bedroom window. 'There! The gun is there – don't you se-see? It can easily fire down *into* the trenches. You must get everyone out—'

And just as they stood there, by the edge of the ornamental lake, a first long raking burst of machine-gun fire came from the window. Once more the girls fell to the ground. The bullets, kicking up a trail of exploding dirt, passed only a few yards away.

'*Now* do you see?' Hetty yelled at her mother.

'Indeed I see it . . . it is *war*!' Frances shouted – and, leaving the girls at the first aid station, she was off then, at the double, to marshal a counterattack on the Shelbourne.

A number of nurses and a doctor were tending those Volunteers who had been wounded. Hetty and Léonie at once offered help. The doctor showed surprise at their presence. 'You should have left here long ago,' she told them. 'All the civilians—'

'No,' Hetty interrupted her. 'I'm Henrietta *Fraser*. She's my Mama, I'm afraid. We're here – and we'll help now.'

'But you must *leave*. It's not your fight – you've no right to risk your lives in this way.' The older woman, though not in the least agitated, was firm.

'We're *staying*,' Hetty told her equally firmly. 'There'd be much more risk – going out on to the streets now.'

The doctor, seeing that Hetty was immovable, simply held out her hand. 'I'm Dr ffrench-Mullen. It's brave of you . . . very. I'm sure we'll all be grateful for your help.'

It was indeed a war that had started now – but one which the rebels could never win. Later in the afternoon, a second heavy machine-gun, set up to the west, on a roof behind the Russell Hotel, started to traverse the other side of the Green – while the first gun in the Shelbourne continued its sporadic depredations, concentrating largely on the bandstand, to general outrage, since a large Red Cross flag had flown from its top almost from the beginning of hostilities.

Frances, arriving back at the dressing station to confer with Dr ffrench-Mullen, was particularly incensed. 'How dare they shoot at wounded men!'

She bristled with righteous indignation, moving off again at once to see what she could do about it. Running over the little Bridge of Sighs, along a makeshift trench, dodging from one flowering bush to another, she came to the trees and railings immediately facing the Shelbourne.

And it was here, in her fury, that she shot the British officer. During a lull in the firing he had emerged from the Shelbourne porch – a big burly man in full field uniform, his chest covered in ribbons, but unarmed. He had ambled across the road, like a sleepwalker, shoulder twitching, straight towards the barbed wire railings. Frances, in the trees behind with several Volunteers, confronted him as he stepped up close to the railings.

'My dear good woman,' the officer told her vaguely, pleasantly, 'you must stop all this at once – they have a machine-gun above you – you will be overrun at any moment. You really—'

Taking out her Luger as he spoke, she shot the man between the eyes, at point blank range, so that, though the bullet crashed straight through, destroying the entire back of his skull, it left only a smallish burnt hole in his forehead. The officer seemed barely hurt at all for a long second, his eyes no more glazed than they had been a few moments ago, before he wobbled a bit, then fell backwards, slowly at first, before plunging with a crash to the pavement.

This was almost the last success of the rebels. By evening, the Green, now reeking of spent cordite, had been enfiladed from all four sides by reinforcements of British troops, their rifles and machine-guns playing havoc with the Volunteers in their half-secure trenches. Only the onset of darkness prevented a massacre.

The girls meanwhile, with the arrival of more wounded at the bandstand, found themselves fully occupied – boiling up kettles on open fires, opening tins of food, cutting the bread and cakes from the van they had driven.

They sweated in the heat, their smart brocade waistcoats long since abandoned, lace-collared blouses open right down their throats now, hair awry and ash-filled – so that when Commandant Mallin paid an encouraging visit to the dressing station, passing by their fires, he looked at them twice.

'Well done, girls – that's great work!' And it was then that he looked again, noticing their ruined clothes. 'I don't think I know you? . . .'

'Hetty – and this Léonie,' she told him shortly, wiping her brow.

'Indeed, but—'

'We're just over from France – for the Easter holidays,' she informed him casually, but in tones of such cutting arrogance that the Commander simply shook his head, mystified, before passing on.

They camped that night behind the bandstand, on rugs near the fires, waking next morning to another balmy day. As the guns opened up at them again from all round the Green with increased vigour, their situation very soon became quite impossible.

Soon after nine o'clock Frances arrived at the dressing

station. 'We are evacuating the Green,' she told the women brusquely. 'Moving to the College of Surgeons.'

'Not before time,' Hetty told her. The girls, though they had had little sleep, were perky enough, getting the hang of things, quite aware of the seriousness of the situation, but relishing it and their small part in the adventure.

'Stretchers then,' Dr ffrench-Mullen ordered. There were some twenty-five or so wounded men in the bandstand now, but only half that number of stretchers available, so that moving them across the Green had to be done in two sorties. And, though again they carried the Red Cross flag in each of these operations, again they were fired upon.

And it was while following behind one stretcher, just before they came to the heavily barricaded exit in front of the big granite College of Surgeons opposite, that Léonie was hit – a piece of shrapnel, a stray bullet, a ricochet, it was not clear. There was just a fizz of metal in the air before she fell, clutching her calf – her skirt almost immediately colouring with dark blood.

Hetty, next to her, cried out. Léonie, fallen right over now, face twisted round, though not apparently in pain, was strangely mute, her eyes closed.

'Léa! Léa!' Hetty knelt over her, thinking her dead.

But Léonie, opening her eyes then, looked up at her in a dazed way. 'I'm all right – can't feel a thing.' But the blood was soaking through the skirt now, flooding out, before Hetty and another Volunteer nurse pulled her gently to the cover of a big flowering cherry near the railings.

'Léonie dearest . . .' Hetty bent over her aghast, as some cherry blossoms floated down over her friend's bloodless face.

'I'm all right, you ninny – it's nothing.'

The nurse, cutting her skirt up the seam, revealed the wound, a bad gash in the calf.

'Not broken, I think – just a flesh wound,' the nurse said. 'We'll take her over next time round – you stay with her meanwhile.' And, taking out one of half a dozen

538

leather tourniquets she carried at her waistband, she applied it expertly just below Léonie's knee, before disappearing.

'Oh, Léa, what have I done? – getting you into all this?' Hetty, quite stricken now, leant over her, close, whispering endearments, furiously pulling at tufts of grass round her head, trying to make a pillow out of them.

'Don't be such an ass!' Léonie told her. 'It's only a scratch – I could be dead!'

Then she fainted.

The College of Surgeons, closed for the Easter holiday, had been rapidly broken into and taken over. A large elongated building, with its two-storeyed granite façade and small windows facing the Green, and an equally stout side wall running back towards the slum quarters behind, it offered an almost impregnable redoubt, which the rebels might far better have occupied from the beginning. It was a natural fortress with ideal fire lines, commanding both the Green and half its approaches, complete with a surgery, medical equipment and spacious lecture rooms. And now, with many more wounded to tend, and Volunteers from other parts of the city who had joined Commandant Mallin's group, it came into its own, prolonging a fight which would otherwise have ended there and then, with a massacre on the Green.

The wounded, on stretchers, were laid out next to the demonstration operating theatre on the ground floor. And here, in the capable hands of Dr ffrench-Mullen and her nurses, they received attention. The other Volunteers, some from rebel positions that had fallen in other parts of the city, increased to over a hundred men and women now, took up positions by the windows, which were soon filled with desks and sandbags, or on the roof, or mustered in lecture rooms on the first floor.

Léonie – the shrapnel removed, wound cleaned, stitched and bandaged by Dr ffrench-Mullen – lay on a blanket next to the unlit coal grate, in one of the first floor lecture-rooms where she had been carried on a stretcher, the walls adorned with medical illustrations – gory posters, charts, blood-red expositions of the human body: the musculature, lungs, intestines, bowels, alimentary and colonic canals. At one end of the room, behind a raised desk, a complete, yellowing human skeleton, disturbed by all the sudden movement, swayed eerily from a coat hanger.

Léonie, a rug round her shoulders, as Hetty tried to start the fire next to her, looked over at the swinging bones. 'Most suitable, I'm sure . . .'

'Oh, God – I'll move it.'

Léonie laughed up at her. 'Why?'

Hetty turned back, surprised. 'You are extraordinary – a bullet in your leg – yet you're so *calm*.' She knelt down beside her again. 'Your Papa will never forgive me.'

'*Us*, remember. It was my idea going into the Green – and, besides, he *always* forgives me . . .'

The noise of gunfire, to and from the College, increased as the day wore on. And there was the sound now – repeated heavy thuds – of some far larger naval guns down by the river. As a result of this shelling, fires had broken out in houses nearby and some much bigger conflagration had erupted in the city's centre, in Sackville Street, around the General Post Office – great grey-black plumes of smoke billowing up into the sky.

The Volunteers, ensuring that they had an emergency exit from the College, were smashing holes in the interconnecting walls to their left, leading through to other houses on the Green. The noise, the heat, the acrid cordite fumes, the falling brick and plaster dust in the building – all soon became intolerable. And the food, with so many more men to cater for, had begun to run out.

Hetty's mother, on a tour of inspection, came into the fetid classroom later in the afternoon, and stopped by the two girls. Her smart green tunic and cocked hat were covered in a fine white powder and an oily smear ran down beneath her right shoulder, from the Mauser she had been repeatedly firing. But her face was flushed and radiant. 'You will not regret it,' she told Hetty as her daughter ladled out the last of an oatmeal gruel she had concocted. 'I'm proud of you!'

Hetty, quite disregarding the compliment, barely turned her head. 'The food is running out – this is quite the last of the p-p-porridge. When will you see the madness of it all? How many more dead and wounded do you need – before you surrender?'

'We are not here to *surrender*,' she told her sharply. 'We can hold this building – oh, indefinitely!'

Frances knew this was not true. Their ammunition, not just the food, was running out – and quite a few of the Mauser rifles, used so continuously, had jammed. On the other hand, they had, just half an hour before, discovered in a locked basement room a whole cache of small arms belonging to the College's Officer Training Corps – some sixty practically unused Lee Enfield rifles, Webley revolvers and a quantity of ammunition. These they were keeping in reserve. And, just then, noticing the wicker basket of carrier pigeons, which they had taken to send messages to the other Volunteers about the city, an idea struck Frances: an idea for a surprise counterattack.

For there was no doubt they needed just such an event: British troops, having thoroughly consolidated their positions all round the Green, and moving from house to house, were already beginning to close in on them. For the rest of that day, at least, leaving aside the secret cache of arms, they had just enough ammunition to keep them at bay. But what if they pretended they had run out, of everything, exhausted all their reserves, material and moral, and then let the British come to them? . . .

She put the idea to Commandant Mallin straightaway. 'You see, we hardly need the pigeons for anything else now. We can send half a dozen off – with the same message: that we are almost out of ammunition, must soon give in. One of the pigeons, at least, will surely be brought down – you see how they have shot down several already? Gradually we cease firing – and leave it at that, dead silence. Then, with all these new Lee Enfields, when they come for us . . .'

Mallin agreed. Messages were prepared and the pigeons, at five-minute intervals, were sent off from the roof of the building. And sure enough the fifth one, blasted from the roof of the University Club on the north side of the Green, fell to earth by the Club steps, to be hurriedly taken inside by a British trooper. The trap was set. And thereafter, until darkness fell, they eked out their rifle fire with the remaining Mausers almost down to nothing.

Overnight, handing out the Lee Enfields to thirty or so of their best marksmen, they set the men, two to either side of the barricaded front windows and the rest hidden behind the roof parapet in a long line. So that, by dawn on Wednesday morning, the College, quite stilled and silent, without any firing as the hours passed, must have appeared ripe for a final assault by the British.

Frances had taken up position by the window in the lecture-room where Hetty and Léonie were, her Lee Enfield resting on the fire bay of mattresses and sandbags, the barrel just poking out towards the Green, the bay offering a clear field of fire from there down to the Grafton Street corner.

And she waited now, in a state of happy anticipation, a spring wound tight – waited, just as she had all those years ago, at Fraser Hall in Domenica, behind just such a mattress, looking out on the lovely tropic garden into the sunset, waiting for the Caribs to attack. She felt old now in this world of violence, vastly experienced in sudden death. She would freely mete it out. She would accept it, just as willingly, herself.

Hours passed without a shot fired in the Green. But by midday, observing the British troop movements carefully with field glasses, the rebels saw them moving covertly, from one building to another about the Green, gradually getting closer to the College for a final attack. They knew, too, from their scouts, that several British platoons had already moved into the Green itself and were hidden now straight across the road from them behind the trees.

At 12.30, on some pre-arranged signal, the British rifles and heavy machine-guns opened up all round them – an intense fire aimed at the College, so that everyone took cover as the hail battered the granite, the mattresses and sandbags. Not a single shot was fired in return. The fusillade stopped eventually and there was silence everywhere, just the noise of plaster falling about the big lecture-room.

Frances got to her feet and peered out into the bright sunshine. There was nothing to be seen, no movement anywhere, the British troops still under cover. Another fifteen, then twenty, minutes went by. Nothing. Perhaps their plan had misfired.

Then, just after one o'clock, the troops came into the open – first running down the near pavements from the Russell Hotel and Grafton Street corners, hugging the cover of the buildings, then, twenty or thirty of them, breaking from the trees and railings in front of the College and storming straight across the road. Suddenly, momentarily, there were some forty or fifty British soldiers in their field of fire – Frances drawing a bead on a sergeant leading his men across the road from the Green.

All the Volunteers opened fire, rapid fire, the British falling like ninepins beneath the brazen blue sky. It was a massacre.

The British retreated in disorder. And thereafter silence reigned again – and it seemed, indeed, as if the College might be held indefinitely.

Hetty, huddled protectively next to Léonie during all this frantic noise and killing, turned to her now. 'All right?'

'Yes, yes – leg's aching a bit, but all right.'

'Oh, God, I can't bear it – I'll get you something,' Hetty almost yelled, rising to her feet. Others among the more badly wounded in the lecture-room were crying, moaning now, as Hetty, distraught, began to wander about the room.

Léonie called her back. 'It's *all right* – just sit down, rest, it's nothing, leg's all right.'

'Oh, Léa, there must be something!' And she went off then to try to find Dr ffrench-Mullen.

While she was gone Frances, leaving her rifle at the window, and brushing some blood from her brow where she had been grazed by a stone splinter, came over to Léonie. 'How are you? I'm so sorry that you should be involved in this – not your fight – and wounded too. You are a brave woman.'

She spoke gently, but with such feeling and concern that Léonie, knowing only her previous sour or arrogant moods, was quite taken aback. She looked up at Frances quizzically. 'I'm all right. And you?' she asked, for lack of anything better to say.

'Excellent!'

'But you can't win . . .'

'Yes, we can! By winning – or by dying. Either way we can't lose.'

'But if you *do* lose here?'

'Oh, I shall be shot – all the leaders probably. But that will be an even greater victory.' Frances bent down then, looking into Léonie's eyes. 'If, when, that happens, you will look after Hetty, won't you? You are so much her best friend. I have meant so little to her, I'm afraid . . .'

She pursed her lips, but then smiled. 'It's been my hope for many years – this revolution!' She gestured towards the Green. 'And I don't regret it for an instant. Not for myself, but for Hetty – she has really suffered more for it, this cause of freedom. Perhaps, with an American mother, you will understand that. You were first, after all, to rid yourself of the British . . . and so may better put my case to her than I could.'

She knelt down now, even closer to Léonie, who could smell the cordite on her clothes, see the sheen in the trickle of blood that ran down her forehead. 'Yes, I regret nothing of this fight,' she said with gentle intensity. 'But to her I should like to have made some amends, and cannot. You may feel, perhaps, you can speak on my behalf.'

Then, before Léonie had time to reply, Frances was suddenly on her feet and gone. Léonie was astonished at this transformation – in a woman, previously so bitter, insensitive, vicious. She was not to know how such

544

a transformation lay at the very heart of Frances's and the other leaders' philosophy: a holy purification through fire. This transfiguration had occurred in Frances now – with the ultimate joy and release of a martyr's death still to come.

When Hetty returned with some aspirin, Léonie talked of this change, of Frances's obvious bravery, telling Hetty most of what Frances had said to her.

'Bravery?' Hetty was scornful. 'Or blind stupidity?'

'But, Hetty, if you believe in something so completely, *is* it just stupidity?'

'If it so damages you, kills you and everyone else – yes!'

'It's a kind of love, too, though – isn't it? All this freedom thing. And that's often blind.'

'Does love *destroy* people, though?' asked Hetty, more defiance than certainty in her rhetoric.

'Oh yes, of course it can.' Léonie winced in pain.

The College, despite further counterattacks by the British, held out for the next three days. The nights were the worst. Then, in almost total darkness and without the distraction of firing, there were only thoughts of pain, death, hunger – for the food, but for some scraps found in houses further along the Green, had quite run out by then.

Hetty lay close to Léonie during these nights, the latter's wound, stiffening and throbbing, growing more painful. And conditions were such in the building now – the airless squalor, the rank smell of death and excretion – that its occupants, beginning to lose all material hope, resorted instead to prayer.

Each evening, with the Angelus, and at intervals throughout the night, a single lantern, low down, casting yellow shadow light over the wounded and dying, prayers were intoned, to and fro across the lecture-room.

'Holy Mother of God, pray for us, intercede for us . . .'

'Now and at the hour of our death . . .'

The prayers rose, taken up by many voices, a silver chant floating over the room, a balm and blessing, as everyone waited for some end on that Saturday night, a great peace everywhere, now that it was quite clear to everyone that there could be no military victory.

But Hetty and Léonie, at odds with this native Irish faith, found an alternative way of prayer, simply by clinging to each other in the frail light. And it was then that another faith came to them – one that Léonie had proposed to Hetty two years before in her convent bed: the faith just of themselves, alive and together, in which a schoolgirl crush, that had become a devil-may-care friendship, now became a hunger, a great mutual need – the single means by which they might be saved, not by prayer but in a chant that they set up silently in each other's arms. The Volunteers had been transfigured, taken on the lineaments of martyrdom, by sacrifice and loss; the girls were changed utterly in this war by gaining a deep love.

The rebels, under a flag of truce, finally surrendered on Sunday morning – some hundred and twenty of them, walking out in good order from the side door of the College into York Street where, having handed over their arms to Captain de Courcy Wheeler and his men, they formed ranks and waited.

Then the dead and wounded were carried forth, on stretchers or in makeshift shrouds, and moved into British army field ambulances, standing by in front of the College. Hetty, next to Léonie on her stretcher, emerged into a pearl-grey morning light, rain in the moist air, a much more typically Irish 'soft' day, the freak balmy summer weather of the week all gone.

One of the British officers by the kerb, noticing their age and the remnants of their fashionable clothes, stopped them. 'Civilians? – are you the two girls from the Shelbourne – caught in the Green that first day?'

Hetty nodded. Then she said, 'I'm Henrietta Fraser. My mother—'

But Dr ffrench-Mullen, right behind Léonie's stretcher, interrupted her, so that the officer did not take in Hetty's last words. 'Yes, these are the two girls caught in the

Green. We took them to the College with us. This girl has a flesh wound, in the calf – should be seen to at once.'

The officer glared at the doctor dismissively for a second. 'Over here then, with that stretcher,' he told two of his orderlies. 'The civilian ambulance.'

Hetty and Léonie glanced back at Dr ffrench-Mullen, Léonie with gratitude in her eyes. Hetty had very nearly got them sent off with the others. 'You ninny!' she whispered up as they both moved off to the front of the building. 'One martyr's enough in the family.'

Finally, accompanying the last of the wounded, Frances Cordiner, with Commandant Mallin, left the College. Walking over to Captain de Courcy Wheeler, saluting briefly, she presented him with her Sam Browne belt, pistol and ammunition.

The Captain, a rotund and moustachioed figure, held the equipment awkwardly for a moment, embarrassed by this confrontation, this surrender by a mere woman, yet taller than he.

'Would you prefer,' the Captain said diffidently, 'I can drive you to the Castle?'

'Captain, I am second in command here – naturally, I should prefer to march at the head of our men, with Commandant Mallin.'

'Very well, if you wish.'

He saluted, watching her go to the head of the waiting lines of men – as Hetty and Léonie watched her from beside the civilian ambulance: Frances, her smart green uniform with its silver buttons all tattered and torn, but walking like a queen.

And it was then, as the Volunteers set off down York Street for Kilmainham jail, that the bystanders who had gathered to watch – upright citizens of the city, their prim wives, bookies' runners, old shawly women, pixie-faced little men, together with hordes of urchins – it was at that moment that all of them, with one voice, set up their jeering yells, catcalls, oaths of hatred.

'G'wan wi' ye – ye crowd of bowsies!'

'Ya rottin' lot of good for nuttin' gutties . . .'

'I hope yees are all hunged – shootin's too good for ye! Tryin' to stir up trouble fer us all.'

'Ye damn shower of Sinn Feiners – shure didn't yees go and ruin me Easther holidays!'

'And why wouldn't ya go and fight the *Kaiser* now – ya lot o' lily-livered, yellow bellies!'

A great wild paean of laughter and malevolence rose everywhere in the street as the men tramped off – pursuing them, a mocking, cackling, raucous chorus of spite and derision that Hetty and Léonie could hear rising up over the city long after all the Volunteer prisoners had disappeared.

Hetty was almost in tears then. 'I can't believe it – all that fighting – for *them*. And that's what they think of it.'

As they got into the ambulance, the now ragged Republican tricolour which had been hanging on top of the College all week was hauled down. It started to rain.

A week later, on the 6th May, Frances was court-martialled and sentenced to death. It was a sentence meted out to all the leaders of the rising, a rebellion now brutally avenged – a set-piece of its kind, theatrical in its intention and effects, going through each appropriate stage of farce, spectacle and tragedy.

7

The sound of the piano – repeated fits and starts from Mendelssohn's 'Spring Song' – could barely be heard from behind the closed double doors of the drawing room. But gradually, the notes put together more competently and confidently, the music, in these still confused but dazzling staccato runs, seeped out into the other rooms and corridors: a vague imprint, a mysterious half presence – like the shadow of some fabulous animal stalking the empty house. In its urgent uncertainty, the music was an appropriate harbinger of a spring that had not yet really come to Summer Hill.

'Can't quite get the right rhythm . . .' Hetty slumped her shoulders, frustrated. 'Though God knows I played it often enough, with old Sister Marie at the convent.'

'You'll get it!' Léonie spoke from her wicker wheelchair. 'You really *can* play well, you know.'

She gazed admiringly at Hetty sitting at the Blüthner Grand, peering at her through the edge of a vase of white narcissi with yellow, crimson-edged cups and blue grape hyacinths set on a small table between them.

'Though this piano isn't good for Mendelssohn anyway. It's a *singing* piano – more for you, soft and sweet! That's its tone, really lovely.'

And, breaking into a different composer's music, with themes which she knew much better, Hetty encouraged Léonie to sing Pinkerton's early duologue with Sharpless from *Madame Butterfly*, her voice rising and falling with sonorous exaggeration and a wittily guyed emotion, flooding the room with a spirited rendering of their argument over Pinkerton's irresponsible marriage plans. '*E un facile vangelo!*' Léonie thundered. They had seen the opera in Paris with the Strauses. It was one of their favourites.

At the end they laughed and Hetty clapped vigorously. 'You *must* go on with your singing lessons, Léa! There'll be lots of good singing teachers over here – the Irish are wonderful singers! . . .' Hetty was flushed with excitement.

'Yes . . .' Léonie was uncertain. 'You really think . . . we'll be staying here?'

'Of course! Why not? We talked to Mortimer in Dublin. And he's coming down this afternoon to arrange things generally at Summer Hill – and I'm sure when your Mama and Papa get here tomorrow they'll agree. You can do *all* the things here you do in France – well, most of them – and certainly the singing. You sang that *Butterfly* duet perfectly!'

'Not as good as your piano in the "Spring Song".'

Léonie turned and looked out over the rain-sodden view. 'Though it hardly looks like spring.'

'No. Not yet – but it will! I *know* it will.' Hetty reached out her hand. 'Oh, Léa, after all that death and disaster in Dublin – when I thought we were gone, too . . . What does it matter, a bit of rain? Just to be alive.'

Léonie reached from her wheelchair and grasped Hetty's hand. The two girls gazed at each other through the cascade of white narcissi. 'Yes,' Léonie said. 'Yes.' Her deep grey-green eyes flickered – an instant smile, as the light brightened for a moment outside the window, a sudden shaft of watery sun illuminating the room.

Léonie suddenly changed the subject. 'Hetty, it's strange, but behind you there, on the wall . . . there are sort of dark patterns, in a certain light – when the sun came through just now, as if there was a mural or something hidden there. Look!'

Hetty turned and they both gazed at the white wall, with the Fantin-Latour flower painting set half-way up.

'Something, yes, those lines here – and there especially.' Hetty stood on a chair and removed the picture. 'Something dark there, a row of dark things. Old wallpaper maybe? Or a mural. Let's see.'

She picked up a silver paper knife from the bureau and started to scrape away at the paint, where the flower picture had been. After some vigorous work, the crown and then the brim of a bowler hat emerged – and further along, as she continued her scraping, another similar hat came to light, on top of a rubicund Irish face, then the bow of a fiddle and the neck of a bottle of stout: a bucolic, bibulous village band, it seemed, was trying, like the spring, to force its way back into life, through the paint, another herald of joy, long-forgotten, emerging from the walls of the old house.

'Hetty, your mother'll be furious—'

'Mama won't be furious here for years and *years*, thank goodness. Look! I don't believe it!' Hetty stood back, displaying her handiwork. 'Not just *one* bowler hat – but a row of them! Playing fiddles and drinking beer. And on the *drawing* room wall!' Hetty considered the matter a moment. 'Unless – it's something of Aunt Emily's, when they thought she was mad and had her locked up. A mural by her, like the ones she has in her bedroom. Looks marvellous.'

'What a house!' Léonie said. 'All sorts of secrets,' she added lightly.

'Nothing but.' Hetty sighed, taking the point more seriously. 'But come on! – let's do some more *Butterfly* before Mortimer gets here.

'Right, I'll do Pinkerton, and you do Cio-Cio San, and we can sing that duet, remember, like we did at the convent – that squashy, sentimental one.'

And so they happily enacted the great love scene, guying it again, Hetty – her histrionic gifts to the fore – putting a narcissus behind her ear, arching her eyebrows oriental-fashion, playing the coy Japanese maiden as she caressed and hit the keys, peeking in and out from behind the vase of flowers . . . while Léonie, with similar mock dramatics, bellowed out all Pinkerton's swelling passion – until, finally, one of the terriers, goaded beyond endurance, started to bark with furious excitement and the girls collapsed in laughter.

Outside, at the hall entrance to the drawing room, Pat Kennedy, the butler, paused at the closed door a moment, listening to the thrilling voices, the soaring music.

He had musical tastes himself – he ought to have enjoyed his eavesdropping. Instead he was doubtful, anxious over something. Before moving on, he hitched his trousers up, displaying for an instant the Webley revolver – once kept hidden in his mattress, but which now never left the holster beneath his waistband.

'But, Mortimer, for all that you are my much older cousin and dear friend . . . it is after all *my* life, my house here. So I do insist I am consulted, that we agree any plans together. I am no longer a child, you know.'

It was over a month since the Rebellion in Dublin when Hetty spoke almost severely to Mortimer Cordiner, down from Dublin to see what he might do over the running of the household and estate, and more particularly to discuss Hetty's future, now that her mother, reprieved from execution at the last moment because of her gender, had started a life sentence in Dublin's Mountjoy Prison.

'Of course, Hetty. I'm not officially *in loco parentis*. Only here to advise, help.' He twiddled his luxuriant beard as they stood in the great hall, below the restored white marble statues of Cupid and Psyche, pondering this formidably assured girl who, when he had last seen her, had indeed been a child.

'Good. Well, let us talk to the others.'

They moved out onto the wide porch – it was another blowy, uncertain late spring day – where the Strauses, Benjamin and Effi, with Léonie in her wheelchair, still not yet fully mobile from her leg wound, were taking coffee. The Strauses, hearing of their daughter's adventures, and with some difficulty and delay making passage from France to Ireland, had finally arrived at Summer Hill the previous evening. Only Aunt Emily and Robert, nearing the end of his school holidays, spent at Summer Hill with a friend from St Columba's College, were absent from the porch; both boys had been out on the river since early morning fishing for trout, Aunt Emily, with her drawing and easel, lost somewhere in the demesne.

'You see,' Hetty said to the assembled company, taking control just as she had with Mortimer a few moments before. 'Where better for Léa and me to stay . . . than here? With the war in France and the awful troubles in Dublin. Though, as you can see, there are absolutely no troubles down here!'

She gazed over the tulip-covered pleasure gardens, the drifts of narcissi and daffodils down the lawn, to the woods above the river and over the blue mountains: the same serene view of arcady.

'Indeed,' Ben Straus agreed. 'But what of *learning*, girls?' He eyed Hetty brightly as he pulled on a small cigar.

'Well, the convent's closed – thank goodness. And, besides, what more should we learn?'

'All the arts and refinements appropriate to young women . . .' Mortimer thought out loud.

'We can surely find some tutor locally, in Kilkenny, to come and teach us sums and history and things – if that's what you're worried about. And as to the other refinements you mention . . .' Hetty looked across at Léonie in the wheelchair. 'We can surely teach each other all that.' She smiled at her friend. She could hardly believe it – it was wonderful to have Léonie here, in her house, but this time without her mother, entirely under her protection.

'But, Henrietta,' Ben Straus spoke slowly, a little sadly, 'what on earth would you and Léa *do* here all on your own together?'

Again Hetty looked out of the window, at the landscape hanging on the edge of summer. 'Why everything – *everything*,' she told him sweetly.

Effi Straus, petite, dark-haired, sensible, put her hand gently on her husband's arm. 'Ben, dearest, it's just you're such a city man yourself, you can't understand country life. There'll be everything for Léonie to get on with here. And you'll miss her, I know – I will too – but we can come visit. And surely, with this dreadful war going on and on, she'd be safer here?'

'Mr Cordiner – what do you feel? I don't want to impose—'

'No imposition whatsoever, Mr Straus. As I said to Hetty, I'm not formally in charge. But I can't see that Frances would object. I saw her last week at Mountjoy – and will be seeing her again when I get back.'

He looked round the company – silent, embarrassed, at this mention of Frances: a ghost at a feast. And indeed it was so noticeable how her absence from Summer Hill had already lightened the mood of every room, every person, the whole air of the house.

Pat Kennedy came on to the porch then, with one of the maids, supervising the coffee clearing and at the same time making enquiries about the wine for that evening's dinner. He addressed himself to Mortimer, as the eldest Cordiner present.

'Ah,' Mortimer twiddled his beard mischievously. 'You must ask Miss Henrietta, Pat – she's in charge here now!' They all looked at Hetty. 'Well, Hetty? The wines – they should be a part of any sensible young woman's education. What would you suggest?'

Suddenly taken out of her reverie she spoke directly to Pat. 'Oh, let us have ch-ch-champagne! – of course, now that we are all here safe and sound, as a c-c-celebration!'

She stared at Pat forcefully as she spoke. And her gaze disturbed the man, just as the girls' singing had done. What was it, he wondered, that made her stare at him in such a knowing, authoritative manner?

Hetty knew well enough why she took this dominant attitude: she remembered watching her mother taking the secret oath to fight the British in his stable rooms years before. If her mother subsequently had become one of the leaders of the rising, there could be no doubt but that Pat was one of the rebels too, as yet undiscovered. She had a power over him there which he knew nothing of. But she would not use it openly yet, for she feared him as well.

Afterwards Ben Straus spoke to Mortimer alone in Frances's study-boudoir off the big drawing room, where Mortimer was going through farm accounts and other household papers, accumulated in Frances's absence.

'I shall expect to contribute to Léonie's keep—'

'Of course not! How many times has Hetty stayed with you in Paris?' Mortimer put his pen down.

Ben Straus had taken to Mortimer at once. In their original views and freedom from stuffy convention they were much in the same mould, men of the world – so that Benjamin felt able to speak quite freely. 'What of . . . Mrs Fraser?' he asked pointedly. 'It's hard to understand . . .'

'Yes, she was always that,' Mortimer replied promptly. 'And very lucky indeed to have been reprieved, along with de Valera. Your country had most to do with it. Lloyd George is scared of American opinion, particularly the Irish there. And, besides, he hopes to get America into the war.'

'I hope not,' Ben humphed. 'Though I suppose it will

surely come . . . But the house here and the big farm – can it run without Mrs Fraser?'

Mortimer smiled, thinking of the Appleton case and the other domestic and farming troubles which, as Frances's legal adviser and only real confidant in Ireland, he had had to deal with over the past years. 'I have to tell you, Mr Straus, that without Mrs Fraser things will run a *lot* more smoothly here.'

'And the girls – what do you really think?'

'I think they'll be fine. I'll be down often enough, keep an eye on things. They'll be fine.'

Later, before he returned to Dublin next morning, Mortimer spoke to Hetty alone, the two of them walking through the formal pleasure gardens and up the terraced lawn – another uncertain, rain-squally afternoon. They had been talking of arrangements in the household – Hetty, remonstrating with him almost over the fate of her Grandmama, still incarcerated in the back wing of the house.

'Yes, I've often spoken to your mother about her. And indeed, years ago, she should have been let out into the light and air. Now it's too late – I've spoken to the new doctor in Thomastown: quite apart from her various heart problems she's almost entirely senile. There's apparently nothing to be done, other than the best attention, which she gets here at home, from old Molly particularly. She can't move—'

'But why did my mother have her put away like that in the first place? It was a m-m-*monstrous* thing . . .'

Mortimer, who knew many of the details which had led to this incarceration, said simply, 'They had disagreements, over the inheritance of Summer Hill – your Grandmama had left it all to your great-uncle, Austin Cordiner—'

'Yes, I've heard something of that – when my uncles died, Henry killed by a snake here and Eustace in that Boer war—'

'Yes, and your mother believed that she had a prior right to the house, as indeed she had.'

'But to lock Grandmama up like that!'

'These family rows – they can be very embittering. Perhaps you can understand? . . .' Mortimer waved his hands in the air, gesturing impotently. 'In any case, it is your mother who must suffer the incarceration now. I fear she will not be released – for a very long while.'

Hetty, far from understanding, was scornful. 'Does she deserve any better? Oh, Léonie has told me: how she spoke to her during the battle at the College of Surgeons – apologizing for her wretched behaviour to me over the years. But no, I c-c-can't understand it! Why, why she should be s-s-such a cruel woman!'

Mortimer, who through Dermot's strictest confidence knew of Frances's affair with the Prince of Wales, of his abandoning her, and how Hetty was their child, thought he understood Frances's behaviour very well. But he could not speak of this to Hetty, and thus show her mother in any better light. Instead he treated the issues vaguely.

'Your mother has been bitterly disappointed in her life—'

'Yes, but *how*?'

'Over Summer Hill here, with her own mother – and later in the West Indies with your father. Oh, and much else. It has driven her . . . in these cruel directions.' He turned to Hetty then. 'But you must know – she was not always like that. When she lived with Dermot and me in London, years ago – what a warm person she was, how happy, enthusiastic, lovely in so many ways.'

Hetty showed surprise. 'How then the cold and ch-charmless person she has always been to me – to everyone – since?'

Again, he could not tell her how, in her own case, it was because Hetty reminded Frances of the Prince, and the disastrous end to their affair, that she so frowned on her daughter.

'Hetty, a person's character can become quite twisted by long disappointment. Do you see? Be sure that it doesn't happen to you.' He gazed into her chilling blue eyes. They had left the pleasure garden now and stood higher up on the lawn, beneath the maple tree which, thirty years before, had held Frances's swing, the stubbed branch still jutting out over the rock and willow garden which had replaced the tennis court.

'Oh, that will not happen to me,' Hetty assured him roundly. 'Disappointments, yes, no doubt – but not that I quite change my character!'

'Good!'

They walked into the rock garden then, suddenly glimpsing Aunt Emily at her easel between the pendent willow branches on the other side, the late sun making delicate yellow patterns through the leaves.

'This, all this, was a tennis court once – I remember so wanting to play on it.'

'Yes, another disappointment of your Mama's . . .'

Hetty chuckled. 'Aunt Emily told me – some man, some rich lord, jilted her here: some "nonsense with men", she said! Aunt Emily hates *men*!' She turned and teased her cousin now. 'Well, I don't hate men – or women,' she thought to add for good measure.

Returning, they stopped by the grotto and artificial waterfall, gazing down at the house bathed in a shaft of evening sunlight, the Virginia creeper just coming into leaf, a vague filigree tracing of green creeping over the façade above the porch. 'And I don't hate Summer Hill either, like I used to. But that's just because Mama's not here. That's awful, isn't it?'

Mortimer bit his lip ruminatively. 'No . . . it's understandable—'

But Hetty rushed on, stricken by the spirit of place, 'It was just here, by the grotto, the day war broke out, that Dermot told me how much the house could offer all of us – me and Robert and Léonie, with him and Mama: married! Just think of it, what "nonsense" that would have been. And yet I believed him – when he said what a future I had here . . .'

Mortimer sighed. 'You, at least, certainly have a future here, Hetty. As to Dermot, well, I have news of him regularly now. I'll send you some of his letters. And he gets the food parcels . . .'

A swirl of emotion overcame Hetty then and she turned to Mortimer vehemently. 'Oh, I do hope the war ends soon. Or he escapes. Why doesn't he *escape*?'

'Perhaps he's tried. But he's in some huge walled castle —'

'I would so like to see him!' Her great eyes glistened.

'So would I. And we will. And the house will have all its promise again.' Mortimer, in fact, was not so sure of any of these things, only managing to hide his doubts in his beard. 'In the meantime, there's me, in Dublin, and Aunt Emily and Elly – and Léonie – here. And the war will be over . . . some day.'

They had started to walk back to the house when Hetty paused half-way down the lawn, beneath the great cedar tree. 'How can there be such peace here – and de-de-death and such horrors everywhere else?'

Mortimer shook his head. 'That's exactly the madness of it all, I'm afraid – which we have to make the real fight against.'

'Because we're not mad, you mean? People like us?'

'Yes, I hope so. Just that.'

Robert and Bertie, his tall bespectacled schoolfriend, were preparing their rods in the porch before going out for a last evening's trout fishing, chattering to Léonie in her wheelchair, when Hetty and Mortimer got back to the house.

'Well, go on! You've never properly told *us*, at least, what it was all *like* in the rebellion!' Robert, already in his fishing waders, his hank of dark hair falling repeatedly over his brow in his excitement, was taxing Léonie. 'We saw *nothing* of it all down here. Do tell us!'

'But, Robert, I *have* told you! It was all . . . just awful! I can't describe it. Here's Hetty – she's much better at describing things.'

Robert turned to Hetty. 'Well? What was the most *awful* thing?'

Hetty looked at him, rather *de haut en bas*. She relished

having done, and been part of, men's violent things, which Robert, with his love of guns and sport, so wanted to experience. 'Oh,' she said grandly, 'so *many* awful things. I think the worst was the nights, the rotten awful smell in the lecture-room, blood and dying and thinking you were going to die next morning yourself when the shooting started again . . . Yes, the nights were worst. Without Léa, I don't know . . .' She looked over at Léonie, smiling quickly, sharing again in an instant all that they had shared in those nights. Robert was spellbound, his bespectacled friend less so.

'Oh, and the *poor* carrier pigeons – I couldn't bear it, when they shot them down. And then, when the British started to *shell* the building, on the last few days, and it looked like the whole place was going to go up in flames . . .'

Robert looked at Hetty with envy and obvious admiration. 'Oh, I *do* wish I'd been there!' But it was Léonie who gazed at Robert as he spoke, in silent sympathy at his frustration.

In the years since St Columba's, Robert had seen little of Hetty. But, their childhood antagonisms largely forgotten, absence had made his heart grow fonder. As for Léonie, ever since she had first seen Robert that day standing like a sentinel on the river bank, he had come in and out of her mind as a vaguely disturbing presence, a distant figure – but all the more attractive for that. Yet Léa saw how very much less distant he was with Hetty and realized how much he liked her; and she felt a pang of jealousy then.

They had had a life together – oh, for so many years before she had met Hetty. And, for a moment, she was jealous of that, too. But then, she thought, they had surely never shared what she and Hetty had experienced – together during those last nights in Dublin. So there was nothing really to be jealous of. And she allowed herself once more to look at Robert as merely attractive and unthreatening.

★

Petrol was rationed, Frances's big Daimler immobilized, so Molloy took the departing company to Thomastown station in the old coach and pair; the girls on the porch waving furious goodbyes, the terriers barking, so that with the general commotion the rooks in the chimney-stacks soared and cawed into the bright blue sky, inky tea-leaves against the sun. A minute later, the girls heard the first white gate clang shut.

Sheila, one of the terriers, jumped up, pawing and stretching herself against Hetty's legs, while Chilly, disturbed by everyone's sudden disappearance, gazed down the drive. After another minute Hetty pushed Léonie into the hall. 'So, all gone,' she said shortly.

'All beginning,' Léonie replied.

Turning the wheelchair towards one of the tall windows, Hetty paused in the shaft of sunlight, bending down close over Léonie's head, both girls silent in the great pillared space.

'That little coloured pane there,' Léonie said eventually, looking at the stained-glass inset at the bottom of the window. 'What is it, I've often wondered—'

'Oh, it's Aunt Emily's – the family arms. And the motto: "Fortune Favours the Brave".'

'Whose fortune?' Léonie asked dully.

'Ours, Léa – ours.'

'That eagle . . . frightens me.' And she shivered, craning round, looking up at Hetty.

'Oh, it's nothing – just like the frigate birds we had everywhere in Domenica: the souls of dead sailors searching for their lost homes . . .'

'That's pretty sad . . .'

'No, it's not! – they find them! They all have homes, just like we have, *here!*'

Hetty turned the chair round as she spoke. And now she wheeled Léonie, slowly at first, as if in some courtly dance, making figures of eight around the pillars. Then, at a gradually increasing pace, speeding past the Flemish hunting tapestry, she ran from the statue of Psyche in its niche at one end of the hall, across to its mate, Cupid, on the other side – pushing Lèonie faster now, the wheels screeching over the marble floor, as she turned the chair in ever-tighter circles, propelling Léonie back and forth in a rising swirl of movement, as if trying to obliterate the immediate past, to set a great distance from that moment of departure minutes before, to reach the threshold of their new life.

They screamed and laughed and sang, the wheelchair a carousel, careering madly about. Then, as it made too sharp a turn, the chair tipped over and Léonie was spilled out, in the middle of the chequered marble floor.

'Léa! . . .'

'I'm all right.' She stood up, quite easily, walked, with only the slightest limp, over to the window, and peered out into the bright sunshine.

'But, Léa . . . your leg?'

'Oh, it's *much* better.' She bent down, eyes once more glued to the little stained-glass pane. 'It's just – I rather liked you pushing me about in that splendid thing, these last weeks . . .'

She turned, righted the chair and, with one vigorous push from her injured foot, sent it careering away into the back of the hall. 'Was that wrong of me?' Hetty, surprised and still breathless, shook her head. 'No? Good. Shall we *walk*?'

Léonie took Hetty's hand and, swinging their arms to and fro, they made a beginning, going out through the doors and into the spring sunlight.

Aunt Emily, from her bedroom studio on the west side of the house, saw the girls move through the pleasure garden, up the terraced lawn, to the maple tree, where they stopped, looking at the rock and willow gardens, Hetty gesticulating at the view.

Taking her sketch-book, Aunt Emily rapidly drew the old maple, as she remembered it more than thirty years before, when Frances was a girl – showing the big branch with its swing leaning out over what had then been the tennis court. And on the swing she put Hetty, in her long, tight-fitting lilac skirt and frilly blouse, with Léonie pushing her – thus predicting, by twenty-four hours exactly, the situation the following morning, when the Summer Hill carpenter, on Hetty's instructions, rigged up just such a swing on another branch. Soon Hetty was pushing Léonie on it, higher and higher, so that Léonie gasped for her to stop.

'Fortune favours the brave!'

When Léonie got off the swing Hetty told her, 'I'd like to turn that dreary willow garden back into a tennis court!'

Aunt Emily, in her now-expanded drawing, had already done just that, colouring her sketch in light and dark green washes, picking out the white lines, the sloping black net – just as it all would have been years before, except that now Léonie was on the swing, feet swooping out over the court in an arc, and Hetty, hands in the air, was laughing beneath the mottled green shadows of the maple.

Hetty, with the run of the house and relishing her control, moved to a bedroom next to Léonie's – taking over the yellow room which her mother had occupied as a young woman, looking eastwards over the valley and the mountains, a pretty, rather faded room now, still with the daffodil-and-primrose frieze running along just beneath the ceiling and the antiquated bathing machine in the small dressing room adjoining, with its water tank mounted on mock bamboo pole supports, rarely used since the installation of the first proper bathroom.

'What a crazy machine!'

'All very cosy, though, in the winter.' Hetty touched Léonie's arm. 'We ought to try it—' And a sensuous complicity grew between them for an instant, before a sudden noise in the next room disturbed them. The grate was full of soot and twigs. 'The rooks in the chimneys.' Hetty bent down and peered up the flue. 'Can't have been a fire here for ages.'

Then something caught her eye and, picking about in the mess, she drew out a blackened silver teaspoon. 'Of course – the thieves!' She pushed her arm up the flue and encountered a ledge a foot or so above the grate. She emerged with a grimy, discoloured glass paperweight – but, embedded in the crystal, as she rubbed it, a beautiful crimson rose materialized.

Again she reached up, searching the ledge. There were several other paperweights there. Finally she brought out a spherical snow-dome, with a delicate ivory model of Summer Hill inside; when she shook it, she set the flakes dancing.

The girls studied the treasures, taking them over to the window, cleaning them more thoroughly. 'The rooks and jackdaws couldn't have taken all these in their beaks – someone must have hidden them here.' Hetty gazed in fascination at the snow-dome, rocking it gently in her hand, letting the flakes wash like a tide over the base of the house.

'Someone may have stolen them then, from about the house, and hidden them there,' Léonie said. 'Secrets, you said,' she went on. 'Nothing but secrets here.'

'Yes.' Hetty was thoughtful. 'Aunt Emily'll probably know – but I'm going to keep these. Especially this!' And she caressed the snow-dome, seeing it somehow as a talisman, an emblem of her new life at Summer Hill with Léonie. This indeed, she thought, was a symbol: the promise of the house incarnate, that promise which Dermot had spoken to her about nearly two years before, when life for all of them would be amazingly, unimaginably lovely, as it would be now, for her and Léonie at least, in *her* house.

Later, in her studio-bedroom, Aunt Emily explained the presence of these little *objets d'art* in the chimney. 'Of course!' she spoke caustically. 'That was your Mama's bedroom, when she was your age – always thieving things about the house, just to annoy!' She glared round at Hetty then in her wide-eyed, mad-happy way.

'But annoy who?'

'Why your grandmother, of course – always hammer and tongs together.' Aunt Emily cackled at the memory.

Hetty was taken aback, not by her mother's thieving

propensities, but by her own apparent inheritance of exactly similar inclinations towards these objects. Was she *like* her mother then – whom she so hated? What a thought . . . So that, in a sudden burst of righteousness, she said, 'Well, I shall have them all put back in the drawing room.' Though she made a mental note not to release the snow-dome. 'Typical of Mama,' she went on disapprovingly, espousing an adulthood she did not yet quite possess. 'Stealing things . . .'

'Typical, yes.' But Aunt Emily spoke with enthusiasm. 'She was a spirited young woman! Gaudy – know what I mean?' she added in her haughty, brogue-tinged voice.

'Not really.'

'Your mother had *character*, girl. And that's the only thing that counts: knew what she wanted – and took it! If only she hadn't taken to all those *men* . . .' Aunt Emily curled her lips sourly.

'What men?'

'*All* men.'

'Were there many?'

'Excuse yourself, girl – *one* man's too much. But she had those Horse Show Johnnies in the Dublin season, that wretched oaf Lord Norton's son, that no-good Fraser chap. Far too many.'

'I never knew that!'

'*Lot* of things you don't know – oh, she was a stunner, all right, lovely girl, if only the men hadn't done for her . . .'

'My father, you mean?'

'Well, he was the worst by all accounts.'

'*Was* he my father, though?'

'Why wouldn't he be?' Aunt Emily looked up at her, puzzled. 'Though, now you mention it, I wonder. Your Mama had *character*, took what she wanted, did things her way . . .'

Hetty, startled by these revelations, felt faint, her vision blurring and shaking: a feeling she had known before whenever she was faced with these strange intimations of her real paternity, the idea that she might have quite another father – a sense that had been with her for so long, that she was a changeling, perhaps; coming from, going towards, some as yet unidentifiable greatness. It disturbed her, yet also gave her a wonderful feeling of secret potential, of immense power – a *will* to power, which she must soon express, accepting her true inheritance.

She was surprised, too, by this new view of her mother, in her great-aunt's praise which, added to Léonie's earlier talk of her bravery and to Mortimer's commendations, seemed to confirm the existence of quite a different woman in her youth: a woman whom she could still hate, yes, but also, in her better features, perhaps emulate. With all this talk of bravery, loveliness, character – did she not already reflect these qualities of her mother's? But what if she had only inherited her worst traits? – as in this need for thieving they seemed to share.

'Am I like my Mama then – I mean her good points – when she was young?'

'Oh, she was more the daredevil! A real case – took the eye out of a tinker once, robbing the Cordiner tombs, with her riding crop! And threw a fit when your grandmother blackened the whole house up after my curious nephew Henry let all the snakes out that killed him – pulled the curtains down, rang all the bells in the place fit to burst, and then stamped off with Elly to London! Oh, she was a real panic, your Mama. I had a lot of time for her. Besides . . .' She ran her fingers over her sketch-book. 'It was she who gave me the run of the place here, when her mother – the old witch – had me locked up in this bedroom! Oh yes, she had character, your mother, and fearless with it!'

Hetty felt chastened, and lessened, by this comparison. She seemed a pale shadow of this daredevil. Feeling the need to assert herself, she blurted out, 'Well, I shall see that Grandmama is moved into the light and air, when the better weather settles. There are to be changes here.'

Aunt Emily cackled. 'Changes, indeed! Of course there will be – just like your Mama, when she got back from that cannibal island! You're so like her, in that way. Always on to change things, when you can't really, no one can. *Just like her!*'

Hetty was now even more determined, like her mother, to assert herself – in whatever bold and impetuous way she could – on the life of Summer Hill.

And she did change things. In a flurry of activity she and Léonie first travelled the house, from attic to cellar, considering every nook and cranny, establishing themselves, as if in a vast new nest. They moved out some of the Georgian furniture, replacing it with heavy Victorian pieces – things Hetty had loved as a child and which her mother had abandoned. They opened rooms which had been long closed, in particular old Sir Desmond's mechanical workshop in the yard, untouched since his death nearly ten years before. They stood among the debris of jagged wood and torn linen, the remains of the biplane which had killed him. Its wooden propellers were smashed, the wicker cockpit seat had been eaten away by rats, the long room was tangled in cobwebs, full of musty decay, yet it was still strangely animate with adventure and hope.

Hetty wiped the thick dust off the linen fuselage, so that the still-brilliant blue lettering emerged: 'ZEPHYR'. Then she pulled one of the control sticks; a wire strained and creaked. 'They fly everywhere nowadays. But he must have been one of the very first.'

'What a *family*, Hetty!'

And Hetty was pleased by the comment – which Léonie felt impelled to repeat when Hetty opened up her Uncle Henry's old museum and work rooms on the top floor – rooms into which she and Robert had stolen through the window, as children. Now, with a key, they marched straight in, finding nothing changed: the same desiccated, slightly medical odour, the partly filled butterfly display case with its last addition, the huge Amazonian Swallowtail still half-secured there; sporting rifles, assegais, military drums and fencing foils, the same snake skeleton in the tea-chest by the ash-filled grate.

Hetty lifted the necklace of vertebrae, terrifying Léonie,

rattling it in the mote-filled sunlight. 'I used to be terrified of this, too. Robert was such a tease . . .'

Léonie gazed through the doorway at the display cases filled with exotic stuffed animals: a porcupine rampant, sad-eyed, frozen lemurs, a malevolently toothy crocodile. 'Did they ever do anything *ordinary* here?'

'We'll do all these things – and more!' Hetty assured her. 'Oh, Léa, that's just what a huge old house like this is *for*! For everything!

She and Léonie hugged each other violently, pressing, swaying together in rising spasms of affection, so that for an instant it seemed their love must catch fire. But at the last moment they drew apart, flushed and breathless, half-annoyed at their restraint.

'No,' Hetty said, gazing at Léonie in frustration. Then, by way of excuse, she went on, 'No, let's not change anything here, leave everything. Unless – we took those.' She picked one of the fencing foils from the wall, flourished it, whipping the air briskly. 'Good way of exercising your leg!'

'A most suitable young lady-like accomplishment indeed! Yes, let's take them.'

'And there's rifles, too – in case the rebels come for us! Dermot showed me how to shoot with them years ago.'

And Hetty, remembering those days, early dawns, star-lit evenings, out and about the estate or by the river with Dermot – when life had opened out for her as a child in all sorts of vivid adventure – was tempted by the idea of some equally wild existence, here with Léonie now, so that she took another foil off the wall, passing it to Léonie, then faced her, flourishing her own foil inexpertly, measuring up to her.

'"Action!" – is that what they say?'

'The brave!' Léonie responded. Both button-point foils were in the air now, as they mimed the start of an engagement, swords meeting with a sharp clash, blades shivering. They glared at each other, mimicking the anger of wicked ladies, true swordswomen.

And for that long moment of confrontation, as their foils

touched, a very different feeling towards Léonie woke in Hetty – one that was not at all tender or protective as it had been hitherto, but another, quite new, dizzy-making urge: a need to hurt, crush, dominate, subdue this young woman, almost as an object, devoid of feeling. Yes, she wanted to possess Léa then, just as she had the paper-weights and the other little objects found in the chimney.

Gazing defiantly into Léa's eyes, she was not to know how her friend, at precisely the same moment, felt an almost identical possessive urge.

Both ashamed of these sensations, they laid the foils down.

'Oh, Léa, I'm sorry . . .' Hetty turned away.

'About what?' Léonie approached her now, concerned – as if determined to rescue, underwrite, confirm something vital which they had both felt in these last minutes – touching her shoulder, turning her head round towards her. 'Probably great fun – these foils – if one knew how to do it.' She gazed at Hetty intently.

'But we don't know how – do we?'

'We can, we *will* though. We can learn, won't we?'

'Yes. Oh, *yes*!' They smiled with relief, that they understood their secret feelings for each other now.

8

'On guard then, Henrietta!' Major Ashley started the lesson in his dry, strident voice. 'No! – hold the foil *correctly* first.' He stopped her, acidly patient. 'Thumb *up*. You don't grip the thing like a *carving* knife: *lightly!* Just thumb and forefinger – the other fingers only used to guide the blade. The doigté is all important – remember the great master Lafaugère: "Hold your sword as if you had a little bird in your hand, firmly enough to prevent its escape, yet not so firmly as to crush it."'

The Major – willowy, distinguished, with ferociously bushy eyebrows over a cadaverous face – took his stick and hobbled across the great hall. Hetty, in a linen culotte and padded body vest, took off her fencing mask. Léonie, similarly clad, stood at the other side of the hall, towards the end of a narrow hessian carpet laid out along its length for some thirty feet.

'No, girl, give it here.' The Major, cynically dispassionate now, showed her how to hold the foil. '*Lightly!*' He balanced it perfectly for a second between thumb and forefinger. Then, with fiendish exultation, his bad leg anchored to the ground, he stamped the other foot forward, lunging sharply. 'Thus – and thus!' he roared, repeating the action. Then he resumed his pitying manner. 'You are not *pig*-sticking, my dear. It is an *art*, this. Do you *hear* me, Léonie?' He had swung round in a trice and confronted her.

'Yes, Major!' Léonie, her mask still in place, did not have to hide her broad smile. It was their third lesson with the irascible, sweet-and-sour Major – demon-faced, arms darting, bizarre, but with a kind and witty heart, a man they had both taken to at once and now almost adored.

'Right, then. Masks on. First positions. On guard!' He issued instructions, rat-a-tat-tat, like a ballet master, as they prepared to engage. 'Feet together, at *right* angles, head and body *erect* . . .' He hit the crucial words with a sharp nasal bark. 'Head facing *forward*, Léonie – not to the side, you idiot girl! – left arm hanging, in touch with the body, right arm and foil in a *straight* line, button six inches from floor – then *advance* – move your *pins*, Henrietta! – short step forward with right foot, then left – the body position not being *changed*, Henrietta, you're not *waltzing* here . . . then *lunge!*'

The lesson proceeded, the pace increasing with vigour, and soon the hall was ringing with the clash of steel as the two girls lunged and parried, stamping their feet on the hessian.

At that moment Major Jack Ashley – an old friend of Mortimer Cordiner's, graduate and keen fencer at Trinity

College, Dublin before joining the British army thirty years before – should have been teaching the girls about Pythagoras or the Crusades. But, for all of them, such academic pursuits, in the past few weeks had proved tiresome. And so, after Hetty had shown Major Ashley the rescued foils from Henry's room, they had instead embarked on these happy fencing lessons.

The Ashleys, the Major and his wife Winifred, came from Dublin, but were now near neighbours at Summer Hill – having bought a small Georgian property across the river from Cloone, after he had been seriously wounded in Flanders the previous year. So, invalided out of the Army, and with time on his hands, he rejoiced in these educational – though now more martial – visits, which Mortimer Cordiner had arranged with him, as tutor for the two girls.

The Major came to Summer Hill three times a week, in a governess trap, driven chariot-fashion, with a dangerously frisky cob, tearing up the long drive in a flurry of gravel. The scheme was entirely seemly, for sometimes Mrs Ashley – a charming, if rather faded and put-upon woman – came as well, and tea was served afterwards, with the best Spode and Georgian silver, demanded by Hetty who had developed a taste for all sorts of extravagant gestures. All this was supervised by Pat Kennedy in his finest summer livery.

For, although many of the estate workers and farm hands had long before volunteered for life – and death – in the trenches on the Western front, Pat Kennedy had not done so, concerned as he was with more pressing military matters at home. The leaders of the Easter rising had been executed and the rest, some thousands including Frances, subsequently imprisoned in Britain. But the secret Irish Republican Brotherhood, together with the remnants of its dependent Army, had almost immediately been reactivated. And Pat Kennedy, one of the few senior members of the Brotherhood still at large, now played a considerable part in this reorganization, meeting secretly with other Republican officers from Kilkenny, or down from Dublin, in one or other of the estate cottages in the village or at outlying farms.

Looking through the green baize door at the back of the hall he had watched the girls fencing and was perturbed by these martial arts so skilfully practised. And, later, as he presided over one of the formal teas, he once again noticed Hetty's knowing glance in his direction. Did she know something then? Had her mother told her about him during that week when they were incarcerated together in the College of Surgeons building? Was he at risk from this sword-slashing Amazon?

In the event the threat which Pat Kennedy feared from Hetty came, a few days later, from quite a different source – in the shape of two British detectives from Dublin Castle, arriving in a small motor insolently and unannounced at the front door, where Pat Kennedy admitted them – seeing them for what they were at once, and almost reaching for his revolver, before they asked to see Miss Henrietta Fraser.

Hetty saw them in the drawing room where, equally impertinent, they lolled on the chintz sofa and smoked cigarettes.

'Yes, of course I was with my m-m-mother most of that week in the College of Surgeons,' she stammered at them furiously.

'We had intended to see you earlier about this—'

'That is your affair. But I have *nothing* to hide, and had nothing to do with the whole business anyway, as you well know. Why, exactly, are you here?'

'We have reason to believe,' the older of the two men said, 'good reason to believe that someone, in the immediate locality, even in the house here itself, is closely connected with the rebels, as yet unapprehended. We have to make our investigations . . .'

Pat Kennedy, his ear to the drawing room door outside, listened intently – and was surprised by Hetty's violent response.

'Why, the idea is pre-pre-preposterous! Who could there be in this house? – with most of the men here away at the war. And, besides, have you not done enough damage already? – with your wicked executions! I did not support the rebels, but you begin to make me wish I had!'

Hetty, in her new mood of regal combativeness, was furious. No, she did not support the Republicans, even now, but she was incensed at these British spies as she saw them, these vulgar nosy-parkers, forcing themselves into *her* house, trying to make further mischief. Of course she knew exactly who they were looking for here: Pat Kennedy. But in her new mood – her new role as châtelaine of Summer Hill – she felt a strong loyalty to everyone in the household. These were her people now.

Quite naturally, and without her really being conscious of the transformation, with the advent of these detectives from London, Hetty became anti-British, champion of the Irish underdog. It was not in any way a political conversion; she neither knew nor cared anything for such matters. It was, more simply, a romantic attitude, which she struck that morning against these two commonplace men – one entirely in line with her new dreams of derring-do, in which she would contest every authority which presumed to set itself against that which she meant herself to impose on Summer Hill.

After more questioning, and some uncalled-for advice as to her own safety in the house, she refused the men permission to interview any of the household or estate staff, telling them abruptly to refer any further enquiries in the matter to her cousin and legal adviser, Mortimer Cordiner, the prominent Dublin lawyer, MP at Westminster, and friend of the Prime Minister.

This news of influence on high somewhat chastened the detectives and they left, though still ungraciously, stubbing their cigarettes out on the porch steps. But Hetty was pleased with her victory over them. It greatly encouraged her in the belief that she now controlled her destiny. Immune from all petty outside interference, she, like her mother before her, now felt in supreme command of the great house on the hill.

While, for Pat Kennedy, the events of the morning and

the conversation he had overheard quite altered his view of Hetty. Far from being a threat to him, she appeared to be on the Republican side of things in Ireland. Perhaps, in that long week at the College of Surgeons, her mother had converted her to the cause?

Léonie entirely supported Hetty in her stance against the police spies. She reminded Hetty of what her mother had said to her at the College – how important Irish freedom was. 'How, my being an American, I'd understand all that better than you. Well, perhaps I do – and perhaps you should?'

'Yes, and I think I do now. Something of it, at least. Certainly one can't have vulgar men like those two running our affairs in Ireland.'

And that afternoon, when the Major arrived, Hetty worked off her ire against the two intruders with a most vehement performance – this time, by way of extending her reach, against the Major himself who, standing anchored to the spot, was taken almost to the limits of his skill by her repeated lunges, sparkling ripostes, feints, remises, and devious false attacks.

'Good! Good, good.' The Major, removing his mask, wiped his brow. '*Quite* the champion . . .'

Hetty beamed.

But there were clouds elsewhere, lurking over the summer view. The first seemed hardly a shadow to Hetty, so that Mortimer, when he next came down, had to insist on its gravity. 'The fact is, Hetty, there must be economies here. Your mother has spent most of her Fraser inheritance – and has not run the estate with any profit since she took over. True, with the war, there's a boom in agriculture, but it won't make up the leeway in the farm accounts, or with the bank, where much is mortgaged.'

Hetty was mystified. 'But my Grandmama – I thought she was very wealthy?'

'She may be. But not a penny of hers can be touched – she instituted all sorts of legal restraints on her account, years ago.'

'And the estate rents, the tenanted farms?'

'They don't amount to much. And many can't pay at all now – sons, fathers, dead or still away at the war. O'Donovan, the steward, has spoken to me. There's great poverty, you know, all round here, just beyond the big gates.' He looked at her gravely. 'Of course not, you can't be aware of that – the *real* life of the country here, how very stricken most people are in Ireland, always have been: illness, debt, every sort of aggravation and deprivation over the years. Beyond these walls . . .' He looked round the gracious drawing room. 'Things are very different . . .'

'Oh yes,' Hetty said. 'I know they are *poor*. I've seen our cottages, inside, too—'

'Those are *estate* cottages, Hetty – the people there are well looked after. You must see others, quite different, no comparison . . .'

And Hetty agreed – she would do just that, a proposal much in line with her new interests in local matters. The other cloud, though, she could do little about. As a result of her mother's rebellious activities in Dublin, and the immense publicity attendant on her act of treason there, Summer Hill had become an almost entirely isolated redoubt. Every Protestant and many Catholics in the immediate neighbourhood and county – from shopkeeper to duke – boycotted Summer Hill and all its inhabitants.

The girls first learnt of this ostracism a few days later. Attending a charity bazaar for the war effort in Thomastown, they had wandered down among the row of stalls set up outside the old church in the high street, glancing at the bric-à-brac and garden produce – all in aid of mittens and woolly socks for the troops at the front – when Hetty realized how the greetings she made to neighbours and vague friends of the family, went quite unregarded. She put this down to mere preoccupation on the part of these county gentry – until she stopped at Mrs Morton's stall, the Mortons of Castleton Hall, the big house of the area, just a mile out of the town, where Mrs Morton, a vigorous, horse-faced Englishwoman, in an ill-cut and unsuitably heavy tweed suit, with a Kitchener brooch prominent in her lapel and a Union Jack over the stall, was selling pots of last year's rather mouldy jam and chutney, together with a variety of home-made sweets and barley sugar twirls.

Hetty fingered a jar of discoloured chutney, thinking not to purchase it. But Mrs Morton, at her most cutting and supercilious, immediately broke in. 'I should be obliged if you would put that down at once. We do *not* sell to rebels here.'

Hetty was so startled she nearly dropped the jar. 'Rebels?'

But Mrs Morton had turned away, searching out her husband, the old Brigadier-General close by, who approached the girls now. 'I'm amazed you have the impudence to show your face here,' he told Hetty – whose face coloured quickly in rage and embarrassment. The General helped himself to the fruits of victory, picking a barley sugar stick from the stall, and the girls left immediately. But Hetty, in her fury, soon recovered, walking head-high back through the row of stalls, where everything had come to a stop now, the prim, self-satisfied, arrogant Protestant community gazing askance at the two girls, who more than held their own in this retreat, looking straight ahead with regal unconcern.

So, apart from the Ashleys' visits, the girls experienced no social life whatsoever that summer – and, even had they been able to, with Mortimer's new economic stringencies there would have been barely the money to support any merrymaking.

The girls were nearly paupers and certainly outcasts. And this state of affairs enraged Hetty, encouraging her all the more in her support of the local people – small tenant farmers, labourers, the real Irish Mortimer had mentioned, whose mean farmsteads and cottages she and Léonie took to visiting and where Hetty, as Frances Fraser's daughter among these Republican sympathizers, was made very welcome.

Here, indeed, she was appalled by what she found. In one cottage, with part of the sodden thatch blown away, on the wilder slopes of Mount Brandon, the girls came upon an emaciated, flushed-faced young woman, not yet thirty, but already widowed and with seven children and an elder brother to support – all of them living in utter squalor, a pig in the parlour, a handkerchief of potato land outside the back door, the children half-naked, filthy, some bow-legged with rickets and open sores, grovelling amidst the pig's feed, a mess of damp peelings and cabbage stalks; the brother, old before his time, a useless figure huddled over a barely smouldering turf fire in the dark, smoke-filled room, a man with a hacking tubercular cough, blood smears on his stubbled chin.

The girls, horrified by the evidence of these trips, did what they could to help, securing medical attention, bringing a little money or parcels of food; but it was all a mere drop in the ocean of this dreadful rural misery.

'And to think of all these rich people sitting in their big houses, helping British troops, but not lifting a finger for their own people, and treating *us* like pariah dogs – it's too much!' Hetty stormed one afternoon as she and Léonie drove back in the trap from a particularly unhappy visit.

'Yes, but what can we really do?'

'Well,' Hetty said, a hard look coming into her eyes, 'these wretched people shall have *more* money and food parcels. And the others, those rich fools, will supply it. Kill two birds! That's what we'll do!'

'How do you mean?' Léonie gazed at her, already excited by Hetty's apparently sure and certain answer to any problem.

'Look!' Hetty pored over the large-scale ordnance survey map of the county later that evening in the library. 'There's lots of big houses – all within easy riding distance of here. Castleton Hall, Brownsbarn, Dangan Mill, Flood Hall . . . Some I know anyway, been there as a child – but we could scout them out beforehand.'

'Riding distance?' Léonie was perplexed.

'Why yes! At night.'

'But what for?'

'To *rob* them of course, you ninny!'

'Of what?'

'Anything we can find – money, silver, jewellery . . .'

Léonie considered the matter, trying to hide her complete surprise. 'But, Hetty . . .' she said at last.

'Why not? They deserve no better. Besides, it'd be great fun. Are you a coward?'

'No!' Léonie said, only half-truthfully.

'So! – "Fortune Favours the Brave".'

'And . . . and if we're caught?'

'We won't be. We'll go over the places first, carefully, in the daylight.'

'But how? You'll be recognized – and everyone absolutely hates us round here anyway.'

'Disguises! We can disguise ourselves – that theatrical stuff here, all those costumes and things in the wicker baskets up in the attics. It'll be tremendous fun!'

Léonie smiled, rather weakly. But then, unwilling to be left behind in any escapade of Hetty's, she agreed. 'Yes,' she said airily. 'Yes, it might be fun.'

'And here's the first place we'll pay a visit to!' Hetty said, happy revenge ringing in her voice. 'Those frightful Mortons.' And she settled her finger on Castleton Hall, seat of this very wealthy English family, whose neo-Gothic pile lay on a rise, amidst extensive parkland, overlooking the river some five miles up-stream from Summer Hill.

It was, however, a place which Hetty had never visited, so that the house and grounds would have to be scouted out first. The annual cricket match, the Hall versus the estate, due to take place there the following week, would give them the opportunity to both see the lie of things and test the efficacy of their disguises.

'What shall we go as?'

'Not two girls anyway. Man and wife?'

'Hardly, we'll look too young.'

'Well, I'll have to go as your beau then – I'm the taller,' Hetty said decisively. 'And you'll be my sweet young thing!'

The two girls were agog as they discussed their plan up in the attic, picking through the great wicker hampers of theatrical stuff. 'But this is all pretty useless,' Léonie said, lifting out a pile of eighteenth-century tricorn hats together with some braided, gilt-buttoned French military jackets. 'It's not a fancy dress ball, is it?'

They left the old costumes, taking with them only a kit of theatrical make-up. Downstairs, they ransacked two big wardrobes, which still contained many of Hetty's uncles' old clothes, and laid out their selection on the floor of Hetty's bedroom.

There were evening and morning dress, town and country suits of every kind – in serge, tweed, worsted, and fine tropical linen. But what was most obviously required, Hetty decided, was the check Norfolk jacket and knicker-bockers, tweed cap, soft-collared shirt, woollen tie, long grey socks and leather brogues – a country expedition out-fit of her uncle Henry's in light cloth, smartly cut, still quite fashionable.

'So?' Léonie asked, fascinated. 'What's the idea? Who are we?'

'We're down from Dublin – take our bicycles, and I can have Henry's old plate camera: doing a summer bicycling tour, taking photographs. Easy!' She started to undress, seeing how the clothes would fit, pushing her legs into the knickerbockers first; they flapped about her calves, until she got the long socks on, and belted the waist. Then she tried the Norfolk jacket. It was almost too small when she buttoned it up, so that her breasts protruded.

'You'll have to flatten yourself there,' Léonie advised her. Hetty took her vest off, standing white-skinned in front of the mirror, while Léonie twisted a narrow linen towel round her chest and pinned it at the back. 'That's better!' Hetty put the jacket back on. 'The trousers need a few tucks in the seams – too baggy – and a bit of shorten-ing. Otherwise, it's marvellous!'

'Yes – even the shoes don't pinch!'

Hetty gazed at herself, full-length, in the big mirror, Léonie behind her, smiling. 'Now the cap!' She set it on her head. 'Your hair – that's the only thing.' Hetty tried to push the fluffy dark locks up inside. 'Have to trim it – and pin it. Give me the scissors.'

Hetty sat down at the dressing table and in ten minutes Léonie had amended her coiffure, brushing the remaining strands sharply up and securing them with a grip. 'There – perfect!' She put the hat back on. 'Now for the make-up – don't quite know about that . . .'

'Here, I'll do it – did it for fancy dress, charades and things here in the old days.' Hetty took the kit and with a Leichner kohl pencil exaggerated her eyebrows . . . then with a powder puff and a box of Crystalessence Talc Shadow she darkened her complexion to a dusty bronze tint. Finally, lighting one of the Abdullah cigarettes she and Léonie sometimes secretly smoked, she stood up and, hands in pockets, strolled about the room meditatively, rocking on the balls of her feet.

'The walk! – it's just right. Just like a man!' Léonie roared with laughter at the transformation. Then, as Hetty stopped by the fireplace, put one arm on the mantelpiece, crossed her legs casually, and looked provocatively at her, Léonie was suddenly serious, stricken in her expression. 'Oh no, Hetty . . .' She rushed over to her. 'You shouldn't – you're too handsome by half!' And she kissed her then – so hard that her own face was smeared when she withdrew, breathless. 'Incredible . . .' she murmured.

And, indeed, Hetty was quite a sight. Masculinity became her. She was a young man now, eighteen or nineteen, a beau most certainly. But there was iron in this dandy: her blue eyes, shadowed by the kohl pencil, glowering down over the ruler-straight nose, the lips supercilious as she compressed them, all this giving her a tigerish air. Her beauty, which at other times could so easily become soft and pliant, had everywhere sharpened and hardened now. She had totally taken on the male role – not only the clothes, but the spirit, too.

It was a fine June day, with a high blue sky and puffy clouds over Mount Brandon. The cricket ground below the red-bricked mansion, overlooking a bend in the river, was circled at various points by leafy chestnut trees, benches of spectators, a striped marquee; cream-clad, tie-belted players made strange patterns in the centre of the greensward, the thunk of leather on wood reverberated in the hot afternoon, followed every now and then by polite applause.

The girls, leaving their bicycles behind the tent, and Hetty with Henry's old tripod plate camera, wandered along the boundary, before taking up a position near the house, setting the camera up, pointing out towards the game.

But then, before they had even begun to establish themselves or their act, a whiskery, red-faced, elderly gentleman approached: Brigadier-General Morton himself. He was eating something again, jaws champing ruminatively, before he noticed them.

'I say!' He admired the camera – by way of more readily admiring, and approaching, Léonie, in bicycling bloomers and a faded poppy-coloured linen jacket. 'That's an old Fox-Talbot, isn't it?' He bent down, inspecting Hetty's camera. 'No shutter – how do you manage to take moving pictures with it?' His eyes strayed from the camera to Léonie's bloomers.

'Oh, I don't worry about that!' Hetty told him, in a throttled voice. 'Just press the button.' And she bent down then, starting to fiddle with the platé camera.

'But, my dear chap – it's a plate camera. It has no button!' he told her, rather irascibly.

'Well, you know, I'm not actually ve-ve-very well up on it all. My grandfather's . . .' Hetty was starting to panic, so that Léonie interjected, flirtatiously.

'What a lovely place you have here!' She ogled the General who at once ceased his interest in the camera. 'Really so beautiful – and the house!' Léonie looked towards the ugly Victorian pile. 'Really lovely! – those stepped gables and corner turrets . . .'

'Indeed!' The old fool beamed. 'Glad you like it.' He held his hand out. 'Morton,' he said. 'General Morton,' he went on, glancing at Hetty, so that she suddenly had to make a response.

'Oh, I am sorry! – this is my friend, Miss Amelia

French. And I'm Cole – Horace Cole, from Dublin. We're on a cycling tour.'

'Not at the war then?' the General said, only half-jocularly, to Hetty. But Hetty had prepared herself for just such an eventuality, taking off the spectacles with which she had supplied herself. 'Afraid not . . . wish I was . . . but these glasses, you see . . . can't see a thing without them!'

'Dear me, well never mind – most *pleasant* to see you both.' His gaze returned to Léonie. 'I'd be honoured – show you round the place, take tea with us later in the marquee – and perhaps I might offer you a little barley sugar meanwhile? I'm afraid I have a wicked taste for it myself.'

'No, no, thank you!' Léonie declined, at her most winning now. 'But would you, though – would you ever? – I should so like to see the house itself. I do so admire the Gothic revival!'

'Why, of course, Miss French – no relation of our former Commander in Chief, are you? I should be only too delighted!'

They left the cricket ground and, crossing the pleasure gardens, entered the drawing room by way of the open windows. Two big black labradors were fast asleep, and remained so until the General roared at them, 'Out! – out, I say – not allowed in here, you brutes!' They had not much to fear from the dogs in the house, Hetty thought, as she glanced round the room. There were some dull pictures, all in a hunting or military vein, and a number of tasteless items set in a clutter on tables and mantelpiece: silver cigarette boxes, china horses, miniature brass cannon – nothing of real value.

'Now, look here,' the General said to Léonie, taking her arm purposefully. 'Come to the library first and let me show you the original plans of the house – *most* interesting.'

They trooped out of the drawing room, across the hall, filled with hunting trophies, down a passageway and into a smaller, darker room, containing few books but with a quantity of popular magazines on a mahogany drum table by the window. 'Yes, we have a number of *very* interesting bits and pieces here – house was designed by Deane and Woodward, the Cork architects, y'know – disciples of Pugin, the House of Commons fellow.'

And then, to the delight of the girls, he took a key from the third drawer down in a small bureau and opened up a big, metal-doored, walk-in safe, behind a curtain in one corner of the room. Following him enthusiastically, they peered inside as he sorted through a number of rolled papers, no doubt architects' plans. But there were many boxes inside as well – tin deed boxes, boxes for silver, jewel boxes, perhaps just money boxes. It hardly mattered, Hetty thought: there were undoubtedly valuable things there. She smiled knowingly at Léonie.

'Now, here we are!' The General extracted a selection of scrolls, bringing them over to the table and unrolling them. Hetty, meanwhile, had wandered over to the windows, one of them half-open in the heat.

They gave out to the side of the building – on to a narrow gravel path, backed by a dark yew hedge, which led round from the front of the house to the lawns overlooking the river. She inspected the window fittings. The usual brass sliding catch, open now, was the only security.

'Now, see this,' the General said proudly, scanning the papers, as if preparing for battle. 'The *original* plans – before we had them amended of course – and then what they came up with! Much more appropriate!'

He displayed the two plans, side by side, as Hetty joined them at the table. One plan was no better than the other, she thought, both seeming even uglier than the house itself.

Pleading the late hour, and the long ride they still had to make to Kilkenny, the girls excused themselves from the cricket tea in the marquee and left soon afterwards, much to the chagrin of the General, who blustered about as they prepared to leave – offering them sugary sustenance for the journey, gazing longingly at Léonie's bloomers as the girls disappeared down the back drive.

'Almost too easy,' Hetty said, as they changed into their

ordinary clothes in a ruined stone barn near Summer Hill. 'All on a plate – knowing where that big safe is *and* the key – and the two dogs as dozy as anything. All we need now is to practise some more night riding – and wait for a moonlit sky!'

And this they did, taking out Hetty's chestnut mare Cinderella and the black gelding Finnegan, which Léonie had always ridden on her visits to Summer Hill: racing each other out along the monkey puzzle alley in the long twilights, then beneath the great overhanging beech trees, which led away into the woods to the south of the house.

They were reasonably accomplished horsewomen already. But during the next week they steeled themselves in practice, riding everywhere about the estate and district – taking the horses out at dawn, just after sun-up, galloping over the water meadows by the river; in the afternoons roving up the gorse-covered slopes towards Mount Brandon; in the evenings going cross-country north to Castleton Hall, planning their route there, so that soon they felt entirely fitted to the task. There was but one matter, Hetty thought – the matter of further disguise . . .

'After all, we don't want to be recognized on the horses, or if they have a lamp or something, suddenly in the house.'

Léonie smiled, pleased to be able to initiate something in the adventure. 'Remember those French Musketeer costumes – the braided military jackets and tricorn hats, up in the attics? Why not be hung for a sheep as a lamb!'

Hetty was charmed. 'Why, of course! – with *masks*, Léa, and foils in our belts!' They shivered with laughter.

Trying on the eighteenth-century theatrical costumes – the dark pantaloons, braided maroon jackets, frilly, open-necked shirts, soft leather boots, and velvet eye masks with elastic bands which they made – they found the disguises perfect.

'Tomorrow then – if the moon is right!'

'It's due full then – or the day after . . .'

*

It was late in June, midsummer's eve, in fact, with twilight until nearly eleven o'clock, the girls knew, as they led the horses silently out of the stable yard, taking them well down the back drive northwards, before mounting and riding off to the ruined barn where they had already left their costumes.

Half an hour later, with a luminous pearl-pink sky showing above the western horizon, they changed their clothes, then each smoked an Abdullah cigarette, waiting for darkness to come. Towards midnight, with just the faintest tinge of pink in the sky now, the moon came up over the hills to the east, a watery pale orb, not over-bright, glazed by high-running clouds, ideal – enough to see their way by, but not easily be seen.

They settled their masks, shook hands, mounted their horses. 'Fortune Favours the Brave!' Hetty said. Though at that moment neither of them felt truly brave at all. A night bird called out, startling them, as they moved off towards the Hall.

As they had carefully planned and travelled their route – so as to avoid moving along the Thomastown road – keeping to the fields or beside the river, all went well until, crossing this main road, they were suddenly confronted, not twenty yards away, by the bright beam of an acetylene bicycle lamp, wavering at them through the soft-lit darkness, as someone rode straight towards them.

Hetty was caught in the lamplight for a long instant – and Cinderella, startled by the dazzle, reared momentarily. But the bicyclist, confronted by this masked and costumed horsewoman, was far more startled. His machine went into a spin, mounted the ditch, and ended in the bushes; the rider, leaving it there, running quickly down the road away from this ghostly vision.

The girls continued. By one o'clock they had arrived by the dark line of chestnut trees which bordered the cricket ground below Castleton Hall. Here, they tethered the horses to a fence, skirted the field, and soon mounted the steps into the pleasure gardens.

The house, unlit and silent, was just a vague silhouette

in the faint moonlight, an eerie castle now, as high clouds scudded across the silver moon.

Tiptoeing over the lawn and round to the side of the house, they came to the yew hedge and the two library windows, some five feet above the gravel path. Hetty had brought a small electric torch and a thin-bladed kitchen knife. Helped up on to the sill and supported there by Léonie, she pushed the knife up in the minute gap between the two sashes, making contact with the sliding brass catch. Then she moved the blade gently, and the catch sprang back, suddenly, with a sharp noise.

They stayed as they were, petrified – Hetty poised dangerously on the sill, Léonie struggling under her weight – for what seemed like minutes on end, listening to the soft wind in the yew hedge behind them. But nothing else stirred.

Hetty, cheek pressed against the glass, began very gradually to bring pressure on the sash. After a minute it slid up easily. Once inside the room, pushing the curtains aside so that the space was faintly lit, they found the key in the drawer, pulled the other curtain aside and opened the walk-in safe. Hetty undid the first of the big leather jewel boxes and peered inside.

It was filled with neatly packed sticks of barley sugar.

And so were all the other jewel and deed and cutlery boxes, as Hetty opened them, one after the other, in frustrated disbelief: packed with sweets of every kind, an Aladdin's cave of sugary delights – nougat, marzipan, toffee, fruit bonbons, Swiss chocolates, bullseyes, mint humbugs, Turkish delight, and whole wooden cases, like ammunition boxes, bought in bulk and stacked on the lower shelves, of 'Army and Navy Stores Best Liqueur Chocolate Selection'.

Hetty, her face distraught in the torchlight, could have cried. Léonie could barely restrain her muffled laughter.

9

'Why don't we just drop it?' Léonie said, annoyed now at Hetty's insistence. 'We weren't caught – put everything back in place in the library – but we *will* be, if we go on with it.'

'Coward!' Hetty spat at her, in her most vindictive mood. 'Where's all your "Fortune favours the brave" now?'

'It's not brave – when you're just stealing things.'

'Wasn't for us! That poor woman, remember? – up in the mountains, coughing blood.'

'Oh, Hetty, be honest. Pretending we're Robin Hood or someone – and we're not. We did it just for fun . . .'

'But it was *such* fun!' Hetty turned suddenly, almost pleading now, making a last effort to take Léonie with her, persuade her to continue with these wild adventures.

But Léonie, older and wiser, and exposing this part of her temperament almost for the first time with Hetty, was not to be dissuaded. 'Yes,' she sighed. 'It was such fun. But the trouble is, Hetty, you're really so *serious* about it all, at heart: not finding anything there, except all those candies – you were furious!'

The girls, one morning a few days later in Hetty's bedroom, with a fresh selection of men's clothes and costumes laid out everywhere, considering another foray, were arguing.

'But of *course* I'm serious,' Hetty fumed. 'All those poor people—'

'Hetty, that's nonsense! It's just theft. And we have money now anyhow, with those dollars Papa has just sent me. We can spend some of that on the cottagers – and there's plenty of food and things here in the house to give them. But if we go on with this burglary thing we'll just be caught and end up in jail, like your Mama, and that'll ruin *everything* for us here, don't you see?'

'Perhaps . . .' Hetty was still not at all convinced.

Though what really annoyed her was her failure to persuade – to dominate – Léonie in the matter.

'And besides,' Léonie went on, sensing this very factor in Hetty's intransigence and trying to placate her. 'There's plenty of other *ordinary* forbidden things to do – where it won't matter if we're caught.'

Léonie tried to join the mundane and the illicit as a working proposition for them. But Hetty saw the contradiction at once. 'Léa, there can't be real fun, unless the things are *extra*ordinary and one *might* be sent to jail for them! That's the whole point—'

'That's just childish. There's lots of other things . . .' But she wasn't sure now what these might be, fingering one of Uncle Henry's linen tropical suits by her chair abstractedly.

'*What* is there?' Hetty rounded on her. 'What can we do? We can't go out anywhere, see people, no social life at all.'

'New people then – new things!' Léonie, seeing how she must make amends in some way for her apparent loss of nerve by offering some fresh diversion, suddenly stood up and taking the tropical linen jacket she went over and held it against Hetty's chest. 'See! It should fit perfectly – we could go into Kilkenny, another bicycling act! – or something?' But Hetty was not to be moved. 'Oh, Hetty, you're so revengeful – relax! You're not giving yourself time to *see* things.'

'Revengeful? Just I hate all these prissy neighbours—'

'Yes, but who *cares* about them? Just let them be. We don't have to fight them, enough wars on now as it is.'

'Perhaps.' Hetty was sullen, still unconvinced, moving away now, walking up and down the bedroom through the shafts of morning sunlight, a caged tiger.

'You're so *restless*, Hetty.'

Léonie was at a loss. But she somehow sensed the real reason for Hetty's restlessness: it was a frustration, not for theft, but of desire. And she sensed, too, how for every moment's inaction in this sun-filled room, the greater the risk was of her losing Hetty, losing her trust, her love.

So, suddenly deciding on something, she picked up the linen tropical suit, took it over to Hetty's bed, and started to undress, climbing out of her long skirt, taking her blouse off, then getting into the new clothes, the jacket and trousers. Hetty, sulking over the other side of the room, fiddling with the snow-dome, surreptitiously glanced over at her friend. But for Léonie, smaller than Hetty, the clothes fitted very much less well. She stood in front of the mirror then, flapping her hands, the jacket cuffs down by her fingers, like a clown.

'You're a fright,' Hetty told her at last, smiling unwillingly.

'Yes.'

'Here, let me try them on.'

Hetty had been tempted, just as Léonie had intended. Léonie undressed again, as Hetty did the same, putting on the linen suit instead. It fitted her very well.

'See, I told you!' Léonie said, standing behind Hetty as she faced the long mirror. 'Now try the shirt and smart striped tie on,' she said, going back to the bed for these additions, before turning again. 'Do it properly! You'll have to take off your vest . . .'

Hetty, encouraged in this charade, half happy again with a tingling feeling of excitement in her stomach, took off the jacket, crossing her arms over then, about to pull off her vest, where it was stuck down into the trousers.

Léonie was behind her once more with the shirt. 'Here – let me.' She undid the belt then, and the trousers fell to the floor about Hetty's bare ankles. Then Léonie pulled her vest up and off from behind, so that Hetty stood there now, her small pointed breasts bare in the sunlight, just in her knickers, with Léonie, only slightly more covered, holding the man's shirt, looking over her shoulder, both facing the mirror.

Léonie smiled into the glass, unbuttoning the shirt meanwhile. Hetty stretched her arms out and back and Léonie pulled the first sleeve on, then the second and Hetty brought her arms to the front then, while Léonie, encircling her chest, did the buttons up again at the front.

But as she did so, starting at the collar, and moving down, her hands, in their fiddle, touched Hetty's breast for an instant. There was a moment's pause, as if this touch might have been a mere accident.

But it wasn't. And there could be no doubt then, a sudden electric charge coursed through them both, a surge of long dammed physical emotion, as Léonie, decisive now and turning Hetty towards her, quickly undid all her handiwork with the man's shirt, taking it off, and embracing her then as they stood by the mirror, kissing her – cheek, chin, neck, breasts.

'Hetty, Hetty – dearest Hetty . . .'

Hetty, giving rein then to that dominant, possessive instinct she had first felt for Léonie weeks before, and soon frustrated by the immobility enforced on them by standing glued together, became almost violent in her attentions, clawing at Léonie desperately, so that Léonie, pulling apart, took her by the hand, over to the big canopied double bed and they lay on the soft eiderdown then, in the sunlight, resuming their love.

'Oh, I so want to hold you close – and yet look at you and *see* you!' Hetty said, shaking her head in wonder.

'Yes!' Léonie gasped now. 'I too – I do, too – just that. Oh, why so long, so long! – to love you like this?—'

'We didn't know—'

'We did! – we must have done!'

Léonie put her hand to Hetty's waist, searching out the buttons on the knickers there, undoing them, then slipping her fingers between the lace and the hip bone, running a finger down her groin, touching her at last in the centre, where Hetty felt her hand like a warm knife moving gently between her legs – moving imperceptibly, gradually.

'Goodness – oh goodness! . . .' Hetty bit her lip, swaying her hips to and fro in the pleasure of Léonie's touch, her own fingers, in just the same way, searching out and finding just the same places in her lover's body.

But then, frustrated again, Hetty almost shouted, 'Oh these wretched bits and pieces, Léa!' And she grappled with the buttons at Léonie's waist – until, almost tearing the fabric away, they ridded themselves of these final flimsy vestiges between them and returned to each other, holding each other, all over, length to length, top to toe, in repeated rising paroxysms – an unbelievable happiness and excitement soon overcoming them.

All their frustrations were over now. They no longer had to hide their need both freely to love or possess each other. This they could do by turns now, see-saw fashion, returning to a balance in the breathless pauses.

If Léonie had taken the initial steps, they seduced each other then, so willingly and well, in scorching fires of rising excitement, learning as they went along, tutored by their nature, finding their roles by sixth sense; Hetty dominant, Léonie pliant, then vice versa, as they embarked that morning – only at the beginning then – on a pleasure they already sensed could end only in something utterly sweet and tempestuous.

So, revelling in the ecstasy, they egged each other on until, goaded beyond endurance, Léonie was first to give in – suddenly arching away from Hetty, becoming rigid, gulping air rapidly, then holding her breath for long seconds, before gasping, stretching, twisting herself violently, eyes tight shut as if in pain – when suddenly, crying out, a feeling of incredible joy burst everywhere through her body, which had no weight now, where she was rising, falling, shuddering in this great flood of fire, suspended in some dark, star-shooting ether.

Falling back, and burying her head in Hetty's breasts, she could say nothing, so drained was she, only convulse in sobs, where Hetty felt Léonie's tears then, as she gradually calmed beside her, moist drops tickling her stomach.

And later, in the same great calm they both shared then, they were equally happy, yet unbelieving somehow, frightened almost, in realizing how they had just now so confirmed their love, yet at the same time had altered it, deepened it, out of all recognition.

Here, certainly, Hetty thought, was no ordinary excitement – something miles beyond mere fun. Was it then wicked? No, such love could not be that. Yet she sensed none the less it was something they should not be caught at. There was a contradiction here which she didn't quite understand.

Robert, down for the summer holidays with his friend Bertie, looked at the girls over the dining room table at luncheon. 'Mean to say you don't *know* about our great push to the Somme?' he asked Hetty in astonishment. 'Started just this month and we took Delville Wood just last week—'

'Oh, Robert, you are such a bore! We don't read the paper down here – much better things to do.'

Robert, who at St Columba's had a map of the Western front, with variously coloured flag pins, attached under his desk lid, where he plotted the course of the war, was dismissive. 'Well you *should* take an interest in it then. It'll be all our bad luck – yours too – if we lose!'

'Well, we *don't* take an interest.' She looked at Léonie for confirmation. But it was not forthcoming. 'Anyway,' she went on, 'you can talk to Major Ashley about it all, next time he comes, till you're blue in the face.'

'Yes, you've taken up fencing . . .' Robert was surprised, almost admiring now.

'And we're splendid at it. But that won't win the war for us, will it?'

Léonie finally spoke. 'Perhaps we *should* take a bit more interest in it all, Hetty. At least, I should, with Mama and Papa in Paris, almost in the middle of it.' She looked at Robert sympathetically. 'Tell us what's happening.'

'Well, Pozières is one of the next main objectives – show you on the map after lunch!' He turned to Léonie enthusiastically, as a tiny *frisson* of division came between the two girls.

'What do you think?' Robert asked Bertie that afternoon; they were out in their waders, upstream from the boathouse, fishing for salmon.

'Of what?' Bertie, quite motionless, had his eye on a

deep black pool, where his dry fly lay, on the far side of the river.

'Of the girls.'

'Hadn't really thought.' Bertie adjusted his spectacles. '*Must* be a fish there.' The heat was just beginning to die above the river. Soon the fish would surely start to rise. 'Try a wet fly, do you think?' Bertie enquired.

'No, I meant – just wondered what you made of them both.'

'Not very well educated,' Bertie said laconically. He was a youth of few words.

'They're extraordinary, though, in other ways – all that fencing they do, yesterday with the Major.'

'Oh, some girls do things like that nowadays – all to do with the suffragette movement,' he said dismissively.

'Might take up the foils myself . . .' Robert, pretending indifference in the matter, tested his friend's reaction.

'Oh, I shouldn't – look bad, just pandering to them.'

'Yes, perhaps. They are strange though.'

'But you've known Hetty for years, haven't you? – practically your sister.'

'Yes. But I don't really know her.'

'Told you – they're young suffragettes. Very common now. Lot of nonsense.'

Just then the girls themselves came into sight, emerging on the river bank from the steep fall of trees, making for the boathouse downstream, with towels and bathing costumes.

Léonie stopped and waved. 'We're swimming! Coming too?'

'Do wish she wouldn't shout like that,' Bertie muttered. 'Frighten the fish.'

But Robert, rather eager to see the girls bathe, moved slowly downstream as he fished during the next ten minutes, so that finally he was within fifty yards of them as Léonie swam off the wooden jetty, splashing about in the water in her long black woollen costume, almost down to the knees, sticking to the skin in a wet, exciting way.

Léonie waved again. But Hetty, sitting on the jetty,

took no notice – which upset him briefly, a tinge of hurt mixed with desire, as he watched her legs in the water. Yes, he thought, she really looked very fine, black moist curls glistening in the sunlight – and really so sporting: fencing – and swimming like that in the river, where no other girls would ever dare! One only swam in the sea.

But she ignored him, untouchable, unobtainable, that was the problem. He could not admit to anyone – hardly even to himself – that he loved her. She dived into the stream then, disappearing, and Robert, rather ashamed of prying, moved back upstream.

The girls, frolicking underwater, could see each other in the clear flow above a patch of silvery stones. Swirling and twining about, bodies glancing, hands touching, they seemed to dance together.

Hetty, watching Léonie – the more expert swimmer – twist and dive so sinuously, noticed how all her usual grace and elasticity was wonderfully released and exaggerated now as she somersaulted in this free-floating element: the sharply narrowing waist, arching back, long kicking legs, the tight bodice of the costume flattening, sweeping over, her firm breasts.

And then, jealous of Léonie's graceful athleticism – and just for the rebellious excitement of it, wanting to taunt and compete with her – Hetty, most of her body still underwater, started to pull her bathing costume off, tugging at the shoulders, grabbing the material away as she trod water, before finally kicking herself out of the rest of it, laughing at her friend . . . then suddenly diving away, a naked Ondine, into the silvery depths.

Léonie saw her in a new light then, as Hetty swooped and fell, trailing bubbles, in these green shallows – her body almost ethereal, so volatile and fancy free that it could not be described, possessed indeed, in any earth-bound manner. And she was jealous of the stream which so confidently embraced Hetty, but divided them, kept them in worlds apart. She longed for Hetty then.

Yes, how much she *valued* every twist and turn in this sensuous body, the lovely ease Hetty displayed, embracing this watery element even more fluently than Léonie herself had been caressed by her in the last weeks. Quite simply, Léonie felt, she adored her. She opened her lips, mouthing the words, 'Je t'aime!' But only clouds of bubbles rose – as both of them, breathless, shot to the surface before returning to the crystal-green shadow-world beneath.

And it was then that Hetty, playing some game, or genuinely caught in the current, her hair trailing out like river weed behind her, began to drift downstream, slipping away from Léonie, her body motionless now as the current took her.

Léonie felt a nightmare surge of horror cutting her to the heart: Hetty was leaving her, a water sprite, her time among mortals over, disappearing now, for ever, back to some cavernous kingdom in the sea . . .

'Come back!' Léonie clawed after her, trying to reach out and pull her back. Out of breath, she rose to the surface, only to see Hetty rocket into the air a few seconds later, smiling broadly.

'You mustn't do that!' Léonie bellowed at her. 'You frightened me – you really did! Thought you were drowning.'

'Oh, Léa, I never meant to—'

'But you did – and you mustn't!' She swam over to her. 'Hetty!' She took her face in her hands. 'You mustn't *ever* leave me like that!'

Later, with her costume restored, sitting on the jetty, and seeing Léonie glance at the boys upstream, Hetty said acidly, 'You do rather go out of your way with Robert.' She had noticed Léonie's vague attentions to him before and was more than a little jealous.

'Oh, Hetty, it's just because you're so . . . well, cold to him, ignoring him.'

'No, it's not – it's just that *you* like him! I can see it.'

'I do like him. Shouldn't I?' Hetty did not reply, lifting her knees right up, drying her toes, then inspecting them carefully, splaying them out. 'You think I shouldn't?'

'Oh, he's such a tease and a bore,' Hetty said at last.

'Not to me he isn't. And, with you, he only does it because he's fond of you – *I* can see that.'

'But I'm too fond of you, for that – for you to think of him,' she said in a low voice.

Léonie touched her arm then. 'Yes, and so am I – of you. But one can just *like* other people as well . . . surely? And our being so happy makes that all the easier, doesn't it?'

'No, I like you *so* much,' Hetty said softly. 'I d-d-don't like you liking other people.' She stammered now, something she had almost entirely ceased to do with Léonie.

'Yes, but I like . . . I love you, Hetty,' Léonie reassured her.

'What do you *really* like in me – and hate?' Hetty took Léonie by surprise with her vehemence, as if her life depended on the answer.

'I don't know – I like everything.' Léonie avoided the second part of the question.

'But *what* – and why?'

'Well, your courage, I think—'

'But you think that just foolhardiness.'

'Sometimes. But, when you're sensible with it, it's marvellous—'

'You can't be sensible *and* courageous!'

'You can! But . . .'

'But what?'

'Depends what it is. Some things aren't worth doing at all. Yet you push and shove and insist on them.'

'I want to be *different* people all the time,' Hetty was more pensive now. 'That's why I push and shove at things.'

'Why not just be *yourself*?'

'But who is that?'

'It's you, you ninny! And, when you're that, you're wonderful. It's just . . .'

'Go on!'

'When you're all those other people – sometimes it worries me. That I don't know you somehow.'

'And that's what you hate in me . . .'

'No, don't hate it. Just don't quite understand – why you want to be someone else. That restlessness, when you have so much in *yourself*.'

The warmth was fading, with hints of twilight.

'Yes, you're so calm,' Hetty said admiringly. 'But what am I? *Who* am I?' she asked then, looking over the river.

'Who or whose? . . . You are mine and I am yours!' Léonie said lightly, finding that her reply had turned into a little couplet. She smiled at her success, looking at Hetty, who had pulled a splinter from the wooden jetty, throwing it out and watching it twirl away in the stream.

'"And when I die in the long green grass
Death will be but a pause.
For the love that I have is all that I have,
Is yours and yours and yours."

I like that poem,' Hetty added, much brighter now. 'Almost my favourite.'

They left the jetty then, going inside the boathouse to change. 'Shall we watch them fish?' Hetty asked, in possession of a real identity for the moment, apparently at ease in the idea that, with their own secure love, they could share their affection – with the two boys, with anyone.

'Yes, let's!' And Léonie kissed her then as they dressed, a tinge of passion rising with the gesture. But she had to repress it, she did not want to upset the balance of calm reason which she felt she had brought to Hetty in the previous minutes.

Léonie sensed then, so clearly, how she had the gift, the knack, the spirit – something, whatever it was – to change this girl's life: she could make her happy. And yet this wisdom brought with it another quite opposite and sad intuition: that she might only be able to share this content with one part of Hetty, whereas there were so many other parts to her, which she could not help her in – roles which this wayward, seemingly orphaned girl had not yet lived.

Living with her, loving her, Léonie felt, was so precious because what thrilled her most in Hetty was what most eluded her: her mystery, lack of identity, what she was not, the person she could become, when she might lose her. And these were things she could not tell her, for it was ridiculous – so to cross bridges before one came to them.

Léonie, in this love, had found herself wonderfully released – in body, but just as much in spirit. She felt a lightness in her life now – a glorious spreading fertility, a quickening sense of God-like certainty and confidence: she could do, she could create, anything. And she wanted these feelings, which Hetty alone provoked, to spread and grow, find anchors in the future. Yet she feared loss in that future. She wanted, in short, to guarantee Hetty's life with her for ever. That was the problem.

Léonie, in the light of the four candles they held, could see the quick shadows of the bats as they dipped and swerved above them in the moist dark air of the caves. She bowed her head, put her free hand up, alarmed at the idea that these animals might suddenly tangle in her hair.

'Here! – we're up here!' Hetty's voice echoed deeply. Léonie with Bertie, some way behind the others, could only just see the wavering candle flame ahead of them, at the top of a rock slope, where Robert and Hetty had stopped at the beginning end of one of the long cave galleries.

Catching up with them, all four standing together with their flickering candles, they found themselves confronted by a solid wall of shiny limestone, a dead end. But Hetty, with her electric torch, illuminated a column of great boulders above and to their right, with a vague opening at the top, forming an almost sheer ascent into another hidden gallery.

'Oh, let's not bother,' Léonie said, realizing this was the worst thing to say as Hetty immediately started to clamber up the narrow aperture above them.

They had made an expedition, with a picnic, in the trap, north of Kilkenny town, to the caves of Dunmore – a great yawning entrance in a field a mile from the main road, which led steeply downwards, through ferns and bushes, into the depths of a flowerless earth, opening out then into a series of limestone galleries, most of which they had already explored, slipping about on the wet boulders, until they had discovered this last obstacle at the end of a chilly cavern.

Hetty having started the climb, the others were forced to follow. 'Come on!' she shouted back at them. 'Bound to be something fantastic! . . .' They all, with varying degrees of effort, managed to climb and pull each other up through the narrowing cone of rock.

At the top they found themselves on a narrow, sandy, pebble-strewn path. It had once been the watercourse of an underground stream, and led forward into the darkness, towards an existing stream, which they could hear rushing in the distance.

They moved up the old water-bed. After twenty yards or so they suddenly felt a breath, it seemed, of damp air, a feeling of space about them. Holding their candles up, they saw they had come into a great nave, a domed, yellowing roof just visible above them.

They stood on a lip of rock. The extraordinary vision lay below and all about them. They were standing on the edge of a saucer-shaped amphitheatre, where stalactites and stalagmites, meeting together over aeons, had formed wonderfully ribbed and coloured pillars, ochre and smoked ivory, frozen cascades which glimmered in the candlelight – pillars as in a cathedral, which ran from floor to roof way above them. The stream they had heard was just visible now, flowing swiftly beyond the pillars, before disappearing into a stygian hole in the furthest rock.

Even Bertie, removing his spectacles, was impressed, as they stood there in the icy air.

'No bats here, no fungus, nothing!' Robert said, awed by the surroundings. 'End of the system – sort of end of the world!'

'No, it's not,' Hetty said. 'Look over there! – there's a passage, a hole, beyond that pillar!' She skidded down the saucer slope to the floor of the cathedral. Then, torch in hand, she moved between two of the pillars, coming to the edge of the narrow, underground stream, close to where it gurgled away into a hole in the rock wall.

'No, Hetty, don't be such a fool!' Léonie urgently called after her, starting to follow, herself slipping down from the rim.

'It's perfectly all right – easy!' Hetty called back.

'No, don't you go – I'll go,' Robert said to Léonie. And he slid down the slope, moving between the pillars, his candle visible before the flame disappeared and Léonie heard a splash.

'Hetty!' she roared. 'Robert – are you all right?'

'Yes, we're fine!' She heard Hetty's voice. 'Just lighting the candle again.' They must have turned some corner now, for no further light could be seen. 'Yes!' They heard Hetty's voice again, but fainter now. 'There's *another* sort of cave here, a drop in the floor, going straight down. Robert! Bring your light here and we can see—'

Suddenly her voice stopped and Léonie heard a cracking, a tumbling noise, of rocks falling, then silence, but for the rushing noise of the stream in the darkness. She started to clamber down the slope. But Bertie held her back. 'No, *don't* hold me!' she yelled at him. 'We must go and see . . .'

They slid down together then, crossing through the pillars, jumping the stream and rounding a corner in the rock face, before they came to a sudden drop in the floor of the narrow cavern beyond. There had indeed been a hole there. But now the declivity was filled with a debris of fallen rock which had almost entirely blocked up the descent. Léonie shouted down. 'Are you all right? – Hetty, Robert!'

But there was no reply.

Hetty's forehead throbbed as she vaguely regained consciousness. Everything was quite dark in her mind. But she was under water, she knew that – naked in the cold black watery depths, swimming about, trying to escape something, with Léonie near her, an equally shadowy figure, twisting and twining beside her. But Léonie was drifting, slipping away from her in the dense flow.

She reached out her hands, tried to follow her, but found herself rooted to the spot. 'Oh, Léonie, Léa! Come back, come back,' she seemed to yell out.

Robert in the pitch darkness next to her – bruised but otherwise uninjured – felt Hetty's cold fingers touch his face. And Hetty, nearer consciousness now, breathed a sigh of relief. 'Oh, Léa! You're there. For an awful moment you were going away, leaving me . . . Please, don't ever go away like that. Oh, Léa, I do so love you—'

'It's me, Robert, not Léonie.' She heard the abrupt male voice.

'Robert?' She could not disguise her disappointment, stretching up, before falling back with a gasp of pain. 'Oh, my side, my hip, I think . . .'

'It's all right – don't move.'

'What happened?'

'We fell – *you* fell. I'm looking for the light.' Robert moved away from her in the darkness, scrabbling about on his hands and knees, looking for the two candles or the torch. Then he realized: of course, he had a box of safety matches in his coat pocket.

He lit one and had a first glimpse of their precarious position. They were perched on a sloping rock floor which, had they fallen a yard or so further, would have sent them tumbling into some bottomless abyss. He lit a second match, turning back then, holding it up to a ragged slope of rock, seeing how a collection of these small boulders, some ten or twelve feet above them, had stuck in the mouth of the drop, almost completely blocking it. But there was no sign of the candles or the torch. And he had only six matches left.

'Well?' Hetty called out.

'Nothing yet. But I've lots of matches. We'll find them.'

But he did not. He lit match after match, until there was only one left. Returning to Hetty he tried to keep the desperation out of his voice. 'No luck,' he said.

'Oh, Robert, they *must* be somewhere. Light another match.'

'I daren't – I've only one left.'

Hetty groaned. Then she twisted in pain. 'Ouch!' Then, even more suddenly, she moved again. 'Robert!' she shouted. 'It's the candle! – I think. But I can't get at it.'

'You idiot!' he told her, running his hands under her in the darkness, fumbling through her skirt, until he felt the candle. His fingers trembled in the deep damp chill, and for agonizing seconds, on this last match, the wick would not take the flame and they thought they were doomed. But at the last moment the candle brightened and very carefully he held it aloft.

The vision was incredible. They had plummeted down into a narrow chamber, some twenty feet high. The sloping floor suddenly fell away a few yards from them, to the pellucid waters of a small pool, how deep they could not tell, though the water, set in a whitish limestone basin, was crystal-clear and tinged with a perfect blue.

Then, as he moved the candle about him, they saw the walls of the chamber. They glittered with every sort of colour and icy fire, decorated as they were with hanging calcite formations – small stalactites, frozen rivulets and excrescences. Most were crystalline, translucent, flashing like diamond pendants; some were a deep gleaming ruby, a few pale blue. And it was as if the flame was circling the interior of some vast jewel box.

'Crystal!' Hetty gasped. 'A crystal cave!'

Robert turned to her with the candle. 'Oh dear – you're cut. And cold.' He took off his coat, wrapping it round her shoulders. Then, with his handkerchief, he mopped her brow where there was a gash just above the hair-line.

'It's nothing. It's my hip that hurts.'

'May be broken – don't move. They'll have gone to get help. Just lie back and I'll see if I can find the other candle.'

'Oh, Robert, what an idiotic thing to do – I do feel such an ass!' she called after him, as he moved about the chamber.

'Doesn't matter. We're alive anyway,' he said a little sourly.

'I thought you were Léonie – so lucky it was you!' She tried to placate him for her earlier error.

'Yes, so you did,' he told her coldly.

'I'm sorry. So glad it was you! Léa would have *hated* it down here!'

'No doubt.' He held the candle up above her head. 'No bats anyway.' Then, some yards behind where Hetty lay, something caught his eye and his expression changed.

Hetty looked up at him. 'What is it?'

'Nothing. Just some . . . can't quite make it out.' He leant forward with the candle and Hetty twisted round.

'Oh, God!' she screamed.

Behind her, in the frail light, she saw the skulls, the ribs and other bones – a collection, strewn about, of hideously broken skeletons.

'Oh, Robert!' She clutched up at him suddenly, violently, so that he felt her hot breath on his cheeks. 'They're *dead*!'

'Course they're dead, idiot. It's perfectly all right.'

She yelped at him then, almost in his arms, pinching him violently in her alarm. 'But that's what's so *frightening*, you ass!'

'Only the bones of some . . . ancient people,' he told her reassuringly, knowledgeably. 'Celts probably – escaping the Vikings when they raided Ireland in the fifth century. They often hid in caves then.'

'Oh, you do find just the right time for a history lesson,' she told him brusquely, regaining some of her attack.

'Well, you were frightened, so I explained. Nothing strange – just old bones.'

'Not strange to you, with all your history books. But *I* don't know all these things.' She shivered, refusing to turn round as he moved to inspect one of the skulls.

'See, it's been pierced – a hole in the cranium,' he told her prosaically. 'Some heavy implement – probably a massacre near by and they buried them here.'

'Don't *want* to know. How long will they be?'

'As long as it takes to get some men – ropes and picks and things. An hour perhaps.'

He returned, setting the candle carefully down between them. There were still several inches left to it. 'Should last out.' He looked at her quizzically through the flame. 'But let's try and get your head up and off the cold stone.' He moved away again, finding a small boulder and propping her head up against it.

'But it's my *legs*,' she moaned. 'They're all cold – all freezing and funny. Maybe if you rubbed them?'

'Nothing to put round them, I'm afraid.' But he started to massage them then, warming them, while she tilted her head back, closing her eyes, feeling some of the circulation return.

'Thanks, that's . . . ah! that *is* better. If I'd fallen in here alone, might have been dead by now.'

'Possibly. But then running away on your own like that—'

'I *told* you already – I'm sorry I was such an idiot.' The warmth began to flow in her legs again now as he rubbed them vigorously.

'Still,' he said to her more kindly, 'you do get up to such madcap things, you and Léonie – one shouldn't be surprised.'

She sensed envy more than condemnation in his tone. 'Don't you ever get up to madcap things – at St Columba's?'

'Not much.'

'Always so serious . . .'

'I'd like not to be. But I suppose . . . I am.'

He had reached her knee and she put her hand down and touched his encouragingly. 'That's nice. And that's what's so *nice* about you, you're so reliable—'

'I don't *want* to be reliable, not all the time.' There was a touch of shame, of anger and frustration, in his voice now, as he urged his hand just above her knee, rubbing her thigh, where she let it roam – until eventually, as his hand rose, she took it and drew it to her cheek. The flesh there was ice-cold.

'Oh, Robert,' she gasped between chattering teeth. 'Come up here – no, *here*, this side away from the bad hip – come and warm me, I'm *freezing* – up here now!'

He slid up beside her then on the rock, putting his whole body along her length, pressing gently round her, circling her with an arm, protectively, and trembling himself then, but from excitement as much as cold, as she pulled him to her. 'Closer!' she said – so that their faces touched in the yellow light and he felt and smelt her breath.

'Oh, that's so close and warm, Robert!' Her voice had deepened now, soft, comforting. 'I'd have frozen – I really would! Frozen alive without you.'

'Yes, well, you won't now.'

And in their trembling embraces then – so entirely innocent and proper – they yet both felt a wonderfully new, illicit and transforming thrill. He had the illusion of loving her, and of being loved in return – while she, for the first time and equally surprised and happy in the event, had the illusion of being possessed by a man. They both cherished their illusions, but could not speak of them.

'Well, you were just so lucky – again,' Léonie told her, as she pushed Hetty down the front drive in the wheelchair. Hetty's hip and thigh bone had been badly bruised, and her ankle, in plaster now, chipped and twisted, nearly broken. She could not walk. She was the invalid now.

'If it hadn't been for Robert . . .' Hetty said, savouring a particular memory of him.

'Yes, so you keep saying.' It was Léonie's turn to feel jealousy.

'Well, he *was* very nice. And, without him, I'd . . . well, I might have died!'

'Yes, I know—'

'You should be thankful to him!'

'I am – I am thankful.'

'You accused me of ignoring him – well, I didn't! Not in the caves . . .' she added mischievously. But Léonie, though curious as to what exactly she meant by this last remark, was not to be baited. Hetty wanted some small revenge. And she accepted that. It was part of their relationship, which was so close that they had begun to prey on each other's absences, on each other's thoughts.

It was, perhaps, too close – and Léonie knew she must resist the temptation to delve and pry. And, besides, Hetty's small revenges were so much an expected part of her, and her disturbed background, Léonie thought: Hetty, because of all the old upsets in her life, always making unreasonable demands or initiations – rushing away in the cave like that; Hetty, always thrusting, pushing, shoving, going over the limit in harebrained schemes. Well, she could not do that for a week or two. Hetty would be more or less immobile. Léonie had her to herself. She could soothe all her hurts, spiritual and physical.

'No, I'm sorry – and I *am* thankful to Robert, *very*. And to you, for being back.' She bent down then and kissed her quickly, on her warm hair, warm and sweet-smelling in the August morning sun.

Robert, with Bertie, in Henry's old work rooms at the top of the house, had noticed the two girls from the window going down the drive. And now, with a pair of Henry's ancient field glasses, he focused on the couple, seeing Léonie bend down, muffling her head in Hetty's hair.

'A crystal cave . . .' Bertie said. 'Love to have seen it!' He was studying a treatize on mineralogy, from a collection of natural history books on a shelf near by. 'What *sort* of rocks, exactly, though? Deep ruby, you say?'

'Yes.' Robert was lost, concentrating on his view of the girls.

'And *translucent* stalactites?'

'Sort of.' Robert turned away from his upsetting vision of Hetty and Léonie. 'I *can't* understand it,' he said to himself, perplexed.

'No, nor can I – when all the other stalactites and stalagmites were just a whitish yellow in the upper galleries.'

'No – I meant . . .' Robert pulled himself together. 'Yes, of course. Well, maybe that book will tell us.'

Half-way down the front drive the postman on his bicycle came towards the girls. He doffed his cap when he neared them and dismounted. Hetty said, 'I'll take the post,' and the man rode away. Hetty shuffled through the letters. There was one for her, a cheap manila envelope, marked 'On His Majesty's Service'. She tore it open. The single sheet of paper, closely written on both sides, was headed 'Aylesbury Prison'. It was from her mother.

August 16th, 1916

My dearest Henrietta,

At last I have gained the privilege of writing a letter – and you shall be the first, tho' I have always been a pretty rotten correspondent and there is at once too much and too little to say. But what I *really* wanted to say was to renew and emphasize what I tried to tell you, and told Léonie, that last day in the College of Surgeons: I do so ask your forgiveness for my many years' neglect of you.

Something snapped in me, changed me completely that week in Dublin (seeing how *really* brave the others were, the wounded and dying there) and made me realize how little life was worth unless one took account of the *unseen* world, as well as the world of liberty, action and so on. And in this way I realized how I had never properly 'seen' you, seeing only my republican vision all these years, and its end in Dublin that week. Tho' I know it cannot actually *be* the end of that, and others will . . .'

Hetty couldn't read the next two lines which had been crossed out, censored.

. . . so, anyway, I want you to know that you are seen now, for the full and fine person you are, as well as in all your trials and tribulations, many of them brought upon you by me, in my selfishness. You will not easily forgive. But perhaps you will come to understand my *acts* these last years – and more importantly my, yes, *spiritual* transformation, if that's not too pretentious a word, for I have so changed, in the light of all those Dublin events – feel a repose in my life that I never felt before, an end of bitterness, conflict with myself and others, with the memory of them . . . We may not have won yet in Ireland – but *I* have won something – different, but quite as precious – a tranquillity and acceptance, where all

I must do now is to prosper it – to this end with Father
Lawrence, one of the prison chaplains here, with whom I
am taking instruction in the Roman Catholic faith, something
I never thought to come to, but which now, so obviously, is
the only real answer for me . . .

There was a little more, in a lighter vein: remarks on
the hollyhocks in the prison garden and the fact that she
had seen a Zeppelin flying over the walled exercise yard
the previous day. The letter ended:

Dearest Henrietta, I miss you and everyone – everything – at
Summer Hill, of course: so much loved a house. But that
apart, and my feelings of sadness over you, I am happy and
content. I am patient, now that I know, now that I *believe*
everything will happen for the best. Give messages to everyone
at home, most particularly remembering me to Elly.
                    Your loving Mama.

Hetty handed the letter to Léonie, saying curtly, 'She
has taken to her dotage – a spiritual dotage!'

Léonie, reading the letter quickly, was equally abrupt,
but to quite another end. 'Oh, that's too hard, Hetty. She's
not a fool. She surely means it all—'

'More's the pity! It's pathetic – a Roman Catholic! –
when she's Jewish. That's their law, you know it very
well yourself – they take the faith from the mother's
side.'

'Only half-Jewish, though.'

'Yes! – and the other half is *Protestant*!'

'What does all that matter – if she finds comfort in it?'

'It's *betraying* again,' Hetty said roughly, bunching her
fingers, just as her mother did when angered, on the arms
of the wheelchair.

'Again?'

'As she did before, always has done, with me and my
Papa – when I'm sure he wasn't!'

'Oh, so you've said to me often enough.' The rest of the
post had spilled from Hetty's lap and Léonie came round,
bending down to retrieve it, before confronting Hetty. 'So
you always say – about your Papa – but there's no proof.
And *why?*'

'No proof! – there would be if there were photographs of him. But there aren't any! She de-de-destroyed all of them, because they would have shown I was *nothing* like him!'

'Oh, Hetty – she probably didn't keep them because he was a bad memory! *You* told me all about that – Mr Fraser, how nasty he was. But you can't really believe your Mama . . . carried on with *other* men?'

'She may have done. Aunt Emily hinted . . .'

'So you've said. But you *know* how she always exaggerates and makes a drama of everything?'

'I feel it,' Hetty insisted. 'He *couldn't* have been my real p-p-Papa,' she said, her voice rising and stuttering with emotion. 'I remember him so well on the island. So nasty and *cruel*!' Tears began to glaze her eyes.

'Well, some fathers *are* just that.' Léonie, kneeling in front of the chair now, took Hetty's hands, gently easing their shaking grip from the arm, cradling them in her own. 'Oh, Hetty, it's common, I'm afraid – bad Papas!' she added mock-mournfully, trying to lighten the convulsing sadness that had come over her friend. 'And I'm just so lucky with mine. But just because Mr Fraser was bad – doesn't mean *you* are bad. Don't you see?'

Hetty did not see. Though it was in just this idea of something rotten behind her, of a flawed inheritance, Léonie sensed, that Hetty's real problem lay.

'But why did Mama *marry* such a bad man?'

Léonie had no ready answer here and admitted it. 'I don't know. But it happens, often enough.'

'But *why*? – when she was so beautiful, gifted. Everyone – Aunt Emily, Dermot, Mortimer – they all say so!'

'There's no real explaining, is there? How can we? We weren't there at the time. Your Papa may have *turned* bad, people do. Just as they can turn good, as your Mama has. Oh, Hetty . . .' Léonie leant forward, embracing her. 'You must forgive her.'

Hetty, immobile against Léonie, looked coldly over her shoulder. 'I will forgive her,' she said, softly but icily, 'when she tells me who my real f-f-father is.'

And Léonie, feeling this deep rage in Hetty, realized it was something she could never properly calm in her. Only an answer to her question could do that– if the question was real at all. Or was it, Léonie wondered, just part of the dialogue in another long-cherished role, among so many, which Hetty had taken on over the years since she had known her, roles to which all this Cordiner family seemed so partial and performed so adeptly: her grandfather playing Icarus with his disastrous flying machine, her mother swapping between violent revolutionary and saint, Aunt Emily with her endlessly imagined pictorial fantasies, her fairy tales saturating the house. And now Hetty, trying to vie with them, or just reflecting this dramatic blood, by giving herself the role of Cinderella – offspring of some romantic, mysterious *alliance*, when in fact she was just the product of an unfortunate marriage.

Léonie had no answers herself here, other than that she saw now, with great clarity, how these factors, real or imagined, were the dangerously shifting bedrock of Hetty's life. She would calm, she would try to stabilize, these subterranean eruptions as best she could.

To this end, during Hetty's enforced immobility, Léonie organized card and paper games for her, with Aunt Emily, Robert and Bertie; or brought objects to divert her – Victorian *jeux* with which the house was filled – when Hetty was alone, sitting listlessly in the drawing room or porch: the stereoscopic cabinet with its exotic photographic views of Egypt and India, in which the Pyramids and the Taj Mahal became startlingly real as Hetty turned the handles; and the Zöetrope, the 'Wheel of Life', which Hetty had played with as a child, now brought out again with its dozens of paper scrolls, each with a succession of individual but slightly altered coloured drawings along its length which, when Hetty spun them in the metal cylinder, peering through the slits in the sides, brought the scrolls to extraordinary life, so that a clown riotously juggled balls, a dog chased a cat helter-skelter, and the fabled cow repeatedly jumped over the moon.

Robert, of course, was not slow to explain matters to her. 'It's really very simple,' he told her one afternoon in the drawing room. 'It's the principle of persistence of vision: your eye isn't quick enough to distinguish each individual drawing as they flash by through the slits. So it merges them all together and the drawings *appear* to move. Quite simple.'

'But it isn't,' Hetty told him sourly. 'It's magic!'

'Nonsense, it's just an optical fact.' He twirled the cylinder dismissively. 'Why, they use the same principle everywhere now, in the Kinematograph machine, only there the pictures are all photographed on celluloid – like in the Kinema houses in Dublin. Bertie and I saw one last term, at the Grafton – and they show them sometimes in Kilkenny, too, at the Theatre.'

'Do they? I'd love to see that! Let's go to one, shall we?'

'Yes – it's all pretty rubbishy stuff, though. But, when you're better, perhaps. Why not?'

But the summer was drawing to a close and, in those last days of August, before the boys went back to school, they were occupied out on the river, or paying purely domestic attentions to Hetty, still largely immobile, her bruises and sprains taking longer to heal than expected. Plans of going to a Kinematograph display in Kilkenny never materialized.

Instead, the new doctor in Thomastown, the bright young Dr Roche, came out several times a week ministering to Hetty, and seeing old Lady Cordiner, too. Hetty had told him, much earlier in the summer, of her plan that the old woman should be moved outdoors in the better weather. But he had advised against it, indeed he had tactfully insisted. 'Miss Fraser, your grandmother is quite past all that, I'm afraid – you have seen her yourself: so gone in age and with her bad heart – it would likely kill her. She should not be moved, I do assure you.' And Hetty had left it at that.

The Ashleys came, once or twice a week, for tea on the porch in the last of the warm weather. Plans were made for the resumption of their lessons in September with the Major – and Aunt Emily continued to fill her sketch-books with endless images, real and imagined, of the household and the glorious summer.

Mortimer came down from Dublin, staying a long weekend, inspecting the accounts, paying bills. The farm still showed no profit. But losses had been stemmed through his economies. And the harvest that year promised well. They would be cutting and threshing the corn earlier than expected and the wartime boom in agricultural prices would make up some leeway in the accounts.

Hetty showed Elly her mother's letter – and Elly, at least, had written to her fulsomely. Hetty merely sent her a short, non-committal note. She had not shown Mortimer the letter, but he had spoken to her of her Mama in any case, tactfully, but generously.

'I shall see more of her in Aylesbury when the House resumes in October,' he had said. 'But already, you know, there is a great ground swell of support for her here in Ireland.'

'Oh, is there? I don't see the newspaper here.'

'Yes, she is much the heroine – she and de Valera, but she especially – quite taken to the hearts of people here. An extraordinary woman!'

'But she is not likely to be set free, of course . . .' Hetty had asked, fearing this but feigning concern.

'No. But she will not be imprisoned for ever, indeed not for too long more at all, I feel. The situation here remains very tense. They will probably declare an amnesty for the Republican prisoners at some point soon, repatriate them all.'

'Oh,' Hetty had said dully.

'Hetty, I know your feelings about your Mama. But you cannot expect her to be away from Summer Hill indefinitely, you know.'

'No . . .'

'And you yourself – apart from the caves, it's all gone well with you and Léonie this summer: Major Ashley has told me.'

'Oh, yes indeed!'

'But soon, I feel – there will have to be other things for you. A winter down here on your own—'

'But I *won't* be on my own! There's Léa . . . and everyone. And we're *so* happy here, and the Major teaches us everything – and Léa's parents are entirely content about it all, too!'

'Yes,' Mortimer had temporized. 'I can see that. All the same—'

'Besides, Léa can't go back to Paris with all those German U-boats in the Channel.'

'Oh – so you do read the newspaper!'

'Robert does, all the time – and he told me.'

'Yes, well, we shall see.'

Then Hetty, sensing his concern and seeing how she might turn it to her advantage, suddenly said, 'But if you're worried – couldn't we use your little flat in Dublin, above your offices, for a while this autumn? Get a singing teacher for Léonie, and I could take proper lessons there. We'd be more . . . supervised in Dublin, safer even,' she added in a most convincingly innocent manner.

'Yes.' Mortimer pondered the matter. 'Yes, that's a possibility. There's my housekeeper, Mrs McCabe – comes in every morning. And Mr Watson, my chief clerk, an excellent man, in the apartment opposite—'

'Oh, let's! It'd be s-s-such a good idea!' Only her sudden unexpected stammer might have betrayed Hetty then – how her thoughts of life in Dublin were not entirely educational, and were far from being for reasons of safety. 'And besides,' she finished, 'we're so boycotted down here by everyone: we really *should* meet some new people!'

Mortimer agreed, promising to develop these plans when he returned to Dublin – and the four of them had tea on the porch after he had gone. Afterwards Robert played croquet with Léonie on the upper lawn, while Bertie, not a gamesman, entertained Hetty, over a debris of teacake, with a reading from *Middlemarch*.

'So, you may come up to Dublin?' Robert, playing laxly so that he might keep pace with the less expert Léonie, had played too carelessly – offering her a most inviting cannonade, which she duly performed, sending his ball way into the bushes on the other side of the court.

'Oh, I *am so* sorry!' she teased him. 'Yes, isn't that nice,' she went on when he returned to the game. 'Dublin – lessons for both of us and a singing teacher for me, maybe. And all the theatres!'

'We . . . perhaps we can meet up there. We have three or four Sunday exeats a term.'

'Of course – I'd like that.' She smiled affectionately at him as he lined up another shot. This time he found himself at an advantage, croqueting her, before taking a further shot which would most likely send her far into the bushes. But he desisted, leaning on his mallet, foot on the ball. He wanted to talk to Léonie about Hetty. But he knew no way of beginning. Léonie sensed his frustration and thought she knew its cause. She liked him for it as she said, 'It's really Hetty you want to see, though, isn't it?'

'No, no – you as well.' He was airy, unconcerned now, addressing his ball.

She smiled at his sudden boisterousness. 'It's her, and why not? You're fond of her – I know.'

'Well, I don't know . . .' He was quite offhand.

'Of *course* you are – you were brought up with her.'

'Ha! Very good reason *not* to be fond of people, usually!'

'Well, you are, Robert! And so you should be. I'm . . . very fond of her, too.'

'Yes,' he said, a touch warily, still fiddling with his mallet. 'Well, that's perfectly natural as well.'

'But you're unhappy about it . . .'

'Oh, no – not at all. Why should I be? Girls – often very fond of each other, so many things . . . in common.'

'Well, yes!' Léonie smiled.

'I meant, well – your being at school together in France and all that.'

'Yes. But it's difficult for you, I see that.'

'Why should it be?' He almost laughed then, striking a more confident note. 'You're not a man, after all!'

'No. But I . . . I monopolize her, perhaps, more than I should – as a man might.' She turned away then, somehow

613

flustered, upset by this admission. 'I am sorry – I can't help it.'

'No, no,' Robert responded in a feigned couldn't-careless voice. 'I quite understand. Very close – and why not? – surviving that awful Easter week together in Dublin and so on. Quite expected.'

'Yes,' she agreed. But the tension was still there in her voice. She turned and approached him, as he stood by the hoop rather crestfallen. In her sudden emotion – about Hetty, about him too – she put her hand briefly on his. 'I *am* sorry, Robert – especially because . . . I like you very much, too.'

He had his foot on the ball, stuck right next to Léonie's then. 'Oh,' he said dully.

There was silence, which Léonie, anxious to lighten the mood, finally interrupted. 'Well, go on then – croquet me! Got me at your mercy!'

And he did just that, with great vigour, sending her ball skimming way into the bushes again. But it made him feel no better, guilty indeed.

'Oh, you brute!' she shrieked at him, laughing.

'I'm sorry,' he told her.

And, seeing his confusion, she came up to him, softening the mood once more. 'Oh, for goodness sake, Robert – we both of us must stop being sorry all the time. What for? It'll all work out all right – promise you, you'll see! Can't but – we're *all* fond of each other. Hetty told me, in the cave, how wonderful you were, saved her life. May not show it mostly, but she really is – she likes you a lot, *really.*'

Léonie had perhaps exaggerated Hetty's affection here. But Robert brightened perceptibly, his rather gaunt features lightening in the hint of a wry smile, his upper lip curling a fraction – his thin face warming now, as if fired by her own candid, affectionate gaze.

It was more than affection that Léonie suddenly felt for him then. She could so willingly have kissed him. She wanted to.

*

The boys returned to school as hints of autumn crept over the landscape. The Virginia creeper above the porch had turned a dazzling orange-red. And now the leaves of the big maple, lacking sap in the first night chills, joined in this fall of the year – a lighter red, a peachy crimson.

The chestnut trees edging the demesne, in the last windless days of warmth, had been faded, drowsy, fly-blown. But now, within a week, with the first of the September winds, the colours turned and the leaves fell, lemon-yellow in the sharpening autumn light. The mornings were dew-laden, the lawns, in the first sunlight, a glittering carpet, covered in gossamers of spiders' webs. By midday, the heat still there in a bright sun, a few late butterflies emerged, flying among the poppies in the orchards beyond the house. The first fruits had ripened quickly here, early Worcester Pearmains and Victoria plums, and Léonie had wheeled Hetty up to the high land one late afternoon to sample them, parking Hetty beneath a laden apple tree.

Léonie reached up and secured a red-veined Worcester, blowing on it, polishing it on her sleeve so that it shone, before giving it to Hetty.

'So,' she said. 'Alone again!'

Hetty did not reply, leaning right back in her chair, head tilted, gazing up between the branches to the twilit blue sky beyond. 'Yes,' she said at last.

'*Fin de saison,*' Léonie said lightly, after another silence.

'Yes. I suppose we'll go to Dublin, shan't we?' Hetty kept her gaze on the sky.

'Yes, of course, why not?' Léonie, arms on hips, also looked up through the branches, wondering what had caught Hetty's attention there. Then she suddenly saw it – a thin scimitar of silvery moon above the apple tree.

'And yet . . . I don't want to leave here now, Léa, not – oh, this summer, Léa – it's not wanting it to go . . .'

'No. But there'll be others.'

'Mama'll probably be here then – not like this one, alone – not *ever* so much again,' she added, without sadness, almost prosaically.

'But Mortimer was right – suppose we can't spend the rest of our lives down here.'

'Rest of *our* lives?' Hetty was suddenly quizzical now, looking down from the tree, gazing at Léonie, who returned the gaze, an equal worry and query in her expression.

'Yes, our lives.'

'That's what frightens me, Léa . . .'

'What?'

'Not having, not being with you, when you're just *there* in the next room – and I can sleep there, or you with me.'

Léonie came towards her, kneeling in the tall yellowing grass in front of her chair, taking her hands.

'Hetty dearest – there are *other* rooms, you know – everywhere, a room together or rooms next to each other, even in Dublin, I'm sure!'

'But other people, too.'

Léonie drew away a fraction, sighing. 'Yes, of course! Other people, other rooms, other voices – there's always that. But . . .' She was suddenly tongue-tied.

'But what?'

Léonie's lips began to pucker as she tried to dam her rising emotion. 'Well, but – aren't we . . .' Her eyes were suddenly cloudy with tears. 'Aren't we everything "other" – *to* each other?'

'Yes, yes!' Hetty cried out, seeing Léonie's tears, and drawing her into her arms, clutching her tightly, so that her head pressed into her breasts, as they comforted each other, desperately, almost violently, trying to calm each other's doubts.

Léonie continued the reading of *Middlemarch* after supper. And later they played cards by a first log fire in the drawing room, when the lamps were brought in; the big, white-globed Aladdin standard lamp set above the Zöetrope on the occasional table beside Hetty.

She turned the cylinder idly, the lamplight falling directly into the interior of this wheel of life, enhancing the dance set free there as the cylinder spun, giving the paper scrolls a golden enchantment. So that, though the images – the juggler, the running dog and cat, the cow –

were blunt, even banal now, to Hetty with much rep-
etition, she none the less gazed at them, mesmerized.
Immobilized over a few weeks in her wheelchair, she
longed to jump into the cylinder – yet then felt just as
strongly that she did not want this. In this mysterious
machine, with its inexplicable movement, its extraordinary
offering and mimicking of real life, she was somehow seeing the very cradle of all her joys and fears.

10

Mortimer, before returning to Westminster that October,
made arrangements for the two girls to take over his top-
floor flat in Crown Alley, a small courtyard of Georgian
business offices off Dame Street, between Dublin Castle
and the river. It was not residential, this legal and financial
hub of the city with its Stock Exchange, City Hall and
magnificent façade of the Bank of Ireland at the other end
of Dame Street. But the girls – helped by Mrs McCabe
the housekeeper, who came for a few hours each morning,
and under the benign, if largely absent, eye of Mr Watson,
Mortimer's celibate chief clerk, who occupied rooms opposite theirs – came to relish these unexpected surroundings.

During the day the streets teemed with hectic activity:
Stock Exchange messengers, clerks, barristers, top-hatted
brokers, journalists from the *Evening Mail* building near
by – all raucously about their business, chattering on the
pavements or skipping between the clanging trams and the
great horse drays rumbling over the cobbles.

But at night, washed in soft gaslight, the quarter was
nearly empty and silent until, towards eight, the crowds
gathered outside the Olympia Theatre not far from Mortimer's offices; and silent once more until, filled with drink,
song and broad wit, the audience was released just after ten.

But the best times, the girls thought when they came

back from the activities about the city, were those November dusks, the lamplighter moving down the narrow alley-way into their courtyard, prodding the gas globes into yellow pools of light above the emptying offices – when soon, they knew, they would have the whole place all to themselves; soon too, at least for Hetty, when they could dress up as smart women, or as man and woman, preparing themselves for some theatrical excitement – emerging from Mortimer's offices an hour or so later, quite transformed, in all sorts of guises and disguises, intent on testing themselves against the city.

And for Hetty, certainly, the dextrous lamplighter was a herald of thrilling change, an unconscious promoter of her hazardous theatricals, the demons that lurked in her heart. The old man was like a stage-hand, Hetty thought, arranging a set, turning up the footlights, illuminating the backcloth and props, in front of which the curtain would rise soon on a performance uniquely hers – and Léonie's – when they would step out into the limelight, magic people then, transformed by every artifice which – as wardrobe mistress and actor-manager combined – she had so painstakingly collected and applied in Mortimer's flat beforehand.

So it was, one evening, watching the lamplighter from the front window six weeks after they had arrived in Dublin, that Hetty – fingering through a collection of her uncle Henry's old clothes and others more recently purchased from a variety of second-hand clothes shops in the city – thought to do something properly rash.

'Let's dress up tonight – and go to the Olympia Music Hall!' She looked at Léonie, just arrived back at the flat, where Hetty had been most of the afternoon, pondering the style and form of the evening's adventure.

Léonie, taking her coat off, gave a sigh of disinclination. 'Hetty, I'm tired . . .'

'Oh, *please*, Léa, I've been *so* thinking about it – all afternoon!'

'But all those rough types . . .' Léonie made the limp excuse. 'See them queueing every evening.'

'But that's just what'll be such *fun* – those rough types. Look!' Hetty picked up a smart, chestnut-coloured, check suit and waistcoat of Henry's, then a fawn bowler and red cravat. 'And I've got that pearl tiepin and spats to go with it,' she rushed on. 'And the silver-topped cane. I'll go as a young Dublin rake, out for a night on the halls. And for you . . .' She bent down to the bed again. 'I've something very quaint! Merry young woman's outfit, cheeky servant style – "Bridey from Rathmines": you can be my sweet young thing again!'

She held up the bits and pieces of Léonie's intended costume – a hand-me-down ensemble of slightly thread-bare green velveteen topcoat, cheap picture hat with papier-mâché cherries round the crown and scuffed, lace-up black bootees.

'Hardly very merry, is it?' Léonie considered the clothes coldly. 'I'm not going anywhere in that tatty stuff.' Then she was even firmer. 'And, anyway, I'm *tired* of being your "sweet young thing".'

Hetty was quite taken aback by her blunt decisive-ness, a quality she had conveniently forgotten in her friend. 'But, Léa, this isn't all of it. There are other things—'

'Besides, if we are playing these charades, why can't *I* go as the man for a change?'

Hetty was uncertain for a moment. 'Well, just I'm t-t-taller than you, that's the only reason.' Then she found her stride. 'But, really, it'd look very stupid if you were the *small* man, out with a *big* woman.'

'Why should it? I've seen *tiny* men out with *much* bigger women, in Dublin. Often.'

'But, Léa, that wouldn't work with us. You'd be far too young-looking a man – to be taking me out.'

Léonie rounded on her vehemently. 'Why can't we *both* go out as young men then?'

Hetty was genuinely astonished. 'Why, Léa, that'd be *awfully* unnatural.'

The two women gazed at each other challengingly. But really there was more doubt in their eyes. Both were confused by these sudden changes and reversals, of sex, age and identity.

'Well, anyway . . .' Léonie flounced away into the front drawing room, taking her coat off, before shouting back, 'I'm not going out in that rubbish – playing the maid or anyone's "sweet young thing". I'm tired of that, so there!'

'But, Léa, wait – wait till you see what else I got for you today!'

Léonie stayed in the outer room. When she had come back that evening to find Hetty fidgeting about the flat, she had clearly sensed a return of that old fierce restlessness in her friend – a frustration over things Hetty so wanted to express: images of a divine discontent in which she, inevitably, would be the empty canvas, the dull clay for these unformed desires, asked to take on some new or old role as lover – pliant menial or *grande cocotte*; saint or slave, the empty page in any case on which Hetty so wished to mark her life, stamping on another all the myriad personae she repressed in herself.

All this Léonie knew or sensed. And generally she had gone along with such fantasies because she loved Hetty and knew how she craved this release. These productions of Hetty's were as life's blood to her which, if the flow was too long suppressed, would poison the whole body with anger, petulance, frustration – and so, equally, poison their relationship. Yet she would not take direction in every aspect of the production – that was nonsense, bad for her and worse for Hetty: the clay, after all, had a life of its own. None the less Léonie returned then, willing to play audience, at least, in this particular performance.

Hetty had hidden the *pièces de résistance* – and now she produced the first from a hanger in the wardrobe. It was a tea-gown, second-hand, but exquisitely sophisticated, shimmery and well-cut, an airy, flimsy *thé-dansant* dress in smoothest crêpe de chine, with puffed sleeves, black-edged *décolletage*, a loose bodice, billowy and free, caught in at the waist, running down to a tight, sheath-like hobble skirt, cut at an angle up one side, so as to display the leg.

Léonie came forward, inspecting it, astonished, fingering the gossamer silk which crackled faintly in her hand. Pre-war, she thought – nothing of this sort was available or worn in the present austerities – but most definitely *haute couture*. She admired it . . . objectively. The pale green silk seemed all the more smooth and glittering in the lamplight: moonlit waters of the Nile.

'See! – it so goes with your eyes.' Hetty held the gown up proudly against Léonie's chest. 'The grey-green and the bluey-green. Oh, Léa, it's perfect. Do try it on at least.'

'But, Hetty, what can you be thinking! – no maid would ever wear a thing like that.'

'What does it matter – it'll be hidden by the topcoat.'

'Then what's the point of wearing it, if no one sees it, knows it's there?'

Hetty was surprised at this point. 'But *I'll* know it's there. And I've got some brand-new underthings to go with it, from Brown Thomas this afternoon—'

'Hetty, you are an idiot! You can't possibly think – piling all those different sorts of clothes one on top of the other – as if I were a clothes horse. I'd be a complete freak!'

'No you won't, the topcoat will hide it all. And, anyway, it'll be great fun – you'll see. Try it on at least.'

'Yes, a clothes horse . . .' Léonie reflected again on the idea, her head shaking with amusement now. 'And all a jumble of things that don't match, one on top of the other, because you don't know *what* you want me to be!' She paused then, chin jutting, before adding bitterly, 'But why can't I just be *myself*? And why can't *you* be . . . you?'

Hetty looked at her, again with genuine puzzlement. 'But, Léa, *of course* you're yourself. And so am I. This is just . . . dressing up. A game. Can't we amuse ourselves any more?'

She spoke in tones of such patient reason, like a teacher

explaining some obvious calculation to a dunderhead, that Léonie, shaking her head again in disbelief, did not pursue the matter. 'All right then, I'll try it on. But I'm not going out anywhere in it, in *any* of it!'

Hetty did not reply, busying herself with the clothes – until finally she said, confidently, quietly, 'You'll see – you'll see.'

Léonie, who had been wearing a tweed suit and flannel blouse, climbed out of her winter clothes, and stood there shivering a moment, just in her woollen underthings, before moving over to the glowing coal grate in the bedroom.

Léonie was uncertain. It seemed in this clothes play as if Hetty was taking some seductive initiative here, just as she herself had done, in something of the same manner, swapping clothes in Hetty's bedroom, some six months before at Summer Hill. Thus she could hardly complain if this were so. Indeed, at another time, she would have welcomed such attentions. Yet, given the present circumstances, there was an obvious flaw in this idea. She cannot wish to seduce me, to undress me, Léonie thought, for she wants just the opposite: to *cover* me with all these clothes.

She was perplexed. But she relaxed . . . stripped off her underclothes, standing naked by the fire, before Hetty, quite clinically, dispassionately, offered her the first of the new silk undergarments, then the others, pausing between each successive covering, observing the rising foundations as a painter might consider the effects of successive layers of colour on a canvas.

Then she gave her the crêpe-de-chine tea-gown, helping her put it on, easing the silk sheath down Léonie's waist and hips, pulling the bodice up, buttoning it at the back. She flounced the billowy silk out, about Léonie's shoulders, neck and breasts, breathing on the thin folds so that they rippled like green waves in the fire-light.

'Don't blow so – you're tickling me!' Léonie, despite herself, was being drawn into the performance, feeling the touch of silk brushing her skin, beneath her arms, at her throat.

'See! With a bit of height from the shoes it'll hang perfectly.' Hetty, totally absorbed now in the creation of this model, scurried about Léonie, pinching in the gown, smoothing the hang, straightening the waist, running her hand down the flanks, adjusting, moulding the silk against Léonie's shape.

Léonie played the mannequin without moving, without a sound. But, as Hetty's hands roved about, she found this more difficult. For it was quite clear to her now, as her skin began to prickle with pleasure: Hetty – unconsciously or not, she could not decide – *was* seducing her, not by undressing, but by dressing her. And that, strangely, seemed even more exciting.

Hetty, finally satisfied, drew Léonie over to the long dressing mirror. 'Just one last thing!' She went to the wardrobe, producing a magnificent turban in brocaded satin, an egret feather at the centre, held in place by a large turquoise stone, and placed it on Léonie's head. It fitted perfectly, a metallic silver crown quite covering her dark curls.

'There!' Hetty was beside herself. 'I knew it'd go. Isn't it wonderful?'

Léonie nodded vigorously, biting her lip. She was speechless, with suppressed mirth, sorrow, love – she could not distinguish the feelings. But finally she said the wrong thing. 'You are a real ninny, Hetty – you had that horrid cherry hat before and that tatty overcoat – and now all this magnificence! But none of that . . . would go with any of this!'

Hetty was crestfallen for a moment. Then she was suddenly petulant. 'Oh, what does it matter?' She waltzed over to the bed and, rummaging furiously all round it, she picked up the other old clothes – the Dublin rake's outfit, the cherry hat and the maid's threadbare velveteen coat – throwing them in the air, all over the place. 'What *does* it matter?' she shouted, suddenly bitter now. 'They're all only *ideas*, Léa – so many, many ideas I have about you!

Don't you see? And they'd *all* suit – you can wear anything and I'm too tall. You could be anything, Bridey or Madame de Pompadour or Scheherazade. And I can't somehow—'

'That's nonsense! You're a *much* better actress – that's the whole trouble!'

Hetty paused in her rampage, looking at Léonie carefully, rather sadly, and quite deflated now. 'But, Léa – I want all that much more f-f-for you.' She stopped again, tripped suddenly by her stammer. Then there was the still, small voice: 'I want everything for *you*, Léa – not for me.'

Hetty turned away then, overcome with emotion, starting to fiddle with her hands, cracking the finger joints. Then she picked up the snow-dome of Summer Hill which she kept by her bedside, and sucked her thumb. Léonie, stricken, saw her wander off into the shadows of the bedroom. She stood up, an odalisque in her oriental headdress and shimmering silk, distraught. She put her head to one side, as if trying to ward off some blow, her eyes screwed up in pain, holding her arms out. 'Oh, Hetty, do come here – *please*. I am so sorry, to be so tactless, misunderstanding everything. *Please* come.'

But Hetty stayed in the corner. So that Léonie swiftly went to her, turned her round and took her in her arms.

'Hetty,' she said, feeling her moist cheeks on hers. 'Oh, Hetty – I want everything for you, too, everything. Love you more than the world – love me . . .'

'That stupid feather,' Hetty said at last. 'It's tickling me . . .'

'I'll take it off, take everything off. *And* I'll go out to the theatre tonight, however you want me – promise I will.'

Léonie removed all her splendid clothes then – and soon she had helped Hetty do the same, before they loved each other again, naked and without artifice.

'The *real* Dublin life!' Hetty exclaimed, excited, a glass of ale in her hand, glancing at Léonie, sipping a cheap sherry, her lips puckered in distaste, as she tried to smile, nervously. 'You look fine. Don't worry!' Hetty added the whispered reassurance.

The two girls stood behind the glass windows of the bar at the back of the stalls at the Olympia Theatre. The lilting music from the small pit orchestra – a Lehar melody sung in an uncertain contralto by a buxom woman – wafted to them as the bar doors swung to and fro. It was a Friday night, one of music hall variety acts, the theatre almost full: suburban men nursing bowler hats with their rapt wives, groups of restless, derisive British Tommies in the back rows, one or two women of easy virtue glancing at the soldiers from behind the glass at the long bar, the intermittent catcalls and whistling of old shawlies, Dublin codgers and urchins just audible from the gods far above.

The misguided contralto finished to ragged jeers and ironic applause. The girls, fascinated, watched the act numbers change, the flash of electric bulbs on either side of the stage, nine to ten, the last act before the interval. A louche Scotsman, in kilt and tam-o'-shanter, knobbly-kneed, with an outsize furry sporran, came on then, amidst a great outburst, and proceeded with a risqué imitation of Harry Lauder, lifting his kilt suggestively as he began to stamp about the stage. Behind the glass the girls could just hear the words of the song: 'Roamin' in the gloamin' wi' a lassie by me side! . . .'

The Scotsman lifted his kilt higher, starting to jig in front of a heather-glen curtain drop, and the house exploded – as his 'lassie' emerged from the wings, an elderly crone, sprigs of heather all askew over a poke bonnet, who lifted her skirts then and, with a simpering smirk, started to scamper about the stage, avoiding the man's lascivious attentions.

The girls forced a smile. It was hot in the bar, the place reeking of stout and tobacco, the great electric globes above the counter fuzzy in the drifting smoke, as the drinkers, attracted now by the excitement on stage, pushed forward round the girls, peering out into the red and gilt auditorium.

Hetty loosened her red cravat, undid the top button of her check waistcoat and, inspecting her vague reflection in the glass, adjusted the tilt of her fawn bowler.

She was dressed as she had first suggested, two hours before in the flat, as a keen young Dublin blade, in a smart chestnut check suit, spats and red cravat, a near gent, out for an evening's slumming in the halls before a bit of slap and tickle later in a jarvey's cab, with Léonie, his little bit of fluff, in the rubbed green velveteen topcoat, cherry hat and lace-up bootees. The tea-gown and turban would await another occasion. They were well enough disguised, Hetty knew. But this was their first occasion in a public bar, cheek by jowl with sharp men and loose women.

Just then two men approached them, pushing in close, viewing the show from the windows: one robust, florid-faced, arrogant in a canary waistcoat, almost bald and narrow-eyed with a few foxy strands of hair over pendulous ears – together with quite a different sort, an elderly, much smaller man, rubicund, a little pixie of a fellow in a loud check suit and bowler.

'I'm afraid not, Mr O'Grady,' the tall man spoke superciliously, in a nasal, suburban English accent, pulling on a wet cigar in a lordly fashion, spewing the smoke out over the bowler beneath him. 'We really have no dates available for you people. The panto's coming up – then right through till the spring we have a hundred and one different acts booked in from England, from the Metropolitan, from Collins' – all booked up, you see!' He bared his discoloured teeth in an ogre-ish smile.

'Ah, Mr Purcell, but a night or two with some of my people – and you'd *really* see something.' The little man spoke with a marked Dublin brogue. He was chirpy, confident, like a bird. Across his pot belly, from one waistcoat pocket to the other, lay the gold chains, heavy and spectacular, of a fob watch. He sipped from a glass of stout, then licked his pronounced cherubic lips. His eyes were unnaturally large as well, great baby's eyes, too big for the pudgy, dewlapped, mischievous face that was quite hairless, smooth and very white, like that of an ivory Buddha.

The Englishman laughed drily. 'But I *have* seen your people, Mr O'Grady – several of your summer seasons out at Bray: know them well – the dwarfs, jugglers and the mangy lion too! Fine for the visitors there, the day trippers. But this is the Olympia *Theatre*, you know. Now, if you'll just excuse me a moment . . .'

The cocky theatre manager drifted away, leaving Mr O'Grady humming a tune, sipping his stout next to the girls, as he gazed sarcastically out at the antics in the Harry Lauder imitation on stage.

'Ah, Holy Mother o' God!' He nodded to Hetty. 'Will ye look at it! Thim two edjits out there – lowest of the low, I'd buy oul' Harry himself, but that's a travesty, that kinda o' codology.'

Hetty, who had overheard the entire previous conversation between the two men, immediately agreed. 'Quite dreadful!' she said, her voice several tones lower, upper-class, dismissive. 'Absolute rubbish.' And then, the devil suddenly rising in her, she told him, 'I and my friend here – we do a far better act.' Léonie, horrified, dared not open her mouth.

'Ye do?' The pixie looked up at the tall, imperious figure, the finely-cut features of the dandy – then at Léonie in the ridiculous cherry hat. He seemed doubtful. Yet he was taken by the poise of the young man, the classy confidence, the arrogant control – above all, by the obvious beauty of the couple. 'And what do ye do?' He fed himself some more stout, raising the glass too high, but then leaning over the rim and dipping into it like a duck.

'Oh, we have a singing act – "Bertie and Bridey" – we do imitations, but *proper* ones: popular tunes, operetta. My friend plays the piano, I sing. And sometimes the other way round. And we dance.'

'Ye *both* sing . . . and play the pianner?'

'Oh yes – *Madame Butterfly* is our great number.'

'A sort of comedy act?'

627

'Yes. But we can do it all quite straight, too. My friend's a proper singer – trained.'

'I've not heard of ye. On the boards before?'

'A little – in London.'

'"Bertie and Bridey" . . .' The little man looked at them, first savouring, then seeming to like, the idea. 'Have ye got iny photographs?' Hetty nodded. 'Well, send thim to me – and come out with your act and I'll look at it. Here's me card.'

He finished his stout then, before touching his bowler and waddling away. Hetty looked at the card. 'Mr Alphonso O'Grady' it said in neat copperplate at the top. But beneath, in fancy mock Gothic capitals, was the bold inscription 'FONSY O'GRADY'S THEATRE OF VARIETIES' – before the copperplate was prosaically resumed. 'Bray Promenade, Bray, County Wicklow, Ireland.'

Hetty giggled. 'What a laugh,' she said. '*Perfect!*'

But was it all so perfect, Léonie wondered later that evening, taking off the servant's clothes back in the flat? Had she – for her tactlessness, her love and in the emotion of the moment – given in too readily to Hetty's sensuous vaudeville fantasies? And had she not made amends for her insensitivity – had not they both done so, as real people, in their love-making afterwards? Léonie thought they had. Yet she retained a sneaking suspicion that, when she had dressed to go out as her 'sweet young thing', Hetty had found this an even more exciting gift.

Had Hetty recovered because she had been indubitably loved – or did her later joy that evening stem from quite another sort of pleasure, much more devious, a victory in which she had subtly blackmailed her, Léonie thought, to change her mind and collaborate in this mimic escapade at the theatre?

Did her subsequent bliss in any case justify all these charades? Perhaps, in the short term. But if they became a permanent sport, a constant condition of their lives together, surely they would lose each other? – for who could love a chimera indefinitely, a will-o'-the-wisp, running from one incarnation to another, when the real person was gradually suffocated, submerged, lost.

Or did she really love Hetty for just these volatile qualities, for her personality thus constantly reborn, a wizard's gift in the girl which, far from destroying their love, would, in this necromancy of changing dross to gold, keep it ever fresh?

Yes – that, she thought, was perhaps the truest answer. But it had, as consequence, another less happy facet. Hetty's love would demand constant changes in her as well. They were both to be players in Hetty's games – and she would keep her only if she continued to fulfil the roles offered her – as she had done just that evening with the maid's outfit. She would be sure of Hetty's love only for as long as she played the marionette. That was the truth, too. And Léonie saw it all then with sudden clarity. Well, so be it. She would allow herself to be used. That was the price she would pay, for she could not lose Hetty. She was forced to recognize then that she loved her more than her own independence and dignity.

Hetty pushed the two single divan beds together, as they did every evening, separating them again in the morning before Mrs McCabe arrived. They were aware now that their sort of love was not an accepted thing. But they saw it merely as a social impropriety; that it was in any way immoral did not cross their minds. Soon they were cosy between the sheets, the lamp out, but the room still faintly lit by the dying embers of the fire.

'Well, all that really was *very* funny . . .' Hetty moved her pillow over, laying her head on Léonie's shoulder. 'Wasn't it? – or do you still really feel bad about it all?'

'No . . .'

'But you do. You're not really my "servant", you know – not at all. I'd just as soon go out as that myself – if I were smaller.'

'Yes,' Léonie whispered non-committally.

'But you're still w-worried?' Hetty put her hand out to stroke Léonie's cheek.

'I just wonder about the whole thing. It's always so much more for you than just "fun" . . .'

Hetty turned away then, lying on her back. She sighed. 'Well, is it?' She thought, and then in a much more confident voice she said, 'Yes, I feel I *control* things when I'm being someone else. And I don't when I'm just being me – when I feel nothing, no confidence at all. But the moment I start copying, dressing up, when I start being someone different – I have a w-wonderful feeling of – sheer happiness, because I've walked into someone else's life, someone who knows *exactly* what they're doing and who they are. I suddenly have *power* when I'm someone else. Do you see?'

'A bit.'

'Oh, Léa, it's because I so want to get away from just being me – the weak, stammering, boring, frightened person I am with just myself—'

'But that's not true! You hardly ever stammer with me – and I love the person you *are*, said it often enough—'

'But, Léa, *I* don't like the person I am – because I'm nobody – don't know *who* I am. So I *have* to be other people. I know I do,' she added rather miserably. 'And it won't hurt you, promise. And better still,' she rushed on, vehement now, 'together we can win that way, Léa – run the world, not let it run us, with my Mama and so on. Oh, Léa, I so much want to *win* with you.'

She embraced Léonie then with a fierce tenderness. 'It's not that sort of winning I mean,' Hetty went on, excited, breathless now. 'Not loving you – in that way. It's quite different and just as exciting – it's *doing* so many different things with you, for you. It's the feeling of a future with you in that way that's so exciting. Don't you see?'

'Yes, I do see that.' Léonie responded at last, an urgency in her own voice now. 'Do see it, because – it's that same sense of loving you that I find almost more exciting than the real thing. Mind loving? – yes. You're in my mind all the time, Hetty – *where*ver and *who*ever you are – that's the really wonderful thing. Just sometimes—' She hesitated.

'Sometimes I can't keep up with you changing all the time ahead of me. And I – I think I'll lose you . . .'

Hetty moved to her, touched her. Yet her passion lay only in her words when she spoke – singing, exultant words surging out like a long-dammed waterfall, words as a sudden last ecstasy in an act of love. 'But you won't lose me, Léa, because whoever I am – it's for you. And because I can't be me, whoever that is, *without* you.'

Yes, they needed each other, depended for their very existence on the unequal ties between them. There could be no meaning, no vivacity, no life for them apart. They were indispensable to each other – like puppet and puppet-master.

Léonie recognized all that. But not Hetty, who in Léonie's arms that night thought they had found a greater and more equal depth of understanding and love than they had ever known before.

The top floor pied-à-terre in Crown Alley – a study-drawing room at the front, with the bedroom, small kitchen and bathroom to the rear – had, in Mortimer's infrequent use of it, become a rather grim and spartan affair: the musty, dark-walled front room filled with a large roll-top desk, torn leather armchairs and foxed prints of Georgian Dublin above piles of old legal books and papers, while the bedroom, when the girls had first come there, had been even gloomier, the divans covered with army blankets, decrepit eiderdowns, the curtains frayed and grimy, dampish.

But Mortimer, seeing an opportunity here for change, and telling the girls to make use of his account at Switzers in Grafton Street, suggested they amend the place in a brighter mode. And they had done so, painting the walls a creamy lemon, buying coloured cretonnes and chintzes for the chairs, proper linen for the beds, together with green serge curtains, and organizing coal fires. So that within a few weeks of their arrival the whole place had been transformed: a joyful cosy nest under the rooftops of Dublin, from where they looked out at chimney pots and steep slate roofs under pale November twilights – or in the mornings, first thing, when they leant from their bedroom window, seeing the glinting gunmetal water of the river Liffey above the alleyway and the puffing smoke from a Guinness barge on its way down-river to the port. Then, as the day gathered itself, with the clatter of trams and the heavy clip-clop of dray horses, the two girls, in dressing gowns, preparing their own breakfast and sitting over boiled eggs, soda bread, and thick tea, thought themselves in a wonderfully independent seventh heaven.

Léonie took singing lessons from a faded, but still technically adept Italian tenor, a Signor Grossi, who had a meticulously tidy studio, with an upright piano, surrounded by many ferns and aspidistras, off Grafton Street, behind the Gaiety Theatre. Hetty meanwhile spent her mornings at Mrs Wallingford's Academy – a crammer's for those few young women anxious to enter Trinity College – in Harcourt Street beyond Stephen's Green. The girls usually met at lunch in one of the more fashionable cafés in Grafton Street, at Bewley's or Cairo's, visited the National Gallery or the bookshops on the quays in the afternoon, with theatres, concerts or visits to the Olympia Music Hall in the evening.

And – though they had no intention of furthering the matter with Mr Fonsy O'Grady – they went to a photographer, too, whose sign they had seen outside a gaunt Georgian building at the end of Harcourt Street: a Mr Waxman, a satyr-like Englishman, small and somehow suspicious, Hetty thought, who wore a dark beret even while he worked, in what must originally have been a garden conservatory attached to the back of the house, the studio of screens, couches and potted palms roofed in by an expanse of glass. They went, from the very start, as 'Bertie and Bridey', meticulously turned out in the dandy's costume and the maid's outfit – Hetty explaining their need of some new 'artistic' reproductions of their act.

Mr Waxman very willingly provided them with such, in a variety of cleverly arranged poses around the potted plants, against a Chinese screen for their *Madame Butterfly* act – becoming quite roused as he worked, encouraging saucy smiles and angles, even suggesting they lie together on the couch, directions which Hetty only partly responded to, mistrusting the man more than ever, refusing him their address, saying they would pick up the photographs later.

They were very good – in an unexpected way. Mr Waxman, in his professionalism (and no doubt reflecting his own doubtful tastes), had succeeded, despite Hetty's resistance, in giving the girls a most provocatively teasing and voluptuous air. The sauciness he had wished for was certainly there and made the more compelling by the obvious class of the subjects: Hetty's classically arrogant features touched now by some devil in the flesh; Léonie's usually rather cosy dark looks somehow exaggerated, filled with a slumbrous sensuality.

Mr Waxman was pleased. 'I'd like to see your act – I do quite a lot of theatrical work as it happens. Are you playing at the Queen's or the Olympia?'

'Oh no,' Hetty quickly retorted. 'Just a holiday in Dublin. We work in England.'

A world of other people suited the two girls. Far from losing each other in it, the sophisticated pleasures, company and surroundings of the great city drew them both out from that all-absorbing, too obsessive regard for each other that had begun to threaten their lives alone in Summer Hill.

Here, developing their tastes, their naturally adventurous temperament leading them to entertainment and education of every haphazard kind, they soon found new facets to admire in and surprise each other with. And they came to love these changes in themselves as much as, before, they had taken to what was basic in their character – a need to venture, join hands, in risks against the world.

Now, in Dublin, they could better understand and express their matrix of attraction for each other, name and promote the growing parts, which together seemed to include all things, the whole gamut of emotion: affection, mutual reliance, a complementary wit and intelligence, bedtime company, a deep love of the heart. For the girls at least, not part of the Irish political tensions seething all round them or of the war in Europe, these were days of extravagant hope and happiness.

Léonie's parents, as closely in touch as the sporadic wartime posts allowed, made her a generous allowance; and Mortimer, on Frances's authority, did the same on a lesser scale, from the estate at Summer Hill. Together, their tuition fees paid and the small flat gratis, they had, after giving Mrs McCabe £3 a week for her work, some £12 left over for all their other needs, food, clothes, books, entertainment. Thus, by comparison with most others in the city, a fair sum of free money was available to them. And they made good use of it – buying modern prints from Combridges in Grafton Street and winter hothouse carnations from the old shawly lady at her stall on the Duke Street corner next to the art shop; and their rooms were always full of fruit, autumn pears and apples, which both girls loved to smell and munch.

They entertained Robert and Bertie, too, twice, on their Sunday exeats from St Columba's College in the Dublin mountains: at lunch in the Hibernian Hotel and a second time transporting them in a cab to the Zoological Gardens in Phoenix Park. Holidays, at Christmas and the following Easter, they all spent together at Summer Hill, the mood of their various relationships largely unchanged in that new year of 1917, when Robert, who would be sitting his university examinations, to read modern history in Trinity College in the summer, was more occupied, perforce, with his books than with Hetty.

In early May all four returned to Dublin, and life for the two girls resumed its largely happy tenor, with the added pleasures now of the coming summer in the city, when in the warmth the girls took long afternoon walks to the very far end of Sandymount strand, watching the yachts and sailing dinghies begin to move, from behind the jetty at Kingstown harbour out into the choppy waters of Dublin Bay.

Then without warning – for Mortimer had been away in London and she still rarely looked at a newspaper – the blow fell for Hetty. Returning home alone one afternoon in mid-June she saw the succession of placards outside the *Evening Mail* building in Dame Street: 'AMNESTY DECLARED' – 'REPUBLICAN PRISONERS TO BE RELEASED' – 'MRS FRANCES FRASER COMING HOME!'

I I

When the two girls returned to Summer Hill in July, they found Frances changed indeed . . . They had welcomed her off the mail boat at Kingstown on her return from Aylesbury prison – before, it seemed, half the population of Dublin, on the pier and later in the city, had engulfed her with a far more vigorous greeting. Mrs Fraser, among the frantic crowds and cheers, had been the heroine not just of the hour, but for days subsequently in Dublin – when she had visited the ruins of Liberty Hall and other sites of the rebellion, attending endless welcoming committees and receptions. And in all this fervour Hetty – rather thankfully – had lost her. But now, alone in Summer Hill, she had time to take full stock of her mother.

Yes, she had changed – but so completely, like a brilliant conjuring trick, that it was unbelievable. She was much thinner, pale-faced, hair unkempt now, with a relentlessly beatific smile, all her previous vivid attack and anger seemingly quite gone. She was not so much saintly, as Hetty had half-anticipated, but had more the air of a plaster saint: like that passive blue-and-white Madonna remembered from Elly's tin-roofed Catholic church in Domenica. Her mother might have been shell-shocked or sleep-walking; her voice had no edge to it, full of dying falls. And, worse, much of what she said seemed largely nonsensical to Hetty – often mouthing platitudes about the 'holy spirit' and the 'remission of sin' in a way which Hetty found embarrassing.

Hetty was appalled by the transformation. Her mother, in her pliant submissiveness, far from gaining her soul, appeared a broken person. If this was the result of 'coming to God' Hetty wanted nothing of it – God had simply crushed this woman's spirit. Hetty, finding no resistance in her mother, felt disappointed somehow. Here was no worthy opponent, as she had half-wanted her to be, just a broken reed, a woman now firmly embalmed in a spiritual dotage.

But Hetty quite misread these initial, outwardly passive signs in her mother as the final sum of things in her – and grew over-confident thereby, especially with Léonie.

Frances felt she had come to God, certainly, the God of the New Testament, all-knowing, loving, and forgiving – forsaking that other righteous, all-powerful and punishing being in the Old Testament of her Jewish ancestry and upbringing. And it was just this apparent transformation which Hetty observed with such distaste. In fact – though neither Hetty nor her mother recognized this – Frances's new creed was not really a true belief at all. It was an act, one which she had unconsciously taken up, as suitable to her recent incarnations as sacrificial revolutionary, imprisoned political martyr, lost leader and heroine of Holy Catholic Ireland. Hetty was not to know, since she did not admit it of herself, how her mother was just as good an actress as she.

Hetty and Léonie – in their rainy indoor affairs and trysts, and since Robert was away for the first part of the holidays staying with Bertie and his family in Co. Kildare – had taken to using Henry's locked workrooms at the top of the house. Hetty, ever since her childhood when she had illicitly played there with Robert, had always enjoyed the secrecy of these rooms, and even more their aura of drama and romance, the musty ether smells and sense of fabulous adventure they contained. And here, among the African assegais and exotic stuffed animals, she and Léonie sometimes met – to talk, to play, to love, entering the rooms along the flat roof, behind the balustrade, by one of its windows.

Here – just as Henry and Dermot had done – they made a world of their own far above and beyond any interference from the rest of the household. Here, too, on the shabby Chesterfield sofa, when the mood took them, they could love each other, as they no longer could at night down-stairs, for Frances had returned to her own bedroom, just beyond theirs on the first floor landing. Here in any case, they thought, Frances, who now showed little interest in the affairs of the house, would never interrupt or disturb them.

But Frances, though apparently only concerned with matters spiritual, had only temporarily lost interest in the house. A month after her return, regaining her strength and temper, she conceived a whole new use for the place, in which the great pile would, she envisaged, play a vital role, become a spearhead of enlightened feminine life in the new Republic – when that came, and the moment could not now be long delayed. Yes, she would start to instruct the young women of Ireland in cooking, house-hold management, arts and crafts. She would clear out and make over the top floors as work and classrooms, for knitting, needlework, weaving, Gaelic lessons and other essential feminine accomplishments. It was a mission aimed initially at the culturally deprived and generally benighted women of the immediate locality, so that their horizons, thus broadened, would allow them, as fit citizens, to enter the coming Celtic Republic.

It was this optimistic plan which she first set out to implement one muggy, thunder-threatening afternoon in August, taking the keys of her brother Henry's old rooms with her – deciding that, yes, these rooms, too, would have to be cleared out. They could no longer be kept as a mausoleum, a shrine to him. It was not suitable, as much for his unfortunate proclivities – his, as she now viewed it, immoral relationship with Dermot – as for the fact that these rooms, as she knew, so reeked of Henry's imperial enthusiasms, from which corrupt source, no doubt, he and Dermot had contracted their most regrettable tastes. In the new Ireland there would be no room for any such aberrations. Henry's rooms would have to go. So, quite forgetting the all-knowing, loving and forgiving Christ of the New Testament, she stamped up the stairs as briskly as the stifling heat allowed.

Hetty and Léonie were in Henry's rooms that afternoon.

They lay, scantily clad, in the thunderstruck air, drowsily fondling each other, the land beginning to boom all round them, the windows rattling as the weather exploded over Summer Hill in great salvoes and jagged, sky-scorching flashes.

They never heard Frances's footsteps outside on the landing, nor the key turning in the lock, as they clasped each other, half in fear, half in pleasure. The girls had brought a basket of early Worcester Pearmains with them, munching some of them prior to the onset of the storm. The remainder lay scattered in front of them. And Hetty had been teasing Léonie with the old snake skeleton from the tea-chest so that this sinister necklace of whitened vertebrae lay on the floor as well, just next to the sofa.

It was the first thing Frances noticed as she stepped into the room, then the apple basket, before a vivid flash illuminated the two girls in their *déshabille*. Frances absorbed all these views – fruit, serpent and fallen women – simultaneously with a most vicious thunderclap right above the house, and put the whole together as an apocalyptic vision, a most patently obvious fall from Eden.

Thunderstruck herself now, all her previous visions of Celtic feminine purity in these rooms destroyed, she viewed the two girls with so grotesquely severe an expression that Hetty smiled. Indeed, already deciding that attack was the best means of defence, she nearly laughed.

'Mama! – what *are* you doing here?'

Her mother, for reply, shook convulsively, bunching

her fingers uncontrollably. She seemed about to levitate with anger, to grow huge in the darkened, light-flashing room. The looming shapes from the jungle of stuffed animals appeared to snap and glower at her. She felt threatened by an overwhelming aura of nature's malignity. And though at that moment she seemed so much the prophet of doom, taking on all the lineaments of her mother, Lady Cordiner, in her fiercest days, she was suddenly frightened, oppressed by what she chose to see as an ultimate vision of evil everywhere about her.

Hetty meanwhile, believing her mother had undoubtedly regained the form of worthy opponent, did laugh at her then – outright. But Frances spun away in the same instant, before her daughter's derision had time to rest on her.

Hetty, on Frances's call, eventually made a tardy appearance in front of her mother, ambling with apparent unconcern into her boudoir later that day. The storm had passed. But Hetty, thinking it would remain in her mother's demeanour, decided she had nothing to lose by taking the initiative again – knowing, too, exactly what line she would choose.

So she said immediately, and with biting reproach, 'Mama, you wrote me several times, from prison, how sorry you were over your insensitive, your difficult behaviour towards me as a child. Yet now you seem intent on renewing it. What can all this be aba-aba-about?'

Her stammer betrayed her confident sally. Her mother, quite composed now, waiting patiently by the mantelpiece, took immediate advantage of the lapse.

'Henrietta, this is no matter of *my* insensitivity, my difficulty – but yours.' She spoke with sad reason. 'You have provoked this, not I. You can have no idea how improper your behaviour with Léonie is. So I must tell you, it is *vicious*.' On these last words, she quite changed, rounding on her daughter, eyes ablaze, lapsing from reason then, storming the heights of all her old insensate fury.

Hetty, pleased by this reaction, regained her poise at once. Now she thought she had her mother where she wanted her – a more than worthy opponent, since it was obvious that she had lost her wits again. Hetty was calm, considered. 'Vicious, Mama? It can't be. I love Léonie.'

'Not love – mere lust.' Her mother moved towards the window, while Hetty stood between her and the door, so that she had the happy feeling of having cornered her mother.

'What nonsense. You cannot feel such for someone loved, who loves you just as much.'

'I shall not debate with with you,' her mother ranted. 'For there cannot be debate over such matters. Your behaviour is wicked, depraved.'

Frances moved to her desk . . . and Hetty advanced a few steps, an animal stalking its prey but not yet quite certain of it. Another show of force was required before a kill – and Hetty had prepared herself for this. 'And you?' she asked with bitter sarcasm. 'You must know of just such love – wicked and depraved – to speak of it, to speak of it so wildly.' Hetty gazed at her mother, letting the words sink in. Frances trembled now, speechless. 'Oh, yes,' Hetty went on. 'For years now you've lied to me – about "Mr Fraser". But he was never my real Papa – I know it. There was someone else. Who was it? And what sort of love was that?' Her mother spun across the room then, slapping her daughter's face. But Hetty remained quite unmoved. 'That's no answer – simply proof of my point: how you have always lied to me.'

Frances, brought up short by this invulnerable girl and the force of her argument, took the only way out she could. She retreated.

'I'm – I'm sorry . . .' She cleared her brow with a hand. 'I lost my temper, for what you say is so preposterous. I will tell you – Robert Fraser *was* your father, but I have never properly spoken to you of him, as I should have done, for the reason that I could not bring myself to think of him myself. It was a rash marriage, taken without proper thought on my part, as a result of my banishment from Summer Hill. He was a brute, in every way as I discovered. Naturally I've not wanted to talk to you of this. But he was your father.'

Her words, Hetty had to admit, sounded convincing enough. Hetty remembered all too well what a cruelly unpleasant man he had been. And Frances, sensing that she had crossed this thin ice with her daughter, took the initiative again. 'And it is just because of my own mistakes – with your father,' she moved towards Hetty now, speaking very earnestly, 'that I must see you do not repeat such folly in the same . . . sphere of the emotions. If you can curb your self-will, Hetty – your most unsuitable, unnatural desires – there is a whole world for you, waiting. But not with Léonie. There is no more future there for you than there was for me with your Papa.'

'But Léonie is *not* like my Papa, not for an instant – never cruel, just the opposite. What you say for you is true, no doubt, but not for me. Léa is wonderful.'

Her mother, seeing the force of this argument but unable to admit it, became agitated again. 'None the less, Henrietta, you fail to see the point: for all his faults, your father was a *man*. Léonie is a *woman*.'

'I see no difference. There are no two sorts of love. If one feels such love at all, for anyone, it is the same kind—'

'Henrietta,' her mother interrupted, playing her trump card, 'you shall see . . . how this is no mere cranky opinion of mine. It will be Mortimer's – and that of Léonie's parents, too, I assure you. You will see,' she added ominously. 'There will be changes. None of us can sit by and see you both ruin your lives in this depraved manner.'

Hetty became alarmed now. What was her mother implying? Then it suddenly struck her. 'Oh, no, you can't do that – you can't part us. Not that, never, *ever*!'

But this was exactly what Frances proceeded to do – writing of the event in Henry's rooms, in suitably veiled terms, both to Léonie's parents and to Mortimer, pointing out to him that, in the circumstances, the use of his Dublin pied-à-terre by the two girls must now be discontinued. To Mr and Mrs Straus she wrote more tactfully still. But the message was clear enough: their daughter was involved in a quite unsuitable intimacy with hers and must therefore return to France at once.

Mortimer in his reply, though he privately thought it all a storm in a tea-cup, was forced to accede to Frances's request. She was, after all, Hetty's mother. The posts to France, with the war, were considerably delayed. There was no immediate reply from the Strauses in Paris. But meanwhile the girls were told of Mortimer's regrets: his flat would not be available to them that autumn, when they had expected to return to Dublin, resuming their studies there. And Frances by now had made it clear to Léonie that she could no longer make her welcome at Summer Hill.

All this alarmed and infuriated the two girls – as much because of their impotence in the matter as for the fact that it seemed inevitable now that they would have to part. Léonie would quite possibly be sent to her Uncle Eli's in New York, while Hetty would remain in what would then be the lonely hell of Summer Hill, cooped up with her frightful mother. For Hetty particularly such a fate was not to be contemplated. She hated her Mama once more, with a barely contained fury; all these monstrous man-oeuvrings simply hardened her resolve. But to do what? Neither she nor Léonie had money. Where else could they go?

Frances soon learnt, in the awful silences and air of bitter resentment about the house, how much the girls resisted her dictates – which gave her added proof of their necessity. She gave no thought as to how they might over-turn them. How could they? Neither girl had yet reached her majority; they had no resources.

'Yes, they'll probably send me to New York,' Léonie said to Hetty quietly one evening. But Hetty shook her head vigorously. 'We'll never let them do that. We agreed, Léa, we'll not be separated, never, ever.'

Léonie nodded. 'But how not?' she asked wanly.

'I've been thinking: there is one way. Remember that little baby-faced man – Mr Fonsy O'Grady? We met him that night at the Olympia Theatre. "Fonsy O'Grady" and his "Theatre of Varieties"?'

'Yes?'

'Well, I found his card.' She held it out then with a flourish, like a magic charm. 'You remember, we told him we had an act together – "Bertie and Bridey" – and he said to come out and show it to him. Well, we will! That's just what we'll do. And he'll give us a job, I know he will – and we'll go away with them on his tours, and they'll never find us!' Hetty, as she spoke, became more and more breathlessly enchanted with the idea.

'But, Hetty—'

'Of *course* it'll work! "Fortune favours the brave" – remember? I *know* we'll win. You've always been so doubtful about the dressing up thing. But don't you see? – this is the very thing that'll save us now – just that!'

Léonie remained doubtful. But suddenly she was moved by something, almost palpable, hanging in the air between them: a gift of faith it seemed, which Hetty had just offered her, which was hers for the taking if she made the same leap into the dark. So she leapt. Hetty's vast excitement, her surging confidence, convinced her, enveloped her. Yes, it seemed obvious now – with Hetty one could do anything. Yes, they would win. Hetty was right. She gazed into her blue eyes, letting Hetty's certainties flow into her like a balm, her flashing beauty and spirit at that moment a sure guarantee that everything would work out just as she said.

'All right,' Léonie agreed, kissing her softly, briefly. 'Yes! – yes, yes!'

There were careful preparations to be made. They would need money – more than the £20 or so of their earlier allowances which they had saved. They would have to practise their act, invent new ones, plan their actual escape from the house – to which tasks they set themselves throughout the rest of August.

Frances was not suspicious of their sudden musical

enthusiasms – indeed she readily agreed when they asked if the grand piano might be moved to the morning room at the back of the house, for here she could keep an eye on them. And the girls spent hours there, with operatic scores and popular music sheets bought in Kilkenny, thumping out renditions and pastiches of the latest songs – 'Tipperary', 'Keep the Home Fires Burning' – together with old music hall favourites, 'Down at the Old Bull and Bush' and 'Knees Up Mother Brown', before refining their duets from *Madame Butterfly* and adding other operas and operettas to their repertoire, flagrantly dramatic passages, which they guyed or sang straight from *The Merry Widow* or *La Traviata*.

'Your tiny hand is frozen . . .' Hetty sang lugubriously, gazing with exaggerated longing at Léonie, before both of them burst out laughing. '*No*, that's just what we mustn't to – that's the whole point – no use unless we do it all *absolutely* with a serious face.'

Hetty loved the whole direction of these rehearsals and showed innate gifts which flowered in the hot August days, as they pursued their variety acts over the piano keys and across the morning room carpet.

For they danced, too, and invented routines against the tinny music from a great horn gramophone – military quicksteps, mimicking strutting soldiers, to the sound of 'The Dashing White Sergeant' and 'Dolly Gray'. And they fenced as well, stamping across the room, creating an act of great brio, foils clashing to the strains of Strauss's 'Thunder and Lightning' polka.

By the end of the month they had got together half a dozen polished and really quite professional numbers – 'Bertie and Bridey', the rakish near gent in loud checks and the maid in the papier-mâché cherry hat who together had such droll and unexpected musical gifts, rendering with tongue-in-cheek vivacity or with genuine emotion a whole range of songs, together with song-and-dance routines, leading to the climax of a dazzling fencing bout, after which, foils dipped, they both practised their final bows and curtsys to an imaginary audience.

Money was a problem in a different key. Hetty eventually decided to steal it – in kind, if not in cash. And so, just as her mother had done twenty years before at Summer Hill, she began to filch small objects about the house – silver teaspoons, gold-topped scent bottles, Baccarat paperweights – soon gathering quite a collection of little *objets d'art* which they would sell when the need arose. As to their actual escape – well, with all the baggage they would need for their costumes, that presented further problems. They would think about it.

They were forced to think about it sooner than expected. At the beginning of September letters arrived from the Strauses in Paris, for both Léonie and Frances. To the latter, Benjamin Straus, ever the man of the world and not to be intimidated by someone he knew to be slightly dotty, was fairly blunt. He wrote that he regarded the whole business between the girls as no more than an understandable *tendresse*. He had perfect confidence in his daughter's good sense in the matter, he went on. 'But of course,' he continued, 'I would not wish Léonie to overstay her welcome in the present circumstances – and have therefore arranged that she go to your cousin Mortimer's house at Islandbridge. We have exchanged telegrams and he is perfectly willing that she stay with him, pending her return to France – a journey which, given the present U-boat situation in both Channels, she will not make until I am certain that it is absolutely safe to do so.'

To Léonie her parents wrote that she should stay with Mortimer – for the duration of the war, if necessary – and that she could resume her singing lessons in Dublin. And her father added a footnote: he was sorry that, as it seemed, her friendship with Hetty would have to be suspended. But he consoled her by hinting that its termination at Summer Hill was the act of an unbalanced woman and that Léonie could surely resume the association at a later date. Meanwhile, with the present situation in France and on the high seas, she would be safer in Ireland. There was no question of her going to stay with her Uncle Eli in New

York. America was already in the war, as much as made no difference, he told her – and any United States shipping across the Atlantic was in jeopardy.

'Well, that's all right for you,' Hetty told Léonie when she had read the letter. 'But I won't be allowed *near* Dublin.' And Léonie had turned to her, saying with soft certainty, 'So what? You'll be near *me*. Because I *won't* be going to Islandbridge. Wherever we're going – we're going together. Remember? We agreed.'

'Yes,' Hetty said simply.

It was Aunt Emily who solved the problem of their escape from Summer Hill. Hetty, as always, often visited her in the studio-bedroom overlooking the hornbeam maze. And she had spoken to her, of course, of her mother's latest wicked machinations, how she and Léonie were to be forcibly separated – just because they were so fond of each other. Aunt Emily had humphed with particular sympathy in her gruff way. Subsequently, with her insights and intuitions, she came to suspect that the girls were planning to escape the house altogether.

So it was that one day, when Hetty arrived in her room, that she found her great-aunt engaged on a most surprising water-colour. She looked over her shoulder at the nearly completed picture. It showed herself and Léonie – and Aunt Emily with her easel and paintboxes – out in the governess trap, the vehicle filled with other luggage, hat boxes and suitcases and Gladstone bags, piled up between them. The trap, careering along a dusty country road, was clearly making this spanking pace towards Thomastown station on the horizon, where a train waited, the engine puffing smoke impatiently into a blue sky.

Hetty was astonished by her aunt's prescience. 'Aunt Emily! – what can you be thinking of? We're not going anywhere like that!'

'Excuse yourself, girl – I'm not *that* much of a fool. Know all about your troubles. It's obvious! You're off somewhere together. And quite right too. Wouldn't stay here a minute longer, with your Mama up to her wicked schemes again. Quite right to get out. And here's the way:

I'll take you both out on a painting expedition, put your baggage and stuff in a ditch beforehand and we'll pick it up on the way to the station. Nothing simpler.'

'But Aunt Emily, why—'

Aunt Emily looked up at her irascibly. 'Excuse yourself again, girl! Haven't I heard it all? – they want you and Léonie out of each other's light. And for why?'

'Why?'

'They want you to have *men* friends, that's the why.'

'I don't know about—'

'Don't interrupt, girl – I know very well that's the reason. And didn't I tell your Mama many times – have *nothing* to do with men, ruination of everything, ruined her. And I've told you the same – and thank God you took the hint. You stick with Léonie – best move you ever made. And that's why you'll both be coming with me in the trap.'

And so it was. A week later, on a sunny autumn morning, with the leaves just starting to turn and a hint of delicate chill in the changing air, the three of them clattered down the drive, disturbing the rooks from the trees about the house.

Hetty looked back at the long house on the hill, disappearing into its haven of trees, a last glint of sunlight on its tall windows before it was gone and only the ragged cawing of the birds reminded her of all that she had loved and hated at Summer Hill.

Léonie, sensing her emotion, took her hand. 'Don't be sad.'

'Oh, I'm not,' Hetty lied. 'We'll come back.'

'Of course you will!' Aunt Emily frisked the horse along, the ends of the red scarf with which she had tied her floppy straw hat down streaming out behind her in the wind. 'You'll be back, one day, just as your mother was – when she skedaddled off to the colonies years ago.'

Hetty was touched by her great-aunt's happy certainties, so that tears did come to her eyes then, and Léonie offered her a handkerchief as they sped out of the gateway.

In just such a manner, on such a day, Frances had

consoled Elly nearly twenty years before, when they, too, had made an equally precipitate exit from Summer Hill. History was almost exactly repeating itself.

Fonsy O'Grady's 'Theatre of Varieties' was just that – a wonderful mix of players and acts: part music hall, part circus, part straight theatre, part knockabout farce, part *café-concert*. The company, as well as its comics, musicians and singers, also included jugglers, clowns, a duo of tight-rope artists, a fat lady, a gypsy fortune teller, a ventrilo-quist, a troupe of acrobatic dwarfs and a mangy lion with its keeper – all brought together by Fonsy's whimsical but most comprehensive view of theatre.

Fonsy had been a fine Dublin comedian himself in the old days. But he had never taken dictation easily – had, indeed, taken more readily to the bottle, which combination, together with his generally wayward approach, had led him to form this haphazard collection of players over the years; he spurned all dull uniformity, insisting only that the acts should be quick, daring, vivacious, original – reflecting his own tastes and abilities here.

With such unconventional ideas he had never main-tained his place in the big Dublin music halls, the Olympia or the Queen's. But he had been more than content to run things his way, on a smaller and quite different scale, with engagements in out of the way places. His passion – without his knowing it – was for the life of the old strolling players, for *commedia dell' arte*, for improvisation, sur-prise, a joyous variety in all things. Theatre for him was only this – and the open road; a date in some small market town in the wilds of Ireland pleased him so much more than anything metropolitan. 'Tents under the stars!' he would shout to his troupe when the beds in some local commercial hotel were all filled. Though he himself would invariably find comfort in just such a place, with his much more hard-headed wife Marjorie, who ran the company's finances. Fonsy O'Grady, in his devil-may-care enthusi-asms, his cherub grace, charity and unconscious identification with the old Gaelic world of wandering minstrels, always seemed like the last of his kind.

And the two girls were lucky in his eclectic spirit. He took to them and their act at once, seeing how, if both lacked finesse, they were equally without any hint of the tired or blasé. Like him, the girls were originals. Yes, they could join his company of players. Their summer season had just closed in Bray – some of the British artistes, employed only for those months, had returned home. They could do with an extra act or two since, from now on, through the winter and spring, they would be touring the provinces, with dates in small theatres and village halls throughout the country, across its length and breadth, from Wexford to Galway, Cork to Sligo town.

The girls had met Fonsy, not in Bray, but at his permanent headquarters – an encampment in the narrow Dargle valley some miles inland from Bray, where Fonsy, years before, had taken over a small farmhouse, set above the thickly wooded slopes running down to the tumbling river. And here, on cleared terraces among the beech and elm, he had set up his troupe. Those that did not lodge in Bray lived in the farm outhouses and then, descending the valley, in wooden huts, some bell tents and a few green-roofed horse caravans.

The rehearsal rooms and general centre for the company were in a stone barn, fitted with sprung boards, taken from an old *celidhe* crossroads dance floor, set over the rough earth. And it was here, with a clattery upright piano, that the girls had given their audition.

Without deceit, they had first appeared before Fonsy in their real personae, the 'Bertie and Bridey' costumes still in their baggage – dissembling only in their provenance. They were first cousins, they explained (and in their dark Jewish colourings there was a sufficient likeness here to justify the claim) – Rachel and Sarah Bauer, with homes in the East End of London. They had started careers there, on the boards of the local music hall, the Theatre Royal, off the Mile End Road. Their act had gone well enough. But they had itchy feet, and had decided to try their luck elsewhere. They wanted to tour, fancy free, to see a bit of the world.

Fonsy saw no reason to disbelieve them. But his wife Marjorie was more circumspect. 'I like them, Fonsy – and the act,' she told him. 'But they're too classy somehow. You don't get that sort in the Mile End Road.'

'Ah, ye might well,' he opined. 'Aren't they a class of a Jew to start with? – and the East End there full of them. And then aren't there all sorts of wimmin doin' queer things these days? – what with the war on and them suffragettes and all.' And since they both liked them – Marjorie, maternal at heart, was without any children of her own – they left it at that.

'You can board with us for the moment,' Marjorie told them. 'Though maybe Bella Lynch, now that old Johnny is gone – maybe you might share with her? – in the big caravan below.'

Bella Lynch was the fat woman who did an act with a melodeon. Her husband Johnny had played the fiddle with her, doing Irish jigs. But he had died a month before.

'Yes – perhaps,' the girls had said, taken at once by the romance of this idea. Bella was a huge friendly woman from Galway with a great scatter of red hair and the trusting blue eyes of a child in a face of unmade dough. She lived in a large, untidy caravan half-way down the hill.

And this, before they set off on their first engagement, was what they did. Bella, in her recent bereavement, was happy to have the two girls as company and distraction, and despite her splendid size there was space enough, at one end of the caravan, where, with a curtain pulled across at night, the girls slept in narrow bunks to either side, covered in thick patchwork quilts which Bella with her delicate nimble fingers – so at odds with the rest of her body – occupied her spare time in making.

The girls, almost immediately, had sent letters to Frances, to Mortimer and to the Strauses in Paris. They were happy and well and *together* – and intended to stay that way, until such time, Hetty told her mother, as she saw fit to change her mind about their friendship. Léonie, with her parents, was entirely open and reassuring, at least as to her present welfare. It had been agreed anyway, as she pointed out, that she should remain in the safety of Ireland for the duration of the war. And she was doing just that. But that safety depended as much on her being with Hetty. She left a poste restante address for her parents to get in touch with her in Dublin. To Mortimer Hetty was equally open – he would understand, she knew. And, when he received her letter, he did.

With Frances it was quite a different matter. On the girls' disappearance, in a flurry of all her old dramatic dictates, she had informed the local constabulary and then detectives in Dublin. At first they had taken notice; a few enquiries were made, a watch was put on railway terminals and ports. But, after the arrival of the various letters from the two girls, the police had relaxed. With the present political turmoil in the country they had many, far more pressing concerns.

Meanwhile, throughout the rest of September, the girls sharpened their act. But much more than that, face to face with the real thing now, they began to absorb all the arts of variety theatre. In the big barn – to the varied sounds of melodeon music from Bella, the thump and cries of the dwarf acrobats, the drum-beats accompanying the tight-rope act – they soon found friends among the troupe. With a fascination which they tried to hide, they watched these acts, spellbound by all the tricks of the trade, anxious now to mimic them, completely to throw themselves into this vibrant new life.

The two tightrope artistes, a Belfast couple, Jessy and Hal Morton, particularly took to them. And so did the stand-up comics, Billy and Tony Whelan, middle-aged men who did a tramp act. But above all it was the collection of dwarfs who really took them in hand – 'The Tumbling Tinies', six small men, two Irish brothers and the rest assortedly from Britain, headed by the eldest brother, Eddy Nolan, hirsute and slightly hunchback, a most deft and vital character who led the troupe in a series of lightning spins, hand-stands, somersaults and whirly cart-wheels across the boards, before he ended the act, juggling balls, atop a pyramid of the other five.

With these people, watching everything they did, the girls began to see the essence of things: immaculate physical control, co-ordination, split-second timing, the need for endless exercise, practice, suppleness. They came to love and envy the skills they saw before them. The world quite changed as you watched them, Hetty thought. With the lovely flash and dazzle of their movements, their perfect balance, poise, timing, the tear-pricking beauty of their acts, these people, the moment they took to the boards, entered another dimension – lost to all the dross of reality, entering a pure, exalted ether where they were suddenly in command of life, towering over it, where they had *won* – which was exactly what Hetty longed for herself.

And so she and Léonie, under the excuse of improving their own act, asked to join in, to learn from them. In woollen tights and leotards, the dwarfs taught them all the knockabout tumbles and routines – banana slides, prat-falls and the art of giving alternate cracking back-handers to the cheek without hurt. With the Whelan brothers they learnt the three-hat trick, in which shabby bowlers, at increasing speed, were passed between them, from hand to head to hand . . . and their conjuring act which followed, with baggy sleeves, from which an endless succession of carrots emerged, apparently disappearing down their throats with equal dispatch. Hetty, by the end of the month, managed several perilously swaying trips across the tightrope – before she began to master even this act.

Until the year before, the company had toured in a large charabanc, with two lorries and trailers for the props, costumes and the mangy lion. But now, with the advent of petrol rationing, these vehicles lay idle in a big hay barn. The company, without the lion, would have to tour this year by train, Fonsy told them – or, for those who wished and had such, by caravans with their horses. Bella, with the persistent encouragement of the girls (who had no wish to be seen at railway stations), was persuaded to adopt the latter transport. Thus Bobs, a sturdy chestnut farm horse, was fed with daily oats and made ready for the shafts – the journey to their first date in Wicklow town, fifteen miles south, at the end of September.

So began enchanted months for the two girls. They ran away into a life they could never have imagined – of comradeship and breathtaking excitement, stress, tears, happiness, stage fright: all these offered and taken from them in a swirl of vivid days and nights, with hectic moves, set-ups, rehearsals, lugging the great wicker costume skips about, plunging around tiny squalid dressing rooms against broken mirrors, with faint candles or oil light to make up with, before the curtain rose, the dross was put away and the magic began: Bella on the melodeon, strutting out centre stage, her black shawl and lovely red Galway petticoats flowing, starting the show with a helter-skelter medley of Irish songs – 'Phil the Fluter's Ball', 'MacGinty's Goat' and 'The Rose of Mooncoin'.

It was a life the girls came to love, and their own love bloomed in it: the open road, tents under the stars, opening the caravan door in some country byway on to yellow-leafed autumn mornings; dawns in mid-winter when Hetty lit the stove, sending woodsmoke crackling up the stove chimney, flooding the air with burning pine wood and later the smell of sizzling bacon; dazzling frost crystals on the leaded window panes, wafer-thin ice on the wash bowl as Hetty plunged her hands into it, the cold stinging thrill on her cheeks as she cleared the remnants of last night's make-up off, while Léonie gave the horse a haybag and Bella commenced her elaborate dressings behind the serge curtain.

Their act – in Wicklow, Enniscorthy and Wexford, as they made their way south – went down well. Fonsy had got them to shorten it, dividing it in two parts, with their fencing bout in the second half of the show, dressed as two Musketeers in braided jackets, pantaloons and long boots, though still clearly women. And this second act, as they clashed and parried across the stage to the frenzied drumbeats and fiddles in the pit beneath them, roused the locals.

'Good – great!' Fonsy told them one evening as they left the small stage in Wexford. And later, in a smoky, whiskey-laden back room of White's Hotel, he had looked at them admiringly. 'Clare to God, I'd like to get the points of thim swords at the throat of Bob Molloy in Waterford – and he havin' just cancelled our date at the Royal there.'

'Why?'

'Ah and hasn't he gone and put in one of thim Kinema machines instead – the curse of life for all of us it is, bein' put in now all over the country, ruining our dates.'

Fonsy morosely fed himself more stout. All the company was depressed that night. The Waterford date had always been a good one.

But Hetty said to Léonie later, 'That's easy – we can get the date back for them.'

'Easy?'

'Yes, the Kinema thing that shows the pictures – just put it out of action. Then they'll want us as a replacement.'

'Hetty, if the police—'

'The police won't do anything. They'll never know.'

The company in any case went on to Waterford, where rooms had already been booked, and in the hopes of finding another venue. Bella parked the caravan in a field half a mile south out of the town on the Dunmore road. Léonie hoped Hetty might have forgotten her threat. But she had not.

'Smart clothes today,' she told her first thing that morning. 'We're going into town.'

'For what?'

'You'll see – tell you when we get there.'

They dressed in their most fashionable outfits – pompous hats and veils, kid gloves and discreet handbags – in the manner of society ladies. Telling Bella they were going shopping, they took a cab to the Adelphi Hotel on the quays near the Theatre Royal just round the corner. Here, over coffee in the lounge, Hetty explained her plan.

'We'll walk round and see the theatre manager, this Molloy person – tell him we are organizing a series of charity concerts in the provinces, for the Society of Protestant Orphans or something, and would like to see round the theatre. We'll do it all very grand and hoity-toity. You keep him occupied and I'll slip away – I'm bound to find the stupid machine somewhere. It'll be at the back probably, in the balcony, and I'll put the kybosh on it.'

'Hetty, it's madness—'

'Léa, Fonsy and the others have all helped us no end. It's the least we can do. Besides, all this Kinema picture show business – it's so cheap and *vulgar*. Locals are much better off without it.'

The manager – a dapper little man, very full of himself – played straight into their hands when, having shown them round the theatre, he suggested they take a look at his sensational new equipment which he had just installed upstairs, in a metal cubicle at the back of the balcony.

'There, now – just look at it!' he told them, puffed up with pride. 'All the way from London – the latest Kalee projecting machine. See—' He pointed out the big drum-spool at the top. 'That's where the film goes first, then right down through this little gate here, past the shutter and lens, then into the bottom spool. Clickety-click! – you'd never imagine it. We've a great Chaplin two-reeler tomorrow night – Keystone Kops, Fatty Arbuckle, Mack Sennett, the lot!'

Hetty noticed the shutter. It was a delicate spinning mechanism, in the shape of a Maltese cross, with four black arms, set between the lens and the mechanical gate. She made eyes at Léonie, gesturing to her to get the manager out of the way for a moment.

'Now, Mr Molloy,' Léonie said with breathless interest, 'I think I understand all that. But what happens out *there*?' She led him to the window of the little cubicle. 'Is that the wall of the stage the light shines on, or just a sheet?'

'Ah, no indeed, Miss – that's a special silver screen, specially treated paint . . .'

The two of them moved away. In the same instant Hetty put her hand into the projector and broke off two of the shutter arms. They snapped in her fingers like matchsticks. She came forward then, joining the others. 'I say,' she spoke in her most gracious Ascendancy voice, 'it really is all *most* interesting, Mr Molloy.'

Mr Molloy's much-heralded Kinematograph performance did not take place that night, nor, indeed, on the four subsequent evenings. Fonsy O'Grady's Theatre of Varieties most conveniently and successfully filled the bill instead.

It was a constant battle and worry for the company on the tour – these new Kinema machines, theatres converted, replaced by hideous picture palaces being set up everywhere in Irish towns, which took away half their audiences when they did play – and, worse, forbade them some dates completely in towns they had performed in for years. Hetty came to despise the whole business of the Kinema which so jeopardized their livelihoods.

'But it is all very *real*,' Léa told her one day.

'But it's *not* real – that's the whole point. Just a childish sort of peepshow. People on stage *are* real, no comparison.'

'They flock to it all the same.'

'Yes, like children,' Hetty retorted petulantly, like a child.

After Christmas they moved on round the Ring of Kerry, towards Limerick and Galway, through isolated towns in the west where there were fewer picture theatres and audiences who still craved their traditional fare. Spring broke in moist, cloudy blue skies over the stony land of Co. Clare: hawthorn blossom flooded sunken hedges along the Shannon estuary and a soft wind blew off the Atlantic in the little seaside resort of Kilkee when they arrived for an Easter date in the ballroom of the Hydro Hotel in late March.

Bella parked the caravan above a sheltered cove behind the hotel, where a huge half-moon of sandy beach ran away southwards. The girls walked it, barefoot, through cloud-dappled sunlight one late afternoon, imprinting their toes on the moist sand, teasing the waves, provoking and retreating from the sea.

'Tour finishes next month in Galway,' Léonie said, scanning the wave-tossed horizon, when they sat down on a rock at the far end of the beach.

'Yes . . . Then Bray and the summer season, I suppose.'

'Summer Hill as well, your Mama – all that. Can't avoid it for ever.'

'Perhaps she'll have changed her mind.'

'Doubt it. But we'll have to do something about it.'

'Probably try and lock me up. I wish I was twenty-one. Oh, Léa, it's all such nonsense! Might as well be twenty-one. We can look after ourselves, make a living, so perfectly well.'

'Yes, but the war won't last for ever. And I'll have to go back to Paris then, see Mama and Papa.'

'I'll go with you?'

'Yes, of course you can.' But Léonie turned then, a query in her grey-green eyes. 'You will, won't you?'

'Yes, Léa – yes!' Hetty turned then, stroking Léonie's cheek gently, before suddenly cupping her face, staring at her for an age, then kissing her briefly on the forehead. 'Oh, Léa, I do so love you.'

Léonie shivered then, involuntarily – suddenly aware of all the endless ramifications of her feelings for this woman, who was the focus for everything she possessed, in herself and in her life.

In the event the British government most conveniently solved the girls' immediate problem when they imprisoned Frances once more for seditious activities, this time interning her, without trial, at Holloway in London.

In April 1918, shortly after Fonsy's troupe arrived in Galway, the Allied war effort began to totter in France, Ludendorff had made his great push. British and French lines were stretched to the limit. More cannon fodder was needed – so that Lloyd George, pressured by Sir Henry

Wilson, the British Chief of Staff, finally agreed to a Conscription Bill for Ireland.

Nothing could have been better calculated to inflame every sort of opinion in the country. For although tens of thousands of Irishmen had volunteered to fight for Britain, there were – understandably in the light of the recent rising and executions in Dublin – even more able-bodied men who had refused to do so. And for the first time the Irish Catholic Bishops, when the Bill was introduced, took the side of these patriots, many of whom were now supporters, not of Redmond's old Irish Parliamentary Party, but of the IRA or of Sinn Fein, its political wing. The Bishops passed a unanimous resolution against the Bill.

It was a sign the remaining revolutionary leaders had long been waiting for. The Catholic hierarchy, as well as most moderate opinion in Ireland, was now behind them at last. Protest and passive resistance to the Bill would start at once. And, if that failed, force would be used again. The feeling in the country that spring was intense – a lit fuse against a powder keg. As one – with De Valera – of the two remaining leaders of the 1916 Rebellion, Frances felt duty bound to come immediately to Dublin, where she was soon in the thick of things. British machine-gunners lined the roof of the Bank of Ireland. Another rising seemed imminent. Frances, quite forsaking her pacifist notions, resumed her role as militant revolutionary once more, involving herself in all the public protests of the moment – while secretly starting to prepare the necessary medical facilities in Dublin in the event of force being used.

Meanwhile the British, aware of these rebellious plans, but unable quite to put their finger on them, or find any cast-iron reason to arrest the leaders, took fright. A trumped-up excuse was needed – and was soon found. The Irish Chief Secretary discovered an entirely imaginary 'German Plot' among the Sinn Fein leaders, and the arrests began. First De Valera and Arthur Griffith were taken; then Frances and a number of others.

This, at least, was news that Hetty read avidly in Galway. So that at the end of the tour, with a month's break before the summer season, she and Léonie returned at once to Summer Hill, on their way through Dublin contacting Mortimer, who joined them a few days later.

'Well, I knew you were both all right,' he told Hetty, as the two of them took tea in the drawing room, after she and Léonie had described their theatrical activities of the past months. 'As did Léonie's parents. We got your various postcards. But *really*, Hetty . . .' Mortimer fingered his great bird's nest beard an instant, looking at her half critically, half in admiration, over his spectacles. 'The whole thing – it really was very rash of you both, you know.'

'But, Mortimer, we had no alternative,' Hetty told him sensibly, but with a happy glint in her eyes. Then she was entirely serious. 'You knew it well – that Mama was quite determined to separate us. And such a hypocrite about it all, too! Having written me those understanding letters from Aylesbury prison, she then quite lost her reason again. And now, worse still, the same madness has taken her back to the rebels – in prison once more!'

Hetty, charmed to be home again, in a home without her mother, was pert and excited – charmed above all by having taken such a victory over her Mama, turned the tables on her mean spirit.

'Yes, well . . .' Mortimer considered things.

'How else can you explain it?' Hetty, switching blame from herself to her mother, spoke with mature concern now, as if they were discussing the problems of a most difficult child. 'So forgiving, reasonable, apologetic – then so vicious all over again?'

'It's difficult for her, Hetty. An unreconciled nature? I believe so. The hurts she suffered herself in the past – she's tried, but been unable to quite erase them. You should be more understanding, now you're older – and certainly so much more experienced! – yourself.'

His eyes twinkled at her over the tea-cup.

'But *what* great hurt? – just that she was banished to the colonies and the house wasn't left to her?'

'Hurt enough! You see, she loves the house – desperately.'

'But why was she "banished", Mortimer? Such a dramatic word – she used it herself to me. What frightful thing had she done?'

Here Mortimer, who knew exactly what she had done, was forced to dissemble. 'Why, rather like you, Hetty! She and *her* Mama spent most of their time at each other's throats. She refused to marry Lord Norton's son, for example, over some little tiff on the tennis court. And then there was the matter of your Uncle Henry's funeral, when she tore down the crêpe and black drapes in the house before ringing the bells all over the place.'

'How spirited of her! But that was long before her "banishment" surely? For she lived with you in London, didn't she? – worked there as a nurse for several years. And then went out to the Boer war, when Uncle Eustace was killed. She was only "banished" *after* all that. So what had she done to deserve it – at *that* point?'

Mortimer, giving himself time to think, turned away, looking into the grate. 'I can't say – exactly.' He returned to his white lies most reasonably. 'Except, at that point, with both of her brothers now dead, the issue of the inheritance must first have come up, when her mother told her she was not to have the house, that Austin and Bunty were instead.'

'Yes, but Grandmama changed her will after that, didn't she – in *her* favour. I wonder how Mama managed to persuade her?'

Mortimer had often wondered just the same thing. 'I don't know. She persuaded her somehow. A most forceful character – all three of you!'

He twinkled at Hetty again. She went to the window, and gazed at the changing April light for a long moment before turning. 'Just "force of character" you say?'

'Yes. A fine quality, if you can direct it – suitably!'

'And I have not?'

'Not always—'

'But, Mortimer!' Hetty, frustrated now, knelt in front of him by the fire, speaking vehemently. 'Mortimer, there *must* be something else to it all. I've always felt it so: my father – that he wasn't my real father, couldn't have been – and that *that's* at the heart of it all. Isn't it? You'd know if anyone did.' Mortimer was most uneasy then. But with his lawyer's skill, he hid every sign of this discomfort. '*Isn't* it, Mortimer? That's Mama's real hurt – and that was the reason for her banishment, for her not inheriting Summer Hill. Because I'm not – not legitimate. There was some other m-man, before Mr Fraser, and Grandmama knew about it, which is why she disowned her – I'm sure of it. Oh, *do* tell me,' she asked then, no longer vehement, pleading softly.

Mortimer sighed. He wished so much he could tell her – despite the enormity of the truth: that indeed she had another and once most real father, that she was, in fact, half-sister to the present King Emperor, George V – for he was entirely aware how most of Hetty's difficulties, her tantrums and unhappinesses as a child, her rash and irresponsible behaviour now, must all stem from this central lie in her life. But he could say nothing of this. Instead he temporized. 'Hetty, I really don't know. But I don't believe—' He paused. 'I don't think it's possible. I believe Robert Fraser was your father.'

Hetty had noticed his hesitations. 'But you think I *might* be right?'

'No. I don't think you are.' He stood up then, outraged and frustrated at his lies, anxious to break off this painful inquisition. 'But in any case, Hetty, we must think of the future, not the past. Your Mama is likely to be interned in London for some time. She knows of your return here—'

'And the Strauses in Paris know we're safely back too . . . so you're not thinking of trying to separate us again?'

'No, of course not. Though I can't, obviously, go quite against your Mama's earlier demand by letting you have the Dublin flat back—'

'But Léa can't return to France yet either with all the

U-boats about. So! . . . we'll stay here . . . till the summer season starts in Bray.'

Mortimer walked over to the window and Hetty joined him. 'Yes, of course you can stay here, Hetty. It's your home after all . . .'

'And I so love it. Without Mama . . .'

Mortimer gave an understanding nod. 'But, Hetty, you must give her that credit at least. Without her earlier efforts with old Lady Cordiner – whatever they were – it wouldn't be your home at all. Austin and Bunty would be living here now.'

'Yes, Austin and Bunty – all that stupid nonsense. Not that I care much for her. She and Austin came here, you know, last time Mama was in prison – to see Grandmama. I wonder why?'

'Oh, Bunty wouldn't have set foot in the place with your Mama here: daggers always drawn, those two!'

'No, I meant – why did she want to see Grandmama?'

'Well, Austin's her brother-in-law. You know – family. And of course Bunty desperately wanted Summer Hill as well in the old days – never forgiven your Mama over that.'

'No, nor me either, it seems. She didn't speak a word to me when she was last here.'

'Indeed . . . Because of course, Hetty, unless your mother changes her will, which I drew up for her last year, this house will go to you. Did you know that?'

Hetty turned to him, astonished. 'No! – No, I di-didn't.'

'Who did you think it would all go to then?'

'I di-di-*didn't* think.'

'Well, in that case perhaps you'd better not tell your Mama I told you. But, yes, of course – it must be yours. There's no one else.'

Hetty felt a *frisson* of stomach-turning surprise, as she laid a hand involuntarily on the tall window shutter. She gazed out over the daffodil lawns, the budding chestnuts, the whole estate around and beyond. She looked at her hand on the shutter, then ran her eye up to the delicately moulded ceiling with its Italianate bas-reliefs, the gilt stucco of cherubs and harps and cornucopias far above her, the white Georgian room suddenly lit by an intense spring light. All this would be hers? But how could it be? She and her mother had hated each other for so long, and with such intensity, the idea that Frances would ever make over such a great gift to her had never crossed her mind.

Yet now the thought of owning Summer Hill suddenly held a startling, an overwhelming appeal. The cold brick and mortar took on a quite different aura, seemed imbued with human qualities, a confiding warmth and promise, nothing to do with her mother but for her alone. Something had been returned to her in Mortimer's words about the will – something lost, like a person, which she had missed all her life. Yes, the great house proposed itself to her now, as an answer to all her hurts, like a lover who would calm all the searching storms in her heart, fill the emptiness there. Then she saw how unlikely the idea was.

'But, Mortimer, Mama hates me so! One doesn't give things – like this, all this – to people one so dislikes!'

'Come, Hetty, you exaggerate, I think. You forget, sometimes she doesn't hate you at all, when she was in Aylesbury prison for example. With her temperament, her feelings are always something of a seesaw, hot and cold. And then – remember – you *are* her daughter. There's absolutely no doubt about that! And it's blood that counts in the end.'

'Anyway, she's barely forty. Won't happen for years. And she'll probably change her will in any case, after what Léa and I have done. So it's not worth thinking about.'

'Oh, but it *is*, Hetty.' Mortimer took her arm as they walked away from the window, stopping by a vase of narcissi on the grand piano. 'That's what a house like this is all about: keeping it in the same family. You'll marry, surely, have children . . .' He paused then, seeing her face sour in an instant. 'You probably will, you know, one day.'

'No . . .' Hetty turned away decisively, frowning, starting to fiddle with a narcissus.

Mortimer, quite aware of the strength of her affection for Léonie, knew he might be treading delicate ground here. But none the less he gently pursued the matter. 'I'm well aware of your feelings for Léonie, and I've never for a moment come between you over that – you know that. But those feelings – why, they don't prevent you marrying one day, Hetty.'

'Oh, but it would prevent me.' Hetty turned, staring at him with a childish intensity. 'It w-w-would, you see, because, well, I'm really "married" to her.'

Mortimer had not seen – and did not see – that. But he hid his astonishment. For him their relationship had seemed a great friendship, the happy maturing of a girlish crush. The idea of their being "married" shocked him momentarily, not for any moral reason, he thought and hoped, but because, looking at this astonishingly beautiful, dark-curled, vivacious creature, he could not conceive that some man, many men in time, would not pay court to her. And that, one day, finding the right man, she would return the compliment.

Yes, in the year since he had last seen her, Hetty had grown up, her beauty finding mature shapes, dramatic curves, a hard suppleness in her limbs, meticulous poise and control – a result, he supposed, of all her theatrical exercises and activities. The puppy fat had quite gone; her high cheek-bones, more prominent now, sloped into delicate hollows, nostrils flaring over thin lips. Her almond-like, Wedgwood-blue eyes gazed piercingly from beneath a more controlled mass of dark hair. She was a woman. Yet the child in her had not quite disappeared, nor the insecurities of that childhood. There was still the stammer. Always precocious, commanding, unreasonable, moody – now these qualities, though they were still present, had softened, were directed by a much more real and relaxed assurance. She had, at the centre, an inviolate calm, Mortimer felt – such as lovers feel. Yes, that was it, of course! He saw it clearly now. They did love each other.

The evidence was perfectly clear, he realized, in all her new radiance.

'Well,' he went on easily, 'there's plenty of time. Meanwhile I should see your grandmother while I'm down here. Will you come with me?'

They went upstairs, down the long landing, up the little Gothic arched stairway, through the great oak door and into the Victorian back wing of the house. Sally, the maid who had taken over from Molly in looking after Lady Cordiner, sat in a wicker chair at the foot of the four-poster bed at one end of the long room. Lady Cordiner, propped up on pillows, lay asleep – still surrounded, in this her last domain, by all the heavy furnishings and mementoes of her own life here: black-bordered photographs of her adored sons Henry and Eustace prominent at one end of the refectory table; the walls covered with banal Victorian prints and pictures; glass-domed wax flowers, Eustace's Victoria Cross displayed in its velvet box, Henry's cavalry sabre on one wall. The room was permanently dark, with thick drapes against the light; it was filled with decay, nothing had been moved or changed in years.

Mortimer and Hetty stood at the end of the bed. 'Her Ladyship has been sleeping *very* well,' Sally whispered to them. 'Like a lamb.'

And indeed the old woman, with her carefully tended white hair and even paler wrinkled skin, seemed the very picture of unconscious repose. But just then she opened her eyes a fraction, clearly recognizing them both, staring at them, before she concentrated her gaze most malevolently on Hetty. Her eyes were bright, red bright in the lamplight, shining out wickedly from the withered mask of her face – just like the Hallowe'en turnip mask, Hetty thought, that her mother had set before Lady Cordiner years ago, when Hetty had gazed down into the bedroom from the hole in the ceiling. Now, seeing the same malice in her grandmother's face, she wondered whether such evil transferred itself between the generations, from one to the other. Appalled at the thought that she, too, might be so infected, Hetty almost ran from the room.

Mortimer joined her in the corridor. 'De-did you notice how she l-l-looked at me?' Hetty stammered.

'Yes,' he had to admit.

'Why should she hate me so?'

'All of us, I think, Hetty—'

'No – just me. Particularly me.'

Mortimer shook his head. 'You must try and forget the past, Hetty.'

'How can I? You said yourself – the past, our family line – that's exactly what a house like this is all about.'

Robert, reading modern history now at Trinity, was down with Bertie for the Easter holidays. He had been annoyed at first, and then dismissive of Hetty's and Léonie's theatrical behaviour. True, Hetty had sent him several postcards. But really, he'd thought, when he heard about it, it had all been a senseless performance – so needlessly antagonizing and upsetting to everyone.

But when he saw Hetty again now – so grown, so composed, fulfilled, happy – he was forced to change his mind about her. Hetty had been *living*, while he only lived in history books. And secretly he loved her all the more for this, as he had loved her before in any case. But that had been a hopeless suit – and must be the more hopeless now, he thought, given Hetty's brazen behaviour and obvious attachment to Léonie.

So he was surprised at the attentions Hetty paid him during the holiday, when she acknowledged him as an equal, as an adult himself now, enquiring warmly about his work, his ambitions – so warmly indeed that the hopes he had had of her were suddenly renewed.

'Oh, I don't quite know what I'll do,' he told her one afternoon, when the four of them were out walking the woods together, Léonie and Bertie ahead of them, making down the valley towards the river. 'I've another two years at Trinity. I'd like to be a journalist, but that's difficult.'

'Teaching perhaps?'

'No . . . Well, I may have to, I suppose. But something a little livelier. Like you.'

'But I've no real gifts, no likely profession.'

'Goodness! – that can't be true: all year with that theatrical company. You must be brilliant!'

'At what?' Hetty was genuinely puzzled.

'At acting, of course. I'd love to have seen you.'

'You can – at Bray. We'll be there this summer. But it's not very much.'

'You and Léonie, you're not going to do that as a career?'

'Course not! Just a way of getting out of Mama's clutches – and staying together,' she added lightly.

'Together?' Robert was rather pointed.

'Yes, of course.'

'But – but that's not really a career either, is it?'

'I don't really expect a career. Léonie'll have that – in opera. Wants to study it properly when she goes back to Paris. And I'll go there, too.'

'And help her?'

'Why, yes – I suppose so.' Hetty had never envisaged any precise details of her future life with Léonie; that she would simply live and be with her was sufficient in itself.

'But you'll surely have to do something else, Hetty, won't you?'

'What?'

'Well, there's lots of new things for women these days. And old things, too – like marriage!'

'Oh, I won't marry.' She laughed. 'Just look at all the unhappiness that brings. Look at M-Mama! And that awful man she married: my "f-f-father". Oh, Robert, you most of all – you'll remember!' She turned suddenly, grasping his arm, eyes clouding with emotion, passionate in her remembrance. 'How *terrible* he was in Domenica: on the beach that birthday of mine – and that night, shouting and roaring drunk with Mama. You remember!'

She gazed at him, longing for his confirmation of their joint unhappiness years before. They had stopped in a shaft of dappled sunlight on the pathway; the others were some distance ahead. Robert, remembering the events all too well, and taking Hetty's impassioned approach as a miraculous indication that perhaps she did love him after all, suddenly grasped her, kissing her awkwardly, before Hetty disentangled herself from the embrace, embarrassed, astonished.

But she had the tact not to show her reaction, letting his embrace seem impetuous evidence simply of his deep understanding. She moved, forward, linking her arm in his, but without any intimacy.

'Oh, Robert,' she said easily. 'It's so nice that we're such good friends now. All those rows we used to have!' She swung on down the path, leading him briskly, catching up with the others. 'So nice to have you, because only you – you alone – know all about our past, right back to the beginning, to talk about it, which makes me feel so much better.'

But Robert was less comforted by this bond of shared memories. He wanted a future with Hetty, not a past. And, if Hetty conveniently repressed her knowledge of this, Léonie could not do likewise. She had seen Robert's embrace.

Later, out on the river, Léonie sat in the stern of one of the boats, watching Robert row over the smooth blue-black water. More than ever now, she was reminded of Robert's feelings for Hetty – knowing, too, how Hetty never thought of him in the same way. And she felt for him then, desperately, but did not know quite how to express it.

'So, you're happy at Trinity?' she asked him, putting all her vivacity and enthusiasm into the banal enquiry.

He sighed. 'Yes,' he said brightly, the tone of voice going quite against his sadness.

Léonie felt stricken by his plight – and by her own part in his disappointment. Suddenly, unable to bear her restraint any more, she leant forward and took his hands, clasping them firmly, so that he had to stop rowing, gazing up at him then with a frustrated tenderness.

'Oh, Robert, please don't be so sad. I so hate it, because . . .' She shook her head, unable to finish the sentence, looking away. But then, turning back, she willed her own eyes deep into his. 'Because you're so good and nice and I'm really so fond of you. I do really like you very much,' she added, speaking with almost painful emphasis.

Robert moved awkwardly on the seat. She took her hands away at last. He stared at her then, half-resentfully, yet half-lovingly, with a surprised intensity as if he were seeing her properly only for the first time. But then the curtain fell and he shut himself away once more.

'Yes,' he said, in a dull voice.

'Yes . . . what?' she asked eagerly.

'I like you too.' He frowned again. But there was no half-smile there this time. His face which, for that one moment before, had been filled with light for her, resumed its set, disappointed form. Yet, Léonie knew something vital had passed between them in that moment when, like a sleep walker, he had woken from his obsession with Hetty and seen her properly.

'Robert,' she said, quickly wanting to do or tell him something of vast importance, but then forgetting what it was.

'Yes?'

Suddenly she knew what it was – and could not say it, just as she had been unable to do it: she had wanted to kiss Robert then, just as he had kissed Hetty back in the woods fifteen minutes before. A kiss of sympathy, she thought. Or was it more of love?

She could not tell Hetty anything of these feelings. But Hetty was not slow to speak.

'My goodness!' she laughed when they were in Léonie's bedroom later that evening. 'You and Robert in the boat this afternoon – clutching and clasping! What *were* you trying to do? Teach him to row?'

Léonie saw the touch of worry and jealousy just beneath Hetty's good humour, but none the less felt she had to make an honest reply. 'Hetty, it's such a punishment for him. I saw you both, behind us in the woods—'

'It's not *my* fault!' Hetty, suddenly annoyed, flounced over to the wardrobe, opening it, running her fingers through Léonie's clothes there, as if trying to avoid the issue by having them both dress up and escape into some theatrical adventure, one of their 'games'. 'Not my fault – I've been as nice as pie to him these holidays!'

'Yes, you have been nice to him, I've seen that – and I know it's not your fault. And that's why—'

'That's why *you've* been trying to comfort him – as usual,' Hetty spat back. She had a mauve silk evening dress in her hand now, and shook it in Léonie's face, as if trying to will her into it. But Léonie did not respond. She would not play that game, any game, just then. Hetty stamped her foot. 'Besides,' she went on even more angrily, 'you can't love people on demand, you know. There has to be a *special* feeling. And that's what you have for him – else you wouldn't be making the running over it. Well, *you* love him, then, if that's what you want.' She paused. 'And you do l-l-love him, don't you?'

Léonie coloured, but was determined to remain calm . . . and honest. 'Oh, Hetty, only a fraction as much as I love you.'

Hetty shook with anger at this quite unexpected confirmation of her worst fears. 'A "fraction"?' she shouted. Then she laughed – a bitter, incredulous laugh. 'A *fraction*? That's enough – that's the beginning of the end then, isn't it?' she almost screamed.

'What absolute nonsense!' Léonie, herself angered now, but equally determined in this instance not to be bullied by Hetty, still managed to control her voice. 'A loving affection – you can have that for someone. Nothing *like* what we have. You're being very childish.'

Hetty fully expected Léonie to come to her then, as she had so often before, to comfort her and make things up. But Léonie did not move. Instead she said in a chillingly calm voice, 'Nothing like that – like *him* – is ever going to take me away from you, Hetty.'

Hetty continued to sulk. Léonie hoped that for once she might make the effort at reconciliation, by confirming a parallel sentiment. But all she finally said was 'yes' in a small flat voice.

'"Yes" – what does that mean?' Léonie was unable to prevent a touch of anxiety in her voice now.

Hetty, sensing her unease, took immediate advantage, resuming the attack. She turned, eyes ablaze with self-righteousness, so much the injured party. 'Yes – well, I mean it's not something I could ever even *think* of doing with a man, *ever*. That's all.'

At the end of the Easter holidays Robert and Bertie returned to Trinity College, the girls rejoined Fonsy O'Grady's troupe for the summer season at Bray . . . and Frances remained in Holloway. The war rumbled on in France, the Allies regaining some of the ground lost earlier that year in Ludendorff's great push. Situations that had seemed so unstable at Easter, at Summer Hill and on the Western front, seemed to regain a balance once more. But the poise was illusory.

After their row over Robert, matters between the two girls had in fact changed considerably. Hetty for the first time had failed to dominate, to have her way with Léonie. Léonie had stood firm in her admission of love, or loving affection, for Robert. She had failed to recant – and, worse, had failed to make things up with her, Hetty felt. Worst of all, Léonie then, and subsequently, had abandoned their 'game'. At the crucial moment in their argument, when she had offered Léonie the mauve ball gown, when if she had undressed and worn it, or not worn it, they could have loved each other and so reached a reconciliation in the best possible manner – at this vital instant Léa had denied her.

This betrayal, as Hetty saw it, began to fester in her soul, a corruption which, throughout that summer and autumn, brought back, indeed increased, all her old poisonous frustrations, her domineering restlessness, so that for lack of mastering Léonie, she punished her in various little theatrical ways – over 'business' in their act, the sharing of a dressing room mirror, promoting a quite unnecessary aggressiveness in their fencing performance. Hetty felt her soul drying out – all the myriad personae there, which before Léonie had so nurtured and responded to, finding no outlet now.

Léonie, whose great gift was to know what was in the minds of others and to love without making unreasonable demands, saw and understood these changes in Hetty – and did everything she could to reassure her. But Léonie had changed, too.

She thought she would love Hetty all her life. But, after the business with Robert, and Hetty's unjust accusations, Léonie felt she could no longer entirely repress her own personality in this love – and this because she wanted at all costs to preserve and not lose it. For something had moved in her heart then, during their row over Robert, spelling out the clear message at last – confirming, insisting on something she had long felt – that, if she continued to give in to Hetty, pander to her every whim, Hetty would use her up, suck her dry, finally turning her into something despised, a slave, and then drop her. So now, a last chance, it was vital to stand firm and not become that slave. They must both grow into a different love, a love that would have to mature if it was to survive. And she said as much to Hetty, as tactfully as she could, during the following months.

'Don't you *see*, Hetty,' she told her one day, sitting among the gorse bushes on top of Bray Head. 'We dress up every evening for our act. And *that's* why there's no need for all our old games any more. We can have a different love now, an even better sort.' She turned, trying to catch her attention. But Hetty's gaze remained fixed on a ship far out to sea. 'You think, because we don't have our games any more, that I love you less? No! Not true – I love you as much as ever, promise you. Just, if our games go on . . . they'll destroy us. You'll come to despise me for giving in to you all the time. And it's not love – just being someone's mirror for ever and ever. And, besides, you have that mirror every day now in the audiences. You don't *need* me for that any more. Please – just need me as a person – I've so often told you – the one I am, am growing to be.'

Hetty, who had nodded vaguely throughout all this, still gazed out to sea. 'Oh, *Hetty!* – we have to change. You know we do.' She took her hand and stroked it. She would have embraced and kissed, made love with her even, there and then, among the gorse bushes. But Hetty, though she seemed to have agreed with all this, remained cold – stone cold in the warm August afternoon.

Finally all she said was, 'Dermot'll be back soon, from that prisoner of war camp. Everyone says the war will be over in a month or so. And that'll be something at least.' She smiled to herself. 'Wonderful! – I've missed him so much.'

Léonie took this sudden unrelated comment as a small piece of revengeful spite on Hetty's part, as indeed it was. But just as much was it a true sentiment. Hetty really had missed Dermot, writing to him regularly, receiving brief POW cards from him sometimes in return. And now, with this sense of the war's ending, she was excited by the idea of seeing him again.

Father, or father figure: all that still mattered to Hetty in Dermot. But in any case he was her great, her greatest friend, as far as men were concerned. She longed to tell him of all her adventures in the years since she had last seen him, the daring child now become an even more daring woman. Hetty, especially in the light of her present impasse with Léonie, was tempted by Dermot once more. And, though she could not admit it for a second, he loomed on the horizon for her that afternoon as someone, aside from Léonie, whom she might set out, as she had once before, to impress, perhaps to dominate, even to love. Had she been able to admit this to herself, she might have added that Dermot occurred to her now not as a substitute father but as a potential replacement for Léonie. But she refused to bring any such honest self-analysis to bear in the matter.

The war ended in early November. By then the girls were on tour again, moving south along the coast, as on the previous year, towards Wexford and Waterford. Frances remained in jail. But the political situation in Ireland, so increasingly chaotic, was such that it seemed likely she would be released soon – for now she was no mere rebel prisoner, but a member of parliament at Westminster.

She and seventy-two other Sinn Fein candidates, many of them also in prison, were elected as Irish MPs in the British general election that December. The mood in the country, quite forsaking Redmond's old Irish Parliamentary Party, had swung round almost entirely in favour of Arthur Griffith's abstentionist Sinn Feiners, who, though elected, would refuse to take their seats at Westminster, forming instead their own illegal government in Ireland. Mortimer Cordiner was one of only a handful of Redmondite MPs who managed to retain their seats at Westminster. Thus he was in London, at his house in Wilton Street, when Dermot returned to England before Christmas.

12

There was another young man returning to London from the war, an Irish-American, who had volunteered more than a year earlier, serving with the Royal Canadian Flying Corps on the Western front. But he went on almost at once to Dublin, taking a suite at the Shelbourne Hotel. Now, immaculate in soft Donegal tweeds, sipping coffee in his rooms overlooking Stephen's Green, he sifted through a portfolio of theatrical photographs which Mr Waxman had brought to show him.

'So, Waxman – up to your old tricks again . . .' The tone was quick and ironic, a New York accent – but touched with another and softer melody, a more cultured Irish tone just discernible in the background.

Waxman, still retaining his black beret, smiled. It was almost a leer. 'Tricks?'

'All these girls – *Irish* girls. How do you manage

to persuade them into these poses! "Holy Catholic Ireland" . . .'

He adopted an authentic brogue for these last words, using the pleasantry as a cover for his keen interest in some of the more daring situations which Mr Waxman had contrived for the girls on his studio chaise-longue.

'Ah, the temptation of the camera, Mr Williamson – you'll know it yourself. They can't resist it, do anything for it, with a bit of encouragement. They're more than willing. You'd be surprised!'

'No, I wouldn't.' Craig Williamson cut Waxman's familiarity dead as he abruptly discarded the last risqué photograph, going on to something more decorous.

'Of course not, Mr Williamson.' Mr Waxman resumed his obsequious stance behind the armchair.

Craig Williamson, though not tall, still appeared lanky. It was his thin face, delicate proportions and fine bone structure which gave him a willowy appearance. And the well-cut tweeds, green silk handkerchief trailing casually from his breast pocket, the soft cotton shirt and hand-made brogues, all accentuated his natural finesse. He was neat, quick, contained, with a darting precision in his movements – an expression steely and dreamy by turns, dangerously chameleon in mood.

In the same way he seemed both older and younger than his twenty-nine years. There was a vast maturity sometimes in his faraway gaze, an air of contemplative understanding. Yet just as often he was filled with a dazzling Celtic boyishness, playing the rogue . . . or promoting a biting, sometimes even a cruel, wit, a deceptively sharp intellect and dominant intent which quite gave the lie to his matinée idol good looks.

'There!' Waxman stooped down and pointed to a new photograph. 'Rather nice, isn't she? A Miss Gilchrist – soubrette at the Queen's Theatre here. She would do well in classical costume,' he added with a judicious smirk.

Craig Williamson looked up sharply.

'Miss Gilchrist has the air of a Dublin seamstress, Waxman. This is *Cleopatra* I'm considering women for. Something considerably more regal is required.'

'Oh, I thought you had already cast her.'

'I had. With Miss Swanson. But she's not available. Triangle won't release her. So I'm considering others – on my way through town.'

'Of course, Mr Williamson.' Waxman was unctuous. 'I know your great affection for Ireland—'

'I have very little affection for Ireland.' He cut him dead again, with bitter emphasis. 'Came by only to see my family.'

'Yes, the big house . . . In Limerick, isn't it?'

'No – County Cork.' Craig Williamson turned away, uneasy for the first time about something. 'Anyway, that's no matter.' He returned to his view of Miss Gilchrist. 'Yes, something considerably more regal, Mr Waxman.'

He stood up then, and with something of a belligerent swagger walked over to the big window. But now the image of the matinée idol was somewhat tarnished: he swaggered, but with a slight limp, as he went to inspect a group of Redouté flower prints on the wall. Reaching out, he took one, of a lovely arum lily, gazing at it, then holding it up to the winter sunlight as if it was a chalice. 'Yes, *regal*, Mr Waxman – like this flower.' He turned, confronting the little man, showing him the print, staring at him with his grey-blue eyes – usually slumbrous, relaxed, but fired now with a vivid enthusiasm. 'This lily,' he went on, 'a pure beauty, grace, poise, *innocence*, yes! But at the same time something dark in the heart, mysterious, a hint of evil. *That's* my Cleopatra. And Miss Gilchrist doesn't quite fit the bill, I'm afraid, Waxman.' As he spoke he was unable to disguise his passion for both sides of the coin in this ideal woman: she was someone equally dedicated to the sacred and to the profane.

'Yes, Mr Williamson. But there are . . . other women. Possible Cleopatras.' He gestured to the portfolio.

'So they said in London. But there weren't.' Craig Williamson returned, disconsolate and bored, to the armchair.

'You've been in London, of course.' Waxman resumed his oleaginous air. 'Your war wound – very sorry to hear about it.'

Williamson brightened, vaguely warming towards Waxman for the first time. 'In some god-awful hospital in Eastbourne actually, laid out with weights and pulleys which did no damn good at all.'

'Yes, you've been away at the war some time, haven't you? What? – over a year?' Waxman, attempting subtle revenge now, had a doubting tone in his voice, implying that perhaps Williamson had been away at the war too long, had lost touch with things in Hollywood, that he might not now be quite the powerful figure he had once been there.

'Yes, a year, Mr Waxman. But patriotism counts more with me . . . than it does perhaps for some people.' He glowered at Waxman before returning to the portfolio, about to dispense with it, thumbing quickly through the final few photographs, before one of them caught his eye. It was of Hetty and Léonie, in their 'Bertie and Bridey' costumes, one of the series that Waxman had taken of them over a year before – the girls, in his skilled hands, at their most decoratively seductive. Craig Williamson gazed at the photograph intently, then at the others, his eyes suddenly alive.

'Who are these two?'

'Ah hah!' Mr Waxman was pleased to have struck gold at last. 'An interesting pair. That one,' he pointed at Hetty, 'not a young man at all, you see: a young *woman*, *dressed* as a man!' He looked at Williamson knowingly. 'Yes, a young woman – though she wouldn't admit it. They came to me straight off the street, dressed like that; said they had a music hall act together, in England. Of course I didn't believe them. Her accent was too good – the tall one – and clearly Irish. And both were too classy by half. Just a pair of mischievous Irish girls – *very* mischievous – up to some elaborate party trick.'

'Yes, Waxman. But *who* are they?'

'Ah, there you have me—'

'I'll make it worth your while.' Craig Williamson showed a nakedly dominant intent now.

'They left no address, picked up the photographs themselves. But I kept copies, they were so good – and I followed them when they left the studio. They returned to an office behind the Olympia—'

'I see, so they were playing at the Olympia?'

'No, no – not at all. I checked that. They went back to a lawyers' office in Crown Alley. That's all I know . . .'

Williamson held up the last photograph, in which Hetty, at her most masculine, in cravat, check suit and fawn bowler, with an arm round Léonie, was gazing imperiously into the lens.

'A *woman*, you say?'

'Sure of it. Just look at the shapes there. That's not a man's chest. Nor the waist – or the behind! – I can assure you of that!' Mr Waxman licked his lips.

'It's the *face* I'm interested in, Mr Waxman,' Williamson told him curtly. 'Can't you see it? That's what I meant by regality.'

'Indeed. But with just that hint of, well, something . . . quite "uncalled for" . . .' Mr Waxman gazed at him with narrow, conniving eyes. 'I can take you round there, if you're interested. The lawyers there will probably know about them.'

'I'll go round there myself – if I'm interested.'

Craig Williamson had concluded the meeting, though he still held the photographs. Waxman gestured at them.

'You'll keep those then?'

'Yes. I'll pay for them.' Opening his wallet, he handed over a crisp five pound note. Then, his expression suddenly hardening, he took out another note, holding it up casually. Waxman showed surprise. 'Come now, Waxman – I'm not quite such a fool.' Williamson moved forward, almost threatening him. 'Will you take the extra money, or shall I adopt . . .?' Williamson, though slight, showed all the aggression of a fly-weight boxer.

'I don't understand.'

'But of course you do. If you'd bothered to follow those

girls half-way across Dublin in the first place – *and* brought me their photographs – then you must know where I can find them. "Mischievous girls" they may be. But they're obviously stage people as well, have some music hall act here. Where is it, Waxman?' He raised his voice. 'The Gaiety? The Olympia? The Queen's?' He dangled the money in one hand, bunching the knuckles of the other.

Waxman was alarmed. 'No, no, not in any of the Dublin theatres – I checked on that. But I'll tell you,' he said urgently, 'they could be with Fonsy O'Grady's troupe. That's the only other music hall outfit here: "Fonsy O'Grady's Theatre of Varieties" – on Bray Promenade. But they'd be on tour now, Wexford or Waterford. They tour every winter, all over Ireland.'

Williamson nodded, handing him the extra money. 'Thank you, Waxman. "Fonsy O'Grady's Theatre of Varieties" – sounds just their style.' He was happy at last as he showed Waxman to the door.

'I hope you won't be disappointed, Mr Williamson.' Waxman made a last sally. 'They're not really actresses, I'm sure of that. Still, that's not really what you wanted them for, was it?' he added quickly, before scuttling out of the door.

Waxman knew something of Craig Williamson's wayward tastes in young women. He had acted as tacit procurer for this most successful Hollywood picture director, on several of his previous visits to Ireland. His family was Anglo-Irish, he thought – the St John Williamsons, weren't they? – from some big house in the west. He wasn't sure where, for Mr Williamson had only hinted to him of his family background. Why would he do more? – when his private interests, when he came here were . . . well, so necessarily private.

Craig Williamson, taking the photographs round the Dublin theatres that afternoon, learnt that, as far as anyone knew, the girls had indeed never acted at the Olympia, the Queen's or the Gaiety. They must, as Waxman had suggested, work for Fonsy O'Grady's troupe, if they worked for anyone. And then the stage doorman at the

Queen's Theatre, who knew several of the artistes in Fonsy's company, confirmed this supposition, after he had seen the photographs. Yes, he told him, he had heard of a comic act, a song-and-dance duo, in Fonsy's company, two women, one dressed as a man. It was supposed to be quite good. Yes, indeed, he said, looking at the photographs, that was likely to be them. But Fonsy was on tour now, the stage doorman went on – probably due to start his annual date at the Theatre Royal in Waterford, which was usually the first week in December.

This suited Craig Williamson very well. He had to go south the following day in any case, to Cork, to see his father briefly. His boat, from Queenstown to New York, was not due to leave for another week – and with all the returning American troops would almost certainly be further delayed. He had time to spare. After Cork he would come back to Dublin via Waterford. Fonsy's company was usually there for a week, the doorman told him.

Returning to the Shelbourne he looked through the photographs of the two girls once more. Was it worth it all, he wondered? So many would think it sheer madness – this chancy pursuit of a mere image. But then he reminded himself how, in the moving picture business, that was exactly what everyone pursued, producers and audience equally: just a photographic image. In his world that was everything.

It was certainly worth it. He had rarely, if ever, seen so startling or tempting a face as the taller girl's – or one so formidably beautiful, the dead straight nose, the classical arrogant lines. And yet so pure, untutored: a face which, if he could get his hands and his cameras on it, might at one blow regain his fortunes in Hollywood – a face so entirely different, at once more distinguished and seductive than any possessed by the picture stars out there now: the banal shop-girl, spit-and-kiss-curl women like Mabel Normand or Mary Miles Minter, the preposterous vamp Theda Bara, the blonde ringlets and cloying innocence of that false child, the World's Sweetheart, Mary Pickford . . .

And, apart from his professional interest in this woman, he was taken by her in a more personal way. The insolent intelligence in her expression, the cool mischief there, appealed to him. Here, he sensed, was a worthy opponent, a valid quarry in his long hunt. And beyond that there was even something more, in those great liquid eyes – a touch of mystery, of hurt, of anguish even – which drew from him a quite different feeling, one which he hardly dared think about, having suppressed it for so long: a sense of protectiveness, the possibility, even, of love.

Yes, something in her expression murmured to his romantic heart, so long overlaid by mere lusts, sad desires, successive failures in the hunt. But in these photographs he thought he heard a voice say to him, 'This one will be happy – this one is for you.'

The chance of finding her in Waterford . . . well, he might be disappointed. Yet she existed somewhere. The photographs proved that. And, since she existed, then he would find her. In that material respect at least, he would win – as he always had. To win: that was the simple motto of his life.

In a dark overcoat, trilby hat and a scarf right up against his mouth as if he was trying to disguise himself, Williamson pushed against the cold December wind, walking into the city from Cork railway station. He passed the Presbyterian church on the corner – knowing it all too well, inside and out, from so many childhood Sundays spent there – before finally turning into the High Street.

He saw his father's grocery shop, with its pretentious rustic wooden lettering: 'W. C. Curtis. High Class Family Grocers & Provisioners'. The shop was half-way down the main street, near the new picture palace where that week Gloria Swanson was starring in de Mille's latest extravaganza *Her Gilded Cage*.

Craig felt a pang of jealous bitterness as he passed the billboards, impatient to be back behind a camera himself, and walked on past the statue of Father Matthew, the great apostle of temperance in County Cork, set in the middle of the wide thoroughfare. Narrow-minded, teetotal Catholics – and a few Presbyterians more prejudiced still; ragged, barefoot children playing by the Mardyke, and dank vegetable shops full of wet cabbages under the misty street lights: the whole city had always been as cold as charity for him. He hated the place.

It was late afternoon and dark, but the windows in the flat above the shop, which had been a chilly home to him for the first fifteen years of his life, were unlit. His mother, Eileen, who years ago would always have been there to welcome him with a pot of Barry's strong tea and a big fry-up, had died almost ten years before.

She had been a Catholic, from Dublin, pregnant with him before her hurried and disastrous marriage to his father, which had resulted in their both disappearing from the capital, moving to Cork and opening the shop there: a misalliance which had resulted in his mother's incarceration upstairs in the flat, feigning invalidism on his father's instructions, so as to avoid meeting the other members of the Presbyterian community in the city. Now there was only his father in the shop. He could see him through the window now, beavering away behind the counter, an area he hardly ever left.

The little bell on top of the door pinged as he entered, moving past shelves filled with the more select brands of jam amd marmalade, jars of sauce, pickles and tins of Colman's mustard. To his right a row of Irish gammon hams hung from the ceiling. He made towards the long pine counter, then hesitated. An insolent county lady in heavy, oatmeal tweeds, was speaking to his father. 'Yes, Mr Curtis – but it must be a *Yorkshire* ham for Christmas. Not these local ones. And I shall need the usual sweetmeats, nuts, dried fruit and so on. Have you any pineapples?'

'I'm afraid not, ma'am. The war, you know . . .'

Craig Williamson almost turned and left the shop – appalled, as he always had been, by his father's obsequious tone and attitude. But his father noticed him just at that moment – a cold, neat figure in a dark tie and wing collar, impeccably dressed, in a white bibbed apron over his pin-striped jacket, a few dark slivers of hair running across a balding scalp, thin moustache, narrow lips, a man already old in his early sixties.

Craig made a covert gesture, to delay their meeting until the arrogant lady had finished her order. He made the sign seem one of pure courtesy. In fact he did not want to embarrass his father – or himself – by making their relationship apparent.

Eventually, the customer gone, his father spoke. 'Michael – Michael Curtis,' he said to his son, Craig St John Williamson. 'The prodigal's return,' he added drily. There was no welcome in his dull, clipped voice, just a tone of tired criticism and exasperation – as there had always been. And once more Craig was tempted to turn on his heel . . . and quit this sad place, filled with so many old lies and familial horrors, this shop with its flickering gaslight, smelling of bacon rind, sawdust and carbolic soap; its memories for him of such hypocrisy; a stinginess and cruelty upstairs, together with a servile respectability and lavish credit for the county gentry downstairs in the shop.

But he could not leave. For, just as he nurtured a frustrated, twisted romanticism in his heart, so, too, in the same place lurked the shadows of Christian honour and duty, all the ineradicable traits of the lapsed Puritan.

In Waterford the following day he took a room at the Adelphi Hotel on the quays, confirming that Fonsy O'Grady's troupe was indeed playing at the Theatre Royal nearby, and going on there that evening. He paid nine-pence for a front seat in the stalls, then a penny for a programme. And there was the act: 'Bertie and Bridey', number six in the first half, the 'The Two Musketeers' – whatever that was – number seven in the second. And the names of the two players in each instance: 'Sarah and Rachel Bauer'. This surprised him. They were Jewish obviously. But had not Waxman clearly mentioned an Irish accent?

Their song-and-dance act, when it came, did not astonish him. Remembering such vaudeville theatre from his days in New York, he found it no more than a routine performance – not amateur, but with too many ragged edges, insufficiently skilled musical backing, and without the proper pacing that would have made it truly professional. One of the girls, the smaller one, could certainly sing – a lovely velvety soprano. And the other – though with no real voice at all, indeed she seemed for an actress to have at moments a strange hesitancy in her voice – played the piano very well. As for their second number, both of them in eighteenth-century French costume as 'The Two Musketeers' – well, it was rousing stuff and the taller girl could certainly use a foil. But it was all more in the way of a fencing exhibition. No, indeed, their performances left something to be desired. But the basic human material there . . . well, that was quite astonishing.

The tall girl, dressed as a man: there was so much more poise, beauty and maturity than the photographs had suggested. Even beneath the bowler and the high cravat he could see the vividly expressive features, all so strongly marked, above all the animal vigour, the spontaneous vivacity of the girl, the thrill she offered in just being alive, which gave her so startling and immediate a presence, a wit or cheek or tender wistfulness, that simply leapt over the footlights, pervading the audience with her spirit.

What she possessed most of all, Craig Williamson recognized at once, was some indefinable quality which, unaware of it herself, she could project, without thought or effort; and, when this happened, made it impossible to take one's eyes off her. No one in the picture business had ever really defined that gift, Williamson knew: a mix of so many natural or identifiable gifts, but essentially something mysterious, untouchable – a radiant spirit, and its most hidden recesses at that, which very few stage people were able to promote, as this girl did now, just by standing there and looking at you.

You could not identify this quality until you saw it. But in his business, when you did see it, you recognized it at once, and your stomach turned over with excitement. Intuition alone told you then, as it told him now: this girl had it – a dazzlingly engaging presence, which drew you like a magnet, something that could never be faked or produced or emulated, a unique, un-put-downable quality given only to the greatest stars in his celluloid heaven.

'No, Mr Williamson. We're not the least interested in working in your "photoplays" or "moving pictures" or whatever nonsense.'

Hetty, at her most dismissive, glowered at Craig Williamson over her untouched coffee cup in the lounge of the Adelphi Hotel where he had brought the two girls after the performance.

Craig sipped delicately, treading the ground with extreme caution. Getting the two girls to the hotel had been difficult enough. Having sent his card up to them, he had hung around in the alley behind the theatre like any stage-door Johnny for nearly half an hour before they finally appeared, surrounded by 'The Tumbling Tinies', a troupe of dwarfs in their minute coats and boots against the cold wind.

To begin with, the girls had refused any hospitality or conversation with him, until he had suggested the dwarfs accompany them to the hotel; where they were now, happily ensconced over drinks, a row of merry gnomes on high bar stools in a room leading off the lounge. At first he had been quite confident the girls would come back with him. They were actresses – theatre people – after all. And the card he had sent up – 'Craig St John Williamson', from the 'William Fox Picture Corporation, Hollywood, Los Angeles' – had always been a sure bait in the past. But they had refused.

'Is this *you*?' The taller girl had flourished his visiting card dismissively in his face as she left the stage door. And 'yes', he had replied, with something of a wicked smile and an exaggerated brogue – 'Tis me! Who else?' – as if they had met before and she was a bad girl to have forgotten him.

And then, as if startled by some sudden barrier in front of her, the girl had paused in her departure from the theatre, staring at him carefully in his red scarf and trilby, momentarily intrigued. Putting his card between her teeth, donning a Russian fur hat and pushing her curls up beneath it, she stared at him.

Something passed between them then, in that first instant in the lamplight outside the stage door – a moment's acknowledgement, as between duellists, of some future engagement. And that, Craig thought, was the real reason she had finally agreed to come with him: she had been tempted, against his roguish impertinence, by the idea of punishing him for his temerity, and by the prospect of an easy victory there.

So that now in the hotel, while retaining some of this wit, he was much more careful in his approach, favouring the other, smaller, dark-haired girl as much as her companion.

'I wish you'd at least consider a picture test. I can fix it up in London, or Dublin – Miss?' He hesitated, looking at Hetty. 'It's Miss Sarah Bauer, isn't it?'

'No, I'm Rachel.' She gestured at Léonie. 'My cousin – she's the Sarah.'

'I see . . .' Craig nodded wisely. He felt somehow he was being lied to. They both looked Jewish certainly, especially the smaller girl. But the taller one had this distinctly cultured Irish accent, Ascendancy Irish – there was no doubt about it. He could spot it at once, for he himself had longed for just such an accent and background, things he so assiduously pretended to now.

'Nice name . . . "Bauer". Jewish, isn't it?' he went on lightly. 'But of course you're Irish. At least *you* are.' He looked steadily at Hetty. 'Not many Jewish people in Ireland, are there?'

'Oh yes, one or t-t-two!'

Now he was almost certain she was lying: that sudden stammer told him something. The girl was not so confident in this alias. But he let it pass. 'Anyway, as I've told you, I'm on my way back to America from the war . . . and

686

looking for people to cast in a new motion picture I'm hoping to start soon.'

'Oh yes – what's that?' Hetty retaliated at her most haughty.

'*Cleopatra.*'

She laughed. 'Well, you're not suggesting I could p-play her, are you?'

'No, you couldn't.' He paused. 'Not yet,' he added.

Léonie chuckled. 'Cleopatra,' she murmured. 'What next?'

Craig turned to Léonie. 'Not beyond the bounds of possibility, you know. You can both act. Your friend particularly: wonderful presence. Need more training, more experience, of course. But it's all there for her, I assure you. I don't return to the States for a week or two. So let me fix up a test?'

'But, Mr Williamson,' Léonie interrupted, sensing clearly how he was making a play for Hetty, excluding her, 'we've neither of us the slightest interest in your motion picture business. Indeed,' she leant forward, confidingly dismissive. 'Indeed, more than that, we – all of us in the company – we actively resent your business a great deal. It's been ruining half our dates in Ireland for the past few years, all these new picture palaces – taking the bread from our mouths. And, quite besides that, it's really such *rubbish* you people produce!'

'Yes, indeed!' Hetty took over, though with less conviction than Léonie had shown. 'Far from working with you, I'd like to destroy all your picture palaces!'

'I'm sure you would.' Craig smiled. 'That's just the vigorous quality I like in you. And woman of your word, no doubt, too. Yes, indeed, you'd do *just* that,' he ran on enthusiastically. 'But, Miss Bauer, even you can't stand against this picture palace business for ever. And, with your great gifts in the same field, why, it's obvious: if you can't beat 'em, join 'em!'

Léonie shook her head, answering for Hetty. 'Not possible. This music hall act is only a temporary business, taken up because we couldn't travel with the war on. But

I'm to study opera soon – in Paris. And my cousin will be coming with me. So, you see, it's simply not possible, even if we wanted to get into your motion picture business, which we *don't*.'

Léonie, having delivered this *coup de grâce*, stood up to leave. But Hetty was less anxious to go.

'Well, thank you for the offer, Mr Williamson. Some other time perhaps . . . I might consider the idea of taking your test or whatever.' She smiled at him briefly. But Léonie was furious.

'Hetty!' she remonstrated with her. 'What can you be thinking of? There's no question . . .' Her voice trailed off. There was silence.

'"Hetty"?' Craig Williamson asked. 'Not Rachel – but Hetty. Short for Henrietta. Not a very Jewish name!'

Hetty was furious now. 'Henrietta is my middle name – and it's none of your business what my friends call me, Mr Williamson.'

She stamped out of the room, Léonie following her. But in her anger she had forgotten her purse on the table, a little blue bead bag. Craig Williamson, opening it very quickly, fingered deftly through the contents, soon finding what he wanted – an envelope with a London postmark, addressed to 'Miss Henrietta Fraser, Summer Hill, Cloone, Co Kilkenny'. He followed the two girls out to the hall and returned the purse.

'You left this behind, Miss Bauer.' He gave her one of his nicest smiles. 'Yes, I do hope you'll reconsider my offer. I'll be in touch with you.' The troupe of dwarfs, leaving the bar, surrounded the girls. 'Why,' he went on, looking down at the tiny men. 'You could *all* come to Hollywood – I'll need just such people, for Cleopatra's Egyptian court!'

Hetty, snatching the purse, turned on her heel without another word.

Craig Williamson returned to the Shelbourne Hotel in Dublin. 'Henrietta Fraser, Summer Hill, Cloone, Co Kilkenny'. Who could she be? It should not be difficult to find out. He spoke to the manager of the hotel, someone sure to be well versed in big houses and great families in Ireland.

He answered at once, but without any enthusiasm. 'Henrietta Fraser – of Summer Hill in Kilkenny? She must be related to Frances Fraser, the Republican rebel who caused such havoc here in the hotel and in the Green in the 1916 rising. She's in jail at the moment. In London,' he added thankfully.

'Are you sure?'

'About the woman Frances Fraser anyway. No doubt. She certainly comes from Summer Hill, a big house down there. One of the Cordiner family. But I'm sure you'll find all the information you want here, Mr Williamson,' he said tartly, handing him the hotel's copy of *Burke's Irish Landed Gentry*.

And there indeed it all was, in nearly two pages of the directory – the Cordiners of Cloone and Kilclondowne, with the latest in that line as a final entry: 'Henrietta Francesca Elizabeth Fraser (b. 1900) dau. of Frances Fraser (née Cordiner) and Bruce Fraser, of Fraser Hall, Domenica (d. 1908)', with her address as the family seat at Summer Hill.

Craig was enchanted by all this information. His boat to New York was delayed. He had more time on his hands. He would go down to Summer Hill, make another approach to the girl. She would surely be there over Christmas – with her 'cousin', if such she was. The whole business of these subterfuges – her male disguise, her alias as 'Miss Bauer' – all this only added to her charm for him. And now this additional factor of her aristocratic lineage, with a great house in Ireland, made her more attractive still. There was no question, he would renew his suit. He would not let her go. He would win. This girl, quite apart from her theatrical gifts, her beauty, represented in her background everything he had ever dreamed of for himself in Ireland: 'Henrietta Francesca Elizabeth Fraser – of Summer Hill, Co Kilkenny'. The idea and its ramifications sent a thrill down his spine.

Leaving the hotel that evening, he saw the billboard by the news-stand in the porch: MRS FRASER TO BE

RELEASED! HOME FOR CHRISTMAS! Buying a copy of the paper he saw the woman's photograph on the front page. Yes, of course, something of the same features – this was the girl's mother! There was no doubt of it.

Henrietta Fraser: daughter of an Irish rebel leader, with some exotic West Indian background to boot, and heir no doubt to a great estate, wonderful comedienne, fencer, outrageous liar, male impersonator and with that clear hint he had had in the Waterford hotel of some unsuitable relationship with her 'cousin' – the mix was almost too rich. The stars in Hollywood, like Theda Bara, had to have such lives invented for them by the publicity departments – and such skills, usually and unsuccessfully, drummed into them. This girl had all this in truth and by nature. Now that the petrol rationing was over, he would motor down to Summer Hill in the next few days.

In normal circumstances – if the two girls had gone to Paris or continued their tour with Fonsy, disappearing into the wilds of Ireland – Hetty would never have had to think of Craig Williamson again. But circumstances changed.

That following day in Waterford Léonie received news from Paris, a telegram from her father: her mother was ill, dangerously so it seemed, with influenza. Léonie, perforce, had to make arrangements at once to return home, booking passage on the boat to England the next morning.

'Of course, you'll come with me,' she had said to Hetty.

But Hetty was unwilling. And later she became adamant. 'Léa – it's rather nonsense: for me to go all that way to Paris, when your Mama only has 'flu. She's bound to recover . . . and you'll be back here anyway in a week or so. And, besides, I *can't* go. I promised to be home next week – for Christmas. Dermot's coming back, remember?' She grasped Léonie's hand reassuringly. 'I just had that wonderful long letter from him. He's expecting me at Summer Hill. I can hardly disappoint him, after four years away. He and Mortimer and Robert – all coming home for Christmas. It's all fixed. And I could never get back from Paris in time, if I came with you.'

Léonie was distraught. 'But, Hetty, we promised to stay together—'

'Of course we did! And we will. But in this case, just for a week or so, we can't. You know we can't. And you'll be back soon enough, of course you will . . .' Hetty was becoming impatient at what she felt were Léonie's clinging tentacles. 'Don't you *see*, Léa?' she added, a touch impatiently.

Léonie did see, but repressed what she saw – preferring to think that Hetty was tactfully dropping her, that she was trying to push her out of her life, as she always suspected she might, using her mother's illness in Paris now as the excuse, and no doubt intending to take up instead with this awful Craig Williamson and his motion picture plans.

Adding insult to injury, as Léonie felt, Hetty more or less forced her on to the mail boat for Fishguard next morning, propelling her up the gangway, into her cabin, so that Léonie was quite frantic when they got there.

'No, Léa,' Hetty tried to calm her, reason with her once more. 'You have to go. You can't let people down in this way—'

'Me letting *you* down? But it's *you* I want to be with!' Léonie nearly screamed.

'No, I meant letting your parents down, your Mama.'

'But . . . you're just as important as they are. More important . . .' She began to sob – as Hetty embraced her. 'Oh, yes, Léa.' She brushed her ear with her lips. 'And you to me. But this time I *have* to stay. And you really have to go.' Hetty's tone was warm enough. But the words, the balance of the phrasing, could not but give a dismissive impression.

'You're just pushing me out of your life! . . .'

'But I'm not – I'm *not*, Léa dearest. Our life – all that we have together – has to include other people sometimes: your Mama and Papa, Dermot, Robert, Mortimer . . . And we can't be so selfish, just with each other, all the time. Don't you see?'

'No! You just want to be free of me – or go off with that man Williamson. I can feel it!'

'No, Léa, no!' Hetty lied.

'Hetty, come with me – we can have our games in Paris, better than we ever could in Ireland.' Léonie's eyes, filled with tears, took on an extra dimension now – of seductive compliance, a yielding submission.

'No, I *can't!*'

'Why can't you, damn you?' Léonie was desperate now. 'I can love you any way we like, any way you want in Paris. As long as you're there, in front of me, in bed with me. *That's* how I love you.'

'But, Léa, you told me once it was your *thinking* of loving me that meant most to you, not . . . doing it. Well, same here. So it won't matter if we're apart for a bit. We can both *think* of loving each other. You said so yourself! . . .'

'Did I? Well I've changed my mind.' Léonie remembered very well this earlier, happier invention of hers – when Hetty could readily be possessed. Now, losing her, she resorted to every deceit, compromise, exaggeration, approaching her in a clumsy embrace. 'I want you so much – *that* way, Hetty, not thinking of you.'

'Oh, Léa – you're being totally self-centred and indulgent about it all.'

The ship's siren rasped, calling visitors off and drowning out Léonie's next words: 'You don't *want* me to love you then.' And Hetty, thinking Léonie had said something else, something happy by way of goodbye, nodded her head vigorously and kissed her before turning away, leaving Léonie sobbing in the cabin.

So Hetty returned to Summer Hill a week earlier than expected. The thought of meeting Dermot soon obliterated the unhappy departure scene with Léonie. He had written her such a lovely letter. She had kept it in her purse, rereading it every so often, and now she was able to remind herself that, without Léonie, here was someone else, clearly in view, who loved her, to whom she might pay court, who would replace Léonie temporarily. For of course Léonie would get over her pettish, possessive anger. It was so unjustified in any case – for had not Léonie in fact abandoned her, leaving her just because of her mother's silly bout of 'flu? So Hetty conveniently argued her quite justified liberation from her friend, without thought for any possible consequence. It was time she freed herself from her a bit; indeed Mr Williamson had seemed to hint as much . . .

But when she arrived at Summer Hill a real setback awaited her. There was another letter from London, this time from Mortimer: Dermot had succumbed to the same influenza epidemic, was ill in bed, and was likely to remain in London for some time. Neither of them could be expected over for Christmas. Mortimer, unaware of Léonie's departure, hoped that Hetty, with Léonie and Robert, would hold the fort at Summer Hill over the holiday season, and that they might then all meet in the New Year.

Hetty was inconsolable. Robert, alone of the four who had already arrived at Summer Hill, did his best to cheer her up.

'It's really awful – I *do* feel for you,' he told her comfortingly. 'But there's nothing we can do about it really. It's some new form of influenza. I read about it – it's to do with the end of the war: all the troops returning from the filthy trenches, packed up like sardines in ships and trains, then seeing their friends and relations at home – so that it's spreading like wildfire. A real plague apparently. Best thing is just to stay put here—'

'We could travel over to London, you and I, and see them there!'

'Oh, Hetty, I know what you feel. But it wouldn't work. Mortimer'll be busy with Dermot—'

'Exactly! So *I* could look after him.'

'And get the 'flu yourself? Look, it'll all soon blow over. Much better to stay here. And besides, now that your Grandmama is failing, we really ought to stay here. You heard what Dr Roche said this morning – she probably won't last long. And, with your Mama away, *someone* has to take charge here. And that person's really you, isn't it?'

Hetty had to agree. Indeed, given the way Robert had so artfully put it, she was pleased to agree, consoling herself finally with the role she could now play – with every good reason – as châtelaine of Summer Hill.

So that immediately, with Elly and old Mrs Martin the housekeeper, she set about directing domestic details in the household, going ahead with all the usual Christmas arrangements – a quiet Christmas, no doubt, though perhaps she might ask the Ashleys to stay over the season. Yes, that was a plan . . . which would save something from the social wreck. She would make the house as bright and merry as possible, decorate it with lots of holly and ivy, even mistletoe, why not? She could kiss the Major under it. And put lots of lamps about – how she wished they had electricity – glittering lights and fires everywhere in these dank, dark mid-winter days. To this end she went to the lamp room with Mrs Martin and Teresa, the maid responsible, picking out a number of extra Aladdin and other taller standard lamps, asking that they be cleaned, filled with plenty of oil and made ready to set about the house.

'Let's light the whole place up!' she said to Mrs Martin, eyes ablaze, like the effect she intended, speaking with such vehement joy that the old housekeeper, remembering her mother's similarly manic fits, thought her touched now in the same way. 'Yes,' Hetty flew on. 'Let's have lights! And music! Let's all eat, drink and be merry! . . . Don't you think, Mrs Martin?'

Mrs Martin, as a staunch Presbyterian, thought no such thing. But she followed her instructions – so that the house that afternoon, when darkness fell and Austin and Bunty Cordiner arrived quite unannounced, was lit by fires and lamps, sparkling like a catherine wheel, as if for some great reception.

Hetty had only the briefest and coldest of words with Bunty, before she and Austin went on up to the back wing to see Lady Cordiner. They, too, had heard from Dr Roche: the old lady was failing. Austin Cordiner, out of kindness, had come to offer what he could in the way of consolatory gestures towards his sister-in-law. But Bunty, as on her previous visit, had another and entirely devious reason. Taking advantage of Frances's continued absence in Holloway, and the fact that, if she knew she was dying, old Lady Cordiner might somehow speak at last, she would make one final attempt to elicit an answer to the question that had so plagued her since she had been denied Summer Hill nearly ten years before.

Who was Henrietta's real father?

If she had sure answer to this, she could then contest Lady Cordiner's subsequent change in her will – and perhaps, even at this late date, by confronting, even blackmailing, Frances with this truth, secure the house and estate for herself, or at least for her descendants.

Both of them sat in Lady Cordiner's gloomy bedroom, Bunty gazing at the withered old lady, propped up on her many pillows, asleep at first. But soon she opened her eyes. And they were bright again when she recognized them. It was clear that she looked on them both without any of the malice she reserved for Hetty.

'How are you . . . dear Sarah?' Austin spoke gently. 'Are you well?' he added awkwardly.

After what seemed an age, she nodded. Bunty particularly was pleased with this response. The old lady, though unable really to speak a coherent word, could nod and perhaps shake her head, at least. She could thus say 'Yes' and 'No' – like a spirit in a table-tapping session. And that would be quite sufficient for her purpose here, Bunty thought. She would speak to her, alone, when Austin left to visit O'Donovan, the farm steward, as he always did on his rare visits to the house.

A few minutes later Austin rose to his feet. 'I'll go and see O'Donovan, dearest. You'll keep her company a bit longer, won't you?' he whispered.

'Of course, dear.' Bunty was at her most charitable and concerned.

But the moment her husband left the room her expression changed. Taking her chair right over beside the bed, starting her interrogation, she looked fixedly into Lady Cordiner's eyes.

'It's me, you *know* it's me,' she began, in a steely but confiding voice. 'Frances is still in prison in England – and we're quite alone here now. We may talk, or I may – about the house, about everything – the things you'd like me to do for you, and about Frances, who so wickedly took the house away from you. But first you must tell me about Henrietta – her real father. It wasn't Bruce Fraser, was it?'

Lady Cordiner tried to speak. But only a dry warble emerged from her lips. 'Just shake your head.' Bunty could barely restrain her impatience. 'Was it Bruce Fraser?' Lady Cordiner shook her head a fraction. 'Was it young Dermot then – out at the Boer war with her?' Lady Cordiner did not seem to understand. But Bunty had come prepared. She produced a photograph of Dermot and held it up to her. Again, after a long moment, Lady Cordiner shook her head.

'Then it must be him.' Bunty produced another illustration, this time in a torn page from an old *Irish Tatler*, a full-page line drawing of the Prince of Wales, done many years before. 'Was it him?' And at this, seeing the drawing, Lady Cordiner nodded her head, not once, but several times.

Bunty showed a huge relief. 'So, the old King's daughter! I suspected as much . . . not legitimate at all. And so Henrietta has no right to the house!' Bunty, her eyes filled with greedy satisfaction, patted the old lady's hand, still staring at her fixedly. 'Well, now I know – I may do something about it!' And indeed, she thought, what damage she could now do with this information – by blackmailing Frances with it for a start, just as Frances herself had obviously done ten years before with the old lady. 'Of course,' she whispered to Lady Cordiner, leaning forward – confiding, arrogant, condescending, all in one glance. 'It all makes sense now. *That's* how Frances forced you . . . into changing your will . . . wasn't it?'

Lady Cordiner nodded once more, her own eyes

strangely alight now, seemingly happy with Bunty's comments. 'Well,' Bunty went on. 'Now we may have the house, just as you wanted, Austin and I – or at least the boys may have it. You'd want that, wouldn't you?'

Lady Cordiner did not nod this time. Instead she seemed to give a smile of assent. She turned her eyes towards the oil lamp on the bedside table, set some distance away, well out of her reach, making a feeble gesture with her arm.

'You'd like the lamp brought nearer?'

Lady Cordiner nodded. Bunty, at her most solicitous now, moved the entire table next to the bed. 'There, you'll see better—'

In the same instant Lady Cordiner, summoning up all her last reserves of energy, reached out with her one good arm and gave the lamp a violent push – breaking the frosted glass shade and chimney, spinning it over on the bedside table, where the oil spurted out across the lacquered surface, immediately taking fire there, flames leaping up in an explosive mix of varnish and paraffin. Bunty, taken by surprise, dithered for a long moment, allowing the fire to get a grip, before finally she picked up one of the crochet-work woollen shawls on the bed and threw it over the flames.

The shawl promptly caught fire, before falling to the floor. Bunty attempted to stamp the flames out, treading and scraping at the burning wool. Within a moment the hem of her dress took fire – and a few moments later the flames, leaping upwards, gorging on the material, had turned her into a blazing human torch.

She screamed then, and started a frenzied, swaying dance about the room, thus encouraging the flames, which soon had a firm grip on her. She thought to extinguish the fire amidst the blankets of the four-poster bed. But that was alight now: Lady Cordiner immobile in the centre, sitting up, perfectly still, a witch in a closing circle of fire, the flames skating over the silk eiderdown, nibbling at her arms, beginning with voracious appetite to feed on her nightdress, the pillows, the shawl around her shoulders.

Bunty, blinded by flame and smoke and in the belief that she was moving towards the door, found herself instead over by the window. She tugged at the velvet drapes, trying to envelop herself in them. But, instead, offering the fire another foothold, the dry curtains flamed in a streak of ascending yellow light, travelling up to the ceiling like the tail of a rocket.

And now Bunty screamed, terrified shrieks, while Lady Cordiner, still conscious, saw her sister-in-law's agony, and smiled, well pleased at her handiwork.

But she saw no more as her eyes closed, the lids seeming to melt in the searing heat rising all about her. The loose folds of skin on her neck and cheeks started to blister and bubble, the little fat left in her face began to crackle – and then, in a sudden tinder flash, her wispy hair caught fire and the old lady disappeared from view in a pall of smoke.

Everything was ablaze now – bed, curtains, floorboards, most of the furniture, the long refectory table with its tasselled velvet cloth, its dusty Victorian mementoes, the silver-framed photographs of Henry and Eustace. Objects sizzled and popped about the room in a series of small explosions. The heat was intense in the sealed space – the air, almost gone now, feeding the conflagration. So that when Pat Kennedy – with Austin and O'Donovan behind him – opened the bedroom door, letting a sudden surge of air inside, they were met by a fireball exploding outwards, which scorched and felled Kennedy and drove the other two men back, before they rallied, managing to return, dragging the butler away with them, and running themselves then, pursued by flames, finding sanctuary in the main house, slamming the heavy interconnecting oak door behind them. In another ten minutes the whole neo-Gothic north wing of Summer Hill was an inferno.

By next morning firemen and the estate workers had finally doused the last of the smouldering timbers. The roof and floors of the north wing had largely collapsed, leaving just the charred walls and gaping windows, the rest a smoking pyre of damp brick and mortar open to the December sky. But, apart from one or two rooms, including Frances's study-boudoir next to the north wing, now a sodden shambles, the men had managed to save the rest of the Georgian house.

The Constabulary were there, picking through the blackened debris. Undertakers had removed the charred bodies of the two women. An ambulance had taken Pat Kennedy, burnt about the face and hands, to the County Infirmary. Austin Cordiner bore up, showing great courage, while the rest of the household stood about aghast. Hetty was with Robert on the front lawn, practically speechless. Then, taking a grip on herself, she said, 'I'll get that telegram off to Mortimer, Mama must be told. Then I'll talk to Austin, see about the rest of his family getting down here.'

The servants, many of whom had had their quarters in the north wing and had lost everything, were still in a state of shock, weeping, being ministered to by Dr Roche and old Mrs Molloy with cups of tea in the kitchen. Teresa, the lamp maid, was particularly distraught – weeping, shaking, in the housekeeper's parlour, where Mrs Martin tried to console her.

'*Of course* it wasn't your fault,' she told her.

'But 'twas I who got out all those extra lamps in the first place, like you said. And I'd just filled her Ladyship's lamp up, right up to the top—'

'You put out all the new lamps in the *main* house, Teresa. And the fire didn't start there. Nothing to do with you at all.' She calmed the girl.

'But how did the fire start then?'

Mrs Martin shook her head. 'An accident – I don't know. But it certainly wasn't you.'

Of course it had crossed Mrs Martin's mind that Hetty's sudden manic enthusiasm about the lamps and fires that same afternoon might have had something to do with the conflagration. She knew very well of the girl's headstrong ways – just like her mother, up to every rash trick when the mood took her. She knew, too, of the enmity between her and Bunty Cordiner – she had witnessed just this during their meeting in the hall only half an hour before the fire had started. And, of course, she had known for a long time how much old Lady Cordiner had disliked her granddaughter and assumed the feeling was mutual. Was it possible? – that Hetty had set the place on fire, getting rid of the two of them in one fell swoop? Anything was possible with the women of this family, she thought.

And this, certainly, was Frances's view subsequently. Hetty had no need to telegram Mortimer. Her mother, released from Holloway the day before, had crossed over to Dublin on the mail boat that night and taken a hired motor down to Kilkenny straight away next morning. She drove up to the house an hour later.

Frances's reaction to the deaths of the two women and the loss of the north wing was not one of sympathy or resignation but of astonishing anger. From the beginning she suspected that Hetty had been in some way responsible for the blaze. And, when she learnt of all the additional lamps and fires which her daughter had commanded the previous day, her suspicions became a certainty: Hetty, in this covert manner, had tried to set the whole house alight. She was, in any case, still furious with her daughter for her behaviour in running off with Léonie more than a year before. So that now, with arson to be added to her crimes, their confrontation later that morning in the drawing room was electric.

'That *I* tried to burn the house down?' Hetty, astonished, was just as angry.

'But of course . . . as your revenge against me! The one thing you knew was truly dear to me – this house!'

'You are insane. Why should I b-burn down our house?'

'*Our* house? Not yours – *ever!*' Her mother loomed at her viciously and for a moment it seemed they might come to blows. 'And further . . .' Her mother stopped inches away from her. 'I shall have you charged with arson. Oh yes – I shall call the Constabulary.'

'They will take no notice of such ravings – least of all from you, a convicted rebel, just out of jail! Besides – and Robert can vouch for this – I was nowhere near the north w-wing yesterday. Only Bunty and Austin went up there.

And it was Bunty who stayed on alone in the room with Grandmama. If anyone started the fire it was *her*! You know perfectly we-we-well how she's always coveted the house, especially since she was done out of it when you got Grandmama to change her will. It was she, if anyone, taking revenge on you, not me.'

They stormed at each other, up and down the long room, just as Frances herself had done, twenty years previously, with her own mother, before her banishment to the West Indies. And now Frances had an identical end in view for Hetty.

'Your behaviour, as I've told you before, is simply *criminal*. But now you have gone too far. If you are not convicted of arson, I can promise you one thing – you will leave this house now, for good and all, never set foot in it again!'

Hetty, deciding to disengage herself from the pointless argument, shook her head and smiled pityingly at her mother. 'Calm yourself. Your threats and theories are all nonsense. We have more important things to do. Austin, for example, we must think of him . . .'

This sensible line of argument only served to infuriate Frances the more. 'How dare you feign concern for a man you have just widowed – you brazen little hussy!'

Frances aimed a blow at Hetty's cheek. But Hetty, far more fit than her mother after the latter's months in prison, caught her arm and held it. Slowly she bent it back, until her mother struggled in pain.

'Madness. Sheer madness,' Hetty remarked casually, letting her go. 'Just like Grandmama – whom *you* made mad. I saw you once, you know, up in that great bedroom, years ago! Oh yes – you had that w-w-wicked Hallowe'en turnip head – and you set it in front of her, with a candle inside, while you just sat there, torturing her. *You* killed Grandmama long ago. You're the criminal, not I. But I'll promise you one thing: you'll not kill me. And another thing . . .' Hetty looked round the room. 'It's *you* who have destroyed this house – just as if you'd burnt it – with your evil temper, your cruelties and ma-ma-mad ambitions for it, your hatreds, your p-p-possessiveness.' Hetty turned now, half-way to the door. 'When I have Summer Hill, things will be very different . . .' With these last words, issued without the slightest hesitancy, Hetty turned and left.

But, alone in her bedroom, Hetty showed none of the same confidence and attack. She collapsed, sobbing, on her bed. Finally, with this fire, these deaths, and the return of her mother, it had all become too much for her.

Léonie, as Hetty chose to think, had dropped her. And Dermot, with just the excuse of some silly bout of 'flu, had failed her as well. Admittedly, there were still Robert and Aunt Emily at Summer Hill. But, even if her mother had not just forbidden her the house, she could not have faced staying with this malignant woman a moment longer. She would have to leave – for London, Paris, anywhere. Her world had collapsed. She could fall no further.

At the nadir of her fortunes, she picked up the snow-dome from her bedside table, shook it gently, and watched the flakes rise and wheel over the ivory miniature of Summer Hill. Something touched her heart in this fairy-tale beauty: drifts of snow, memories of childhood. There was an inviolate solace there, embedded in the crystal, beyond all corruption. And a proprietorial feeling for her in it, too – a confirmation of security, power and long tradition, of which she was part. That could not be taken away from her. The house was hers. And, just as she had told her mother, one day she would return and repossess it. Of course she would! Summer Hill was the essence of her life; no one could ever deprive her of that. Here alone – in these bricks and mortar – was something that would never betray her.

And at that moment she regained some of her old confidence – and with it, she realized, came something even better: a burning, surging feeling of anger, then a godlike distancing and independence from all these setbacks. She was immune from them. What should she care for her mother's madness, the frailties of her friends? All that was a waste of time and spirit now. You could not in the end really trust others – could only rely on yourself. And she need not be dependent on anyone now. For it was she, after all, who had the real character, vigour, talent, beauty – she who could make her way perfectly well without them all.

'Let them all go hang!' she said, speaking to the little crystal globe – pure, undefiled emblem of all her hopes. 'Fortune Favours the Brave,' she added, speaking slowly and decisively, her tears drying, a wonderful feeling of command sweeping over her. She would run things her own way from now on. She would win. She stood up, went to the wardrobe and started packing a suitcase, taking the snow-dome with her, placing it carefully, protecting it between the thickest clothes.

Craig Williamson, in the back of the chauffeur-driven Daimler, looked about him as the car wound up the long drive. A pale sun had emerged, running in shafts across the valley, before it reached the great house, spotlighting it among the semicircle of dark trees. He was excited, avaricious for the grandeur of it all. Every prospect pleased him here. This was exactly the sort of great house and estate – a dream of classic ease and order – for which he had always longed; a landscape which, at one fell swoop, would wipe out all the drab, penny-pinching memories, the chilly cruelties and indignities of his own childhood in Cork.

Then, he saw the men, still gathered about the blackened remains of the north wing. Seeing the destruction, he stopped the car near the archway into the yard, and got out to investigate. A constable stood near by.

'What happened?'

'Ah, a terrible blaze altogether.'

'And casualties?'

'I believe so . . .' The constable was not more forthcoming.

But another man approached him now, tall and elderly, with a prophet's beard. 'I'm O'Donovan, the steward.

You'll be from the insurance people—'

'No, in fact—'

But Mr O'Donovan did not hear him. They both turned then, as part of the wall, high up, collapsed, falling inwards with a great crash, so that the man hurried away and Craig, accepted now as someone who had business in the place, was left on his own. He walked up over the lawn towards the south end of the burnt wing, where it joined the Georgian house, stepping over damp rubble. Soon he found himself looking through a gaping hole in the brickwork, giving straight on to the sodden remains of Frances's boudoir.

Charred and broken furniture lay beneath drifts of fallen brick and plaster. Tin deed boxes poked out among the damp paper and splintered glass. Stepping gingerly through the hole, he surveyed the desolate scene inside.

His boot slipped on a morass of damp plaster, hitting one of the deed boxes, half-buried beneath it. The lid, he saw, had buckled in the heat, leaving the box partly open at one end. Then, just next to the lid, something caught his eye, a flash of light in the mess of plaster. He bent down. It was a brooch-watch, barely harmed, an exquisite Victorian timepiece, set in a gold case with a blue glazed enamel face, the pin-clip inset with diamonds. Turning it over, he saw the engraved dedication: 'Frances. From Alix and Edward. Christmas, Sandringham, 1898.' And, beneath that, a miniature coat of arms, three ostrich feathers above the legend 'Ich Dien'. Then it was suddenly clear to him: 'Alix and Edward – Sandringham – Ich Dien'; the watch must have been a gift to Mrs Fraser from Edward VII when he was still Prince of Wales.

He held it in his hand for a long moment, tempted by something – not to steal it, no, but by some other feeling, some sixth sense, which he could not identify.

Then, sensing that someone was looking at him, but unwilling to let the watch fall and disappear again among the smoking debris, he pocketed it adroitly. Looking round, he saw a woman gazing at him. She was dressed in travelling clothes, framed above him in a broken, smoking arch that had once been a doorway into the room. Her face was quite expressionless, without distaste or interest at his presence: a hard, tear-streaked mask. Craig, composing himself, settling his red scarf about his throat, took off his trilby hat.

'I *am* sorry,' he said, looking at the destruction around him, then back at the broken face. There was nothing of the rogue, the actor, no irony in his voice now. The tone was heartfelt. 'Can I help – in any way?'

Hetty considered the offer for what seemed an age. Then, with the same hard tone in her voice, she said, 'Yes – yes, you can. I want to go to Dublin. That's your c-c-car, isn't it?' She gestured towards the yard. 'Can you take me to the station?'

'Of course, I'd be pleased to. But I'm going back to Dublin myself. I can give you a lift all the way.'

'W-wait for me then. Don't let them see you. Leave the c-car where it is. I'll join you in a minute.'

Hetty said goodbye to Robert, then to Aunt Emily. Robert tried to dissuade her.

'It's madness, Hetty!—'

'No! I'd go m-m-mad if I stayed here—'

'But your Mama'll cool down!'

'She won't! She's going to have me charged with arson—'

'Take no notice of her ravings. Where'll you go anyway?'

'London, see Mortimer at least. Then Paris, to Léonie. There's no p-p-*point*, don't you see? I can't stay. Mama's told me to get out, tried to hit me. We'd both come to blows. It's impossible. Best to go away for a bit. But I'll be back.'

Aunt Emily, bewildered by the fire, was much more enthusiastic in her old mad way. 'Paris? – I'll come with you. There's a decent enough hotel, near the shops in the St Honoré, just round the corner from our Legation there, a most accommodating manager as I remember—'

'Not now, Aunt. Another time. It's Léonie, you see. Her Mama's very ill.'

'Ah, Léonie, of course. As long as you're not running off with some man . . .'

'Of course not.'

She kissed her aunt – as she resumed the drawing she had started that morning, a most spirited sketch, Hetty saw, of the north wing in flames, violent yellow streaks soaring up against the darkness; an entirely realistic painting, except for the clear shape of a face in the swirling pattern of leaping flame and smoke, the features of Lady Cordiner, an evil genie rising from the ruined wing, spiralling away, with a headdress of sparks, into the night sky.

Hetty left by the back door. And, as she left, running along the basement corridor and raising her hand, she touched all the room bells, in a line above her head, pushing each one vigorously as she passed, so that the house came alive suddenly, with a joyous, sparkling sound, rising through the floors and stairways, flooding the house with challenging melody.

Hetty, on the journey to Dublin, gradually, in fits and starts, but gathering confidence against the man's attentive and sympathetic demeanour, explained the whole situation to Craig Williamson. So that by the time they arrived at the Shelbourne she had agreed to take a room there herself, at least for that night, and talk further of his propositions.

She was surprised at her change of heart about the man. But then, she argued conveniently, she simply had not known him before. And indeed this was true in quite another way. In her theatrical experience she had not expected, nor so far encountered, anyone so apparently civilized, sophisticated, intelligent. She had loved all the rough-and-tumble of the music hall, the deep camaraderie she shared among her friends there. But this man, part of the same tradition, showed a refinement and sensitivity that was quite new to her.

Above all – the moment she had stepped into the luxury of the Daimler – there was the clear feeling that she had entered a world, not so much of money, which meant little to her, but one of power, which at that moment in her life meant everything.

They dined in the hotel restaurant that night. Wartime austerity was over, there was Veuve Clicquot champagne with the Galway oysters, before the filet mignon.

He wore a smartly cut dark suit – with a double-breasted jacket of a sort she had never seen before – and she felt frumpy in the few clothes she had taken quickly from Summer Hill. He raised his glass, his hair a dark sheen in the lamplight. 'The future: yours – and mine.'

'But I haven't said I'd take that p-p-picture test.' Despite the hesitancy, she returned his look calmly.

'No, you haven't. But hearing your story I think you should. Now's the time – for change.'

'Here?'

'In California.'

She eyed him carefully, putting down her glass, avoiding the issue raised by this implied invitation. 'You think – a test – it's w-worth it?'

'Not really. But you are. That's the real point I made – about California. You should come there with me.'

He studied her then, waiting for a reaction, looking into her blue eyes, an air of incipient fun visible for the first time that day. But she said nothing, joining him in a trial of wills, looking at him coolly in return. By way of response he leant back then, instead of forward, allowing distance to emphasize the authority of his words.

'Test or no, Miss Fraser, you have the qualities that make motion picture stars.' Then, dusting his lips with a napkin, he added casually, 'I can make you a star.'

She laughed. 'As easy as that . . .!'

'No. A lot of hard work – and mostly yours.'

'And you're so c-c-confident?'

'Oh yes. I am. Have to be. Done it before.' He spoke in an abrupt staccato, slightly fretful now. 'It's my business, my life, you see. Think I'd risk it over someone I didn't believe in?'

'No. You wouldn't. I can see that.'

'And I can see the same thing in you, too, Miss Fraser,' he retorted sharply. 'You're *just* as ambitious – for something.'

They smiled, the first intimation of some real understanding passing between them. 'Besides . . .' Craig leant forward into the lamplight then. 'Now the war's over, the picture business in America is really going to go places. You think it's just a thing of nickelodeons and hucksters, a pastime for the lower orders. Well, that's true. But it's a lot more: an art – a real art – as well as a huge money-spinner. And remember that as well, Miss Fraser: now that your mother's pushed you out, how did you think you were going to live? On the charity of your friends in London or Paris?' He took the Veuve Clicquot from its cooler, half-filling her glass.

'Live?' She was genuinely curious.

'Yes. Money – this sort of thing.' He tapped the bottle.

'Oh, I don't need that – have no real t-taste for it.'

'Clothes?' He looked at her pointedly. 'You like clothes, don't you? Love the whole dressing up thing – I saw that in Waterford.'

At this Hetty admitted distinct interest. 'You mean they pay people – I mean really *pay* them – to be in your moving pictures?'

'Mary Pickford, when I left Hollywood last year, was getting ten thousand dollars a week from Zukor's Famous Players . . . And, besides, the whole business is about clothes – and dressing up . . .' He lingered invitingly on these ideas for a moment. 'You should see Gloria Swanson's wardrobes in de Mille's pictures.'

'Ten thousand dollars a *week*?' she asked. Craig nodded. 'But that's *thousands* of pounds, isn't it?' He nodded again. 'Fonsy O'Grady paid most of us ten *shillings* a week!'

'Well, he didn't have a big audience, you see. You don't understand – everyone, the world over now, pays to go see moving pictures. That's why they call the actors stars,' he added with some irony. 'Everyone, everywhere, sees them.'

'But wha-what is it – and why do you think I have it – that makes them that?'

'Listen,' he told her. 'What you have is half a dozen characters churning about inside you trying to get out. It's obvious! – that stammer and telling me you were "Miss Bauer" and dressing up as a *man* at the drop of a hat and all that aggressive sword play you go in for: your general kicking against the traces! And that's the cause of half your troubles – with your mother, your friends, that nice girl friend you tell me dropped you and skedaddled off to Paris. They don't know who you *are*, what to expect next, can't rely on you. But that sort of response, that invention, is just what's required in motion pictures – *if* you can discipline it, get rid of the purely wayward elements . . .' He looked at her quite severely now. 'So you have that. And you can *act* as well, as long as you don't have to do too much speaking, with that . . . attractive hesitancy of yours, which you won't in motion pictures, because they're silent. But the real thing you have, well . . .' He gestured vaguely. 'You can't lay hands on it. Some quality, some secret, nobody quite knows what – you can't put it into words. No more than I could tell you why exactly this champagne tastes so good.'

'Oh, I can,' she broke in enthusiastically. 'It's fizzy and dry and d-d-delicious!'

He smiled. 'Well, there you have it, near enough. That's just what you taste of as well. Get that on the screen – and that's what'll make you a star.' He raised his glass again, looking at her steadily over the bubbles. 'So, you'll come with me to California then?'

'I might – I may.' There was nothing of the tease in her voice. She still had genuine doubts.

'Your friend, Léonie . . . That's the real problem, isn't it? She's more than just a friend, isn't she?' He touched her hand quickly. 'I understand,' he went on. 'It's tough, these break-ups.'

'Oh, no – it's nothing.' But Hetty's expression gave the lie to her words. And Craig, seeing the lie, took advantage of it by lying himself. 'Well then, you don't have to worry about that.' He looked at her with a mature knowingness. 'She's the one who left you – you don't have to worry too much about her.'

'No.'

She was grateful for his quick support. But then she felt awful, a great yawning horror opening up inside her, for this betrayal of Léonie – until, as if he had sensed this, she thought, he broke into her thoughts and calmed them once more.

'No, you can't worry about Léonie,' he said softly, the devil's advocate now. 'We all lose friends sometimes that way. We grow away from them, to places they can't follow. It's tough. But what can you do? Deny your own life, all the gifts there? Well, that'd be crazy! Because you have *so much* there. The truth is there's really no future for you in that relationship – you've grown beyond it, towards every other sort of future, which you *can* have, just waiting for you, out there, in Hollywood . . .'

He had brought her to that high hill then, and shown her the view on the other side, the limitless plains where the beasts of pure self-will and unfettered ambition were free to roam – in pursuit of every egotistical fulfilment and worldly achievement, encouraged to feed on every exotic pleasure, pursue every vanity, forget every old friend. He had shown her this amoral vision, and she had taken it in, he was sure of that. He would let her sleep on it.

That night, in her room, Hetty weighed her opportunities with Craig Williamson. Yes, the man reeked of power: that was the most exciting thing about him – not the power of birth or class, which she was entirely accustomed to, but a force quite new to her, without those inherited trappings or constraints, a power that operated from scratch and without scruple, in the real world: a confidence and command which stemmed not from great houses or inherited wealth but from sheer arrogant will, character, talent, quite free from the constraints of ordinary life or from any emotional commitment there.

And, in these hours of deep bitterness and betrayal, Hetty, sniffing at the hems of power, found the aroma infinitely sweet, intoxicating, drawn by it, seeing clearly how, if she could come to feed off the same magic elixir, she need never again find herself at the mercy of her demented mother, or suffer the vagaries and disappointments of her friends. She could revenge herself on all that – and all the other earlier injustices of her life, putting herself finally beyond reach of hurt and pain.

Yes, that was what Craig Williamson offered her – what she had always wanted for herself, she openly admitted now: the power, without any inhibition, to impose herself on life, on others, on an 'audience' – something on which Léonie in the end had quite failed to collaborate with her. But here, against this new mirror, with this man so obviously taken by her, she could give free rein to her *true* personality. It was so obvious! Craig Williamson, given the nature of his motion picture business, expected this from her, and had said as much. He *wanted* everything which Léonie had tried to frustrate or deny in her – all the many conflicting people trapped in her soul.

Indeed, this was the essence of the whole business: Craig Williamson was offering her the person she really was. He had already half done so – prodding her, long dormant from her chrysalis, into the life she was born for. And she had basked in these first intimations of change, making hesitant wing-beats in these glorious new colours, testing herself in the balmy airs. Now she would go the whole way, leap into that bright world and fly, become that completely changed being, accept her destiny.

Something finally snapped in her. She could not sleep, tense with a euphoric mood of vast energy, ruthless intent. She sprang out of bed and started walking to and fro. Yes, she had done with all this temporizing, these compromises – with her mother, with Léonie and Dermot. She had done her best there. But it was useless. At worst these people, like her mother, were utterly malign; at best, though with good intentions, no doubt, they quite failed to see the real purpose of her life – which was to be free to express these gifts she had been born with; a task, she saw then, in which she must now serve herself alone, a discipline which she must ruthlessly pursue, forsaking her past, as part of the cost, part of the debt she owed to her talent. Craig Williamson saw all that. The others did not. It was as simple as that. She made the firm decision then: she would go with him to California.

In his own bedroom Craig Williamson considered the day. It had gone well – all the chances had fallen his way. The girl was as good as his, he thought. Though he was equally aware that his future success with her would need patience, clever handling, many wiles on his part. But she was worth every effort, every scheme. The relaunching of his Hollywood career, his whole future there, could well depend on this woman. He knew well what a jungle it was over there. A year away from the cameras, and others had jumped into your place, they were *happy* to do so and to forget you, and you could well be finished. But with such a woman, a hidden star in your pocket, you had the one thing no one could resist out on the coast: you possessed the raw material which sustained all their lives in that shallow, dream-obsessed suburb – a rare, deep vein of gold which, when mined and minted through the alchemy of the camera, turned to dollars. It was as simple as that. And that was the sure, indeed the only, means towards any resurrection in Hollywood: dollars.

epilogue

'Fresh woods, pastures new' – for Hetty in Hollywood.

Hetty's story is continued in *Return to Summer Hill*. Ahead of her, as Craig has guaranteed, lies a glittering new life as a silent-movie star. The past is dead, he has told her. She must come into her true estate now, which is not Summer Hill but her own unique talent.

But the past never dies. And least of all for Hetty, who has too many anchors there for her ever to escape that other, true inheritance of hers: the world of Summer Hill and all her old loves there – Robert, Dermot, above all Léonie. In *Return to Summer Hill* these ghosts revive, when Hetty must confront them, accept her past, and go forward into real maturity. Her trials to this end is the story of *Return to Summer Hill*.

When Hollywood gold turns to dross, and Hetty's life among the rich and shallow in Nice, Paris and London during the late twenties becomes increasingly dissolute, it is the great house in Ireland – despised by Hetty for so long – and her former friends there which save her. But her past is still full of secrets, of questions, of relationships lost but not dead, where Hetty must find real answers now: to her love for Léonie – and for Robert and Dermot; when she must, too, come to terms with her mother Frances. Above all, she must learn who her real father is.

These are now the tasks of Hetty's life, a journey which takes her into the arms of a latter Prince of Wales, to a final showdown with Craig, to new relationships with all her old friends. It is a story, too, which brings Léonie to France as a British agent in the Second World War and then brings Hetty to Auschwitz. . .

But, finally, *Return to Summer Hill* is a story of survival, a voyage through disaster into light, a tale of secrets answered, of love resolved.

Pamela Belle
The Moon in the Water £3.99

Thomazine was born heiress to the lands and fortune of the Neron dynasty, and she was born under a dark and troublesome star. Orphaned at ten years old, growing to womanhood among cousins, she met the headstrong Francis and they both dreamed of the mystic unicorn. The sweep of the times was against them. Francis was banished and imprisoned, Thomazine forced into loveless wedlock, and the onrush of beating drums and naked steel heralded England's Civil War.

'Masterly . . . vivid tapestry of a family saga, richly crowded with flesh-and-blood people' ROSEMARY SUTCLIFFE

The Chains of Fate £4.50

The blood-red tide of civil war ran deep over the land, and Thomazine became the wife of a man she would learn to hate, believing her Francis to be dead. When she learned the truth – that Francis lived – Thomazine rode north on a mission hung with the chains of fate. Those chains weighed down her journey as she moved through land occupied by enemy soldiers, found the man she loved at the price of deserting her own child, and lost Francis again to the cause of Montrose . . . Time and again Thomazine and Francis would be torn apart, yet one day, the chains of love must prove stronger . . .

Alathea £4.99

Surviving family tragedy, the threatening attentions of her jealous half-brother, the devastation of both the Plague and the Great Fire, and forsaking marriage for her career, the beautiful, headstrong, gifted Alathea grows up into fame and fortune, and is the mistress of a notorious rake.

But the destiny of this fiercely independent artist is as yet unfulfilled, and in time the wheel will come full circle for Alathea, child of dreams and truths and Unicorns . . .

Pamela Belle
Wintercombe £4.99

'A lovely warm tapestry of a book, weaving together suspense and drama with a bittersweet love story and a richly detailed account of life in an English Manor House during the Civil War.
ROSEMARY SUTCLIFFE

Civil war has raged, her sombre husband has been away for two years and young Silence St Barbe, Mistress of Wintercombe has enjoyed a peaceful time with her children.

This sheltered world is shattered when enemy Cavaliers, led by the sadistic Colonel Ridgely turn tranquil Wintercombe into an unruly, drunken garrison.

But for Silence a more subtle threat dawns as handsome Captain Nick Hellier attempts to unlock the chains of her fragile Puritan heart.

Herald of Joy

'A fitting sequel to *Wintercombe*, setting out as a richly detailed and delightful family chronicle and quickening into an unputdownable adventure story, in which it is such a pleasure to meet Captain Nick Hellier again' ROSEMARY SUTCLIFFE

England lies quiet after the ravages of Civil War. But in Somerset, at Wintercombe, the death of George St Barbe will change for ever the course of events, leaving the rest of the family with uncertain, uneven destinies . . .

For his widow, Silence, it is a time of freedom and of longing – for reunion with the dashing Captain Nick Hellier. For their children, too, promises and pitfalls beckon: Young Nat claims Wintercombe as his own, and Rachel, like her mother before her, falls victim to an arranged marriage.

Fate unfurls across the breadth of the nation. With Captain Hellier at his side, Charles II invades England to claim his throne. And Silence's daughter Tabby weaves a rope of intrigue that will draw Nick back to Wintercombe . . .

To meet Silence . . . To face the future.

Jean Stubbs
A Lasting Spring £3.99

'The winter of war is over and gone. Still I must hope for a lasting spring . . .'

On a May afternoon in 1945, a woman waits in a Manchester teashop for a stranger to walk through the door. That stranger will be a man she hasn't seen for nearly two years, her husband coming home from the war.

While she waits, her thoughts go back over twenty years of growing and fulfilment, of love and loss, of happiness and heartbreak, of peace and war.

Faces from the past are like ghosts in the sunlight . . . the first lover who betrayed her newly wakened passion, the step-brother who became her best and closest friend, and her husband who brought her a glimpse of the springtime so long in coming . . .

A Lasting Spring is Jean Stubb's most important novel to date . . . tender and passionate, rich in incident and character, wonderfully evocative and suffused with warm nostalgia. Here is a novel of ordinary men and women living and loving through extraordinary times . . . a splendid chronicle of all our yesterdays.

Anita Burgh
The Azure Bowl £4.99

Here begins the rich and compelling saga
Daughters of a Granite Land

For Alice Tregowan, daughter of a wealthy mine owner, the Cornish estate of Gwenfer still holds the dreams of a past long buried: the wealth and privilege she sacrificed in her fight for freedom . . . and love.

But for la Blewett, daughter of a drunken and penniless miner and Alice's childhood friend, Gwenfer is the symbol of all that she could never have; and all that she will struggle to gain in her relentless quest for wealth and vengeance.

From the sweeping landscape of rugged Cornwall, to the brothels of Victorian London and the grim tenements of turn of the century New York, theirs is a story of passion and conflict, of courage and desire.

The Golden Butterfly £4.99

This is the second book in the rich, and compelling saga

Daughters of a Granite Land

Juniper Boscar, beautiful, spoiled and fabulously rich, is the charming and dangerous Golden Butterfly. A woman who captivates everyone she meets, yet a woman whose allure can only be measured by the heartbreak and destruction left in her wake.

Juniper Boscar, heiress to a fortune, yet burdened still by dreams of a past long-buried among the ancient gravestones of Cornwall. Only Polly Frobisher, neglected daughter of the actress Francine, holds the key to Juniper's torment – and to the secret of the azure bowl, the dramatic symbol of two destinies for ever linked by tragedy . . .

From the sheltered wealth of New England to the rugged beauty of Cornwall, from the glittering society of the 1930s London to the terrors of war-torn France, *The Golden Butterfly* continues the saga which began with *The Azure Bowl*.

Anita Burgh
Distinctions of Class £4.99

From backstreet girl to Laird's Lady,
A woman follows her star.
For better, or for worse . . .

'Jane sat alone at the back of her private plane.
She had a decision to make: one which could
change her extraordinary life, once again'

Jane dared to dream as she grew into a beautiful woman in a
dead-end world of mean streets, but she never dared dream that
one day she'd be the laird's lady, wife to Alistair Redland, future
Earl of Upnor.

When that impossible dream became real, she had to wake one day
and find her love match wrecked on rocks of class pride and social
prejudice.

So in cloistered Cambridge and elegant Italy, Jane built her life anew.
Always desirable, wherever she went there were men who knew
just how desirable.

Until her star of destiny drew her north again, to the Highlands where
a twist of fate lay ready to seize again her dreams and test again her
courage . . .

Distinctions of Class is a compelling story, a remarkable novel from
the pen of an exciting new author, reflecting more than a little of
the real life of its creator, Anita, Lady Burgh.

Lynda La Plante
The Legacy £3.99

At a Welsh pithead at the turn of the century, a gypsy girl, a romany princess driven out by her people, waited for the pitman father of the bastard son in her arms.

When he emerged the black coal seam, he turned away and walked off with his pals to the pub, while her curse echoed after him down the hillside . . .

A vast and panoramic novel . . . possessed of a spendid narrative sweep . . . its pages teeming with compelling characters . . . its richness stemming from the age-old traditions of the romany people . . .

The Legacy is the first part of Lynda La Plante's splendid saga of four generations of a bloodline tainted by a romany curse . . .

After the death of Freedom, his sons are despatched by fate in very different directions. While Edward goes up to Cambridge . . . Alex goes into a remand home . . . and on to prison . . . serving his time for a killing he did not commit.

It was not until twelve years after the end of *The Legacy* that the brothers met again . . . standing at their mother's graveside.

Lynda La Plante continues her magnificent saga in *The Talisman* . . . following the curse down through the third and fourth generations.

Lynda La Plante
The Talisman £3.99

The long dark skein of the romany curse runs down to the fourth generation . . .

The sons of Freedom Stubbs meet again at their mother's graveside, twelve long years on.

Edward . . . the first born son, brutally born of his prizefighter father's trade and his razor-sharp wits honed by a Cambridge education. He inherits not only the dark romany looks, but the powers and dangers of second sight – *the curse of Midas* . . .

Alex . . . the second son, his colleges the prison cells where he paid for a crime he didn't commit, his talent the ability to manipulate and shape his brother's Midas touch into a powerful empire . . .

Evelyn and Juliana . . . the fourth generation, born to wealth beyond dreams, heirs to a legacy in the long shadow of a romany curse . . .

The Talisman completes the vast and compelling saga that began with *The Legacy*. The story that originated in the pit villages and prize rings of years ago, moves on through the mineral mines of South Africa and the fashion houses of Paris to the boardrooms and brothels of modern London, tracing a dark curse down a bloodline tainted by darker secrets . . .

All Pan books are available at your local bookshop or newsagent, or can be ordered direct from the publisher. Indicate the number of copies required and fill in the form below.

Send to: **CS Department, Pan Books Ltd., P.O. Box 40, Basingstoke, Hants.   RG21 2YT.**

or phone: 0256 469551 (Ansaphone), quoting title, author and Credit Card number.

Please enclose a remittance* to the value of the cover price plus: 60p for the first book plus 30p per copy for each additional book ordered to a maximum charge of £2.40 to cover postage and packing.

*Payment may be made in sterling by UK personal cheque, postal order, sterling draft or international money order, made payable to Pan Books Ltd.

Alternatively by Barclaycard/Access:

Card No.

Signature:

Applicable only in the UK and Republic of Ireland.

While every effort is made to keep prices low, it is sometimes necessary to increase prices at short notice. Pan Books reserve the right to show on covers and charge new retail prices which may differ from those advertised in the text or elsewhere.

NAME AND ADDRESS IN BLOCK LETTERS PLEASE:

....

Name ————————————————————————————

Address ————————————————————————————

————————————————————————————

————————————————————————————

————————————————————————————

3/87